ALSO BY MELISA TORRES

PERFECT BALANCE GYMNASTICS SERIES
I've Got This
Nothing Better Than Gym Friends
Dance is the Secret Event
Brothers Have Talent, Too
The Kip
Score Out
Courage to Fly
Season of Change

PERFECT BALANCE GYMNASTICS OPTIONALS
New Challenges
Strive for Excellence
The Comeback

PERFECT BALANCE GYMNASTICS WORKBOOKS
Goal Setting Journal
Overcoming Mental Blocks
Perfect Balance Gymnastics Coloring Book

MOM AND DAD LOVE ME SERIES
Mom and Dave Love Me the Same
What if Santa Can't Find Us?

PERFECT BALANCE GYMNASTICS OPTIONALS COLLECTION

NEW CHALLENGES

STRIVE FOR EXCELLENCE

THE COMEBACK

Written by Melisa Torres
The Optionals Collection Published by Dancing Water
Cover art by ezarago
Edited by Clara Somers Editing Services
Edited by RFK Bookworks
The Comeback reviewed by sports medicine doctor,
Dr. Daniel C Herman, MD, PhD
ISBN Hardback: 978-1-958613-31-3
ISBN Paperback: 978-1-958613-30-6
ISBN ebook: 978-1-958613-32-0

TABLE OF CONTENTS

New Challenges

by MELISA TORRES

CHAPTER 1

"What did you decide, Paige?" Trista asks me. We just finished our Level 5 season and my teammates and I are at dinner celebrating our second-place win at our State Meet only hours ago. I surprised everyone, including myself, by staying on beam for the first time all season and scoring a high enough all-around to advance to Level 6. Trista is asking me if I am going to, in fact, move to the Level 6 team.

"I'm not sure yet. I didn't expect to score out today," I answer honestly. She continues to look at me expectantly so I elaborate, "I think I'm just going to see how training goes over the holidays and if I can get my layout on floor." The thing about gymnastics is that not only do you have to score out of a level to get to the next one, you need to be able to do the harder skills in the next level. I'm so close; I might be ready in January for Level 6. Competition season for Level 5 is in the fall and for Level 6 it's in the winter. So either I move fast and compete Level 6 in six weeks or I wait an entire year. I frown to myself and then add, "Since I'm older, I'd rather not wait until next year." Trista seems to accept this answer and she turns to our teammate Lucy.

"Lucy?" she asks, posing the same question.

"I . . . I'm going to do Level 6," Lucy stammers. "Even if I have to do the back walkover on beam. I'm ready for Level 6," she says. Lucy is the best Level 5 on our team. She is just struggling with her back handspring on beam, which is a Level 6 skill. Technically, it's a nice to have Level 6 skill.

Level 6 is a big change because we get to create our own routines. We will have certain requirements we need to include in our routines, but we can still play to our strengths. Level 6 through 10 are called optionals because we have the option to do what we want. I'm happy to leave compulsories behind. I had a hard time with compulsories. All of us had the exact same routines. For me, some of the required skills were really hard.

"You are totally ready," Savannah says, agreeing with Lucy.

"You'll get your back handspring," Trista adds, and Lucy gives her a little smile of confidence.

"I'm going to kind of miss compulsories," Lucy admits.

"You will not!" Trista shrieks.

Then the girls all start talking at once about compulsories versus optionals. Maybe I should go immediately to Level 6. The girls training in the Level 6 and 7 groups are more my age. I look around at the table. As much as I love these girls, they are two or three years younger than I am. I'm in seventh grade while Trista, Carmen, Alexis, and Marissa are in fifth grade. Lucy and Savannah are in fourth grade. They are like sisters to me and I enjoy being their leader, but I'm also ready to train with girls my age.

I think about my situation as I watch Lucy's younger sister, Rose, join us at the table. She squeezes into Lucy's chair making me giggle. I hate that we are going to be splitting up. From what I can tell Lucy, Savannah, and Alexis will be moving to Level 6 and Trista, Marissa, and Carmen will be staying in Level 5.

And what will I do? I really want to move to Level 6 but gymnastics isn't that easy. I may have scored out today, but I do not have all of the requirements to compete Level 6. I wonder if my coaches, James and Melony, will even give me the choice to move up? Trista asked me what I am going to do as if it's all up to me. It's not all up to me. My coaches have to agree that I'm ready. I look down the long table to where our coaches are eating with our parents. I wonder if my score today will mean that they'll invite me to move up. I could see it going either way.

After dinner we file out of the restaurant with a lot of good-byes and 'see you Tuesday!' But I know I may not see some of them at my next practice. We will split up from here. I go along with the jovial goodbyes, but a part of me is sad at the reality of our group never being the same again.

Once we are in the car my mom immediately turns back to me. "James invited you to train with the 6s and 7s next week," she divulges.

"He did? Just like that?" I ask, surprised.

"Well, he thought you could try their workouts until the new year and then decide what you want to do," she explains.

"So, I'm not officially moved up?" I ask.

"I don't know, pumpkin, I just know he said, 'have Paige come in on Monday to the six-seven practice and see how it goes' and I said that you would like that. Did I speak too soon? Is that not what you want?" she asks, confused.

"No, it's fine," I assure her. "I'm just not sure if I'm on the Level 6 team or if this is some sort of trial."

She is quiet in response so my dad pipes up. "He said he wanted you there to see how it goes. What is there to debate? You scored out today, right?"

"I did. But I don't have a layout on floor or bars," I explain.

"Well, duh," my younger brother, Jason, pipes up. "It's a test. And you better pass."

Leave it to my brother to get right to the heart of the matter. He's right. I'm invited to practice, but not officially on the team.

It's a test and I better pass.

The following Monday at school I can't focus. All I can think about is that I'm going to practice today with the Level 6s and 7s. Half of my teammates aren't going to be there. What will the girls in the optionals group think when they see that I can't do a layout on floor or a back handspring on beam? In the past I've always moved up with my teammates. I've been with the same girls since Level 3. I've been with the same coach for that matter. Will James be coaching the Level 6s and 7s? Or will it be Katie? I know Katie is in charge of the optionals teams, but does that mean she coaches all of them? The upper optionals are there almost every day. They must take a lot of Katie's time. How did I not think to ask who is coaching the lower optional teams?

It doesn't matter anyway, I realize as I tap my pencil faster on my desk. I would want to be in the optionals practice today no matter who was coaching. It would have been nice to know. I sigh and look at the clock. Ten more minutes until lunch time. This day is crawling by. I look back down at my paper. I'm supposed to write something about what we just read. What did we read? I flip over the paper on my desk and reread the story that I didn't retain the first time. It's a terrible story about ocean garbage and I dread writing something about it.

Finally, the bell rings and I shove my blank paper in my backpack and head out the door to find my friends. I've been going to this school since kindergarten, so the transition to middle school hasn't been as bad as it must be for other kids. We have a homeroom which is two hours and then we rotate to our other four classes. That was an adjustment, but other than that, it feels the same. Most of all, I have the same friends.

I find our table in the cafeteria and flop my backpack down to dig out my lunch. Abigail quickly joins me followed by Katherine.

"I hate having science before lunch; it makes me nauseated," Abigail declares.

"It wasn't that bad," Katherine comments.

"What did you do today?" I ask, pulling out my lunch and setting my backpack on the floor next to me.

"All our teacher can talk about is how we're going to dissect frogs. It's so gross," she answers.

"I don't know what you're going to do when we actually get to the part where we really do dissect it," Katherine comments.

"Be absent that day," Abigail says smartly.

"How was your weekend?" Katherine asks me. "Didn't you have a big meet or something?"

"Yes, we had our State Championships. We placed second," I answer with a smile.

"Out of how many?" Abigail asks.

"I don't know, a lot. At least ten teams."

"Did you win the all-around?" Katherine asks, not really understanding how hard that is to do in gymnastics.

"No, but I scored out," I share.

"What does that mean?" she asks.

"It means I can go to the next level. Today in fact," I add.

"You don't have tryouts or anything?" Abigail asks. Abigail and Katherine are both dancers and they are always trying out for one team or another. I don't really get it, probably how they don't get gymnastics.

"No tryouts. We just have to get a certain score in Level 5 and the new Level 6 skills before we can move up. Come to think of it we sort of do have tryouts. It's just usually called testing day or an intrasquad."

"So you're not doing that this time? You just move up today?" Katherine asks.

My stomach sinks as I think about her question," I don't know."

"Paige, how do you not know?" Abigail laughs.

"I'm invited today or this week, I think, on a trial basis. I'm pretty sure I have to get some skills to stay," I finally admit out loud.

"Sounds stressful," Abigail says.

I don't comment creating an awkward silence, which is rare for our threesome. "Wanna see the dance we made up this weekend?" Katherine asks.

I nod yes and she pulls out her phone. I watch the two of them on the little screen and their silliness makes me laugh. I feel lucky to have these two friends at school. It seems like I had so many friends when we were little and our group got smaller and smaller as we got older. I ended up staying friends with Abigail and Katherine because we live near each other and we all like to dance when we hang out together. Although, I haven't done much hanging out with them since I moved up to Level 5.

"Now that your competition season is over are you going

to be able to hang out this weekend?" Abigail asks, looking up from the video.

"I don't know, maybe. I think I might be going right into another season," I admit.

"You don't seem to know much about your new Level. Find out today and let us know," Katherine orders.

She's right. I don't know much about my new level.

CHAPTER 2

I walk into the gym in my favorite red and gold leotard with my gold shorts and a sweatshirt zipped over the top. My curly red hair is pulled back in a low ponytail. I wear either a low pony or double buns because I do a back extension roll on beam. The high ponytail or single bun get in the way and hurts my head. I walk upstairs to our team cubbies and see Savannah there stuffing a sweatshirt into her cubby.

"Think we'll get to use the optionals room?" I ask her pulling off my sweatshirt and throwing it in my cubby. We *are* working out with optionals today.

"I'm not sure, so I figured I'd use this," she answers, referring to our personal cubbies we earned back when we got our kip in Level 4. I nod in agreement and put my shoes in my cubby.

"Are you nervous?" she asks me.

"Yes. Are you?" I ask her.

"Yeah. And it was weird coming here without Trista," she admits.

"I bet." Trista and Savannah are neighbors and Trista has been on our team since Level 3. It will be odd not to have some of our teammates here. We are silent as we walk downstairs and into the training area for our new practice.

Katie, the Optionals Coach, sees us as soon as we push through the glass doors. "Paige and Savannah!" she exclaims, and we walk over to her. "Welcome to optionals! We'll start running in a few minutes when everyone is here. For now, let me introduce you to the team." She yells over to some girls who are on the trampoline and they trot over to us. "These are my only returning Level 6s, Riley and Victoria. This is Paige and Savannah." The girls politely say hi and quietly observe us.

"Oh look the rest of my new 6s," Katie exclaims. "Over here girls!" she yells. "Alexis and Lucy, this is Riley and Victoria," she repeats.

We all say hi again and then Katie tells us to run ten laps. As I'm running I notice my former coach, James, over on bars with the little Level 3s. I give him a wave as we run by and he waves back. It's weird that he's not coaching us. I'm a little nervous about being trained by Katie. I've seen her with the Level 8s, 9s, and 10s and sometimes she seems intense.

By the time we finish our ten laps the rest of the lower-level optional team has arrived. "Stretch lightly while I introduce everyone again. Then we'll do complex."

The girls flop into splits and start chattering amongst themselves. I turn to my old teammates Alexis, Lucy, and Savannah and they seem as unsure as I do. As the oldest, I used to be the leader of this group. But it seems weird to still act like their leader when I have no idea what to expect and I'm no longer the oldest. The 6s and 7s look like they are all

10

in middle school like me. Alexis, Lucy, and Savannah seem young for this group.

"These are our 7s over here," Katies says to us, standing near four of the girls. I listen as I switch to my left splits. "This is Aubrey," she says walking over to a girl and pointing to her as she adjusts her splits, "Brooklyn, Payton, and Maya. Girls these are your new 6s; Savannah, Alexis, Lucy, and Paige." We say an awkward hi making Katie chuckle. She tells us we have five more minutes to stretch whatever we need to before complex. Then she walks away and into the coaches' office.

We quietly do as she says, stretching our legs, backs, wrists, and necks.

"What school do you guys go to?" Peyton asks.

Alexis answers first, "I go to Mountain View Charter," she answers.

"What grade?"

"Fifth," Alexis answers.

"Are you going to stay there for middle school?" Brooklyn asks, knowing that Mountain View goes all the way up to eighth grade.

"Yeah, all my brothers go there. Except my oldest brother," she adds.

"I go to Hilltop Elementary," Savannah supplies.

"What grade?"

"Fourth,"

"Wow! You guys are young," Brooklyn comments.

"I'm in seventh grade," I say, saving my teammates from feeling bad for being young. "I go to St. Mary's."

"That place is supposed to be hard. Is it?" Maya asks.

"I don't think it's that bad, but I don't know any better. I've been going there since I was little."

"And what about you?" Peyton asks Lucy.

She shyly says, "I don't live near here. I go to Reagan

Elementary downtown. I'm in fourth grade, like Savannah."

"We're all in middle school. Snowcap Canyon Middle School and Mountain View. Your brothers might know Peyton and Maya," Brooklyn says to Alexis.

"Stand up for complex!" Katie yells as she walks back to us.

The girls stop talking and do as Katie says, standing up and forming three lines on the floor for complex. I'm nervous as I get in line. Last summer I trained with the Level 6 and 7s when my teammates were at different gymnastics camps. I wasn't expected to do everything in the complex. Today I feel like I should be able to do everything Katie calls out if I want to be a Level 6. Am I officially a Level 6? I don't even know. I was just invited to workout with them. Is this like an interview? If I can't cut it, do I go back to the Level 5s?

I look at my teammates who are also here at their first day of Level 6. They have instinctively lined up behind me.

"Let's do three lines of three. Lucy or Savannah, come over here to Aubrey's line." I see Lucy and Savannah exchange looks and without a word Savannah slowly walks over to the back of a line of Level 7s. Lucy, Savannah, and Alexis are as nervous as I am. I don't know why. The three of them scored out weeks ago and even had time to start learning their floor routines over the last few weekends. Clearly, they are going to stay in this group.

"Handstand walks!" Katie yells. We are starting with handstand walks? Usually James starts us with handstand forward rolls. I take a deep breath, this is optionals. Level 6 and up is serious business I think as I kick up into a handstand and walk on my hands about ten feet before I step down.

"Count your falls; ten push-ups for each fall. Do them when you get to the other end of the floor," Katie instructs.

I quickly kick up and make it another ten feet before

12

falling. By the time I get to the other end of the floor I have fallen three times, so I start my thirty push-ups. Thankfully other girls fell too and are doing push-ups. I notice Brooklyn and Peyton are standing talking while the rest of us are doing push-ups. Which must mean they made it across the entire floor. Impressive.

As girls finish their push-ups and start standing up Katie calls out front and back walkovers and my line begins without me. By the time I finish my push-ups Alexis, who was at the back of my line, is starting her turn. I jump up and get ready to take my turn doing walkovers.

My walkovers are terrible because I have bad shoulder flexibility. Katie knows this and doesn't say anything. I get through them as best as I can. As soon as I finish she says, "Power hurdle round-off back handspring!"

Usually we warm-up with just the power hurdle round-off and then on the next turn we do the round-off back handspring. Apparently, in this group, they skip that step. Thankfully, I can do round-off back handsprings with no problem and I breeze through that skill and so do my teammates. Then she yells, "Round-off back tuck!" Wait, what? *A round-off back tuck with no back handspring?*

I'm glad I'm now at the back of my line as I watch Lucy, who is at the front, pause and think about what Katie just said. Of course, Lucy takes her turn and does a perfect round-off back tuck. Then Alexis steps up after her and does a decent back tuck out of her round-off. I stand at the edge of the floor. It's my turn, but I can't move.

"You can do the round-off back handspring again if you want Paige," Katie yells over to me, obviously aware of my hesitation.

I look over at her and she smiles at me, making me brave for the moment. "Can you spot me?" I ask. She nods and walks over to my side of the floor.

"Have you ever done a tuck out of a round-off?" she asks me. I shake my head no. "You're going to love it. Remember, feet behind you on the round-off to set," she says, and motions for me to go. I take a deep breath, power hurdle, round-off, and set (as she reminded me) so that I go up instead of back. I reach up, lift my knees, feel her hands on my back and waist, see the ground, and land. "No problem," Katie says, as I land safely.

I look up in shock. "That *was* easier!" I exclaim.

"Good, because it's probably going to be your series on beam."

A round-off back tuck on beam? That sounds exciting and scary at the same time. I quietly nod and get back in line to wait for the next skill. She has us do front handsprings, front handspring dive rolls, aerials, leaps, switch leaps, and front tucks. Then she calls out a few odd combinations 'just for fun' like hitch kick aerial and round-off straddle jumps. I liked trying the different dance and acro combinations.

By the time complex is over I am beat; and we are just beginning. Katie tells us to grip up and go to bars. We go upstairs to get our grips. Alexis, Savannah, Lucy, and I stop at our Kip Club Cubbies while we watch our new teammates continue to walk to the far side of the room and through a door that says 'Optionals.'

"Do you think we go in there?" Alexis asks.

"Our stuff is here," Lucy points out.

"Yeah, but we're Level 6s now," Alexis persists, "shouldn't we put our grips on in there?"

All three of them look at me. But I'm not sure what to do.

"I can ask Katie about it," I slowly say as I watch Savanah pulling on her pink wrist bands. "Let's just grip up here for now," I suggest, not at all sure if that's the right answer. Barging into the optionals room where we haven't been invited seems weird.

Just then Maya pokes her head out. "You guys can come in," she yells over to us, making several parents turn their heads. "Grab your stuff," she adds in a lower voice.

The girls look at me and I shrug, "We can put our grips on in there," I agree. We grab our grip bags and walk over to where Maya is holding the door open for us.

I have only been in this room once before. There is a desk along the wall where we entered. Across from us there is a big window that looks down on the parking lot. Along the other two walls there are lockers and in the middle of the room there are chairs, a bean bag, and a table. The girls are standing by their lockers putting on their grips.

Four of the lockers are decorated with our names on them. One for me, Lucy, Alexis, and Savannah. They carefully cut our names out of construction paper and taped them each to an empty locker.

"Wow," Alexis says, and I see the girls smiling at us.

"This is so nice!" Savannah exclaims.

"But what if I don't end up competing Level 6?" I ask Maya.

"Oh, you're stuck with us now," she says unconcerned. "Even if you don't compete, you'll stay in our group and work Level 6 and 7 skills," she reasons with confidence.

What she says makes sense. I smile a small smile and walk toward my locker and open it up. It is empty and clean inside so I set my grip bag down in it. "Thanks you guys," I say to them as I pull out a wrist band.

"It was fun," Brooklyn admits, "I like projects like that."

"It was fast though. We had to have Katie let us in yesterday," Aubrey says.

"I'm glad you did," Lucy says, opening her locker.

"Okay, we better hurry, we've been up here longer than usual," Maya points out and we quickly finish putting our grips on and run back downstairs for our bars workout.

CHAPTER 3

Katie has us warm up on bars similar to how James does, with push away kips. It's weird to have someone besides James coaching us. I look across the gym and watch him with the Level 3 girls on floor. They are sharing the floor with two other classes of recreational kids.

"Paige, you're up," Katie says to me. I look back at the bar in front of me. I jump into my glide kip and do three push-away kips. I hit my feet on the third one. I try so hard not to, but it still happens.

"You're going to have to have abs of steel to keep those legs up," Katie comments, "I can help you with that." Great, I have a feeling that is going to equate to rough conditioning. "Other than that, pretty good." I'm in a support position after my third kip and I nod in acknowledgement.

When I jump down she says, "When you're done warming up go to the pit bar and work flyaways without the tap swings before it."

"Out of a cast?" I ask her.

"Yes, start in a support position and swing down and flyaway. If you need to do the flat backs at first, that's fine."

I nod and get back in line for another set of push away kips. I forgot that Level 6 doesn't have tap swings in front of the flyaway. How am I ever going to do that? It sounds scary. I look over at James again. I wish he was coaching us.

I finish my push away kips and head over the pit bar with my old Level 5 teammates. The original Level 6s and 7s are told to do three of each half of their bar routine. The first intrasquad is in a few weeks, just before Thanksgiving. They are already doing routines.

"We have some serious catching up to do, huh?" Lucy asks as we walk up to the pit bar.

"Looks like it," Alexis agrees.

"We don't have to compete this season," Savannah reminds us. "We can just train Level 6 all year and compete next January."

"Is that what you're doing?" Lucy asks her as Alexis climbs up to the pit bar and starts pumping a few swings.

"I don't know," Savannah admits. "James said it was an option for me, but I can tell my mom really wants me to compete this winter."

Alexis swings into a kip and looks down at Savannah from her support position on the bar. "What do *you* want Savannah?"

"No talking up on the bar!" we hear Katie yell over to us. Alexis quickly takes her turn by pushing out, swinging down, letting go of the bar, and falling to a flat back. She did the timer drill rather than the actual flyaway.

"Have you ever flipped it out of a cast?" I ask her.

"Yeah," she says as she climbs out of the pit. "I did a few with my mom at summer camp. It's been a while though."

I nod and watch Lucy climb up. She swings, does a kip, cast, and a perfect tuck flyaway into the pit.

"That was beautiful. I didn't know you could do those," Alexis comments, sitting on the edge of the pit.

"We learned them both ways at Salt Lake Gymnastics," Lucy says. Lucy came to our gym in the middle of the Level 5 competition season. I realize now that when she came here we were only working routines and I have no idea what optionals skills she may already have.

"Do you have all of your Level 6 skills?" I ask her.

"I think so. I'm not sure which ones are Level 6 versus 7, but I'm pretty sure I have everything I need for Level 6. Except the back handspring on beam," she reminds me.

Lucy had her back handspring on beam a few months ago. But when James saw that she was doing it with her wrong hand in front he made her change it. Changing a skill is difficult; worse than learning it the first time.

I watch as Savannah easily does a flat back drill out of a cast. Now it's my turn. I know I can at least do the drill. I climb up to the high bar over the pit and do a pull up, pull over to get up. Then I pause in a support position thinking about what I need to do. I need to push away, like in a baby giant, but then at the top of the swing let go for a flyaway. I take a deep breath, cast and push away from the bar. I swing down and as I come up it feels too scary and fast to let go, so I decide to hang on. I swing up and back doing high tap swings.

"Let go!" I hear Alexis say.

On the second swing I let go and fall to a flat back. Of course, letting go on a tap swing is what we have been doing all season.

Disappointed, I climb out of the pit and watch Alexis jump up. She climbs up to the high bar, tap swings, kips up

19

and pauses like I did.

"You've got this Lexi," Savannah says to her.

Alexis pushes away, swings down, and lets go at the top of her tap swing. Even though she keeps a straight body, she rotates a little father than falling straight to her back. She gives a little squeal as she lands in the pit on her upper shoulders with her feet up like a candle stick.

"You could have flipped that one," Lucy comments.

Alexis says something, but she is muffled within the foam squares of the pit. We wait for her to wiggle into a sitting position. "That was scary. I don't want to flip just yet." She climbs over the foam squares making her way to the edge of the floor where we are standing.

"You'll get it fast I bet," Lucy insists as Savannah jumps up for her turn.

We do this three more times. Savannah doing perfect drills, Lucy doing beautiful flyaways, Alexis over and under rotating her flat back, and me not letting go at all. I sigh, I wish James was here. He would know how to help me.

"Go smaller Paige," Katie says to me as she walks up.

I look at her, "What?"

"Go smaller on your cast so it doesn't feel out of control. After you get used to a flyaway out of a cast you can slowly try it out of a bigger cast," she explains.

I nod, acknowledging that I heard her and wait for my turn. She gives Alexis a similar correction about controlling her cast so her flatback is controlled. Then she compliments Savannah and tells her she can flip her flyaway when she is ready. I notice she doesn't offer to spot; she simply tells her she can do the skill when she's ready.

"Lucy, have you done these on the regular set?" Katie asks, referring to the set of bars that are not over the pit. Lucy nods. "Then what are you doing over here?" she asks.

"You said for all the new 6s to go to the pit, so I did,"

Lucy explains.

"Yes, but you trained a little differently at Salt Lake Gymnastics," Katie says. "I'm guessing you have some of your Level 6 and even 7 skills." Lucy quietly nods in agreement. "Next time speak up and I will keep you with the returning 6s or even the 7s, depending on what we're working on."

"Okay," Lucy agrees, but I can tell she's not sure about it. I can't say I blame her. She just got used to us and now she may have to train with a whole new group of girls.

"Who's up?" Katie asks.

"I am," I answer and quickly get up to the high bar using a pull up, pull over.

"Kip up next time," Katie instructs when I get to a support position. I nod, knowing that is going to be so much harder. "Now, just do a little cast. Control your swing into a nice and easy flat back."

I take a deep breath and cast small, push back, and swing into a fairly slow tap swing. She's right, I feel more in control. My feet barely make it up to horizontal and I let go and float down into the pit with a flat back.

"There you go, Paige," Katie says, sounding pleased.

Maybe Katie isn't so bad after all.

After bars we have an uneventful vault rotation. The four of us who are new are vaulting onto mats. We are doing Tsuk and Yurchenko drills. The other 6s and 7s are doing Tsuk and Yurchenko entries. They vault up onto the table and have a large stack of mats behind the table. The official Level 6 and 7 vaults are entries, or timers, for the bigger Level 8 vaults.

Katie informs me that with my shoulder flexibility, or lack of, I should be training Tsuks, which I already figured.

"Do you want me to keep doing the Yurchenko drills?" I ask her.

"Nope. That's the beauty of optionals. You get to spend

21

your time developing your strengths. Stick with the Tsuk timers."

I nod and get back in line.

I look over at the table where the girls are vaulting and I wonder how fast we have to transfer from drills to timers. It's November and the first optionals meet is in January. I feel like we are expected to make this transition fast and right now it's feeling overwhelming.

When we are done with vault Katie tells us to rotate to floor. I get a drink of water and head to floor where James is waiting for us. I walk up to him and ask, "You're coaching floor?"

"Yep. Katie is with the upper optionals and I'm done with the Level 3s. I coach the end of your workout."

I'm relieved. James knows where I am in the process of learning a layout and he is a good spotter.

The girls don't seem surprised to see James as they get to floor. It must be something he does every week. I never thought about what James was doing when we weren't training with him.

"Hi ladies. Katie said you already did complex, so let's start by doing tucks and front handsprings on the diagonal. And two dance throughs each."

"We don't have floor routines yet," I remind him.

"I have mine," Lucy pipes up.

"Okay, yeah, Lucy has hers she brought from Salt Lake Gymnastics. But we don't," I say gesturing my hand to Alexis and Savannah.

"Yeah, we do," Savannah pipes up.

I turn to look at her, "You do?" I ask.

"Yeah, we've been coming in on Saturdays and Sundays to learn them," she informs me.

Wow, I knew they started learning routines, but I didn't realize they had their routines.

"You both have one?" I ask. They nod with a bit of sympathy in their eyes. I turn back to James, "Correction, I don't have a floor routine," I tell him, feeling left out and a little foolish.

"Don't worry Paige, you're a great dancer. You'll learn your new routine quickly. It won't be a problem. For today, do five of your front tumbling pass and five of your back tumbling pass."

"What are my passes?" I ask, trying not to get frustrated. How does everyone else know what's going on and I don't? It was easier when we were all training the same skills. At least I knew what I needed to get.

"Your back tuck for now, and hmm, let's try some bounders with you. We should get rid of the front handsprings as soon as possible," he thinks out loud.

"What are bounders?" I ask, but he doesn't hear me. He has turned to Lucy, Savannah, and Alexis and is giving them instructions.

They all have the same passes. They are to work round-off back handspring layouts and front handspring dive rolls.

As they all walk to a corner to warm up James turns back to me, "Why are you frustrated Red?"

"Everyone else knows what they're working. When did those three get routines and I didn't?" I sulk.

"Paige, I didn't know if you would score out of Level 5. All three of them had to score out before Melony created a routine for them. You'll catch up," he says unconcerned. He sees my frown and continues. "This is what you have been waiting for! Optionals is going to be great for you. We can pick skills that you're good at. Your shoulders won't hold you back anymore!"

His speech helps me calm down a little. He's right, I've been hoping to make it this far for this very reason. To have options.

"Today, instead of working front handsprings I want you to try front tuck, front tuck."

That sounds hard. And fun.

"How?" I ask curious.

"Go get your steps and do a front tuck landing about two feet in front of the pit. When it feels good, do a second one into the pit. I also want you to try punch, punch, punch front onto an 8-incher. Put the 8-incher along the edge. You won't be using the diagonal for these."

"Okay," I say, and turn to go get an 8-incher. I pull one off the stack by the stereo and throw it on the edge of the floor. I do as James says and stand with my arms over my head and hop on two feet in a punch. When I get two or three good ones in front of the mat I try to flip a front tuck onto the mat. I land on my bum on the very edge and roll back onto the floor.

"What are you working?" Lucy asks.

"Punch, punch, punch-front," I answer getting up.

"We used to do those." Of course she did. "Try starting your punches at the edge of the mat and work backwards to get your steps."

I nod. It's good advice. I start with the mat at my heels and punch away from it to see how far I travel. Then I turn around and go back the other way and this time I land on my bum in the middle of the mat.

"That's it Paige, keep your arms up and bend at your chest, not waist!" James yells at me from the diagonal.

I nod to indicate that I heard him, get up, and try again. It is kind of fun to be working something that no one else on my team is working. Maybe I am going to like optionals after all.

I'm grateful James is coaching us, even if it's only for a few rotations a week. He always seems to know how to coach me.

24

CHAPTER 4

When I walk up to our table at lunch Abigail and Katherine are hunched over Katherine's phone. I take a seat across from them.

"What are you guys doing?" I ask.

"Trying to pick out a song for a dance we're going to make up today," Abigail answers.

"That sounds fun," I say digging in my backpack for my lunch.

"You can come, but we know you have practice," Katherine adds.

"Actually I don't," I say, pulling out my lunch and setting down my bag.

"You don't?" they both say.

"What happened?" Abigail asks.

"I don't have practice on Tuesdays anymore because I changed teams," I explain.

"So you are officially on Level 6?" Abigail questions.

"Yeah, and they workout on Monday, Wednesday, Thursday, and Saturday."

"You passed the tryouts!" Katherine squeals, "Why didn't you tell us?" she asks.

"Because I wasn't sure. But I think it will stick. I'm not going back to Level 5." James is right, optionals is a good place for me and I shouldn't go back to Level 5, even if I don't compete in January.

"Well, that's cool," Abigail says. "You have Fridays off now," she points out.

"And you can come over today! Oh please, you never hang out with us anymore," Katherine pleads.

She's right. I don't see these two as much as I did when I was younger. I always eat lunch with them but outside of school I have been spending most of my time with my gym friends. "I'll ask my mom when she comes to pick up Jason and me."

Satisfied they both go back to picking out music for their dance they plan to create this afternoon.

When school is out I find Jason and we stand on the edge of the curb waiting for our mom to pull up. When we see her I walk up to the passenger window, "Can I hang out at Katherine's today?" I ask.

"Oh, pumpkin, that would be great!" I frown, she's a little too excited. She thinks I spend too much time with my gymnastics friends and worries that they are not my age.

"You know the Level 7s are my age," I sass.

"I know Paige. It's just that school friends are important, too."

I open the door for Jason and tell him I'll see him in a couple of hours.

"I'll have Dad get you on his way home," my mom says. I nod and shut the door. Then I turn back to find Katherine waiting for her mom.

When her mom pulls up all three of us pile in the car and Katherine and Abigail immediately start chattering about who they got paired up with in science. My mom is right; it is good to have school friends who are my age. The thought makes me feel a bit like a traitor to my gym friends. They are good friends, even if they are younger.

When we get to Katherine's house her mom says she needs to finish up some work and tells us to help ourselves to a snack. Then she disappears with her laptop. Katherine opens the pantry while Abigail takes a seat at the kitchen counter. I follow her lead and take a seat next to her.

"Do you have Oreos?" Abigail asks.

"No we ate those yesterday," Katherine says, leaning into the pantry. She's standing on one leg with her foot against her ankle.

"Graham crackers?" Katherine offers.

"No," Abigail decides, clearly comfortable in Katherine's house.

"Oh, here are some Pop Tarts in the back!" Katherine exclaims and comes out of the panty with a box of Pop Tarts.

"Are you happy you got paired up with Quinn?" Katherine asks Abigail as she opens the foil packet.

"Yes and no," Abigail answers. "I'm glad I get to talk to him every day, but it's a little stressful to do projects with him. I mean, what if I mess up?"

"You're supposed to do the projects together. There's nothing to mess up," I point out.

"I guess," she says. "But I want him to know I'm smart."

"Of course he knows your smart, you've known him since kindergarten," Katherine points out.

"It's different now," she says.

I'm not sure I understand how it's different. We have all known each other forever at St. Mary's. Of course Quinn knows Abigail is smart and is probably happy to be her partner because she is nice and funny, too.

Katherine puts the pastries in the toaster and taps her fingers on the counter while she waits.

"Who did you get paired with Paige?" Abigail asks me.

"Trey," I answer.

"Oh my gosh, Trey is so cute!" Abigail gushes.

"Yeah," I agree. "We've been friends since second grade. Doing the projects together will be easy."

"You should make him your boyfriend," Katherine says, handing us each a Pop Tart on a napkin and turning to put one in the toaster for herself.

"How do I do that?" I ask.

"I don't know, just ask him, I think," she answers.

"That would be weird. And it might make him feel weird and then our projects wouldn't be easy," I decide.

"Then Abigail you ask Quinn," she directs.

"No way, he can ask me," Abigail determines. "Besides, you go first. If you know how all this works, you get a boyfriend first and tell us how it goes down."

Katherine is quiet as she pulls out her snack from the toaster.

"I'm just not that interested in anyone at our school," she deflects and I start laughing.

"What! What's so funny!"

"Of course you are. You always have been. You're just as scared as we are on what to do about it," I call her out in a way my teammates would do. Straight forward and to the point.

She walks over to the family room just off the kitchen and plops into a stuffed chair. "It's just that I have cramps so bad I can't see straight much less think about what to say to a boy."

"Cramps from what?" I ask. They both turn and look at

me like I'm crazy. "It's not like we've done any exercise today; not even in PE. We just learned about the rules of badminton."

"Are you serious, Paige?" Abigail says, recovering first.

Suddenly I feel embarrassed that I don't know what they're talking about. I'm not sure if I should pretend I know what's going on or come clean that I'm confused. I decide to stay quiet and see what they say.

"Paige," Katherine says, sitting up, "have you not gotten your period yet?"

Ohhh! That's what they're talking about. Duh, how did I miss that? "No, not yet."

"Might be a while, you're so thin. Isn't that, like, a thing for gymnasts?" Abigail asks.

"I don't know," I answer. I really don't know; all of my teammates are younger than me. I guess my old teammates are younger than me. Some of my new Level 6 and 7 teammates are my age. I wonder if I'll ever be close enough friends with them to ask them when they got their period, or if they have gotten it yet.

"I think it's a thing," Abigail repeats. "I got mine the summer between 5th and 6th grade."

"Wow," I say. That's so young. I had no idea she was dealing with something so grown up.

"Don't worry Paige, you're not exactly that far behind. I just got mine six months ago," Katherine explains. "My mom says that's why the cramps are so bad. Because my body is still getting used to it."

"What does it feel like?" I ask.

"It's huuuurts," she moans rolling to her side in the chair and tucking her feet up.

"Like a stomachache?" I ask.

"No, like a dull ache all over my tummy and back. I don't know how to explain it," she says. "I'm so glad we

29

didn't really do anything in PE. That would have been impossible."

"Why?" I ask.

"Because I just don't want to move. I want to sit right here and not move," she declares.

How the heck am I going to do gymnastics when I get my period if I'm not going to want to move? Hopefully Abigail is right and it's a gymnast thing to not get your period.

"It's not that bad for me," Abigail offers. "Everyone is different. For some reason I don't have hardly any cramps and my period is only a few days," she shares.

"Lucky," Katherine says.

Abigail regards her for a moment and then asks, "What are we going to do if all you're going to do is sit there?"

"We could paint our nails," Katherine suggests. "I have some new colors; one that's iridescent."

"I'll get them," Abigail says leaving the room to go get Katherine's stash of nail polish.

"What can I do?" I ask, seeing that Katherine is truly in pain.

"Why don't you get some paper towels so we can paint our nails right here and I don't have to move."

I nod and go to the kitchen and grab the entire roll and bring it back to the family room where Katherine is sitting. Abigail comes back with a shoebox full of nail polish.

We have a great time picking colors and painting each other's fingernails. I try the iridescent one. It turned out to be gray that shimmers purple when it's in a certain light. I can't wait to show it to my teammates. Katherine went with dark blue and Abigail did hot pink with sparkles over the top.

By the time my dad texts me that he is out front, Katherine and Abigail have moved on to their toes.

"My dad's here," I tell them and stand up and go over to

my backpack.

"Oh, bummer. We'll get to your toes next time," Katherine announces.

"Sounds good," I say, slinging my backpack over my shoulder.

"Bye guys, feel better Katherine," I say.

"I will," she says, admiring her toes.

"See you tomorrow," Abigail says and I head out.

I climb into the car and my dad asks what we did.

"Painted our nails," I say holding out my gray iridescent fingernails.

"Wow, so trendy," he says surprised.

I admire my fingers, "They are, aren't they?"

CHAPTER 5

I'm having a great beam work out. All the other girls are working routines since they have an intrasquad soon. Even Lucy, Savannah, and Alexis have a beam routine. They are doing what Katie calls a routine A with a back walkover and when they stick five of those, they do three of routine B with the back handspring in it. Savannah and Alexis have their back handspring on high beam with a few mats stacked underneath. For now, Katie is letting them do their routines with the mats or on the medium beam.

My assignment is five back extensions rolls on high beam and round-offs on low beam. Today I feel ready to take my round-offs to a higher progression. I was so caught up preparing for Level 5 State Meet the last few weeks that I haven't had much time to focus on the round-off. I was doing them on low beam without really realizing that they are ready to go up to either the medium beam with mats or the high beam with mats. When the mats are stacked up they seem the same to me.

I ask Katie if I can try them on a high beam with mats. "Do them on the medium beam since the girls are running routines on the high beams," she answers.

"Okay, can I have mats?" I ask.

"I don't think you need to, but do whatever you need to do to feel comfortable," she replies and turns her attention back to the high beams.

"I can help you," Brooklyn offers.

"Thanks," I say, surprised at the offer.

"I need the medium beam too and mats would be good," she says.

"Are you already done with routines?" I ask her.

"No, but I will be done with my five A routines soon and I need the medium beam to warm up my new series," she explains.

"Is the series in your B routine?" I ask her as we walk over to the stack of 8-inchers over at floor.

"Yes, I really want to compete it this season," she adds.

"What is your current series and what is the new one?" I ask her.

"In my A routine I do a back walkover back handspring. My B routine has a back handspring series," she says.

"Seems like they are both hard but I bet once you get one you'll get the other," I comment as we pull off a mat and start dragging it over.

"Sort of, the back handsprings are just faster, which can be scary if you're off at all," she shares. "I see you're working round-offs. I think you'll be the only one on the team doing those."

"Yeah, I can't do back handsprings," I admit. Rather than asking me why, like most people do, she just nods in understanding as we slide the mat under the medium beam.

"Do you want one more?" she asks me.

"I kind of do," I hesitantly admit.

"Good, me too!" she says, making me laugh. We walk back to the stack of mats and drag one more over. "You compete back extension rolls, right? They seem way harder than a round-off," she points out.

"Seems like it," I agree. "It was my only option in Level 5 since I couldn't do back walkovers. The round-off feels easier, but I think if I don't make it, the falls are going to be worse."

"Totally," she agrees as we straighten the second mat under the medium beam. With two mats under the beam there is about a foot of space under it, making a round-off on the medium beam doable. "Who's up first?" she asks me.

I hesitate for a moment. Brooklyn is quietly eyeing the beam. "I can go," I say, and slowly climb up. She nods and goes over to a low beam to warm up her series. I stand up on the beam, walk to one end, turn around, and take a breath. I raise my arms and all I can see is the space between the beam and the mat. The mats aren't high enough to completely keep me from crashing. It's not like I can step down to them. "Maybe I need one more," I mumble and drop my arms.

"You can do this Paige!" I hear Katie yell over to me from three beams away. I look over at her not convinced at all that I can do it. "Think about the hand placement and twisting right over the top of the beam."

I look back at the beam. No getting out of it now, my entire new team is watching to see what I'll do. I raise my arms again and decide to go. I think about my hands and popping to my feet. I land with one foot on and I fall to the side onto my feet on the mats below. My heart is pounding so loud in my ears. I did it!

"Who-hoo!" I hear Savannah yell.

"That was high!" Brooklyn adds.

"Way to go for it," Alexis says.

"Thanks," is all I say as I climb back up. I want to go again before I lose my nerve.

"I did my round-off on the medium beam!" I exclaim as I open the car door and get in. "Oh I forgot," I say, shutting the back door and deciding to sit up front. I'm finally big enough to sit up front with my mom.

"No fair!" I hear Jason yell as I get in the front.

My mom ignores him and says, "That's great pumpkin. Is that one of the skills you need by the end of the year?"

"No, but I think I can compete it if I get it. I'm not clear on what things I'm working that are required for Level 6 skills versus what skills are nice to have. But Katie seems to know all of it. I'm sure she'll tell me as we get closer."

"Seems like we're pretty close," my mom muses as she turns out of the parking lot.

"And I almost did bounders today on floor!" I continue, not deterred by my mom's comment about the time crunch.

"What's a bounder?" she and Jason ask at the same time.

"A front tuck right into another front tuck," I answer.

"I was able to do them onto a mat today. I mean, I landed on my bum, but I did them."

"Do you think you'll be ready in six weeks?" my mom asks.

I turn my head and smile at her. "I really do! Optionals is so much easier for me. Well not easy, but not as impossible as compulsories felt sometimes. I can play to my strengths. I can avoid doing anything that requires shoulder flexibility. James said it would be better for me. He was right. He's always right."

"Well, good. Because Katie emailed me today and asked

if you could stay after on Saturday or come in on Sunday to get a floor routine."

"Yes! You told her yes, right?"

"I told her I would talk to you. A week ago you didn't even know if they would have you on the team. I didn't know what to say," she admits.

"I know. But now I finally get what optionals is all about and I think I can do it. Can I get a routine mom? Please?"

"You're sure this is what you want to do? It's a much bigger commitment. Increasing from nine hours a week to twelve is a lot," she reminds me.

"It's what I want," I confirm.

"Okay. I'll email Katie back and see what time Melony can meet with you."

"Thanks Mom. If you weren't driving I would hug you," I say, making her laugh.

When I walk into the training room on Thursday I see James is standing with Katie on the floor waiting for us.

"Are you coaching us today?" I ask him as I walk up.

"Yes indeed. There are no compulsory girls in the gym on Thursdays so I help Katie with optionals," he explains.

"You never get a day off?" I ask.

"I get mornings and Sundays off," he offers. "Except on meet days."

"Where are my girls?" Katie mumbles, referring to her upper optional girls I saw running upstairs as I was walking in. I assume they are taking their time getting grips on. I know the upper optional girls start before we do and end after we do. I wonder how long their workouts really are.

"How long are they here?" I ask her.

"The 8s are here four hours, the 9s and 10s for five," she answers.

"Wow, and I thought coming for three hours at a time was a lot. I get hungry after only three hours."

"Bring snacks and eat them when you put your grips on," Katie says absently before walking away. Presumably to go tell her girls that their break is over.

"Hi ladies," James says, greeting Maya and Victoria. "Why don't you start running. The others can catch up."

We run in silence as the rest of the team trickles in. The gym seems different without any compulsory kids here. There are more rec kids in their absence.

"Come stretch over here, so these classes can get started," James says to us. We follow him to a corner of the floor and start stretching. "We will stay on this half of the floor and start with pit tumbling and then come back to floor for routines at the end of practice." This statement gets a loud groan from the girls. "I don't know what to tell you. The entire floor won't be open for a while. It's good conditioning to see how you throw a set at the end of practice anyway." The girls are silent and I'm glad I don't have a routine yet.

He tells us each what pass we are working into the pit and which pass we are to work when we get out of the pit and tumble back the other way. Most of the girls anticipated what they are to work and give him a quick nod and line up.

"Half of you line up here and half at that end so it rotates smoothly," he instructs. Then he turns to me. "Layouts into the pit and punch, punch, punch fronts headed back. The mat is already there for those who need it."

"Okay," I agree and I get in line to tumble into the pit. For my first turn I just do a round-off back handspring in front of the pit to get my steps. Then I do the punch front drills on the way back. They are hard for me and I land the punch front on my bum. On my second turn tumbling into the pit James tells me to do the back tuck. Since I had to compete a round-off back handspring back tuck in Level 5, it's not a problem to do it into the pit.

"That was a little lower than usual, wait for the set," James corrects me as I climb out of the pit. "Do you want to do a layout on the next one?" he asks me.

I'm a little hesitant to do a layout after only one warm-up, but I realize I have some serious catching up to do if I'm going to compete so I nod yes.

"I'll spot," he offers.

"A big spot?" I ask, as I climb out of the pit and stand next to him.

"I guess it has been a while since you've done these. Was it the summer?" he asks me and I nod. Once the Level 5 season started last September, we stopped working Level 6 skills and focused on Level 5 routines. "Okay, big spot it is. You'll be fine. Nice tight set and pull your toes instead of your knees," he instructs.

"Toes," I say.

"And stay hollow," he adds.

"Toes and hollow," I repeat, and walk over to take my turn on punch fronts.

"Aubrey, are you twisting this one?" he yells over to the next teammate in line.

I'm thinking about the layout when I do my punch fronts and, of course, land on my bum. I'm going to have to learn to focus on more than one skill at a time. This group works hard and moves fast.

I get back in line for my turn at the pit and I watch Lucy do a beautiful layout with a tiny quarter turn at the end. I watch James laughing and talking to her. My guess is he told her to try a half twist and she was a bit cautious on her first attempt. I can't say I blame her. Then I watch Victoria do a layout with a half twist and I can see what James was trying to get Lucy to do.

It's my turn and I repeat James' corrections in my head before I take my turn. Tight, set, toes, hollow. The same thing as the back flip, just a little straighter.

"Layout!" James yells to me and I nod.

I run, do a round-off back handspring, set, pull my toes and I try to stay hollow but I feel like I'm not flipping very fast. I can feel James' hand on my back lifting me up and helping me flip. I panic that I'm not going to make it around so I bend at my hips in a pike position, which then speeds up my rotation and I over rotate into the pit.

"The first half was right, why did you pull it into a pike?" James asks me.

I struggle to sit up in the foam squares. When I finally do I answer him, "It felt so slow."

"It was a little, but I had you."

"I don't remember it being so slow last summer," I admit.

"It probably wasn't. You've grown a lot, so it's going to flip slower unless you set better," he replies.

"What?" I ask, as I stand up out of the pit.

"You need to set better," he repeats.

"No, about the growing."

"Paige, you've grown at least two inches in the last four months. Layouts are a straight body, so the taller you are, the slower it flips. It's just physics," he adds, unconcerned. "Are you twisting?" he yells to Aubrey who is waiting for me to get out of the way to take her turn.

It's just physics, I think as I step out of the way so Aubrey can take her turn. It doesn't feel like physics. It feels unfair, I think as I watch petite Aubrey do a perfect layout full.

CHAPTER 6

"Oh my gosh, I finally feel better," Katherine says, plunking down in a chair across from me at lunch. This time I know what she's talking about.

"It lasts that long?" I ask, surprised and curious.

"Like three days that are impossible, and finally today I no longer have cramps. I'm still having my period. I'll be done by Sunday," she says, pulling out her lunch.

"A week then," I summarize.

"About a week," she agrees.

"I'm so glad it's Friday," Abigail says walking up. "I hate when teachers give homework on Fridays," she complains as she sits.

"You should be used to it by now. This place always assigns weekend homework," Katherine comments.

"What are you guys up to this weekend?" I ask them.

"Making up a dance tonight for dance company tryouts. You should join us," Abigail exclaims.

"Yeah, Paige. You used to be so good at making up routines with us. Didn't you say you don't have practice on Friday's anymore?" Katherine points out.

"I don't have practice," I say slowly.

"Yay!" Abigail cheers.

"But I was planning to go to PNO," I add.

"Remind me what that is. I remember you told us, but I forget," Katherine says.

"It stands for Parents Night Out. The parents drop off the kids and the kids play on the equipment for the evening," I explain.

"Sounds kind of babyish. I mean, aren't you allowed to stay home alone now that you're in seventh grade?"

"Well, yeah, I can stay home alone. I don't go just so my parents can have a night out. I go because it's fun to play on the equipment and work skills I don't usually get to work."

"You've been there all week. Don't you want a night off? You could hang with us."

"Pu-leese. Your choreography is the best! We miss it!"

I have been at the gym three days this week, which I am used to. Tomorrow I have my first Saturday morning practice for a new fourth day. Maybe I should rest up for the morning.

"Maybe," I say. As I start to cave, I remember Trista, Marissa, and Carmen. I promised my former teammates I would see them at PNO.

"Don't look so glum. I promise we're fun," Abigail says, noticing my torn expression.

I look up and smile, "I know. You guys are great. I would be lost at school without you."

"You'd be eating by yourself, that's for sure," Katherine teases.

"No, she'd probably get Trey to come over here and eat with her."

"What?" I say, surprised she pulled that name out.

41

"He's your lab partner, right?"

"Oh, yeah. Yeah he is."

"I've seen how he looks at you."

"Ooh, we can text him tonight and see if he likes her."

"Let's stick to making up a dance," I suggest. Thankfully, this redirects their conversation away from Trey and back to their dance tryouts.

It probably would be good to have a break before tomorrow's practice. I wonder if Alexis, Savannah, and Lucy are going to PNO tonight or if they decided to rest too? If I skip PNO, how am I going to explain my decision to my gym friends?

"How's the new level going anyway?" Katherine asks me.

"Good. I have a new coach for part of the time, so that's weird," I admit.

"It's more hours?" Abigail asks as she pulls out a baggie of cookies.

"Yeah. I went from nine to twelve hours a week," I say proudly.

"So are you exhausted?"

"So far it feels the same because I've only gone three days this week. Tomorrow morning is my fourth day."

"So you can't sleep over?" Abigail asks.

"Probably not," I confirm.

"Man, I think you should ditch gymnastics and do dance with us. There's more time to hang out."

"Not if we were good like she is. We'd have that many hours if we made the dance teams we tried for last fall," Abigail points out.

"You guys are good," I laugh. "We'll create something amazing for you tonight and you'll make this team."

When I get home from school my mom has to immediately take Jason to soccer practice. Well, not that immediately because he takes forever to find his shin guards and indoor soccer shoes. Usually, I go with my mom to take him and then she drops me off at practice. I don't have Friday practice anymore so I decide to stay home.

Once they're finally gone and I hear the garage door close, I flop into an overstuffed chair. It's kind of nice not having practice on Friday. I sit down and realize my body is tired and sore from working new skills all week. The house is so quiet. I wonder what I should do. I don't want to do homework just yet; I have until Sunday night anyway. Maybe I'll read.

I hear my phone ping from inside the front pocket of my backpack. Thankfully my bag is leaning against my chair and I don't have to get up. I lean over, unzip the front pocket and pull my phone out. It's a text from Trista's mom, which probably means Trista since she doesn't have her own phone yet.

> Mrs. Thompson/Trista:
>
> Hi Paige, Trista here. We are not going to Open Gym after practice. We're going to grab dinner and head back to PNO. Can't wait to see you!

Oh man, I have to tell her I'm not going. I really am torn. On the one hand, I want to see Trista, Marissa, and Carmen. But on the other hand, I don't want to be worn out for tomorrow's practice and I want to hang out with Abigail and Katherine. What do I say? I hold the phone, wondering what to reply.

Me:

Not going tonight, maybe next week.

Then I stare at the phone. I can't imagine Trista will take no for an answer that quickly.

Mrs. Thompson/Trista:

What?! Why?

Me:

Tired, big week.

The minute I send that excuse I regret it. Trista will be mad if she finds out I lied or am not telling the whole truth.

Mrs. Thompson/Trista:

I heard you need to pick out floor music choices. We can just sit and do that? Not wear you out? We have some ideas for you.

Me:

Sounds fun, but I told school friends I would hang out with them.

I stare at the phone and no reply comes back. I know I just hurt her feelings. I'm the one that told her nothing would be different and that we'd see each other at PNO. And here we are at the very first PNO since our team split up and I'm already blowing it off.

My phone continues to be blank, making me feel incredibly guilty. I want to make sure she's not mad at me so I send her one more text:

Me:

What floor music did you have in mind for me?

I hold my breath waiting for it to ping back. When it does I feel relieved.

Mrs. Thompson/Trista:
>Ballet music. Fancy music.

Her answer makes me laugh out loud.

Me:
>You mean classical?

Mrs. Thompson/Trista:
>Yes. From a ballet. Wanted you to hear it tonight. I can have Savannah's mom email it to you.

Me:
>Okay. Thanks Trista.

Then I think to add.

Me:
>You're a good friend.

Mrs. Thompson/Trista:
>Yeah, yeah. Have fun tonight. See you Wednesday.

Wednesday is the only day we are in gym on the same day. I set my phone down and lean back in the chair. This stinks. Why can't we all move up together like in other sports? I notice Jason's team all moves up together with their grade level. I feel my eyes flutter shut and I realize I really am tired from this week. Then I hear my phone ping again. I pick it up and look at it. It looks like I got an email. I open up my emails and see it's from Debbie, Savannah's mom. That was fast. Trista is probably at Savannah's house right now.

I open the email and see there are three music files. I open the first one and it is beautiful, classical, and fast. I don't know if I can move that fast. There's an annoying part in the middle where someone says 'sample' over the top of the song. I have to listen a few times to hear the music during the interruption. I click on the second one. This one sounds similar, but not as fast. It sounds like it's from the same song, but a different section. I click on the third one and it is a recognizable Nutcracker song. I giggle, Christmas music would be kind of fun. But I think I like the first two. I glance up and read Debbie's message:

> Paige,
>
> You are such a beautiful dancer we thought these songs would be perfect for you. I can tell your mom what website to buy them from if you like any. The first two are from Swan Lake and the last one is from the Nutcracker.
> Debbie

I had the Nutcracker one right. Swan Lake; I think I like those two the best. I listen to all three of them again. Maybe Abigail and Katherine can tell me what they think. Although, it just won't be the same as my gymnastics friends weighing in on which music they like for me. They know where the tumbling passes would be and what kind of dancer I am in gymnastics. I sigh, maybe I should go to PNO. I hate this.

My mom comes in from the garage, "Are you going to PNO tonight pumpkin, or do you need to rest?"

"I don't know," I moan.

"Maybe you should take a break from the gym tonight so you can have a good practice tomorrow," she reasons as she shrugs out of her coat. "Man, am I glad it's Friday."

"Am I supposed to bring music?" I ask her.

"Oh yeah, Katie emailed me a few days ago. Sorry pumpkin, I've just been so busy. You know how it is this time of year." My mom is a graphic designer for a marketing company. Every year she says all her major holiday projects will be done by Halloween, but they never are. "She gave us some websites where we can listen to samples," my mom continues. "You're supposed to bring your three favorite and I guess you decide with Melony tomorrow. And did you know you are staying after practice tomorrow? To work on the routine?"

"That part I knew. I didn't know I had to bring music choices. Debbie knew though," I comment.

My mom laughs, "That woman knows everything."

"She even sent me some songs I might like."

"That was nice. She's probably been listening to music for Savannah for months," my mom says.

"Yeah, probably. They're pretty cool. Here, listen." I play one of the Swan Lake songs from my phone.

When the song is done my mom says, "Oh Paige, that is beautiful. It would fit you perfectly."

"It might," I agree, "But can you give me the website and I'll listen to some of the other choices at Abigail's tonight."

"Sure. You're going to Abigail's?" she asks.

"She and Katherine are hanging out and asked if I could come. Can I?" I think to ask a little late.

"Of course," she smiles, pleased I'm not ignoring my school friends like I did all summer and fall.

47

CHAPTER 7

I arrive at Abigail's house with my phone fully charged and the website bookmarked so we can listen to floor music. They are dancers; they can weigh in.

I knock on the door and hear "Come in!" I hesitantly open the door.

"Hello?" I yell as I poke my head in.

"Back here!" I hear Abigail yell. I walk all the way in, past the entry way and kitchen and into the living room beyond that. I find Abigail and Katherine standing in front of a phone that is set up on a stand and facing them at almost their height.

"Hey Paige! Maybe she could record us. Would that be better than the stand?" Katherine asks Abigail.

"Not necessarily because people bounce and shake and get funny angles. Plus if we keep the stand she can join us."

"Join you for what?" I ask.

"We're doing a TikTok video," Abigail explains.

"With the dance you made up for tryouts?" I ask.

"No, we haven't even started that yet."

That surprises me as I sit down behind the camera. "Aren't tryouts on Wednesday?" Maybe I have the week wrong.

"Yeah, plenty of time," Katheryn says as she walks up to the phone. "Okay, ready?" she asks Abigail and she nods.

She touches the phone and music comes on. Katherine backs up to stand next to Abigail and they start dancing in place. Their upper body is moving, but their feet are planted. It is the oddest-looking stand-in-place dance. I can feel a giggle bubbling up and I cover my mouth so I don't interrupt their video. A few seconds later they stop.

"That's it?" I ask, surprised at the brevity.

"We could go longer but TikTok likes short videos," she explains.

They immediately crowd around the phone to see their recording. They talk through the parts they like and don't like and then decide to try again. I watch them record the dance three more times, and honestly, all three versions look the same to me. But on the last one they squeal with delight that they nailed it and they happily post the video.

"Let's pick another one so Paige can join us," Katherine says, scrolling through her phone.

"Actually, I was hoping you guys could help me."

"Sure, what is it?" Abigail asks.

"I have to pick floor music by tomorrow," I say excited. They both blink at me and I realize they have no idea what a big deal this is. I have waited years to get my own unique music. "It's a big deal. The first time I get to pick. Can you just listen to a few with me?"

They nod and sit down on the big fluffy couch with me. I find the website and look at the menu. "There are tons here. Where should we start? Show tunes, hip hop, jazz, classical, soundtracks."

"Hip hop," Katheryn says. I click on the hip hop button and a huge list of songs come up. I start reading them off and the girls recognize most of them and ask me to play several. I select one and hit play. The instrumental version of the song comes on and I start trying to visualize how it would look to a floor routine.

"Why does it sound so funny? Why isn't she singing?" Abigail asks.

"It has to be instrumental," I explain.

"Well, that stinks. Her voice is what makes that song rock. Try another one." I click on another song we all know. But with the lack of singing, she's right. The song is kind of flat.

"No, that sounds wrong, too." I click to another hip-hop song and it has the same problem. It sounds all wrong without the artist. "Maybe let's try another genre. One that is instrumental to begin with," I suggest.

I click on soundtracks and these make Abigail and Katherine much happier. But they spend each song trying to guess what movie it's from instead of telling me if it would make good floor music.

"But which one should I pick?" I ask them.

"They're all cool. I like the Spiderman one, but that might be just because I like the movie," Katheryn admits.

"Tom Holland is so hot."

"Right? Did you see that dance he did on YouTube?" Abigail says, picking up her phone and pulling up the video for Katheryn to see.

This is a disaster. They have no idea what they are listening for. Why did I think I could pick out floor music with non-gymnasts? I sigh. I must decide by tomorrow. I don't have time to do this with my teammates.

I think about the email Debbie sent me. My teammates

have already been thinking about my floor music (and theirs) for months. I bet they were listening to music for Savannah when they found songs that might work for me. I can envision Savannah and Trista listening to music endlessly.

"Hey guys, will you listen to one more?"

"Sure hold on." They are still huddled around a phone watching a video. When the video is done they look up expectantly at me.

"Okay, what do you think of this one for me?"

I press play on one of the Swam Lake songs. The girls are quiet as they listen. They are much more captivated than they were with all the other songs. When it is over Katheryn says, "Tchaikovsky's Swan Lake. Pas de deux. A beautiful piece Paige; I think you would rock it," she says in all sincerity.

"How did you know the song?" I ask, pleased she likes it.

"Duh, we have taken ballet for like, ever. And Swan Lake is my favorite ballet of all time. Even though it's kind of weird. I love the music and when all the dancers become swans."

Of course, I should have known they would know a ballet. "You really think I could pull it off?" I ask, playing it again.

They are quiet as they listen again and finally Abigail says, "Totally. That one is perfect for you." I smile to myself. Trista and Savannah knew all along.

We spend the rest of the night scrolling through TikTok, picking out a video to copy, learning the choreography, and recording it. I don't really understand the point but it was silly and fun and made my friends happy.

I am still worried for them that they have to create something by Wednesday but they don't seem concerned about it, so I stopped bringing it up. I'm so used to planning ahead with gymnastics and being the leader with my team that I have to try to step back and just hang out when I'm with Abigail and Katherine.

By the time my mom texts me that she is on her way to get me they are talking about boys and who they should text.

"You know their numbers?" I ask, surprised.

"They're in the school directory," Abigail teases.

"Really?" I ask.

"No, Paige, don't use that! You'll get their parents. We have some numbers from the yearbook signings last year and from asking," Katherine explains.

"Asking? You ask boys for their number?" I ask flabbergasted. I would never have the guts to do that.

"It's helps when your lab partners and you can make up a reason to need his number," Katherine says, teasing Abigail.

"It worked," Abigail a says with a smirk.

I don't know what to say and thankfully my phone pings.

"My mom is here," I say standing up.

"Do you have to go so early? We're just getting to the fun stuff."

"I have practice in the morning," I say, half bummed and half relieved to leave before they start texting boys.

CHAPTER 8

The next morning I walk into Perfect Balance excited about practice. I'm pumped to stay after and work on my floor routine. We run our laps and are stretching when Katie comes up to us with a clip board.

"Who is staying after for floor dance?" she asks. Savannah, Alexis, Lucy, and I all raise our hands. "My newbies, good. All of you need it," she says unapologetically. We know we do. The other girls got their routines in August, when we were starting our Level 5 season. "Anyone else?" she asks looking up. "Madame Julia will be here and the new 6s aren't ready for her. So any of you who can stay and work on the fine details with Julia should do so." Madame Julia is our ballet teacher. She is very picky when it comes to dance execution.

"I can stay," Maya says. A few of the other girls murmur that they will text their parents and see if they can stay.

"I told you guys last week," Katie says, frustrated.

They remind me a little of Katherine and Abigail procrastinating on making up their dance routine when I was there to help them and give new ideas. Now my new teammates have a chance to get help with Madame Julia and they are dragging their feet. I wonder if it's a teenage thing.

"The more you prepare now, the better you will score in January," Katie reminds them and they say nothing. "Keep stretching until James gets here. He'll decide where you start," she instructs. Then she leaves to coach the upper optional girls who have been vaulting.

"James is coming?" I ask.

At the same time Savannah asks, "How early do they get here?"

"Yes, James coaches us on Saturdays," Aubrey answers, "There are no compulsories on Saturdays. And Katie coaches the upper optionals the entire time."

"Unless he's at a meet," Peyton points out.

"Yeah," Aubrey agrees, "but meet season for compulsories is over."

"They get here an hour before us and stay an hour after," Brooklyn answers Savanah as Peyton and Aubrey keep talking about James' schedule.

"Wow," Savanah says under her breath. I can tell this rattles Savannah a little, but instead of saying anything she turns to me and asks, "Did you like any of the songs we picked out?"

"I think I like one of the Swan Lake ones," I share.

"I knew it!" she grins. "That one is perfect for you!"

"Can we hear it! Play it on the gym stereo," Brooklyn encourages.

"It's on my phone," I say.

"You can grab it when we go up to put grips on," she points out and I nod.

"Good morning ladies," James says walking up with a

cap pulled down low over his eyes and coffee in hand. "What event do you want to do first?"

The girls call out four different events and James decides we are starting on beam. I think he already knew that because it doesn't look like he even heard us. I don't care how groggy he is, I'm just happy he's here to coach us this morning. Saturday morning may be my favorite workout of the week.

Saturday morning workout was the worst. Frist of all, we started on beam and my feet were still cold and every round-off stung. James let us stay in sweatpants or leggings, but, of course, we have to have bare feet for beam. Then we went to bars and the cold stung my hands and I got two rips. I haven't had a rip in a long time. James said it was from the increase in hours this week. Apparently my hands aren't used to it. Vault went okay because by then the gym was a little warmer, or I was, I'm not sure which. I never thought about how when we come in after school it is the warmest part of the day in Snowcap Canyon. Mornings here are cold. I'm going to have to wear long sleeves next week.

By the time we get to floor I finally feel warm. Most of the morning recreational classes are over by now and we have the entire floor to ourselves. The upper optionals have been waiting for the floor to be empty, too. I see them come over to floor as we are walking over. Uh-oh James and Katie didn't coordinate and now there are too many of us on one event.

"Five lines!" I hear James yell and that is when I realize we are all going to do floor together. With this many kids? I am supposed to do what a Level 10 is doing?

Wildly intimidated I get in line behind Peyton and I

notice that my former Level 5 teammates all get in line behind me.

"Complex ladies. If you cannot do what I call out, do a modified version."

"Round-off back tuck! For my littles, do either a round-off or a round-off back handspring. The modification is your choice!"

Girls start doing sky high round-off back tucks. *Littles?* We are the littles now. With no Level 1-5 girls present, we are the littles. I look back at Savannah, Lucy, and Alexis and they are tiny compared the rest of the girls lined up. Peyton has taken her turn and I am up. I decide to do just the round-off and, of course, nobody cares. I turn and do a second round-off because I have room. When I get to the end of the floor, I get back in line behind Peyton. I look around at this big group of high-level gymnasts and I have to say, I like being one of the little ones for once.

"Front handspring!" James yells out.

We continue like this for another twenty minutes. Some of the skills James yells out are impossible, but there's always a smaller version we can do. And some of the combinations he calls out are fun to try. When we're done, I'm curious how this many girls are going to train floor. James announces we are tumbling on the diagonal and along two sides for tumbling drills. In addition we are to rotate to the red tumble strip and then over to trampoline. I notice no one is tumbling into the pit today.

"No routines either?" Brooklyn asks.

"Let's take a break from them. Maybe dance throughs at the end for conditioning," he muses.

I know by now to work punch fronts along the side where there is an 8-inch mat set out for us. For my turn on the diagonal I work layouts. Both Katie and James are spotting kids on the diagonal tumbling and I love the different passes the girls are doing. It's hard to work out when you just want to stop and watch.

I rotate to a diagonal corner and take a deep breath. Should I warm-up with a tuck or go straight to the layout? Thankfully James is standing at the other and of the diagonal and he holds up a fist, indicating a tuck. I nod and run and do a round-off back handspring back tuck. It's okay, but it felt sluggish. James must have not noticed because he just nodded and said, "Layout the next one. Let me know if you need a spot."

"I need a spot," I say quickly, making him laugh.

"Okay, do your bounders on the tumble track, front halves on the trampoline, and then come back over here for your layout," he instructs. The multiple stations keep us moving and I'm tired by the time I get back to the diagonal. I wait to catch James' eye and he holds up a straight hand indicating I am to do a straight body back flip, a layout. I nod, take a deep breath, and go. I do a round-off back handspring, and my take-off feels funny. I know better than to stop. I have to keep going and do the best I can. I pull my toes and try to stay hollow. I feel like I'm in slow motion and I'm not going to make it around. Thankfully, I feel James bumping my back, helping me get some height. I still feel low so I bend in the hips and change to a pike position rather than a layout. This change helps me flip faster and get to my feet. I land on my feet with my weight back on my heels. I fall on my bum as James stumbles past me after he sets me down.

"Why'd you pike halfway through?" he asks, coming back to where I'm picking myself up off the floor.

"It felt slow," I say, standing up.

"It was slow, but I had you,"

I nod, feeling silly I piked it. "Why's it so slow?" I ask him.

"Your back handspring is not the best technically so you're going to have to have a great set and nice hollow body to make it around," he says.

"But I've always had a bad back handsprings. This felt different," I try to explain.

James shrugs, "You're growing Paige. You're going to have to work through the changes and learn this skill despite the challenges," he says. His words seem unsympathetic, but his face is looking at me with pity. I have never seen that look before.

"But I've grown before and I never felt this . . . slow," I say.

"Well," he hesitates, "this time your center of gravity is changing."

Then he motions for the next girl to go and I step out of the way. I know I'm supposed to go over and work my punch fronts along the edge. I don't move. I need to know what he's talking about.

Lucy takes her turn doing a perfect layout and I wait for James to turn back to me.

"What's my center of gravity?"

He waves for Savannah to go and says, "Hang on." Savannah does a nice high layout and I'm not sure why James is even standing there for her. He gives her a quick correction and turns back to me.

"So Paige, when boys and girls are children all of them have their center of gravity between their shoulders, right here," he says, pounding a fist against himself just above his chest. "When girls go through puberty their center of gravity moves lower, to about their hips. This can be good on beam, because your balance is closer to the beam. It is not great for floor. You will have to get more height in your set to get your hips high enough for a flip. It's biology and physics."

"Biology and physics," I repeat, surprised by this new

information about my body. Does it really change that much?

"It's also gradual, so you should still be able to do your skills." When I don't say anything he asks, "It has been gradual, right? Not a drastic change?"

"No, not drastic," I agree.

"You are strong Paige. You just have to use those legs and be more technically correct with your set."

"Okay," I agree. "I'll set."

I'm a little overwhelmed by this information but his answer satisfies me enough to walk away and over to my front tumbling. Now I'm behind Savanah and I watch her do a front handspring into a dive roll onto the mat. Then I do my front tuck into a dive roll onto the mat. She waits for me and we walk over to the tumble track together.

I am deep in thought over this center of gravity thing and Savannah doesn't seem to mind the silence. She starts her tumbling pass on the tumble strip. I take my turn doing front tucks. Then we make our way over to the trampoline. I have a great time here attempting front twisting. Soon enough I forget about my problems on the layout until it is time to rotate back to the diagonal.

I wait for James' signal. He is telling me to do a layout again. I take a deep breath and go. This time I think about my set, pulling my toes, and staying hollow rather than bending in the hips. I can feel James bump and catch me.

He nods when he sets me down. "Better."

"Still slow," I complain.

"I know. You're just going to have to work through it."

Through what? Feeling sluggish?

I don't say anything and go over to my front pass. My front pass is feeling weird too, although not as odd as the layout. Maybe back tumbling just isn't my thing.

The rest of floor is the same. I don't have a bad work out; I just feel like I'm not improving. Maybe I'm just tired

59

because this is my fourth workout this week and I'm used to only three. Either way, I'm glad when James announces it's time for conditioning. As we start conditioning Melony comes over and pulls me, Savannah, Alexis, and Lucy from the group to work on our routines.

She turns to my teammates and says, "Do five of each leap pass to warm up and then do five of each dance section. We will run dance throughs after I am done here with Paige." They nod and get to work.

"Do you have music choices?" she asks me.

"I have three, but I'm hoping you like my favorite one," I share.

"Let's hear it," she says. I pull up the email, click on the song, and hand my phone to her. The Swan Lake song comes out tinny on my phone but I see Melony break into a big grin.

"This is perfect for you," she says as she turns up the volume. "Madame Julia is going to love it," she adds.

"I like it better than the others," I repeat. She hands the phone back to me.

"I'd still like to listen to your other choices," she says, handing the phone back to me.

I pull up another song and hand her my phone. It's the other Swan Lake song. "This is similar, what's the third one?"

I reach over and click on the Nutcracker song. "Oh, I love this!" she exclaims. I stand there nervous that she's going to make me use the Nutcracker song when I like the Swan Lake one. She is intently listening to the song and I am holding my breath to see what she says. "Beautiful choices. I could create something for you from any of them. You pick," she says handing back the phone.

"Really?" I say relieved.

"Of course, you're the one that's going to have to listen to it a thousand and one times."

"Pas de deux then. The first Swan Lake one," I confirm.

"Perfect timing!" Melony exclaims as Madame Julia walks up. "Listen to Paige's music," she says, playing Swan Lake again.

Madame Julia listens quietly and then says, "Perfect for Paige, the dancer *and* gymnast."

"I agree," Melony says. Then she instructs Madame Julia on who she will be working with. "Maya is here to work with you and I think Brooklyn has stayed, too. They both need work on making everything in their dance bigger."

Madame Julia nods and goes over to where Maya has been working turns.

Melony looks at me, "Let's pick out your leap pass," she says.

Melony has me try several different leap combinations to see what I'm best at.

"When your split leap gets to 180 degrees it will be so pretty with your toe point," she comments.

We finally decide on split leap, split jump. Then she leaves me to work one and a half turns in front of the mirror while she helps my teammates with their dance. Turns are much easier for me than the leaps. I do turns until I have rug burns on the ball of my foot.

"Melony, do you want me to work something else?" I ask over to where she is helping Savannah with a dance sequence she doesn't seem to be getting.

Melony looks over to me and says, "You can be done for today. I will have some of your routine ready for you on Monday." I nod and walk over to Alexis.

"Are you about done?" I ask her.

"I think so. Either way, my mom is going to be here soon because we have to drive to a basketball game that is a few hours away." Alexis has four brothers. All of them except Drew play basketball and baseball. Drew is a gymnast like

61

us. I search the gym and see Drew on the trampoline. He must have been here all morning. First with the boys' team and now just hanging out waiting for Alexis.

"Okay you four," Melony says walking over to us. "You can be done for today. Work on the dance at home. Paige, work on your splits." Then she looks around at the empty gym and adds, "Stretch while you wait for your parents."

We talk a little in our splits as we wait for our parents. My teammates are excited about my music and for me to get a routine.

"Trista is going to be excited when I tell her you picked one of the ones we picked out," Savannah says.

"You guys listened to a lot didn't you?" I guess.

"Tons. And whenever we heard the classical stuff we thought of you."

"Thanks, I really like it. I didn't think I was going to score out of Level 5 so I wasn't listening to music at all."

"They've got your back," Alexis pipes in. "Debbie has been listening to music since Savannah was a Level 3," she teases.

Savannah laughs good naturedly and then says, "Turns out it was a good thing."

"Yeah, totally," I agree.

When I get home from practice I flop into a chair in the family room. I am so tired. Beyond tired.

"Do you want some lunch?" my mom calls from the kitchen.

"Not really."

She walks into where I'm sitting and looks at me for a moment. "You look beat."

"I feel beat," I agree.

"Level 6 is hard, huh?" she comments.

"Yeah. But it's more fun. I get to work different skills."

"Why don't you go lay down and rest. You can eat after a little nap," she suggests.

I would like to just sit right here. Unfortunately, my brother bounces in with a stack of cards and asks if he can do a magic trick.

"I think Paige is going to rest," my mom says saving me. "Why don't you perform the trick for me?"

He runs over to her and tells her to pick a card. I drag myself out of the chair and up to my room before Jason sees I'm gone. Now that my mom mentioned it, a nap sounds like a good idea. I don't know why I'm so tired. Today's workout wasn't that much harder. I didn't even do conditioning. Usually I workout three days and go to PNO. This week I did three days plus Saturday morning. It's not that different, so why do I feel so drained? I walk to my room and fall onto my bed. I don't even bother changing out of my leotard and sweats. I roll to my side, pull my blanket over myself, and drift off instantly.

When I wake I don't know what day it is. I look out my window and see afternoon light streaming in. Oh yeah, it's Saturday afternoon. I sit up, or evening? How long was I asleep? I reach over and turn my nightstand clock toward me. Four o'clock. Wow, I slept for several hours. My head hurts from being in a ponytail all day. I reach up and tug the rubber band out. My red curly hair sprays every which way. I run my hand through my hair, making it feel better but probably making my hair crazier.

I hear my stomach rumbling and realize I'm starving. I wander down the hall and find my mom doing laundry.

"Well hello sleepy head. Do you feel better?" she asks.

I nod. "I'm hungry."

"I'm sure you are. We had turkey sandwiches for lunch. I made you one and put it in the fridge," she says, reaching into the washer and moving clothes to the dryer.

"'kay," I say and shuffle off to find the sandwich. I make my way down to the kitchen. The house is quiet which means Jason is probably playing video games. I yank open the refrigerator door and find a plate with a sandwich sitting under plastic wrap. I pull it out along with some orange juice. Then I search the pantry and find a mini bag of chips.

I sit at the counter and slowly eat my lunch. My mom comes down a minute later and pours herself a glass of juice.

"I got an email from Melony saying I needed to go online and buy your music," my mom comments.

"Yeah, we picked my music today."

"That's exciting, can I hear it?" she asks.

"It's on my phone," I look around. I don't even know where I dropped my gym bag. I still feel a little disoriented. "Why am I so tired?" I ask my mom.

"This was a big new week," my mom answers.

"Not really, my practices were still three hours each. I feel spent." I try to explain.

"I think you're growing." She comments.

"Why does everyone keep saying that?" I ask in frustration.

"Nothing to get frustrated about; you're twelve. This is when kids have growth spurts," she comments, unconcerned.

"I don't want a growth spurt," I pout, making my mom laugh.

"Of course you do. You don't you want to be 4'10" your whole life," she points out.

"Maybe I do," I grumble. "At least a little while longer anyway," I qualify.

"Let me hear your music again," my mom says, smartly changing the subject.

"You already heard it and I don't know where my gym bag is," I huff.

"I'd like to hear it again. You bag is by the door where you dropped it," she comments as she takes a sip of her juice.

"I don't feel like getting it," I snap at her. Why am I being so rude?

My mom looks at me over her cup. She nods and walks out of the room. Now I feel like a jerk. The worst part is that I want to share my music with my mom. I think she'll like it. Now what do I do?

I get down from the counter and go over to the front door to where my gym bag is flopped on the ground; just where my mom said it was. I rummage through and find my phone. I wander around the house until I find my mom folding laundry in her room.

"Mom," I say and she turns to me but doesn't say anything. I tentatively walk in farther. "I'd like you to hear my music," I say.

"I'd like that too" she says, pairing socks together.

"Sorry I was a jerk," I add.

She looks at me, holds my gaze and says, "Thank you."

It's an awkward silence for a moment and then she adds, "Paige, I know you're going through a lot with the new level, growing so fast, and trying to juggle school. But no matter how hectic things get, you still need to respect your mom."

"I know," I say, and I do. I honestly don't know what came over me.

She nods satisfied and picks up another pair of socks and says, "Let's hear it." I smile and scroll through my phone to Debbie's email. I find the right Swan Lake song and play it.

"I think that will fit you really well," she comments.

"I do too," I agree. "I bet Madame Julia will even help me put in a few real ballet moves," I speculate.

"We have to buy it?" she asks. "To get a version that

doesn't say 'sample' right in the middle?"

"Yeah, Savannah's mom sent the link and everything. After we buy it, we have to email the download to Melony and she will put it on the gym phone," I explain.

"And you're sure this is the one you want?" she asks me. "You listened to other choices?"

I smile, "I did. And I'm sure."

CHAPTER 9

It's the week of Thanksgiving so I only have school Monday and Tuesday and practice Monday and Wednesday. I'm hoping I can work on my floor routine this weekend. Melony got the music from my mom and said she would start creating something right away. She is aiming to have a routine for me by the holiday weekend. We usually go to my Aunt Jennifer's farm for the Thanksgiving weekend. Maybe Melony will finish it and I will have time to learn it before we go out of town. Sometimes my birthday falls on the Thanksgiving weekend. I haven't looked at a calendar, I wonder if it does this year.

"Why the frown?" Katherine says to me as she plops down at the cafeteria table across from me.

"I was just wondering about our Thanksgiving plans this weekend," I share.

"We're skiing," she says. "We're staying in Park City for the entire weekend. My favorite part is the hot tub on the back deck."

"You're getting a hot tub?" Abigail asks, having caught only the last part of Katherine's sentence.

"No, we're going to a cabin in Park City with a hot tub," she clarifies.

"Lucky. I'm going to my grandma's house in Oregon," Abigail shares.

"That sounds fun," I say, wondering why she sounds bummed.

"It can be. But it can also be boring. She doesn't allow electronics so we have to, like, do puzzles and play board games the entire time," she complains.

"Not even movies?" Katherine asks in horror.

"Yes, movies, but only in the evening and everyone has to decide together so no guarantee the group picks a good one."

"Geez that's strict," Katherine says.

"Four whole days. At least my cousins can be cool," she admits.

"What about you, Paige? Are you going to the farm?"

"I'm not sure this year," I say slowly.

"What's not to be sure about?" Abigail asks me, taking a bite of her sandwich.

"I think I need to stay and work on my floor routine. Or rather, learn my floor routine," I explain.

"You can't take one weekend off?" Katherine asks.

"It doesn't seem like a good idea. I'm so far behind. All the other girls, including the other new Level 6s, have their floor routine. We have a mock intrasquad this Wednesday that I can't even participate in. By Christmas I'm supposed to be ready at a real intrasquad."

"That's a month away," Abigail points out.

"Is it a lot to learn in a month?" Katherine asks, trying to understand.

I nod, "It feels like it," I say.

"What do you have to get? Don't give me that look. Abigail and I did gymnastics before we decided to focus on dance. We aren't totally out of it," she reprimands me.

"Okay, I have to get my floor tumbling passes, my dismount on bars, and . . . and I guess that's it," I realize as I think about it. My vault is a Tsuk timer, which is really just a half-on. On bars I need to learn the flyaway from a cast, on beam I can keep doing my back extension roll, and on floor I need a layout. I'm not sure if I'm doing the bounder this season or not. I should talk to James or Katie. Or whoever is making my routines because I should know this.

"That's not that bad; you could take a Thanksgiving vacation to your aunt's farm," Abigail decides.

Maybe I could. Then again, everything in gymnastics is harder than it seems. At least for me.

The rest of the school day drags along. Teachers are frantically wrapping up units before we go on break. I keep thinking about the skills I need and how maybe I'm closer than I realized. I think I'm feeling behind because I don't have routines yet. Whenever beam or floor routines are assigned, I'm given a separate assignment. That brings me to the very reason I should stay, to learn my floor routine. I wonder if I can stay; I haven't even asked my parents. Would my entire family miss Thanksgiving so I can learn a floor routine?

When school gets out I find Jason at our usual spot. We stand by the curb to wait for our mom along with tons of other kids. It seems chaotic but the pick-up line is fairly organized. Cars roll up in the inside lane, pick up kids, and move to the outside lane. The cars have the last name of the children in their visor and as the car rounds the corner a teacher announces the name in a microphone and those kids run up to the front of the curb to be picked up. Our mom is later than usual to pick us up and I see her car round the corner before our name is announced.

"Green!" we hear as I take Jason's hand and walk to the curb. My mom pulls up and we quickly climb in. We know to chat after we're seated and buckled since she has to pull away from the curb quickly to let other parents in.

Since we're a private school, there are no buses. Every single kid has to be picked up in a car. Unless they walk, but very few kids live nearby. Most of my classmates are scattered all over the Salt Lake Valley. I'm lucky Abigail and Katherine live close to me. I think that's why we became friends. Our parents were able to get us together outside of school because we live near each other.

When we're finally leaving the parking lot my mom says, "How was your day?" I stay silent knowing Jason will answer.

"We got a classroom lizard!" Jason exclaims. "No one can decide on a name. I think it should be Lizzie."

"Your poor teachers," my mom says.

"Nuh-uh, they love it. Lizzie already likes my teacher the best. We vote on a name Tuesday. Is tomorrow Tuesday?" he asks.

"Yes. Tomorrow is Tuesday. You have school and then we're on break," she adds.

"Then I think we get a party tomorrow too," he says.

"Yes you do. Remember, you're having a Thanksgiving dinner at lunch. I have to send you with cranberries," she reminds him. Then she turns to me. "Are you doing anything in homeroom for Thanksgiving?"

"No, they don't do anything fun in seventh grade," I sulk.

"Oh, pumpkin, it's hard to grow up," she teases.

"When are we leaving for the farm?" I ask.

"After work on Wednesday. You're going to have to

watch Jason on Wednesday while we're at work."

"When do we get back?"

"Probably Sunday afternoon so I have time to do laundry and settle in before another week of work begins."

"What about practice?" I ask.

"You can miss practice or we can leave right after practice."

"But when am I going to get my floor routine?" I ask, starting to panic. I know I was just thinking everything was going to be fine, but now I'm frustrated no one asked me about this trip.

"When we get back. The gym is closed anyway," she says.

"Not for optionals. It's never closed for optionals."

She turns and looks at me, surprised. "Do you have practice?"

"Well, no. I don't know. I mean, I thought Melony said she was going to have my routine ready."

"And it will still be here when we get back. Paige, it's four days. What's the big deal?"

"The big deal is I'm so far behind!" I cry.

"I doubt that. Melony said you were doing great."

I huff, not sure what to say. "Well, I feel behind. The girls are doing an intrasquad on Wednesday and I'm the only one not participating because I don't have routines."

"Paige, we knew this would be a push. You decided to fast track and go straight from Level 5 to Level 6. One month ago you thought you were going to be in Level 5 another year. Give yourself a break. Be realistic," she adds.

Be realistic. I think about that silently as we drive. Jason changes the subject back to himself and tells us that he did a magic trick at recess. He's not supposed to bring his magic supplies to school, but clearly he did. My mom must not be listening too closely to him because she hasn't gotten mad at him yet.

"Let's talk to Melony or Katie, or whoever we need to after practice today, okay? See what they think. If they think you need to stay maybe we can work something out."

"And make all of you miss the farm? That's not fair!" I yell.

"Paige, you are testing my patience."

I slump in my seat, "Sorry." I say. I really am sorry. I want to go to the farm and enjoy Thanksgiving. I also really want to learn my floor routine so I can catch up.

"How far away is the farm?" I ask, thinking maybe we can go back and forth.

"Two and a half hours," she says, giving me a sideways glance that says, 'I am not driving you to practice that far away.' "Let's just see what Melony says about your routine today."

"Okay," I agree.

"Maybe we should have talked to your coaches sooner. I didn't really know what to expect when you started training with the optionals group. I didn't know you would want to do the intrasquad. It all seems so fast."

"Yeah," I agree. "I think that's why some kids, like Marissa, are waiting until next season to do Level 6."

"How are Savannah, Lucy, and Alexis dealing with it?" she asks me.

"They all scored out before I did, so they had time to learn floor and beam routines. Honestly the skills aren't a big change from Level 5 to Level 6. I think they'll be ready on Wednesday," I explain.

"So it's mostly the routines that you need to learn?" she asks trying to understand.

"I forgot my cards at school! Turn back!" Jason yells.

"Jason, I told you not to bring your magic toys to school," my mom chides.

"Turn back, please!" he begs.

"They'll be there tomorrow. And if they're not, then that's a good lesson for you to leave that stuff at home," she says, unbothered by the crying that has started in the back seat.

I can't stand it! "I have an old deck," I tell him.

His crying stops, "You do?"

"Yes. You can play with it tonight," I promise him.

"You spoil him," my mom whispers to me as the wailing stops.

Maybe. I need him to be on my side if I ask my parents not to go to the farm this weekend.

Chapter 10

At practice that night we start on beam. After a short complex we are assigned five stuck routines and then work B skills with any left-over time. Katie calls me over, presumably to give me my non-routine assignment.

"The intrasquad is tomorrow. Obviously you will not be able to do beam or floor since you don't have routines yet. But you can do vault and bars if you would like?"

I see she is waiting for me to answer, "I don't have a bar routine either," I point out.

"You can just do the Level 5 bar routine without the tap swings or the baby giant. You can add a sole circle or something if you want."

"I . . . I've never done a flyaway out of a cast," I remind her.

"You did it in the pit on to a mat last week didn't you?"

"Yeah, the pit. Not on the competition set."

"You are just off of season, which means you're still

conditioned for a full bar routine. Just do a small cast into the dismount and I can spot you through the flyaway," she reasons.

I'm silent so she adds, "Or James can spot you."

"He'll be there?" I ask hopefully.

"He coaches compulsories on Wednesday, but I'm sure he can come over and spot you. And he coaches you guys on bars today as soon as the 3s are done with practice. You can try it then. I know you're used to James and that I'm pushing you pretty fast." I don't say anything so she finally wraps up her crazy idea with, "We can see how today goes and then decide."

"Okay," I agree.

"And your Tsuk entry is a no-brainer. You can do that tomorrow."

"Yeah," I agree. That I can do. One event. I guess that's better than nothing.

"Stick five back extension rolls, leaps, jumps, turns on high beam and then stick five round-offs," she instructs, abruptly turning my attention back to beam.

I nod and move to go to a beam that is open. "Oh and Paige," she calls back to me. I turn and wait. "Melony said she has a beam and floor routine for you. If you're in town you can learn both this weekend."

I don't know what to say so I nod and continue to the beam and jump up. *If I'm in town.* Do I ask my family to stay in town just for me? That seems crazy and Jason would never forgive me. He loves the farm and the horses and our cousins. So do I.

I reach up and do a back extension roll and, shockingly, I stick it. I could rarely make these a few weeks ago. But I made it at State Championships and something clicked. I can make them a lot now.

"Those are so pretty," Brooklyn comments from the end

of the beam where she is waiting for a turn.

"Thanks," I say and step up to do another one.

"I've never seen anyone except you do those on beam," she adds.

"That's because most people can do a back walkover," I remind her, but I am secretly happy with her compliment.

It takes me almost the entire work out to stick five of everything. I feel good about all of my beam skills. All I need to do is string together my skills with some dance and I'll be ready for the next intrasquad.

After beam we rotate to floor and, like beam, everyone is asked to do one full routine, two dance throughs with runs (for conditioning) and three of each pass. Katie has to call me over again for my own assignment.

"Four of each tumbling pass and three of each leap pass and your one and a half turn."

"Um, Katie?"

"What are my tumbling passes?" I ask, feeling super dumb, but I really don't know. I can't do bounders yet, or my layout. I'm not sure if that means I can't compete floor until I get those skills or if I compete easier passes that I can already do.

"Round-off back handspring layout or tuck for your back pass and front tuck for your front pass," she answers.

"Front tuck? I can do just the tuck for an entire pass?" I ask.

"You can. I'd like you to get that bounder as soon as possible, but the front alone is fine for now," she explains.

"It seems easier than Level 5," I point out.

"In some ways it is. Some kids don't stay in Level 6 very long," she comments.

I watch Lucy tumble by with a huge layout, "Like Lucy," I comment.

"Like Lucy," she confirms.

"Look Paige, you are going to do fine in Level 6 once you get your routines. James says you catch on to dance faster than most kids. You'll be doing routines just fine. You basically have all of your skills. We just need to get that layout on bars and floor and you are good to go."

"It just feels so close," I admit.

"I know we are pushing you fast, but it's that or wait an entire year and I think that you would get bored," she shares. I nod in agreement. "Work bounders after you're done with your assignment." With that I know she is done talking and needs to spot some of the girls on their tumbling passes.

I get started with warming up my layout pass first. I start with back tucks and when I am ready to do the layout I ask Katie to spot. I've never had Katie spot me before and I am nervous. I stand on the corner and tell myself it is exactly like having James spot. Except she is so much smaller. Can she really bump me up the way James does? I run and do a round-off back handspring back tuck. I feel Katie bump me and I go way higher and rotate much faster than usual. I'm not ready for the landing. I can feel Katie grab my waist to help me on the landing, but I have too much rotation. She sets me down and I fall back to my bum with a bounce.

"I thought you said you were doing a layout," she says confused.

"I did. I meant to," I stammer as I stand up.

"You have to commit to a skill before you go or you'll hurt something," she says.

"Okay, I promise," and she nods and turns to her next tumbler. I'm just glad she doesn't know that I changed it because she was the one spotting.

I do my front tuck in the other diagonal and my leap pass along the edge of the floor. Then I stop and wait while Aubrey does a floor routine.

The 7s seem to know her routine and know when they

can leap or tumble around her.

"Sixes, watch and learn her routine so you don't have to stop while she is going!" Katie yells out to all of us.

When Aubrey is done, it's my turn to do another layout. Katie sees me in the corner and motions for me to go. I know she knows she needs to spot me but since she doesn't do the hand motions like James I yell, "Layout?"

She nods and motions again. I know I can't stand here all day. Girls are standing behind me waiting to tumble. I take a deep breath and decide to do it this time for real.

I run, do a round-off back handspring, set, and pull my toes instead of my knees. I feel Katie bump me and I try to stay in a tight hollow position. I see the ground and feel her catch me just before I land.

"Beautiful Paige!" she says as soon as I land. I grin; it felt good! "Keep doing it like that and you will be doing them on your own in no time," she adds.

"Thanks," I say. I'm able to finish my floor assignment and I'm relieved I don't have to have the bounder to be able to compete. I think I may actually be able to pull off Level 6 this winter.

After floor we head up to the optionals room to put on our grips. It's still weird to go upstairs and walk past the Kip Club Cubbies. I see Trista, Carmen, and Marissa's names and I'm little sad to not be on the same team as them this season. I look up at the optionals door and remember that Level 6 and 7 train together, so likely we will all be together again next year.

We go to our lockers and have a quick snack as we pull on our grips.

"Are you going to try your flyaway without the taps?" Lucy asks me as she opens her locker door.

I feel my stomach tighten, "I don't know. I mean, I want to do something besides vault. I just don't feel ready," I admit.

"This gym is more about pushing you than waiting for you to be good and ready," she points out.

"Good and ready sounds nice right about now," I pout.

"Trust me, sometimes waiting stinks, too."

"Yeah, I guess so," I concede.

She shuts her locker door and has one grip on and the other in her hand. "On the flyaway, just do a tiny cast and pretend it's your third tap swing. It only gets scary when you do a giant cast into it. A big cast is harder to control."

"Pretend it's my third tap swing," I repeat.

"It worked for me when I was first doing them," she says pulling on her second grip.

"She's right," Brooklyn jumps in. "Do a small cast at first. Katie will throw you through it if you don't have enough height."

"So you're doing vault and bars tomorrow?" Savannah asks.

"Vault for sure. I'm undecided on bars," I tell her.

"You'll catch up," is all she says as she puts her empty grip bag in her locker. "Especially on floor and beam."

I don't know what to say to her vote of confidence, but I appreciate it. Maybe I will catch up on floor and beam once I have routines. The girls start filing downstairs to go to bars. I'm excited, nervous, and not at all sure how my bar workout is going to go.

After practice Melony has called the new Level 6s, Alexis, Savannah, Lucy, and I, into her office to order competition leotards. I'm giddy as I walk in. I did my flyaway out of a cast. Okay, it was a baby teeny tiny cast, but still I swung down and let go. Thankfully James was coaching bars because I was much more likely to go for it with him. I am starting to trust Katie, but maybe not enough for my first flyaway out of a cast. Anyway, I did it! As long as James spots me in the intrasquad on Wednesday I will be fine.

"Okay, girls, Katie is busy coaching the upper optional team so she asked me to help her order comp leos for you. These are the child large," she says pointing to a pile of long sleeve leotards sitting on her desk. "These are adult extra small," she gestures to a few laid over her chair, "and this one is adult small, which probably only Paige needs to try this one." I look up when I hear my name. Why am I being singled out as needing the biggest size? Then I look at my young teammates. They are only fifth graders, of course I'll need a bigger size. Still, I feel so large these days.

"Try on what you think is the best fit and I want to see it before we order," she instructs.

Alexis, Savannah, and Lucy grab for the first two piles and I grab the one adult small to see how it will fit. I don't remember what size my last leo was. I think a child large, but come to think of it, it was getting pretty tight.

"Are optionals still getting the leo with the one snowflake on the side?" Savannah asks.

"Yes, Levels 6, 7, and 8 get that one; 9s and 10s change every couple of years. They've worked hard to get where they are so we like to let them switch it up more."

Savannah nods and then we all file out to go up to the locker rooms to try on our sample leos. I listen to the three of them try on one size and then swap and try on another and then trade back again.

I'm standing in my adult small that fits perfectly, ready to go down and show Melony. "You guys better decide on something to go show Melony," I say.

I watch them swap sizes again and finally they are ready to go down with me. The sample leotards are black on the bottom with swirls on top. In my opinion, they aren't nearly as pretty as the Perfect Balance snowflake leos.

When we get to the bottom of the stairs and walk into the office, Savannah's mom is there talking to Melony.

"Hi girls!" she greets us. "Don't you four look darling in those leos!" she exclaims.

"Come over here so I can see," Melony instructs us. We walk over and she immediately says to me, "That looks perfect Paige. How does it feel?"

"Good. Better than my old one," I admit.

"Is it the small or extra small?" she asks in front of everyone.

"Small," I croak feeling so much bigger than my teammates.

Melony jots my size down on a piece of paper and moves over to tiny Lucy. "This may be a little baggy on you. What size is it?" she asks her.

"The child large," Lucy says, making me feel gigantic.

Thankfully Savannah's mom, Debbie, turns to me, "I hear you're getting your floor routine this weekend."

"Maybe. Well, I don't know," I stammer.

"Melony says it's done. I imagine you will want to learn it as soon as possible," she points out. She's not wrong. That would be best.

"We might be going out of town," I share.

Her eyes widen, "Really? When you are trying to pull together four new routines in six weeks?"

"Mom," I hear Savannah say to her mom in a warning tone.

"What? I'm not trying to be rude. It's a lot for anyone." Then she turns to me, "Paige, honey, if you want to stay with Savannah and I over the holiday we would love to have you.

I can bring you here Friday, Saturday, Sunday, whatever you need," she offers.

"Really?" I ask, surprised at her generosity. "What about Thanksgiving?" I ask.

"Oh, don't worry about the holiday. It's just going to be Savannah, me, and Savannah's grandma. You would make it a perfect four. We do a simple turkey dinner and watch movies."

I stand there thinking about it. It would be great to learn my routine this weekend. Then again, I would be bummed not to be with my family for Thanksgiving or my birthday. I'm pretty sure my birthday falls on Thanksgiving weekend this year. I need to ask my mom.

"Melony, when would you be able to work with Paige?" Debbie asks.

Melony is examining Alexis' leo and absently responds with, "Any day except Thursday," she says, tugging Alexis' sleeve.

"You can do Sunday, right?" Debbie asks, knowing that some people in Utah don't work on Sunday.

"Yep, Sunday is fine. Alexis you are between sizes so let's size up to the adult extra small."

Debbie turns to me and says, "You could work on it a couple of times!"

I nod, warming up to the idea.

"Talk to your mom and let me know," Debbie says when I don't say anything.

"Okay," I agree.

My mom and Alexis' mom both come into the office and Melony starts talking to them about our new competition leotards. Mainly they are discussing price and Melony takes their credit cards. A few minutes later Lucy's mom comes in and Melony goes through the entire process with her.

"Custom leotards usually take six weeks. If they are late

the girls can start the season in their Level 5 leos."

As the girls and moms select sizes, Melony makes a note of what she is going to order each girl. When it's my turn to make a decision with my mom Melony jots down my size and then looks up. "I have a floor routine for Paige. Are you guys in town this weekend so she can learn it?" she asks my mom.

"We are out of town this weekend."

"I told Paige she can stay with me," Debbie offers, jumping into the conversation. She sees my mom's confused expression and explains more. "I can take her to the gym Friday and Saturday to work on it. Sunday if she needs it."

My mom turns and looks at me questioningly. I don't know what to say so I give a little shrug. "That's a very sweet offer, Debbie," my mom says. "We'll talk about it as a family tonight." That answer seems to satisfy Debbie and the moms go back to talking about a book McKell, Lucy's mom, was telling them about.

When we finally get out of the gym and into the car my mom instantly says, "You don't want to miss the farm, do you?"

"I don't know," I admit.

"You love the farm," she says quietly.

"I know," I agree.

"Your birthday is on Friday this year," she says.

"It is?" I ask. That makes missing the farm so much worse.

"You are okay missing both?"

"I don't know," I say, feeling so very conflicted.

CHAPTER 11

After a lot of deliberation, and my dad going nuts that I would consider missing Thanksgiving, we finally come up with a compromise. We are all going out to the farm today after practice as originally planned. We will have Thanksgiving tomorrow with Aunt Jennifer and Uncle Justin's family, play on the farm Friday and Saturday, and then Saturday afternoon my mom and I are going to drive back to Snowcap Canyon. I will work on my routine with Melony on Sunday morning. I'll get to be with my family for my birthday before my mom and I come back early.

Melony said the Level 6 routines are short and I could probably learn it in one day. I'm happy with this compromise because I get the best of both situations. I get to spend most of Thanksgiving at the farm and still get my floor routine over the weekend.

Today is an easy workout since we are doing the practice intrasquad. There are no judges today, just Katie. It's still stressful to do new routines in front of all of your teammates. I feel a little lame that I am only doing two events.

We aren't competing in Olympic order like we would at a meet. We're rotating how we normally would in practice, which means beam first. While my teammates warm up on the high beams Katie tells me to work on my skills on low beam.

"Oh, Paige, I was thinking about you last night. If you don't get your round-off on high beam you're going to need a series. Try handstands right into your back extension roll."

"I thought I could just do my back extension roll if I don't get a round-off," I say, confused.

"It's not a flight skill. You need either a series or a flight element," she quickly explains and turns back to her athletes warming up on high beam.

I need a series or a skill in flight. Optionals is complicated. How would I do a handstand into a back extension roll? I decide to try it on the out-of-bounds line along the edge of the floor. I kick up into a handstand, then I step down making sure to step down with my feet together so I can go right into my back extension roll. My back extension roll is a mess, but I connected it. I try again, this time making sure the handstand is straight so my back extension roll is straight. Almost! This is kind of fun.

I do a few more and Katie tells me to take them to low beam. I nod and go to a low beam that already has panel mats on either side of it. I do the handstand just in front of the panel mats so my back extension roll is at the mats. It's much harder than on the line on the floor. I sigh, this is going to be as hard as the round-off.

Before I'm able to do another one Katie calls us over to give us our order for routines. Of course, she does not name me since I'm not doing a routine. I know I am expected to sit and watch my teammates perform their routines.

We all sit in a row on a low beam facing the high beams. Riley is waiting by a high beam to salute Katie. I watch as she salutes and begins her routine. I notice she does a back walkover back handspring. A series and a flight skill. I wonder why she isn't Level 7. Maybe another event is holding her back.

I watch the rest of the Level 6s closely to see what they have in their routines. Riley and Victoria, the two returning Level 6s, both do a back walkover back handspring. Alexis and Savannah both do a back handspring and Lucy does a back walkover back walkover. Lucy will replace that series with a back handspring soon.

Aubrey, Brooklyn, Peyton, and Maya, the Level 7s, all do a back handspring series. I'm definitely the outlier doing back extension rolls and round-offs. On the one hand I think it's kind of cool my routine will be different. On the other hand, I understand it means my skills are harder. I don't have a lot of choice; my shoulders will just not allow my hands to get close enough for a back walkover or back handspring on beam.

Katie comes over and talks to us about how the beam rotation went. There were several falls and she talks about how we just need to 'put in the numbers' meaning we have to do a lot of routines in practice so we don't fall in meets. Then she tells us to grip up for bars.

I head upstairs with my teammates to get my grips. I'm extremely nervous for bars. I look out the parent viewing window as we pass it to get our grips. I see James on floor with the Level 4s and 5s and I hope I can pull him away to spot me on bars.

I need to remember to do a small cast and pretend it's the third tap swing like in Level 5. I remind myself this over and over as I get my grips on and follow my team back downstairs. We warm up with push away kips as usual. Then

86

we each do a first half, last half, and one routine.

When I am ready for my last half I ask Katie if I can call James over to spot me on the flyaway. She nods and then yells over to him. Melony is coaching with him so he can leave for a moment.

He comes over to the bars, stands under the high bar, and nods to me. "Out of the cast?" he asks, double checking what he is spotting. "Yes, out of the cast. No baby giant, just kip, cast, flyaway," I answer.

"Piece of cake," he says, stepping closer to the high bar. I kip, squat on, jump to the high bar, and do my long hang kip. *Small cast*, I think as I cast out of the kip and push away to swing down into the fly away. *Just like the third tap swing.* When I see my toes come up I let go and I feel James' hand on my back as he bumps me up harder than usual. Even with the bump I barely make it around to my feet. I land short and take a few huge steps forward.

"That was a little too small," James comments.

"But too big makes the tap swing feel out of control," I counter.

"Too small and you won't make it around," he points out. I sigh and nod. "You'll find the sweet spot. Call me over on your full set," he says and walks back over to floor. I watch him go and feel dumb that I have to have him come over here at all. I should be able to have Katie spot. Not today though. Today is enough new stuff and Katie doesn't seem to mind.

When it's my turn again, Katie calls over to James. He trots over and asks, "Full set?" I nod and he gets into place under the high bar. He motions for me to go. I begin my very basic Level 6 routine. Kip, free hip, kip, squat on, jump to high bar, long hang kip. I'm too nervous to cast bigger like James said, so I cast about the same as last time and I do a flyaway about the same as last time, too.

After I take my huge step forward James says, "Fix it next week. For today you are good enough to do a routine in the intrasquad." I smile with relief.

"Paige, you're fourth up," Katie says to me.

"Okay," I agree and walk over to the chalk tray. I watch as the rest of my teammates finish warming up. I start getting nervous as I stand and wait.

"Let's have you guys sit over here," Katie says gesturing to a panel mat sitting on the floor near the bars.

"Can I pull one more over?" Maya asks and Katie nods.

We all sit in a row on two panel mats and I see Savannah is first and Lucy is chalking up. I watch as Savannah does the same routine as I do with higher casts, clear hips, and a strong layout flyaway. Then Lucy does the same routine, only she pops up to handstand on her casts using the straddle up way James taught her.

Then Katie and Aubrey move the bars slightly farther apart for Riley, Victoria, Alexis, and I. Alexis does a clean routine and then it's my turn. As soon as James is ready Katie salutes me.

"You've got this, Paige!" I hear someone, maybe Maya, yell as I salute back. I'm glad I get to do this routine. I jump into my kip and begin. I do a clean kip, clear hip, kip, squat on. I don't even hit my feet on floor as I swing under for my second kip. I jump to the high bar and swing into a long hang kip and start thinking about my cast. *Not too big, not too small.* I cast a little higher than I meant to, but I'm able to pike my body and slow down my swing a little. *Third tap,* I tell myself and when my feet come up, I let go. I can feel James spot me lighter than before, but I land just fine. I finish and turn to salute Katie. Then I look up at James to see him beaming.

He gives me a high five, "Nice Red."

He tips an imaginary hat to Katie and runs back over to

his Level 4s and 5s.

I did it! I walk over to sit on the panel mat and Victoria gives me a quick high five as she passes me to the chalk tray. I sit down and Savannah whispers to me, "That was a great flyaway."

"Thanks shrimp," I say, using an old nick name. I notice it makes her a little red and I realize maybe I should ditch that nick name and just call her Anna like everyone else.

I see Katie salute Riley and I watch as she does our same routine, only she swings almost to handstand out of her casts and clear hip. And, of course, her flyaway is a layout. Victoria's routine is similar.

Then we watch the Level 7s. Their routines are similar except they have added giants. That looks like a really difficult skill and I'm glad I have at least another year before I have to worry about it.

Brooklyn finishes out our rotation with a beautiful bar routine complete with giants and stalder swings. We are told to put our grips away and go to vault. I'm happy that I'm doing vault and bars today. At least I'm doing half the events which feels a little more like I belong here than just doing one event. Mostly, I'm happy bars is over and all I have left to do is a half-on entry. Then I can sit back and watch my teammates' floor routines.

We quickly warm up vault with two sprints and two vaults. Then Katie puts us in order by size and vault so moving the equipment is easier for her. This puts Alexis and Savannah first. They don't seem to mind as they both do half-ons, or Tsuk timers. I know both of them are working Yurchenkos, but that is a harder entry and my guess is they're not ready yet.

I do my half-on after Alexis and then we watch Lucy and the returning Level 6s and the Level 7s all do Yurchenko entries. That vault looks crazy hard and I'm glad my shoulders make it so I never have to do that vault. For once, I'm grateful for my impossibly tight shoulders.

The girls are excited as we rotate to floor. Floor is where optionals is really fun. I'm familiar with my teammates' routines by now, but it will still be fun to sit and watch them.

"Paige, I want you to work back tucks and front tucks while they warm up," Katie instructs. I nod and join my teammates in the corner of the diagonal. They have been instructed to do two of each pass. I will tumble until the rest of my team is ready to compete.

I get in three of each pass before the rest of the team is ready. Katie tells us where to sit and the girls line up in order of competition. I sit at the very end since I'm not competing. As I watch Alexis walk onto the floor and wait to start her routine I feel better than I did during beam. I successfully did two routines today. More than that, I know when I get a floor routine, I will be a strong Level 6 on floor. I'm good at dance and floor has always been my best event. I wonder what Melony has come up with as I watch Alexis' pretty Beauty and the Beast routine.

Alexis finishes and Riley pops up. I watch Riley, Victoria, and Savannah closely. All of their routines are very different and I'm pretty sure Melony created all of them. She's good. She knows how to tailor the routine to the individual girl. I can't wait to learn mine on Sunday. I happily watch the Level 7s perform. Like Level 6, their routine is only two tumbling passes. The big difference is that their tumbling passes are harder.

"Do they have the same routine as last season?" I ask Riley who is sitting next to me on the other side of Alexis.

"Yes, we keep the same routines for Level 6 and 7. Of course, they change for Level 8 because upper optional routines are so much longer," she explains.

"They look good," I add.

"Yeah, they're ready," she agrees.

That is what I need. To be ready.

CHAPTER 12

As soon as practice is over I hurry out of the gym as quickly as possible. My family is driving to my aunt's farm tonight and we are going straight from my practice. I jump in the car and my brother thoughtfully hands me my tablet.

"Thanks," I say, taking it from him. It's not that my tablet is that important to me, but it's the ultimate gift from my brother. He loves video games and since my mom limits his time each day, he loves road trips.

"We can play the entire drive," he reminds me. I nod and try to hide my grin.

I buckle up next to Jason and notice my mom isn't in the front with my dad. "Where's Mom?" I ask.

"She went up early since we needed to drive two cars anyway," my dad replies.

"Why do we need two cars?" I ask.

He glances at me in the mirror and says, "So you can go

back early on Saturday."

"Oh," I say, feeling bad I'm inconveniencing my parents so much. "Can I have something to eat?" I ask him.

"Right here," he says, passing a plastic container back to me. I open it up and find my mom's fancy macaroni and cheese. I breath in the smell and realize it's still pretty warm. It's a little messy in the car but I manage by holding it up under my chin. I am starving. Why am I so hungry? I can't seem to get the food in fast enough.

"How was the intrasquad?" my dad asks.

"Good," I say around a mouthful of food.

"Did you do vault and bars?" he asks, knowing that bars was a maybe going into the day. I nod since I'm chewing. Without a word he hands me a bottle of water and I take a long drink.

"I'm so hungry!" I exclaim.

"I see that. Maybe we need to send you with a bigger snack," he suggests and I nod in agreement. "You're growing," he comments with pride.

"When do we get there?" I ask.

My dad chuckles, "That's supposed to be Jason's line." I look over at Jason engrossed in his game and I know I won't hear a peep from him until we get there. "The weather is clear so it should only take us a couple of hours," my dad answers. When I don't say anything he adds, "Mom said they have a big surprise for you for your birthday." I love when my birthday falls on the holiday weekend. I get to spend my birthday with my cousins. It's like a 4-day birthday party instead of one afternoon.

"I wonder what it is," I comment.

"Thirteen is a big deal. I bet Jennifer went all out," my dad guesses.

I smile thinking about that as I finish the last of the pasta. I set the container at my feet. Then I lean back in my seat and look around. I guess I can't read because it's dark. I pick up my tablet and plug in my earphones. I decide to listen to music and watch the videos. As I relax into the seat I feel extremely tired. I find myself unable to keep my eyes open any longer.

When I wake up I'm in the car and Jason is still playing games next to me.

"Are we almost there?" I ask.

"Yes, only about five minutes," my dad answers.

We arrive only a few minutes later. I get out of the car and start grabbing bags while my dad has to break the news to Jason that we arrived and he has to stop playing games.

My aunt bursts open the door and my cousins come flying out behind her. I see my mom step out onto the porch, happy to see we made it. Chloe and Noah barrel toward us for hugs, Grace is a teenager so she hangs back and waits for the commotion to die down before she greets us.

At age eleven, Chloe is a year and a half younger than me. Noah is the youngest at age nine, a bit older than Jason. They hug all of us before we can get to the steps of the house.

I look up at my Aunt Jennifer and Uncle Justin on the steps of their idyllic farmhouse. It's white with a porch that wraps all the way around it. Since it's dark all we can see are the front steps, the front door, and a swing just to the right of the door. But I know from coming here before that the deck wraps all the way around and there is nothing but fields on all sides with a view of the massive Rocky Mountains from the back.

"Welcome to the J&J Ranch," my aunt says, giving me a hug. "You've grown!" she exclaims stepping back to take a look at me. We haven't seen them since early summer. I haven't grown that much since then, have I?

I hug her back and when she moves to Jason I greet Grace. She is a year older than me and she has fiery red hair like mine, only hers is straight. Our parents loved to take pictures of us together when we were babies because the color of our hair was so similar to each other and unusual from everyone else.

"Hi Grace," I greet.

"Hey," she says without much emotion. I don't take offense to Grace's greeting. She is shy. She likes horses better than people. By tomorrow she'll be talking. Once she remembers she likes us.

"Let me help you with your bags," Uncle Justin says, going to our car and lifting bags out.

"Grace, show the kids to the bonus room," Aunt Jennifer instructs.

Whenever we are here all the kids sleep on the floor in the bonus room. Not that there isn't enough room in their bedrooms, we just like to all be together. I grab my bag and follow Grace even though I know exactly where to go.

Once we are settled in the bonus room and my parents are settled in the guest room, Aunt Jennifer invites us down for milk and cookies before bed. This is an unusual treat for Jason and I and we immediately accept.

There's a lot of chattering going on in the kitchen at once. My mom asks me about the intersquad and I fill her in on my two events. My dad is talking with my aunt and uncle about their new horse, Noah is talking to my brother about doing archery tomorrow, and Chloe starts telling me about new kittens.

"New kittens?" I ask, perking up.

"Yeah, sometimes the cats have a litter in the fall. It's rough on the babies, but they are in the barn, so they should make it through the winter."

"How many?" I ask.

"Five."

"I'd love to see them," I say.

"Tomorrow," her mom interjects. "You can feed them at first light."

"How did she know what we were talking about?" I ask.

"She hears everything," Grace answers. "Best to be quiet." I look at Grace and nod. Maybe that's why she likes to be quiet.

"What is new with you?" I ask Grace.

"Eighth grade sucks. But other than that, the new horse, Marshmallow, is cool."

"I can't wait to see her," I say, sincerely.

"It sounds like you guys have a big day planned. Finish up your cookies and let's get to bed."

I finish my cookies, put my milk cup in the sink, and follow the kids upstairs. I'm used to just Jason and I in the house. The five of us feels a little chaotic.

By the time we get in our jammies, teeth brushed, and sleeping bags out I'm exhausted. The boys have decided to sleep in Noah's room, probably so they can sneak games, which is fine by me. I'll have time to catch up with Chole and Grace.

"How's gymnastics?" Chloe asks, fluffing her pillow and settling in for the night.

"Good. Hard, but good. I'm in a new Level now," I share.

"That's cool. It looks scary. Is it scary?" she asks.

"Sometimes," I admit. But then I think about the sport they are into and I add, "No scarier than jumping horses I suppose."

They both like this comment as we lay down in our bags. We are too tired to say much more.

"Kittens in the morning," Chloe reminds me.

"Kittens in the morning," I agree. "Good night."

They both say good night and I quietly look up at the ceiling. I'm glad I didn't stay back with Savannah and her mom. Being here and thinking about something else for a moment feels good.

CHAPTER 13

I wake up to light streaming in through the front windows of the house. The bonus room is empty. Chloe and Grace must be up.

I get up and rummage through my bag to find fleece lined jeans and a waffle long sleeve shirt. I know I'll be outside today. I also know it will be cold. After I dress I head downstairs to a bustling kitchen. My mom and Aunt Jennifer are busy preparing for our Thanksgiving dinner.

"Happy Thanksgiving, pumpkin!" my mom exclaims when she sees me.

I rub my eyes and mumble Happy Thanksgiving back. "Where is everyone?" I ask.

"The dads are feeding the horses, the boys are feeding the dogs, and the girls are waiting for you to go feed the kittens."

"Oh. I'm last up?" I ask, a little embarrassed.

"You must have needed the sleep. Your mom has been

telling me how hard you've been working on your gymnastics."

"It has gotten hard, but I like it. Where are the girls waiting?"

"They're on the front porch swinging. No rush; have some breakfast first. Those kittens can wait," she says, handing me a bowl of oatmeal with apples cut up and cinnamon sprinkled on top. "You can take that outside," she says.

I take the bowl and spoon she is offering me and walk out the front door onto the porch. To the left Chloe and Grace are swinging on the bench swing.

"You're going too fast; I'm going to spill!" Grace exclaims.

"Morning," I say, startling them and hopefully breaking up the fight that is brewing.

"Morning," Grace says jumping up. "Let's sit over here Paige."

"No," Chloe whines, "I won't pump too fast, I promise!"

"There's not room for three anyway. We can sit on the rocking chairs or stairs," Grace decides.

Chloe sticks out her lower lip and swings her legs up onto the bench so she is taking up the entire thing. I walk over and sit in a rocking chair while Grace takes the one next to me.

"I can't wait to meet the kittens. Have you named them all?" I ask Chloe.

This brightens up her mood and she straightens, "I've only named one Peek-a-boo because he likes to play peek-a-boo. The mom is named Mama because she always seems to have kittens. I'm waiting to learn the personalities of the others before I name them."

"Can I name one?" I ask.

Chloe thinks for a minute and says, "Only if the one you

name likes you."

"Fair enough," I decide and dig into my oatmeal.

After we're done eating we take our dishes into the kitchen. Aunt Jennifer hands us two cans of kitten food and we head to the barn.

We walk across the yard and it's bitter cold even though the sun is out. It looks like a beautiful day, but the air has an arctic breeze. Without a word, all of us walk a little faster.

When we enter the barn the horses sense us and whiney their greetings. The girls say hi to each of them by name as they pass their stalls. When we get to the other end of the barn there's a ladder leaned against the wall heading up to the loft. Chloe scrambles up the ladder and I follow her with Grace behind me.

The loft has hay bales stacked everywhere and a small path to walk. I hear faint meowing in the far left corner. Chloe skips the path forward and heads left where there's a small space to walk. She knows exactly where Mama is located. I follow Chloe and sure enough in the back corner curled against a bale of hay is the mama cat with several kittens around her. Some are nursing and some are wandering around crying in a high-pitched meow.

"Oh my gosh, they're so cute!" I exclaim.

"You should have seen them a few weeks ago," Grace comments, sitting down next to the mama cat. "Hi Mama," she says. The cat looks up in acknowledgement of our greeting. She doesn't seem to mind we are there.

"She knows you guys?" I ask.

"Of course," Chloe says, setting out bowls spaced several inches apart. Then she hands me a can and a fork, "Here scoop one out and the kittens will come running." I take the can from her and scoop the mushy stinky kitten food into a bowl. Sure enough as soon as the kittens hear the sound of my spoon scooping the food into the bowl they come running. They smoosh all their heads into the bowl as they frantically eat. They're so crowded I can't finish putting food in the bowl.

"Greedy little guys," I say laughing.

"If you fill this bowl we can move some of them over here so they aren't so crowded," she comments.

I move over to the second bowl and I'm able to empty out the can in that bowl without any of the kittens even noticing. Once I'm done Chloe grabs one of them and sets her by the second bowl. I do the same with a sweet little black one.

I watch them as they eat. There are three tortoiseshell kittens, one that is all black, and one that is white with black tipped ears and black fur around her blue eyes. I reach down and pet them while they eat.

"You haven't named four of them?" I ask.

"They've been hard to tell apart so I was waiting to watch their personalities. That way I know who is who later."

"They're probably old enough to name now," Grace says.

"Should we stay and play with them?" Chloe asks.

Grace shrugs, "If we go back to the house mom is going to make us peel potatoes."

Chloe smiles, "Naming them it is then." She reaches over and pulls a few pieces of hay out of a bale and hands us each one. I take mine wondering why she gave it to me. I don't say anything; I just twirl it between my fingers.

The black kitten walks away from the bowl and Grace immediately starts swishing her piece of hay back and forth on the ground in front of the kitten and she immediately pounces on it making us laugh. When another kitten is done eating Chloe does the same. They are so curious and playful.

The white kitten stops eating and walks toward me. I move my piece of straw back and forth just how Chloe and

Grace did. The white kitten doesn't pounce like her siblings. She squats down behind a bale of hay, peeks her head around the corner, and watches my piece of straw from a safe distance.

"Am I doing it wrong?" I ask.

Chloe looks up from playing with the two kittens to see who I am entertaining and says, "No, she's just a cautious one. Keep doing it. She'll play when she's had time to think about it." I do as she says and keep swiping my straw back and forth. I notice her eyes are following the straw closely. I slow it down a little to see what she'll do. Her face is focused and her ears are turned forward. I look over and Grace and Chloe both have two kittens playing with them and I can't even get this one to engage. I look back at my cautious kitten and decide not to give up on her. I move the straw forward and back then side to side. I see her focus narrow in even more when I move the straw side to side. Then out of nowhere she pounces! She catches me off guard and pulls the piece of hay out of my hand.

"Hey! That's mine!" I exclaim trying to grab it back. She puts a paw on it to keep it in place.

"She's good when she decides to pounce," Chloe comments. "She's faster than the others."

"We can call her Flash," Grace comments.

"No, that's not good enough," I decide..

"Once you name enough animals, anything is good enough."

"I've never named an animal," I admit.

"Then you should do all of them!" Chloe exclaims.

I look up, "Really? You guys don't mind?"

"We have lots of chances, especially since we name the chickens."

"Okay," I agree looking over at the other four kittens playing with Chloe and Grace. "The black one should be

Noche," I comment referring to the word night in Spanish.

"Night?" Grace says, getting it right away. I nod and look at the tortoiseshell kittens.

"They look like messy paintings. Maybe Picasso?" I muse.

"Or Sunset, to go with Noche," Chloe suggests.

I laugh, "That's so silly."

"Pet names can be super silly. Even horses."

"This little lady looks like a puff of snow," I say referring to my cautious kitten who is back to hiding behind a bale and watching me intently. "Snow Queen, Snowflake, Snowball, Snowfluff . . ." I muse out loud.

"I like Snow Queen or maybe even Snow Lady."

"You know she's not going to stay white, right?" Grace says.

"She's not?" I ask.

"No. She has the markings of a Siamese. We have a Siamese Tom around here that gives Mama a half Siamese kitten once in a while. Look at her blue eyes and black markings on her face and ears. Those are Siamese markings. Her coat will darken with age."

I pick her up from her hiding place and put her in my lap. She wanders around on my legs, not wanting to cuddle. I pet her snowy white fur and am sad that we all have to grow up and change. "That's too bad," I say stroking her.

"We have Peek-a-boo, Noche, Snow-something, what about this one?" Chloe asks, picking up another tortoiseshell-colored kitten.

"This is harder than I thought," I say laughing. "Should we let Jason name one?"

"Sure," Chloe says, setting her down.

"We should get back. Mom will be mad if we avoid chores for too long," Grace decides.

We agree and give all the kittens one last good-bye and

head back down the ladder to the main level of the barn.

Grace was right. As soon as we walk back into the house Aunt Jennifer puts us to work peeling potatoes.

"Do the chickens need feeding?" Chloe asks hopefully.

"The boys are doing it," Aunt Jennifer comments.

"They'll be out there forever," Grace says, knowing their trick.

Aunt Jennifer doesn't say anything and just goes back to work on whatever dish she is making. I'm guessing she doesn't care how long they're gone as long as everyone is doing some kind of chore.

We work quietly for a while. The kitchen is warm and smells like Thanksgiving. The Turkey has been in the oven all morning and I watch as my mom opens the oven and bastes it.

My cousins and I are each sitting on a chair with a bucket in front of us and a pile of potatoes on the kitchen counter. We are peeling them over the bucket and then putting the peeled potatoes in a huge bowl sitting on the table.

"Do we seriously need all of these?" Grace complains.

"I like leftovers," Aunt Jennifer comments. "Plus potatoes always look like more before they're mashed."

"Can we go outside when this is done?" Chloe asks.

"Once you guys get most of the potatoes peeled you can go play and send the boys in. They're not going to get away with not doing kitchen chores on Thanksgiving."

This satisfies my cousins and we don't say anymore as we hunker down and peel potatoes. I notice the girls are faster than me. They've done this a lot more than I have. I think the last time I peeled potatoes was last Thanksgiving. I rarely help my mom in the kitchen and I'm a little embarrassed to admit it. I hope they don't see how slow and uncoordinated my peeling is compared to theirs.

I look over and watch Grace expertly rotate the potato around as she peels. I think I would get my finger in the blade if I did it like that. I'm finally done with my first potato and I put it in the giant bowl Aunt Jennifer set out. I notice three potatoes are already in there. My guess is that Grace already did two and Chloe one before I got one done. I try not to worry about it as I reach for a new one to peel.

"Shall we put on music?" My mom asks.

"Alexa, play holiday music," Aunt Jennifer commands. Instantly Christmas music comes on. This house is a weird combination of old and new. The animals, farm equipment, and the barn all seem out of the past. Yet Aunt Jennifer has technology in her house that we don't even have yet.

"Are we allowed to have Christmas music before Thanksgiving?" my mom teases.

"As far as I'm concerned, Thanksgiving is for getting together with family and kicking off the season."

"Does that mean we can get a tree tomorrow?" Chloe asks, setting down a peeled potato on the table and picking up another one.

"I think so. I'll have to double check if your dad got a permit," Aunt Jennifer comments as she dumps ingredients into her giant electric mixer and turns it on.

"What does he need a permit for?" I ask.

"For cutting down a tree in the mountains. They don't want them to be over harvested at the holidays so they give permits for certain areas. Some years we don't get one and have to go get our tree in town," Grace says wrinkling up her nose as if that is the most awful way to get a tree.

I laugh, "I take it you like the ones from the mountains."

"Yeah, they're the best."

"They smell so good," Chloe chimes in.

Our moms start talking about what they want to decorate tomorrow and it sounds like a lot. I enjoy listening to them planning along with the Christmas music in the background. Christmas at the farm is fun. I have some great memories here of snowed-in white Christmases.

My peaceful thoughts are broken by Jason and Noah slamming through the front door.

"Perfect timing!" Aunt Jennifer yells.

"We can't help. Jason just had to come in to pee!" Noah yells back as they run by. "And I'm getting my bows," he adds.

"Yeah, you girls will definitely have to tag them in when you get about halfway done," she decides.

At the mention of the restroom I decide I should go before we get the green light to be done with potatoes and can go outside. I set my potato down and head to the bathroom off the kitchen but realize Jason is in there so I head upstairs to Grace and Chloe's bathroom. I step in and shut and lock the door.

When I'm finished I go to wash my hands and the soap dispenser is completely empty. I look around for more soap, but that is the only dispenser in here. Mom keeps her extra soap under the sink; maybe Aunt Jennifer does too.

I crouch down and open the cupboard under the sink. I see two baskets under the sink and soap lined up to the right of the baskets. *Bingo*, I think as I reach for the soap. As I am grabbing the soap I notice that the basket is full of pads neatly lined up in yellow wrappers. Grace needs pads? I look at the basket next to it and it has colorful fabrics folded into little squares. I wonder what that is? I take one and as soon as I hold it up, I realize it is a pair of brightly patterned underwear. Embarrassed that I grabbed one of Grace's underwear I try to fold it back up just how I found it and put it back in the basket. Why does she have underwear in the bathroom?

I stand up with the soap, set it on the counter and begin

to wash my hands. I can't decide if I'm insulted that I haven't gotten my period yet or glad. I feel like my friends all know something grown up that I don't know.

I head back downstairs wondering what getting your period is like. Abigail and Katherine talked about it a little, but I didn't feel like I could ask them questions. Maybe I could ask Grace. When I walk into the kitchen Grace and Chloe are gone and Noah and Jason are in their place.

"Where'd you go?" my mom asks.

"To the bathroom."

"Grace and Chloe headed back outside. The boys are going to do the rest."

I don't need any more explanation than that as I turn and grab my coat by the door and head outside. We play tag outside until we are called in for dinner.

Thankfully there's a kids table. Aunt Jennifer and Uncle Justin invited a bunch of adults over for dinner that don't have family in town. The adult table looks formal and intimidating. The kid's table is more fun, in my opinion. It's just the five of us and most of the time Jason entertains us with his off-the-wall jokes.

We are done much earlier than the adults and we're excused to go play. Since it gets dark early this time of year, we have to come up with something to do inside. We go up to the bonus room where our cousins teach us a made-up version of billiards. Instead of using pool sticks we just push the balls around with our hands. Since Noah seems to have established rules, he teaches them to us, and the game is pretty fun.

When Noah is about to beat us all our parents call us down for pie. We run down the stairs and sit only long enough to eat warm homemade pie. Then we run back upstairs to start a movie and fall asleep altogether in the bonus room.

It was a great Thanksgiving.

CHAPTER 14

The next morning I'm the last one to get up again. Which is a bit of a bummer since it's my birthday.

I head downstairs and when I walk into the kitchen there is the usual morning bustle but on the wall there is a banner that says, 'Happy Birthday!'

"Good morning birthday girl!" my aunt says coming over to give me a hug.

"Thanks," I say, happy she remembered.

"I love it when your birthday falls on Thanksgiving weekend and we get to celebrate with you," she exclaims.

"Is that my birthday girl?" I hear my mom say, coming in from the front porch.

"Hi Mom," I reply. She is bundled up from being outside. I'm guessing she was out there having a quiet cup of coffee.

"How's my teenager?" she exclaims.

I smile, "The same," I say. I really do feel the same.

"You are absolutely not the same," my aunt interjects. "Look how tall you are and filling out just like a lady." *Filling out?* What does that mean? I don't want to fill out. I want to be the same.

"Where are the others?" I ask.

"Noah and Chloe went to deliver some bales with Justin. Jason and Grace are feeding the horses."

"Can I feed the kittens?" I ask.

"You sure can. Breakfast first," she says, scooping scrambled eggs onto a plate for me.

I quietly eat and when I am almost done I ask, "Where's Dad?"

"On the porch reading. I think he's waiting to wish you a happy birthday," my mom says.

"Okay," I say and take the can of kitten food Aunt Jennifer has opened and is handing to me. I go to the door and pull on my boots. Then I put on my coat and decide to grab a beanie hat from the rack.

I walk outside and sure enough my dad is in one of the rocking chairs looking at his phone. He doesn't look up when I step out so I walk a little closer.

"Oh, hi pumpkin," he says, using my family nickname. "Are you too old for me to call you pumpkin?"

"No," I say, shaking my head. "I'm the same," I repeat.

"Well not entirely. You're thirteen today. Holy cow, when did I get so old that I have a teenager?"

I'm silent because I don't think I should agree with him that he's old. "We're going to have a great day," he decides. "Are you headed to feed the kittens?" he asks, seeing the can in my hand.

"Yeah, they're so cute, you should see them," I brighten a little.

"I can't get up that ladder," he teases. "You enjoy those kittens birthday girl," he says.

"Thanks Dad, I will."

I turn and walk down the porch steps and across the yard to the barn. It's another crisp day and I wonder how Mama and her kittens stand it. I get to the barn and find Grace teaching my brother how to feed the horses. For once he is being serious and calm. They turn when they hear me and Jason whispers, "Happy Birthday."

"Why are you whispering?" I ask.

"Because we are being quiet and calm," Grace says and winks at me. In that moment she looks just like my mom.

"Oh, got it," I whisper back. "I'm just going to feed Snow Queen and the rest of her court," I say heading to the ladder.

"Going with Snow Queen, huh? Even though she'll be darker in a few weeks?"

"I think so," I say as I head up the ladder awkwardly using the sides of my hands since one hand is carrying the can of kitten food and the other hand has a spoon and bowl. I finally make it up and head back to Mama's corner. Sure enough she is in the same spot she was yesterday and kittens are meowing around her. Mama must not ever get any sleep.

"Hi Mama," I greet her, setting down the bowl. "I'm here to give your little ones some extra food," I explain as I scoop food out of the can and kittens come dashing over.

"I'm not sure why they act so hungry. You seem to feed them just fine," I comment. She looks at me with the wisdom of a mother and sets her chin on her paws.

I sit down cross legged and pick up a piece of straw. All the kittens are busy eating the food I brought so I twirl it between my fingers while I wait. I can't believe I'm thirteen today. I don't feel thirteen, whatever that is supposed to feel like. All the other teenagers I know, like Grace, and even Abigail and Katherine, seem so much more sophisticated than I am. I hate that I'm growing so much. I didn't think it was that much, but it's all anyone can seem to talk about. I have noticed tumbling is harder. I wonder if my older Level 7 teammates, Brooklyn or Maya, went through a growth spurt too. I should get to know them. I feel like I've gotten thrown into this group so fast I haven't really gotten to know the other girls. That and I feel safe with Savannah, Alexis, and Lucy so I haven't talked much to my new teammates.

Snow Queen finishes her meal and walks toward me with curiosity. I swipe the straw on the ground in front of her and she cautiously watches it. Then her brothers and sisters join us until they are in each other's way and I decide to pick up a second straw and play with that one a little way away. They make me laugh as they stalk and pounce with very little coordination. Even funnier is how they run into each other. After a while Snow Queen retreats and climbs into my lap. I drop the straw to pet her. She purrs for a brief moment, then falls asleep.

"I see the adoration is mutual," I hear Grace say from behind me. I look over and smile.

"She is sweet," I say. "Where's Jason?"

"He wanted to go do some archery with my brother. My dad promised to show him."

"Is that safe?" I wonder out loud, making Grace laugh.

"My dad will help him. Do you want to ride?" she asks.

"I'm not very good, remember?" The only time I ever ride is when I visit my cousins.

"I can put you on Honey Bear, our gentle mare," she assures me.

"Okay. If you think Honey Bear can do all the work," I agree.

"You play with the kittens a little longer, I'll tack up," she says.

She stands up and leaves the loft. I notice the other kittens have worn themselves out and are cuddling together to stay warm as they take a nap. My mind wanders again as I pet the tiny animal in my lap. It is relaxing to be here; maybe I shouldn't go home early. No, I really want my floor routine. I need to be able to do routines in practice like everyone else. I hope Melony makes up something good. Maybe we should have asked Madame Julia to make up my routine. After all the music *is* from a ballet. Then again, she might put things in there that I can't do.

"You ready birthday girl?" I hear Grace call up. "Set the kitten down and let's go!"

Reluctantly, I pick up Snow Queen and set her down on a little bed of hay. She meows at me to let me know she is not happy to be disturbed.

"Sorry little one. I'll be back," I say and stand up.

I climb down the ladder from the loft to the main part of the barn. When I get down Grace is waiting for me and without a word I follow her to the other end of the barn where two horses are waiting bridled and saddled. She unclips the reins where Honey Bear is waiting and hands them to me.

"This is Honey Bear. Just hold these and walk with her. You can follow us," she says as she goes over and unclips her white and gray mare.

"What's her name?" I ask, as she begins to walk with her horse next to her.

"Marshmallow," Grace answers. Honey Bear patiently waits and when it's our turn she starts to walk. I think she's walking me out of the tack room, not the other way around.

I watch the white horse in front of me and smile, Marshmallow is a funny name. I look at Honey Bear, she does have a beautiful light brown coat, but not really the color of honey. We follow Grace out into the yard and she walks us over to a tree stump. Honey Bear knows where she's going and she walks over and stands right next to the tree stump.

"You are going to use this stump as a step stool. Stand on here. Now put your left foot in the stirrup, your hand on the saddle, and pull yourself up. You remember, right?" she asks me.

I nod. It has been a while, but I remember. I do as she says and put my foot in the stirrup, my hand on the saddle, and I swing myself up and onto Honey Bear. Grace hands me the reins, which I didn't even realize she was holding.

"Thanks," I say, taking them.

"You remember how to tell her what you want, right?" she asks and I nod yes. Not because I remember that well, but because I have a feeling Honey Bear is in charge. I look down. It's so much higher up than I remember.

Grace easily swings up onto Marshmallow's saddle without using the tree stump. Then she looks at me, "Ready?"

"I think so," I say hesitantly.

"We'll just take a little walk around a few fields, you'll be fine," she reassures me sensing my slight nervousness.

She makes a little click sound to Marshmallow and she starts walking but Honey Bear stays still. Then I remember I have to make the same clicking sound. I awkwardly try making the clicking sound and Honey Bear starts walking, creating an odd rocking sensation. After a few steps I get used to it and click again telling her to speed up. We catch up with Marshmallow and Grace and walk beside them. I glance at Grace; she has a content expression on her face as she looks out at the fields. The wind picks up her hair and waves it behind her. Her name is perfect for her.

We walk along quietly for a while and as I finally get comfortable she says, "Do you want to trot for a bit?"

I remember that trotting is fun so I nod. She says, "Use a little heel with your click," and she is off, leaving Honey

Bear and I behind.

"Well, girl, do you want to stretch your legs?" I ask her. She continues to plod along without a comment. I'm worried I might hurt her if I use my heels too much so I lightly tap my heels into her side and click. She walks a little faster, but not much.

"Come on Honey Bear, lets catch them," I say and try again with a little more force as I click louder. This time she gets the message and we are off. I can feel my hair lifting with the wind and Honey Bear's strength. The air we are running through is cold and sharp. The sky is vivid blue without a cloud in sight. If it weren't for my breath puffing in front of me and my hands turning red, someone watching us might think it's a summer day.

We trot the length of a field and when Grace turns a corner she slows down. We catch up to her and Honey Bear slows down without me really doing anything.

"How do you feel?" she asks me. Her cheeks are rosy and her hair is tangled and I know she loves it out here.

"Wonderful and cold all at the same time," I admit.

"Oh sorry, I should have gotten you gloves," she apologizes. "We can head back. If we walk it's not as cold."

We walk along the edge of the field and I can see their farmhouse in the distance. It looks like it came right out of a storybook with the white and blue trim, the two levels, and the porch with rocking chairs. The barn next to it is a classic red with white trim.

"Do you like growing up here?" I ask her.

"Of course. I feel cramped when we visit you guys. Even in that big house of yours," she comments.

"But we have a pool," I tease, referring to the community pool in our neighborhood.

"We have a lake."

"We have a mall."

"We have horses."

"We have gymnastics!" I cry.

She laughs, "You got me there. I don't think we have a gym nearby for miles."

"You don't, my mom and I looked into it last summer to see if I could workout a few days at a local gym. There's nothing."

"Really? I didn't know that. Is it that bad if you miss? Is that why you're going back tomorrow?" she asks.

"It was not a big deal when I took off a week last summer. I can miss days. I just don't like to," I admit. "I'm going back tomorrow because I'm getting my first floor routine."

"Your first? Haven't you been competing for a few years now?" she asks confused.

I explain to her the difference between compulsories and optionals and how this will be the first routine that is uniquely my own. I tell her how the Level 5 season runs right into the Level 6 season and how I am rushed to be ready.

"Sounds stressful," she concludes.

"Maybe, but I love it."

"And I love the horses so it's a good thing my mom is my mom and Heather is your mom," she says, making us both laugh.

"Grace?" I ask.

"Hmm?"

"What's it like to get your period?" I ask.

"Whoa, where'd that come from?" she asks as her horse comes to an abrupt stop. She laughs, "I didn't mean, whoa to you! Sorry Marshmallow," she says, leaning down and rubbing her neck. She clicks Marshmallow back to a walk and catches up to us, since Honey Bear didn't stop her pace.

"You haven't gotten it yet?" she asks me. I shake my head embarrassed. It's my thirteenth birthday and I haven't gotten my period. What's worse is I am relived. "How do you know I've gotten mine?"

"I saw your supplies under the cupboard in the bathroom," I admit. "Sorry, I was looking for soap," I quickly add.

She nods in understanding, thinks for a second and says, "I don't know how to explain it. It's not really a big deal. The pads can feel lumpy. Sometimes your stomach hurts."

"My friends at school said that about the stomach hurting. But how does it hurt?" I ask.

"Like a dull ache. Not sharp. It's weird."

"Weird," I repeat, not at all sure I get it.

"Chloe says she doesn't get cramps at all and that hardly anything happens. That's why she can wear the period underwear."

"Chloe!"

"Yeah, she got hers a few months ago."

"But Chloe is only eleven," I say, still in shock.

She shrugs, "My mom said that's normal for kids today." Then she looks at me, "Hopefully you'll get yours soon so you can get your boobs."

"Boobs?"

"Yeah. Both of us started growing our boobs after we got our periods," she shares.

"I don't want boobs!"

"Why not?"

"I think they might throw me off or get in the way. I don't know, they just seem inconvenient for a gymnast," I explain.

"Just wear a big ol' sports bra. You're related to us. They won't get that big. We are all slender with like size Bs. Getting your actual period will be a bigger problem," she says.

"How so?"

"What will you do? What do gymnasts and dancers do when they get their period? My pads would be way too big and Chloe's period underwear are huge. How would you hide all that?"

"I don't know!" I squeak in panic. Now I really don't want to get my period. Ever.

"Do you have any older girls on your team?"

"Yes," I answer. "For the first time in my gymnastics career there are older girls on my team."

"Ask them," she says.

"I hardly know them."

"You asked me out of the blue," she reminds me.

"You're my cousin. I've known you my entire life and you have to stay friends with me," I counter.

"True. Could you ask your mom?" she wonders.

"I guess," I say, disappointed I didn't get much more out of her than Abigail or Katherine.

Maybe it's time to talk to my mom.

CHAPTER 15

We get back from our ride and Grace teaches me how to untack and care for the horses. It takes almost as long as the ride, but I can tell Grace doesn't mind the work. Hungry now, we head inside.

The other kids are in the kitchen asking for lunch. Everyone is talking at once, which is common for my family. My uncle is preparing lunch for us and my aunt is baking and telling him he's in the way.

"I'm making your birthday cake with love!" she trills at me. I smile, a little embarrassed at all the attention.

"Are you sure your favorite isn't chocolate cake?" my uncle asks. I shake my head no.

"She loves the butter cakes Justin. You have to wait for your birthday for chocolate," she reminds him.

Uncle Justin shuffles us out on the porch for lunch telling us we need fresh air. Grace and I sit on the swing bundled under blankets. Jason and Chloe are smooshed into a rocking chair and Noah is eating on the steps insisting that he isn't cold.

I take a bite out of my sandwich as I watch the sky darken and the clouds roll in.

"It's a good thing we got our ride in this morning," Grace comments. I agree and pull the blanket tighter around me.

"What'd you guys do this morning?" I ask the others.

"Archery," Noah answers and stands up and starts pacing along the deck. I assume it's because he really is cold. "Jason's pretty good," he adds making my brother beam.

"I'm ready to go in," Chloe says standing up and heading inside. Noah immediately follows her without a word.

I look at Jason all alone on the rocking chair, "Do you want to join us?" I offer.

He shakes his head no and says, "I'm better than Noah at archery."

I doubt that but I say, "Nice. Did you show Dad?"

"Yeah, he was there. He's terrible," he shares twisting his face up making us laugh. "I'm serious!" he yells as if he is mad at us. But one thing is for sure, if Jason has caused the laughing he can't stay mad. He gets too delighted with himself.

"You better teach him how to do it then," Grace says. He nods, satisfied we believe he is the best. Then he stands up and heads inside.

I look at Grace as we swing, "Should we head in?" I ask her.

"Let's wait just a minute. I smell snow. It's going to come down any second. I love the first snow."

"It's already snowed this year," I remind her.

"I mean the first snow that comes down in a storm before things get whipping around," she explains.

I look out at the calm looking empty and brown fields. The sky is gray and gloomy. We swing quietly for a while and watch as the gray gives way to a white sky and then, just as Grace predicted, snowflakes begin to swirl around. They aren't really falling so much as swirling. It's like they came out of the middle of the sky instead the clouds above.

"Where'd they come from?" I ask.

"It's cool, huh?" she replies.

"I like the farm more and more each year," I comment.

"Why do you think?" she asks.

"I don't know. Middle school is hard I guess. The kittens are nicer to me," I say, making Grace laugh.

"Animals are great. I might like them better than people," she admits.

Just then we hear the screen door slam and we turn and look to see my mom holding two mugs. "I thought you two might like some birthday hot chocolate," she says handing us each a mug.

"Thanks Aunt Heather."

"Thanks Mom," I say, taking the mug. It immediately warms my hands. The whip cream on top is swirled perfectly and it has sprinkles on top.

"Why does she get sprinklings?" Grace says in a teasing voice. She holds out her mug that has the whip cream but is, indeed, without sprinkles.

"She's the birthday girl!" my mom exclaims. Then quickly adds, "Jennifer told me it was a new tradition, is that not right?"

Grace laughs, "It is. I'm just messing with you."

My mom smiles in relief and says, "I'll let you two get back to your teenage talk." She sends me a wink and walks back into the house.

Teenage talk. "I don't feel like a teenager."

"Why not, you are one. As of today."

I give Grace a look. She immediately knows what I am scowling about. "Your period? Who cares? It doesn't define how mature you are. You do," she says, sounding very adult. "My mom didn't get hers until she was fourteen," she continues. "When did your mom get hers?"

"I don't know."

"Have you guys talked about it at all?" she asks.

"Not really," I admit.

"Maybe that's why you're so worried."

Maybe. Or maybe I'm worried I'll get my period at practice, or worse, a meet. I'm worried I won't have the stuff to take care of it. What do gymnasts use anyway? It feels like this big secret that everyone knows and no one knows. Kind of like when we do mass in Latin once a month at school. We all kind of know what's happening but at the same time, we don't know the details.

"I'm worried I'm going to keep growing," I finally share.

"Why?"

"Gymnastics has been getting harder lately. I think it's because I'm getting bigger."

"Didn't you just move up like two levels in a year?" she asks me.

"Yeah."

"Maybe that's why it's hard."

I think about this as I watch the snow swirl around. I take a sip of my hot chocolate and wonder about what Grace just said. Maybe gymnastics is harder because I'm trying to be ready for Level 6 so quickly. Maybe I should have taken the extra year like Marissa chose to. Except I like the flexibility of optionals where I can create routines that play to my strengths. Or rather, avoid my weaknesses.

I watch the snow shift from swirling to coming down in larger flakes. I'm glad my mom and I are heading back tomorrow because I think once I have my routines maybe I'll feel better. I look at Grace, a little sad to leave early.

"Mom said we could watch a movie since it's snowing out," Noah calls, poking his head out of the house.

"It is getting cold out here," Grace says and I nod in agreement. We untangle ourselves from the blankets and stand up. Grace hands me her mug and collects the blankets to take inside.

"Mom says Paige gets to decide the movie since it's her birthday," Noah adds.

I don't really care what we watch, but it will be fun to have final say.

The snow doesn't let up after the movie so we start a puzzle up in the bonus room. The five of us get along shockingly well as we sort all 1,000 pieces and began to make the frame. That's the thing about cousins; you don't take them for granted as much as siblings. You tend to be nicer to them when you play so there are less fights.

"Hey guys!" Aunt Jennifer yells up to us.

We look up from our puzzle and Chloe yells back, "What?"

"Wash your hands and come down for dinner!" she yells.

We reluctantly stop what we're doing and disperse to the two bathrooms upstairs to wash our hands. As we are walking down I smell my favorite dinner, spaghetti and meatballs. When I get to the dining room there are now balloons to go with the sign, gifts on the table, and a cake.

"Wow, thank you," I say to all the adults, because I know it was a team effort.

"Happy Birthday pumpkin," my mom says coming over to give me a hug.

"Do the presents now!" Jason exclaims.

"Let's have dinner first while it's hot," Aunt Jennifer says, setting a salad on the table.

"Wait," my mom says picking up the salad Aunt Jennifer just set down. "Pictures first."

We take pictures with me and the cake, banner, and cousins and then we are allowed to start dinner. As usual, everyone is talking at once. Grace is reporting on the horses, Jason is talking about wanting to do a magic show, the adults keep talking about remembering their thirteenth birthday, and Chloe and Noah keep arguing about who gets the flower on the cake. I smile to myself, it's a perfect dinner.

When we are done with dinner Uncle Justin dims the lights and everyone starts singing Happy Birthday while Aunt Jennifer brings me the cake with thirteen candles. As soon as they are done singing I pause to think of a wish. I wish for a successful Level 6 season. Then I take a deep breath and blow out the candles.

My mom takes the cake and starts cutting it and serving pieces to everyone while Aunt Jennifer moves me to the family room to open gifts. Uncle Justin and Noah stay in the kitchen to clean the dishes. They make it clear I can't open their gift until they are done. I sit down in the family room and there are three packages sitting on the coffee table in festive birthday wrap with red, yellow, and green balloons.

The first one is a pair of stud earrings with my birthstone from my parents.

"Every teenage girl needs a nice pair of earrings," my mom says.

"Thanks Mom," I say and put the earrings on. The second gift is a book and a deck of cards from Jason and the third gift is a beautiful red and white workout leotard from my parents.

"We're so proud of how hard you've worked. A new leotard seemed appropriate," my mom says with pride.

"Thanks Mom," I say again, reaching over to hug her.

"Ready for our gift?" Chloe squeals with excitement. I

look at the coffee table and there are no packages on the table. I look at her confused.

"Grace is getting your present," Aunt Jennifer says.

"Hold on! We want to see this!" Uncle Justin says as he and Noah come in from the kitchen to watch me get my present.

"Ready?" we hear Grace yell from outside and Aunt Jennifer yells back that we are ready.

As Grace walks in the door with a brown box everyone is very quiet, which for this group, is rare. Grace slowly walks across the room and hands me the box. When she puts it in my lap I can feel it moving. It can't be.

I lift the lid and there is Snow Queen meowing away with a green bow around her neck. She sees I have lifted the lid and pops her head up with a loud indignant cry making the group laugh.

"Really?!" I exclaim, lifting her out of the box.

"Grace said you two hit it off," Aunt Jennifer beams at us.

"Mom?" I ask, in shock that I can really have a kitten.

"I think you are responsible enough to handle her," my mom says with a huge grin.

I snuggle her to my cheek and try not to cry. This is the best birthday ever!

CHAPTER 16

The next day the snow is coming down so we don't ride. We do visit the animals since they still need to be fed. I, of course, opt to go to the loft to check on Mama and the rest of the kittens. I kept Snow Queen with me in the bonus room last night. She cried and cried until she wore herself out and fell asleep at my feet.

Now she is tucked under my arm as I climb up the ladder. "Why don't you hang out here today with your mom and siblings. I'll come get you before we leave this afternoon." I set her down and she slowly walks to her siblings. They seem not to have noticed her absence. "You knew. Isn't that right Mama?" I ask the mama cat. She looks at me warily. "I'll take good care of her," I promise.

I sit down and start scooping the food in a bowl. At the sound of my scraping all the kittens come running. "I'm going to miss you guys."

Once they are done eating, I play with them while I

listen to Jason, Chloe, and Grace talk to the horses below. The horses are cool, but somehow I feel more at ease with the kittens. I'm a little bit sad to leave this afternoon, but I'm excited to go home and learn my new floor routine. Plus, I need to get back home to work on homework, too. There are a few projects due before Christmas that I have put off. I wonder how long they will really take.

"Paige?" I hear Grace yell up to me interrupting my thoughts.

"Yeah?" I yell down.

"We are done here; do you want to go back in with us?" she asks.

"Yeah, just a sec," I answer, standing up. "Mama, kittens," I acknowledge them. "Snow Queen, I will be back for you this afternoon." She is busy trying to bite off her green ribbon and doesn't respond. I take pity on her and reach down and untie it. "There you go. See you later."

I climb back down the ladder. My cousins and brother are waiting for me at the bottom. Without a word we tighten our coats and walk back to the house together.

"Can we go sledding?" Jason asks.

"There aren't any hills, silly," Chloe says.

"Oh yeah," Jason says, sounding deflated. "I'm used to our neighborhood," he comments.

"The mountains are a little farther for us," Grace comments. "You're right though, this would be perfect sledding snow," she says trying to make him feel better.

"We can still make snow angels," I say running and jumping onto a fluffy section of snow sitting over the grass in the yard. The others follow me and pretty soon the front yard is full of snow angel imprints and we have snow down our backs.

Noah hears the ruckus and, not wanting to miss the fun, comes out and joins us. I look up at the gray sky with snow coming down, I take in a cold crisp breath, and move my arms and legs to create a new angel. When my neck can't take the cold any longer I sit up. My angel mark looks pretty good. I look over at Chloe, "The trick is getting up without ruining it," she says, also sitting up.

We both carefully stand up and step out of our angel imprint without ruining it with footprints. "Mom, look!" Chloe yells to her mom who has come out onto the porch to see what all the commotion is about.

"'Tis the season," Aunt Jennifer says.

Noah bounces up, "Can we go get a tree now?"

"The snow is too bad today. We'll go up tomorrow," she comments.

I realize I'm going to miss the fun of picking out a tree tomorrow and probably decorating it. I wish I could be two places at once. Or, if I'm wishing, I just wish their farm was closer to us. Or maybe that a gym was out here. Then we could just move here. Although, I don't think my parents care much for the farm, even though my mom was raised on one.

"I'm sad I'm going to miss getting the tree," I comment.

"Then stay!" Chloe squeals.

"We'd love to have you and your mom stay one more day," Aunt Jennifer adds.

I shake my head. They don't get it. I don't say any more about it in fear that Aunt Jennifer talks my mom into staying.

We spend the day playing games and working on the giant puzzle. The afternoon arrives quickly and before I know it my mom tells me to go pack up to go home. I reluctantly pull myself away from the puzzle I am working on with my cousins. I wonder if going back a day early is worth it as I stuff my clothes in my bag and roll up my sleeping bag.

I hear the other kids talking about what movie they want to watch tonight.

"We could watch a Christmas one. Thanksgiving is over and we're decorating tomorrow," Chloe reasons.

I sigh and stand up, grabbing my pillow and bag. I sling my bag over my shoulder and walk over to my cousins and brother.

"You're leaving already?" Grace asks. I nod and she gives me a hug. Chloe and Noah do the same. Jason just gives me a fist bump. He's decided lately that he's too old for hugs.

"Bye, Jay," I say and grab a hug anyway. He wiggles out of it but doesn't complain.

"Don't have too much fun without me," I say even though I know they will.

I head down the stairs and they go back to their puzzle. I walk outside and find my mom and dad packing the car. I hand my mom my bag and she puts it in the trunk.

"Ready pumpkin?" She asks.

"Hold on," I hear Aunt Jennifer say, as she walks down the stairs with a cat carrier in her hand. "Let's go get your little girl," she says to me.

I happily grab the carrier and head to the barn with my aunt to get Snow Queen. "I was hoping she would forget," I hear my dad grumble under his breath.

As I walk across the yard I worry about Mama as I take one of her babies away. I stop and turn to my aunt, "I don't think I can do it."

"What?" my aunt asks, surprised.

"I can't take her from Mama," I explain.

My aunt laughs and walks over to me, takes the cat carrier, and says, "You city kids. She'll be fine. They will be going off on their own soon anyway." She strides toward the barn. I stand rooted to my spot.

"I can't do it," I say. All I can see is Mama cat watching me take her baby.

Aunt Jennifer stops and turns back to look at me. "I'll do it. She'll understand, I promise." She doesn't try to talk me into coming with her, she just walks to the barn with the carrier swinging at her side. I watch her disappear into the barn and although I am curious to see how Mama takes it, I can't move. I stand and wait for what feels like forever. Hopefully Aunt Jennifer is explaining to Mama that Snow Queen is going to a good home.

Finally, my aunt emerges from the barn with a loudly meowing Snow Queen in the cat carrier. She walks up to me and hands me the carrier.

"She's crying because of the carrier. I know she's happy to go with you. Grace told me about how you two bonded." I tentatively take the carrier, still feeling bad about Mama. "Trust me, her life will be better with you. Some of them won't make it through the winter."

"Then why don't you bring them in?" I ask.

"As much as we would love to, it would just be too many animals inside. Farm life is different, Paige," she explains.

I nod as if I understand, but I don't. I walk to the car and I see my mom is waiting by the car to hug her sister goodbye. I climb into the front passenger seat. I settle Snow Queen in my lap and quietly tell her everything is going to be okay. I don't think she believes me though because she won't stop yowling.

CHAPTER 17

We made it home from the farm with plenty of time to have a relaxing evening. We had to stop at the pet store on the way home to get Snow Queen kitty litter, cat food, bowls, and a few toys. Once home, I let her explore the house. Mom and I decided to put her box in the laundry room and her food in the kitchen. I sat with her in the laundry room until she discovered her box. Then I scooped her up and took her to my room. She meowed and meowed probably feeling so out of place without her mom and siblings. Eventually, she wore herself out and fell asleep on my bed. It didn't take me long to join her and fall asleep, too.

It's now Sunday morning and I'm getting ready to go to practice and I hate to leave her. "I'll be back in a couple of hours. I think we are going to have to lock you in the laundry room so you don't get lost," I try to explain to her.

She's not listening as she sniffs my dirty clothes basket. I put on the new leo I got for my birthday. Now that we're home I'm so excited to go to the gym and get my routine. I dig through my drawer of leos, shorts, and leggings. I decide to put on leggings. It's Sunday; no classes will be going on so the gym will probably have the heat on low.

Then I put my hair in a single fluffy ponytail, throw a sweatshirt on, pull on my fuzzy boots and I'm ready. I scoop up Snow Queen and carry her down the hall to the laundry room. I set her down and she immediately makes a run for the door. I have to pick her up again, place her in the middle of the room, and quickly shut the door. I can hear her meowing behind the door, making me feel terrible.

"I'll be back soon!" I yell through the door to her.

I run down the stairs and I find my mom quietly having a cup of coffee and doodling designs in her notebook.

"Morning mom," I say, making her look up.

"Good morning pumpkin," she greets. "Are you ready for this?"

"So ready," I say, grabbing a banana.

"Do you want anything else?" she asks me. I think about how I'm growing so much, maybe I shouldn't have more than a banana. Then my stomach growls.

"Yeah, maybe some toast or something." As much as I want to be small, I don't know how anyone ignores their stomach.

"You may have to eat this in the car," she says, putting a piece of bread in the toaster. I look at the clock and agree.

"How is Snow this morning?" she asks me.

"You mean Snow Queen?" I ask.

"I thought I would call her Snow for short," she says, I frown thinking about that nick name. I'm not sure.

"She's not happy about being in the laundry room. But I think if I leave her to roam the house I won't find her when I get back."

"She's pretty tiny and could get lost. I think you're

right," she says, pulling out my toast, putting butter on it, and handing it to me wrapped in a napkin.

"Thanks," I say, taking it appreciatively.

"Shall we?" she asks.

I nod, "Are you staying?" I ask, with my mouth full of toast.

"I thought I would. I have my book."

"It will be more exciting than your book," I tease her as we walk to the garage.

We get there a few minutes before Melony and the gym is locked. We are the only ones in the parking lot. My mom and I are quiet for a moment. Maybe I should ask her what I'm supposed to do about wearing a leotard when I get my period.

I remain silent, trying to get up the courage to talk to her when I see Melony pull up. My mom probably wouldn't know the answer anyway. I mean, she wasn't a gymnast. Then again, she is a mom.

Without a word, my opportunity is over as we both step out of the car.

Melony greets us as we hustle to the door. The sun is out, but the air is cold and snow is on the ground. As we are entering the gym I see a couple more cars pull up.

"Who else is coming?" I ask.

"Oh, I invited Savannah and Lucy to work on their routines this morning too. All of you just haven't had as much time with your routines," she says.

Since we have the gym to ourselves, I don't bother going upstairs to the optionals room. I pull off my boots and toss them in a cubby in the lobby. Lucy and Savannah walk in with their moms behind them.

"Good morning," I say.

"This is going to be fun," Debbie says, super bubbly for first thing in the morning. "Let's grab a chair from the coaches room so all three of us can sit in the training area," she says disappearing into the training offices.

"Come on in girls," Melony says. "It's a bit cold, but I just turned up the heaters. Why don't you run a little and we'll get started."

Lucy, Rose, Savannah, and I start running. As soon as we round the first corner Savannah asks me, "How was the farm?"

"Awesome! I got a kitten!"

"You did?" Lucy exclaims.

"Yeah, for my birthday," I explain.

"It's your birthday?" Lucy asks.

"Yesterday."

"How old are you?" she asks.

"Thirteen."

"Wow," she huffs as she runs. "How does that feel?"

"I don't know. The same I guess."

"What does she look like?" Savannah asks.

"Who?" I ask, getting lost in all the questions they are firing at me.

"The kitten!" Savannah exclaims. "I can't believe I haven't talked my mom into a kitten," she marvels.

"Oh, she's so cute! She is all white with black ears and face, and blue eyes."

"What's her name?" Lucy asks.

"Snow Queen."

"I can't wait to meet her," Savannah says.

"We should have brought her," I say, regretting leaving her in the laundry room.

We slow down on our last lap and stop in the middle of the floor. Since this isn't an official workout we skip our jumps and sit down in our splits to stretch.

"How was your Thanksgiving?" I ask my teammates.

Savannah shrugs, "Quiet. Just my mom and my

grandma. I think my mom was bummed you didn't stay. She likes people. On Friday we had a friendsgiving. A bunch of her friends from college and work came over, so that was nice for her. Honestly, I liked the quiet day better."

I nod, understanding Savannah. She likes to be social, but it seems like she likes small groups better.

I turn to Rose, who has been quiet all this time, "What are you working today?"

"I think I have to stay on floor with you because James can't come in today. So probably my round-off back handspring, back handspring. I need to clean up my form on the second one."

"Are you guys ready?" Melony asks, walking up to us. We nod and she starts to give instructions. "Lucy and Savannah, ten of each of the dance skills in your routine in front of the mirrors while I work with Paige. When you are done, I'll watch a dance through and tell you what you need to work on after that." Then she turns to Rose, "Rose, since you are off season I want you work on getting your steps into the pit."

"How do I do that?" Rose asks.

"Start on the edge of the floor in front of the pit and do your round-off back handspring from there. See how far it is and then try doing a round-off back handspring punch into the pit."

Rose lights up at this idea and runs over to the edge of the floor by the pit. Lucy and Savannah walk over to the mirror and begin working their dance skills.

Melony looks at me and smiles, "Ready?"

I smile back, "Ready."

"I have had so much fun creating this routine for you. Some parts might be challenging, but if you don't get it, we can change it."

"I'll get it," I say, confident in my ability to dance.

"I think so too," she says walking over to the gym stereo at the edge of the floor. She plugs in the gym phone and scrolls down to where it says, *Paige's music – Swan Lake*. She looks at me and says, "Let's listen to the first few eight counts so you have the rhythm in your head before I teach you the first section." She turns on the music and I remember how much I love it. "Listen to how it starts slow and flowy," she says.

We are quiet for a minute while we listen. Then she starts it over and counts over the music so I can hear the counts. I nod and she starts it again and says, "You're going to be still for the first eight and come in on the one of the second eight count."

"Okay," I say with confidence. I can hear the counts well and I know what she means.

"Let me teach you the first sixteen counts then," she turns off the music and walks a few feet away and I follow her.

"I want you to start here facing the corner," she says and shows me my starting pose, which is very beautiful with my arms in fourth position and my back toe pointed behind me with my legs straight. She has me do some flowy arm movements before I slowly move to the corner.

I learn the sixteen counts quickly and I love what she has put together so far. It's very balletic in its movement, which is what I wanted.

"Practice that first part into the corner while I have these two do dance throughs for me," she instructs.

I do as she says and practice my new dance section from the beginning to where I get myself to the corner ready to tumble. I am dying to try it to the music but Lucy is playing her music right now.

As soon as she and Savannah are done, I ask, "Can I try it to the music?"

"Five times at least," Melony says and walks over to check on Rose's progress.

Lucy hears this and asks, "Want me to turn it on for you?" as she walks over to the stereo.

"Yes please," I say getting into my starting pose.

"I like it already," she says as she presses play.

I do my sixteen counts, but not quite right and without a word I start again and Lucy starts the music over. We do this several times until Melony comes back.

"Thanks Lucy, I'll take it from here so you can go work leaps," she says, taking the phone from her. Lucy nods and gets back to work. Melony looks at me, "Let me see it to the music and we'll move on."

I show her the sixteen counts to the music and this time I get it. The moms clap and cheer from their chairs just inside the training area. I grin and do a pretend curtsy, making them clap louder.

Melony just says, "Over here," and she walks to the other end of the floor to where I would end my first tumbling pass. Then she shows me a few poses into my leap pass. Then a few more poses and I am to my second and final tumbling pass.

"That was fast," I say.

"I put a lot of dance at the end so that will be what judges remember," she wisely says.

"Good call," I say, knowing that my dance ability far exceeds my tumbling skills.

"Let's learn to the end of your second pass today," she decides.

"I can learn all of it," I plead.

"Probably, but I find it ends up cleaner if you learn a little at a time. Besides knowing through the second pass is enough to do it in practice and get your floor conditioning up."

I agree, but I'm bummed. I thought I would leave today knowing my entire routine. The Level 6 and 7 routines are so short I shouldn't have to split it up.

"Besides, I'm not entirely sure about a few of the dance moves until I see how the first half looks on you," she explains.

"Okay," I say so morosely that she starts laughing.

"Paige, you have most of your routine. Don't be disappointed. You have something to work on in practice now. That was worth coming in for," she reminds me.

She's right; it was. I do my partial routine to the music several times. It surprises me how it does wear me out more than the Level 5 routine ever did. The movements are harder and after the first tumbling pass the energy level is higher and faster.

"That's enough for today Paige," Melony finally says to me. Then to the group, "Girls, stretch it out and then you can go!"

We happily sit in a circle stretching. Since this is a voluntary workout we don't have conditioning nor is Melony telling us what to stretch. She is over talking to the moms.

"Your routine is beautiful," Lucy says as we sit down.

"Thanks," I say with a grin.

"Do you like it?" Savannah asks.

"So far," I say, "But I'm sad I didn't learn the entire thing." I admit.

We are silent for a brief moment before Rose says, "I can't wait to be in optionals." This makes me smile. I remember that feeling so well; being stuck with the monotonous compulsory routines. With that one statement Rose made me grateful to have even half of a routine. Because it's *my* half; no one else's.

CHAPTER 18

That afternoon I practice the first half of my routine over and over in my room. When the sun goes down my mom pokes her head in.

"Why don't you come down for dinner pumpkin," she invites me. I stop what I'm doing and think for a moment. Now that she mentions it, I am hungry. I look at Snow Queen curled up on my bed.

"Okay," I say, "But what if she wakes up? She still doesn't know the house very well."

"Bring her down. She can explore the kitchen."

I look at my white ball-of-fur kitten and I hate to wake her; but I hate the idea of leaving her more. I scoop her up and carry her down to the kitchen. She wakes and meows at me and it feels like she is saying, 'Now where are you taking me?'

I set her on the family room couch which is just off the kitchen. She immediately walks back and forth on the couch and cries.

"Let her be, she's just getting used to the house," my mom says, pulling containers of Thanksgiving leftovers out of the fridge that we brought back from the farm. "Here, make a plate of your favorites," she instructs.

I walk up to the counter and take one of the plates she set out and I fill it with mashed potatoes, stuffing, and corn. I go to put my plate in the microwave and my mom plops a piece of turkey on my plate.

"You need protein to grow," she justifies.

I don't say anything, but continue to the microwave asking, "How long?"

"Start with 45 seconds and then let's take a look."

I set the microwave and watch my plate through the window going in circles.

"What if I don't want to grow anymore?" I ask her.

"What?" my mom asks confused as she piles her plate with something from every container.

"You said the protein will make me grow. What if I don't want to grow anymore?" I repeat.

She stops mid scoop and looks at me, "Why wouldn't you want to grow?" she asks perplexed.

"Because I'm a gymnast. And I'm tired of being the tallest on the team and of people telling me how tall I am."

"Oh pumpkin, I had no idea that bothered you," she apologetically replies. I shrug and keep watching my food. "First of all I hardly think five feet is tall."

My food beeps and I look at her, "But everyone keeps telling me how tall I'm getting."

"That's because you grew a lot in a short amount of time. That doesn't mean you're a tall human being. Look, Paige, you aren't going to be a gymnast forever and you are going to want a little more height."

I'm not so sure about that, I think, as I reach up and take my food out. I walk it over to the counter and sit down while she heats up her food. I poke at the meat on my plate. If the protein represents growth, then I don't want to eat it.

"What's wrong with a tall gymnast anyway?" she asks.

"Nothing, I guess. It's just hard," I admit.

"What's hard?" she asks.

"Everything. Mostly floor. Tumbling has gotten really hard for me. Skills I already have feel like I'm just learning them. They're awkward and clunky."

"I had no idea. You had such a great workout today," she points out.

"That's because I was just doing dance today."

My mom frowns as she brings her plate around and sits next to me. Then she turns to me with a very serious expression.

"Paige, growing is part of life. I'm sorry it's making gymnastics difficult, but in the big picture of your life, you want to be the height you were meant to be. You don't want to cut out food or dislike your body because it's not the norm for gymnasts."

I look down and stab my rubbery microwaved turkey again. She sees me do it and says, "Plus, protein is energy and strength, too. You need energy to be able to do gymnastics in the first place."

"Can't I just stop growing for now?" I whine.

This is where Jason would have laughed or made a joke. Since he's still at the farm the mood remains solemn and my mom is intently looking at me.

"I'm sad you feel this way pumpkin. You need to stay healthy and let nature help you grow to the size you were meant to be."

"Am I going to get my period soon?" I ask, surprising both of us.

"I imagine so. I guess I've been so wrapped up in my

own stuff I haven't talked to you about it."

"It's okay," I say. "Grace and Chloe both got theirs. I talked to them. Well, to Grace."

"I see," my mom says, sounding a little hurt. "Chloe, too?"

"I thought that was crazy, too!" I exclaim.

"Girls are getting it younger these days," she comments.

She takes a bite and finally says, "Do you have any questions for me? Or did Grace answer them all for you?"

"What do I do when I get it? I mean, about gymnastics?"

"I imagine you will have to learn to use a tampon."

"What's that?" I ask.

"I'll get you some at the store tomorrow and you can see. But basically, you put it inside your body and it absorbs the bleeding so you can do sports or swim and forget you are having your period at all."

"So, it like, goes inside?"

"Yes."

"Gross."

"It's not gross; it's your body. Your body does so many amazing things, this is just one more. Your body is preparing to create babies if you want them. Don't you think that's kind of cool? Your body can create a human!"

I pause and think about what she said. It is kind of amazing when she says it like that. But babies seem so far away, why does my body have to get ready now?

"Does it hurt?" I ask.

"It can. It's more uncomfortable," she says.

I sigh, "I don't want to get it," I decide.

My mom laughs, "You can't stop it pumpkin. It's just one of those facts of life."

She is quiet for a moment. I decide to follow her lead and eat in silence. It's not hard to be quiet. We're so used to Jason talking all the time that when he's gone we struggle to make dinner conversation.

"When do you think they'll get back?" I ask. I thought my dad and Jason would be back from the farm by now.

"Dad said not until late. I guess they had a fun morning cutting down a Christmas tree."

"Lucky," I sigh. "Can we watch a movie?"

"Yes. Actually, I have an idea of what we should watch," she says with a grin.

"What?" I say.

"It's a surprise. You clean up here, I'm going to see if I can find what I want to watch," she says, getting up from the counter and going into the family room to pull up movies on the TV.

I look at the mess out on the counter, it looks bad but shouldn't take too long to clean. I rinse off our plates and put them in the dishwasher. Then I put away the food containers in the fridge. When I'm done with the kitchen I text Katherine and Abigail that we are back from Thanksgiving. I think of Snow Queen and text them that I have a surprise to tell them at school tomorrow.

Katherine:
Did you get a boyfriend?
Abigail:
Did you get your period?

I laugh, they both seem equally unlikely.

Me:
I'll tell you tomorrow.

Based on the questions they fired back at me, they might be disappointed by the announcement of Snow Queen.

"Are you ready for a great movie?" my mom sounds

happy with whatever we are going to watch. We settle into the family room and my mom already has a streaming app up on the TV.

"What are we watching?" I ask.

"Freaky Friday," she says, pulling a blanket up over us.

CHAPTER 19

I get to our lunch table before Katherine or Abigail. I sit down and pull out my lunch and my phone and start to scroll through my pictures. I decide on one from my birthday where she is still wearing the green bow.

"What's the big news?" Katherine asks walking up.

I extend my arm out and turn my phone to her so she can see the picture of Snow Queen.

"Oh my gosh, she is darling! Is that the news? Is she yours?"

I nod, "Her name is Snow Queen."

"What is it? I want to see!" Abigail demands walking up to our table. I show the picture to her.

"Why are we looking at this kitten?" she asks.

"It's Paige's new kitten!" Katherine exclaims.

"Really? She's your news?"

"She is," I say turning the phone back to me to look for another picture. I scroll through and land on one from last night when we were watching the movie.

"A kitten *is* big news," Abigail decides. "You'll have her forever."

"I hope so," I say as I hold out another picture. They are less interested this time so I put my phone down and pull out my sandwich.

"How were your Thanksgivings?" I ask. They both tell me about their weekends. Abigail visited her grandma's house in Oregon and she told us about how they shopped and went to the movies. Katherine went to Park City with her family for a ski trip. "The snow was just okay this early in the season. The hot tub at the house was amazing though," she shares.

"How was the farm?" Abigail asks.

"Awesome! That's where I got Snow Queen."

"Who's Snow Queen?" Abigail asks.

"The kitten. Keep up."

"The kitten. My kitten," I confirm. "There was an entire litter in the loft. They were so cute. I wish I could have taken all of them home."

I tell them more about the farm; the mama cat, her kittens, and horseback riding. I even tell them about the snowstorm and the giant puzzle.

"Your weekend sounds better," Abigail decides.

"Maybe I can bring you guys out to the farm sometime," I say. Grace would love these two. I'm not sure what Chloe would think and Noah would probably be annoyed. Maybe not. "Or maybe I could bring Grace out here and you guys could meet her," I amend.

"When do we get to see this kitten?" Katherine asks.

"Yeah! Let's come over today!" Abigail decides.

"I have practice today," I remind them.

"Oh yeah," she says, her face falling.

"I don't tomorrow though," I quickly add.

"Ask your mom if we can go home with you tomorrow," Katherine tells me. I nod just as the bell rings for us to go back to class.

As I'm walking back I wonder what it must be like to be Katherine and Abigail. They get to do whatever they please every day after school.

That afternoon, as I'm getting ready to go to the gym, I talk to Snow Queen about where I'm going and how long I'll be. I make sure to remember my phone because it has my floor music on it . . . and pictures of Snow Queen.

Practice starts on beam. The beam assignment is five stuck routines. As usual, Katie calls me over to give me my separate assignment.

"You are pretty set on beam Paige; you just need beam dance and a series or a flight element. How is the handstand back extension roll combination going?"

"It's hard, but I can do them sometimes on low beam," I share.

She nods and says, "Keep doing them there. If you have to stop between the two skills in the intersquad, you have to stop."

"What happens if I stop?"

"You get a deduction for not having a requirement," she explains. "I want you to attempt the series ten times on the low beam and five on high beam with the stop. Then five of everything in your routine and you can spend any remaining time on round-offs."

"Okay," I agree. It's a big assignment that will definitely keep me busy while everyone else is doing routines.

I decide to start with the version on high beam where I

step down and can stop if I need to. I can do a handstand and I can do a back extension roll. Doing them connected can't be that hard. *Except it is hard* a little voice says in my head. I shake my head to get that thought out and lift my arms for my handstand. I kick up to a nice tight handstand and step down into a lunge. A lunge does me no good. I can't connect anything with my feet apart like this. I sigh and try again. I kick up to a handstand, step down one foot and then the other one, staggered but right next to the first foot. I stand all the way up, pause for a second, and squat down into my back extension roll. I am crooked and step down off to the side of the beam. I am smiling because I think I can do this, I almost connected it.

"Keep your arms moving the entire time!" I hear Katie yell at me from a few beams away.

I nod, I know I paused. I step up again. This time I pause a little less, but I'm off to the side. The following time I pause longer and almost make my back extension roll. Adding a handstand is harder than it seems.

By the time Katie comes over my head is starting to hurt from so many back extension rolls. She silently watches a few. I do my three best ones (still a pause, still off to the side) while she is watching.

"I think you can get that. What do you think?" she asks me.

"By when?" I ask.

"Christmas."

"I can get it," I say with more confidence than I'm feeling.

She nods and says, "I saw you rubbing your head. Go on to five of everything in your routine and if you still have time then round-offs."

Even though I don't have a routine, per se, I know what will be in it. I have to have a full turn, a leap pass, mount, dismount, a series, and a jump combination.

"What's my mount?" I ask Katie, realizing I don't have one to work.

"Melony will decide when she creates your dance. Speaking of dance, how did the floor routine go?" she asks.

"It's awesome, the dance is really pretty."

"I'm sure it is. I imagine Melony will use a lot of the dance from your floor routine for beam. You can learn it this weekend."

I make a note in my head that I will probably have to come in extra this weekend. I don't mind. Aside from leaving poor Snow Queen, I don't mind.

"A beam is open," Katie says to Maya as Lucy jumps down and heads over to the low beams.

"Done with your five, Lucy?" Katie asks. She and Lucy start talking about what extra skills Lucy can work. I jump up on a beam to work my leaps, turns, and jumps. My back extension roll series is cool, but it's hard. Can I get that by Christmas?

How are Savannah and Lucy so far ahead of me in their preparedness for Level 6? *Because they are better than you* my voice says. When did my voice get so mean? My voice used to be so nice and encouraging.

"Paige, focus!" I hear Katie say to me. How does she know? I miss James. As much as I'm getting used to Katie, I miss James.

"Eyes on the end of the beam!" she yells at me. *Focus. Focus*, I can do that. I fix my eyes on the end of the beam and focus on my split jump, split jump.

"Beautiful! Do it like that every time!" she yells. I give her a tiny nod of acknowledgement and go again. I know it's another good one and I hear Katie give a few claps and walk to the next beam. Thank goodness for dance elements. They save me every time.

"Paige you have got to pull your toes to make it around," James tells me. We are on the last rotation of the day. James is working with us because he is done with the Level 3 practice. Katie is working with the Level 8s, 9s, and 10s on beam. I was so excited to have James coaching us, unfortunately my floor rotation is not going as planned.

We don't have access to the entire floor yet. Two classes are using half of the floor and we are tumbling on the other half. James told us we would run routines at the end of the rotation. I'm excited to show my teammates the first half of my routine. That's the only thing keeping me going in this miserable workout.

"What are your passes?" James asks me.

"Layout and front, front," I answer.

"And your first meet is in a month?" he asks.

"About. We have our final intrasquad before Christmas break and our first meet is the first weekend in January."

"What is your back up plan?" he asks me.

"I don't know." *A back up plan? Back up to what?*

"I'll talk to Katie," he says.

"About what?"

"You need a plan B if this layout doesn't become more consistent."

"You think I can't do it?" I ask, feeling my eyes prickle hot. James has always believed in me. I have never had him question if I could make a skill. There are skills he knows would be physically impossible for me, like a back walkover on beam. That was different, he believed I could do the back extension roll instead.

"Paige, you are a very talented athlete and you work

hard. I believe you can get these skills. By moving up form Level 5 to 6 in the same year, you gave yourself very little time to prepare. A back up plan might be a good idea."

I lift my chin, "Then why hasn't Katie mentioned it?" I ask defiantly.

"Because Katie has five optionals teams she's trying to keep track of," he fires back at me.

"She lost track of me?" I say, trying even harder to keep my watery eyes from giving me away.

"Not exactly, I bet she's just waiting to see what you do at the intrasquad. I think it would be a good idea for you to have an A and B routine on floor."

"A and B?" I ask. Out of the corner of my eye I see Maya motion for James to spot. He nods and motions for me to move off to the side of the floor and waves for her to go. He spots her, gives a correction, and turns back to me.

"Work both layouts and tucks today. Then work both bounders and single front tucks," he instructs.

I nod. Ironically, that's what I'm already doing. I do several back tucks when I warm up for layouts and I'm not even doing bounders. I'm doing front tuck, stop, front tuck into the pit. The gut punch is hearing that James thinks I need a back-up plan.

I slowly walk back to my place in line to tumble back up the floor to the other end. I run and do a lame punch front. I land in a deep squat, which is uncharacteristic of me. What is wrong with me? Why is my tumbling so low? My front tucks used to land so light and airy and never in a deep almost bum hitting squat.

"Flip on the way up Paige!" James yells to me. I nod as I walk back in line, but I don't turn to look at him, I can feel my face burning in embarrassment. When did I become bad at floor? When is this rotation going to be over? And here I was excited to do floor today. I fumbled through an entire work out only to be miserable at my favorite event.

I just want to go home and see Snow Queen, or hang out with Katherine and Abigail, or workout with my old Level 5s. I wonder what Trista and Carmen are doing tonight.

After another several miserable tumbling passes the recreational kids finish their rotation on floor and we get the entire floor for the last fifteen minutes of practice. Normally we would be conditioning by now but James decides we will do floor dance throughs as conditioning.

"Ladies, one dance through each with three sprints per tumbling pass. Push-ups and V-ups along the edge of the floor while you wait for your turn. Three sets of ten and then stretch."

It's an easy assignment as far as conditioning goes and we're all smart enough not to say anything and to just get to work.

I'm not sure if I'm supposed to do my half routine or not. I quietly do my push-ups as I watch my teammates huff through dance throughs. James pauses the music when they get to a tumbling pass and they sprint along the diagonal three times rather than doing a tumbling pass. When I get to V-ups everyone has gone except for me.

"Paige, didn't you learn your routine this weekend?" James asks me.

"Half of it."

"Come on up," he motions for me to get up. "Let's do the half you know. Something is better than nothing."

I slowly stand up, nervous and excited to do my routine for my teammates for the first time. I walk to the corner and stand in my starting pose and James starts the music. As soon as my music begins the entire gym stops. All the kids and coaches recognize the new floor music and they want to see a new routine. I do the dance Melony taught me to the corner and when I pause to tumble James pauses the music and I run across the diagonal.

"Great music," I hear Maya saying and it makes me smile a little as I run back the way I came. When I'm done with my three sprints I get in a lunge as if I finished my first tumbling pass and James plays the music. I listen closely to hear when to start dancing again. I do my dance and leap pass and make my way to the next corner. I sprint again, end in a lunge, and then drop my arms and look at James.

"That's it. That's all I know."

He pauses the music, "That's most of it anyway. Great routine Paige. It will be a judge pleaser for sure. Good job today. Go stretch with your teammates."

I don't say anything to him, I just turn and go to where my teammates are sitting along the edge of the floor. I sit down in my splits and my teammates immediately start talking.

"I recognize that music. What's it from?" Victoria asks.

"A ballet," Savannah answers.

"Which one?"

"Swan Lake," I supply.

"It's beautiful. It looks so good on you," Riley says.

"I wish I could dance like that," Alexis comments.

"Thanks," I say, a bit embarrassed by all the praise.

"Paige likes ballet class. That's what it looks like when you pay attention in ballet class," James says walking up and dropping a panel mat in front of us for over splits.

Embarrassed and pleased, I put my foot up on the mat James brought over and slide into over splits.

"I can't wait to see the end," Maya says.

"When do you learn the rest of it?" Savannah asks.

"I'm not sure," I stammer.

"Try for tomorrow," James advises. "I would text Melony and see if she can meet with you before or after the Level 4s and 5s tomorrow."

"Text Melony?" I ask. I've never texted a coach before.

James nods, "Get it done as soon as possible so you can start conditioning for a full set. I'll give your mom her number before you leave." Then he starts talking to Brooklyn about her tumbling passes. In usual James fashion he walks around and adjusts our splits while he chats. I do miss him, even if he doesn't fully believe in me anymore.

CHAPTER 20

I sit in the car eating a snack as my mom rushes me from school to the gym so I can work with Melony on my floor routine before she coaches the Level 4s and 5s. It's Tuesday, my day off from practice. This won't feel like practice though. Learning dance is easy and fun.

Jason is chattering the entire drive and when my mom pulls up to the gym I jump out without a word.

"How long do you think you'll be?" she asks as I'm getting out.

"Probably only an hour because the Level 4s and 5s start practice in an hour," I answer.

"We'll just go get a snack and come back then," my mom says. I smile and shut the door, happy to leave Jason's chatter.

I walk into the gym and head straight to the bathroom to change. Then I come out and throw my stuff in a cubby in the lobby, not bothering to go up to the optionals room. The gym isn't busy yet, so the lobby is quiet.

"What are you doing here on a Tuesday?" Suzanne, who works at the front desk, asks me.

"I'm here to finish learning my floor routine."

"I saw that yesterday. It looks great so far. I can't wait to see the rest of it."

"Me either," I say.

"Go on in. Melony is in the office. I'm sure she'll be out soon," she says.

I do as she says and head out into the training area and warm myself up. There is one pre-school class going on and a couple of privates. It's too early for much else, as most kids are still in school.

I'm sitting in my splits when Melony comes out a few minutes later.

"I'm so glad you could come this early. I think we can knock this out today since you learn dance so fast." She sits down in her splits next to me. "There's a lot of dance in the last part."

"I'm ready," I say standing up.

"Great, warm up with a dance through of what you know so far," she instructs.

"With or without music?" I ask.

"Let's do one of each."

I do as she says and do a quiet dance through without the music. Then she turns on the stereo and I do a dance through with the music, which feels so much better.

Melony teaches me the dance after my second tumbling pass. She choreographed pretty and graceful movements that aren't particularly difficult. Then she teaches me a jump combination, shows me where to do my one and a half turn, and teaches me the ending pose.

"That's it?" I say, surprised we're done.

"That's it. Level 6 and 7 floor routines are about half the

length of the upper optional routines," she explains.

I knew that. I've been watching the optional girls with envy for years. I just expected it to feel longer once I was the one doing it.

"Plus dance comes easy for you. For some girls it takes a lot more practice to learn and remember their routines. Let's do the second half to music a few more times," she says, walking over to the gym phone. "Start just after the leap pass." I easily do the second half three more times.

"Are you ready for a full dance through?" She asks.

I smile and nod. Of course I'm ready! I can't wait to do the entire thing! I look up to the parent viewing area and I see Jason and my mom are there watching. Well, my mom is watching. Jason is playing video games on his tablet. She sees me look up and waves.

I give her a little wave as I walk to my starting corner. I get in my starting pose and wait for Melony to play the music. I have to concentrate to remember all the dance movements. The music helps me remember what I'm supposed to be doing. I forget a small part after my leap but find the music again for the poses before the tumbling pass.

When I'm done Melony claps as she walks over to me.

"That looked great! Let's just go over the part after the leap."

I nod while I'm catching my breath. That took more energy than I thought it would. And I didn't even tumble! Imagine how it's going to feel when I put it all together. I keep my concerns to myself as I watch Melony show me the steps again. I repeat them behind her. It helps to do them while she is doing them and I see where I got confused.

"I think I've got it," I say.

"Do it a few more times. Then let's do one more dance through before I have to coach team," Melony instructs.

"It's already time for them to start?" I ask, shocked.

"We've been at it for almost an hour. Time flies when you're having fun," she says over her shoulder as she goes to the stereo to play my music.

I do the segment I struggled with two more times before I feel ready for a final dance through.

As I stand in my corner waiting for the music to begin, I hear the lobby has gotten loud. Classes are starting to come into the training area. The door is swinging open and closed as kids are streaming in.

When my music starts I try to forget the chaos in the lobby and focus on my routine. The music is so powerful and beautiful I have no problem forgetting everything around me and focusing on my dance. I run across the diagonal during my tumbling pass. It crosses my mind to look up at my mom, but I have only eight counts to get to the corner and keep dancing. I get in my lunge and immediately hear the music where I dance again. Then I have my leap pass, more dance, run across the diagonal, one and a half turn, dance, jump, ending pose.

I did it! I have my very own beautiful amazing Swan Lake floor routine!

"That was totally awesome!" I hear someone yell.

I drop my arms from my ending pose and turn to see who it is. Trista is standing there with a huge grin on her face. "I mean it. Totally awesome, Paige."

I'm so happy to see her! "Thanks," I say.

"I'm so glad my mom dropped me off early so I could see that. You should do it one more time so Carmen and Marissa can see it."

I turn to Melony and give her a questioning look.

"Sure, you can do one more while they're running laps around the floor. But then we need to be done. The gym is way too busy this time of day for us to take up the entire floor."

"How have you been?" I ask Trista, as Melony goes back over to the stereo.

"Good. I have my layout on floor. Bars is still the bane of my existence," she says dramatically.

"I miss you guys."

"We miss you, too. Seeing you only one day a week stinks."

"Maybe the summer schedule will be better," I say, hoping it will be true. I really do miss Trista, Carmen, and Marissa.

"Hi Paige. What are you doing here on a Tuesday?" Marissa asks, as she walks into the training room and onto the floor.

"Getting her amazing floor routine," Trista answers.

"Oh, do we get to see it?"

"While you are running laps," I answer.

"How are you?" she asks.

"A little overwhelmed," I answer honestly.

"I bet. I knew it would be too much for me," Marissa says maturely.

"Level 4s and 5s, start running!" Melony yells and then turns to me and yells across the floor, "You ready?"

I nod and walk over to my starting spot, excited and nervous to show my friends my new routine. As I'm standing in my starting pose I see Carmen out of the corner of my eye walk in and it makes me happy that all of my former teammates will see my new routine.

When the music starts, I stop thinking about who is in the gym and force myself to think about the dance. Thankfully the music is so specific and clear, I can remember what goes where.

I do a much better job with the dance before the leap pass, I flub the one and a half turn, and I enjoy the dance at the end. When I'm done my former teammates are clapping as they run their laps around the edge of the floor.

"Great job Paige," Melony says to me. "I want you to go home and do it at least five more times so you don't forget."

"I won't forget," I promise.

"Do it anyway. It's a time-honored tradition to drive your family crazy with your new floor routine," she says. Then she puts her hand on my shoulder, "It's a beautiful routine Paige. I put some difficult dance in there and you learned it with no problem."

"Thanks," I say, a little embarrassed.

"Why don't you stretch with these girls before you leave," she says, gesturing toward the Level 4s and 5s. "I have to talk to Katie before she gets started with the upper optionals."

I happily do as she says and join my friends.

"That was beautiful," Carmen says as soon as I sit in my splits next to her.

"Swan Lake fits you," Marissa adds.

"Thanks guys," I say, surprised I'm a little out of breath.

"The judges are going to love you," Trista says.

"I hope so," I smile. I miss these three. "I miss you guys," I blurt out.

"We miss you, too," Carmen says easily.

"Next season we'll be together. When we are 6s and you are a 7. It will be okay," Trista says. I can tell she has told herself this a lot.

I nod, "You're right. It will be."

"Paige!" I hear my mom loudly whisper to me. I look up and she is looking around the glass training room doors and motioning for me to go.

"I have to go. It was good seeing you guys. Have a good workout," I say, as I stand up and walk to my mom.

As I'm walking out, Melony comes out of the coaches room. "Over and over again tonight, okay?"

"Okay," I agree, knowing that won't be a problem.

"Great job today," she adds.

I feel pleased with myself as I walk out of the training area. I'm going to be able to compete next month after all. I can do this!

"Your routine is gorgeous," my mom says as we walk out of the gym.

"I think so, too," I agree. "I have to practice it tonight so I don't forget it."

"It's a lot to remember," she comments as we get into the car.

"Can I invite Katherine and Abigail over?"

"I thought you just said you had to practice," my mom says confused.

"I do. I want to show them. They're dancers, they'll get it," I say. "And they are dying to see Snow Queen," I add.

"If you text them right now I can pick them up on the way home."

"Can I have unlimited game time then?" Jason pipes up.

"Why would you get unlimited game time?" my mom asks him.

"Because Paige is getting friends over."

"Jason, that makes no sense. You can have friends over if you want, but no extra games," she tells him.

He slumps back in his seat and keeps playing while he can. He knows when he gets home he has to put it away.

Abigail and Katherine are able to come over. In fact, they were already both hanging out at Katherine's house so we only have to make one stop.

"I thought you didn't have practice on Tuesdays," Katherine says as they get in the car and she sees me in a leo and sweat pants. "I can't keep up," she says squeezing in the back seat. They are in the back with Jason, while I sit up front.

"I can't wait to see your kitten!" Abigail exclaims.

"I don't usually have practice on Tuesdays. I was learning the rest of my floor routine today," I explain.

"Do we get to see it?" Abigail asks.

"I have to go home and do it over and over again, so yes, you get to see it."

"Where will you have room? It's too cold outside for anything," Katherine asks.

"We can push the couches to the walls in the family room," my mom says. "It won't be as big as the real floor, but it should work, right Paige?" she asks me.

"It will work. The dance doesn't have to take up a lot of space. As long as I remember the pattern in my head."

We pull up to the house and the girls are talking over the top of each other arguing over who gets to make up my next floor routine.

"I am going to be a famous choreographer, so it should be me," Abigail says.

"That's fine, because I'm going to be too busy designing clothes," Katherine fires back. While they are arguing I run up and get Snow Queen from the laundry room and bring her down.

As soon as I walk into the family with her the girls immediately stop what they are saying to fuss over Snow Queen.

"Awe, she's so cute!"

"I love her blue eyes!"

"I love her white paws."

"Can I hold her?"

I hand her over to Abigail, even though I know it won't last. Snow Queen immediately squirms out of her grasp and falls to the floor, which is where she wanted to be in the first place.

I go to the cupboard and get her treats and toys out so the

girls can play with her. We sit on the floor giving Snow Queen all the attention for a while. We run feathers across the floor and when she gets tired of that we try a toy mouse. When she gets tired of the mouse we give her treats. Then she finally climbs in my lap and falls asleep.

"She's an awesome birthday present," Katherine comments.

"She is," I agree.

"How are we going to see your floor routine with her in your lap like that?" Abigail asks.

"Maybe I can move her," I say, gingerly lifting her up and trying to stand at the same time. Of course, I wake her and she is not happy about it. I immediately put her on a pillow on the couch. She stands up, looks at me, and saunters to a different pillow.

"Shall we move these?" Katherine asks, referring to the couches.

We move the two couches, a chair, and a coffee table to the walls at the edge of the room. Snow Queen just looks at us while we move the couch she is sitting on.

Once the room is cleared of furniture I begin to figure out what my pattern will be. Abigail and Katherine plop on the couches and wait.

"Okay, I think I've got it," I say. I hand Abigail my phone. "Here, just hit play. I have it connected to the speaker, already."

She nods, "Tell me when you're ready."

I go to my pretend corner on the other side of the room, raise my arms, and say, "Ready." Abigail hits play and almost instantly my music begins. I do my beginning dance and where I'm supposed to tumble I just walk across the room.

"This is when I tumble," I explain.

"We got that," Katherine says.

I wait for the music in a lunge. When the music catches up to me I continue on with the dance, leap, more dance, and the last tumbling pass. Then I do a terrible turn and do the final dance sequence, my jumps, and ending pose.

When I'm done I look expectantly at my friends.

"That was great!" Abigail says.

"You have some classic ballet in there. Where did you learn to do that?"

"From the ballet classes at the gym. We have a real Madame from the Salt Lake City Ballet."

"I can tell. You even have pique turns in there."

"I do? I don't actually know what that is."

Katherine stands up, "It's this move," she says demonstrating a turn sequence that I have in my routine.

"Oh, what's it called again?"

"Pique turns," she says.

"They're fun," I admit.

"They totally are. Ballet has its moments."

"Let's see it again," Abigail requests.

"Really? You want to see it again?"

"Yes."

"Good, because I'm supposed to practice it a lot," I admit.

I do my routine at least five more times. Katherine and Abigail are much more useful than I thought they would be. They correct me on my pique turns and my one and a half turn. They criticize my arm positions on some of my moves and they tell me to get my chin up. They could be gymnastics dance teachers someday.

"Can we make up something new now?" Abigail asks.

"Yes, I'm beat," I say, and flop on the couch.

"What song," Katherine asks and starts scrolling through her phone. Pretty soon all of us are looking at music on our phones trying to find a good dance song. We play several for each other but can't seem to decide.

The girls absently start talking about school and homework. I'm exhausted, I'm glad we didn't find a song. I'm happy to sit here and listen to them. Snow Queen sees me and comes over to my lap and curls up.

"Paige, you look a little pale," Abigail says to me.

"I think I'm just tired. I've been going non-stop since last week. I don't know how I'm going to get through practice tomorrow."

"Can you take a day off?" Katherine asks.

"Not really, not this time of year. Unless I'm sick for real. I'm not though; just out of steam I guess."

"She's right. You don't look so good."

"Gee thanks," I say with sarcasm.

"Oh, here's one!" Abigail says, having found the perfect song. Thankfully they've forgotten about me and my exhaustion.

Am I really that pale? I would get up and look in the mirror, but Snow Queen is sitting on me. I didn't think I was pushing myself that hard, but maybe I am.

Katherine agrees that the song Abigail found is perfect and they quickly throw together a routine. I stay on the couch. I blame Snow Queen even though we all know the real reason is I just can't seem to find the energy to get up.

.

CHAPTER 21

I'm excited to get to practice and show my teammates my compete floor routine. I'm feeling better than last night, but still kind of off. I have a weird headache and belly ache. I better not be getting sick. I don't have time to be sick. I only have a few weeks before the second and final intrasquad.

We go to bars first and I have a decent practice. Katie is spotting me on flyaways and I'm becoming more comfortable with having her there rather than James. I'm really just piking my flyaway rather than laying out, but it's progress.

"Keep that hollow body position you have when you let go. Stop bending in the hips," Katies says to me.

I know I'm bending in the hips. I just don't see how I'm going to get around to my feet if I stay straight.

"Why don't you go do a few into the pit. Remember what it feels like. Throw a mat in if it feels good."

I'm happy to go to the pit so I can learn this skill

correctly. The downside is the pit bar can get lonely. I readjust my grips as I walk by the beams and across the floor to the pit bar and take a deep breath, this is the only skill I need to have a decent Level 6 bar routine. I can do this. I climb up to the bar, do a few tap swings and a tuck flyaway to warm up.

"What are you working?" Lucy asks walking up. I look at her from my position buried in foam squares.

"Layout flyaways," I answer.

"For a second I thought you were doing double back timers," she replies.

"Yeah, right," I chuckle climbing out. "I have to get the layout first."

"I thought you had your layout?" she questions.

"I sort of do with James. I hold back with Katie," I say quietly as I get out so none of the coaches will hear me.

"I know how hard it is to change coaches," Lucy says with sympathy.

"I can't imagine changing gyms." When Lucy came here she was quiet and never complained. Looking back, it must have been a big change. "Why are you over here?"

"I'm done with my assignment so I get to work double back timers."

"Wow, are you allowed to do that in Level 6?"

"It's not for Level 6 or even Level 7. Katie wants me to work them for Level 8."

"Do you think it will throw off your layout?" I ask.

"I don't think so. The body positions are so different. I don't think it will make me over rotate my layout."

I wasn't even thinking about over rotating, I was thinking more about forgetting which body position to do. I watch Lucy jump up to the high bar and pump into a long hang kip. Then she stops up in a support position on the high bar, takes a deep breath, casts almost to handstand, swings down and does a nice high tuck flyaway. Instead of landing on her feet she scoops her feet and lands on her back in the pit. Doing one and a quarter flips.

"That looks easy Lucy!" Lucy smiles as she hears Katie from across the gym.

"She doesn't know I did these at camp. I didn't want to say anything in case I forgot how to do them."

"Looks like you remembered."

"Yeah, I'll be able to flip it if she comes over and spots," she says.

"I can't wait to see it," I say and jump up and swing into my flyaway. Inspired by Lucy's beautiful flyaway, I decide to really try to stay hollow for the layout. I tap three times, see my toes, let go, stay hollow, and easily flip to my feet.

"Good Paige, now from a cast!" Katie yells over to me.

"How does she see everything?" I ask Lucy.

"Everything," Lucy agrees.

I eventually do my layout flyaway from a cast in the pit, but it is still a little piked. I think I pike to make sure I get it around. I'm going to have to get more brave on these.

After bars we go to beam and all the girls are doing full routines while I'm on low beam working handstand back extension rolls.

Katie gets everyone started on their assignment and then comes over to me. "You have a couple of choices on the back extension roll series," Katie says to me.

"What is that?" I ask, curious.

"You can do a handstand step down like you've been doing or you can do a handstand straddle down into in."

"Staddle down?"

"Here let me show you. Shannon Miller did it beautifully in '96," she says, pulling out her phone. She pulls up the routine she is thinking of and shows me. Sure enough a tiny Olympian is doing a perfect handstand. Rather than stepping down out of her handstand she brings it down controlled to a straddled sitting position and immediately rolls back into a back extension roll. Then out of that handstand she does another one.

"She does two!" I exclaim.

"I know, so rare. And she did them perfectly."

"Can I see again?" I ask. She nods and hands me the phone.

"When you're done watching, try some handstand straddle downs on the medium beam. Use a sting mat for your first several."

I take the phone and am mesmerized by Shannon Miller's back extension rolls. I go to the floor and kick up to a handstand and try my press down. I could never press up to handstand, but I did get pretty good at straddling down. When I feel good about that, I go get a sting mat and drag it over to the medium beam and throw it over. When I step up I pause for a second, not sure how this is going to go.

"Do the handstand in front of the mat, then straddle down onto it and roll on it," Katie instructs.

I do as she says and kick up to handstand with my hands on the beam just in front of the mats. I straddle and try to control it down, but at the last second I plop down on the sting mat. I do this a few more times until finally I do one that is controlled and rolling back out of it is easy.

"That's it Paige!" Katie exclaims, "Just like that, do it again!"

Motivated by Katie's excitement I immediately do it again. I'm able to control it down again and roll back.

"Push up into that back extension roll. Don't be shy," Katie says.

"Okay," I say, standing next to the medium beam. My back is aching, I wonder if I jarred it plopping down onto the beam the first few times. "May I get a drink?"

Katie absently nods and I turn to the drinking fountain. I have a water bottle upstairs, but I don't want to go all the way up. I just need a second to see what is going on with my back. I hope I'm not hurt. The ache is deep inside my back, I must have been in less control coming down than I thought. I take a drink and walk a little hoping it will go away. It doesn't go away, but it doesn't hurt so bad that I need to stop either. I go back to my medium beam determined to get this combination.

I climb up, pausing for a moment to think about what I need to do. Tight handstand, control it down, and go right into the back extension roll that I have been doing for over a year. I raise my arms, kick up into a tight handstand, straddle and in a controlled movement lean my shoulders forward a bit, roll my hips so I straddle down smoothly. As soon as I touch the beam, I roll back and push up into a handstand and fall off to the side.

"That's it! Do you like that way better?" Katie asks me.

"It's faster, so pushing up into the handstand is easier. Controlling it down is hard," I admit.

"You decide which is easier for you," she says. "Try the other way and see."

"Right now?"

"Yes."

I jump up and kick to a handstand, step down, and roll into a back extension roll. It is harder to push up into the handstand because I'm moving slower. I fall off to the side and look at Katie. She looks at me, waiting for me to speak.

"Tough call. The speed of the straddle down helps, but I can't always control it down."

"Keep working both then," she says, turning to the group and yelling that we have five minutes.

I jump up and do a few more before we have to rotate. Katie tells the team to go get a drink and go to floor, then she walks over to me.

"You'll get your beam routine this Saturday," she informs me.

"Do I need to stay after practice?"

"No Melony can come work with you during practice. You'll be able to do routines next week."

"What about my series?" I ask, referring to the handstand back extension roll.

"You can just do the handstand back extension roll with a pause in routines until you're ready to connect it," she comments, unconcerned.

She walks with me to the lobby so I can get a drink. "I know it's all very fast, Paige. You're doing well. You'll find success this season," she says matter-of-factly.

I wish I was as confident.

I look out the parent viewing area as I pass it to the optionals room. The Level 4s and 5s are here, which means James will not be with us on floor. I have to start trusting Katie. She has done nothing to make me feel like she can't spot. In fact, she spots the upper optional girls. I'm just used to James.

I go into the optionals room and over to my locker. The rest of my team is already there, finishing up a quick snack and closing their locker doors. I quickly get out my drink and a sports bar. I take one bite of the sports bar and all of a sudden I don't want it. I can't be sick. Not only am I behind in the gym, but my school is so tough that missing a day or two means a ton of homework. I take a quick sip of water and set it back down then follow my teammates out of the room and back down into the training area.

Katie is ready on floor. There are no upper optional girls in the gym on Wednesdays so we have Katie for the entire rotation.

"Two of each tumbling pass. One routine with your first

pass, one routine with your second pass, and one dance through," she announces.

"Paige, I want you to do one dance through, and one routine with one pass. Whichever one you want." I know she is giving me an easier assignment because my routine is new. But I do not have the luxury of several weeks of dance throughs like my teammates.

The girls spread out to the different corners and Katie announces that someone has to start a routine so we can get through everyone before practice is over. Brooklyn volunteers to start with her dance through while everyone else tumbles.

I warm up with a round-off back handspring and feel pretty good. Then I do a round-off back handspring back tuck and it is terrible. My set must have been off because I landed really low.

"Snap down more out of that back handspring and get your chest up for your set," Katie tells me. I nod, grateful for the correction. I knew something was off.

I go to the corner and wait for a moment while Brooklyn is dancing.

"That diagonal can go while she is in this corner!" Katie yells at the other corner. "You should know her pattern by now!" she reminds us.

Aubrey from the opposite diagonal tumbles while Brooklyn dances near my corner. Then Brooklyn runs to the other end of the floor where her tumbling would be and dances along the side of the floor so Savannah in our corner knows to tumble. She does a beautiful layout. When did that get so good? Savannah, Lucy, and Alexis have really improved since we've been with the Level 6s and 7s.

Brooklyn's music ends and it's my turn to tumble. I think about the exact correction Katie gave me. Usually that works and I can make the correction. To my surprise I do another really low back tuck. It just felt wrong and my back is throbbing. Maybe I really did hurt myself doing those klutzy swing downs on beam.

"Who wants to go next?" Katie calls out, scrolling down the gym phone.

"I will!" I volunteer. I have been dying to do my routine for my teammates and my tumbling is a disaster right now anyway.

"Great, Paige it is," she says, finding my music as I walk to my starting corner. My teammates stop tumbling and Katie doesn't yell at them this once. It is an unwritten rule that the gym is allowed to stop for new floor routines. When my music comes on I can tell the entire gym turns to watch. This time I have a full routine to show them.

I have a great time with the music and my ballet moves. I improved a lot last night working with Katherine and Abigail and I am happy to show it off.

When my music ends the gym claps, which surprises me a little.

"Beautiful Paige. Now we just have to get you conditioned in a month to add the tumbling. Who's up?"

Savannah volunteers to go next. Since the gym has seen her routine several times, everyone goes back to work.

I decide to go to front tucks. I don't want to go back to terrible back tucks again. My front tucks are unusually low. What is going on? I get no correction from Katie since she's watching Savannah's dance through.

I finish my three front tucks and I have no choice but to go back to back tucks. Now Alexis is doing her routine. I watch as she moves through her routine and I know when she leaps along the floor that I am safe to take a turn. I run, do my round-off back handspring, back tuck. Only instead of making the back tuck around, I land short and immediately put my hands down, ending on my hands and knees. I sit back on my heels. I feel woozy and out of sorts.

"Paige, are you okay?" I hear Katie ask. She sounds far away. I look up and see her closer to me than I would have guessed.

"Paige?" she asks, putting her hand out to help me up. "You're a little pale, everything all right? Did that one rattle you?"

"I'm off," I say slowly. "Something's wrong."

"Go get a drink and sit down. Did you eat a snack? Did you eat lunch today?" she asks me with her hand still on my arm.

"I think so," I say. Come to think of it, food hasn't sounded good all day and I'm not sure what I've eaten.

"Maya, go get Paige a granola bar from my office and sit her down," she orders, passing me off.

Maya grabs my arm and leads me to one of two chairs in the training area. Once she has me sitting she disappears in the coaches office and comes back out with a granola bar.

She hands it to me and says, "Trust me, you want to eat. I tried it for a while and it just made my gymnastics worse, not better."

"What are you talking about?" I ask, taking the bar she is holding out to me.

"You stopped eating, right? That's why you're landing short and are so pale."

What? I shake my head, "No, that's not it."

"Could have fooled me. Paige, you look great. You're just growing. Don't sabotage yourself, okay?"

"Okay," I agree, even though that's not my problem. Although, to be fair, it did cross my mind these last few weeks. Today wasn't intentional though, I just didn't feel like eating much. I sit and eat my granola bar while I watch my teammates run routines.

"All okay over here?" James asks. The Level 4s and 5s

are on beam, right next to where I'm sitting. I nod, embarrassed that everyone thinks I've been starving myself.

He pauses and looks at me for a moment with those sharp gray eyes. "Better take care of yourself if you want to be a high level athlete."

"I will. I promise." He nods and goes back to his team.

I watch the Level 4s and 5s playing around with new skills since they're not in season. Should I have stayed with them? Carmen jumps down from a beam, catches my eye and waves. I give a weak smile and wave back.

I want to get back to my workout, but I feel so gross. I lean forward and put my elbows on my knees and my face in my hands. Maybe I'm just tired. I have worked out every day since Sunday. Usually I would rest on Sunday and Tuesday. I don't feel like I worked that hard on those extra days, but maybe I did. Maybe this is what it means to be in optionals. Hard work. I better keep up if I'm going to compete in the intersquad in a few weeks. I need to finish this workout even if I feel crummy.

I decide to go to the restroom and then get back to work. I stand up quickly and get woozy again. I grab the back of the chair for support and stand still until it passes. Maybe I do need to call my mom. *What a royal bummer*, I think as I walk to the bathroom that is off of the training area. I push open the door debating in my head if I should stay for the rest of the workout or call my mom and go home. I sit down on the toilet and look down and to my surprise I see bright red blood spots in my underpants. Oh my gosh, my period! What do I do? I don't have any pads with me. Would pads even work in a leotard? I should have put pads in my gym bag. How much more blood is going to come out? Will it make a mess if I go back to practice? I have to go home. I feel awful anyway. I wad up a bunch of toilet paper and stick it in my underwear. I'm grateful I'm wearing black workout shorts today. I stand up and go to the sink to wash my hands. I look in the mirror and see that Katie was right, I am pale. Is all this misery because of my period? The loss of energy and wooziness? The tummy ache? It all makes sense now.

I finish washing my hands, dry them off, and leave the bathroom. There is a girl outside waiting for me. Hopefully I wasn't in there too long. I walk over to Katie.

"How are you feeling?" she asks me when I walk up.

"Not great," I answer honestly. "Can I go home?"

"Of course, get some rest," she says, with real sympathy. She must think I'm either coming down with the flu or I'm starving myself.

I want to get out of here before any of my teammates ask me what's wrong. I quickly turn and go out of the training room and into the lobby. I walk up to the optional room to get my phone and text my mom.

Me:
> Not feeling well. Can you come get me?

Mom:
> Of course. What's wrong?

Me:
> I got my period.

Mom:
> Be right there.

CHAPTER 22

I look at my phone and for the first time I realize that all women, including my mom, know what this feels like. They are all in on the secret and they don't tell kids. Is everyone caught off guard like me?

I pull out my sweatshirt and sweatpants and throw them on. Then I worry that blood may seep through my black shorts onto my light gray sweatpants. Do I put them on anyway, or leave them off? I take my sweatshirt back off and tie it around my waist. I put my water and snacks in my gym bag, throw it over my shoulder, and shut my locker.

Do the older girls leave pads in their lockers? Or tampons? I'm tempted to look but then I realize I already know; they must leave supplies here. That's probably why Katie gives the older kids lockers instead of cubbies. I leave the optionals room and quickly walk through the parent viewing area. There are more parents on Wednesdays since the upper optionals aren't here and there's more room in the gym for recreational kids. Thankfully, none of the parents pay attention to me. I make it downstairs and walk through the lobby and outside. I know waiting in the cold December air is not the best idea for a sick kid. I'm not sick . . . I'm . . . I'm . . . a woman.

It actually feels good to stand in the cold. I didn't realize I was heating up in there. I feel my cheeks and they are warm with a small fever. Or is it from panic? Or embarrassment? I'm not sure which. I try to slow down my breathing. I focus on watching the puffs of air as I breathe out into the cold air. The slow breathing calms me. My head feels better, my stomach still feels icky, and my back aches. I'm worried I hurt myself doing those handstand swing downs on beam.

After about ten minutes I see my mom's van round the corner and enter the parking lot. I step closer to the edge of the curb as she pulls up. As soon as the car stops I climb into the front passenger seat.

"I'm so sorry pumpkin. Did you have stuff?"

"No," I say as grumpy as I feel.

"I'm sorry, we should have put some pads in your gym bag."

"I don't see how pads will work. All lumpy under a leo."

"It depends on the pad and how heavy you are. How heavy is it?" she asks me.

"How should I know? I didn't sit and watch! I just left."

"Okay. We'll figure it out. Start with a medium pad and depending on how fast you go through it we can go bigger or smaller."

"What if I am . . . heavy, as you call it? What do I do at practice?"

"You wear tampons."

"Those seem difficult."

"Paige, there are lots of female athletes who go through what you're going through. They wear tampons and it will feel like you're not even having a period."

"What about the light headedness and tummy ache? That will still remind me," I say surly.

"Do you have a headache?"

"Yes and I got light headed a couple of times. And my tummy hurts."

"Oh pumpkin, I'm sorry. We can go home and make you feel more comfortable."

"I think I hurt my back today, too. Probably because I was feeling off."

"You did?" she asks, flicking a surprised look at me before turning back to the road. I tell her about the back extension roll and how I am trying to connect it to a handstand by swinging down the then rolling back.

"I must have slammed down harder than I thought because it hurts deep inside."

"Your lower back?" she asks.

"Yeah," I say, feeling the ache even more acutely now.

"I think that's cramps from your period."

"In my back?!" I exclaim.

"Yes, you are feeling your uterus."

I think about that for a moment, "At least I'm not hurt then. That's weird it hurts all the way back there. Why does it hurt so bad?"

"Your uterus is squeezing, working for the first time. You're getting sore. Like a sore muscle."

"Does it get better then? If it gets stronger?"

"Yes, actually. Periods usually get easier as you get older. They can be unpredictable for young people," she admits.

I'm silent as I take in all this information. Now I understand why Katherine was so miserable before. I feel bad I wasn't more sympathetic.

We pull into the garage and as soon as we're inside the

house my mom disappears and comes back with two boxes of pads (two different sizes) for me to keep in my bathroom. I immediately grab clean underwear and go to my bathroom. I take a pad out of the box, unwrap it, and see that it has paper on the back. I peel off the paper to reveal a sticky strip and I stick it to my underwear. That was easy. I wash up and go back into my bedroom to finish changing. I pull on my fuzziest most comfy sweatpants and throw on my favorite hoodie and head downstairs.

I'm hungry, but nothing sounds good. My back aches and I just want to curl up in a ball. I walk to the couch and do just that. It seems so weird to be home so early. I'm not sure what to do with myself.

"Where's Jason?" I ask my mom.

"At a friend's house." I never thought I would miss him. Now would be the perfect time for his silly magic shows.

"Where's Snow Queen?" I ask.

"She's right here drinking water. I'll bring her to you when you when she's done."

"How long until dinner?"

"A couple of hours. Are you hungry?"

"Not really. Sort of. I don't know," I answer.

"Why don't you call your friends to see if they want to come over and hang out or watch a movie. There's not much to do on a dark winter day," she suggests.

"My friends are all at practice," I comment, rolling my eyes.

"Not all of them. What about your St. Mary's friends? They'll understand."

"My phone's all the way upstairs," I wail.

"No it isn't, silly. You dropped your gym bag by the garage door," my mom says, walking over and picking it up. I watch gratefully as she walks it over to me and drops it in my lap.

"Thanks," I murmur, zipping open my gym bag.

"It's the least I can do," she says and walks away.

I find my phone and text Abigail and Katherine on a group text.

Me:

Do you guys want to come over?

Katherine:

Don't you have practice?

Me:

I left early.

Abigail:

Everything okay?

Me:

I guess.

Katherine:

Tell us.

Me:

Come over.

Katherine:

What can we bring?

Me:

Something that will make my stupid cramps go away.

Abigail:

You got your period today!

Katherine:

Welcome to womanhood!

Me:

Gee, thanks. Just come over.

Abigail:

I know what to bring.

Katherine:

Abigail, can you come get me? My mom's not home.

Abigail:

You are close enough to walk.

Katherine:

But I don't want to.

Abigail:

    Fine, see you in 5.

I set my phone down and lean my head back. They distracted me from my pain while I was texting them. Maybe my mom is right, I need to hang out with friends. I hear my mom walking back in and she has a blue square of fabric in her hand that has a electrical cord attached to it. She goes to the wall next to me, plugs it in, and says, "Sit up."

I sit up and ask, "What are you doing?"

"Giving you a hot pad for your back," she says, as she slips it between the couch and my lower back. "Now lean back onto it." I do as she says.

"I don't feel anything," I say.

"Give it a sec," she says. "It will help. Here," she says, holding out a pill for me.

"What is this?"

"Ibuprofen. It will help with your headache and back pain. I promise."

I nod, I'll take all the help I can get. "Will you please get me water?" I ask as nicely as I can. I know I'm pushing my luck with being a spoiled lazy child, but I really, really, don't want to move away from this chair.

"Of course, thanks for asking nicely," she says and goes to get me the water. I sink back into the chair and adjust the hot pad for a minute.

"Ooh, I feel the warmth now, it does fell good," I say, leaning back into the hot pad.

I feel like a big baby. I never knew a period came with so much discomfort. They didn't tell us that in health class. Come to think of it, they didn't tell us nearly enough in health class. I am starting to understand the value of girlfriends. I'm glad Grace answered my questions and wasn't embarrassed to talk to me about it.

My mom hands me a glass of water. I take it from her, swallow the pill, and hand it back to her.

"Keep it here," she says setting it down on the coffee table next to me.

"What else is going to change?" I ask quietly.

"You'll probably fill out more, keep growing," she says.

"What do you mean by 'fill-out'?" I ask. Aunt Jennifer used that phrase, too.

"You know, develop more in your chest, your hips may widen a little, your muscle may bulk up a bit."

"I don't want to be bigger," I wail.

"Paige, it's okay; you're growing up," she reminds me.

"It's not okay. Gymnasts are supposed to be small," I point out.

"Says who? Have you seen the college girls lately? They are regular sized people. Super strong fit people, but still regular."

"They're all 5'2"," I counter.

"But they are *women* who are 5'2". What gave you this idea that you have to be small?"

"I don't know," I say toying with the cord on my heating pad. "I guess because my teammates are small. And it was easier when I was small. I can't do a back tuck anymore," I try to explain.

"You're changing fast, I'm sure you just need to adjust."

I don't say anything to that. I don't know what to say. Adjusting is easier said than done. Thankfully the doorbell rings, ending our conversation.

Abigail and Katherine come in with what feels like boundless energy.

"You look like crap," Katherine says.

"Katherine!" Abigail chides.

"It's okay. We're here to save the day!" she announces holding up a heating pad.

"Got it," I say. "But thanks."

"Your mom is on it," she says.

Katherine sits on the coffee table and faces me while Abigail takes the chair next to me. Katherine plunks down a canvas bag and starts pulling out junk food.

"We don't know what your PMS foods are yet so we brought everything."

"PMS?" I ask.

"Premenstrual Syndrome."

"Why pre? The uncomfortable part is happening now."

"For some people it's a few days before," Abigail says.

"What is it for you guys?" I ask.

"During," Abigail says.

"Both before and during," Katherine admits.

"Let's see, we brought you potato chips," she says pulling them out of her bag, "chocolate, and red licorice. We don't know if you crave salt, sugar, or chocolate."

I think about it a moment. Nothing sounded good earlier, but now the chips look amazing.

"The chips," I say.

"Salty it is," she says handing them over.

"Oh and we brought you this," Abigail says, pulling out a flier and handing it to me.

I take it and see it's a flier from health class that they printed out. "Your Body and Your Menstruation," I read. "You guys are hilarious," I say, setting it down. Although, secretly, I might read it later. Katherine stands up and walks over to the couch across from us.

"So you couldn't make it through practice today, huh?" Katherine asks.

"No," I say. "I don't know how I'm going to go tomorrow either. And I need to go. It seems like growing is making me worse."

"Dance can be like that," Abigail pipes up. "It's not that

you are worse. You just have to readjust your balance and timing for your new body. Your muscles remember the skills."

I nod. It's good advice, but gymnastics seems so much harder to adjust to than dance. I tell them about my tumbling pass and how I feel slow and off.

"And I'm nowhere near getting my flyaway," I admit. When I say it out loud all of sudden I can feel a wave of strong emotion wash though me.

"What's a flyaway?" Abigail asks.

"I don't know . . . " I start, but choke on my own tears. "I don't know if I can do this." The tears that came out of nowhere start streaming down my face. "Why am I crying?"

"Oh, honey, it's just all part of it," Abigail says like an old woman. She grabs the bag they brought and produces a box of tissues and hands it to me.

The absurdity of them knowing I would need a box of tissues make me smile a little as I take the box from her. I open the box and can't seem to get the first tissue out which for some reason frustrates me, making me cry further.

"I can't get it!" I yell, in frustration and throw the box at Abigail. She catches it, pulls out the first tissue and hands it to me. I can tell my friends are trying not to laugh. "What?" I growl.

"You just have it bad."

"Have what bad?"

"Just all the symptoms that go along with getting your period."

"I don't think so. I think I'm just under a lot of pressure to do a level I clearly have no business doing," I say, falling deeper into my self-pity.

"Who is pressuring you?" Katherine asks.

"No one. Me. My coaches. Maybe. I don't know. I decided to do this by January and it's almost January," I finally explain.

"Seems like everyone is just helping you because you said you wanted to do it."

"Shut up," I say, making them laugh, even though it's not that funny.

The girls stay for another hour or so keeping me company. My emotions get more under control when we talk about other things, like school, clothes, and their dance classes. They show me some funny TikTok videos to cheer me up and it does help.

I learn to keep my mind focused on them and what they are talking about because anytime I think about gymnastics I start to feel the tears well up. I really don't want to cry again.

When Katherine's mom texts that she was coming to get them, I feel drained.

"Keep the bag, you can restock it and give it back to me when I need it," Abigail says. I nod and start to get up to walk them to the door.

"No need," Katherine says, pushing me back down. "Stay in your cocoon with your hot pad."

I sit back down, "Thanks guys."

"See you tomorrow!" Abigail sings as she walks down the hall to my front door.

"Congratulations on becoming woman!" Katherine tosses over her shoulder, making me grin. I'm lucky to have them as friends.

"What makes you a woman?" Jason asks, walking through the front door. I have no idea what to say to him.

"She's thirteen now," my mom says, saving me from any explanation. "That was sweet of your friends to come over and keep you company." She says, pulling out a TV tray and setting it in front of me.

"I can eat in here?" I ask surprised. My mom is a big stickler for dinner time as a family.

"Dad's working late and you don't look like you want to move. I figured, just this once." I watch her go back into the kitchen and come back with a bowl of soup and bread and set it down on the tray.

"I'm not sick," I comment looking at the bowl.

My mom straightens up and looks at me, "You don't have to be sick to enjoy soup on a cold winter day."

Good point. I nod and whisper, "Thanks." Because even though I'm not sick, I sure don't feel myself.

Chapter 23

The hard wooden chairs that are attached to our desks seem extra hard today. I squirm in my seat and cannot get comfortable. My back hurts like crazy and I'm starting to get a headache. I'm so worried that the pad I'm wearing won't work that I'm wearing gymnastics shorts under my plaid skirt. I used to wear the shorts under my skirt all the time when I did gymnastics at recess. When I started sixth grade I didn't need to anymore because we no longer had recess.

Last night before bed, I pulled out the pamphlet Katherine and Abigail brought over as a joke. I read the entire thing to see if I ignored information in fifth grade when we had the maturation class at school. The pamphlet explained all the things that are happening in my body and how I would continue to change and how I need deodorant. But it didn't say anything about all the weird symptoms. Maybe that's why Katherine and Abigail found the pamphlet funny, it only tells half the story. They need an asterisk in there that says *for all useful information talk to your besties.*

I manage to make it through the day and as soon as I get home I toss my backpack on the floor and fall to the couch. How can I possibly do gymnastics feeling this way?

My mom finds me curled up on the couch when she comes home in time to take me to practice. Usually I am dressed and ready for practice when she gets home and we run out the door.

"Maybe you should stay home today," she says.

I lift my head and look at her. I agree with her, I should stay home. I'm not sure how I'm going to catch up at this rate and that thought bothers me as I lay my head back down, "Yeah," I say.

"I'll text Katie," she says.

"Just tell her I'm sick," I mumble. I wouldn't put it past my mom to tell her exactly what is going on. That thought embarrasses me. I think about it for a moment. I guess Katie knows what I'm going through. It would be more embarrassing if she had to call James.

I hear my mom come back in the room, "I sent Jason over to play with Will and Dad is going to be home late again so it's just us girls." She sits down next to me and starts rubbing my back. "I'm sorry it's so painful for you." I don't say anything and after a moment she gets up again, "I'm going to get you an ibuprofen. When was the last time you had one?" she asks me.

"Yesterday," I mumble.

"Well, no wonder. Let's help you a bit with your cramps," she leaves again and comes back with a little maroon pill and a glass of water. I sit up and take it without question. "Do you want to watch a movie?"

"How am I ever going to catch up at the gym if I stay home to hang out with friends and watch movies with you?" I ask.

189

My mom starts rubbing my back again, "It's not always going to be like this. You'll learn how to manage your body. What activities make you feel better, which healthy foods help, that kind of thing."

I think about this for a minute. "Sometimes I wish I was a boy," I admit.

"I think all girls think that at some point. Especially when it comes to their period and childbirth. We can't change it, so I like to think about what I like about being a girl," she says.

"The clothes," I smile.

"And make-up," she says.

"We can wear dresses or pants."

"We have good friendships."

"We have better hair," I say making my mom laugh.

"See, it's not all bad," my mom says. "What do you want to watch?" she asks me.

"On a week night?" I ask. Usually we are not allowed movies on week nights.

"Of course, finish your homework first and then, yes, let's watch something fun. It's just us girls, so we can watch whatever we want," she says with enthusiasm. Jason usually picks the movies on our Friday night movie night, so this is a fun treat.

"Let's see what Rom-Coms they have," I say, getting into the spirit.

We pick a romantic comedy that was released straight to streaming. It's a cute show, but my mind keeps wandering back to gymnastics. How am I possibly going to catch up if I have to take several days off each time I get my period?

"When do you think I'll start to feel better?" I ask my mom.

"The worst part is the first three days. Hopefully by tomorrow you'll feel better."

"We don't even have practice tomorrow," I sulk.

"Then you will for sure be able to go on Saturday," she predicts.

This satisfies me enough to focus on the rest of the movie.

My mom was right, I do feel better today. It's Saturday and I haven't been to the gym since Wednesday, when I left practice before it ended. My only concern is that I'm still bleeding enough that I need a big pad or a tampon. A small pad, or panty liner, would work in a leo, but I think I need more protection than that. Thank goodness our gym allows workout shorts over our leos whenever we want. The only exception is we have to take them off for intrasquads and meets.

My mom bought me a box of tampons, knowing it was one of the few answers for athletes. I told her I don't know how to use them and she told me to read the directions in the box. So that's what I'm doing now. I have the directions spread out on the bathroom counter. The instructions include pictures. While the pictures are totally something Katherine and Abigail would make fun of, I'm glad to have them. I take a deep breath and decide to try.

After three failed attempts I'm frustrated and trying not to cry. How hard can this be? She makes it look easy in the picture. I start panicking that I'm going to be late for gymnastics and that makes everything worse. A few more attempts and I throw the instructions across the small room and bury my face in my hands.

"Paige, are you okay in there?" I hear my mom asking through the door. I must have been in here for ages.

"No!" I yell back. "I can't do it!"

There is a pause. "Can you wear a light pad? One of the panty liners?"

"No!" I yell back in frustration.

"What do you want to do? Keep trying or skip today?" she asks.

Skip today? I can't miss another day. I feel good, small cramps and more energy than I've felt in days. I look up at the ceiling. I really hate this. I walk over and pick up the instructions again.

"I don't want to skip," I yell in frustration.

"Okay, Paige, try to relax. Take your time. It's no big deal to be late once in a while. You can do this."

I take some deep breaths and try to relax. I can do this. I can do back flips for crying out loud, I should be able to do this. I take a deep breath and clam myself down. I try one last time and, to my surprise, I'm successful. My mom is right. Once the tampon is in, it doesn't feel like anything. I quickly wash up, shove the instructions back in the box, and throw the box under the sink.

"I'm ready!" I announce.

"You did it?" my mom asks.

"I did it," I say with pride opening the bathroom door. For once I think I just did something before Katherine and Abigail. I'm pretty sure neither of them have worn a tampon yet. I probably wouldn't have either if I wasn't determined to go to practice today. "Am I going to feel it?" I ask my mom.

"You shouldn't," she says. "The biggest thing is to remember to take it out."

"How do I know when to take it out?"

"Take it out after three or four hours or when it's full."

"How do I know when it's full?"

"You will start spotting. Are you wearing a panty liner?"

"A what?"

192

"One of the lighter pads," she says, walking into the bathroom and grabbing one of the boxes. "You wear one of these with it."

Without a word I take the box from her and shut myself back into the backroom.

CHAPTER 24

My teammates are happy to see me when I show up for Saturday morning practice. I didn't realize they were worried about me when I abruptly left on Wednesday. I'm sticking to the story that I had a little tummy ache and no one seems to question it or care. They're just glad I'm back.

As soon as we finish warming up Melony pulls me out of the group to teach me my beam routine. She took dance movements and poses from my floor routine and choreographed them into my beam routine. She lets me choose if I want to do my back extension roll first thing or after a leap pass. I decide to do the leap pass first, then the back extension roll. After that I just have jumps and a full turn. The routine was fast to learn but I'm not sure I'm actually going to remember it. I ask Melony to record me doing it on my phone so I can go home and memorize it. Everyone else is doing routines that seem second nature to them. I want mine to get like that. Melony and I stay over on the beams working on my routine for the entire bars rotation. While I need to work my flyaway, I need a beam routine more.

"What's your dismount?" Melony asks me after watching me do a full dance through of my new routine.

"Front tuck."

"How about a dance through with the mount and dismount?"

"Let me warm up the front tucks," I say. I do about three front tucks off the end of the beam. They are a pretty simple skill if you can do front tucks on floor. The only hard part is being ready for the landing. I feel good about knowing where I am and glad I have a new dismount this easily.

When the bars rotation (that I missed altogether) is over, my teammates join me on beam. Katie announces five stuck routines and five of everything we fall on. It dawns on me that I can actually do this assignment today.

"Paige," Katie calls over to me, "do a cartwheel where the round-off goes."

"We didn't put in a round-off," I admit.

"Are you planning to learn it?"

Not in less than three weeks! "Yes."

"Then choreograph it in and do a cartwheel for now. When you get the round-off you can replace the cartwheel." I stand there a little dumbfounded. There are now two skills in my routine that I am nowhere near doing and I don't know where to put the round-off. Or cartwheel really, because that is what it's going to be for a while.

"Where should I put the round-off?" I squeak.

"Melony!" Katie yells past a few beams to where Melony is helping Lucy.

Melony looks up and Katie yells, "Can you add a round-off to Paige's routine?"

Melony looks at me, nods, and goes back to helping

195

Lucy. When she is done she comes over to me.

"A round-off in the routine, huh?" she says walking up to me by the low beams.

"Guess so," I sulk.

"It's actually smart because then you don't have to rework the entire routine when you get that skill." I don't say anything because rearranging dance seems minimal. "This is optionals, you can change your routine whenever you need to."

I do like that, but just when I feel like I have a handle on Level 6, I get pushed to do more than I feel like I can do.

"Don't look so down. You can do a cartwheel right?"

"Of course," I say. A cartwheel was in the Level 4 routine, she knows I can do it.

"Then this is no big deal. Where should we put it? In the end? After your series?"

I think about it for a moment, "After the series," I confirm. Melony does some movements on the low beam, trying to figure out how I can gracefully move in and out of the cartwheel. Then she turns to me and teaches to me what she just created. Then I put it all together doing a dance through on low beam.

"That's exactly it. Want me to record it?" she asks and I nod and run over and grab my phone that was sitting on a panel mat nearby. "After this you should go put your phone away before someone steps on it," she comments, taking the phone from me.

I do the new dance through on the low beam while Melony records it. On the first try I totally forgot the new section she taught me. Melony is nice about it and shows it to me again. I try again, this time I get it right and Melony gets it on video.

"Got it. Now go put your phone away and do five more so you can start to commit it to memory. Then work on your series," she instructs.

I do as she says and run up and put my phone away. It feels good to have a beam routine. Now I can finally participate in the all-around at the next intrasquad. *Not if you don't have all your skills* a rude voice in my head reminds me. That makes me run back downstairs faster so I have time to work my series on beam before we rotate to floor.

I end up doing my five dance throughs on high beam and both Savannah and Brooklyn comment on how pretty my routine is, which is nice of them. I was also able to get a few tries of my handstand swing down to back extension roll. I'm still doing it on the medium beam with the sting mat thrown over the beam. I think I can actually get this skill in the next few weeks. It definitely seems easier than a back walkover back handspring, even though everyone else says the opposite.

By the time the beam rotation is over, I'm tired of beam. I've been here for two rotations and I'm ready to go to floor.

On floor my back tucks feel better and I'm happy I can finally participate in the assignment with everyone else. As I walk by the mirror to get from one corner to the other I am surprised at what I see. I feel like my legs are so much bigger than they used to be. Thicker. When did that happen? I will myself not to stop and stare as I walk by and see a person I don't even recognize.

I get to my corner and I can't seem to concentrate. I decide to do my front tuck first. I'm not in a good place mentally to do back tumbling right now. I'm rattled by what I saw. I take a deep breath and run and do a nice front tuck.

"Paige are you ready?" I hear Katie yell over to me. I look over and nod to her. "Are you starting with the dance through or the last pass set?" she asks.

"Last pass," I tell her. I love that in optionals my last pass can be my front tumbling where compulsories my hardest pass, the back tumbling, was always at the end of the routine. Now I can switch it up and do my layout (or back tuck) in the first pass and my front tuck in the last pass.

I hardly need to be warmed up to do a routine with a front tuck at the end, which is probably why Katie called on me to go early on. The Level 7s need more time to warm up their passes.

I stand in the corner and wait for my music to start. I enjoy the dance and try to show off my movements. I'm surprised to find myself a bit winded as I stand in the corner before my front tuck. I take a deep breath, run, punch, do my front tuck and barely land it. I do my end dance and when I hit the ending pose I'm shocked at how tired I am. Without asking I walk over and get a drink.

That was hard. Harder than I expected. Then I smile to myself because I am doing routines.

At the end of practice I'm waiting in the lobby for my mom when Katie walks up, "I told your mom to come a few minutes late because I'd like to speak with you. Come on in," she says motioning for me to go into the coaches' office.

She wants to speak with me? Oh no, what if she has decided I shouldn't compete this season?

I enter the office with a horrible feeling settling over me. All this hard work to sit out this season. She pulls her chair from around the desk and motions for us to sit next to each other.

"How are things going Paige?" she asks me.

"Fine," I answer, not sure what she is asking.

"What happened at your last practice?"

"My last practice?" I ask, not sure what she is talking about. My last practice I did everything I was told.

"When you left early. Everything okay?" she presses.

I am not about to tell her I got my period so I just nod.

"Are you eating well?" she continues.

198

I nod again.

"Paige, you look wonderful and healthy. I hope you are not cutting back on your eating because you don't like how you are changing."

I'm a little offended she thinks I'm not eating, but she hit a bit of a chord on the part about me not liking how I'm changing.

"I'm eating." I say. She looks at me and so I confess, "but I don't like how I'm changing."

"Why not? It's all perfectly normal," she reminds me.

"Not for gymnasts," I say, starting to choke up. "They are little and cute."

"What gymnasts are you talking about?" she asks.

"Savannah, Lucy, Alexis, ... and the old version of me," I crack out, starting to cry.

"Oh, Paige, you can't do that," she says, reaching over and putting her hand over mine. "You are comparing yourself to young girls. You are becoming a woman. There are lots of grown women who are successful gymnasts." I sniff and nod, even though I'm not sure I believe her.

She stands up and shuffles through her desk and pulls out a gymnastics magazine. "Look at our Olympic Team. Grown women," she says, holding the magazine out to me. I sit up and look at the picture she is holding out. She is right. I wipe a tear off my face. Those girls are my size or bigger. "I know the stereotype for gymnastics has historically been that gymnasts must be small and prepubescent to be successful. That is just not the case anymore. These girls have proved that. The college girls have proved that. Look over here, look at these posters," she says, walking over to the wall that has four college posters on it. "Stand up and look at them, Paige," she orders.

I stand up and walk up to the wall. I examine the Utah poster, then I walk over to the BYU poster, then Utah State, and Southern Utah. The gymnasts in the pictures all have broad shoulders, breasts, muscled arms, and strong thick legs. They are beautiful. Their skin is clear and their smiles are bright. They seem comfortable in their intricate sparkling team leotards.

"They're pretty," I say.

"Yes, and that is what you are becoming. A beautiful fit strong woman. You cannot compare yourself to children."

I nod. I don't say anything because for some reason the tears are coming back. The silence stretches between us. Finally, Katie adds, "So please let yourself grow and keep eating healthy, okay?"

I turn and look at her, "I promise I'm eating. But thank you for showing me these pictures." She stands up and walks over to me and gives me a big hug. I swallow my tears and hug her back.

CHAPTER 25

By Sunday my period is over and I feel lighter than I have felt all week. I can't wait to get back into the gym to learn my series on beam, my layout flyaway on bars, and my layout on floor. The list is intimidating, but I think I can do it. I have seen how much Alexis, Lucy, and Savannah have improved since we moved up to Level 6 and I think I'm only slightly behind them. It's a bit embarrassing to be behind kids who are two years younger than me. That's how gymnastics is sometimes. I mean, Maya is older than everyone else and she doesn't seem to mind. It's also weird to not be the leader anymore. Peyton and Maya definitely are the leaders of Level 6 and 7. Maybe when they move up to Level 8 next year and my old teammates move up from Level 5, I can be the leader again.

I look out my bedroom window at the wind and gray clouds. I miss my old teammates. Savannah is having a Christmas Party Friday night with all the Level 6s and some of the 5s. I'm looking forward to it. The only thing that would make it better was if Katherine and Abigail were there. It's a bummer how school friends and gym friends are separate. Unless you are lucky like Savannah and Trista, who go to the same school.

I spend the day catching up on homework. My homework isn't intended for me to do all in one day at the end of the week. I have been so busy with gymnastics, that that has been the only way to keep up.

After several hours I'm finally done with homework and I think about texting Katherine and Abigail. But I don't think I can handle all their chatter today. I decide to text Grace. I wish the farm was closer. It seems like the perfect place to be on a quiet cold day like today. The farm makes me think of Snow Queen and I call for her. She is usually active in the early morning, but a bit sleepy this time of day. I wander out of my room looking for her in her favorite sleeping places. I find her in the family room sleeping in a ray of sun coming through the window. Smart little kitty. I sit down next to her and lean against the couch. She wakes when she sees me, stretches, and rolls over to show me her belly. I pet her belly and she stands up and crawls in my lap. Then she kneads my legs for a moment and finally lays down. I pet her and enjoy the warmth with her. I notice her coat is, in fact, turning gray like Grace said it would. She's not as cute as she was even a few weeks ago. I sigh, it's a bummer to grow up.

I think about how my week went as I prepare for Savannah's party. The week flew by both at the gym and at school. At St. Mary's we have several projects we have to finish before the Christmas break and at the gym we are all trying to put our routines together before our intersquad held just before Christmas. I'm just glad I have routines to do at all. Katie hasn't said anything to me, so I assume I'm allowed to compete in the all-around at the intersquad.

I step into my only winter dress and reach around and zip it as far as I can. I stand in front of the mirror debating how I want to do my hair. It would be fun to keep it down since my teammates never see it that way. Savannah told us this party would be fancy and to wear a dress, or at least sparkles. I smile to myself as I pick up a sparkly head band. I think I will do both.

I step into my black ballet flats and go find my mom so she can zip me. I find her in the kitchen sitting down, peeling an orange. She looks up when I walk in.

"Don't you look beautiful," she says, setting down her orange on her napkin.

"I couldn't zip it all the way," I say, walking to her so she can help me. I turn around as she wipes her hands on the napkin, stands up, and faces my zipper. When she zips it, she gets stuck where I did, at my mid back.

"Pumpkin, I don't think I can get this to zip."

"What? No way, I just got it this last spring in the post season sale."

"I know, but you have grown so much."

"Taller, yeah, but wider?"

"Let me try again," she says, bringing the zipper down and tugging on the dress near my waist to make the zipper perfectly straight before she tries again. "Hold this," she says to me. I reach around to my back and pull the dress down and hold it straight. I feel my mom pull the sides together as close as she can. She slowly zips it up and I can feel it getting very tight as she passes my lat muscles. Then it gets easier as she gets to my shoulder blades. I let out a breath when she gets the zipper all the way up.

"That may not hold," she says, making me feel like a cow. "Why don't you bring a back-up dress? One of your summer ones you have that is stretchy jersey material."

"Because it's a winter Christmas party," I point out.

"Maybe bring a pair of jeans and a fancy sweater?" she suggests.

"Can I pick something out and leave it in your car? If something happens you can bring it to me?"

She pauses for a moment so I give her my best pleading expression. "Oh, alright. As much as I hate driving up and down the hill for no reason, I will do it for you. And it's just a precaution. Now that you are in the dress, it looks like it fits."

"It pulls really tight if I move my arms forward," I say, bringing my arms up and in front of me. I feel the seams straining.

"Then don't do that, silly. Now go get your back-up clothes," she says.

Back-up clothes. When I bought this dress last spring I never dreamed it wouldn't fit this winter. I go to my room and grab my favorite jeans and my only sparkly sweater. I haven't worn it since last Christmas, but it's stretchy material, so it will fit.

I take one more look in the mirror. I look nice. I don't look as crammed into the dress as I feel. I look at the jeans and sweater in my hand and decide I can wear it with the same shoes. I find my mom again who is waiting by the garage door with her purse and keys in her hand.

"Ready?" she asks.

"Ready," I say. I follow her into the garage, climb into the front seat of the car and throw my clothes in the back.

We drive mostly in silence, my mom goes over a few rules about manners that I already know. I'm trying not to move and rip my dress before we get there.

When we arrive, my mom walks me to the door, which she doesn't need to do.

"I want to say hi to Debbie. I'd like to thank her," I roll my eyes, but don't say anything as she follows me up the walk. Thankfully their driveway and path to the door are shoveled because my ballet flats aren't really made for snow.

When we get to the door Savannah answers it. She looks darling in a white tulle dress with rhinestones dotting the skirt.

"Welcome!" she says, and I can tell she is already having the time of her life.

"Hi Savannah," my mom says, "is your mom around?"

Savannah nods, looks over her shoulder, and motions her mom to the door. Debbie walks up and enjoys the small talk and thank yous from my mom as I walk in.

"Bye pumpkin, see you in a few hours!" I wave good-bye and she leaves, taking my back-up clothes with her.

After she leaves I finally take in the room. The living room just off of the entry way is where the girls are sitting around a beautiful tree with red, blue, and gold bulbs. Trista, Carmen, and Marissa are sitting on one couch and Lucy and her sister, Rose, are sitting on the other. I walk over and take a seat by Lucy.

"Hi Lucy," I say quietly.

"Are we the only 6s who are going to be here?" she asks me.

"I imagine they will all be here," I point out. "But you know the others from the fall," I remind her.

"I do, of course I do. I just wasn't on the Level 5 team for very long before I moved up and these girls know each other really well."

"They do, they have been training together for years."

"Did you see the tree?" she asks me, changing the subject.

I look at it more closely, and I see that the theme is gymnastics. There are ornaments of gymnasts, grips, and trophies. The gold bulbs have a design on them making them look like a gold medal. Some of Savannah's medals are looped over branches, adding to the gymnastics theme.

"Perfect for this crowd," I say, relaxing Lucy a little.

Savannah comes in and sets down a tray of crackers and cheese saying, "Have a little snack you guys, and when everyone gets here, we'll start."

"Start what?" Lucy whispers to me.

I shrug, "Knowing Debbie, it will be good."

We hear the doorbell ring and Savannah flounces to the door to greet Alexis. The moms chat for a moment while Alexis comes in and takes off her coat. She is in a darling dress of midnight blue with little cap sleeves and a square neck line. I look around at everyone and I love that Savannah told us to dress up. I rarely get to see these girls in school clothes, much less in fancy clothes.

Before Debbie has time to shut the door Riley and Victoria arrive. The moms talk while Savannah greets them. "I'm so happy you guys came!" She grabs Victoria's arm and pulls her in. "You guys know Victoria and Riley, right?"

"We know them from PNO," Trista says.

"I'll remind you of names anyway. This is Trista, Carmen, and Marissa. And you know these guys," she says gesturing to Lucy and I. "Oh, do you know Rose? Rose is Lucy's sister."

Victoria and Riley say a quiet hello and we make room on the couch for them to sit.

"What's your favorite event?" Trista asks them, breaking the ice. The girls easily start talking about gymnastics and I can see Savannah visibly relaxing. She must have been worried about mixing these two teams.

When Debbie shuts the door she turns to us, "You girls

look so cute. Let's get a picture before we start." She lines us up on the stairs so each of us can be seen. The girls are excited and a little chaotic. I notice Marissa is the one to settle them down. We finally get a good picture and then Savannah sits us down to tell us about our game.

"I have names of famous people on these sticky labels. You each get one on your back and you have to figure out who you are. You can only ask yes or no questions, like, 'Am I an Olympian?' stuff like that. And you can only ask one question to each person. After one question you have to find someone else. There's a prize for whoever guesses their person first and smaller prizes for second and third. I promise you will love them!"

The girls all start talking at once and Savannah and her mom are trying to figure out how to get us our sticky notes on our back without anyone seeing the names. They also want us all starting at the same time so it's fair.

"We could line up like march-in and you could put all the sticky labels on us and we start at the same time," Marissa suggests.

"Great idea, Marissa," Debbie says. Then she turns to the rest of us. "Girls, line up shoulder to shoulder like you are being announced before a meet."

"Do you want us small to tall?" Riley asks, making us laugh.

"Sure, why not?" Debbie says.

We shuffle around for a minute and in a shockingly quick amount of time we are standing small to tall, shoulder to shoulder. I am on the end as the tallest. It has been a while since I've been the tallest. I look down the row at all the girls in their Christmas party dresses. They are all thin and petite. I bet none of them had trouble zipping up their dress today.

Savannah steps forward with her sticky labels ready to give us each a name and her mom stops her, "Don't you want to play?" she asks.

"No, I'll help people," she says, and begins to walk along our line, peeling off stickers and sticking them on our backs.

As soon as Savannah passes Trista I see her lean back and look at the stickers on both people next to her. "They're all gymnasts!" Trista exclaims. This admission makes me feel much better about the game. I don't know famous people like Katherine and Abigail do. I do know gymnasts. Savannah finally gets to me and sticks a label on my back.

"Okay, go!" Savannah says. Girls immediately start asking each other questions.

"Am I an Olympian?"

"Am I on the current national team?"

I hear all these questions when Carmen turns to me, "Am I an elite or college gymnast?" I lean over and look at the sticky on her back. Peng-Peng Lee. She was both.

"You have to ask me a yes or no question," I remind her.

"Was I a college gymnast?" she asks.

"Yes," I confirm.

"Was I a college gymnast?" I ask.

She looks at the name on my back and pauses. "Um, not was," she says.

"Currently I'm a college gymnast?" Since I didn't ask a yes or no question she just gives me a little smile.

Hmm, a new college gymnast, so she didn't get famous that way. Maybe a recent Olympian.

I walk over to Trista, "Am I an Olympian?" I ask her.

She looks at my back. "Sadly no, but you should have been."

"Trista!" Savannah yells at her for giving me an extra clue.

"What? I can't help it, she should have," Trista justifies unapologetically.

"Ask me a question," I tell Trista, so she doesn't get in further trouble and disqualified from our game. As she's thinking of a question I turn her and look at her back. Jordyn Wieber.

"Let's see, I know I'm an Olympian. Did I win a gold medal?" she asks.

"Yes."

"Team or individual?" she follows up.

"You have to ask someone else."

"Oh yeah," she turns to Alexis, "did I win an all-around gold medal in the Olympics?"

Alexis looks and she says, "Nope. sorry."

"Hmm, team medal then," Trista thinks aloud.

I smile to myself. She'll get it soon. I better focus and think about my gymnast. She's not an Olympian, but she is in college now.

I turn to Alexis, "Did I go to worlds?" I ask.

She turns me, reads my label and says, "You sure did."

Worlds doesn't really narrow it down. This is hard.

"Can I do a triple double?" Victoria asks me. The only females that can do a triple doubles are Simone Biles and Jade Carey. I look at her label: Jordan Chiles.

"No," I say. She is close. Jordan was on the same team as Simone and Jade. I need to think of a good question. All I know is I was at worlds.

"Did I win the all-around at worlds?" I ask her.

"Yes," she confirms. I won worlds but I'm not an Olympian so I'm not Simone. *Think Paige think.* Other gymnasts won worlds before Simone came along.

"Did my floor routine go viral?" I hear someone ask.

"Am I a college coach now?" someone else asks.

They are asking good questions. Then it pops in my head. Morgan Hurd won worlds when Simone took a year off.

"Do I wear glasses?" I ask Rose.

"Yes!" she says.

"Am I Morgan Hurd?" I ask Carmen.

"Yes! Paige got it! Paige got hers!" she yells.

"Everyone stop for a second!" Savannah yells and the girls stop chatting and look over. "We need to see if Paige won and if she did we can keep going for second place.

Savannah walks over to me. "Who do you think you are?" she asks.

"Morgan Hurd."

"Paige is first place winner! You guys can keep going for second." The girls start frantically asking questions again. Savannah looks at me, "You can still answer their questions. That's what I'm doing; it's fun."

"Did you think of all the names?" I ask her.

"My mom and I did."

I nod and Alexis walks up to me with a question, "Am I an announcer?" she asks. I look, Nastia Lukin.

"Yes," I say.

"Am I Nastia Lukin?" she asks.

"Yes!"

"We have second place!" Savannah yells and the room gets more frantic as the girls are getting closer to knowing their gymnasts. I smile, this was a good idea. Only these girls would be able to answer yes or no questions about gymnasts.

"Am I a mom?" I hear someone ask.

"Yes."

"Am I Chelsea Memel?" she asks.

"Yes!"

"Am I an Olympic All-Around Champion?"

"Yes!"

"Am I Suni Li?"

"Yes!"

The third place winner sounded like a tie to me. The

game is technically over, so girls start giving each other huge hints.

"You were an Olympian, but not for the US. But you did college in the US."

"Wait, what? I have no idea."

"Yes you do. Think about it."

"Where did I do college."

"No way that's way too easy."

"The game is over!"

"Fine, UCLA."

"Oh! Peng-Peng!"

The girls are so excited when they guess their gymnast even with heavy hints and more than yes or no questions. Once everyone guesses their gymnast the girls settle down and Savannah gives us our prizes. I get a gift bag with hair ties, wrist bands, and a key chain with a gymnast on it. Leave it to Savannah's mom to make everything gymnastics themed. She knows this group.

I look up from my gift bag and see everyone is talking about the gymnast they had on their back and how they figured it out. I've never seen these girls so talkative.

"Okay girls, time for dessert!" Savannah's mom announces, coming in with a tray of cupcakes. Savannah passes out plates and napkins and the girls are not shy selecting a cupcake.

We are quiet for a brief moment while everyone eats their treat.

"How is your flyaway Alexis?" Marissa asks, breaking the silence.

"I think I'll be ready by the intersquad. I'm doing it on the competition set onto an 8-incher. I think I'll be landing them on the 4-incher soon."

"They are so pretty," Lucy adds.

"What about you Lucy?" Marissa continues, "How are

your back handsprings?" We all know Lucy has been struggling with her back handspring on beam since she had to change which hand she puts in front.

"It finally doesn't feel funny and my landing is getting consistent. I'm not sure if I'll do it in the intersquad, but I know I'll be able to do it this season."

"So you're doing them on high beam?" Trista asks.

"Yes, with 8-inchers," Lucy explains.

"Only two," Savannah interjects.

"How's it going for you, Paige?" I'm silent for a moment. My flyaway is the same, my tumbling is the same, and my vault is the same. "I'm adding a handstand to my back extension roll," I share, finally landing on something new that I'm doing.

"That sounds hard," Carmen says, and I smile at her. Marissa continues to ask the girls gymnastics questions to keep our conversation going. As I listen, I realize two things. One, my teammates are ready for the intersquad. And two, Marissa is the new leader of the Level 5s.

CHAPTER 26

For the next two weeks I work hard in the gym to get my new Level 6 skills. Unfortunately I am not very close. A week ago Katie pulled me aside and said I needed to be clear on my A and B routines. She told me to start running full routines with a tuck flyaway on bars and a back tuck and front tuck on floor. Then when I'm done with an assignment I can work my new skills and eventually run the new skills in my B routines. I agreed with her, what else could I do? The problem is that it has been taking me the entire rotation to complete the assignment with my A routines. I never actually get to my B routines, or even the skills in the B routines. The upside is that I have been doing my A routines well all week.

I just finished my last workout before the Level 6/7 intersquad tomorrow. Katie has given us a pep talk about how we are ready. Now that I have routines and I'm doing basic skills in them, she is right. I am ready. Sadly, I have the easiest skills of all the girls on the team. I found the downside of optionals. Everyone can see it if you're behind. In compulsories we all had the same skills so it felt more even. You either had your skills and got to compete or you didn't. Tomorrow I will be competing with baby skills compared to my teammates.

"Why so quiet, Pumpkin?" my mom asks.

I turn and look at her in the drivers seat. I sigh, "My routines feel dumb."

"Dumb? They look beautiful to me."

"But they are simple Level 5 skills. I didn't learn anything new."

"Were you expecting to in six weeks?" she asks.

"Yes," I pout crossing my arms. "I'm training more hours. I have Katie coaching me. I have been coming in extra. I thought I would at least have my layout flyaway or my layout on floor. Something!"

"You've been growing so much," my mom starts.

"Don't finish that sentence. I'm tired of everyone telling me how big and fat I am!"

"No one said fat!" my mom exclaims.

"What are you saying then?"

"That when you grow you have to learn to do your skills with that new height."

"And weight!" I fire at her. As soon as the car comes to a stop in the garage I jump out and slam the door and run up to my room.

I plop on the bed and Snow Queen comes scrambling out from under the bed. "Sorry girl," I say, knowing I scared her. I slide off the bed and sit on the floor to be next to her. She looks at me with skepticism. "I didn't mean to wake you from your nap," I try again. She looks at me and decides to walk over to me. I reach out and pet her. I stroke her silky coat that is now gray and black along the back. She purrs and rolls back over, stands up, and walks into my lap. We sit in

214

silence for a while. Well, I am silent, she is purring up a storm.

I hear a knock on my door and Snow Queen launches out of my lap as my mom peeks her head in. "Can I come in?" she asks. I nod and she walks all the way into my room and sits down on the ground next to me. We are silent for a minute. Then she says, "It concerns me that you think growing into a healthy woman means that you are fat."

I roll my eyes and lean my head back, "Mo-um."

"What? Help me understand. Because to me you are perfect."

"I'm just . . . just . . . not the same," I choke out.

"Of course you aren't. You aren't supposed to be the same. You are a thirteen-year-old girl becoming a woman."

"What if I don't want to be a woman?"

"We can't stop these things, Paige. It's life."

"I feel so heavy. So huge."

"I imagine a sport in flight like gymnastics you notice every change in your body. That doesn't mean there is anything wrong with your body. You are just changing."

"It feels wrong," I sulk.

"I am sure it feels weird and different." she says, tucking a curly strand of hair behind my ear. "You should see how you look doing your floor routine. It's stunning."

"But I don't do anything in it!" I wail. "And I look gigantic!" I add.

"Gigantic? Compered to who? You look the same as your teammates."

"No I don't. Savannah, Lucy, and Alexis are tiny."

"Paige, Savannah, Lucy, and Alexis are fifth graders. They are eleven and you are thirteen. You can't compare. Look at girls your age, the Level 7s. You are exactly the same size."

"I guess I don't think of them as my teammates yet."

"Well they are. Even if you weren't their size, there is still nothing wrong with you. You are exactly the size you are supposed to be. You have to stop comparing, Paige. It's not healthy."

We are quiet for a moment. I know my mom is right. I can't seem to tell her. I feel stuck in my bad mood. I feel gross inside.

Snow Queen wanders over to my mom and gives her a little bump with her head as an invitation to pet her.

"Do you still think Snow Queen is cute?"

"Of course I do! What kind of question is that?" I exclaim.

"Even though she's bigger and no longer white?" she asks.

"Mom, don't be silly," I say picking up Snow Queen. "She's still my sweet kitten."

My mom leans over and kisses my head and says, "And you will always be my sweet pumpkin."

"I walked right into that one," I say to Snow Queen.

"You aren't fat," my mom says.

"I know."

"Good. I need you to know and remember. Be confident and stop comparing yourself to others."

"Okay," I say without looking up. I feel dumb. I know I'm not fat. I just hate talking about my new size.

"Do you want to invite Katherine and Abigail to the intersquad?" she asks me.

"I though Grace and Chloe were coming for winter break."

"They are driving out tomorrow, but they won't be able to make it in time for your intersquad."

That's too bad, I was hoping to have friends there who don't know gymnastics very well. I guess Katherine and Abigail won't know that my routines are lame and lacking hard skills.

"Why not?" I say. "Mom? Do you think I should have stayed in Level 5?" I ask.

My mom takes her time answering and finally says, "From what I can tell you are between the two levels. I don't think you would have been happy staying in Level 5 any more than you are in Level 6."

"Maybe gymnastics doesn't make me happy anymore?" I wonder out loud.

"Only you can answer that pumpkin. But I do think you should participate in the intrasquad before you make any big decisions."

She kisses me on the forehead again and stands up. She quietly leaves me and a disappointed Snow Queen who was loving the attention.

I stand up, scooping up Snow Queen with me. I climb into bed and try to get Snow Queen to stay with me. She wiggles out of my grasp and jumps off the bed. I roll to my side and think about my options.

I could quit and do whatever it is Katherine and Abigail do after school. I could skip this season and just train skills all year. I could swallow my pride and compete. I've never been the best, so why is being the clear worst bothering me so much?

I reach for my phone and text Abigail and Katherine:

Me:

Do you guys want to come to my intersquad tomorrow?

Abigail:

What's an intersquad?

Katheryn:

What time?

217

Me:

    2 and it's a practice meet at Perfect Balance.

Katherine:

    I'm in if we can catch a ride.

Abigail:

    Can I bring Quinn?

Katherine:

    What? Is it that serious that you are doing stuff outside of school?!

Abigail:

    I just told him I'd hang out tomorrow.

Me:

    It's fine. He may think it boring though.

Abigail:

    Doubt it, plus, hanging out is usually boring. This will be better.

I close my eyes. Bringing middle school boys was more than I bargained for, but that's Abigail for you. Our text thread turns into a conversation about boys. I can't contribute much so I end up reading their banter until Katherine addresses me directly.

Katherine:

    Paige, my mom can take us if yours can bring us home.

"Mom! Can you bring Katherine and Abigail home tomorrow after the intersquad?" I yell.

I wait a moment and hear, "Yes!"

Me:

    She can bring you home.

Katherine:

    Awesome, can't wait!

I set my phone down and lay back on my bed. I guess if I'm quitting or moving to Level 5, I'm not doing it until I attempt Level 6 in an intersquad.

CHAPTER 27

Katie decided to have us come in Saturday afternoon for the intersquad so we would have the gym to ourselves. As I walk up to the viewing area, the gym seems almost eerie. It's usually bustling with kids, coaches, and parents. I walk through the quiet parent viewing area and into the optionals room and over to my locker. I take off my sweats, wad them up and stuff them in my locker. I take a deep breath and realize I'm nervous. I'm not nervous of the skills I'm going to be doing. They are all skills I have been doing for a while. I'm nervous because for the first time I'm doing my own unique routines. What if the other girls think my routines with Level 5 skills are silly?

Too late now a voice says to me. I sigh again, grateful no one else is in here. I grab my water bottle and head back downstairs.

I go into the training room and see a few of the girls are already here. Since the gym is empty they didn't bother going up to the lockers, they just dumped their bags inside the training room doors.

I quietly join them and sit down in my splits. It's all the upper optional girls, Levels 8, 9, and 10. I don't know these girls well, but since we have the same competition season, we are doing our intersquad together. I'm excited to watch their routines and am intimidated for them to watch mine.

"Good morning, ladies," I hear James say as he walks up. I'm relieved to see James here.

"Are you coaching optionals this season?" I ask hopefully.

"There are a lot of you this morning, so Katie asked for me to help out," he explains.

"What events?" Kayla asks.

"Bars and Floor. Who needs a spot in their routine and which passes?" he asks. I listen as the girls tell him which pass they would like a spot on, double backs mostly.

"What about you, Paige?" he asks me. "Do you need help with your first pass?" he asks, referring to my back tuck. Or maybe he thinks I'm doing a layout. I should be by now.

"No, I'm just doing the tuck," I answer.

He nods and surveys the group. Most of the girls have arrived by now. "Ten laps ladies, then come back and stretch."

We stand up and start to run around the floor. This is a big group when you add in the upper optional girls. I look up at the parent viewing area as I run and I see it has filled in with parents who have come to watch.

We finish running and one of the Level 10s leads us in an organized stretching routine. We take up the entire floor and it is fun to be part of such a big group. When we are done we break into five lines and do a quick and basic complex that is, again, led by the Level 10s. When we're finished we go over to Katie to be told what events we are starting on.

"Thanks for warming us up Kayla. Girls, this is Jill and this is Sarah, they will be judging you today." My stomach sinks as I realize we have actual judges here. "They are going to help us make sure we have all the requirements in each routine and tell us what we need to work on. Upper optionals start on vault, lower optionals start on bars. 6s and 7s, go grip up," she tells us.

We walk over to the doors of the training area to get our grips. Some girls left their gym bags by the entrance of the training areas, some in the cubbies in the lobby, and some put their bags upstairs like a regular practice day.

Lucy and Alexis follow me upstairs, I assume their grips are in their lockers too.

"Are you nervous?" Alexis asks Lucy.

"Not as much as I thought I would be," Lucy tells her.

"You just seem quiet, but then again, you're a quiet person," Alexis observes.

"I'm glad to start on bars," I say, as we reach the top of the stairs. When we see all the parents in the training area our conversation stops and we walk quietly to the optionals room.

We can hear the moms murmuring about warm-ups and what skills their daughters will be doing. Well, the moms that know the names of the skills. Savannah's mom knows stuff like that, my mom doesn't.

We walk into the optional room and over to our lockers. "Should we just grab our bags and take them downstairs since no one else is here today?" Lucy asks.

"Might as well," I agree. We grab our bags and head downstairs where we sit with the rest of our team by bars to put our grips on. We watch as James moves mats around and prepares for our bars rotation. He is talking to the judge, Jill, while he moves mats. Then he gets her a spotting block to sit on. Once he has her settled with a clipboard and a water, he turns to us, "Push away kips!" he yells.

We get in two lines at the competition bars for push away kips to warm up. Once we are done with kips we each do a first half, second half, and full set.

My tuck flyaways are consistent and I am finally comfortable doing them out of a cast. I'm just embarrassed I'm the only one doing a tuck flyaway. Savannah, Alexis, and Lucy all have their layout flyaway. I go over to the chalk tray. There is nothing I can do about it now except to do the best routine I can.

Once we've all done a full set James tells us our order and gives a piece of paper to Jill. I can see it has a grid with our names on it. I assume it's to keep track of our scores rather than using score cards like she would in a meet.

"Level 7s are going to start us off. Sixes, you can sit down," James tells us.

We walk over to the panel mat that James set out and we sit down facing the bars. I sit down, loosen my grips, and watch the girls on the Level 7 team learn their order. They are standing around the chalk tray quietly talking to James. While I wait for them to get situated I look up to see if my family has arrived on time.

I find my mom and wave. I spot Abigail and Katherine next to her. I notice no Quinn; probably for the best. I wonder what they are going to think of all this. At the very least they should have fun watching the Level 10s. As I'm scanning the parent viewing area I spot Trista, Carmen, and Marissa.

"Our 5s are here," I whisper to Alexis.

Alexis, looks up and waves to the girls and says, "That was nice." I smile to myself; it was.

We watch as Brooklyn steps over to the low bar, salutes our judge and begins. As soon as Brooklyn lands I hear girls cheering over at vault. I turn over my shoulder just in time to see one of the 10s do a beautiful layout Tsuk.

I look up to see if Abigail and Katheryn saw her and I see they are busy talking and completely missed it. I shake my head, maybe they won't be impressed by the 10s. Trista and Carmen are clapping furiously, I know *they* appreciated that vault.

I turn back to watch Aubrey take her turn. Aubrey and the rest of the 7s do clean routines that swing just a little higher than ours. When they're finished they take their seat on our panel mat and we get up and go to the chalk tray.

James comes over to us and gives us our order. He has me go first, then Savannah, Alexis, Lucy, Riley, and Victoria. I do a quick kip clear hip for my one-touch and then chalk up and wait to compete. I stand by the low bar and watch my teammates finish their one touch.

James sets out the springboard for my mount and comes over to me. "Swing tight and clean. Get those shoulders in front on your casts," he says. "I've seen them get pretty high lately," he says, making me smile. My casts have gotten higher. They aren't to handstand yet, but they are above the required 45-degree angle.

He steps away from me and immediately the judge salutes me. I salute back and step up onto the springboard. I take a deep breath and jump into my glide kip. I cast above 45 degrees and go right into a decent clear hip circle, then I swing down into another kip. I pike on, jump to the high bar, kip, cast. The cast feels big, I swing down and right into my tuck flyaway. I let go at just the right time and, to my surprise, I stick the landing.

I turn to the judge and salute that I am done. She gives me a nice smile and looks down at her notes. James comes up to me with a big high five. "That was nice and clean. You'll score well," he says. I will? But I didn't really do anything. I walk over to the panel mat, tugging off my grips as I walk. When I sit down, the 7s congratulate me on a good routine.

We are using an old-school scoring stand. The judge is putting up the scores herself before she turns to the next routine. She flips up a score and then turns the stand for me to see. An 8.5. Wait, what? I look at her to catch her eye to see if that score is meant for me, but the judge is already saluting Savannah.

How did I get an 8.5? I didn't do anything. I don't go to handstand on my casts or clear hips, and I did a tuck flyaway. Maybe she meant 7.5. I can ask James after the meet. I watch as Savannah jumps to the high bar, casts to handstand, and does a big layout flyaway. She is arched in the air and she takes several big steps on the landing, but at least she did the layout.

She gets a high five from James and comes over to sit with us. I give her a side hug as she sits down. "You're getting pretty good at bars Anna," I say.

She smiles, "It's fun," she says as she peels off her grips. We watch as the judge turns Savannah's score toward us, 7.70. That can't be right. Thankfully Savannah doesn't ask me what I got and we go straight to watching Alexis.

The rest of our rotation moves quickly since bars is a fast event and we only have one judge to wait for. The upper optionals have come over from vault and are putting on their grips as they watch Victoria, our last routine.

When Victoria is done we walk over to vault. Our judge, Jill, comes with us. The judges will talk to us about our routines at the end of the meet. Therefore, we need the same judge watching us for all four events.

We work with Katie to set up vault. The upper optionals vault with only 8-inch and 4-inch mats behind the vaulting table. We vault with huge mats behind the vaulting table so we need to set them up.

We help Katie push the port-a-pit in place behind the table. Then we throw two more 8-inchers on top. When we are done setting up we run back down the runway for a quick sprint warm-up and then we each do two vaults.

Katie tells us our order and this time we are sorted by the type of timer we do rather than Level 6 and 7. The girls doing Yurchenko entries are first. Katie wraps the springboard with the yellow square mat made to go around the board. Then she stands partially on it as she waits for her first Yurchenko vaulter to go.

Lucy is the only Level 6 doing the Yurchenko entry. I think she practiced it more at her last gym before she came to Perfect Balance. Alexis is doing a front handspring entry and Savannah, Maya, Brooklyn and I are doing Tsuk entries. The five of us sit on floor and watch our teammates.

They all seem to score in the same 8.0 to 8.8 range. Then it's our turn. Their vaults go so fast that Katie says we don't need a one touch vault. We line up in the order Katie tells us and we are ready.

I am to go after Maya and Brooklyn, which is intimidating because I'm sure their form is better than mine.

Both Maya and Brooklyn do clean half-ons and it's my turn. Vault gives me no jitters. It has always been easier for me and this is one area where my new height and weight seem to help. I salute the judge and step onto the runway. I run, hurdle, and punch. I think of twisting in my shoulders while driving my heels like Katie and James have taught me. I do a half turn up onto the table and try to block and pop to my feet on the mats behind the table. I try to keep my momentum moving and fall to my back after my feet hit. The fall at the end seems forced, but hopefully the judge didn't notice. Falling is part of the skill that helps us rotate. Eventually we will do a flip to our feet without the mats behind the table. I stand up and salute Judge Jill.

When I climb down Katie is there to walk down the runway with me for my second one. "Good form and drive on the front half. Keep that momentum on the back half. Think of rotating to your back rather the landing on your feet and falling back," she says. So much for no one noticing.

I nod and stop at my spot on the runway. Katie gives my shoulder a squeeze and steps away from me. I turn and the judge is still looking down calculating my score. Then she looks up at me. She sees I am looking at her so she salutes and I salute back. I step onto the runway.

Keep moving I think to myself. I run and do a vault basically the same as the first one. So much for keep moving. It's harder than it sounds.

Katie greets me with high fives and goes to Savannah to talk with her before her vault. I have no idea what kind of score I'll get on vault and I'm pleased with a simple 8.0. I look up at my mom and friends in the parent viewing area and I'm glad they came. It makes it more like a meet.

After the rest of my team finishes their vaults we rotate to floor and the upper optionals go to beam. We know to go to different corners and to start tumbling on the diagonal. James is with us on floor and Katie went to beam. I'm glad he is here because I know he'll step in on my back tuck if I don't set well.

James doesn't time us like in a meet but just tells us to do one good version of each tumbling pass. I do my front tucks first. It only takes me two tries to feel good. Then I go on to my round-off back handspring back tuck. They feel okay today. Not as sluggish as they have been in the past. Maybe it's the extra adrenaline or maybe I'm finally getting used to my new height. Whatever the reason, I'm glad it feels okay.

I walk over to James when I'm done. "Are you done warming up the tumbling?" He asks me and I nod that I am. "Then warm up your leap and turn along the edge while you wait for the rest of your team to finish."

I do my leap pass along the edge of the floor. By the time the rest of the girls are done I'm more than ready to compete floor. I'm excited to do floor today; even my lame tumbling can't diminish my excitement to perform my very own floor routine.

I look up to the viewing area and I see my dad and brother have joined my mom and my friends. They came straight from Jason's indoor soccer practice. I'm glad they didn't miss floor.

James gathers us together and gives us our order. I notice he has the 6s going first and then the 7s. We sit down along the floor and Alexis starts us off. She has a pretty routine performed to a Beauty and the Beast medley. Alexis is clean and precise and I can tell she is getting more comfortable with her routine. She does a clean layout on her first pass and a front handspring dive roll for her second pass.

Next up is Savannah, who also has her layout and front handspring dive roll. Savannah is performing a peppy and fun routine to the Zombie's movie music. She looks like she is having fun on floor, which makes up for her less than perfect dance lines. Then Lucy is up and I start getting nervous. Why would James have me go after Lucy? She is so good. Her tumbling is amazing and her dance is fun and engaging. As Lucy does a perfect layout I begin to get nervous. Then I watch her dance to her music from the movie Home with an energy I cannot imagine having on floor. My team starts clapping to her music and I look around at everyone enjoying her routine. I stand up to get my blood moving and watch Lucy prepare for her second pass. I walk to my corner as I watch her do a beautiful front handspring front tuck.

Tough act to follow.

I get to the edge of the floor as she is walking off and I give her a high five. "Great routine," I say, and I mean it.

James greets Lucy and murmurs something to her before coming over to me. "You ready?" he asks me.

"My dance is. My tumbling is questionable," I admit.

"You are doing perfectly acceptable Level 6 passes. Own it and show off your dance."

Since I don't really know what is acceptable for Level 6, I don't argue with him. All I know is that all of my teammates do harder skills. He pats my back and moves away from me so Jill can see that I'm ready. There's not much I can do about my tumbling now. All I can do is show off my pretty new floor routine and hope my friends and parents like it.

Judge Jill salutes me, I salute back and walk onto the floor. It's nice and comfortable to do a routine in our own gym. I feel only mildly nervous as I take my starting position. My music starts and I do my dance into the corner, take a deep breath, and run for my first tumbling pass. I do a typical round-off back handspring back tuck. Typical is good considering all of my challenges lately. When I land I am so happy to have done a nice high back tuck. Even more surprising is how my teammates are cheering for me. They know how hard these last several weeks have been for me. I smile and keep going. I enjoy the music and dance of a routine that fits me far better than compulsories ever did. I do my leap pass, dance, pose in the corner and I pause for a moment before my second and final pass of a simple front tuck. I run, punch, and do a clean front tuck with a stuck landing. I do my brief dance sequence and prepare for a one and a half turn. I'm proud of this because most Level 6s do just a full turn. I complete a perfect one and a half turn, dance, do my jump combination and hit my ending pose. I salute the judge and walk off the floor.

My teammates give me high fives and Lucy says, "I think that's the prettiest routine I have even seen."

"Thanks Lucy," I say sitting down next to her.

James walks over and gives me a quick high five and says, "Great crowd pleaser," and then turns to Riley who is next.

I turn and watch the judge intently. I have no idea what to expect. My tumbling is so basic, it could be bad. She adjusts the numbers, turns the stand to us, and then salutes Riley. I can hear my teammates cheering for Riley as she begins, but I'm too shocked to join in. The stand says 8.85. That doesn't seem possible. There is nothing in my routine. Savannah and Lucy got a point lower than me and they were doing way harder stuff. I look up at my mom and she silently claps for me when I catch her eye. I wave at her and my friends and turn back to Riley. I'm not sure how I got that score. I don't think I deserved it. Katie said the judges are going to go over our routines and scores for us at the end of the intrasquad. I'm interested to see what she says.

We enjoy watching the 7s compete on floor and then we head to beam. The upper optionals are not done with beam yet, so we warm-up on the two beams farthest away from the beam they are competing on. We make sure to warm up as quietly as possible. I do each of the skills in my routine once, a dance through, and I'm ready.

I finish slightly before my teammates so I stand next to James and watch the Level 10s compete. They are so good. I can't imagine doing a back handspring on beam, much less three in a row. I look up at my family and friends in the viewing area and they are riveted. I'm glad the 10s are here to make the intrasquad more interesting for everyone who came today.

The last girl competing beam dismounts. The upper optional girls talk to Katie for a moment and then walk over to James.

"You guys ready to end strong?" he asks them. They all

answer something different at once making him laugh as they walk over to floor together.

Katie comes over to us, "How was floor?"

We are silent for a moment and finally Maya says, "We all hit, so it might be time for B routines already." The girls laugh and I notice they are good natured about skills they haven't gotten yet.

"Alright, how about a one touch on the competition beam and we'll begin." We walk over to the far beam and each take a quick turn in the order we're going to compete. I'm third up, which is perfect in my opinion. I can rest after my one-touch and get my head together, but I also don't have to wait too long.

I watch Brooklyn and Maya start us off. They each fall on their series. At least they're doing a series. Now it's my turn to do my puny routine that has no back walkover and no back handspring. *You have a skill no one else can do* my little voice reminds me. That's true, no one else can do a back extension roll on beam. I stand by the beam as Katie walks up.

"Enjoy it up there. You have a clean routine, show Jill that."

"Thank you," I say. She smiles at me and moves away.

Judge Jill salutes and I salute back. I do my simple mount of splits and stand up. I do a nice leap pass, pose and then I kick into a nice tight handstand. I step down and try to do my back extension roll as quickly as possible. I make the back extension roll, but it was definitely not connected to the handstand. I have never connected it so I didn't really intend to. Happy to have made the back extension roll I do a pose, my full turn, and cross steps to move me to the end of the beam. Then I do a clean cartwheel, my jumps, and turn to do my dismount going the other way. My dismount is a simple front tuck and I land it well.

I turn and salute the judge with a big grin. I stayed on! That's something to be proud of.

Katie comes over and give me a high five, "Beautiful. You are going to be a fun beam worker to train over the years." I dip my head, surprised at her compliment.

I go over and sit next to my teammates. They all congratulate me for staying on and then they turn to Alexis, who is next. Alexis has to wait for the judge to figure out my score before she can go, and it is an unusually long wait. Finally, she stops writing, takes the score stand, fiddles with the numbers, and turns it toward us. She is saluting Alexis I see my score. 9.15. What? That can't be right. I look around in confusion. I want to be excited about my scores, I just can't let myself be excited because I don't believe they are right. What is going on?

I look up at my old teammates in the parent viewing area. Marissa gets my attention and holds up a piece of paper with says 33.85 in big black letters. Then she gives me a thumbs up.

Is that right? A 33.85? Did I really just get one of my best all-around scores in a Level 6 intrasquad? James always said I would do well in optionals. Can I believe these scores? I look up at Trista, Marissa, and Carmen. They seem to believe it.

I watch as almost all of my teammates fall on beam doing their new skills. I guess that's what an intersquad is for, to try new skills and get the jitters out.

When our group is done on beam, floor is not even half way done. The upper optionals have longer routines than ours by almost double. I'm glad they aren't done because I love watching them. We sit along the edge of the floor to watch the show.

I see Katie and Judge Jill talking out of the corner of my eye. I'm sure she has a lot to say about us and I'm dying to hear what it is. I sigh; she will talk to us as soon as the upper optional girls are done with floor.

I watch Kayla, a Level 10, salute the judge and start her routine. Kayla has grown since I've been watching her in the gym these last few years. In fact, she is kind of tall. I watch her open with a beautiful piked double back. She smiles bright as she runs into a complicated leap pass. Kayla is like the college girls on the poster Katie showed me. She has broad shoulders, a chest, and muscled arms and legs. She is bigger than me, and yet, I think she is gorgeous. I look at Alexis sitting next to me. Maybe I do need to stop comparing myself to younger girls. I'm growing into a gymnast like Kayla.

I look up at my friends and family again and see they are engrossed in the floor routine going on. I smile to myself; I can't blame them. These girls are inspiring. I relax and try to enjoy the last three routines.

CHAPTER 28

As soon as the upper optional girls are done competing in our intersquad, the judges gather us around them in two groups. The upper optionals sit down in the middle of the floor with Katie and we are ushered to sit over by beam to listen to Judge Jill with James.

"Great meet today! I would say you are all ready for a successful optionals season. Your coaches have asked me to go over each event and tell you where I took deductions. We will go in Olympic order. Vault was solid over all. Most of my deductions came from the body position off the table."

She continues to tell us how vault judging works. I learn that most of my deductions were from not blocking off the table. Then she moves on to bars.

"In Level 6 your casts need to be above 45 degrees. All of you did that and some of you even went to handstand. I love seeing the handstands but the girls that went to handstand had major form breaks, causing a lot of deductions." Then she points to me, "Paige, is it?" I nod nervously. "Paige has all of her casts above 45 degrees and she had no form breaks in her cast, so she had less deductions than someone who maybe went all the way to handstand."

She continues talking about the requirements in Level 6 and I learn that my tuck flyaway is worth the same as a layout flyaway. I did not get a deduction for doing the easier dismount. My scores are starting to make sense.

Judge Jill moves on to beam. She talks about the basic requirements and deductions. Then she turns to me again, "Are you planning to connect the handstand to the back extension roll?"

"Yes," I say, even though I'm not sure if I'll ever get it.

"Good. You're getting a deduction for not having a connected series or a flight element." I nod, this is not news to me. I know I need to have one or the other. "Your leaps are almost 180 degrees and your turn is very controlled. I had very few deductions for you other than that requirement."

Then she turns to Lucy and gives her specific feedback on the requirements in her routine. I don't exactly hear what she's saying because I am shocked and pleased that the score she gave me is what she meant. I really did earn a 9.15 on beam.

After a long discussion with the Level 7s on their beam scores she finally moves to floor. She addresses us, the Level 6s, first.

"All of you met the requirements. Most of your deductions came from leaps, jumps, and turns. Spend time on your dance, it will vastly improve your score." Then she talks to a few of the girls about some big deductions on leaps that can be easily corrected.

"My favorite routine of the day was Swan Lake," she says turning to me. "It was clean with beautiful extension and lines. You were a joy to watch. That routine should score well for you all season."

"Thank you," I squeak out. *Favorite routine of the day?*

"I know we put a lot of value on the tumbling and you guys are trying to reach goals and move to the next level. But remember, to a judge, the tumbling is only half the routine. You must work on all of it."

She talks a little more to specific girls. All I can hear is *favorite routine of the day* over and over in my head. Here I thought I was going to be the scrub of the day. The lowest scorer, the girl who should consider sitting out of the Level 6 season.

"Thank you for your insight," James says. "We'll get working on everything you shared with us as soon as they come in on Monday." Then he turns to us, "Ladies you are free to go. If you want a print out of your scores, come to my office in five minutes and I will have them for you."

Immediately girls pop up and start talking, heading to their gym bags, and finding their parents. Parents have come down from the viewing area and are talking with kids in the lobby. I walk out into the lobby and find my parents and friends.

"I don't know what you were worried about," Katherine says, throwing her hair over her shoulder. "You were, like, one of the best ones on your team."

I laugh at her comment and say, "I don't know about that, but apparently my routines score well."

"Great job today pumpkin," my mom says, giving me a hug.

"Thanks Mom," I say, hugging her back. I turn to my friends and thank them for coming.

Katherine was right, I don't know what I was worried about. So I grew. So what? I can still do Level 6; and do it well. My routines aren't what I thought they would be, but they still score well. My body is not what I want it to be, but I noticed today that I look like the upper optional girls. I still look like a gymnast, just an older gymnast.

Maybe my mind has it all wrong and I need to just enjoy gymnastics and not try to be like anyone else.

"I really liked that backwards roll to handstand thing you did on beam," Abigail says. "No one else did that."

I smile, "No one else does. My gymnastics is a little different."

"I like it," she says.

"So do I."

STRIVE FOR EXCELLENCE

by MELISA TORRES

CHAPTER 1

I float around in the pool on my favorite raft while I watch my friends jump off the diving board. Of course, they don't just jump off the way regular kids would. They are flipping or twisting or both because they can. I turn my face up to the sun and let it warm my cheeks.

"I'm sad summer is ending," I admit to Savannah, who is laying stomach down on a towel at the edge of the pool.

"Me too," she says, sitting up onto her forearms. "But with school starting we begin our new fall training schedule at the gym." It seems weird to be calling it fall when this is only the second week of August and it's 95 degrees out. "You'll finally get to be with us," she adds. My stomach sinks with excitement and fear at the reminder.

Last fall I scored out of Level 5, but rather than choosing to move up with my teammates, Savannah, Alexis, Lucy, and Paige, I decided to stay back in Level 5. The Level 6 season began a few weeks after the Level 5 season ended and I just didn't feel ready. I had fun training in the off season all winter and spring. I got so many of my new Level 6 skills, like my layout on floor and bars and my back handspring on beam. My coaches, James and Melony, told me I could train Level 6 over the summer since I was finally ready.

I chose to stay Level 5 just a little bit longer so I could finish out a chess season. To be honest, I love training with Trista and Carmen. I'm not excited to leave them behind in Level 5. They still need to compete this fall and score out before they can move to Level 6.

"Marissa! Judge this one!" Trista yells right before she does a back layout off the diving board. She over-rotates causing a huge splash. I wait for her to come up before I give her my score.

"8.5! Your form was good in the air, but your entry was terrible," I tell her.

"I know. I have trouble with that," she agrees swimming over to Savannah and me. She gets to the edge and holds on to the rim of the pool with one hand so she doesn't have to tread water.

"Are you ready for tomorrow?" she asks me.

"Which part?"

"Which part are you nervous for?"

"School probably more than gym. We've worked out with the 6s and 7s before," I remind her. "Katie's not too bad."

"Of course she's not bad," Savannah pipes up. "Our workouts are the same, just a little longer. We even get a snack break."

"School then," Trista confirms.

"Yeah, I'm nervous I won't find my classes or be able to open my locker."

"Didn't you guys do all that on Friday?" Savannah questions, referring to an orientation we attended.

"Yes, they talked to us a lot about school rules and then we walked to our classes. We get our lockers tomorrow. I guess we figure it out then," Trista surmises.

"Do you have a lock you can practice with?" I ask her.

"No, do you?"

"Yeah, my mom got me one."

"Can I try it?"

"I'm jealous you guys are going to be at the same school," Savannah sighs. "No gym together; no school together."

"We still live next door, Savannah," Trista says, pulling herself out of the pool. Then she leans over and grabs my innertube and pulls me to the edge.

"What are you doing?" I laugh.

"You need to get out and get me that lock so I can learn how to open one."

"You're more nervous than I am," I observe. She looks at me and I can tell she is thinking of flipping my tube and dumping me out. "Don't do it."

"Do what?" she smiles.

"I can read your mind. You were thinking of dumping me," I remark, climbing out.

"I only thought it," she grumbles, making Savannah and me laugh.

I grab a towel next to Savannah and wrap it around me. I smile at Trista; it will be fun to go to the same middle school as her. I went to Aspen Elementary while she and Savannah were at Hilltop. Both schools feed into Snowcap Canyon Middle School. Savannah is starting fifth grade tomorrow at Hilltop. She won't be at school with either of us this year.

I squeeze the water out of my long black hair because dripping hair makes the biggest mess when I go inside. Then I quickly dry my legs enough to keep from slipping on the tile. I rewrap the towel around my waist and head inside. I run upstairs to my room and grab the lock off my nightstand and run back down.

When I step outside, I see most of my team is done swimming and are laying in the sun. I sit next to Trista and teach her how to use the combination lock.

"And you are sure this is how our locks will be?" she checks.

"Yes, all of them go right, left, right," I confirm. She frowns and takes the lock from me and tries again.

As I watch her try again and again, I get more nervous thinking about tomorrow. In fact, I am nervous about the entire school year. I want to get straight As and have a successful Level 6 season. I think I can do it. I have all my required Level 6 skills and I usually do well in school. I know I can do it; it's just that the unknown of both middle school and the optionals team is making me nervous.

"I did it!" Trista squeals excitedly holding up the open combination lock.

I smile at her, "Then you're ready."

"Yeah, right," she says, clicking the lock shut and trying again.

"What are you wearing tomorrow?" she asks, surprising me because Trista is not one to care much about clothes.

"Probably my pleated skirt," I answer.

"My sister says I need to step it up, but I'm not sure what that means. Maybe it means a skirt," she pauses and looks up. "I don't even know if I have a skirt."

"Just wear what you feel good in," I advise, repeating what my mom told me and hoping it works for Trista too.

"You sound like my mom," she comments, popping the lock again. "I think I've got it," she remarks, setting the lock on the towel next to her. "We'll miss you at practice on Tuesday," she adds quietly.

"You'll be with us in November as soon as your season

is over," I say.

She looks at me with a very serious face, "I hope so. I don't know which I'm more nervous for, middle school or the new season," she finally admits.

Me either.

CHAPTER 2

"Do we have to hold the signs?" my sister, Vanessa, protests.

"We always do the first day of school signs," my mom replies, handing us both a sign to hold in front of us for our annual picture.

"Now that we're both in middle school, I think we're too old," Vanessa pleads.

My mom makes a sad face. "I need to remember what grade you're starting," she says a little sadly.

"Fine," my sister gives in, adjusting the sign that says '8th grade' in front of her.

I look down at mine and realize '6th grade' is upside down. I turn it around and smile for the picture.

"You guys are going to have so much fun!" my mom exclaims and snaps the picture.

We hand her back the signs and head into the garage to get into the car. My mom pulls out and heads to Logan's house. He is a friend of mine from chess. His mom and my mom got to be friends over the summer attending our chess tournaments. They arranged a carpool for school. My mom will be driving us to school and Logan's mom will drive us home.

As we pull up, we see Logan out front enduring first day of school pictures too. When he sees us arrive, he grabs his backpack and runs over to us with a quick wave to his mom.

He gets in back next to me and says, "Thanks for getting me out of any more pictures."

"Oh Logan, your mom just wants to document this day," my mom defends.

"At least you didn't have a sign," my sister points out.

"What classes do you have?" I ask him. He pulls out a printout with room numbers written on it. I should have thought of that. Instead, I have a map with my classes and the period number next to it indicating where I am supposed to go. Vanessa helped me with it so I think I'll be okay. I really hope I don't get lost.

We compare schedules and learn that we have English and math together. At least I'll know someone.

"Can I see your map?" Logan asks. I hand it to him. He studies it for a moment and hands it back to me. I can tell he's as nervous as I am.

We ride the rest of the way in silence. Then my mom tells us where to walk across the street to wait for Logan's mom after school. She pulls into the long line of cars waiting to drive up to the side of the school. I get increasingly nervous. I hope I can open my locker. She slows to a stop and Vanessa gets out and starts walking without a word. I wait for Logan to get out and I slide across the seat. He at least gets out and waits for me.

"Bye, Mom!" I exclaim as I climb out of the car.

"English is first," Logan says as I slam the door behind

me. "We can find it together."

I nod, grateful to have a friend. As we start walking, my mom rolls down the window and yells, "Have a great day!" I smile; she can't help it. At the entrance I see Vanessa is, in fact, waiting for us.

"I knew she would do that," she laughs, falling in step with us. "I just wanted to get a little bit away from the car," she explains.

Logan and I follow her into the school. We enter the busy main hallway and I notice that the kids are big here. Logan and I end up having to walk single file to squeeze through the crowd. At a smaller hallway entrance, my sister turns to me and says, "Most of the 6th grade classes are down this one. I probably won't see you all day because my classes are upstairs and our lunches are at different times."

"Okay," I say.

"Have a good day and I'll see you after school." Then she turns and heads down the main hallway to the stairway. Logan and I turn down the hall, and sure enough, the kids in this hallway are much smaller. They are busy looking at maps and schedules too. I feel much more at ease with all the other 6th graders.

Logan and I find our English class and head in. Our desks don't have names on them like in elementary school. Our teacher tells us to sit anywhere and that we will get seat assignments when the bell rings. We find seats in the back next to each other, but we don't bother talking.

I wonder where Trista is and how riding the bus was for her. I know I have science with her, which means I will get to see her this morning.

The bell rings and our teacher walks to the front of the room. She welcomes us, takes roll, and tells us briefly about English and Language Arts class (ELA). Then she tells us that we are lucky we have ELA first because it is the class where we get our computers and lockers. She passes out a paper to each of us with a locker number, combination, and computer number. Then she walks us all out into the main hall to find our lockers and practice opening them several times. I look at the combination on my sheet of paper. 22-7-12. I can do this: right, left, right. To my relief, I get it open on the second try. I look around and Logan's locker is down the hall pretty far from mine, which is a bummer. I wonder where Trista's is going to be.

When everyone has had a chance to open their locker, our teacher marches us all back to the classroom. Then she passes out our laptops and tells us they are going to be ours for the year. She tells us how to care for them and how to get onto the school website.

It's a little overwhelming to learn all our assignments are going to be turned in online. To my shock, she tells us we have run out of time and we will learn how to use the website more tomorrow. Then the bell rings and everyone goes every which way. "Do we take our computers with us?" I ask my teacher.

"Yes. They go to every class and home with you."

I shove it into my backpack and pull out my map and schedule. I pick up my backpack and it is incredibly heavy now with the computer in it. I look at my schedule; history is next.

Out in the hall there are kids everywhere. I know my class is in this hall, but where? I look at the number on my schedule and the numbers by the door. Are they going up or down? As I tentatively walk down the hall, I hear the bell ring again. What? How am I possibly late for the next class?

I panic a little and I walk as fast as I can down the hall. The numbers are going down, it must be the next one. I find my room, slip into class, and take a seat. Several kids are sitting and several are still coming in. I wasn't the only one who wasn't fast enough. I sigh as I set my backpack down next to me. This is going to be a long day.

CHAPTER 3

History was uneventful; the teacher seemed nice, but I don't know anyone in that class. Science is next and I'm so happy to see Trista. We immediately find seats next to each other. "Did you get your locker open?" I ask her.

"I haven't gotten mine yet. When do I get it?"

"In English class," I tell her. She glances at her schedule in her hand.

"At the end of the day," she states and stuffs her schedule back in her backpack just as the teacher starts talking. Unfortunately, our teacher immediately starts with a seating chart and moves us. At least science sounds like it is going to be interesting. We are going to get to work with mini robots on Fridays. When the bell rings, we find each other and walk out of the classroom together. I'm grateful Trista is in a class with me right before lunch because we can walk to the cafeteria together.

We walk in silence down the sixth-grade hall, which is

rare for Trista. She must be feeling as overwhelmed as I am. When we get to the end of the hall and turn down the main hall, it is a crowded smorgasbord of what feels like the entire school. I know it's only sixth graders because each grade has a separate lunch. There are a lot of kids at this school.

"Did you bring your lunch?" Trista asks me, leaning close and raising her voice to be heard over all the kids. I nod that I did. "Good, then we don't have to stand in that line. We can just find a table."

My backpack is so heavy with the laptop in it. I wonder if I should put it in my locker. I look to where my locker is located and there are so many kids swarming around there that I don't know how I would even get to it. I give up on that idea and follow Trista into the cafeteria.

"Should we find Vanessa?" she remarks.

"Eighth graders have a different lunch time."

"Oh, bummer." She picks a table and sits down. I take off my backpack and sit across from her.

"What classes did you already have?" I inquire.

"I start in history, Spanish, and then science with you," she answers pulling out her lunch bag. "Are you excited for practice?"

"I haven't had time to really think about it. Yes, I guess so. I'm also a little sad I won't be working out with you and Carmen anymore."

"We'll join you after the Level 5 season," she declares with confidence.

"I'm nervous to be coached by Katie," I admit.

"She's subbed for James before," Trista points out.

"Yeah, a day here and there is fine. But I've noticed she doesn't spot very often. If she does, she won't allow spots for very long like James does."

Trista thinks about this for a moment, "That's true, I never noticed though."

"Can I eat with you guys?" I look up and Logan is standing awkwardly by our table holding a tray in his hands.

"Sure," I scoot over to make room.

"I can't find my friends anywhere," he frowns, looking around the room. I follow his gaze and see the massive number of kids. I can understand how he couldn't find his friends. "How did you guys find each other?"

"We had the class before this together," Trista explains, as he sets his tray down and sits next to me.

"That was lucky," he observes as he picks up a mini corndog and dips it in ketchup.

"I'm Trista," she introduces herself, looking at him curiously.

"Logan," he says and pops the corndog bite in his mouth.

"We play chess together and we're in carpool together," I explain to Trista.

"Oh yeah, I've seen you at the pool," Trista realizes, placing him.

"If it was Aspen Acres pool, then probably. What class do you have together before this?"

"Science," we both say at the same time.

"Do you like science?"

"I don't, Marissa does," Trista answers for me.

He laughs, "So you guys know each other pretty well then," he guesses.

Trista tells him how we know each other from gymnastics. As I listen to her, I realize I am relieved to have friends with me on this overwhelming first day of school.

Vanessa finds me after school walking out of the sixth-grade hall. We leave the building together and head to where we're supposed to meet Logan's mom. Logan finds us outside and falls in step next to us. We are silent for a few paces before Logan asks me, "Did you know there's a Chess Club?"

I stop. "There is?"

"Yeah, after school on Tuesdays," he tells me.

"I have practice Tuesday," I say automatically. Then I remember that was my Level 5 schedule. We trained on Tuesday, Wednesday, and Friday. Now my new Level 6 days are Monday, Wednesday, Thursday, and Saturday. "Wait, I don't have practice on Tuesday."

"So, you could come?"

"I don't know," I hesitate. I have learned that when I take on too much, I end up not good at anything. Well, I don't end up bad, just not as good as I want to be. But really, what harm could one day a week of chess really be? I stayed in Level 5 over the summer to play chess. I assumed I would have to give it up this fall as a Level 6. Maybe I don't need to if chess is at my school. "I need to think about it."

"Well, don't think to long because they start next week."

I nod that I heard him as we walk up to his mom's car. Vanessa hops in the front seat as we climb in the back. I let Logan and Vanessa talk to Mrs. Watson all the way home. I am too busy thinking about if I can do chess, Level 6, and still get straight As.

When we get dropped off at home, Vanessa and I let ourselves in. We make a snack of milk and graham crackers. Vanessa asks me about my classes and we learn that I don't have any of the teachers she had in 6th grade. Then she walks over to the family room, flops on the couch, and opens her laptop.

"You have homework already?" I don't have any homework yet. I just have some papers Mom or Dad need to sign.

"Yep, honors classes don't waste any time," she affirms, logging in.

"I'm going to change," I say. My mom will drive up just in time to take me to practice. I am supposed to be ready. I head up to my room. I feel relieved I survived the first day of school. I'm excited to start training with Level 6 today. As sad as I am to leave Carmen and Trista behind, I'm happy to be with Alexis, Paige, Savannah, and Lucy again.

I select a flowered leotard and black shorts and get dressed. Then I pull my hair back into a ponytail and run downstairs to find my gym bag.

Just as I find my gym bag, I hear my mom honking outside. I run to the front door where our shoes are in a big bucket. I find my flip-flops and throw them on. Even though school has started, it's still warm and sunny, like a summer day.

"Bye, Vanessa!" I yell as I run out the door.

I climb into the back seat and my mom asks me about my first day of school as she backs out of the driveway. I tell her I have Logan in a class and Trista in another class and that is it. I know some of the other kids from last year, but not well. I tell her I got my locker open, but I only got it open when we were practicing as a class. I didn't have time to try it the rest of the day. My mom listens and then asks if I have homework as we pull up to the gym.

"Just some forms you have to sign and that's it," I tell her, as I get out of the car. "Bye, Mom!" I exclaim. She tells me to have a good workout as I shut the door. My mind is already on my practice. I'm excited to be in optionals today.

CHAPTER 4

I walk up to my Kip Club Cubby upstairs and stuff my gym bag in just as Victoria, a Level 7, walks up.

"Oh, you get to come in here," she invites, gesturing to the Optionals Room. I thought maybe I would, but I wasn't sure. I smile and grab my gym bag and follow her to the Optionals Room. Savannah let it slip yesterday that they had decorated a locker for me. I'm excited to see it.

When we walk in, I look at the two walls of lockers and sure enough, in the middle of the far wall there's a locker with my name on it. It's decorated with letters in purple construction paper, my favorite color. "This is awesome!" I exclaim as I walk over to my locker.

I open it up and see that it's empty and clean inside. I set my gym bag down.

"Oh, I wanted to see your face when you saw it," I hear Savannah's disappointment as she comes in.

"Oops, sorry. I just didn't want her putting her stuff out there," Victoria explains.

"It's okay," Savannah says, crossing the room. "Welcome!" she smiles, opening her locker a few over from mine.

"Thanks. How much do you guys hang out in here?" I ask them.

"Not that much; the upper optionals tend it use it more. Some of the girls come straight from school and hang out before their workout starts at 3:30," Victoria explains.

Since it's almost 4:30, it explains why they aren't in here; they have already started training.

Victoria turns to Savannah, "Did you bring extra snacks?" Savannah nods.

"Why do you need extra?" I inquire, taking off my T-shirt and stuffing it in my locker.

"I'm staying the extra half hour with the Level 7s today," she shares.

"Are you doing Level 7?" I ask surprised. She smiles and ducks her head, "Wow, good job, Savannah."

"It's basically the same; we just stay until 8:00 and you guys are done at 7:30."

I'm happy for Savannah, but a little bummed that just as I move up, she is moving up too. "Everyone else too?" I question.

"Just me and Lucy," she answers, knowing I'm wondering about our old Level 5 team. "Alexis and Paige are competing Level 6 again. Unless Alexis gets her giants, then I think she'll move to 7."

I sigh; at least I will know girls in my rotation. I toss my shoes in my locker as Paige, Lucy, and Brooklyn come in. The chatter moves to first day of school news and excitement about who has moved up.

"Payton and Maya are down there with the Level 8s," Aubrey announces.

"I wonder how it's going for them," Paige comments.

"Let's head down you guys," Victoria suggests. "It's almost 4:30."

We loudly file out of the Optionals Room, through the parent viewing area, and downstairs. The girls know to start us running laps even though no coach is here to tell us to do so. Then we do chassés, skips, and high knees. I follow along and am a bit winded by the time we are done.

Then the girls take a small corner of the floor and stretch. We know more classes will be coming in soon so we don't take up too much space while we stretch.

"How was your first day of school?" Aubrey asks Paige.

"I don't start for another week," Paige comments.

"Lucky," Victoria says.

"It's not so lucky when I'm still in school two weeks after you guys in June," she comments, changing legs in her splits.

"How was it for you guys?" Victoria looks at us.

"I'm at the same school so it was no big deal," Savannah admits.

I remain quiet until Savannah turns to me expectantly. "Mine was . . . overwhelming," I admit.

"Yeah, Trista said she didn't like it," Savannah says. I'm not surprised Trista didn't love our new school or that she already talked to Savannah about it. "She said she didn't like the hassle of getting to six different classes."

"Hi, girls," Coach Katie greets, walking up to us. "Does everyone know each other?" she asks, knowing today is my first day in this group. We nod at her. I know all of these girls. I was either with them when they were in Level 5 or I trained with them in the summer. Sometimes our summer groups are small because kids are on vacation. When that happens James and Katie like to put the Level 5s up with 6s and the 4s down with the 3s.

"Good, nice to see you, Marissa," she says to me. I don't

257

know what to say so I just smile at her. "We are going to start with complex and then beam. So, stand up and form three lines on just these two strips. Leave that strip for the classes that are starting."

We get in our lines and I'm not worried at all. I have done complex with the Level 6s and 7s lots of times over the summer. We would warm-up together and then split into groups. The only difference is that Katie seems to skip progressions. Like instead of starting with round-offs, we go straight to round-off, back handsprings. We also do more leap-gymnastics combinations, like round-off, straddle jump or hitch kick, aerial (I have to do a cartwheel).

After only about fifteen minutes of complex, Katie tells us to go to beam. I thought we would split up, but with only nine of us in this group and Katie as the only coach, I guess it makes sense to stay together.

We do a simple complex on beam that Brooklyn, a returning Level 7, leads us through. Then Katie tells the Level 7s to go to low beam and the Level 6s to stay on high beams.

"Sixes, ten of your leap passes and jumps. Then ten of your series or flight element that you can do on high beam. Ten dismounts. Then you can go to the low beams and work your new skills the rest of the time. Sevens, stick ten of your new skills on your current progression then do ten on the next progression. Then come to high beam and do the high beam assignment I just gave out."

Everyone immediately gets to work. Katie calls me over. "Do you have a beam routine?" she asks me.

"No, only floor," I confirm.

"Okay, we have plenty of time for Melony to help you with that. And what is your flight element?"

"Back handspring," I tell her.

"Where do you have them?"

"Medium beam."

"Good, and your dismount?"

"Cartwheel, back tuck,"

"Your jump combo?"

"I don't really have one. We just worked several different combinations all summer,"

"Which one is easiest for you?" she grills.

"Probably split jump, straight jump," I answer. It was the Level 5 combination which is why I think I like it. I have done it a thousand times.

"We might want to change that, but we don't have to change it today. Do you remember the assignment I just gave the 6s?" she asks, and I nod. "Good, get started and when you are done work your back handsprings on the medium beam."

The assignment feels like a long one, but the girls seem to get more skills done in a shorter amount of time than the Level 5s. I guess they are just older and more serious.

I get up on the beam and decide to work my jump combination first. When I am done with ten, I warm-up cartwheels for my dismount. There are four high beams and four of us. We do not stop to rest until some of the Level 7s come over and are waiting for a high beam.

I need a rest so I do a dismount off and let Riley take a turn on the high beam. I look around and Savannah and Lucy are working hard on their back handspring series on the medium beam with mats. When did they get so good? It seems like they have both improved a ton in the eight months since they have been on the optionals team.

Riley jumps down and I get up again. All I have is three more dismounts and leaps. I wonder if I'm supposed to do back walkovers too. When I am done with dismounts and leaps I ask Katie about the walkover. She tells me to just stick three on high beam to keep the skill.

After I stick my three, I go over to the low beams to

warm-up my back handsprings. They are consistent and pretty easy for me, but it still took me all summer to get them from the low beam to the medium beam. I'm glad Lucy and Savannah put mats under the medium beam, that will make it a little easier for me today.

By the time I'm ready to do my back handsprings on the medium beam, I'm a little tired. This group works more intensely than the Level 4s and 5s. Maybe because the skills are bigger? Or maybe because Katie is the coach? Whatever the reason, I'm already tired and I have three more events after this.

"Can I join you on this medium beam?" Alexis asks me. I smile and gesture her to the beam. It has been so long since I have worked out with Alexis, I am happy train with her again.

"What are you working?" I ask her.

"Back walkover, back handspring." I noticed Lucy and Savannah were working back handspring, back handspring, which is probably why they are training to compete Level 7 this winter.

I climb up onto the medium beam and step my feet together, raise my arms, and do a nice, clean straight back handspring.

"Those have gotten really good. I haven't seen them in a while," she compliments. I smile as I step up to do another one. When I stick that one, I jump down; Alexis walks up, high fives me, and jumps up for her turn. This groups hardly has time to talk but I like how I feel when I workout with them.

I stick eight back handsprings before it is time for us to go to vault. I have four months until the Level 6 competition season. Working out at this rate, I will be ready for sure.

CHAPTER 5

Paige and I are waiting outside for my mom to pick us up. We carpool to and from practice since we both live in Aspen Acres. Today she didn't catch a ride with us because she was back-to-school shopping.

"How was your first optionals practice?" she asks me as my mom drives up.

"It was great, even though I am beat," I admit, climbing into the car.

"Yeah, it takes some getting used to; they don't mess around in that group." I nod in agreement. "It looks like you have all of your skills already," she comments. "You're in much better shape than I was when I moved up," she shares.

Paige chose to move to Level 6 last November right after the Level 5 season ended. I can't imagine how stressful that must have been for her to only have a month before her first Level 6 meet in January.

"Your season turned out okay, didn't it?" I question.

STRIVE FOR EXCELLENCE

"I scored okay, but I just didn't have a lot of the skills that most Level 6s have. This season will be so much better," she declares.

I'm not sure what to say so I decide to change the subject. "How was school shopping?"

"Not as fun as you might think, since we wear a uniform," she shares as my mom pulls up and we get in. "It was more about trying sizes on at the uniform store. But I get to wear whatever shoes I want. I had fun picking those out."

"What'd you get?"

"Combat boots for fall, fuzzy boots for winter, and flats for spring."

"A uniform sounds kind of nice," I comment. It seems so practical and easy to know what you are going to wear every day.

"It is sometimes, but it also gets boring." We are silent for a moment before she says, "How was school for you today?"

"It was fine, I guess."

"Do you have classes with anyone you know?"

"Yeah, I have first period with Logan, third period with Trista, and then a few people I kind of know from Aspen Elementary in fifth and sixth period."

"That's a good start."

"Do you have any advice for Marissa?" my mom chimes in as we turn onto Paige's street. Paige is in eighth grade now; it's good question to ask her.

"Um, use your planner and your locker," she advises as we pull up to her house. She gets out and says, "See you Wednesday," before slamming the door and walking up the drive to her house.

"Sounds like good advice," my mom comments.

"Yeah," I agree, thinking about how I can't even figure out how to get to my locker much less use it.

262

"Do I need to buy you a planner?"

"No, the school gave us one. I have a bunch of papers you need to sign tonight," I tell her. She nods as we pull into our driveway. I'm so tired from such a big day that I just want to eat and go to bed.

"Let's eat first. Dinner is waiting for us," she comments parking the car and getting out. I drag myself out of the car and follow her into the house. My dad and sister are in the kitchen talking about her first day as they spoon broccoli beef stir-fry from a large wok onto their plates.

"Just in time," my dad says. "We were starving so we thought we would get started. We knew you guys would be here any second."

I walk to the sink to wash my hands and then I grab a plate and fill it. I sit at the counter next to my sister. Our counter seats four people at the kitchen island. Sometimes we eat there instead of at the table. My mom tries to get us to the table for dinner, but it doesn't always happen.

I'm starving! I dig in as I listen to my sister continue to talk about her day. She is happy with the music teacher and excited about history and art class. "What about math?" my dad inquires.

"Math was fine – easy," she says. She's like me; numbers come easy for her. I don't think she finds them as fun as I do though.

"How was your day, Marissa?" my dad asks.

"Fine," I answer.

"Did you like your classes?"

"I guess," I shrug. I'm not sure if I like my classes. It's too early to tell. I was mostly worried about getting to the correct classes on time.

"Anything interesting happen today?" he presses, clearly not satisfied with my evasive answers.

I think for a minute. I better give him something decent

or he'll keep asking me. "I got my locker open, I found all my classes, and I have a class with Trista."

"That's a successful day," my mom smiles encouragingly. I shrug slightly in agreement and go back to my food. I finish before everyone because I was starving and because I talked way less than Vanessa.

"May I be excused?" My mom sees my tired face and nods.

I drag myself upstairs, shower, and fall into bed. How am I going to do this for four more days this week?

"Place your parental consent forms in the basket as you walk in," I hear my teacher instruct as I walk into class.

The papers!

I totally forgot! I didn't get any of them signed. I needed one signed for each class. I just missed homework for six classes. How did that happen? I have never missed homework in my life!

I told my mom I needed her to sign papers and then she forgot. I sigh; I know I can't blame her. I forgot. I ate dinner and crashed. At least tonight I don't have practice and I can remember to get them signed.

"They are due Wednesday, but I have reward tickets for everyone who turns them in today."

"What do the reward tickets do?" I ask Logan, and he shrugs and walks over to his seat. I notice when he gets to his desk, he opens his backpack and gets out his signed papers.

Not a great start for me, but at least it isn't a real assignment. I get through the morning a little easier than yesterday because I know where all my classes are. I finally get to my locker at lunchtime and dump my notebooks from the first three classes. Now my backpack isn't so heavy.

Trista is leaning against the locker next to me waiting for me before we go to the cafeteria.

"How was practice yesterday?"

"Hard. I mean, it was the same three hours that we are used to, but it just felt a little more intense," I admit.

"Is it Katie?"

"Or maybe just at this level the girls are more serious," I suggest. As soon as I say that I feel terrible. "Not that you aren't serious," I hastily add.

She is quiet for a moment and then says, "Maybe it's because you have more skills to learn. And as soon as you get a skill, you start working on another one."

"James lets you guys move on to Level 6 skills," I point out.

"Yeah, but we can't actually compete them," she counters.

"Whatever the reason is, I'm tired and sore," I complain, shutting my locker, spinning the dial, and picking up my backpack.

We walk into the cafeteria just a little later than yesterday and it's a zoo. We struggle to find a table and are zig zagging through full tables with kids yell-talking.

"Marissa," I hear my name being called out and I see Logan. He is sitting alone and he looks relieved to see us. We quickly walk over to him and sit down.

"We need a regular spot," I say, as I sit down.

"Should we make it this one?" he suggests.

"Sure," we both agree.

"Keep your eye out for Nate," Logan says looking around the cafeteria. "He ate alone yesterday."

Before we have a chance to look for Nate, Logan spots him and waves him over. Nate looks relieved as he sits down.

"This place is crazy," he grumbles as he sits. "I'm glad I

found you today," he says to Logan.

We are all awkward for a moment and then Trista pipes up, "I'm Trista, and this is Marissa."

"Hi. Yeah, I know Marissa," he says awkwardly. I look around and notice very few tables have a mix of boys and girls at them. It is so comfortable with Logan that I didn't think much about it yesterday.

"What class did you come from?" Trista asks.

She immediately puts Nate at ease and I am grateful for Trista's outgoing personality. We talk about Nate's classes and find out he has a lot of the same teachers and classes that we do, just in a different order.

Lunch goes by fast and before I know it the bell rings for fourth period. Trista and I walk together out of the cafeteria and then we have to split off to go to our separate classes. As I am walking to class, a girl I hardly know (I think her name is Blair) starts walking with me.

"So, is, like, he your boyfriend?" she asks.

"Who?"

"Logan. I saw you at a boy-girl table."

"So?" I retort.

"So, are you like, dating?"

I stop walking, "Dating?" What is wrong with this girl?

"Yeah, I mean, you were eating lunch together," she points out.

"I'm aware," I say. I get to the door of my classroom. "This is my class," I utter and slip away from her.

What the heck was that? Am I dating Logan? How do you even date when you are eleven? Happy to be away from the nosy girl, I quickly find my seat and get out my laptop.

"You should've just told her yes," Vanessa comments when I tell her about the weird questions from Blair. Logan's mom dropped us off at home. Vanessa opens the fridge and asks, "What do you want? Salami and cheese? Or there's some apples. We could have them with peanut butter?"

"Apples and peanut butter," I decide and walk to the cabinet to get the peanut butter. She gets out the apples and cuts them while I spoon peanut butter onto a plate for dipping. Then we both sit down to the counter.

"I forgot to have Mom sign my forms for each class last night," I comment as we start eating.

"You have to do that stuff right away because it's easy to forget," she comments.

"Did you remember all yours?"

"Yeah," she says, picking up an apple slice.

"Why didn't Mom just sign mine when she was signing yours?" I wonder.

"Because you were at practice," she garbles around a mouth full of apple. I frown at that. I guess I better get out the dumb papers and make sure my mom or dad sign them tonight. I dig through my backpack and pull out my different folders for each class.

"It helps if you put them all in one place," my sister advises, eyeing my six folders scattered all over the counter.

"They're for different classes," I point out.

"I'm telling you, use one folder for homework."

I look at all the folders in front of me and feel overwhelmed. "How do you keep track of it all?"

"Check your online school account every day, use a planner, and have one homework folder," she says. As if it were that simple.

CHAPTER 6

I survived the first week of school and the first week of practice. Well, almost the first week of practice. Today is my first Saturday morning workout. I feel so much better walking into the gym rested and ready for practice rather than coming in after school. The gym is empty when Paige and I arrive.

"At least it's not cold," she comments as we walk into the Optionals Room to put our bags and shoes away.

"Do you like Saturday morning workouts?" I ask her.

"Yes. They're a little more relaxed and we tend to work new skills more on Saturdays. The only problem is it makes going to PNO harder. I like to rest on Friday nights."

Our gym holds Parents Night Out every Friday. The point is to just play on the equipment, but team kids come to work skills. We used to always come together as a team back in Level 3 and 4. Now that Paige mentions it, there are less Optionals kids at PNO. Now I know why.

"I'm glad I'm not the only one. Last night I didn't want to do anything. I just laid on the couch and watched the show, *The Floor is Lava*."

We head back downstairs and when we enter the gym, we see Katie is there flipping on lights. "Good morning, girls," she greets us. "Hang out for a couple of minutes and you can all run together." We nod and sit down.

I sit with my legs in front of me in a pike position. I reach my hands to my feet and lean my head down toward my knees. It feels good to stretch my back and hamstrings. Thankfully, the conditioning is not much harder than I'm used to and I'm only mildly sore.

"Good morning, ladies," I hear the distinct voice of James.

"You coach us on Saturdays?" I exclaim.

"When compulsories aren't competing, I come in from time to time. Thought I would see how you are coming along, Riss," he says, as he walks over to me and pushes me down in my pikes.

"I was enjoying a nice easy stretch," I protest.

He ignores me and says, "Katie's upper optionals group is getting big. She probably needs to hire someone before my compulsories season starts."

"When is their first meet?" Paige inquires.

He stops leaning on me and walks over to her and adjusts her pancake stretch. "Early September," he replies. "They have about two weeks to get their act together."

"They're ready," I confirm, thinking about how my former teammates have been running routines all summer.

"For the most part," he agrees. "How was school this week?"

"I haven't started yet," Paige says, and he turns to me expectantly.

I shrug, "Annoying."

"Really? I thought you liked school," he comments.

"Middle school is just a lot," I say, trying to help him understand that I like learning, but that I don't really like this new format for school.

"If anyone can handle it, Marissa, it's you," he declares with a confidence I don't feel.

"There's enough of you to get started!" Katie yells over to us from where she is moving mats around at vault. I look around and she's right; several girls have arrived since we've been talking to James.

I stand up to run with both the lower and the upper optionals teams. I look at James, "What events are you coaching?" I ask.

"Bars and maybe some floor," he answers.

I nod and start running around the floor. James on bars today will be helpful. My bar routine is basically the old Level 5 routine, except with no tap swings before the flyaway. I learned a layout flyaway over the summer and I'm trying to get my casts and clear hips up to handstand. I also want to add in another skill to make it a little more interesting.

After we run and stretch we do complex with all the optionals teams, Level 6 to Level 10. I have to modify most of what Katie and James yell out for us. We finish just before nine o'clock when all the recreational kids start arriving.

Katie decides lower level optionals (Levels 6 and 7) will start with James on bars and that she will start with upper optionals (Levels 8-10) on beam. I'm happy with this great start to my first Saturday workout as I run upstairs with my teammates to go put our grips on.

"The only problem with doing bars first is we don't need our snack yet while we are up here," Victoria mentions.

We quietly get our grips out and put them on as we run back down the stairs.

James has us start with push away kips. I have gotten pretty good at these because we did them in Level 5 too. When we are done warming up, he gives us his assignment.

"Clear hips on this bar with me," he instructs, pointing to a bar that has a spotting block under it. "Flyaways on that set, handstand pirouettes on the floor bar, and back extension rolls to blind change down the cheese mat."

Back extension rolls with grips on? Does that seem weird to anyone else? I watch as two of my teammates start over on the cheese mat drill. They take their fingers out of the grip and tuck the top temporarily in the wrist band. Okay, I can do that.

I decide to start with James on clear hips. He is already up on the spotting block when I walk up. He motions for me to go and I know what to do. I do a kip cast and he helps me all the way up to a handstand. Then I lean my shoulders forward and come down controlled. When my body gets parallel to the ground, I lean my shoulders back into a clear hip. On the back side of the clear hip, James grabs my legs and pulls me up to a handstand. Then I control it down again, only this time into a glide.

"You could have done a second one," he says when I come to a stop under the bar.

A second one? I stand up and look at him quietly. He continues, "It's time for you to do two or three clear hips in a row. Especially while I'm spotting." That sounds hard, but I nod my head as if it is something I can do. I go to the chalk tray, chalk up, and walk over to the flyaway bar. I easily do a tuck flyaway to warm-up.

"Those have gotten good," Alexis comments as I walk toward her at the floor bar station.

"Really?" I ask, a little surprised.

"Yeah, you used to let go a little early and land short. Now you land nice and high."

"Thanks," I say with a grin. She's right; my flyaways have improved. "I think I like them out of the cast better."

"That took me a while to adjust to, but now I think I like them better too." She kicks up to a handstand on the floor bar, switches one hand, then rotates her body halfway around and ends on a solid handstand facing the other way and then she steps down. She gives me a smile and heads over to the other station which is the back extension rolls down the cheese.

We rotate through the four stations three times before James announces it's time for us to work giants. "Paige and Marissa, take off your grips and go to the strap bar, the rest of you to the pit bar."

I start walking toward the training doors that lead upstairs as I take off my grips. "You can leave them down here," Paige suggests to me. "We can take them up when everyone else goes up. We'll get more turns in that way."

I do as she says and walk to the strap bar with her. We slide a spotting block under the strap bar to help us reach it.

"Everyone else has their giants?" I ask as Paige stands up on the spotting block and straps herself in.

"Basically. Alexis does them with a spot. Everyone else can do them on their own." Then she slides her hands to the middle of the bar, drops off the spotting block, and starts pumping tap swings as high as she can go.

Paige easily gets herself high enough to swing several giants before she slows herself down. Once she is hanging, she swings her legs over to the block, stands up, then moves her hands over, and unstraps herself.

"Those look good, why aren't you over there?"

"I always arch too soon and fall over on the back side. I go so early James or Katie can't help me over. I need to work on body shaping at the right time."

"Giants are hard, aren't they?" I observe, climbing up

next to her and strapping myself in.

"I think so," she agrees.

It seems like everything in optionals and middle school is hard.

CHAPTER 7

I happily spend Saturday afternoon reading by the pool. My mom comes out with two glasses of lemonade. She hands me one and asks, "You don't want to get in?"

I shake my head. "I'm pretty tired."

"I guess it has been a big week," she says, sitting down next to me. "Want to talk about it?"

"There's not much to talk about. School is just . . . not fun," I say, unable to explain it to her.

"Not fun," she repeats. "But you like learning."

"I know. But we aren't learning very much. And I miss recess," I admit.

That makes her chuckle. "Give it time, peanut; school is just getting started. I'm sure you will be learning interesting things in no time."

I don't disagree with her to be nice, even though I'm not so sure. "There's a Chess Club at school," I tell her.

"Really? I'm not sure you have time for that."

"It's on Tuesdays."

"It's a lot, Marissa. Remember what happened when you took on too much before?" she reminds me of the summer before Level 4 when I got really behind in the gym because I was doing too many things. Since then, we have been really careful to make sure I am not doing too much. That's a big reason I stayed with the Level 5s over the summer. It allowed me to participate in chess while still being successful at gymnastics. When I started school and Level 6, I told the rec center I could no longer do their chess classes or tournaments. Now here I am, a week later, asking to do chess again.

"I remember. But it fits my schedule so I think I can do it."

She leans back and takes a sip of her lemonade. "I love that you have several interests. School is most important. Just make sure you keep schoolwork as a priority."

"I will. School is easy, Mom. I'll be fine."

Chess Club gave me something to look forward to at school. I made it through the day, and, per the fliers taped all over the school, I am headed to room 1135 for Chess Club. I find it down a seventh-grade hall I've never been to before. I see the classroom with kids already inside setting up vinyl chess boards.

"Hello," the teacher greets as I walk in. "Are you looking for Chess Club?" I nod that I am. "Then you found the right place!" I walk the rest of the way in and he asks my name and grade.

"Marissa, and I'm in sixth grade."

"Nice to meet you, Marissa. I'm Mr. Belsky," he says.

I hesitate, not sure if I should set up a board or sit and watch the game that just got started.

"Why don't you set up this board with me; I'm sure a few more kids will trickle in. Once everyone is here, I can tell you more about what we will do this year."

I do as he says and start setting pieces out on a board that he laid out.

"Have you played before?" I stop mid-set up with a bishop in my hand.

"Of course."

He laughs. "Some people come here to learn to play. I take it you are serious?"

"I mean, I'm competitive," I share, setting the bishop on his starting square.

"Do you know your rating?"

"No," I say, looking up. "What's that?"

"It's just a way for us to know your skill level. It's okay if you don't have one. A lot of kids don't bother to get a rating until high school."

"How can I get one?" I ask, picking up the rook.

He laughs and says, "You are going to do well here, Marissa; I can tell."

I don't know what to say to that. Thankfully, I don't have to say anything because Logan walks in and Mr. Belsky goes through his greeting all over again. After Logan briefly introduces himself, he sits down at the board I just set up. Without a word we start playing.

I enjoy playing Logan; he has a solid opening game, but I have a better closing game. I have to be very careful in the beginning. It's hard today because kids keep coming in and talking with Mr. Belsky. I slip up in my distraction and Logan gets my knight. He knows I like having both knights on the board.

"I was distracted," I grumble.

"This is a middle school team, better step it up," he teases. I don't have a good reply so I take his rook instead.

"Eye for an eye," he mumbles as he stares at the board.

As Logan is contemplating the board, Mr. Belsky interrupts us. "I think everyone who is interested is here. I want to tell all of you briefly about Chess Club."

We all stop playing and turn toward him to see what he has to say.

"This group is for kids who enjoy playing chess or who want to learn. We get together every week to play the game as well as to improve our game. I will try to give you pointers when I play against you. There will be a tournament at the end of October. Our team will be made up of six kids and one alternate. Seven of you will get to go to represent Snowcap Middle School. I will have the exact date of that event soon. Some kids don't want to enter a tournament and some do. Either way is fine, just let me know. For those that want to attend, we will hold a tournament among ourselves to see who the top six kids are."

When no one says anything, he continues, "Okay then, play on. If your game ends, the winner can play me."

I really enjoy my game with Logan, even though he wins. Logan goes over to play Mr. Belsky while I wait for another game to end so I can play someone else.

I watch the three other games in progress. These kids are pretty good, but nothing spectacular or intimidating. I enjoy seeing their different strategies. As I am sitting there watching a sophisticated chess game, I realize I am having fun at middle school for the first time.

CHAPTER 8

"How is middle school going?" Alexis asks me at the chalk tray the next day.

"It's okay. They have a chess team," I add.

"Is it during school?"

"After school. On Tuesdays."

"You got lucky there," she comments, knowing we only have Tuesdays, Fridays, and Sundays off.

"I know. Super lucky because it's the only fun thing about middle school so far. How is it going for you?"

"It's not much different because our school is K through eight. But I do have to rotate for science and math now. I can't imagine doing that for all my classes."

"It can be overwhelming," I admit.

"I bet," she says and heads over to the bar for her flyaways.

We are at the end of our bar workout. We really don't have much time to talk at practice with the exception of the occasional chalk tray conversation. I like Alexis; I should see if she wants to come over and swim this weekend. It will be too cold to swim soon. In fact, I should have the entire team over. Do I invite my new team? Or my old team? Or both? Both would be a lot. I hate that we are split up like this.

I sigh as I watch Lucy do giants on the competition bars. Katie is standing on a block, spotting her, but I can tell she can probably do them on her own. I guess we all learn at different rates and it can't be helped.

Katie tells us to go put our grips away and head to floor. I do as she says and sneak a few bites of a granola bar while I'm in the Optionals Room putting my grips away. Then I follow my teammates downstairs and to floor. We do complex on only half the floor while we share with the Level 4s and 5s. Then we warm-up our tumbling on the red strip while the Level 4s and 5s run routines. They had their intersquads already and they have a meet this weekend. It's odd to think they are officially in season now. I watch as Trista does a beautiful floor routine.

"Marissa, you're up!" I hear Katie yelling, bringing me back to my workout. "What pass are you doing?"

"Layout!" I yell back. She knows I mean a back layout since I can't do a front layout yet. I run and do a round-off, back handspring, layout. It feels high and floaty and I have no problem seeing my landing and coming down controlled. The red tumble strip is bouncier than the regular floor. It's fun tumbling over here once in a while.

"Those are looking very nice, Marissa," Katies praises. I smile; grateful things are going so well in the gym. "When they are done with routines and doing conditioning, we will do dance throughs. Your music is on the gym phone, right?"

"I'm pretty sure. My mom emailed it to Melony. She had it when she taught me my routine."

"Then it's there. It's been a while; do you remember it?"

I nod. Of course I do! I love my routine! My first optionals routine. Melony created it for me at the end of summer when we decided with James that I was going to forego the Level 5 season and train with the 6s starting when school began. Getting a floor routine is seriously the best part of moving up to optionals. My routine is to *Silverwood* by Billy Hammer. It is slower than most music therefore I must be more careful and intentional with my dance. I love that it has violin in it as a nod to my hobby of playing violin. When my mom and I were sitting listening to all the options on the website, we both perked up when we heard this song.

"I could play it for you live at meets!" my sister teased.

"It has all the other instruments though," I commented.

"Don't be so serious, Marissa. It would be fun!" she argued, and then I felt bad that I always have to be so literal.

"Okay, two more like that and you can move on to your front pass," Katie instructs, bringing me back to the present.

I walk over to the trampoline for my turn there. I have fun trying to do front layouts. When I'm done with my turn on trampoline and I'm walking to get back in line at the tumble strip, I wonder what my front tumbling pass is. I have been doing front handspring, dive rolls and front tucks at practice. Which one goes in my routine? When it's my turn I do a front handspring to warm-up and then I ask Katie, "What's my front tumbling pass?"

She laughs. "Sorry, I should have told you. Sometimes there are so many routines to keep track of I forget you can't read my mind. Let's have you do the front handspring, dive roll and move it to a front handspring, front as soon as possible."

With that, James yells over to her that he and his team are done with floor and we take over while they go to conditioning.

"Everyone do two dance throughs. Leaps along the

edges while you wait. And start memorizing routines!" Katies yells.

"Savannah, you're up," she says, queuing up the music. I guess since we aren't tumbling we don't need to warm-up, but it seems like we are jumping into routines fast. I watch as Savannah walks to a corner and strikes a starting pose.

"What does she mean by memorize routines?" I ask Lucy who is standing next to me.

"She wants us to know each other's routines so you'll know when you can tumble during workout," Lucy explains. Know when to tumble? I must look confused because Lucy continues, "We have limited time during a floor rotation so when someone is running a routine we still need to tumble the diagonal. If we are only tumbling between routines, we would never finish our assignment."

"We have to tumble when someone is doing her routine. I guess I remember watching the upper optionals do that," I comment.

"The person doing the routine has the right of way. It's up to us to know her routine and know when she's not going to be on a diagonal long enough for a couple of us to tumble."

It's funny, I've watched the optional girls do several floor workouts and they do tumble during each other's routines. I never thought about how they had to memorize each other's patterns to know when to go.

"Marissa, do you want to go?" Katie yells over to me from the stereo.

"Sure," I agree, excited to do my routine for my teammates. When I learned it on Sundays with Melony, only Victoria and Riley were there because they were getting new routines too. Lucy, Paige, Savannah, and Alexis are keeping their routines from last year. They have never seen me do this routine. I walk over to the corner I picked with Melony as my starting corner. I stand in my starting pose with one hand on my hip and the other one down to my side. While I wait for my music to begin, I notice that the gym has gotten quiet. On Wednesdays all the compulsory kids are here and there are several classes since the upper optionals have the day off.

"Whoo-hoo, Marissa!" I hear Trista yell just before my music begins, making me smile. As my music comes on, I lift my arm that was straight in a sweeping circle up over my head and tilt my head back. It is such a graceful movement and I love that my routine starts this way. Then I step to the corner, do one more pose, and pause to tumble. Instead of tumbling, I run down the diagonal to the opposite corner since this is just a dance through.

The entire gym really has stopped to watch! It's common when new music comes on. We all listen to the same floor music all year so new music is noticeable in the gym. Since all eyes are on me, I try to show it off. I run into my leap pass, more dance, and to the next corner. Then I run across the diagonal and stand in a lunge waiting for my music. Then I do my one and a half turn and ending pose. For fun, I salute Katie while my team claps.

"That routine is beautiful!" Savannah says.

"Way to show it off," Alexis chimes in.

"That will score well," Paige comments.

I don't respond because I am breathing hard. I grab my sides to puff in and out. I look up and see Victoria has noticed my labored breathing. She pats me on the back and says, "Welcome to Optionals. Why don't you go get a drink?"

CHAPTER 9

It's weird to be in the stands for the Back-to-School
Bonanza Meet. I competed in this meet for the last three
years, in Level 3, 4, and 5. Today I'm here to watch the Level
5 team compete, mostly Carmen and Trista. I do know the
other girls since I worked out with them over the summer.
But I have been friends with Trista since Level 3 and Carmen
since Level 4. Savannah's mom brought Savannah, Alexis,
and me. She is sitting with us making lively conversation.

"Just when I know what to look for in the Level 5
routine, they go and change them," she complains.

"I like them though, they look more fun," Savannah
comments.

"My mom thinks these routines will help kids progress
to optionals better," Alexis says. Her mom was a Level 10
and college gymnast. Sometimes she even coaches private
lessons for the upper optional girls. I have a feeling Alexis
will be a coach someday too.

"Do we know their rotation order yet?" I ask the group.

"I think its bars, beam, floor, vault," Alexis observes.

"Trista will like that order," Savannah comments.

"Do you guys need a snack or anything?" Debbie, Savannah's mom, says as she stands. "I'm getting a drink." We all say we don't need anything. She gives us a skeptical look and walks down the bleachers to the concession stands. This is a small meet held in a local gym. The concession stand consists of young gymnasts selling snacks out of the gym office.

We watch warm-ups quietly for a moment before I finally say what we are all thinking. "Do you think they'll score out today?"

"They both are more than capable of it. It's just a matter of sticking their routines," Alexis determines.

"Or just staying on," Savannah adds, meaning no falls off the equipment.

I don't say anything to either comment because I think their assessments are correct. They both need to have solid routines. They can wobble or have a small mistake, but nothing else.

"This is just the first meet," I finally say. "If they don't score out today, they can at the next one in a few weeks."

We all know that as soon as either of them score out, they will be allowed to get a floor routine and can plan to train with us as soon as their season is over in November. I know they are both dying to get floor routines. In compulsories every gymnast has the same music and routine. In optionals we all get to pick our own music and have our own routine. It's a huge deal.

"I just hope they either both score out or both don't." Savannah whispers. Leave it to Savannah to see the emotional side of the situation. "It would be rough for the person that is getting left behind."

"No one will be left behind," Alexis affirms. "They will both score out before the season is over." I completely agree; they are both more than ready to join us in Level 6.

By now they are done warming up on bars and the meet director is announcing the teams. We quiet down and listen. There are only four teams here so it will be a quick meet. We stand up for the National Anthem and I'm reminded that soon it will be us standing down there listening to the National Anthem before a meet. January is our first meet. I smile to myself; I think I really will be ready, at least with my A routines.

We sit down and Savannah pulls out a notebook that I can tell is to keep track of their scores. I don't say anything as I watch James put them in order to compete. It looks like Trista is up first. She likes to go first and I'm willing to bet she requested it. Trista walks over to the chalk tray and is silently chalking up.

"I wish I could be over there with her," Savannah says. "This is the first time she has been in a meet without us."

"She has James," Alexis says as we watch her walk over to James for some last-minute instructions. In meets he doesn't always give pointers. Sometimes he just talks to help you feel comfortable.

"I didn't miss anything, did I?" Debbie asks, coming up the bleachers and sitting back down next to us. She hands us a soft pretzel to share. Even though none of us requested it, we happily split it apart and start eating.

"Trista is about to go," Savannah answers her.

"Oh, I better get my phone out," she says and quickly gets her phone up and recording just as Trista salutes.

We watch Trista swing through a nice, clean bar routine. Her casts are above horizontal and her form is clean. When she jumps to catch the high bar, I see James step close to stand there for her dismount. She must be doing the layout; I can't believe I didn't know she was doing that today. Sure enough, she does a nice layout flyaway.

"Whoo-hoo!" Alexis yells and claps when she lands.

"Way to go, Trista!" Savannah yells.

"That was really nice and clean," I comment. "She will score well."

"I can't believe bars is becoming a solid event for her," Alexis says. Trista used to hate bars, but you would never know by watching her routine today.

"Good start," Debbie states, putting her phone back into her pocket.

The rest of the new Level 5s look good, but nervous. They are swinging hesitantly and a little slow. It makes me realize how far we have all come in a year.

Finally, Carmen is last up on bars. We watch as she salutes and jumps into a clean glide kip. Her casts are a little higher than Trista's, but her form is not as tight. Again, I am shocked at how much she has improved since last season. I realize I was with these girls all summer, but until I stopped to watch a routine in a meet, I didn't notice how good they've gotten. I think they're definitely ready for Level 6 this winter.

I watch as Carmen does a nice, high tuck flyaway and sticks the landing. We clap and cheer for her, hoping she can hear us across the gym. James gives her a big hug and she walks over to her teammates for high fives.

"That's so easy for her. She should do the layout," Alexis comments.

"There's Andrea and Maria," Debbie says, pointing to Trista and Carmen's parents at the other side of the bleachers a little way up. "Let's go sit by them," she suggests, standing up.

I look up and see a bunch of parents wearing Perfect Balance T-shirts. How did we miss seeing them when we came in? I stand up and follow Debbie up the bleachers and over to the Perfect Balance parents.

We get settled before they start beam. We let the parents talk while we watch beam warm-ups. The girls look confident and ready. They should be; they have been running these routines all summer.

In a matter of minutes, Trista is standing by the beam ready to salute the judge.

"Trista is up," I tell the parents. Often times parents can't tell the difference between warm-up and competition, especially in a capital cup format. It helps if we alert them. Andrea, Trista's mom, immediately stops talking and pulls out her phone.

"I'll record it, you enjoy watching," Debbie tells her. Andrea nods and murmurs her thanks as Trista salutes the judge.

We watch Trista begin her routine with confidence. I'm enjoying watching how much she has improved in her dance with our ballet teacher, Madame Julia. Trista is having a great routine. Just as I think that we watch her wobble and fall on a full turn.

"Oh dear," her mom says. We hold our breath as we watch James talk to Trista.

"Can she still score out?" Savannah wonders.

"She needs a 32?" I verify, and Savannah nods.

"She needs an 8.0 on each event. Depending on how much this sets her back, she could make it up on floor with an 8.5," I determine.

"The only problem is the new routines," Alexis points out.

"Why?" Savannah whispers as we watch Trista get back up on the beam.

"Well, with a new set of routines the coaches don't know what the judges are looking for yet. This is the first season on this set. Last season was James' eighth season with those routines. He knew how to get us to score well."

"Aren't they always just looking for straight legs and pointed toes?" I tease.

"Yes, but also, where should her passé have been on the turn? How long does she have to hold the scale? Stuff like that," she answers seriously, not understanding that I was teasing her.

"Isn't all of that in the new code?"

"Yes, but it's a lot for the coaches to remember. Especially for a coach like James at a smaller gym who is coaching all the compulsory levels."

"Was your mom ever a judge?" I ask Alexis, knowing that she has all this extra insight from her mom.

"She did judge before we were born. She coached back then too," she confirms.

Trista dismounts and puts on a brave smile, but I can tell she is very disappointed. We clap and cheer for her, but it feels hollow. We all feel her disappointment.

"She has the entire season," I hear Debbie say to Andrea.

True, she has the entire season, but Trista is not a patient person. She is not going to like it if she doesn't score out today; not one bit.

CHAPTER 10

Alexis was right, the scores were a lot lower than in past seasons. Coaches, judges, and gymnast were all getting used to the new routines. Neither Trista nor Carmen scored out.

We quickly say hi to the Level 5 team before awards and leave. Debbie drives us all the short distance home.

"We're a little late," Debbie mutters as she runs a yellow light.

"Late for what?" I comment.

"Oh, Alexis' mom wanted her back at a certain time," she stutters.

"Then why are we driving up to my house first? We can drop Alexis off if she's late."

"Marissa, you are too smart for your own good," Debbie chuckles.

"I texted my mom, we're good," Alexis quips, turning red.

What is going on? I look around the car and everyone

looks awkward in the eerie silence.

"When is their next meet?" I ask the car in general.

"I think in just two weeks," Savannah answers. "Cedar City, maybe? Or maybe it's the Capitol Hill meet. I can't remember. Trista showed me their meets, but I can't remember the order."

"They will score out next time," Alexis predicts with confidence. I hope so. I hope Trista is not too down on herself at school on Monday. Sometimes she can get crabby when she's frustrated.

We pull up to my house and I'm surprised to see cars in the driveway. Maybe my mom has her Mahjong friends over or something.

When Debbie stops the car, everyone gets out, which confuses me because I thought I was just getting dropped off. It seems rude to ask what they are doing. I quietly walk to my front door with Savannah, Alexis, and Debbie oddly following me.

My mom knows I am expected home so I assume the door will be unlocked. I push open the front door and I'm greeted with a loud, "Surprise!"

I am shocked at the scene before me. My mom, dad, and sister are standing in the entry way with a sign above them that says, 'Happy Birthday.' There are silver and purple balloons on either side of them.

I put my hands over my mouth in surprise. Oh. My. Gosh! A surprise party! For me!

"Say something," my sister prompts.

"No wonder you guys were being so weird in the car!" I exclaim and everyone laughs. We walk the rest of the way in and I give my mom a hug. I know she was the master mind behind this.

"Thanks, Mom," I grin.

"It was Vanessa's idea," she replies.

I turn to Vanessa and she is standing next to her friend, Sarah. "I figured since it's a couple of days early you would never guess," she explains.

"Thanks, Vanessa," I say.

My mom ushers us all the way into the house to the living room. I see Paige, Lucy, Riley, and Victoria are there along with a shy Logan standing in the back of the room.

I greet the girls with a hug. When I get to Logan I'm not sure what to do. Rather than a hug I say, "Chess later?" He agrees with a slight movement of his chin and a smile. "Thanks for coming," I say.

"Your sister said there would be cake," he teases, making me laugh.

I survey the group. Everyone is talking loudly as I observe them. The only people missing are Trista and Carmen. I am certain they will be here after awards. I'm not sure what to say to everyone so I stammer out another thank you. My mom helps me out by telling everyone Vanessa has a game for us.

"Sarah and I have Charades!" Vanessa announces holding up a box.

"Sarah will be captain of the purple team and I will be captain of the silver team."

"How about Paige, Riley, Victoria, and Savannah with me. Lucy, Logan, Marissa, and Alexis with Sarah," my sister announces.

"I'm not so sure Logan and Marissa should be on the same team; they will trounce us," Paige points out.

My sister pauses at this thought, then she shrugs, "Oh, well, it's her birthday party."

We split up into two teams. One team sits on the couch and the other team across from them on the two oversized chairs. Of course, some kids just sit on the floor since the chairs can't fit everyone.

My sister explains how one player on a team will read a card and try to get their teammates to guess the correct word or phrase. They will see how many they can guess in one minute. Each card is worth one point. When the time is up, the next team will go.

"Who will keep score?" Riley asks.

"Marissa should," Paige decides. Vanessa hands me a pen and pad of paper she had sitting by the box.

"Purple group first? Who wants to start?" Vanessa shouts.

When no one says anything Victoria surprises me by saying she'll go first. "My cousins have this game," she shares, standing up and opening the box that is sitting on the table between the two teams. She takes out an hourglass timer and sets it on the table, then she selects a card from one end of the stack. "Are you guys ready?" she prompts her team.

"Yes!" they yell. She flips over the timer, glances at the card in her hand, and starts hopping around the room.

"Bunny rabbit!"

"Tots classes!"

"Peter Rabbit!"

Victoria looks at her team in frustration and decides to try something else. She looks at her belly and pretends to open something in front of her belly.

"Kangaroo!" someone yells.

"Yes!" she yells, setting down the card and picking up another one. I look down at my notepad and give them one point. I look up and she is already onto the next card, acting out a baseball player even though her team doesn't seem to be getting it. This game moves fast; I'm going to have to give the notepad to someone from the other team when it's our turn. I don't think I'll be able to do both.

"Baseball player!" we hear someone yell from the

doorway and we see Trista and Carmen have arrived. I jump up and greet them.

"Hi, hurry in here," I usher them in. "I guess you are on their team, Trista, since you just helped them get that point."

"Time's up," Paige says, and we all see the hourglass has run out of sand. "It might have been up for a while; we may want to use a timer on someone's phone instead."

We get Trista situated on the purple team and Carmen on our silver team. We use Sarah's phone as the timer so it will beep at us. Then I hand over the score pad to Paige and our team is ready to begin.

"Marissa, you go first," Trista says. I stand up feeling a little nervous. It's one thing to play this game with my family, but it's a another to play it in front of friends. Then as I walk over to the table, I repeat the word *friends* in my head. These are my friends; they like me even if I can't act out a kangaroo or whatever I get on my card.

"Ready?" Paige asks me, holding the timer.

"Ready," I confirm.

She presses the timer and shouts, "Go!"

I grab a card and it says 'shark.' I quickly start doing the hand motions to the Baby Shark song that was popular a few years ago. My team guesses it right away. I set the card down and quickly grab another one. This one says 'table.' I know I can't point to a table so I decide to be the table and I get on my hands and knees.

"Cat!"

"Dog!"

I shake my head no and point to my back.

"Back!"

"No pointing," my sister reprimands.

This isn't working. I get up and sit on the edge of the couch. I mime the outline of a table. I act like I'm picking up a drink off the table. I start to pretend to drink.

"Drinking!"

"Lemonade!"

I laugh as I hear the timer beep that we are done.

"Table!" I tell them.

"Oh, that's what you were outlining," Sarah says.

I set the card down. "Yeah. We got one," I tell Paige for score keeping. And I walk over to sit down. That was more fun than I thought it would be and I can't wait for my turn again.

We play twelve rounds, as Vanessa had planned, because it's my twelfth birthday. By the time we are done, our stomachs hurt from laughing so much. As the rounds went on, the guessing got sillier and sillier.

"Pizza's here!" my dad announces, walking through the front door with a stack of five large pizzas in his arms.

"Perfect timing! That was the twelfth round," my sister announces.

"Who won?" Trista questions.

Vanessa holds the notepad to her chest and says, "The silver team, of course!"

I have no idea if we won or not, but Vanessa announces our team as the winners.

We all gather in the kitchen and my mom starts passing out paper plates.

My dad lines up the pizzas on the kitchen counter and starts opening the boxes to all our choices. Two cheese, two pepperoni, and one combo, which I assume is for my parents.

The kitchen is loud as kids are getting plates, pizza, and napkins before they sit down at the kitchen table. There are so many of us that some kids are at the table, some at the counter, and Sarah and Vanessa are all the way in the family room.

My friends have saved me a spot at the middle of the table. I sit down and start eating. The room is finally quiet as we eat dinner.

"How did your meet go?" Riley asks Carmen and Trista.

"We didn't score out," Trista shares with scorn in her voice.

"It was your first meet, you will," Alexis says.

"How were the new routines?" Paige asks.

"They are fun; I like them better even though they don't score as well," Carmen admits.

"The coaches just don't know them as well yet is all," Alexis explains.

We are quiet for a moment and Vanessa turns to Logan who has been silent most of the party. "How is soccer? Any more tournaments?"

"A couple more," he says. "I think our last one is early November."

"You play year-round?"

"Our tournaments and games are spring and fall, but yeah, we train year-round."

Then he asks Vanessa about violin and Sarah and Paige start talking about school. The silence is gone and my friends are getting along great. It makes me happy.

"Are you guys ready for cake?" my mom asks.

We say that we are and my dad turns out the lights. Then my mom walks in with a round cake lit with twelve candles. She sets it in front of me. It is a chess-themed cake with a knight piece on top. Everyone is silent and waiting for me to make a wish.

Straight As and 9.0s in optionals, I think and blow out my candles.

I don't get them in one breath; there are two stubborn candles that don't go out right away. Everyone claps anyway.

My sister turns the light back on and I start taking candles out of the cake. I get a better look at it. It has a checkerboard on top in purple and white and the words

'Happy Birthday Marissa' in black. I grab the chess piece on top and lick the frosting off the bottom.

"Now we can't use that one," Logan teases.

I smile and set it with the candles, "Sure we can! It'll be our lucky piece."

"The bakery didn't know how to do a gymnastics cake so we had to go with your second favorite choice," my mom explains.

"But we have gymnastics plates!" my sister sing-songs bringing over a stack of pink plates with gymnasts doing various poses on them.

"Perfect!"

CHAPTER 11

I wake up on my actual birthday to my mom rubbing my back instead of my alarm. "Happy Birthday, peanut," she whispers. I roll over and smile up at her. She's already dressed for work and she smells like coffee.

"It's so much nicer to wake up to you instead of my alarm," I murmur, stretching my arms over my head.

"I figured," she says.

"Can I stay home from school since it's my birthday?" I plead.

"Nice try; you still have school and practice today," she reminds me. We are quiet for a moment and she says, "I can't believe my baby is twelve. How did you get so big?"

I sit up, "I don't know. I don't feel twelve."

She smiles at me, "You will." Then she gives me a hug and kisses me on the head.

"Thanks Mom," I say and get up and pad over to the bathroom.

"I'll meet you downstairs," she shouts after me.

When I finally make my way downstairs, I'm dressed and ready for school. My family kept up the birthday banner from Saturday since today is my actual birthday. There are three presents sitting out on the kitchen counter.

"Presents!" I exclaim. "Can I open them now?"

"Whatever you want. You can open them this morning or tonight after practice. Or some of both," my dad says.

"I'll open the book now," I decide, sitting up to the counter. My family laughs at my assumption there is a book in the stack of presents. I'm right though, as my sister passes me a book.

I tear open the purple wrapping paper to find the new *Wings of Fire* book. I thank my parents and give them both hugs.

"You're welcome, kid," my dad smiles. "Happy Birthday."

"Thanks, Dad."

"Okay, peanut, you have to eat fast so we aren't late picking up Logan," my mom prods.

"Happy Birthday!" Trista exclaims as soon as I walk into science class.

"Thanks," I say.

"What are you doing to celebrate?"

"We celebrated on Saturday. You were there," I laugh.

"Yeah, but is your family doing anything else?"

"I have a few presents when I get home. And my mom might make her homemade egg rolls for dinner. That's about it."

"That's cool," she says, sitting at her desk. Our desks are

one row apart so as soon as class fills in we can't talk anymore.

When class is over, we pick up where we left off as we leave and head to lunch.

"What do you think the presents are?" she asks.

"I got a book this morning. And there was a big box. I'm not sure what it could be."

"What did you ask for?"

"I didn't."

"You didn't?" she stops so fast a kid almost bumps into her as she gapes at me.

"What?"

"How do you get what you want if you don't tell your family what you want?" she wonders as we resume walking.

I think about this for a moment as we enter the buzz of the cafeteria. "I guess I just know that my family knows me and will pick out something I'll like."

"Wow, that's some serious trust," she marvels as we sit down at our table.

"What's serious trust?" Logan asks, sitting down.

"Marissa just lets her family pick out her birthday presents without giving them any hints," she explains.

"Oh yeah, today's your birthday! Happy Birthday!"

"Thanks."

"I don't see the problem," he says to Trista. "She got a ton of stuff on Saturday."

"But not from her parents. Parent gifts are the best," she insists.

"What was the best gift you ever got from your parents?" I ask her.

"A Simone signed leo," she answers.

"That is a good one. How come I've never seen it?"

"I'm afraid to wear it."

"Who's Simone?" Logan asks, making us both groan.

I guessed right. After practice, my mom had homemade egg rolls and rice waiting for me. My family ate dinner while I was at practice, but they waited to have leftover cake with me.

"Do you want your presents before or after cake?" my mom asks.

"Before," I decide.

My sister walks over and hands me one large heavy box and one light box. I open the light box first and it's a beautiful black and purple tie dye hoodie. "Wow, this is so cool!" I exclaim holding it up to myself.

"Do you like it?" my mom smiles.

"I love it. I can't wait for it to get colder so I can wear it." I mean it too. It is such a beautiful purple with the striking black in contrast. The tie-dye pattern looks unusual with only two colors. I know it is going to be my favorite hoodie all winter.

"Open the big one," Vanessa prompts.

I set my sweatshirt down and pull the big box toward me. I rip open the paper to find a cream-colored box with no indicator of what's inside. I carefully open the box, remove a layer of tissue, and inside is a stunning glass chess board. Instead of black and white squares, it has clear glass and frosty glass squares.

"Oh wow," I breath as I pull out the board. "This is amazing."

"You worked so hard on chess over the summer, we wanted you to have a nice board you can keep forever," my dad explains as I gently lift out the board and set it on the counter.

I remove another layer of thin foam and under it is another box. I open it and all the glass pieces are sitting in individual little rectangles. I carefully start pulling them out and setting them on the board.

"Can I see the queen?" Vanessa requests. I pluck the queen out of her box in the middle and hand it to my sister. She turns it in her hand and then sets it down.

"Will you play me?" I ask my dad.

"If you go easy on me," he says with a wink.

I grin back and keep setting out pieces. I think Trista is wrong. Letting my family pick out what to get me without having any idea whatsoever made these presents amazing. I loved the surprise and thoughtfulness of them. I can't wait to beat my dad using my new chess set.

"Ready?" I ask him and he nods, already in full concentration.

CHAPTER 12

"I think you can move that up to high beam today," Katie announces, referring to my back handspring. This makes my stomach both sink and flutter.

"I'm still using mats," I sputter in surprise. I'm standing on the medium beam and I have an 8-inch mat under it.

"You can have mats under the high beam too," she comments. "I'll spot the first one," she offers. Katie rarely offers to spot because she believes we should be ready enough to move up progressions on our own. I nod, knowing I need to take her up on her offer. I jump down and slowly walk over to the high beam that has four mats under it. I climb up, not sure what I think about doing this skill right now.

Katie climbs up onto the mats under the beam and looks up at me. "Do it exactly the same as you have been. They are technically correct. It's just a matter of getting used to them over here."

I nod at her. *Exactly the same.* I'm good at that, I compete like that. In fact, I don't know how some athletes change their gymnastics so much from practice to competition.

"And focus," she adds, seeing that my mind has wandered.

"Okay, exactly the same," I say to both of us as I turn to face the front of the beam. I step together, raise my arms, feel Katie's hand on my back, and before I can think any more about it, I jump back into my back handspring. I land with both feet on the beam and I feel Katie's hands on my waist steadying me a little on the landing.

"Great job!" she shouts, reaching up to give me a high five that I have to reach down to connect with. "How did it feel?" she asks.

"A little scary . . . but also, similar to the medium beam," I admit.

"Two more and then you don't need me," she says. I take a deep breath and step together again to prepare for another try. This time I am off to the side and Katie can't save it. I land on my feet on the mats below.

"That one you jumped crooked. Reach back evenly when you jump," she corrects.

I nod; I'm not sure what happened on that one, except that I didn't stop to think or square up my hips over the beam. I step up to go again; this time I pause before lifting my arms allowing myself time to think. I take a breath, step together, reach up, and think about jumping and reaching back evenly. I feel Katie's hand on my back and I go. This time I jump straight and I land it perfectly square and solid.

"Nice job," Katie says jumping down from the mats. "Take a break and then do a few more." I do as she says and jump down, letting Lucy take a turn on the beam with mats for her series.

I can't believe I just did it! I just did back handsprings on high beam! I am scared to go up there again without Katie, but for this tiny moment I want to enjoy this feeling of accomplishment. I watch as Lucy hesitates before her series.

"Those look good," I hear Paige say to me as she walks up. "You aren't going to have any problems in Level 6 this season," she assures me.

"Thanks," I smile at her.

As soon as I get home from practice, my good mood ends as I think about my homework. I miss elementary school with only one teacher. When you have one teacher, she knows how much homework she has assigned. In middle school, it is pure luck if you have no homework or six classes worth of homework. I flip through my planner; not entirely sure I wrote everything down today. I try to think back to my day and what I'm supposed to do in each class. I have math for sure, but that's easy. Do I have English homework? Was I supposed to read something?

I hear the microwave beep and I look up from my planner. My mom gets the plate out of the microwave and slides it across the counter to me.

"Do you have a lot of homework?" she asks.

"I don't think so," I answer vaguely. I look at my plate of chow-mein (brown noodles, pork, and veggies) and I realize I am ravenous. I slide my planner out of the way and dig in. My mom hangs out with me while I eat.

"How was workout?" she prompts. I tell her how well it's going. That I did my back handspring on high beam with mats today and that I have a few different choices on tumbling passes. I can compete the front handspring, dive roll for sure, and maybe even a front handspring, front. She follows me on the back handspring on beam part, but I think I lost her when I started rattling off front tumbling passes. It doesn't matter; she knows the gist of the story is that I am doing well in Level 6.

"So, it didn't hurt you to stay in Level 5 over the summer," she surmises.

"I don't think so. And by not competing Level 6 last winter, I had more time to get my new skills. I think it was the right decision."

We are quiet for a moment and we hear Vanessa practicing her violin. It makes me wince a little as I realize I haven't practiced much since school started. At least I'm not in orchestra anymore and don't have to learn at the same rate as other kids. Chess and gymnastics are enough. I feel so lucky chess landed on an afternoon I don't have practice.

"I'm headed up to get ready for bed," my mom says. "Turn off the lights down here when you're done," she tells me.

Bed? Is it that late already? I look at the clock above the pantry and sure enough, it's 8:30 at night. I guess with practice going until 7:30, by the time I get home and have dinner, it's 8:30. I sigh, finally full. I take my plate and rinse it off and put it in the dishwasher. I feel tired. Too tired for homework. Most of the assignments are only five or ten points anyway. It won't be a big deal if I skip a few homework assignments here and there, especially since I get As on tests.

I grab my planner, stuff it in my backpack and head upstairs for bed. I listen to Vanessa play as I head to bed. I'm a little jealous she has gotten so good.

CHAPTER 13

I'm doodling on the edge of my notebook while my teacher drones on about the book we are going to be reading. I've learned that if I draw a gymnast in the very corner of my notebook in various stages of a skill, that when I flip the pages, she looks like she's moving. I'm not very good at drawing her. I have to do simple skills like giants. I finally have six frames and I begin to flip the corners and it looks like she just did a giant. Pleased with myself, I look up and see everyone else now has their laptops out. I wonder what we have moved on to. I quickly grab my laptop and try to figure out what is going on. I watch for a moment and see that people are pulling up their grades. *How do I do that?* I wonder as I sign in and put in my password. Now what? I see kids exclaiming over their grades, but how did they get to that page? I scan the room and finally see bullet point instructions on the whiteboard and I quickly follow them.

I find where to pull up my list of classes with my grade

next to each one. And then I see it, sitting there as big as you please, a D. I can't believe I have not one, but two Ds! I have an A in art, a B in history, a C in science and math, and a D in English and Spanish. How did this happen? Especially in science and math. I get 100% on all the tests.

I feel nauseated as I realize I have to tell my parents my grades. Vanessa has been getting straight As since she started middle school two years ago. How does she do that? I know she's as busy as I am with violin and orchestra and even a social life.

How did I let this happen? I realize my grades are up on my computer for anyone to see. Embarrassed, I quickly shut my laptop. I look around and see most kids are busy looking at their own grades. I sigh in relief that no one saw mine.

"See where you might have zeros on assignments you need to turn in. Look for low tests scores that you can retake," our teacher is explaining. I see kids clicking on their grades to dig deeper into why they have the grades they have. I should be doing that too, but I can't bring myself to open up my list of grades again. "You can stay after school to retake tests; forgotten assignments need to be turned in by the end of the quarter."

When's the end of the quarter? I frantically start rifling through my backpack to find my planner. I know my teacher made us write down the end of quarter at the beginning of the year. I wrote it down but didn't pay any attention to what it meant. Quarters began and ended in elementary school and they didn't mean much.

"Nothing but As, huh Marissa?" Logan teases me on his way to the class pencil sharpener.

"Yeah," I laugh nervously.

"I figured," he says, not catching my sarcasm or panic. He just assumes I have all As because I'm smart. Apparently, that's not enough anymore. I pull out my planner and flip through it. I see 'end of quarter' written on a box in mid-October. Okay, I have time. I wonder how many assignments I need to make up. I want to know, but not enough to pull up my incriminating list of classes again. Thankfully our teacher tells us to quickly write down what we need to take care of and pack up our laptops because the bell is going to ring soon. I make a show of writing in my planner, but I'm not writing anything useful. I just jot down, 'figure out what you need to turn in.'

Then I close my planner and shove it and my laptop into my backpack as the bell rings.

"What's with you?" I hear Trista demand, breaking me out of my trance.

"What?" I play dumb, even though I heard her.

"Did you have a bad workout yesterday?" she presses.

"Actually, I had a good workout. Really good," I smile.

"What'd you get?"

"I did my back handspring on high beam."

"Nice," she grins, reaching up her hand for a high five.

"What are we celebrating?" Logan asks, sliding into the seat next to Trista.

"Marissa got her back handspring on high beam last night," Trista tells him.

"With mats," I add.

"What's that?" Logan asks at the same time.

"If I had a phone, I would show you," Trista pouts.

"I have one," Logan says, pulling his phone out of his bag. They huddle over it together while Trista tries to find a video of someone doing a back handspring on beam.

I quietly eat my lunch until Logan looks up. "You can do

that?" he asks.

"What are you looking at?" I laugh.

Trista turns to the phone to me, showing a video of Savannah doing a perfect back handspring on beam.

"Yeah, but with a few mats under the beam and a little sloppier," I admit.

"Just say yes, Marissa," Trista says turning the phone back to her and Logan. "He probably wouldn't be able to tell the difference anyway. You did it. That's what matters."

"I did," I confirm.

"That's pretty cool," Logan admits. "You're good at everything, aren't you?" he teases.

I don't know what to say to this because I know that he thinks I have straight As. I don't have the guts to tell him the truth so I just shrug.

Being good at school was something I could count on. I would just show up, half listen in class, take tests, and get an A. I better figure out how to get As in this new place because getting Bs are not an option. Getting a C is out of the question and a D is mortifying.

Vanessa gets As; I better ask her what I need to do. She could help me. Would she help me without telling Mom and Dad? What will Mom and Dad think? School is the most important thing to them. Oh my gosh, will they make me quit gymnastics? No, they would never do that. I don't think.

I remember some of the upper optionals girls talking about grades in the Optionals Rooms one night. They were saying what grades they needed to maintain to stay in gymnastics. That must be a family rule, not a gym rule. And what did they say they needed? A 3.0? A 3.5?

"What's a 3.5 grade average?"

"Half As and half Bs," Trista answers. "I only know that because that is what my sister has been trying for in high school."

"Oh," I breath, realizing that with Cs and Ds I don't even have a 3.5. Probably best to keep this to myself, just in case. I can get my grades up before my parents see them.

"When do grades go home?" I inquire.

"At the end of the semester, whenever that is," Logan says. "I think it's in our planner. Why all the questions, Marissa?" Logan asks.

"No reason, I just want to understand is all," I lie.

He eyes me suspiciously and then turns to Nate and asks him if he can hang out after school.

I watch them. Maybe I could tell Logan. He's a good student, maybe he could help me. Except he thinks I have better grades than him and that school is easy for me. I don't want him to know the truth.

Now that it is cooler end-of-September weather, I have my light jacket in my locker. It helps me remember to go to my locker at the end of the day. I grab my coat, glad it's Friday, and head outside looking for my sister and Logan.

I find Vanessa talking to some friends and when she sees me walk up she tells them goodbye.

"Where's Logan?" she asks.

"I don't know. I thought he would already be here. I took forever opening my locker," I admit. She looks over my head.

"There he is, let's go," she says, starting to walk to our carpool meeting spot. I wait for Logan and he falls in step with me.

"Happy Friday," he greets.

"No kidding," I agree.

"Practice tonight?" He can never get my schedule right.

"No, tomorrow morning," I comment. "What are you doing this weekend?"

"I have a soccer tournament," he says. We are silent as we walk. Then he asks, "How'd you do on Harper's test?"

"Dunno," I pout. I'm afraid to look.

"I don't know why I ask, of course you got an A," he says, kicking a pebble down the sidewalk.

I want to confide in Logan that I don't actually have good grades. But I'm worried about what he might say, what he might think. I'm getting pretty buried in some of my classes. He may be the only person who knows how to help. I take a deep breath to confess that I am not the perfect student he thinks I am when Vanessa yells, "Hurry up you slow pokes!" and Logan picks up his pace to the car.

I guess he can go on thinking I'm a perfect student a little longer, I decide as I trudge to the car.

Logan's Mom drops us off and we let ourselves into the house. Vanessa starts opening the cupboards to try to figure out an after-school snack.

"There's a note here from Mom," I discover, turning the note on the counter to face me.

"What's it say?" she asks.

"It's a list. We have to empty the dishwasher, the trash, and switch the laundry," I tell her. She comes over and looks over my shoulder.

"No, *you* have to empty the dishwasher and trash and I have to switch the laundry," she corrects. The list does have our names next to each item, but her list is shorter.

"Yours is easier," I fuss.

"No it isn't because switching the laundry includes folding the dry clothes," she counters.

"Fine," I concede and sit down at the counter.

"It will be nice to have some of this done before she gets home, since it's Friday," she says, setting out a sliced pear and some cheese slices.

We eat silently for a while and when most of the snack is
gone Vanessa goes upstairs to switch out the laundry like the
note instructed. Of course she throws a "don't forget your
list," over her shoulder as she leaves. As if I am a little child
that needs reminding.

I walk over to the dishwasher, open it up, and slide out
the bottom row. I start putting away the plates and singing to
myself. A song on the stereo would be better than me
singing. I walk over to the TV and turn it on. Then I scroll to
the music apps. I select one, but then I have trouble selecting
a genre. I finally land on Top 40 and set the remote down.

"What are you doing?" Vanessa demands.

"Getting music," I answer, plopping on the couch,
engrossed in the video that came up to accompany the song.

"But you aren't done," she says.

"With what?"

"Marissa!"

"What! Why are you yelling at me?"

"The dishwasher," she huffs.

"Oh yeah." I get up and walk back to the kitchen and
pick up where I left off on the bottom rack of dishes.

"You aren't done with laundry yet, are you?" I retort.

"With starting a load, yes, but the towels I need to get
out aren't dry yet. I came back down to get my backpack."
With that she lifts her backpack and walks out with a "Don't
forget the garbage." Which is super annoying.

I finish the bottom rack and move to the top rack. I put
away a few glasses when a terrible old person song comes
on. I walk over to the family room to press the skip button.
The next one is just as bad so I hit skip again. Apparently, if
you hit skip three times you get a commercial that you can't
skip. I sit down to wait out the commercial. I look down at
my fingernails and realize they need trimming. I go upstairs

to get the nail clippers out of Mom's room.

I go back to my room, grab my garbage can, sit on my bed, and start clipping my nails. About halfway through, Vanessa pops her head in. "What are you doing?"

"Clipping my nails," I answer, even though it's obvious.

"No, I mean why did you abandon the dishwasher?"

"Oh, I forgot," I shrug.

"Seriously, Marissa? You can't finish anything," she says in frustration and storms out. I don't know what the big deal is. I was going to go back to it. Or was I? I kind of did already forget about the list.

Now I feel bad, because when this happens, sometimes Vanessa just finishes the job.

I throw the clippers on my desk and hurry downstairs. Sure enough, Vanessa is emptying the last of the dishwasher.

"Why are you doing that? It's my chore," I remind her.

"Because I wanted the list done by the time mom gets home," she says in a condescending tone.

Guiltily, I get the garbage can out from under the sink and take it out to the garage. I come back in and I'm careful to remember to put a new trash liner in the bag. I forget that one a lot. Why am I so much more forgetful than Vanessa? I used to think it was because she was older, now I'm not so sure.

CHAPTER 14

It's October and our first intersquad will be just before Thanksgiving. Then we will have another one just before Christmas. Our first meet is in January. It feels far away until I try to do full routines.

I notice as we are stretching at Saturday morning practice that James is not here today. "No James today," I comment to Melony.

"No, compulsories are in season."

"But they don't have a meet today," I counter. Or do they? No, Trista would have told me at lunch yesterday.

"No, but he works a lot of long weekends when they are in season. He's just taking a break today."

I never thought about it, but she's right. James would have to stay at a meet for the Level 3, Level 4, and Level 5 sessions. That is a long day.

"Good morning!" Katie greets walking up to us where we're stretching. "Classes are about to come in. We need to decide what event we're starting on."

My teammates start yelling out their votes of what event they want to go to. Of course, all four events are called out. Which is not helpful to Katie at all.

"You know you guys can't do floor until the classes clear out at the end of practice," she reminds us.

"Beam?" Melony suggests. "Since I will be over there anyway with Marissa," she says to Katie. Me? Why will she be over at beam with me?

"Good idea," Katie agrees. "Marissa," she calls out to me and looks around. When her eyes land on me she says, "You need a beam routine." Oh yeah, I do need a beam routine. I wait for her to say more.

"Melony is going to create a routine with you today. The rest of you will do beam with me. Riley, lead us in a quick complex. Classes will be here in ten minutes."

We do as she instructs, a quick complex on floor to warm-up and then we go to beam and do an even quicker beam complex. I love Saturday workouts; they seem to move faster.

As soon as we're done with complex, I walk over to the low beams to work with Melony. I'm excited to finally get my beam routine. I hope she puts some cool poses in it. I wonder what my mount will be. I step up onto a low beam next to where Melony is looking at the Code of Points.

"Marissa! Time for a beam routine!" she announces. "Are you excited?"

"Yes, but not as excited as I was with floor," I admit.

"Sure, new floor routines are the best," she agrees, flipping a page in the binder.

"Do you have any ideas already for what you want to do as a mount?"

"No." I didn't know I got to pick out my mount.

"Alright. Would you prefer a safe mount that gets you up

there and gets you started, or a risky mount that gives you difficulty right out of the gate?"

"I . . . I'm not sure. What are the pros and cons?"

"Well, mounts are a fun way to get difficulty. But if you fall it may rattle you for the rest of the routine. Would you be able to recover and finish your set if you fell at the beginning?".

She is looking at me like she already knows the answer but wants to see what I will say. Well, I tend to compete exactly how I practice. If it's a mount I can do in workout, I'm sure it's one I can do in a meet. I have only fallen in a meet on beam once, and while I was rattled, I was also able to get back up and finish a decent routine.

"I don't think a fall early on would rattle me," I decide. Then I grin and say, "Let's do the difficult mount."

"That's what I was thinking too," she smiles. "Here are some mounts you're allowed to do in Level 6. You are only allowed to do As and Bs. Look at the list of Bs and see what you think of them." I take the book from her and sit down on the beam. She sits next to me as I look closely at the pictures.

In optionals, each skill gets a letter identifying its difficulty level- A being the easiest and J being the hardest. Level 6s and 7s can only do As and Bs. Level 8s can do As, Bs, and Cs. Level 9 can do As, Bs, Cs, and one D in each routine. Level 10s can do up to Es. The rest are for Elites, who are the rare athletes training for the National Team.

All the A mounts are a simple jump up or splits onto the beam. I flip the page to look at the Bs.

"A leap up onto the end looks fun," I say. "Or the straddle jump," I add, scanning the pictures on the B column.

"They are," she says with a grin. "And you can add to it as you get better at it."

"How?"

"Well, it could become your entire leap pass in Level 7

or 8.”

"This will be my mount forever?" I ask, realizing that this is a big decision.

"It doesn't have to be. But if you go to all the trouble of learning it and competing it, you might as well build on it. On the other hand, if you hate the stress at the beginning of your routine, we can do something different next year." With that explanation, she stands up and takes the book from me.

"Let's assume you do that mount. You would end here, facing this way," she explains, standing on the end of a low beam. "Let me teach you a routine from here."

I stand up on the beam next to her on the end just like her and she shows me a few walking poses into a leap.

For the next thirty minutes she creates a beam routine. She makes it up as she goes. She asks me questions like, "Do you want your back handspring at the beginning or end?" Depending on how I answer, she gets me to certain places on the beam using dance poses. Most of the poses she took from my floor routine. I love this because the poses are familiar to me and unique from everyone else's beam routine. It is 'my style' she insists. Really, it's the style she created for me.

When I finally think I have it, she and I do a dance through of the entire routine on low beams next to each other. I like the order of it. I mount, do my leap pass, then my back handspring. Then I do my jumps, a few dance poses, my full turn, and I dance to the end for my dismount.

"Do that dance through three more times while I go make sure with Katie that we have everything in the routine that she wanted you to have," she says, walking away.

I nod and start over at the end of the beam where I would complete my mount. Most of the routine is made up of dance and leaps. The only things I'm skipping for a dance through are the back handspring, mount, and dismount.

When I'm just about done with one dance through,

Melony comes back and silently watches me do my second dance through. Then she corrects me on two of my poses that I wasn't doing quite right.

"Let me record this last one and we'll move on," she says. She holds up the gym phone and I start again. During this dance through I forget what I'm doing after the back handspring and Melony has to stop recording to show me. "Start over," she instructs, holding up the phone again.

I take a breath and start again. This time I remember the entire thing and even do a little cartwheel at the end for my dismount.

"That is so pretty on you. Do you like it?"

"Yes, especially the parts that are from my floor routine," I share.

"Good. I'm sending this video to your mom."

Melony starts scrolling through the gym phone for my mom's number. All of the team parents are in there. "Okay, sent. I told her it was for you to study."

"Last turn and then bars!" we hear Katie yell.

"Except for you," Melony says to me.

"But we just finished," I point out, confused.

"We need to figure out your mount. Go grab a springboard from vault and drag it over here," she says. Skip bars? I feel like I'm getting away with something. I don't dislike bars, but it is hard and playing around with mounts sounds way more fun.

I walk over to the vault runway where springboards are lined up along the wall. I pick one of the softer ones, pull it away from the wall, lean it against my back, and drag it across the two runways over to the high beams.

"This one," Melany says, pointing to the first beam at the edge of the floor. "That way we are using the least amount of floor and disrupting the classes less."

I do as she says and drop the board at the end of a high

beam. Just then, Katie brings over a spotting block and slides it under the beam. "Thought I would help you while the girls are putting grips on," she says.

"Thanks," I say.

"I like the idea of a leap mount for you. You have the nerves for it from what James tells me. The block will help you try several ways to see what you like. Maybe even a sting mat," she thinks aloud.

"I've got it," Melony says and heads over to the medium beam that has a thin mat draped over it.

"How is the rest of it?" Katie asks.

"Good. I like the order she put the skills in," I articulate.

"She's good at what she does. The fun thing about optionals is we can adjust as we go. If you don't like something or want to change the order, speak up."

"Okay," I agree.

"Alright, I've got to set up bars. Holler when you have a favorite mount you want to show me," she instructs as she walks away.

Melony throws the sting mat over the beam where the block is. Between the sting mat and the block I can be way off and still not get hurt. I would just step down. Melony leans over and adjusts the springboard in front of the beam, "Let's start with straight jumps," she tells me.

She tells me to run and hurdle, like on vault, but slower and more upright. Then I am to punch and just go straight up and land on the end of the beam with two feet.

Sounds simple enough. I run, punch, and get scared at the last minute. I purposely go off to the side landing on the block and fall off to the side.

"I guess I didn't mention, go straight."

"It was a little scary," I admit.

"Hmm, let's try something else." She pulls the block out from under the beam and drags it to the floor. Then she puts the board in front of it. "Do a few onto the block and I'll be right back.

This looks much easier. I run, punch, and easily do a straight jump onto the block. That was fun! I'm walking back when Melony comes back with a roll of athletic tape in her hand. She tapes a line on the block. "Here's your beam," she says. "Try again."

I walk back to where I can get a little run. I see the line on the block; I can do that. I run, punch, and do a perfect straight jump onto the line.

"There you go! A few more," she exclaims. I do a few more just like the last one and then she tells me to try a tuck jump. That ends up being scarier, but I can do it. Then she tells me to do a straddle jump, which I find easier than the tuck jump.

"Wow, that's pretty," she says. "Okay, now try off of one foot into a leap."

I go back to try that variation. I can't figure out how to launch off the springboard on one leg. Melony starts laughing. "It's okay to step on the board. Just think step, step, leap. Your second step is at the top of the board."

I try it several more times before I can finally leap up to the block. It's still more awkward for me than the two foot take off. "I think I like the stretch jump the best."

"Do you want to try them on beam?"

"I think so," I admit, feeling nervous, but more confident than that first try.

She moves the block back under the beam while I move the board. She adjusts the sting mat over the beam while I walk a few yards away to start. Then she stands back and waits for me.

"Start with the stretch jump," she says. I nod in agreement.

I run, punch, and go straight up. I have to bend my legs a

bit to make it. I land on the beam and fall off onto the block. I'm happy I connected to the beam.

"A good start. A few more of those," she says.

I end up doing several more and they feel pretty good. However, none are good enough for me to ask to do a tuck jump or straddle jump. I don't even really want to do the split leap. The beam is higher up than the block. It feels a lot more difficult.

"That's enough for today. Their bars workout is almost over. Just do strap bars for the rest of the workout. Don't waste time gripping up."

I agree; I love strap bars. Strapping your wrists onto the bar makes it so much easier to swing giants.

"I want you to work on your beam dance at home tomorrow, okay?"

"I promise," I agree.

"Great job today. Now go get a drink and go to bars."

I nod that I heard her and head over to the drinking fountain because I don't want to walk up to my locker when I don't have much workout left. Right as I walk to the front of the gym, I see Trista and Carmen walk through the training doors.

"Hi guys, what are you doing here?"

"Floor routines!" Trista squeals.

"You are both for sure doing Level 6 this winter?" I ask.

"I mean, we both have to score out, but that is the plan," Trista confirms.

"You will," I declare, and I mean it. They both just need one good meet. And the season is early still.

"Why didn't you tell me yesterday?" I pout. This is a big deal; Trista would have told me.

"We didn't know until last night. James called us and talked to our parents. I guess Melony finished our routines. The coaches decided we might as well learn them on a weekend that we don't have a meet."

"It's a bit of a gamble," Carmen comments.

"No, it's not; you two will score out," I insist.

"Marissa! Bars!" Katie yells over to me.

"Coming!" I yell back, a little embarrassed.

"I have to go. I can't wait to see your routines," I say and run off to do a few turns on the strap bar before conditioning.

CHAPTER 15

At dinner on Sunday night my mom asks me about school and I don't know what to say. I'm afraid she's going to look at my grades. I push my food around and finally say, "I got an A on a math test."

My mom smiles but Vanessa gives me a look. So, I decide to partially come clean. "I have a few zeros I need to take care of."

My mom frowns, "Zeros? How did that happen?"

I shrug, "I forget to submit the work. Like the science videos – I watch them, but then I forget to submit the questions." This is true, but only partially true. Is it lying when you leave information out? I look over at Vanessa and she is quietly eating, leaving me to drown alone.

"You know, Marissa, getting a zero is like two Fs," my dad pipes in.

"What?" I look at him. Two Fs?

"Think about the math," he explains, "an A is 90%, a B

80%, and so on. An F is 50%. But a missing assignment is 0%, pulling your grade way down. If you have a 100% going in a class and turn in an F and get 50%, then you get a C in the class at 75%. But if you turn in nothing that zero brings your 100% down to 50%, an F."

"That's assuming everything is weighted the same," I point out.

"Yes, for the sake of the example, I am assuming everything is weighted the same. But you see what I am saying? You're good at math, Marissa, think about how damaging one zero can be on your grade."

I'm embarrassed to admit I'd never thought of it like that before. "One zero is like two Fs," I repeat quietly.

"Yes. Fix those zeros no matter how small they seem."

"Some of them are pretty small, like five points," I say, defending my bad decision making.

"It still adds up," he insists.

"Can you make them up?" my mom inquires, probably sensing that there are more zeros than I'm telling her.

"She has until the end of the quarter to make up zeros," Vanessa pipes up.

"How do you know?" my mom asks.

"They are easy on sixth graders and it's school policy that they have until the end of the quarter to turn in missed work or retake tests. By seventh grade, teachers lock out assignments and you have no such luck."

"There you go, Marissa. You have time to turn in anything that's missing. Do you want me to help you make a list of what you need to take care of?" my mom offers.

"I can do it," I mumble. I really don't want her looking.

Thankfully, the conversation turns to music and Vanessa. I silently eat my dinner hoping the discussion doesn't focus on me again.

On Monday, we start on vault. I'm still training both half-ons and Yurchenkos. We are rotating between doing vaults up onto the table with mats behind the table and doing entry drills on the floor. I am doing half-ons onto the table and Yurchenkos on the drill station. I notice Paige is doing the half-ons both places, Alexis is doing front handsprings on the table and Yurchenkos on the drill. Everyone else is doing Yurchenko entries both places.

"You're going for hand fronts?" I ask Alexis as we stand in line after doing our drill. "Yeah, I like going forward so much more. I know where I am and it just makes sense to me. Since my front tumbling is solid, Katie thought I might be good at handspring fronts on vault."

"It looks fun," I admit.

"Do you like going forward?" she asks me.

I think about it for a moment. "I like both," I finally answer.

"Lucky you," she smiles, and then she steps onto the vault runway to take her turn. I watch as she does a beautiful front handspring timer. I step onto the runway for my half-on entry.

"Look under that arm, Marissa," Katie instructs as I fall to my back. "You have good power. These will be fun to flip."

"Flip?" I ask, climbing down off the mats.

"Sure, we can do it on a Saturday into the pit. We have to have a little fun, even during season."

"Katie?" She looks over at me waiting for my question.

"What's my bar routine?"

"Just do the Level 5 routine without the baby giant or the tap swings," she explains while watching Savannah take her turn.

"Too far back on the board, Savannah," she says as Savannah jumps down.

"Yeah, my steps were a little off," Savannah agrees. "And I did the round-off really far back."

"Do an extra one at the drills before coming back over here. And I want to stand there for the next one," Katie says.

Savannah nods. When she walks away, I resume our conversation. "Can I add anything else in?"

"To bars?" she clarifies.

"Yeah, that seems like a short routine."

"Trust me; on bars short is good. But, sure, you can add something. Do you have stalders?" I shake my head no. "Sole circle?" No again. "Let me think. We can find something fun and useful."

"Useful?"

"A skill that will help you with another skill on bars later on," she explains. "I'll think, you go vault."

I walk over to the entry station. She is going to think of something for me. I wish talking to my teachers was this easy.

"Marissa, can you do a pike-on?" Katie asks me.

"Yeah," I answer from over at the chalk tray.

"Okay, come over here," she says to me from the low bar. I do as she says while she steps up onto a panel mat to spot me. I stand in front of the bar to wait for her to tell me what to do. "I want you to do a pike-on and then switch your hands. I'll help hold you there while you regrip."

"Switch my hands?" I repeat.

"Yes, to a front grip. Like how you did in the front single

leg circle in Level 3, remember?"

I think back, I did do a front grip then. "Okay," I agree slowly as I step up onto my panel mat. "Kip first?"

"Always," she confirms.

I nod and jump into a kip, pike-on. Just as she said she would, she holds onto my forearm with one hand so I don't fall forward. Her other hand is on my back so I don't fall backwards. "Switch your grip to a front grip," she tells me.

I slowly let go of one hand and turn it to a front grip. She starts laughing, "The other one too." I slowly turn my other hand. "Okay, now fall forward," she says. That sounds a little scary. I stay there in the pike with my hands all awkward and I don't move. "I've got you," she assures, gently pushing me forward. I feel myself fall over the front of the bar, Katie grabs my waist as I swing forward and under the bar. As soon as I am under the bar, my feet pop off and hit the ground. I'm still hanging onto the bar, but in my awkward grip.

"That's it!" Katie exclaims. "Just keep your feet on long enough to swing back to this side, switch your hands back, and glide into a kip."

"When do I switch my hands?" I ask confused.

"Put your feet back on the bar," she orders. I hang from the bar and put my toes on. Katie pushes me up to the side of the bar where I started, then she holds me suspended in my pike position parallel to the floor. She holds me there and says, "now switch your hands back to a regular grip."

I do as she says and she lets go of me. My toes fall and I swing under the bar into a glide.

"There you go. Now just kip out of it and you have your skill."

I let go and stand between the bars and turn to look at her.

"What's it called?"

"It's the first half of a front sole circle. Stopping three-fourths the way around is not really a specific skill. But it will help you with front giants," she explains. My face falls a little that my skill is nameless. She laughs and says, "We can call it a front sole circle. Now go try some on the floor bar onto the mat. Stand in the pike with a front grip and fall to your back. Make sure to tuck your head," she adds.

I nod, happy to have a skill to spice up my bar routine, even if it doesn't have a name.

CHAPTER 16

I enter the classroom for Chess Club with relief. Logan and Sienna are already there. I drop my backpack in a chair and watch their game for a moment. It looks like Logan is trying a new opener.

When another student, Amelia, walks in, I motion for her to join me at the next table over. A board is out, but the pieces are not set up yet. We start setting them up quietly and I'm not sure what to say to her so I start with her name.

"It's Amelia, right?"

"Yes. What's your name?

"Marissa."

"Oh, yeah. Sorry, I'm bad with remembering names and faces. Facts I can remember, but faces are tough."

"It's okay, it's a lot of new people. Are you a sixth grader too?"

"Seventh," she answers.

"Oh," I say, letting out a sigh. "I'm so glad to be here

and that school is over for today."

"It gets better," she comments.

"What?"

"School. It gets better," she repeats.

"How?" I grumble, setting up my back row of pieces.

"You just get the hang of it, I guess," she says, setting up her final pieces. Then she pulls a chair over and sits down.

"What was the hardest part for you last year?"

She frowns for a minute, "Are you cool with me starting since white is over here?" she asks, gesturing to the chess pieces sitting in front of her. I agree and she moves a pawn out. "For me it was finding people to eat with. Finally, I just started going to the library as soon as I was done eating. I would read and get away from the craziness of the cafeteria."

I think about that for a moment while I move out a pawn. The cafeteria is crazy. I'm lucky I have Trista, Logan, and even Nate to eat with. "You can eat with us," I offer.

She smiles and moves out her knight. "We have different lunches," she reminds me. "It's okay, I've met people here at chess club and we eat together. It's better this year."

"What school did you come from?"

"I moved from Idaho. I didn't know anyone," she shares.

"That must have been tough," I empathize, moving another pawn so I can get my bishop out soon.

"I don't recommend it."

We are silent as the game progresses. Neither of us have strong openings, but she has a solid middle game. I need to get better at my openings. I need to ask Logan about that; he seems to know how to improve.

She surprises me with an aggressive end game and before I know it she has me in check.

"Good game," I acknowledge.

"You too, what's your ranking?"

"I don't know."

"She doesn't play online," Logan pipes in. I look over at Logan with my eyebrows raised. "She doesn't have time because she likes to do all the things."

"You do too! What about soccer?" I demand.

"It's my only other thing," he defends and turns back to his game. Sienna doesn't stand a chance.

"There's a website where you can play online. After you play a certain number of games you get a ranking. You might like it."

She tells me the name of the website and how it works. Instead of writing down what she's telling me in my planner, I wonder why Logan didn't tell me. I mean, I know I'm busy, but shouldn't I decide if I have time for something or not?

Amelia has set up the board for a new game and is waiting for Logan's game to finish so we can trade. There are only the four of us today. Usually there are more kids here.

"Where is everyone today?" I wonder.

"The eighth graders have end of term projects due before parent teacher conferences next week," Mr. Belsky answers.

Parent teacher conferences. I wonder if my parents are planning to come. Maybe they don't know about it. Who am I kidding, of course they know about it.

"What do they talk about at parent teacher conferences?" I ask Amelia.

"Mostly your grades. And if one is low, how you can fix it. They also talk about how you are doing in class in general. But only if something serious is going on. You'll probably fly under the radar."

Our grades. They talk about our grades. I feel sick. No, not exactly sick – I feel really warm. I need to get my grades up now. Today. Or tell my parents what is going on. I don't know how to do either.

A few nights later, after dinner, my dad is working on laundry; Mom and Vanessa finished the dishes and are sitting in the family room reading. I take the garbage out and then decide to go to my room to get my book. When I come back down with my book in hand, Vanessa is gone.

"Where's Vanessa?" I ask.

"She decided to go take a bath," my mom comments looking up at me. I stand at the edge of the room hesitating. Now would be a good time to talk to her.

"Are you going to come read with me?" she invites. I don't answer. Instead I hesitantly walk into the room a little further.

"Mom, I need to talk to you," I finally admit.

"Okay," she pauses, closing her book.

"My grades aren't good," I finally say out loud.

"What do you mean?" she asks confused.

"I mean, you will not have very much fun at my parent teacher conferences." She peers at me, looking extremely surprised. "It's not going to be fun," I repeat.

"Well, what happened, peanut?" she frowns. "Do you need help? A tutor? Or maybe less time at the gym?"

"No!"

"Don't get mad. I just want to help you. We can fix this together; I just need to know how this happened."

"I don't know! I'm just not as smart as you thought," I yell and plop down in our big fluffy chair next to the couch where she is sitting.

"Marissa," she chides me. "Of course you are. I have a feeling this has nothing to do with your intelligence. What is going on?"

"I'm not sure. I test well, it's the homework that's

making a mess of things."

"Are you *doing* the homework?".

"Most of the time. But I don't always turn it in."

"Why?"

"I don't know! I forget, I guess."

"Let's look at your classes online," she suggests. It's the sentence I have been dreading since I realized I am drowning at school.

I grudgingly go and get my laptop. I sit next to my mom and fire up my computer. Then I log in to my school account. I click on my list of grades, then I turn the screen to my mom.

Mom quietly looks at the list. "Two As, two Bs, and two Cs," she announces. We are quiet for a moment. I am grateful I turned in enough assignments to get the Ds up to Cs. "May I see more details on the Cs. Let's see what the problem is."

I click on science, where I have a C, and a list of each assignment comes up.

"You have mostly As in this class," she says, grabbing my laptop and pulling it closer. "You have As on all your tests and quizzes. And you have As on your homework. The problem are these two zeros." She determines, looking up at me. "Can you turn them in?"

"Yes," I say. "I did them a while ago, but I keep forgetting to turn them in."

"Do you want me to email your teacher? Can we send it to her electronically?"

"No, you aren't supposed to get involved, and yes, it is supposed to be electronic. The problem is that it's so late the assignment is closed."

"Closed?" she questions.

"Yeah, like after a certain date you can't turn it in."

"But you just said you could," she points out, confused.

"I can. I just have to talk to my teacher and then she

opens it up. At least that's what they say they will do for sixth graders. Apparently, not for seventh and eighth."

"Why wouldn't they just leave it open then?" she mumbles to herself.

I shrug. "To humiliate us," I pout.

"Well, why don't you try to remember tomorrow, and if you don't, we can talk to her about it at parent teacher conferences."

"Okay," I sulk.

"Let's look at another class," she says clicking on Spanish, the other C.

"All As here too," she mumbles, scrolling down my list of assignments. "And three zeros. Marissa, these zeros are killing you."

"I know."

"If you know, why aren't you turning everything in?"

"I forget," I mumble.

"You forget to do the homework, or you forget to turn it in?" she presses.

"Both," I admit. I want to confide in her that I have a hard time getting homework done before gymnastics and that I'm too tired after. But I don't want gymnastics to be the problem and have her thinking I should quit. I know school is much more of a priority to my family than gymnastics. If my grades are slipping; gym will go. That thought makes my heart sink and I push it away as fast as it came.

"Let's write down all the assignments you need to turn in."

"Okay," I agree.

"Get your planner. Or at least a piece of paper," she instructs.

I go to my backpack and pull out my homework notebook. We are supposed to keep all homework notes in this notebook. I never do because I never seem to have this notebook out during class. It's all so overwhelming. I quickly flip it open so she can't see I have hardly written in it at all.

"Okay, let's start with first period," she says and clicks on my first class. We write down what's missing for each class and it's a list of about ten items. Most of them are small, silly assignments. Almost all of them are items I didn't finish in class and was supposed to finish at home. A few of them were straight homework assignments.

"I'm surprised you aren't getting classwork done," my mom comments.

"They move really fast. Aspen Elementary wasn't like this. I just listened in class and took the tests and did fine. At this school, there are so many little tasks and assignments. I wish they would just teach and test."

"They are teaching you study skills. Which clearly, I need to help you with."

"I don't need to study; I always get As."

"On tests. Marissa, you need to learn to organize yourself and get all your work done. You are going to have to be more disciplined if you are going to continue with gymnastics. Gymnastics requires a lot of time. You have to manage your time so school doesn't suffer."

There it is 'if you are going to continue with gymnastics.' I knew it would come up. I look at my hands. How did this get so out of control? School has always been easy for me. I never even had to think about it. I just did well. Kind of how I hardly need to think about math and numbers; they just make sense to me.

"It's extra work for no reason," I complain.

"Learning is not *no reason*," she counters. "Now, go down that list and highlight the ones you haven't done yet," she tells me.

I look at the list. Most of the assignments I have done. I just need to upload them to the teacher or finish something small. I highlight the ones that aren't done and put a dash mark next to the ones that are partially done. Then I push the notebook toward her.

She stares at my list and finally says, "Finish these that aren't done. Then we'll get these assignments open after talking to your teachers on Wednesday. If you can remember to talk to them before then, even better. Okay?"

"Okay," I agree. I pull my laptop back over to me and get going on the few assignments that aren't actually done. As annoyed as I am that I have to sit here on a Sunday night and do homework, I feel a little relief. My mom knows. And she's going to help me fix it.

Hopefully, it's not too late.

CHAPTER 17

"My 6s and 7s, grip up!" Katie yells. Finally. I am so excited to get to bars. We did our vault rotation with the upper optionals team while the gym was busy. Now we are breaking out into a beam and bars group. James is done coaching compulsories so he'll be able to work with us on bars while Katie coaches beam.

I'm used to Katie, and so far, I have had no problems training with her, but I prefer James. He lets us work skills that are specific to each of us. It feels like Katie wants us all to learn the same skills. Either that or she just has too many gymnasts to keep track of.

I follow my teammates up to the Optional Rooms to put our grips on and grab a quick snack.

"I hope we still get to work giants today," Savannah comments.

"Why wouldn't we?" Alexis asks, opening her locker and pulling out her grip bag.

"My mom said we will probably be doing routines soon and not have time for giants," she explains.

"That's not really how Perfect Balance works," Lucy jumps in.

"What do you mean?" I inquire.

"Well, at my old gym, once season started its was pretty strict and focused on routines. Here, if you finish your assignment, then you can work your new skills."

"That's true," Savannah concedes.

"And if you get the skill, they let you throw it in your routine right away, which is a little crazy," Lucy adds.

"You'll still get to do giants," Paige concludes. "Maybe not as much, but you'll still get to work them."

"And we'll get them this season," Alexis predicts, determined to get the skill she has been tirelessly working on all summer.

"We will," Lucy agrees.

"Of course you will," Alexis teases Lucy. "I wasn't trying to convince you." Lucy just smiles and pulls on her grips. She can do her giants over the pit bar and over the competition set with a spot. She has not tried them without a spot yet. We all know she can do it.

I am so far away from getting a giant. I can only do them on strap bars. I have never done them on a regular bar. Thankfully, it's not a Level 6 skill and I don't have to worry about it for another year. I quickly eat my baggie of almonds, take a swig of my water, and start pulling my wrist bands on. I'm fast with both my grips and my snack because I'm excited to go to bars with James. I want to work my new front sole circle.

I'm the first one to have my grips on and shut my locker, indicating I am ready to head back downstairs. My teammates see me and start putting their stuff away and shutting their lockers too. "You guys ready?" I ask them.

"Almost," Riley says, taking one more bite of her granola bar. "You guys go ahead. I'll be right behind you." We start filing out and by the time we get downstairs to the chalk tray she has caught up to us.

James is busy moving mats and setting up stations. "Push away kips and then come see me."

Without a word, we finish chalking up and split into two groups for the push away kips on the low bars. When girls finish a set and jump down, James tells them their assignment. It sounds like first halves and second halves. Savannah is right; we are starting to work on routines more.

I finish chalking up and walk over to my favorite set of bars. I jump into a kip, push into a cast, swing down into another kip, push away, and into my third kip. These are getting easier for me every day. When I jump down, James is by my set of bars.

"What's your routine?" he asks me.

"I think it's just the Level 5 routine with a front sole circle."

"Can you do a fly away out of a clear hip?"

"I don't know, I've never tried," I admit.

"Okay, try those first. Try clear hip right into a fly away."

"Can I try them in the pit first?" I request. He nods and then keeps going.

"Katie also wants you to do front falls in a front grip on the floor bar. She said you did them last workout."

I nod. "Then the front sole circle with me on the low bar." I smile in relief. I was worried I wasn't going to get to work those today when he threw the clear hip on high bar thing at me.

"Why clear hips on high bar?"

"To even out your routine. If we do a clear hip and your sole circle on the low bar, all you have left for high bar is a kip and flyaway. I think you should do your sole circle on the low bar and the clear hip on high bar."

Okay, makes sense. I'm pleased my routine will be a little different from everyone else's. That is the fun of optionals. Floor and beam we all have unique routines, but sometimes bars feel all the same. At least in Level 6 and 7. By Level 8 they start becoming different from each other.

"So, what is my routine then?" I ask him. I see he is wanting to talk to Alexis who just finished her warm-up kip. He waves her over to him then turns to me.

"Kip, pike-on, front sole circle into the switch grip, kip, pike-on, jump to high bar, long hang kip, clear hip, flyaway," he instructs.

I visualize what he just said in my head and I like it. I look up at him and he is waiting for me to say something. "Sounds good, Coach; I'll be at the pit bar."

"Atta girl," he cheers and turns to Alexis.

I decide to grab a piece of block chalk to take over to the pit bar. I chalk up as I walk across the floor over to the pit. I climb up to the bar, pump a few swings into a kip, and stop in a support position on the bar. Clear hip into a flyaway. Hmm, maybe I need to warm-up the flyaway first. I cast and push away from the bar, swing down, and let go in a tuck flyaway. Okay, the next one I can add the clear hip.

When I climb out of the pit, Lucy is there. "What are you working?" I ask her.

"Just warming up giants before I take them to the comp bars," she says as she jumps up to the pit bar.

I watch her pump tap swings and kip up to a support position. I pick up the chunk of chalk on the ground and add some chalk to my grips while I watch her. She casts to handstand and easily does three giants. After the third one, she pikes to slow her swing, then she lets go when she is under the bar and floats down into the pit.

"Those look so easy for you," I comment.

"They are over here," she agrees, climbing out of the pit. "I get nervous when I'm on the regular bars."

I nod, I get it. Each step is harder and often times scarier than the last.

I jump up to the bar, kip up, and stop. Clear hip into a flyaway. I can do this. Just like doing it out of a cast. I push down into the bar into a cast, drop my shoulders back into a nice clear hip. I come around the bar in what feels like an above horizonal position and swing down way too fast for a flyaway. When it is time to let go for my flyaway, I can't do it. No way, that was super out of control. I swing back down and let go falling feet first into the pit.

"That was exactly it, just let go," Lucy says, rubbing chalk on her grips.

"It felt too fast," I admit.

"Can you make it if you slow it down? How strong is your flyaway?"

"Pretty strong I think."

"Then slow it down. Maybe ask James, but that's what I would do," she muses, jumping up to the bar.

"Riss! If it's too big, pike down!" James yells over to me from the spotting block at the high bar.

I look over and nod. Lucy was right, slow it down.

Alexis walks up breaking my thoughts of my clear hip. "Hey," I greet her as we watch Lucy do three more beautiful giants and fall into the pit.

"James wants you over there," Alexis relays to Lucy as she climbs over the foam cubes in the pit.

"Already?" Lucy squeaks, panic evident in her voice.

"Lucy, they're perfect," Alexis points out.

Lucy doesn't say anything to that as she stands up out of the pit. "Maybe, but they still make me a little queasy when I go over there."

"It's just nerves," Alexis tells her.

Lucy laughs, "I know! That must mean I'm not ready."

"Naw, it just means you're doing hard things," Alexis counters.

"Thanks," Lucy says with sarcasm as she walks back over to James.

Alexis smiles at me, "She'll be fine."

"What are you working?"

"Same as you, clear hip to flyaway," she answers. "I may have a longer first half like you. That puts my clear hip or giant at the end."

"You don't know which one?"

"Clear hip for now, hopefully giants soon. I did them over there with a spot," she says.

"Do they scare you?"

"Actually no, for some reason. Not like beam is scary, it's just hard. I can't seem to get the body positioning right."

"Don't say that or we'll have a ton of hollow body conditioning," I comment as I jump up.

"I know, right?" Alexis laughs as I kip up.

This time I decide to do an itty-bitty clear hip and then I can swing down into a flyaway. I cast small, clear hip small, swing down into a slow tap swing, and I let go early because I don't think I have enough swing to wait for my body to go all the way up.

I land in the pit leaning forward and fall to my stomach in a belly flop.

"You connected it!" Alexis yells, finding the bright side. I laugh and climb out.

CHAPTER 18

"Stop pacing," my sister commands.

"I hate that I am missing practice," I grumble.

"You hate that Mom and Dad are going to find out you don't really do homework," she counters.

"What do they talk about at these conferences?" I ask, looking at her sideways.

"They tell Mom and Dad how brilliant I am," she teases. I roll my eyes. That is definitely not how my meetings are going to go.

"Here's Mom! Let's go," Vanessa shouts. We run out the front door as she pulls up. Vanessa quickly locks the door behind us.

"Dad is going to meet us there," my mom tells us as we climb in. "Vanessa, your first meeting is at 4:30, and Marissa, our first one is at 4:40."

"How are you going to do that?" my sister asks, buckling up.

"Dad is going to your meetings and I'm going to Marissa's," she explains. I feel a little relief hearing this. Mom is more aware I've been struggling and has even been helping me. Dad would be flabbergasted and maybe even embarrassed.

I'm quiet as we drive to school. Vanessa is sitting up front quietly chatting with our mom. I don't really listen as I lean back and look out the window. I would much rather be at practice.

When we get there, we wait a few minutes in the car for Dad to pull up. Mom's phone pings. "He's here, meeting us by the front door. Just in time," she says, getting out.

We pile out and walk to the front doors. I am dreading this. My dad is waiting; he opens the door for us and we follow our mom in. The school is crowded with kids, parents, teachers, and administrators. Our principal is standing right at the entrance and greets us.

"Good evening, Li family. Is this your youngest?" she reaches out and shakes my parents' hands.

"Good evening, Ms. Lopez. Yes, this is our sixth grader, Marissa," my dad introduces.

"Nice to meet you, Marissa," she greets me. "Do you enjoy school like your sister?"

"Not as much," I reply, getting a friendly laugh from all of them.

"Sorry we can't chat, Ms. Lopez, we have a meeting at 4:40," my dad explains.

"Go, go, I won't keep you. Great meeting you, Marissa. I look forward to great things from you."

Just peachy. Great things from me. Everyone talks about

how hard it is to be the oldest, but I think youngest is worse. If your sibling is perfect, then everyone expects you to be perfect too. Or what if she was a delinquent? Then everyone would expect me to be naughty too. But when you're the oldest no one knows anything about your family and you just get to be you.

We walk by the gym and it's full of tables with clubs and information about the school. "We can hit that after," my mom comments to no one in particular.

"Meet you back here; we have to go," my dad says, ushering Vanessa toward the upstairs where most of the eighth-grade classes are.

My mom looks at me, "Where is first period?" she asks. "I scheduled them in order so I could see how your day goes."

"English is first," I say and lead her to my English class. When we walk in, my teacher is at her desk, talking quietly with other kids and parents. The rest of the people there are milling about, looking at some of the poems Mrs. Young put on the wall and reading papers she has put on a back table. I notice everything we are supposed to show our parents in the room is on the opposite side from her desk so that we are all away from the conversation she is having with each student.

"Where do you sit?" my mom asks, and I show her my desk toward the back of the room. "Can you see from here?" I nod but don't say anything. I'm too nervous to talk. "What friends do you have in this class?" she continues.

"Logan," I mumble.

"Oh, that's right. You both can walk together from carpool drop-off. Do either of you stop at lockers?"

"Sometimes," I answer vaguely. The interrogation is annoying. My one-word answers probably won't end it.

Then I see my teacher stand up and say goodbye to the parent and student she was talking to. She looks down at her notebook and then looks up at me.

"Marissa, you're next."

I reluctantly walk over with my mom behind me. When we get to her desk, she introduces herself to my mom and shakes her hand. Then we all sit down.

"Well, Marissa is a joy to have in class," she begins. "She can be quiet at times, but when she does speak up, she is very thoughtful and well-spoken."

"That sounds like Marissa," my mom smiles.

"Let me pull up her grades for you," Mrs. Young says turning to her laptop.

"As you can see, Marissa does very well on tests but has trouble turning work in. It's causing her to have a B- in my class, which is much better than it was a few weeks ago." Then she turns the computer to my mom to look at all my missing assignments.

"Marissa," she addresses me, "You are very smart, we just need you to turn in your work."

I am silent. What can I say?

"We have been working on cleaning up those zeros," my mom shares. I look at her, grateful she is talking for me. "Did she talk to you?"

"No, what did you want to tell me?" Mrs. Young asks me.

"I, um, I finished the reading questions and the thought journal. But I need the assignments opened up so I can turn them in," I manage to request.

"I can do that for you," she turns to her computer and types on it for a minute. "Okay, both are open until Friday night. Try to get your poem turned in too. That would take care of your zeros and really bring up your grade."

We are all silent for an awkward moment and I think we are done. Then my mom says, "Is it normal for sixth graders to be forgetful and have trouble turning work in?"

"For many kids the transition to middle school is tough. Marissa is very bright but distracted. She has a hard time paying attention in class. I see her daydreaming or doodling in her notebook. I think that is when she is getting behind."

"Like maybe ADHD behavior?" my mom ventures.

"What is that?" I jump in, not liking how this conversation is going.

"Attention Deficit Hyperactivity Disorder," my mom answers. *Disorder?*

"I'm not a doctor or counselor, but it might be something to look into," Mrs. Young says. "I have noticed it's harder to catch and diagnose in girls, especially bright children who do well even if they're only partially paying attention." My mom is silent so Mrs. Young continues. "It's common for girls not to be diagnosed until later when organizational skills become more imperative for success."

"But I'm super focused at gymnastics," I blurt out.

My teacher smiles a gentle smile at me and says, "Sometimes kids with ADHD can have hyper focus for things they enjoy and we lose their attention on things they don't enjoy." That shut me up because she just described me perfectly.

"What can we do?" my mom asks.

"You can stop by the school counselor's office. She can give you an evaluation form to take to a pediatrician." Then she turns to me, "Marissa, you will be successful no matter what. Just try to focus during class, get those assignments turned in, and you will get an A in this class."

"What is the name of the counselor?" my mom inquires.

"Mrs. Jones. She will be in the cafeteria with a table. Maybe make an appointment with her if you think you would like to learn more about Marissa's learning style."

My mom nods and stands up, ending the meeting.

"Thank you, Mrs. Young," she says and shakes her hand.

347

I murmur a thank you to my teacher and we leave.

Out in the hall my mom pastes on a smile and says, "Where to next?"

Every meeting is the same. Marissa is daydreaming and not doing in class what she's supposed to be doing. Or Marissa is bright and tests well, but she is not turning in her work. Then we apologize and request they open up the assignments online so I can turn them in. Some teachers give me until Friday, others all the way to Sunday. Either way, I have a ton of work to do this weekend. I'm deflated as we walk to the cafeteria to check out the tables and meet my dad and sister. I bet my mom is wishing she went to Vanessa's meetings.

The cafeteria is abuzz with action and it makes me forget for a moment about my pathetic meetings. There is a table for the PTA and tables for choir, basketball, soccer, volleyball, lacrosse, flag football, after school skiing sign ups, mountain biking, a writing club, an art club, and of course, a table for Chess Club. There's a table with information on becoming a certified babysitter and another one asking for volunteers for community trail clean up.

"You are so lucky to go to a school with so many options available to you," my mom comments. I don't say anything. I'm already doing chess and gymnastics, and clearly, even that is proving to be too much for me. "Do you want to check out any of these tables?"

"No," I mumble. I know I'm in a sullen mood and it's not my mom's fault. In fact, it's absolutely my fault. Why didn't I just do my homework?

"Let's go over to the Chess Club table. You can

introduce me to your friends," she says, trying to cheer me up. I agree and we weave through all the people and get to the far side of the room where Amelia is monitoring the chess table.

She greets me by name and introduces herself to my mom. "What can you tell us about Chess Club that Marissa doesn't already know," my mom says.

"Well, we have a tournament about every other month starting in November." She hands my mom a flier. "And we encourage our members to join this online site. We can play each other from home and get national rankings."

"Did you know about this?" my mom asks me, skimming the flier.

I shrug. "Yeah," I seriously don't know why I'm acting like this. I just can't seem to snap out of it and my mom is being so nice.

"Okay, thank you, Amelia," my mom says, "We'll put the tournaments on the calendar and hopefully Marissa can go to some of them." She turns to me, and since I don't say anything, we leave the table. Thankfully, we run into my dad and Vanessa. She has no interest in looking at any of the tables since she's in eighth grade and already knows what the school offers. Plus, she is happy with the music program at school.

"How did it go?" my dad asks us. I can tell my mom is not sure how to answer this. Finally, she says, "All of Marissa's teachers told us she is incredibly intelligent, which we knew. We'll fill you in on the rest at home. Why don't you guys go get some cookies? I'm going to stop by the counselor's table and ask her a few questions."

"The rest?" my dad says to her retreating back. He turns to me with an eyebrow raised. "Marissa?"

"Let's just say she found out I'm not Vanessa," I explain and quickly start walking toward the table with cookies.

"Why are you bringing me into this?" I hear Vanessa protesting as they follow me through the crowded room.

Once at home, we go about our usual dinnertime routine. I notice my dad has not said a word about my teacher meetings. He is waiting for us to say something. To my mom's credit, she is ignoring it for now as they both bustle around the kitchen to get dinner on the table.

When we finally sit down, my dad can't stand it any longer. "Who wants to tell me what's going on?"

"My teachers think I have ADHD and that's why I'm not doing very well," I blurt out. The surprise on my dad's face is so extreme it's almost funny.

"What?" he stammers, shocked.

"Not one teacher said that Marissa," my mom reminds me. "Her teachers did mention that she daydreams a lot, has trouble staying organized, and struggles to turn in assignments. I am the one that asked about ADHD."

"What did they say when you asked about ADHD?" my dad responds.

"They said to get a doctor's opinion."

"If a doctor tells you she has it, what are you supposed to do about it?" Vanessa inquires.

"Then we look into how to best assist Marissa," my mom answers.

"Will you, like, get special treatment at school?" Vanessa wonders.

"No," I deny immediately feeling like something is wrong with me.

"Maybe," my mom admits.

"Like what?" I ask.

"I'm not exactly sure, but maybe extra time to turn work in and finish tests. I don't know, Marissa, that's what we have to figure out."

On the one hand, that sounds nice. On the other, I don't

want to be treated differently. I wonder if I really have a problem. Was I just being lazy? I'm not sure which answer is worse.

"What are the next steps?" my dad asks logically.

"We fill out an evaluation form, her teachers fill out a different evaluation form, and Marissa fills out a questionnaire. We take all of them to a pediatrician to determine a diagnosis."

He turns to me, "What problems have you been having, Marissa?"

"Um, I guess I'm unorganized and don't turn in stuff. But I test well. I thought my tests would make up for it."

"Is gymnastics getting in the way?"

"No!" I yell.

"You don't need to get upset. I'm just pointing out that your hours increased when school started. Maybe it's too much?"

"It's not. I only added Saturdays," I defend.

"Middle school is a lot harder," my sister comes to my rescue.

"Of course. Of course it is," my mom agrees. "We won't be making any big changes until we know exactly what is going on," she adds, looking my dad in the eye.

"In the meantime, you have a lot of homework to do in the next few days."

After dinner, I escape to my room without doing any chores. I flop on my bed and look up at the cream ceiling. I can't decide how I feel about this possible ADHD thing. It would be nice to know why school is so much harder for me this year. Maybe getting help (whatever that means) would be good. However, I don't like the idea that there is something *wrong* with me.

CHAPTER 19

Tap, tap, tap. "Would you stop?" Vanessa snaps, clearly irritated.

"Sorry, I just have to get this done before practice."

"Then get it done and stop tapping your stupid pencil."

I sigh, toss my pencil down, and go upstairs to get changed for practice. I was worried my parents wouldn't let me go today. They must feel bad that I missed yesterday. I pull open my leotard drawer and stare for a moment at all the bright colorful patterns. I can't wait to be in the gym today and forget about all my problems. I select my favorite purple leo with rhinestones down the front.

I quickly change into my leo, pull on booty shorts, and throw on a sweatshirt. It has been getting colder outside so I decide to put on sweatpants over my shorts. I pull my hair back into a thick ponytail and I'm ready. Except I don't want to go back downstairs and keep working on my impossible pile of homework. I look at the clock. Mom will pull up in fifteen minutes and honk. I'll just stay up here until then. I plop on my bed and stare off into space. What happens if there is something wrong with me? Does that mean gymnastics and school is too much? I already gave up orchestra so I could focus on gymnastics; I don't want to give up chess or gymnastics. I could give up violin, although I kind of already have. If it came down to it, my parents would not hesitate to pull me out of both to get my grades up. School is by far the most important thing to them. Not just school but being good at school. Getting As. I have to have As in this family.

I hear the honk and I'm surprised fifteen minutes already passed. I run down the stairs and out the door to my mom's waiting car.

"Hi, peanut," my mom greets me.

"Hi," I say, throwing in my bag and climbing in after it.

"Before we get to Paige's, I want to talk to you real quick. I called Katie today."

"Oh no," I say, sinking low into my seat. Why, oh why, did she call Katie?

"I told her you have a lot of homework tonight and need to leave early."

"That's it?" I ask as we pull into Paige's driveway.

"That's it. We aren't making any big changes until we meet with a doctor."

"Why do I have to leave early? I can get it all done tomorrow," I promise her, even though I'm not really sure.

"Marissa, better to give yourself a little more time tonight rather than having to cram tomorrow. This is how you got in this pickle in the first place. I think you have fallen into a bad habit of procrastination."

Before I can argue with her about my bad habits, Paige gets into the car. We both greet her and my mom proceeds to tell her I will not be carpooling back with her tonight since

I'm leaving early.

"I have too much homework," I explain.

"The end of the term is the worst," she says, immediately understanding. "Thankfully my school always has everything due Saturday night so I can catch up on the weekends."

"Why Saturday?" I ask. "Why not just Sunday, the end of the weekend."

"I guess we're supposed to be busy with church stuff on Sunday. It's a Catholic school after all."

We are quiet for a minute and then she says, "You'll probably only miss conditioning. You're plenty strong as it is."

I don't know about that, but I appreciate Paige trying to shrug off my need to leave early as no big deal. I hope Katie does the same.

I love my new bar routine. It's just different enough. In fact, I love all my routines! We are starting to put everything together in preparation for our intersquad before Thanksgiving. On bars I was able to do first halves and second halves. My second half I did over the pit because I'm still learning to connect the clear hip to the flyaway. My first halves I can do on the competition set. Katie reminded me to switch my hands faster into my front grip for my front sole circle. Other than that, I think my first halves are pretty good.

We are on beam now and our assignment is three stuck A routines on high beam and three B routines on a low or medium beam. In addition we must stick five of each skill (A and B skills). My A routine has a back walkover, back walkover, and my B routine has the back handspring in it. I'm now able to do my back handspring on a high beam with three mats. That beam is so busy today that I decide to just do my B routines on the medium beam.

"Marissa," Katies says; I turn and wait for her correction. "I get why you are doing routines on the medium beam. But when you do your five back handsprings I want them on high beam."

I nod in agreement. "And I feel like we need to maybe challenge you on a new leap pass," she pauses and thinks. "When you are done, play around with some split jumps and wolf jumps instead of the stretch jump."

"Okay," I agree.

"In your mount, do straight jumps in your A routines and straddle in your B routines. If you ever finish the entire assignment or stay for Open Gym, I want you doing punch fronts up onto a block. Make sure a coach is there for your first few."

I swallow, sometimes she overwhelms me. "Okay," I squeak.

When my mom comes to get me at the end of the beam rotation, I'm having so much fun I really don't want to go. I'm missing vault and conditioning. At least I'm not missing floor. The Level 4s and 5s are in season and get the priority on floor tonight.

When my mom taps on the glass training doors, Katie simply yells, "Marissa, time for you to go!"

"Where are you going?" Savannah asks.

"She has schoolwork to complete. School comes before gymnastics," Katie says, sounding so much like my mother. "Great job today, Marissa; that beam mount is going to be gorgeous."

I smile, "Thanks."

"See you Saturday," she waves.

The other girls chime in, "Bye, Riss, see you Saturday!"

I wave and walk out of the training area. That wasn't as

bad as I thought it would be.

"Let me just go get my stuff," I say to my mom, and I run up to the Optionals Room to get my gym bag and clothes.

At home, my mom pulls up a chair next to me.

"Mom, I don't need you next me the entire time," I complain.

"I just want to see what you have to do and then I'll leave you to it," she explains. I can tell by her defensive tone that I might have hurt her feelings. I don't know how to make it right so I just pull up my account on my laptop.

"Here is everything," I say, scanning the list of assignments in red.

"Which one is most important?"

"How should I know? They're all red," I snap in frustration.

"Marissa, there is no need to get like this; I am trying to help you."

"I know," I sigh. I'm such a jerk.

"Do you know which one is due first or maybe which one is worth a lot of points? I am trying to help you prioritize."

I put my elbows on the table and my face in my hands, "I don't know, I don't know, I don't know," I wail.

"Oh Marissa, it's going to be okay," she assures me, rubbing my back. "Deep breaths and let's take this one at a time."

I breath in and finally look up, "Okay."

"Okay. One at a time. We can do this," she says, turning the laptop toward herself and clicking on the first assignment.

We work on the first assignment, and I'm pleased that it only takes about fifteen minutes. While I am uploading it, my mom gets up and makes herself some tea. Then she comes back around to sit next to me as I pull up the next assignment.

"Oh, I did most of this one in class," I remember, taking a look at the history comprehension questions. I answer one last question and submit that assignment.

Once I'm on a roll, chugging through the assignments is pretty easy. My mom quietly sits and drinks her tea as I make my way through the list.

"Last one! We have only been working for an hour and a half," she points out.

I click on a science video I have to watch. We watch a ten-minute video and I answer questions. As soon as I hit submit, my mom sits back and says, "That wasn't so bad."

It really wasn't, but I feel silly admitting it. I stare at my screen with only green assignments; it feels good.

"Shall we start dinner?" my mom asks as she gets up and walks around the island to the kitchen. I nod and look at the clock.

"I could have stayed at practice," I comment.

"I'm not so sure," she disagrees, opening the fridge and pulling out vegetables. "You're tired by the time you get home and seem to shut down when you think about homework."

I am silent at that observation. "Do you think if I keep up, I won't have to leave early again?" I implore.

She walks over to me and sets three bags of veggies down.

"Of course. Marissa, if you keep up with school, gymnastics will not suffer. I think the key for you is to not let yourself get behind."

I'm not sure how I keep getting behind, but she's right. I can't let it keep happening.

CHAPTER 20

"Why can't I bring my violin? It's part of my costume," I tell my mom. It is Halloween morning and I'm dressed as Martie Maguire, the violinist from the country band, *The Chicks*. She is an amazing artist and dressing country is fun. It's the perfect costume. I have on cowgirl boots, jean shorts (even though I am going to freeze), and a fun long sleeved, flowered button-down flannel shirt.

"That's an expensive violin, Marissa," my mom argues. "It is too nice to get banged up at school."

"But without the violin I just look like a cowgirl, not a country artist," I plead.

"Don't we have an old one?" Vanessa points out, walking into the room wearing a red T-shirt with an M on it. She and Sarah are going as M&M candies.

We stop our arguing and look at her. "Yes, we have the small ones from when you were younger," my mom answers slowly. She turns to me, "That would work. Good idea,

Vanessa."

"How little?" I ask, suspicious of this idea.

My mom is walking out of the room and headed to the basement stairs. "From when you guys were in pre-school; you had to have smaller violins," she answers me as she walks down the stairs.

"That will seem too babyish," I say to my sister.

She shrugs, "You weren't going to win that argument with her. A small violin is better than nothing. Because you're right, you go from being a Chick country star to just a cowgirl without it."

I don't say anything as we wait for my mom to come back up. I grab my lunch and shove it into my bag.

"What if Sarah doesn't show up as the other M?"

"It's just a T-shirt; she will."

"You can take this one," my mom declares, walking back into the kitchen and handing me a small child's violin. I take it from her, grateful I can still pull off my costume. "We need to go or you guys are going to be late for school."

We pile into the car and head to Logan's house. Now I'm nervous about my costume. What if no one else is dressed up? Logan comes outside in jeans, a T-shirt, and a red leather jacket. I know he is dressed as someone, but I'm not sure who.

"Who are you?" I ask as he gets in.

"Hold on, you'll know when I show you the rest of my costume," he says, buckling up. My mom backs out of the driveway and he shows me an old portable tape player that says Walkman on the side. "See? Now do you know?"

"No, sorry," I admit. He frowns and secures the Walkman onto his belt. Then he lifts his backpack and it has a small stuffed Groot tied to the back.

"Oh! You're the guy from Guardians of the Galaxy!"

"Star Lord, yes," he answers, relieved I finally got it.

I expected school to be a little different today, since it's Halloween. But our teachers go about our lessons as if it's an ordinary day. There's no party, no parade, no candy. Of course, with so many kids dressed up, we are louder and more talkative today. We don't get as much done which translates to more homework. In my opinion, homework on Halloween is just mean.

When I walk into science class, I see Trista and she looks great. She is dressed as Wednesday from the Adams Family. She has the black long-sleeved dress with the white collar, black tights, black chunky shoes, and perfect braids. She has put dark eye make up around her eyes that really drives the costume home.

"Your make up looks great!" I exclaim, walking up to her.

"You are such a great rock star!" she fires back. She only knows who I am because I told her at practice who I was going as.

"Thanks. But seriously, who did your makeup?"

"Madison, of course," she says, referring to her older sister.

"Did she dress up?"

"No, she might for a party tonight though."

"You all should be working on your starters," our teacher reminds us. Of course, no one is, but her announcement does get us to stop talking and sit down.

Lunchtime is great fun because we get to look at all the cool costumes. Some kids went all out, some kids didn't dress up at all, and some kids dressed up as a group. Trista and I make our way through the crowd and find our usual table. Logan walks up as soon as we sit down. "Hey, Star Lord," Trista greets him.

He grins widely and turns around so she can see Groot on his backpack, "You have a baby Groot! That is so awesome! I would've dressed up as Gamora if the green wasn't so hard to do."

Logan sits down and shows her his Walkman, "And I have this; it even works."

"Where did you get it?" she wonders.

"My grandpa had it; it even has one of my mom's old tapes in it," he says proudly.

"Can I listen?" she asks, and he hands her one end of the headphones. She puts it to her ear and he presses play. The Walkman loudly clicks into action, rotating the tape inside, sending music to Trista's ear bud.

She listens for a minute, intent on the music. "Who is it?" she asks, handing it back to him.

"Some band called Erasure."

"It was kinda cool."

"Hey, guys," Nate greets, sitting down with his tray. Nate is in his regular clothes with a Jedi robe on top. "They gave us Halloween candy today," he says and picks the handful from off his tray and throws it into the middle of the table for us to grab.

"Are you a specific Jedi?" Trista asks.

"Nope, just part of the order," he cleverly quips. "Wednesday?" he asks her, and she grins. Then he looks at me, "Cowgirl," he surmises. Finally, he turns to Logan, "And Star Lord, of course. Nice."

I point to my violin, "Not just any cowgirl, I'm a Chick from *The Chicks*!"

"So, a music star?"

"Yes," I answer, disappointed that most of the people who knew who I was where teachers and a few of the girls in eighth grade. Oh well, I still love Martie and I'm glad to be her for Halloween. She is such an amazing artist.

"Are you guys trick-or-treating together tonight?" Nate asks us.

"No, since we live farther away from each other, our parents talked us into just going with kids in our neighborhood. I'm going out with Savannah who lives next door to me," Trista answers.

"I'm going with Paige, a teammate that lives by me, and my sister and her friend," I answer. "What about you guys?"

Logan is quiet while Nate says who he is going out with in his neighborhood. "Logan, you can come with us. We will be walking right by your house," I offer, sensing he has not made arrangements with friends.

"Thanks," he smiles, "Maybe go to my street first and I might join you."

We spend the rest of lunch guessing the costumes of the other kids in the cafeteria. The kids are more creative in middle school. There are a lot of anime characters that I don't know. As a gymnast, sometimes you miss some of the pop culture going on. We are so busy training that we aren't always online watching what the other kids are watching. Regardless, it was a fun lunch hour and I'm bummed when the bell rings for us to go back to class.

CHAPTER 21

Vanessa and I are making a snack when my mom calls from work to tell me she is taking me to the doctor this afternoon. I remind her that I have practice and she insists that we need to do it today.

"I didn't have a choice on the day, Marissa. Your pediatrician has a cancellation and I took it. Otherwise, we would have to wait until January."

"I would rather wait a few weeks than miss practice," I complain.

"It's November. January would be months, not weeks," she counters. Then she sighs and says, "This is important, Marissa. We need to get to the bottom of whatever is going on."

"Nothing's going on. Middle school is just hard," I whine, getting defensive.

"Marissa, I know it's hard. But it let's just see your doctor. Okay?"

I am quiet for a minute. I feel like I might cry if I say anything.

"Bring your gym bag and leo and you can go to practice late if we finish up with the doctor early," she finally concedes.

"Okay," I choke out.

"I'll be there in twenty minutes. Finish your evaluation paper, grab your gym stuff, a book, and be ready when I honk," she instructs.

"Okay."

"Let me talk to Vanessa."

"She wants to talk to you," I say, holding out the phone to Vanessa. I abandon my snack and head upstairs to get stuff for practice. I open my drawer and wonder if I should change now. Then I remember Mom said to just bring it. I grab my PBGA workout leo and stuff it in my gym bag. Then I throw in a sweatshirt and a pair of sweats. My hair bands are kept in a drawer in the bathroom, but I look around my room and find one on my nightstand. I grab it and put it on my wrist. I pause to think. That's all. I look at the clock on my dresser and see I have a few minutes to spare. Then I remember that I need to fill out the evaluation form before the doctor appointment. What did I do with that? I just had it yesterday.

I locate it under a pile of books and it's a little wrinkled. I smooth it out and sit down at my desk. It asks really simple questions like 'My thoughts get interrupted when I hear a noise.' Of course they do, doesn't everyone's? I circle *agree*, which is one of only three choices, *agree*, *sometimes*, and *disagree*. I go to the next one, 'Do you find it difficult to sit for longer than 15 minutes?' I go to school, don't I? *Disagree*.

I am finishing the last question when I hear my mom honking. I grab the sheet, pick up my gym bag, and run downstairs. I quickly shove on my fuzzy boots that are sitting by the front door.

"Bye, Vanessa!" I yell over my shoulder. I am out the door before she has time to give me a response. I run down the drive and get in the back seat of the car. "Hi," I greet my mom.

"Hi, peanut." She smiles at me before looking behind her and backing up while I click in my seat belt. "Hopefully, this will be fast and we can get you to practice," she says. "I called Katie and told her you would be late," she adds.

"What did she say?"

"She said okay," my mom replies.

"That's it?"

"Katie knows you would be there if you could. We have to take care of this."

"Did you tell her I'm flunking out of school and we're trying to figure out why?" I sass.

"I told her you had a doctor's appointment and that's it. I told her you might come in late. But maybe we take tonight off and go do something, just us?" she offers, glancing in the mirror.

I'm surprised at this offer. My mom is usually so busy we don't do outings on school days. I don't know what to say. I want to go to practice, but I don't want to hurt her feelings.

"Maybe," I mutter.

Then she asks me about school and whether I'm all caught up on my assignments. I sure hope so; it's all I did the entire weekend. I tell her I'm pretty sure. I'm not going to commit to being sure when everything seems to constantly change on the assignment pages.

We ride in silence for a while. "How far away is it?" I ask, trying to calculate how late I'll be to practice and whether it would be better to do an outing with my mom.

"Marissa, you have been there a thousand times. It is Dr.

Flores' office."

"Yeah, but I never paid attention to how long it took to get there," I admit.

"We'll be there in five minutes," she tells me.

"But how long total? And where are we in relation to Perfect Balance?"

"Oh, I get it," she catches on. "Practice starts in about thirty minutes. We still have the appointment and the drive over there will be another fifteen minutes. You may only miss one event. Or you can take a day off. Let's just see how long this takes. And let's focus on this appointment."

I look outside. It's a gloomy and dark day. It has looked like it's going to rain all day, but it hasn't yet. The sky looks like it's holding back emotions. I sigh; I can relate.

When we pull in, my mom says, "Grab your paper and your book."

"I didn't bring a book," I tell her.

"I told you to bring a book," she says annoyed.

"Well, I forgot," I grumble, frustrated as I get out of the car.

I'm walking into the building when my mom looks at me and sees I'm empty-handed. "Go back and get your paper," she orders and beeps the car. I run back, open the door, get my paper, and jog to get back to her.

We walk in and she checks me in while I take a seat in the waiting area. She joins me and we don't have to wait long before they call me back. My mom follows me to an exam room. The medical assistant takes my temperature, blood pressure, and gets my height and weight. Then we wait in the exam room.

There is no clock anywhere in here and I wonder how long we've been waiting and what event they started on at Perfect Balance.

I'm a little nervous and I'm not sure why because my

mom is right. I have been in this office a thousand times. This is the only doctor I have ever been to.

Finally, we hear a little knock on the door before Dr. Flores comes in. I really do like Dr. Flores; she has been my pediatrician since I was a baby.

"Hello, Marissa, how are you?" she greets me.

"Good," I say, even though maybe I'm not.

She sits down at her computer and scrolls through my chart. Then she turns to me and says, "Tell me about school."

I'm at a loss for what to say. I am silent and she waits patiently for me to answer. "It's easy and hard at the same time," I finally manage.

"How is it easy?" she pushes.

"Well, I don't feel like I'm learning that much. I mean, I don't have to worry about tests and stuff. If a teacher talks about something in class or we read something in class, then I can answer questions about it on the test."

"No surprise, we've always known you have a good brain. How is it hard?"

I look to my mom and she stays quiet. I guess I'm expected to answer.

"I don't know," I mumble.

"Homework is a challenge," my mom finally shares.

Dr. Flores nods at my mom and turns to me, "Why do you think that is?" I am about to answer that I am busy with gymnastics, but I think better of it. If I give that excuse, then my mom will not hesitate to take me out of gymnastics, or at least off of the competition team.

"I can't seem to remember what I'm supposed to do at home," I finally answer. "Like, I know I have homework, but once I'm home it doesn't seem important. Especially since I know all the stuff from listening in class."

"And you're in sixth grade?" she clarifies and I nod. "Do you have the questionnaires?" she asks my mom.

My mom hands her a manilla envelope, "One from each of her core teachers and one from her father and me."

I hand her my wrinkled-up paper and she chuckles. "What?" I ask.

"Just that if you are presenting with ADHD traits, this wrinkled paper is the first indicator. They always get turned in like this," she explains.

I frown; I'm not happy to be a cliché.

She quietly reads all the evaluations. Then she looks at me. "Well, Marissa, according to all the people who know you best, you are displaying some attention deficit behaviors. You are not showing hyperactivity though, which is probably why we haven't caught this before now."

"What does that mean?" my mom asks.

"ADHD is Attention Deficit Hyperactivity Disorder. Based on the answers here, hyperactivity doesn't seem to be a problem, but staying focused and organized does. You don't have to be both for a diagnosis. Based on these evaluations, you are a classic case."

I have a *disorder*? Me? A disorder. I have always been the smartest and best student in the room. How is this possible?

"But I'm a good student," I blurt out.

"You are a smart student that has probably never had to study or do homework before," she guesses, eerily on point. "I'm guessing you skated by in elementary school on your big brain. Now that middle school has assignments and projects, your attention deficit is more noticeable."

"What do we do?" my mom questions.

"First of all, Marissa, lots of kids and adults have ADHD. We just need to help you find the tools you need to be successful." Then she turns to my mom, "I recommend a combination of meds, therapy, and coping skills, like study skills."

They talk for a while of all the different medicine options, then she talks about seeing a therapist and starting a behavior modification program at home. It sounds like a lot of time and effort to deal with.

"Can I still do gymnastics?" I whisper, terrified that trying to resolve this new problem is going to take up all my time.

"Of course," Dr. Flores assures me. "In fact, gymnastics is probably a huge help. It teaches you focus, fitness, and probably burns off some steam."

"I have never been unfocused at the gym," I point out.

"People with ADHD have an ability to focus when they are challenged or interested in the topic," she counters. So much for pointing out a flaw in her diagnosis.

I sit back in my chair and continue to let them talk. I can tell my mom is not too sure about meds. Dr. Flores loads her up with pamphlets and information on different types I can take. Then she gives her two different business cards for therapists and another flier with a list of classes on study skills. Just when I thought she was done overloading my mom, she gives her a list of books on ADHD. By the time we walk out my mom looks overwhelmed.

We walk out of the office in silence. I don't like the idea that there is something wrong with me. Disorder. Can't they think of a better name? Like Inattentive People. Or Too-Smart-for-Boring-School-People, TSBSP.

"Can't I just go to a school that has really hard stuff in class and no homework?" I plead when we get in the car.

"Maybe you can start a school like that someday. For now, we have to work within the system we have. Which is for you to get the tools and skills to focus long enough to do homework."

"How late am I for practice?" I ask. I'm done thinking and talking about ADHD. I'm ready to see my friends at the gym and work on skills I want to learn.

"You'll be about an hour late once we get there," she predicts.

Chapter 22

I come into the gym from my doctor's appointment anxious about how much practice I've missed. Turns out I only missed complex and beam. We still have bars and floor. I'm super bummed I missed beam. But I probably need to work on bars and floor more.

Gymnastics makes me forget all my problems. I get to focus on something I enjoy – challenge myself on new things, see my friends, and workout so hard I fall into bed at night. The sense of accomplishment when I learn a new skill is so much greater than getting an A. Don't get me wrong, I like As; they just come easy. At least on tests, lately they haven't been easy in my overall grade because of stupid homework.

At the gym, and especially now in optionals, I get to set goals and work on learning something I want to learn. I'm so excited about both my front sole circle and my beam mount because they are my things. I should find something cool to do on floor. Although we are so close to season now, my unique floor skill will have to wait until next season. Maybe a cool leap combo or something.

I'm able to do my flyaway out of the clear hip with James spotting and an 8-inch landing mat. James says I'm ready to do them on my own, but it doesn't feel like it to me. My front sole circle is coming along. I'm able to easily swing forward and change grips on the other side and swing into a kip.

On floor we do first halves and last halves. The floor workout is getting harder and harder. I'm nervous for when we have to do a full routine. I know it's coming soon. We are doing dance throughs where we run three times when there is a tumbling pass. According to Lucy these are harder than full sets. Hopefully, she's right.

I've memorized the routines of all the Level 6s and 7s. I can easily tumble in between routines now. It seemed like such a funny thing to learn; I now see the practicality of it.

By the time we are done with our floor workout there isn't much time for conditioning. All we have are pull-ups and leg lifts. It is the first time I get to really talk to my teammates since I arrived mid-workout.

"Where were you earlier?" Savannah asks as she spots me on my leg lifts.

"I had to go to the doctor," I share, lifting my toes up to the bar.

"What for? Just your shots?" I know Savannah is not trying to be nosy; she genuinely cares. I wonder if I'm supposed to be ashamed of my disorder, or if it's not a big deal. I don't answer during my leg lifts and Savannah probably assumes I'm working too hard to talk. Finally, I finish my ten and decide these girls won't treat me differently no matter what the doctor says about me.

I let go of the bar and fall to my feet. I turn to Savannah

and say, "My doctor said I have ADHD," I share.

"What's that?" she asks, climbing onto the block and jumping to the high bar. She swings down and I stop her swing so she can do her leg lifts properly.

"It stands for Attention Deficit Hyperactivity Disorder," I explain.

"My brother has that," Alexis comments.

"So does mine," Paige pipes in.

"Really? Which brother?" I ask, since Alexis has four brothers.

"Ethan . . . and maybe Drew. Mom says gymnastics wears him out so much she's not sure yet."

I think about that as I hold Savannah's lower back.

"How is Drew doing with middle school?" I inquire. Drew is a year older than me. If he really has ADHD he must have struggled last year like I'm doing now.

"Fine. But we go to the charter school until eighth grade. It's not that much different yet. Not like how it is for you guys. Ethan said it was a big change going to the high school from our school," she shares.

Savannah jumps down and it's my turn again.

"What does it mean?" she asks.

"I told you, Attention . . ."

"No, I mean, why is it a thing?"

"Oh, I'm struggling in school," I admit.

"That doesn't sound like you. You're the smartest person I know," Paige says as she jumps up on the bar next to us while Alexis holds her back.

"Smart yes – organized and focused, no," I explain.

"So, what do you do?" Savannah wonders.

"Learn how to be organized, I guess," I say, climbing onto the block for my turn. I jump up and do my leg lifts.

"If anyone can figure out how to get organized, it's you, Marissa. You are logical and practical. You'll find a system,"

Paige encourages.

I don't say anything as I do my leg lifts. The conversation changes to a dance coming up at Riley's school. I haven't figured out where she goes yet, but I don't think it is Snowcap Middle School. I haven't heard of my school holding any dances.

"It's really more like a social at the school," she clarifies. "There will be food trucks and basketball and soccer and music. So maybe dancing. I'm not sure."

"You should for sure check it out." Paige encourages.

"Find out if kids from other schools can come," Alexis requests. "Then we can all do that instead of PNO. Might be fun."

I quietly finish my ten leg lifts and jump down. Savannah climbs up and this time she has pull ups. I'm surprised I told these girls about my . . . what? Problem? Disorder? Secret? I don't even know what it is, but I'm glad they didn't really make a big deal out of it.

We finish our leg lifts and pull ups a few minutes before practice is supposed to be over. Katie tells us to quickly stretch.

We stretch our splits, arms, and shoulders. Then we head upstairs to get our bags and wait outside for our parents. Paige's mom pulls up and we get in the car.

"Hi girls, how was practice?" she asks.

"I did my round-off on high beam!" Paige exclaims.

"You did?" we both exclaim.

"Yeah, with two 8-inchers," she shares.

"It counts," I inform her. "I'm sorry I missed it." Paige has been working so hard on her round-off for what seems like forever. I'm glad she'll be able to compete them this season.

"You'll see it Wednesday," she says, confidently.

"Well, that's awesome! I can't wait to see it."

"Is there something new you are working on?" Paige's mom asks me.

"Back handspring on beam mostly. And front handspring, front. I don't think that will be ready for season."

"It might," Paige counters. "And you can compete it even if you get it mid-season."

"That's what I'm worried about," I admit, making them both laugh.

When I get home, I realize I needed the break from talking about ADHD. I walk into the kitchen and yell that I'm home. I see an entire stack of library books about ADHD on the counter. Break's over.

CHAPTER 23

I haven't said anything to anyone at school about my ADHD. School isn't as safe of a place. Even though Logan and Nate have never given me a reason not to trust them, it's just not the same as the gym.

"How was practice last night?" Trista asks.

"Good. I think I'm going to be able to do my bar routine before the intersquad," I comment.

"Always a win," she remarks, pulling out her sandwich. "I hate the new routines."

"Yeah, it stinks you had to learn new ones."

"You lucked out. Moving up just in time. I just don't know how to maximize my score with these routines or what the judges are looking for," she admits.

"Talking gymnastics again?" Logan teases as he sits down.

"Always," Trista grins.

He sits down next to her and says, "Nate is buying

school lunch, we won't see him for a while." I look up at the school lunch line and it winds around the entire cafeteria. He's right, it will be a while.

"Then you're lucky you have us," Trista teases good-naturedly.

"Sometimes," he agrees and pulls out his lunch. "I have to do math in the library after I eat and will probably miss Nate all together."

"Then he's lucky to have us too, otherwise you would both miss each other and be eating alone," Trista teases.

"Are you ready for table tryouts?" he asks me.

"Table tryouts?" I repeat, confused.

"Yeah, to see which table level you play at the tournament," he reminds me.

"Is that today?" I ask, caught off guard.

"Next week," he chuckles. "Study. If you do, you could make fifth or sixth table, which is really good as a sixth grader."

"So, wait, it's all grades? How does it work?" Trista asks.

"We have a mini tournament for just us," Logan begins.

"Like an intersquad?" Trista interrupts.

"I guess," Logan pauses, then he continues. "We see who the best players from our school are from one to eight. The number one person plays first table, which means they will play the number one player from other schools. Number two plays second table against number twos from other schools and so on. We get six tables," he explains.

"But you said you go out eight places," she astutely points out.

"Two alternates," he explains, taking a bite of his sandwich.

"And you think you're top six?" she asks, turning toward me in her chair.

I shrug. "I don't know. I've beaten almost everyone on the team and almost everyone has beaten me."

"She's top six," Logan answers for me.

"Wow, that's awesome, Marissa!"

"I haven't made top six yet, Triss," I laugh.

"You will!" they both say at the same time, making our entire table erupt in laughter.

I smile at my friends. I'm lucky to have them.

"What's so funny?" Nate asks walking up.

"Trista and Logan share the same brain," I say as Nate sits down.

"That line is the worst," he comments.

"We know!" Trista and Logan exclaim in unison again, making us all laugh even harder.

When the bell rings and I'm making my way to my locker, a girl steps in my way. "So, like, which one do you like?"

"What?" What is she talking about? I need to get around her so I can get to my locker and get to class before I'm tardy. I don't need to add a tardy to my list of problems at school. I step to the side, but she blocks my way.

"Logan or Nate? Which one? You can't have both."

What is this girl talking about? "Excuse me, I need to get by," I mutter and sneak past her. That was so weird. What is wrong with some of the kids here?

I hear her murmuring to her friends about me having two boyfriends. Boyfriends? Is that her problem? I can't believe this is the second time this has come up. The kids here are weird sometimes. Well, she can think whatever. I have to get to class.

I wasn't nervous for our school chess tournament, or intersquad, as Trista calls it, until Logan mentioned it. I probably should get on the website everyone keeps talking about so I can earn a ranking. Or I need to at least get on there to practice. I'm sitting at the kitchen counter after gymnastics practice trying to finish my history homework. I click over to the chess website, surprised it isn't blocked. I see all sorts of fun options. I can play games against the computer or I can find friends and play against them. I wonder if Logan is on here.

I click on "find friends" and get a pop up blocking me from talking to strangers online. I guess that makes sense. I click on a level 1 game to play the computer. I quickly beat the computer and advance to the next level. I wonder how Logan is playing other kids in Chess Club. I continue to play games and move up levels quickly. Maybe I'm better than I realize. On about my fourth game my mom walks in.

"You're still at it, peanut?" my mom asks tenderly. I quickly click over to my history homework and immediately feel guilty.

I can't speak or I will give myself away.

"It seems like your homework is taking you much longer than it should. I talked to the counselors today and they said you shouldn't have more than twenty minutes for each class. No more than two hours. Do you get distracted?"

I nod. If you count getting bored and clicking over to chess games, then yes, I get distracted.

"We'll get to the bottom of this and get you the help you need," my mom says. This makes me feel terrible because I'm the one dorking around and making my homework take forever. "I made an appointment with a therapist for next Tuesday so you don't miss practice."

"Tuesday?" I panic. "I can't miss Tuesday!"

"Marissa, that is the only day you don't have practice, I

thought you would be happy with that."

"I have my chess intersquad that day," I explain. "It's how they choose the ranking for the tournament!" I squeal in frustration.

"Marissa, I can't keep up. I assumed gymnastics was your priority."

"It is. Just this once chess is more important. Please mom. I don't have anything on Fridays," I plead.

"She's not in her office on Fridays," she frowns. "Marissa, I want to get you help as quickly as possible. You should not be spending hours after practice on homework. You need to go to bed. This is silly," she says in frustration.

Now I feel really bad for sneaking on to the chess website. She thinks I have been doing homework this entire time. I can't bring myself to tell her the truth. I have already been full of disappointments.

"I'm basically done," I say closing my laptop. "I'm done," I repeat.

"Bedtime?" she asks me, reaching out her hand.

"Bedtime," I confirm and take her hand and we walk upstairs.

Once in bed, I lay in the dark wondering if I really have a disorder, or if I'm just stubborn and lazy. Every time I go to do homework, I end up doing something else. If someone did that in the gym, neither Katie nor James or even Melony, for that matter, would tolerate it.

Of course, gymnastics is fun, so that probably doesn't happen very often.

Maybe school is harder than I realize. No, that's not it. Why is it so easy for Vanessa? It doesn't seem very fair. Then I remember my mom's words, *no one promised you fair*. I sigh and roll over to my side. I see my medals on the wall. I think about the meets I won because I was consistent, not because I was the best. No, things are rarely fair.

CHAPTER 24

My mom agreed to push back my appointment one week so I could participate at chess. She has always been helpful in letting me do all the things I want to do.

I reminded my mom about the online chess site. She helped me connect with my school chess group so I could play kids I know. I spent a lot of time online on Sunday playing my Chess Club friends. What I learned playing my classmates is that Logan has gotten good. Or at least he is good when he has unlimited time to make a move. I might be better at speed chess.

The room looks a little more official than usual. The boards are set up with timers next to each one and a notepad at each chair. I look at our teacher setting pencils out at each notepad.

"Hi, Marissa," Mr. Belsky greets me.

"Am I early?"

"A few minutes, did your teacher let you out early?"

"I guess she did," I agree. Or at least she didn't keep talking after the bell rang. And I didn't stop at my locker. I have gotten bad about not stopping at my locker and my backpack has gotten heavy. I go to a chair and drop my bag in it.

"We are going to draw for starting spots. We don't have very long so they're going to be fast games."

What if I don't make a table at all? There are about fifteen kids in Chess Club, which means half won't even be going to the tournament. Kids start rolling in and Mr. Belsky tells them we are going to have a quick meeting before we start. We gather around him by the white board and he begins to explain how this tournament is going to work.

"This is so exciting, our little qualifier. Here is how it is going to work. Since some kids don't have a ranking from online, we are just going to draw names to get started. Then we will rotate seats from there. We are going to play six ten-minute games. The usual scoring: five points for a win, zero for a loss, three points each for a stale mate, two points if you run out of time and your opponent gets three points.

"When a game is done, do not move any pieces or rotate seats until I come and look at your board and write down your score. At the end of six games, I will let you know which six of you will be representing the school chess team. We will also have two alternates. All of you will get T-shirts and I encourage you to come to the tournament and cheer for your teammates.

"Okay, let's draw numbers." He holds out a bowl full of white slips of paper. "The bowl has two of each number. Once you have your number, go to the table with that number to start."

"If you drew the number with a star in the corner you are playing with the black pieces. You will play three games each color. Five minutes per person on their side of the timer."

I draw number four and walk to the tables that are set up while he continues to give us directions.

As I get to table four, Sienna walks up. I know I can beat her, even though she is a seventh grader. I don't know her speed game; my speed game is pretty good. I can make fast decisions.

"You may begin," Mr. Belsky says. Instantly the room is quiet with the exception of pieces moving and timers clicking. I have no problem staying focused on my game; I'm determined to beat her. Sienna has a better start than I anticipated, but I still put her in check and raise my hand.

Mr. Belsky comes over and looks at our board, writes our points down, then tells us where to rotate next. The people playing black stay sitting and the people playing white move one chair down. He assures us that halfway through we will switch the board around so no one will have the advantage. White has a small advantage by going first.

I move one seat down. I see Logan is on my same row a few seats up. That means I probably won't play him. I'm kind of glad; I don't want to have to beat him. I think my speed game is better than his.

The hour goes by very quickly and I end up with three wins, two losses, and one stale mate. I don't know if I made top eight, but I know I am one of the best sixth graders. Logan is too, I'm sure of it.

Mr. Belsky gathers us together again to tell us our scores.

"Let me start with our number one player for today. With an impressive score of 23, Eli!" Eli goes up and stands at the front of the room next to Mr. Belsky and gets his team T-shirt to wear at the tournament. I'm sure Eli is an eighth grader. This is going to be hard.

Then he announces second table: another eighth grader;

third table: a seventh grader; fourth table: another eight grader; and fifth table is another seventh grader. Then he says, "We have the rare occurrence of a sixth grader on the team as sixth table – Logan Watson." Logan proudly walks up and gets his T-shirt. I have mixed emotions. I'm happy for Logan but bummed I didn't make the team. I thought I had a good chance.

"First alternate is Marissa Li, our only other sixth grader on the team. Second alternate is Sienna Hall."

I walk up to the front and take the T-shirt he hands me. As I walk by, Logan high fives me and I smile. At least I get to go to the tournament as an alternate player.

"To the rest of you, come get your shirts. I hope to see you at the tournament cheering on your team. Keep coming to Chess Club and you will have another chance to make the team next time."

We are free to go and Logan immediately finds me. "I'm stoked we both get to go!" I see this means more to him than to me. I'm glad things turned out the way it did. We grab our backpacks and walk out to wait for his mom to pick us up.

"I knew Eli was going to be first table. He's so good, I've never beaten him. Have you?" he asks me.

I think about it. "No, I don't think I have.'"

"He has an amazing end game. I can never finish him off early enough to beat him. I do better online. His ranking is 1000. Can you believe it?"

I smile at him. "You will be ranked that high when you're in eighth grade," I point out.

"I hope so," he says as his mom drives up.

CHAPTER 25

The therapist's office is fancy, not like the counselor's office at school at all. We are in the waiting room where there is a sleek, tall desk, plush waiting chairs, plants, and a fish tank. There is no one at the desk but the therapist said to just wait and she would come out and get us.

As promised, she comes out and greets us, "I thought there might be no one at the desk on a Friday at four."

My mom stands up and shakes her hand and says, "Thank you for coming in on a Friday just for us."

"It was no problem, I had some work to catch up on anyway," she comments. Then she leads us back to her office.

It has two stuffed chairs and a couch. I sit on the couch with my mom. The therapist takes a chair across from us and introduces herself.

"Marissa, why don't you tell me what's going on?"

I'm surprised she is addressing me so I turn to my mom.

My mom says, "You can tell her, hon."

"Um, I have ADHD, I guess," I say slowly.

"What does that mean to you?"

"It means school is hard and it shouldn't be."

"Why shouldn't it be?"

I'm embarrassed to say, 'because I'm smart.' The room is quiet for a moment before I finally answer, "Because it usually isn't."

She looks at my mom.

"Marissa is a very intelligent child and up until now, she didn't have to work to get perfect grades. It looks like in middle school she is going to have to work for it, study, and turn in homework. It seems with her ADHD this will be harder for her."

"Is perfect important?" the counselor asks me.

Again, I'm surprised by the question; my mom looks surprised too. "I think it is," I admit.

"Hmm," is all the therapist says. "Let's start with understanding your mind and what it means to have ADHD and how you learn differently."

She tells me how different people's brains process or take in information. I have to admit, when she talks about people with ADHD having trouble filtering out a lot of things going on at once, I can relate. She also talks about impulse control problems, that one I can't relate to. Does that mean I don't really have this and everyone is going down the wrong path?

Then she talks about being distracted or daydreaming, procrastinating, and making excuses to yourself to get out of difficult thinking tasks. Okay, that sounds familiar.

She continues to talk about focus, or lack thereof, and I have to interrupt.

"I focus when I'm at gymnastics." She pauses and nods.

"I assume gymnastics is something you really enjoy?"

"Yes," I confirm. She looks from me to my mom and says, "Kids with ADHD are really good at focusing on something when they enjoy doing it."

"And I focus on chess," I mumble.

"I'm glad to hear it, Marissa," she says kindly. "Since you can focus on gymnastics and chess, then getting some extra tools to help you focus on school shouldn't be too difficult."

"I'm okay at school, I think," I admit. "I just lose focus and interest on homework," I tell her honestly.

"Alright, let's put some things in place to help you with homework," she decides.

She talks to me about writing things down and to my mom about a reward system for me when I do homework each day.

When our time is almost up, she asks me to go back to the waiting room while she talks to my mom. I reluctantly leave the room. If they are talking about me, shouldn't I be allowed to hear everything they are saying? I sit down in a fluffy chair to wait for them. I stare at the fish tank and almost instantly I'm mesmerized by a little teal fish darting in and out of the fake towers and rocks. I wonder if he knows he's not really in the ocean. Then I see a bright yellow and blue guy join him in his pattern. Fish tanks are kind of cool.

"You ready?" my mom asks me as she walks out of the office into the waiting room with me.

"What did she need to talk to you about?" I ask, hoping my mom will share every detail.

"She wanted to talk to me about options of meds for you."

"Meds?"

"Yes, sometimes kids with ADHD take medicine to help them focus."

I think about that for a moment. I'm not sure I have that

much trouble focusing. It feels like my mom and doctors and teachers are making a huge fuss over nothing. "What does Dr. Flores think?" I wonder.

"She says that some kids can learn enough skills to not need meds, but most kids with ADHD do need them. It is like your frontal lobe is asleep; the meds just wake it up."

"Wait, part of my brain is asleep?"

"Kind of. It's more like off the job, not filtering incoming stimulus like it should." I don't say anything so she continues. "I'm reading a book right now on the pros and cons. We'll see Dr. Flores next week and see what she thinks."

"Do I have a say?"

"Of course, you have a say," she assures. "But as your parents and doctors, we will also do what is best for you."

I think everyone is making a fuss over nothing. I focus during gymnastics and chess. I focus during class, most of the time. I just think homework is a waste of time. And I forget about it because it's so dumb.

This ADHD thing feels like it is spiraling out of control with doctors, therapists, books, and medications. All of it seems over the top.

"Is all this necessary?" I grumble as we walk to the car. "Can't I just work on turning in my zeros like we were originally doing?"

"Marissa, your teachers expressed a genuine concern. Your doctor reviewed all the information. This is your diagnosis. I am just getting you all the help you need so you can be successful."

"It's so much," I complain.

"Right now it seems like it because we are just learning about you and what you need."

It all sounds fine and good, but it feels like all we are doing is missing practice. Good thing I didn't make one of the first six chess tables for the tournament. It would mean I would have to practice chess more and I don't even have time for gymnastics.

"Mom, I made alternate for chess," I tell her. I can't believe I forgot to tell her. We have been so busy running around to appointments.

"Alternate for what?"

"For the chess tournament. I am one of only two sixth graders going," I tell her.

She puts her arm around me and hugs me to her side, "That's wonderful, peanut."

I smile; meds or not, I still made the team.

CHAPTER 26

Saturday afternoon I sit down on the couch next to my sister. We both have our laptops out. I set mine on the coffee table in front of me and she keeps hers in her lap as she pulls up the school website.

"Do you use the calendar?" she asks me.

"What calendar?"

"Oh my gosh, Marissa, your teachers didn't show this to you?" She pulls up the familiar schedule page. There is an icon for each class. Then she clicks on a tiny button that reads, "month view" and a calendar opens up. It has assignments written on certain days in green with a few in red. "There are all my assignments and the day they are due."

I look at it closely, that is really cool. In one glance, I can see an overview of when everything is due. "What do the colors mean?"

"Green means it is an open assignment and red means it's closed and overdue."

"You have overdue assignments?" I exclaim in mock shock.

"Not really, those are extra credit," she assures me. "Pull yours up, let's see."

I take my laptop and set it on my legs and log into our school website. I get to my class page and look around for that tiny link she showed me.

"Where is it?".

"On the left."

I scan the left side of the page and finally see it, "It's so tiny," I mutter when I finally spot the link that reads, 'month view.' I click on it and up pops a calendar with all sorts of assignments on it. I am shocked to see all my assignments in one place.

"This is so much easier!" I exclaim.

"Right? I can't believe you have been functioning without it for so long." She peers over my shoulder and I'm embarrassed for her to see how many of my assignments are red. Especially since I have been trying to get missing assignments under control.

"Why do you have so many unopened messages?" she asks me.

"What?"

"You have eighteen new messages."

"How do you know that?"

She leans over and points to a little icon of an envelope on the left of my screen showing a tiny blue bubble with an 18 inside the bubble. "Those are your unread messages and you have eighteen."

I stare at the little envelope bewildered.

"Click on it," she instructs. I slide my finger over the touch pad of my laptop and click on the icon. Up pops a list of messages from my teachers. I scroll down the messages. They are all reminders of my missing work.

"They have been messaging me?" I whisper. I feel so silly. All this time I was so upset at my teachers for not trying to help me. But here are eighteen messages from them trying to get through to me.

"How did you not know about this?" my sister reprimands.

"I don't know. I didn't know we had a messaging system on here," I admit, my voice going up slightly in panic.

"Where were you the first week of school? They go over all of this constantly," she reprimands.

"I don't know!" I yell, exasperated. Why do people keep asking me that? I was there. But I must not hear every little thing my teachers say. Sometimes they get so boring I tune them out.

"Don't yell at me, I'm trying to help you," she fires back at me.

"I know. I know, sorry. It's just overwhelming."

"Why don't you go through those messages and I'll get us a snack." She sets her laptop on the coffee table in front of her and gets up. I go back to my messages. I pull my computer a little closer and start reading my messages. I start with the oldest ones. Most of these don't matter anymore because I have since done the assignment or missed my window to do the assignment.

But the last three are helpful. They are newer assignments that I thought I turned in, but my teachers are saying I didn't. How do I figure out what happened? I sigh, and realize I am grateful Vanessa is here to help me with these mysteries.

She walks up with a plate of cheese and crackers. "What'd you learn?"

"That I need your help chasing down these last three assignments. The rest are so old they don't matter anymore," I admit.

"If you start checking this daily you will be in much better shape," she advises, putting a piece of cheese in her mouth.

"Thanks for helping me," I say in all sincerity.

She nods and turns my laptop toward herself to see what we have to track down. I flop back into the couch; this is going to take longer than I thought.

In the end, Vanessa helped me figure out that the three assignments didn't upload when I tried to upload them. Maybe my wifi was off, or the system was down, or something, but they didn't make it. I had all the assignments saved so we uploaded them again. Then she showed me how I could look to see if they made it.

She also taught me how to make my own list of things to do from the calendar online. She felt that the calendar had a lot of stuff on there that is done in class and can be confusing when doing homework.

"Why does it have class stuff?" I ask.

"So that if you're sick you can just log in and see what you missed," she explains. "It's nice when you're sick. But it's confusing when you aren't sick and are doing stuff in class."

"What do you do?"

"At the end of each day I write down in my paper calendar what wasn't done in class. What I need to do at home."

"Where do you write it?"

"I put it here, on the day it's due. That also helps spread out the assignments and looks less scary."

"You put it on a weekly calendar?" I ask her, looking at

her paper planner.

"I like it better than monthly. There's more room to write."

I get out my paper planner. I have never actually used it. A few times teachers made us write in them the first week. After that, I kind of forgot about it.

I flip to the current week, then I look at the calendar.

"Don't you want to list them on the calendar the day before they're due?" I check with Vanessa before I write anything down.

"Almost everything is due at midnight so you can do them the day they're due. I think writing stuff down on the day before would be confusing. You can always work ahead."

I nod in understanding and start writing in the assignments across the week on the days they are due. It takes me a minute to sift through what will be done in class. Once I'm done, I see I only have four things that will not be worked on in class.

"It's not so bad," I say, looking at the things written in my planner.

"Right? Way better when you write down only what has to be done at home. But still check each day because when you don't finish something in class, it becomes homework. Those are the tricky ones."

I look at my week coming up and it doesn't feel nearly as overwhelming as what I have been experiencing all school year.

"Now, let me show you the modules. It's basically the same thing as the calendar. It is another way to see your assignments. Some teachers put assignments there and forget to put them on the calendar. You have to check both."

Great, just when I was feeling better about this, she throws another step at me. I take a cracker and try to focus on what she is telling me.

"How often do you check both?" I ask around my cracker.

"Every day, Marissa," she says as if I'm brainless.

"Got it," I reply, trying to save some of my dignity. I remain silent the rest of the time she is showing me the modules.

"What do kids do that don't have older sisters?" I wonder.

"They listen in class," she says with a sideways look that looks so much like our mom. As much as her motherly looks annoy me, I am grateful for her help so I keep my comments to myself.

I reach up and knock on the door while my mom waits in the car to see that I get in. I hear running feet and then Trista swings open the door. I turn and wave to my mom and walk inside.

"How long do we have?" she asks.

"She says she's coming back to get me in an hour. It will probably be more like two though because she loves Target on a Sunday," I answer, following her up to her room.

"Cool, what do you want to do?"

"It's too cold to play gymnastics," I reason, looking around her room.

"We could go back up to your house for that," she suggests, knowing there is gymnastics equipment in our basement. "But maybe we try to find something here before we start asking for rides."

She goes to her closet and at the very top are a few games. "Do any of the games looks fun?" she asks, turning to me. I scan the titles, all the usuals.

I plop on the bed and lean back, "I don't really feel like a game."

She walks over to the foot of the bed and looks at me. "What's going on with you?" she eyes me.

"I don't know. Nothing. Everything." I moan.

She sits down. "Start with something."

"Good one," I laugh.

"Seriously though, what's up?"

"I'm just, I'm just not who I thought I was," I finally admit. It sounds so dumb and hurts so much all at the same time.

"Who do you think you are?" Trista asks confused.

"You know- the smart one."

"You're still smart," she says, rolling her eyes. "Marissa, how can you possibly doubt that?"

"Because I don't get As anymore," I wail. "And I have to study and not get zeros."

"Aren't the zeros the worst?" she chimes in. "I'm humming along in a class with my little A or B and then, wham! One forgotten assignment and I'm all the way down to a D. It's so mean," she complains.

"Right? So mean," I agree.

We are quiet for a moment until I have the courage to tell her more. "It's more than that, Trista," I whisper.

She waits so I continue. "I have been diagnosed with ADHD."

She rolls her eyes again and says, "If anyone here is ADHD, its me."

"I'm serious, Trista. And you're just loud, that's different."

"Aren't kids with ADHD usually disruptive, that's not really you," she observes.

"A lot of kids with ADHD can be disruptive. I don't

396

have that, but I still have other traits, so it counts," I explain.

"Oh. So, what's the problem?"

"It mostly means I get distracted. I have a hard time focusing on what's important, that kind of thing," I shrug. "Middle school means I have to study now and that's hard for me."

"Welcome to the party. Most of us have been studying all along. What have you been doing?"

"I was just listening halfway in class and getting As," I admit.

"And now you can't?" she clarifies.

"Now I can't."

"I still don't understand the problem."

"Trista, I'm not me! I'm not the perfect, smart one," I yell.

She frowns, "I still don't see why not."

"I'm just not! How can I be perfect when I have a disorder? I hate that word by the way. *Disorder*. Like there's something wrong with me."

"But there is, isn't there?" she asks, making me crazy.

"You're not helping," I laugh.

"Marissa, who said you had to be perfect?" she exclaims. I'm silent so she continues. "I know you are a machine when you compete and never fall. But one of these days you will. What then?"

"I did fall. Remember? I was mortified."

"But why? We all fall," she reminds me.

"I don't know. I guess I never had before so everyone expected me not to," I try to explain.

"No, we didn't," she fires back at me.

"It's . . . it's, it's my thing, okay? Other than that one time, not falling is my thing."

"Yeah, but you're a Level 6 now. Your skills are getting harder and you *will* fall."

"And get Bs," I add while we're listing my future failures.

"I don't see the problem," Trista presses.

"The problem is, I'm not me."

"You mean not perfect?"

"Same thing."

Trista frowns for a minute and says, "That's not how I think of you."

"How do you think of me?" I ask, very curious to hear her answer.

"You're my friend who is logical, serious, and kind. You like gymnastics and chess and the color purple. That all seems more you than someone who is perfect all the time."

I smile at her very sweet and accurate description. "Thanks, Trista. I needed that."

"Now can we play?" she asks, done with our heartfelt moment.

"Rummikub," I say and she grabs the game off her shelf.

CHAPTER 27

I successfully talked Trista into coming to the chess tournament with me Friday after school. She doesn't really like chess, but she likes me and Logan, so she agreed to come. My mom dropped us off at the host middle school and went shopping with Vanessa. Apparently, they need to find a new dress for her next concert.

"It looks nice out. You think it's going to be warm, but you step out, and it is so cold!" Trista exclaims, tugging her coat closer together

"It is beautiful," I agree, looking at the blue sky, the colorful leaves, and the mountains that have a good amount of snow on them already.

"You think I'd be used to it by now," she mumbles. Trista moved here from California three years ago, but she still has California blood and always squeals at the cold weather.

We pick up our pace in the brisk fall air so we can get in

the warm building where the tournament is being held. We get to the door and there is a sign telling us to go to a different door. Without a word, we hustle around to another side of the building and see signs for the tournament. When we finally get inside, the warmth hits us, burning my cheeks a little.

"This way," Trista says, pointing to a sign that is instructing us to go down a hall and into a gym. There are four rows of tables. Each row has six tables, one for each of the six players on a team.

"That's a lot of chess boards," Trista marvels, taking in the twenty-four tables kids are setting up chess pieces on.

"I think that's our section," I say, pointing to an area of the bleachers that has a hand drawn sign with the name of our school taped to the wall.

"No one is here," she observes, following me.

"It's not exactly a spectator sport," I remind her. We walk over to our section of the bleachers and sit down about halfway up.

"Actually, let's go a little higher so I can see the boards better," I suggest. Trista just nods and we walk up a few more rows and sit down. "This is better," I decide, pulling out my binoculars.

"You are such a nerd," she says to me.

"You love it," I reply as I look through my binoculars. I can see the boards and pieces easily. "Logan's board six. I don't know if he will be at our end or the other end of the room."

"Wouldn't they put the best players by us so we can see?" she reasons.

"You would think, but who knows. We are either by board 1 or board 6."

Since no games are going on I set down my binoculars and see my teacher is gathering the team together. He looks up at the bleachers. Seeing me, he waves me down. As an alternate, I'm surprised he wants me over there.

"It looks like my teacher wants to talk to me," I say hesitantly to Trista. I feel bad leaving her.

"Go, it's fine. I brought a book," she says, waving me away. I smile, grateful for her independence.

I walk down the bleachers and over to my team. I'm wearing our school chess T-shirt, even though I probably won't play. I notice that other teammates not in the tournament are in their T-shirts too.

"Thanks for coming everyone. Where is my board one?" he asks. Eli raises his hand and our coach gives him pointers about the first school he is going to play. "To the rest of you, this team has weak openings but can finish the game well. Try to get them in check early. They also like to run the clock down, be careful of that."

I'm impressed Mr. Belsky has knowledge about the style of each team. "Where are my alternates?" I raise my hand. "Good morning. It looks like everyone is healthy. But sometimes kids get sick mid-tournament and we would need you to step in. Stay in our section of the bleachers so I can find you if I need you." I nod in agreement.

"To the rest of you who came to cheer us on, thank you! It helps your team more than you know. Okay, hands in, ready? Go Snowcap!"

"Go Snowcap!" we repeat. Before I go back up to the bleachers, I study the score board behind the judge's table. It's scored like other tournaments I've been to. Five points for winning, three for stalemate, and zero if you lose. If you run out of time your opponent gets three points and you get two. All six kids on each team play seven times. The games are limited to sixteen minutes, eight per player. I bet most of them finish before that. I notice middle school kids are less patient and basically like speed chess. It will be interesting to see how they play in a tournament.

I head back up to the bleachers. "St. Mary's school's coach is a grand master," I tell Trista.

"What does that mean?" she asks, looking up from her book.

"It's like having a coach that was an Olympian," I try to explain. "Or at least a coach that was a college gymnast."

"Does that mean you guys are in trouble?"

"It might. That would be so cool to be trained by a grand master," I say as I sit down and pick up my binoculars.

Trista leans over and whispers, "What are you looking for?"

"I'm just making sure I can see the boards and the pieces," I whisper back. Since nothing is happening, I lower the binoculars and turn to Trista. "How's gym going?"

She seems a little surprised by my quick change of subject and just shrugs. "It's good, I can't believe my season is almost over," she admits.

"So, you scored out?" I ask, surprised I haven't heard about her scoring out already. Or have I just been in my own world?

"Not yet, you saw at the first meet that I fell on beam. The other meets I have been so close, like within tenths of a point."

"You have a meet tomorrow, right?"

"Yes, we leave tonight after my dad gets off work. I'm already packed, which is why my mom let me come here this afternoon."

"Where is it?".

"St. George. We compete tomorrow afternoon."

"You'll score out tomorrow," I state it as a fact.

"I plan to," she grins, but I can tell she's worried.

"How are your Level 6 skills?"

"That has never really been the issue. I always just

needed to score out," she reminds me. "I have my layout on floor, of course. I have been competing my layout on bars. Beam is iffy, but I can do back walkover, back walkover if I have to."

"And vault?"

"Vault is vault, we can all do the timers," she comments.

"You really are ready for Level 6, aren't you?"

"Just have to score out," she grumbles, putting her elbows on her knees and her chin in her hands.

"And you will join us this winter?" I ask, "Or wait until next year like I did?"

"I don't have other stuff like you, Marissa. I will move up as soon as James lets me."

"But you'll finish the season, right?"

"Yeah, it will be fun. For the first time competing is not this huge stressful thing. I actually feel solid in all my skills."

"Me too."

She looks at me. "Impressive."

I lean into her. "Stop," I say, and we laugh.

"When are they going to start already?"

"This must be how parents feel at gym meets," I say, looking around for Logan.

"For real," Trista agrees.

We are silent as we watch the teams gather around and an adult finally picks up the microphone. The announcer introduces the seven schools and reminds us of the rules and the scoring. Then she points out the scoreboard, which is just a whiteboard with a grid of the names of the teams down a column and the row across the top with the table number. In the middle are squares for the score they get at each game.

We watch as each school takes their seat down a row.

"The best are at the top, farthest away from us," I comment.

"That's dumb," Trista blurts out, making me laugh.

"I agree, the number one table is the game we want to watch and it's farthest away," I complain, picking up the binoculars. "I can't even see it that well because of the other tables lined up in front of it."

"At least Logan is close," she says. I pull down the binoculars; he's close. That will be good.

We watch as all the players shake hands and get their games started. It is silent in the room with the exception of the clicking of timers as kids make their first moves and click the timer over to their opponent. There are so many games going I on, I can't seem to focus on any one game. I wish I could see the number one games better.

My attention moves over to Logan. He has a solid position in his game but his opponent is no slouch. Their game is going to be a while. A few hands are raising to indicate a game is done or the players have questions for the officials.

The officials go over to those tables, look at the game, write down the score, and tell the kids they can move the pieces to set up the next game. I see they set it up with the white on the opposite side of how the last game had it.

"Why are they switching the sides the pieces are on for the next game?" Trista asks me.

"I guess because white has a slight advantage. And if that school doesn't move down a row and stays on that row, then they have a disadvantage. Interesting."

"Did your tournaments do that?"

"No, I never competed for a team though. We just drew for white or black. Honestly, it doesn't really matter unless you are at grand master level," I assure her.

"This is serious stuff then," she surmises, leaning back on the bench behind her.

"Or trying to be," I giggle. We watch again in silence until I see that Logan almost has his opponent in check.

"Logan's about to win."

"Really?" she asks, sitting back up.

"Done," I predict as he moves his rook over, trapping the king. Logan stops the time and his opponent extends his hand in a gesture saying he knows it is over and good game. They shake and then Logan raises his hand to get an official over to look at the game.

"Wow, you called it," she says. We watch Logan stand up and we start clapping.

"Way to go, Logan!" Trista calls out and he looks up and smiles shyly. Trista turns to me, "How did you know?"

"That he was about to win? I just know the game. Just like you know when someone is going to land correctly in gymnastics. You know what you're watching for."

"Tell me what I am looking for."

"Really?" I smile; my sister gets so annoyed when I chatter on and on about chess.

"Yes, otherwise this is going to be a long afternoon," she drawls.

"Fine," I laugh. "So, you win by getting the other person's king. But he is not the most powerful, the queen is,"

"Of course," she interrupts.

I smile, "Of course. Then there is the castle, called the rook; the pointy one, called the bishop; and the horse, called the knight."

By now most games are ending and I absently watch how our team did as I continue to explain the basics to Trista. She is avidly listening making me wish I had brought my travel set and I could just show her.

We watch as Logan moves over a row along with the rest of the kids from our school to play their next game. I continue to explain the game the best way I know how as we watch kids shuffle around and scores go in boxes.

"This game has been around forever, hasn't it?" she

asks.

"One of the few ancient games left, like mahjong," I say.

"Let me guess, you know that one too."

I laugh. "I do, actually."

It was a fun afternoon watching my team play chess and bantering with Trista. I'm a little bummed I didn't make one of the tables. I'm aware that I haven't been practicing chess the way Logan has. He's been playing other classmates online as well as reading strategy books.

We are watching the last of the seven games. Logan must be tired because he is making some silly mistakes. I don't look through my binoculars anymore; I know he is going to lose this one. I shake my head to myself, not sure how he lost his edge.

"What is it?" Trista asks me.

"Logan is going to lose this one," I predict.

"How do you know?"

"He lost his queen and a rook. He loves to have two rooks or the queen with a rook to close. I'm not sure he can put her in check without them."

"The rook is the castle?" she asks.

"Yeah."

"Well, at least he won more than he lost," she says, trying to find the positive.

I smile at her. "He did, but it's not his best."

"Do we always have to be?" Trista raises an eyebrow at me.

"What do you mean?"

"Do we always have to be our best? I mean, can't he have off days?" she presses.

"Maybe when you're practicing, but not in competition," I answer.

She looks at me, "Have you always been like this?"

"Like what?"

"Like, I don't know, expecting perfection?"

"I don't expect perfection," I defend.

"It makes sense, you never goof up at meets. I thought you were just lucky or a really calm and collected competitor," she continues.

"I am," I say.

"Or maybe a mistake isn't an option," she pushes.

I look at her and she looks at me. "It isn't," I finally say.

She lets out a breath, "Wow, Marissa, you've *got* to lighten up."

"Why? It's why I'm good at stuff."

"You are, but it seems stressful," she observes. "Marissa, you are allowed to make mistakes and not be perfect. In practice and meets. And violin and school for that matter," she declares.

Who made her in charge of what I am allowed to do? How I am allowed to think? I know she is trying to be a good friend, but it's kind of annoying.

"They're done, let's go talk to the team," I say, standing up and making my way down the bleachers. Trista follows me and I'm glad our conversation is over.

CHAPTER 28

I know I need to check my homework, but I just don't want to. It is such a drag to have to do homework on the weekend. I begrudgingly find my backpack in the family room and pull out my laptop. I lug it over to the kitchen counter. Once I have it open and trying to connect to the internet, I decide to get my planner. I'm going to use it the way Vanessa showed me. I walk over and dig through the notebooks in my backpack until I find my planner.

I settle in at the counter. Why does school have to be such a drag? Can't we just learn while we are there?

I start with my missing assignments. I click on to the button that takes me to the list of all our assignments and the grade for the quarter so far. I see I have a C in science class. Why do I have a C? I look down at the list and see I am getting 100% on almost everything. Then I see it, all the way at the bottom. Two assignments with zeros next to them. I read what the assignments are. I remember them. I started both of them, I think I even finished them. I didn't turn them in because I thought I could do a little better and then I forgot about them. I click to my saved files, and sure enough, there are the two assignments I have missing. I read the little paragraph I wrote. I was right, it's not great. It is certainly better than an F, but not great. Do I just turn it in or fix it?

I hate this; there are so many assignments I can't really do my best work. If I do, I will be here all day. I decide to see how many zeros I have before I decide if I am going to turn them in as is or fix them and make them better.

I click into each class and the outcome is about the same in each one. I have a B or C or even D because of missing assignments. Most of the missing assignments I have started or even finished. I didn't like them so I never turned them in.

What am I going to do? I put my elbows on the counter and my face in my hands. Trista was right; I'm wasting so much time trying to be perfect. I need to just turn in all this stuff and I'll bring my grades ups to at least Bs.

"Are you okay?" I hear my mom ask as she walks in.

I look up. "I don't know," I wail.

"What is it, Marissa?"

"I have to either turn in garbage, or if I turn in good work, then I get too far behind and have zeros. I'm not sure which to do," I moan.

"That seems so extreme, does it have to be one or the other? You can't turn in mostly good work?" she asks me.

"Not if I don't want to be here all night," I whine.

"You have tomorrow," she reminds me.

"Mom! I'm serious, It's like they want me to do bad work."

"Who is they?"

"My teachers!"

"May I see what you're talking about?".

I turn my list of assignments to her. "These are all the

assignments I have started but not finished."

"I thought you were caught up on your zeros," she mumbles.

"I get caught up and new ones pop up. I can't seem to finish stuff in class," I admit. "I don't know, it just takes me longer than other kids."

"May I see some of your assignments that are half finished?" she requests.

I pull up one of them and turn the computer to her. While she is reading, I go to my green folder and flip through papers until I find a science page half finished. Then I grab a math page that is done, but I didn't show my work. I set those papers next to her.

She looks up at me, "Marissa, what you wrote is good. Why didn't you turn it in?"

"Because it's not good enough. I was going to clean it up a little. Add a closing paragraph."

"Something is better than nothing," she mumbles and picks up my math paper. "This is done, why didn't you turn it in?"

"I didn't show my work."

"Why?"

"Because I did it in my head. I was going to add in the blah, blah of showing my work later."

She doesn't say anything but picks up the third paper. Then she takes off her glasses and looks at me.

"Marissa, your perfectionism is getting in your own way," she finally says.

"You're the one that wants me to be perfect," I pout.

"I never said that."

"But you expect me to be like Vanessa,"

"I never said that either."

We are quiet for a minute. I'm embarrassed at my failure in school and I'm not sure what excuse to throw out next.

"Yes, I expect you to do well in school because I know you can. I also know you have gymnastics and violin and chess and that you are not exactly like Vanessa. We are learning that your brain works differently."

"It's different alright," I agree, trying not to cry.

"Marissa, turn this stuff in! Even if it's not perfect. Getting a B or C is better than a zero. A zero is two Fs, remember? You are trying for 100% and getting a 0%. It makes no sense."

"I just always think I'm going to get to it and then I don't because the work keeps piling on."

"That's why you have to turn it in when it's due, even if it's mediocre."

"I hate that."

"Marissa, what do you do in a meet when you're not ready?"

"I'm always ready," I sass back, even though it's not entirely true.

"I think in Level 5 you were ready and it seems like you will be ready for Level 6. But remember when you were slow to learn your kip. What did you do?"

"A lot of hoping," I retort. She looks at me and I know that's not the answer she's looking for. "I did my best."

"And what happened?"

"I fell on my first kip and made my long hang kip," I answer, remembering back to that very scary intersquad.

"You fell. Why are you afraid to fall in school?" she asks, with her head tilted to the side.

"Because I'm supposed to be smart!" I yell at her.

"Oh, peanut," she says, taking my hand. "You are smart. And no grade can ever take that from you. Don't let grades define you. They are to help you see where you can do better. They help teachers see if they are doing their job. They help me see if you need additional help at home. It's just a

411

measurement for all of us. It does not define you."

I am silent as a few tears escape and I quickly swipe at them.

"Do scores define you in gymnastics?"

I sniff, "No, but it sure is fun when you get a good one."

"Have we ever expected you to get all tens?"

"No," I laugh at that silly idea. "But Mom, if I don't get school under control, aren't you going to take me out of gymnastics?"

She frowns. "Not take you out, per se, but maybe see if we can cut back your hours."

"But then I won't be able to do Level 6!" How did I get into this mess?

"Marissa, based on this work here," she says, holding up my papers. "I think you can do both. Let's just go down the list and turn everything in.

I swallow my tears and nod. I turn the computer back to me and say, "Where do we start?"

"How about with the most recent assignments that aren't locked yet. Then we can see what's left."

She gets up to get herself a drink as I scroll through my missing assignments in each class and find all the ones that are still open. She sits back down with me and makes me turn in all my half-done work. I really dislike turning in lousy work, but I do it.

Once all of it is turned in, and I have check marks next to everything in my planner, I look up at her and say, "Now, what?"

"Now we don't get behind like that again."

"No, I mean about my grades."

"We wait. Your teachers will update them in the next few days."

CHAPTER 29

"I scored out!" Trista yells to me as soon as I walk near the door to science class on Monday.

"Oh, awesome! I knew you would," I exclaim walking into class with her. "Did Carmen?"

"Yep, it was a great meet. And it was so warm down there," she says, referring to St George.

"I wish I could have been there," I say, setting my bag down at my desk.

"It was a little far to just come and watch."

"I know," I agree.

"What was your best event?" I ask. Before Trista can answer, our teacher tells everyone to be seated. I do what she says, knowing Trista will be able to fill me in at lunch time.

I take my seat and the teacher starts talking about the new unit. All I can think about is that Trista and Carmen will get to workout with us now. I know they plan to move to Level 6 as soon as their Level 5 season ends. I wonder when that will be. If I remember right, we were done last year before the Thanksgiving holiday.

I pull out my planner and flip through the calendar to look at the dates. I should write my meets in here. I flip to the to-do page and make a note for myself to get the meet schedule from my mom. My teacher stops talking and the classroom gets noisy as everyone begins opening their backpacks and pulling out their laptops. I am guessing my teacher just asked everyone to do an assignment. I have no choice but to pretend I know what's going on and pull out my laptop too.

I start to panic for a moment because I don't know what I'm supposed to be doing. I look to the kids on either side of me and it looks like they pulled up the school site and went to the class page. I do the same thing, and thankfully, I easily find our in-class assignment listed right at the top. I read the instructions and get to work.

After class, Trista quickly makes her way over to me and picks up our conversation right where we left off. "My best event was floor of course. Then vault was a close second." I nod to indicate I am listening as I try to fit my laptop in my backpack. My backpack is stuffed to the limit since I rarely stop at my locker. "Bars were fine. Not great, but not bad either." I finally get my backpack shut and zipped. I stand up and start walking out of the class; Trista walks in step with me. "Beam was solid. Well, maybe not solid. I did wobble a lot but I stayed on."

"That's awesome, Trista, truly," I say. "When will you start working out with us?"

"After State Meet. We won't workout with you until our season is over."

"Did you do your layout on bars?" I ask her about one of the few upgrades you can do in Level 5.

"No, James and I decided to play it safe until I scored

out. I'm planning to do it at State though."

"When is State?"

"The weekend before Thanksgiving."

"Wow, coming up. Our first intersquad is the week of Thanksgiving. The day before actually."

"I know. James talked to Carmen and me and told us we would miss that intersquad. He said there was another one though. Is that right?"

"Yeah, the first Saturday of winter break."

Trista lets out a breath, "So we have a month to get ready for Level 6."

"You already have all the skills," I remind her because she looks a little pale. When she doesn't say anything I add, "Maybe focus on State first."

We enter the cafeteria to the usual chaos and make our way to our table.

"Well, I'm excited for us to workout together again," I add as we sit down.

Logan hears this and asks why we get to workout together. We explain to him what scoring out means and why we will get to be on the same team again.

"And I thought soccer was complicated," he murmurs.

I can tell Trista's elation is gone and is replaced by some other emotion. Anxiety? Fear? Maybe overwhelmed? I'm not sure, but I decide to change the subject. I ask Logan about soccer and he says he has one more game before his season ends.

"Then what do you do?"

"What do you mean?"

"You said you play year-round. What do you do when it snows?"

"We train at an indoor soccer arena."

"Oh, that's cool, like an indoor pool," I say, trying to picture an indoor soccer field.

"I guess. It isn't real grass and the field is smaller. It's a faster game indoors, but you don't run as far."

"What are we talking about?" Nate asks, sitting down with his tray.

We repeat Trista's news for him and how Logan is ending his soccer season soon. I feel bad Nate misses so much just because the lunch line is long. He doesn't seem to mind. I think we are all just grateful we have a group to eat with.

CHAPTER 30

Paige and I walk into the gym early Wednesday morning. Since we don't have school the Wednesday before Thanksgiving, Katie likes to hold the first optionals intersquad that morning. Then we take a break for the 4-day holiday weekend.

I remember watching Paige do this last year and I feel like I've come so far. Trista said she was coming to watch our intersquad. I wonder if any of the other compulsories girls will be joining her.

I rub my hands together as I slowly walk up the stairs to the Optionals Room. Despite the freezing cold gym, I like competing in the morning. I open up my locker and set my bag inside. I sit to take off my fuzzy boots and I decide to keep my socks on. I can at least keep my feet warm while we run and stretch.

Maya and Kayla come in and give us a groggy hello as they walk to their lockers. I've never been in this room when it has been so silent. I look at them again and they look sleepy. I look at Paige and she tips her head to the door indicating that we should leave. I shut my locker and follow her out of the room. When we get out into the parent viewing area, she says, "It looks like they needed a few more minutes of sleep."

"Hi, girls!" Debbie greets us, reaching the top of the stairs with her hands full of boxes. Savannah is behind her loaded down too.

"Let me help you," Paige says, stepping forward and grabbing a box from Debbie.

"Thank you, sweetheart! I brought coffee and donuts for the parents this morning," she explains, looking around for a place to set everything down. I quickly scan for the table we use for dinner at PNO. It is folded and leaning against a side wall. I run over to get it. Savannah sets down her boxes and comes to help me.

"Your mom is so thoughtful," I tell her as we open the legs on the table and set it upright.

"She's also extra," Savannah smiles.

"You love it," Debbie says, unphased, as she sets her boxes on the table. "Thanks, girls. There's enough here for you when you're done."

"Save me a chocolate," Paige requests.

"Sprinkles," Savannah chimes in and they look at me.

"Maple, if you have it," I say.

"Done. Now go warm-up," Debbie says, hugging Savannah before she runs into the Optionals Room to set her bag down.

We run down the stairs as more teammates are coming up. We hear Debbie greet each of them by name and they tell her what doughnut they want saved for them.

"The heat is on," Katie tells us, walking out of the coaches' office. "Warm-up together when everyone gets here," she continues, skipping a morning greeting and getting right to business. "I will stay here to greet the judges."

"Debbie brought coffee," Paige offers.

Katie looks up from some papers she is holding. "She did? That was brilliant. I'll send the judges up if they want some."

We nod and head into the gym.

"Do you have any events you're worried about?" Paige asks me.

"Not really, I'm doing all my A routines. They have skills that are solid for me. The B routines are when it might get nerve-wracking."

"I'm feeling good too."

We sit down and stretch as we wait for everyone else to get here. Maya and Kayla come down talking quietly. Savannah is close behind them. They sit down with us and Kayla asks us if we feel ready.

"I think I'm ready. Is there anything I should know that is different in optionals?" I inquire. Kayla is a Level 10 and I have looked up to her since I started gymnastics.

She thinks for a minute and finally says, "In optionals you can cover up your mistakes."

"Cover up mistakes?" I repeat.

"Yeah, because the judges don't know what you are going to do. In compulsories, if you are supposed to do a back tuck and you balk and end up doing just the round-off, back handspring, the judges know. And you get huge deductions. In optionals, they don't know what you are going to do. Only you know your mistakes so cover them up and pretend it's what you meant to do."

"Thanks," I say, appreciating the advice.

Our group gets louder as the rest of the teams arrive.

"We can probably get started," Kayla decides and stands up.

Kayla leads our running, stretching, and complex. Then Katie comes out with the judges and Melony. Katie introduces us to the judges and decides to start us on floor and beam. That way if we run late and classes come in we will at least be done on floor.

"We ran into that problem last year. Let's do floor first. Level 8s, 9s, and 10s go to floor. Do two of each pass and then let me know your order."

Then she looks at us. "My 6s and 7s, to beam. Same thing, two of each skill and come to me when you're done."

I go over to the two chairs that are in the training area and throw my sweats on the chair. We don't have time to go upstairs. I'll put them away when I go up for grips before bars.

"Good idea," Riley says and throws her sweats on top of mine.

We walk over to the beams and get to work. I start by warming up my leaps, jumps, and turns. Then I jump down and let someone else up. James comes in and starts setting up a mat for dismounts without a word. Then he pulls a block over for the judges.

"We are going to compete on this beam. Warm-up your dismounts here," Melony shouts out to us. I look at the beam and no one is over there. I decide now is as good a time as any to warm-up my dismounts. I walk over, climb up, and get to the end of the beam. I ask Melony to stand there for the first one. She walks over and says, "You don't need me here, but I will do it today since you're warming up quickly."

I do my two dismounts and get back over to another beam to warm-up my back walkovers. While I am waiting for a beam, I watch floor. They are tumbling in the diagonal, trying to get in two of each pass before we start.

My team is quiet as we warm-up. I look up into the viewing area and I see Carmen sitting next to Trista eating a sprinkled donut. I smile and wave.

"Marissa, a beam is open," James tells me. That snaps me back to warm-ups. I jump up on a beam for one last turn.

By the time I am done and ready to compete so is everyone else.

"Okay, ladies, let's start with Level 7s on this event. Victoria, Riley, Savannah, Lucy, Alexis, Paige, and Marissa."

I can't decide how I feel about being last, but since I can't do anything about it, I try to tell myself I am happy with the order.

I sit next to Savannah and we watch Victoria go stand by the beam and wait. Watching my teammates compete in optionals is more fun than compulsories, especially on beam and floor. We watch as Victoria starts her routine. I know she is nervous about competing her new back handspring series. She does her series but falls out of the second back handspring. I can tell she is happy she did the series in the first place and is not upset about the fall.

Then Riley does her new series too. She sticks it but falls on her new leap combination. You can definitely tell we are at the beginning of our season.

Savannah is up next and she does a nice back walkover, back handspring series. She makes the skill but wobbles and falls after her feet connect. Like Victoria, I think she is happy she is going for the skill and even made it before falling off. We call that a 'clean fall.' She will get credit for completing the skill and have a deduction only for the fall.

Lucy is up next. Although she looks nervous, she throws her back handspring series. Lucy falls with a grin on her face because she's happy she threw the skill. Then Alexis is up and she does a back walkover, back handspring. These are hard for Alexis and she falls too. I feel bad my teammates are having such a hard time.

I watch as Paige walks over to the beam. She and I are the only Level 6s today. By the next intersquad, Trista and Carmen will be joining us.

Paige does a clean and beautiful routine with a round-off as her flight element, which looks so hard to me. She is working on a round-off, back tuck. That combination along with giants are keeping her from Level 7. She will get both; I know she will.

As Paige prepares to dismount, I stand up and walk over to the competition beam. I give Paige plenty of space as I watch her do her front pike dismount. The team claps for her, but we don't give out hugs like we do at a meet. I hold up my hand for her as she walks by me and we high five. She had a great routine that she can be proud of.

I take a deep breath standing by my beam. I watch as the judge adds up Paige's score and then hands it to Drew, Alexis' brother, who is working the score stand for us today. "Marissa is next," the judge says to James.

"This one is a Level 6 too," James tells her and she makes a note on her clipboard.

Then she looks up at me and says, "Marissa?" I acknowledge that I am, in fact, Marissa, and I salute her back. Then I turn and walk over to where I need to start my mount.

I take a deep breath, run, punch, and do a straight jump up onto the beam. I love my mount, but it doesn't look like much for how hard it is. When I add to it someday, it will be cool though. Then I do my leap pass across the beam. They are clean leaps, even if they aren't very split. I do my dance poses and easily do my back walkover, back walkover. Then I do my jumps, full turn, and I am done. I dance my way to the end of the beam for my dismount. I'm done and I stayed on!

I pose before my dismount and then I do my cartwheel,

back tuck off the end of the beam.

I salute the judge and turn to a happy coach.

"It's going to be a fun season for you," he predicts. "Time for bars."

CHAPTER 31

We head upstairs for our grips and our parents know not to talk to us as we pass the parent viewing area. We quickly grab our grips and head back downstairs. Parents and gymnasts generally don't have a chance to talk during a meet and the point of an intersquad is to emulate a meet.

"Why aren't we just switching to floor?" Savannah asks.

"Upper optionals aren't done yet," Victoria answers. "They have as many girls as we do and their routines are longer."

I look out the window as we walk back down and see they are waiting for Kayla to compete.

"They're not even halfway through," Paige points out as we run down the stairs.

James comes over to talk to us while we put our grips on. "Alright ladies, we want to warm-up pretty fast. One set of push away kips to get you started. Then one first half, one second half, and one full set. I will stand there for all dismounts."

We nod, and girls start walking over to the chalk tray. I secure my second grip in place and follow my teammates.

"Warm-up on either set; we are competing on this one," James instructs, pointing to the set that has a mat under the high bar for all of our dismounts. He has the judge situated on a spotting block to the side of the set we will be competing on.

My only concern on bars is my clear hip into my tuck flyaway. I am relieved James will be standing under the high bar for all dismounts. Usually I am fine, but sometimes I don't have a very high clear hip and my swing into the dismount is slow and wonky.

My first dismount in my second half is fine and I'm feeling better. I chalk up and watch my teammates who are competing giants for the first time struggle with nerves and making them around. It seems like the big jump is not from Level 5 to Level 6, but from Level 6 to Level 7.

I watch as Savannah and James have a serious conversation. Then she comes over to the chalk tray.

"Are you okay?" I ask her.

"I'm not making my giants around and they scare me over here," she admits.

"What will you do?"

"No giants today. Basically, a Level 5 routine," she murmurs quietly.

"You have several more weeks, Savannah. And even another intersquad," Paige says, catching the end of our conversation. Savannah puts on a brave smile and nods in agreement.

"Who's up?" I hear James yell, and I run over to do my full set.

Once we are all warmed up, bars competition will go by extremely fast. I am up first so I don't even sit down. I add a little chalk, readjust my grips, and stand by the low bar.

The judge, who has been waiting for us to warm-up, immediately salutes me. I salute back, take a deep breath, and begin. I jump into my kip, pike-on, front sole circle, kip, pike-on. *So far so good*, I think as I jump to the high bar. I swing into a long hang kip, cast, clear hip, *(here we go)* out into the tap swing. I swing down into my dismount, controlled but barely high enough. I let go for my dismount, feel James bump me in my flip, and I land on my feet. I turn and salute the judge. Then I look at James. "You were going a little slow and you let go early," he explains.

I'm bummed he had to help me, but it sounds like I would have landed very short if he hadn't. "Overall good routine. Nice and clean. We just have to get that clear hip to flyaway more consistent and you'll have a solid bars season."

I nod, and I know he is done speaking with me and ready to go talk to Paige.

I walk over to my teammates as I take off my grips. I sit down to watch the rest of the girls, but I don't say anything. I can tell they are all thinking about what they need to do.

Paige does a clean routine that I can tell she is almost bored of. It will be good for her when she adds in her giants. Then Savannah does her routine, also without giants. I can tell Savannah is extremely frustrated and I miss her happy smile. Lucy and Alexis are wracked by nerves since they are doing their giants by themselves today. I'm proud of them for competing the skill even though Alexis falls on hers. Victoria swings a nice routine and lands a beautiful layout flyaway. Overall, I think bars was a successful rotation. It is still pre-season; my teammates will make their skills by January.

When the rotation is over James turns to us. "Take off your grips and leave them over here, ladies. Let's not waste time this morning going back upstairs." We do as he says and leave a pile of grips on the floor along the wall by the doors into the lobby. "We'll go to floor next," he announces.

The upper optionals have not been done for very long. They are only just now warming up beam. I can't believe how much faster we are.

"Their meets must take forever," I comment to James as we walk over to floor.

"Not really, there are less kids in the higher levels so they sometimes finish even before you guys. We just happen to have a big upper optionals team this year." I look over at them. I guess it is a big group. Maya and Payton moved up to Level 8 and no one graduated or quit last year.

"Two of each pass and let's start," James yells to the group, snapping me out of watching beam.

Floor is by far my favorite event to watch my teammates compete in. Everyone has a different routine that fits her personality and I love it. Lucy is up first with her spunky routine, then Savannah with her sweet one. Paige and I are up after them. I'm nervous to compete after Paige; she is a tough act to follow. Her dance is so beautiful and classic. No wonder our ballet teacher, Madame Julia, loves having Paige in class. I stand up when she finishes her last pass and walk to my corner.

This routine is easy for me, at least the passes are. I still have to concentrate on the dance to do it the way Melony intended. I wait in my corner. James doesn't have time to come over to talk to me this time and it is honestly okay. It's not a real meet and I'm not worried about any of my skills. I watch the judge calculate Paige's score and hand it to Drew. Then she turns to me and raises her arm. I salute her back and walk to my starting corner. I stand in my pose waiting for the music to start. When the music begins, I feel calm. The music helps me know what to do. I dance to my corner and easily do my round-off, back handspring, back tuck. Then I do a decent leap pass, a dance sequence, and I'm already to my second and last pass. I run and do a front handspring, dive roll. Then I stand up, do my one and a half turn, strike two poses, and end.

I turn and salute the judge. That was easy, maybe too easy. I probably need to add the layout soon.

James gives me a quick high five and goes over to Alexis who is up next.

I happily watch the rest of the routines. It almost feels like I'm done with the intersquad since all we have left is vault. My vault timer is easy for me.

In fact, this has been the easiest intersquad I have ever had. In Level 4, I didn't even have all my skills; in Level 5, I barely had my skills in time. Does this mean I am finally ready for a season, or that I'm not pushing myself? Maybe I could have added a few B skills to my routines today. It looks like everyone else is trying some on at least one or two events. I am doing A routines on every event today.

I look up at the parent viewing area and Trista gives me a wave and a thumbs up. I give her a weak smile. I may look perfect today, but am I really doing my best?

CHAPTER 32

After the intersquad, my parents rush Vanessa and me home so they can get to the grocery store before the Thanksgiving crowds get there later today.

"Kay, I can do it on my own," my dad volunteers.

"But I'm preparing some special dishes and I need the right ingredients. You get what you need for the turkey and I'll get what I need. The girls can stay home."

"You just seem to be on overload," he comments.

"A little, but I want to go," she says as we pull up to the house.

"Can we go in the hot tub while you guys are gone?" I ask.

"Straighten your room first, then you can. Grandma and Grandpa will be here tonight," our dad answers.

"Oh, and change the sheets on the guest bed," my mom adds.

"Then we'll never get to the hot tub," I whine.

"Marissa, we all spent our morning at your meet when we really should have been home preparing for guests. You need to jump in and help now. Changing the sheets is a small thing."

"Okay," I agree, feeling guilty now that I understand my meet is probably why my mom is wound up.

"We've got it mom; anything else?" Vanessa, Miss Perfect, volunteers.

"Putting the sheets on the guest bed and straightening your rooms is enough until we get back," our mom answers.

My dad pulls up to the house and Vanessa and I jump out. We walk to the house as they pull away. We use the code on the front door and let ourselves in.

"Do you want to change the sheets first or do rooms?" she asks me.

"I need to eat something first. I'm starving," I say, walking to the kitchen.

"Fine, but then, Marissa, you have to help me."

"Okay, okay, let me just eat something. Start on your room and I'll be up." I open the pantry door and stare at the shelves to see if something good presents itself to me. Sometimes having an older sister is like having a second mom. In good and bad ways.

I reach for a box of crackers and eat them as I walk up the stairs. I can't remember how messy my room is. How much will Grandma and Grandpa really be up here anyway? I walk into my room and see that I need to make the bed, get some clothes off the floor, and probably straighten up my desk.

I sit on my bed and think about my morning. I easily hit all four events, which feels really good. I have always loved doing exactly what I set out to do. Although, last state meet I fell on beam and as embarrassing as it was and how horrible it felt at the time, no one treated me differently. I was still

430

part of a winning team and my teammates understood. It was the first time I wasn't perfect and nothing terrible happened. Today I was perfect again and it was a little blah. Compared to my teammates who were trying new skills like their series and giants, I was hardly trying at all. It felt a little lame. Don't get me wrong, I don't envy the nerves some of my teammates had while competing a new skill for the first time, but I do envy that they are pushing themselves and adding new skills.

Maybe perfection means you can't have both. If you are going to be perfect, it has to be easy. Although, Level 3, 4, and 5 weren't easy for me so much as they were set routines. I knew exactly what I had to do. In Level 6, you can do your basic routine or add to it. I'm not sure when it is right to add something.

I set my box of crackers on the nightstand and lay back on my bed. I think I need to try for my B routines by the next intersquad, even if it means not being perfect. No one else was today, why do I have to be? *Because that's your thing* a little voice in my head says. *No*, I argue with myself, *it's Vanessa's thing; she can be the perfect one.* Besides, I already blew it at school.

"Are you done yet?" I hear Vanessa coming down the hall. I quickly sit up, but not before she pops her head in and sees that I was laying down.

"You haven't even started!" she sputters.

"I was thinking," I try to explain.

"Now we're never going to make it to the hot tub."

"Yes, we will. Look, I'm working on it right now," I say getting up. I stand up and look at my room, not sure where to start.

"Let's just make the bed so that's done before they get back," she demands and leaves my room. I follow her to the guest room where our grandparents will be staying.

Our mom has left clean sheets out on the bed. Vanessa picks them up, sets them on the nightstand, and begins stripping the bed. I walk around to the other side of the bed to help her.

"Are you excited?" I ask her.

"Of course, I love having them here," she says, unhooking the corner of the fitted sheet.

"They always bring cool stuff," I say, pulling the sheet back with her. We get the fitted sheet off the bed; Vanessa wads it up and throws it into the hall. Then she picks up the folded sheets. She finds the fitted one and tosses it on the bed. It takes us a minute to figure out which side goes up. Once we do, we secure it onto the mattress on our respective sides.

"Why is mom so stressed out?"

"She always is when Grandma comes, especially for Thanksgiving."

"Oh, I never noticed," I admit.

"Not surprised, you've always been in your own world," she says, flicking out the flat sheet. I watch it billow down to the mattress.

"Why does everyone keep saying that?" I grumble, grabbing a corner of the sheet and pulling it up to the top of the mattress.

"Because it's true," she says, like only a sister would.

I feel dumb if I really have been out of it. Or have I just been a kid? I don't know what to say so I remain silent as we add a blanket and pull up the bedspread.

Vanessa throws a pillow and pillowcase at me and I start to shove the pillow into the new case. "Do you think I should be on meds?"

She looks up surprised. "For ADHD?"

"Yeah."

"I guess if you need it. I think that's a question for

Mom." I shake the pillow the rest of the way into the case. "I don't think there's anything to be ashamed of though," she adds.

"Did Mom talk to you about it?"

"No, but I heard her and Dad talking," she admits.

"And?"

"And they seem worried. They are reading a lot of books and talking to a lot of people."

"I think everyone is making a big deal of nothing," I admit, throwing the now encased pillow up on the bed. Vanessa adds the decorator pillow and smooths out the bedspread.

She leans back and surveys the bed. Satisfied with our work she says, "Come on, let's hit the hot tub."

"What about my room?"

"I'm going to let Mom deal with you and your room."

It might be bad if Mom comes home and finds my room is a mess and I'm in the hot tub. "I'll just straighten up a few things and meet you down there," I decide.

I walk back to my room and survey it from the doorway. Maybe if I just get the clothes up off the floor, that will help. I pick up clothes from the floor and throw the obviously dirty stuff in the dirty clothes. A few of the sweatshirts on my bed aren't very dirty so I shove them in a drawer and quickly make my bed by pulling up the comforter and calling it good. I leave it lumpy with no throw pillows on top, but it looks good enough.

I quickly change into my swimsuit and run down to meet Vanessa. She is just getting the cover off the hot tub when I walk outside.

"That was fast," she says.

"It wasn't that messy."

She gives me a look but doesn't comment. Instead, she says, "I grabbed you a towel."

"Thanks," I say, dipping a toe in; the water is perfect. Not too hot and not too cool. I step in and lower myself down. Then I scoot over so Vanessa can use the steps.

"You looked good this morning," she says. "Trista tried explaining everything to me, but I don't get it. I just know you stayed on and looked 'clean' as you guys call it. Your teammates were all over the place."

"They were doing harder stuff, that's why," I explain.

"That's what Trista said too. Shouldn't they be ready though?"

"Well, they were, with their easier routines. A lot of them put in the harder skills today."

"Did you?"

"No"

"Why not?"

"I wasn't ready, I guess," I mumble. I hold my hand out sideways on the top of the water and let the bubbles collect on the edge of my palm.

"There you guys are," my mom peeks outside. "Did you make the bed?"

"Yes," we answer.

"And clean your rooms?"

"Yes," we confirm.

She gives us a skeptical look and then says. "Okay, when you're done soaking, shower and clean up for their arrival. I also got flowers you can arrange and put in their room."

"Fancy," Vanessa says, making me laugh.

"You can do the flowers; I'm probably going to have to clean my room some more," I admit, knowing my mom is not going to accept the half-done cleaning job I did.

CHAPTER 33

My mom was too busy making dinner to notice my room. I cleaned it to her standards anyway. Or at least I tried.

When I finally get down to the kitchen, I find my mom and sister there assembling pot stickers for tomorrow's appetizer.

"Oh good, you're here. Will you set the table?" she asks me.

"Sure," I agree. I see my dad's comfort dish of brown angel hair pasta with butter and jasmine rice on the counter. "Where's Dad?"

"He went to the airport to pick them up. We'll eat as soon as they arrive," my mom answers.

"What are you making tonight? Besides the pot stickers."

"The eggrolls and peeling potatoes. I can do both stuffings tomorrow."

Our family makes a traditional Thanksgiving dinner

along with a few Chinese dishes. When my mom says both stuffings she means the American stuffing along with a Chinese stuffing, called lapxiang. I like lapxiang better, it has short grain sticky rice with sausage, so yummy.

I grab plates from a cupboard and place them around the table. I remember to get six plates instead of the usual four. As I am setting the table, I hear my grandparents come in from the garage. As soon as they enter the house, Vanessa and I run over for hugs, my mom right behind us.

"Oh my dears, look how much you have grown!" Grandma exclaims.

Then we move over to Grandpa, who hugs us absent-mindedly, while he asks my mom how she has been.

"I have presents for you girls," Grandma sings before she is even all the way inside the house. "Where is my bag?" she asks Grandpa.

"Carl is bringing them in from the car," grandpa says. Right on cue, Dad comes in with the bags and is heading for the stairs when Grandma stops him. "Let me get in there really quick to give the girls their presents."

"Mother, you don't have to bring them something every time," my mom pleads.

"Yes, I do! Let me spoil them, Kay," she says. They go through this every time my grandparents visit and Grandma always wins.

My mom sighs as Grandma goes over to Dad and grabs a smaller bag off his shoulder, telling him the rest of the bags can go up to their room. Grandma comes over and flops her bag on the couch and rummages around for a minute before she finds two small velvet bags. She hands one to me and one to Vanessa.

"Thanks!" we both exclaim, eager to see what she brought us. I pull the drawstring open on the bag and pull out something wrapped in tissue. I quickly unwrap it to find a beautiful hair clip with a pink flower made of stones, gold trim, and gold leaves. It has rhinestones sprinkled between the flower and leaves.

"It's beautiful, Grandma," Vanessa gushes, turning hers over in her hand. I look to see hers is purple. Feeling envious of her purple one, I start scheming to trade her later.

"Thank you, Grandma," I say. "How do you use it?" I wonder, opening the clip.

She comes over to me and gently gathers my hair together like she is going to do a ponytail, but instead of securing it with a band, she twists it, then lifts the twist along my head and slides the clip in as she holds the twist to my head.

"There, what do you think?" I reach up and feel my hair in the twist.

I run to the bathroom to look, turning from side to side in the mirror. It looks very grown up.

"So beautiful," Vanessa says from behind me. I move out of the way so she can see herself. I look at the back of her hair, knowing that is how mine looks too.

"Do you think we can get them like this again?" I ask her.

"We'll have to practice."

"Do you want to trade?" I whisper.

"You are so predictable. I knew you would want the purple one."

"Do you like the pink?"

"I do, but we have to wait until grandma is gone to trade."

"Girls! Dinner!" we hear my mom yell for us.

"You know she's not done giving out presents," Vanessa says as we walk out of the bathroom.

This is going to be a fun weekend.

Vanessa was right. Before the night was over, Grandma gave us each a new dress, a sweatshirt, and Hello Kitty school supplies. My mom keeps grumbling that she's spoiling us. We know all we have to do is have good manners and Grandma wins the argument.

The morning of Thanksgiving is uneventful. It's too cold to go outside, but there is no snow yet for winter activities.

Mom and Dad spend the day cooking and shooing Grandpa out of the kitchen while we play games with Grandma. She is the best person to play games with because she lets us pick out whatever we want to do. She even plays three games of chess with me. Something that no one else in my family will do anymore.

"Girls, go get dressed; our guests arrive soon," my mom instructs. I leave my game with Grandma and do as she says. Most of our large extended family is in San Francisco so my parents invite friends over who, like us, don't have family in town. I know she expects us to wear a dress or skirt for dinner. I pick a simple gray skirt and mauve sweater. I don't bother with tights since we are home and won't be going out in the cold. I slip on my black slippers, since we don't wear shoes in the house. I brush my hair and run back downstairs to finish my game with Grandma.

When I walk downstairs it smells so good. I realize I should probably abandon my game with grandma and help Mom with dinner.

"What can I do to help?" I ask my mom as I enter the kitchen.

"Perfect timing, Marissa. Can you take this tray and offer them to our guests?" she asks, handing me a tray of pot stickers. I see my dad has left the kitchen and my mom has allowed my grandpa to help her finally. "Just set it on the coffee table and come back in for napkins."

I walk into the living room and find my dad talking to four adults I vaguely remember from last year. I set down the tray and hurry back to the kitchen for the napkins. When I come back in, my dad reintroduces me to his friends and I politely say hello. They ask me how school is and I lie and tell them it's fine.

"What do you enjoy besides school?" One of the women asks.

"Gymnastics and chess," I answer.

"Wow, you like difficult hobbies," she observes warmly. I never thought about it like that, but I guess I do.

"Her school even has a chess team," my dad says as Vanessa walks in. Vanessa is introduced and asked the same questions, giving me a chance to sneak away. I would rather help my mom than make small talk.

I go back into the kitchen and my mom and grandpa are hovered over the turkey as they determine if it's done. It is a golden brown and looks done to me.

"What else can I do?" I ask my mom.

She turns and smiles. "You can stir the gravy." She quickly gets out a small pot, puts in the juice from the turkey, adds corn starch, and hands me a spoon to start stirring. I know to stay here and slowly stir until it thickens. I watch as the kitchen is a flurry of activity while they get all the dishes ready at the same time.

Just as my gravy is ready, my mom declares it is time to get all the dishes to the table. My sister, mom, and grandpa start taking trays and bowls to the table. She grabs my pot. "Looks great, peanut," she approves and pours it into a gravy boat. "Here you can take this out and I think we are ready."

I carefully take the gravy into the dining room and set it down. The table is impressive. We have everything. Turkey, mashed potatoes, stuffing, lapxiang, egg rolls, pot stickers, and cranberry sauce.

My mom invites everyone to sit. Since Vanessa and I are the only kids, we sit with the adults this year. I sit down, eyeing the homemade pot stickers. This is going to be a good dinner.

Vanessa and I are quiet through most of dinner as we let the adults talk. After dinner my mom tells us to play violin for our guests. I'm so rusty that I only do a few songs with Vanessa and she does a few more on her own.

It is fun to play for people though, because they think we are good, even though we are just okay. After our guests leave we are back in the kitchen. My dad carves the rest of the turkey so we can save the meat for leftovers. Then he takes all the bones and boils them, making a broth. The broth will be added to jasmine rice to make a soup called jook. We'll eat the jook for the next several days.

Finally, when the kitchen is clean and the leftovers put away, my dad invites my grandparents to watch the video of my intersquad. I wish they had been in town for it, but this is almost as good. I don't realize how proud my parents are of us until they start gushing to my grandparents.

After we watch my routines, my parents put on a family movie, but only Vanessa and I end up watching it. My parents are on their laptops looking at Black Friday deals, Grandma is reading, and Grandpa falls asleep on the couch.

Today was a big day; I am looking forward to relaxing and playing mahjong and chess over the next three days.

CHAPTER 34

The month of December is here. I'm finally getting the hang of using the online calendar at school and writing in my planner. I must still be missing what teachers are saying in class because I'm surprised at what I find in the assignments online when I get home. I also still struggle to finish assignments in class. I've been casually asking Trista, Logan, and Nate if they finish in class. It seems like everyone has enough time for almost everything except me. I've decided to talk to my mom about it, but I haven't found the right moment yet.

Carmen and Trista are working out with us now that their Level 5 season is over. I can tell they are cramming to get used to their routines before our next intersquad.

I have been trying to upgrade my routines. I want to push myself in the same way I see my teammates pushing themselves. I'm so close to having my back handspring on high beam. I plan to do it in my routine at the intersquad.

Katie lets me do them in my routine with two mats under the beam, but I'm only allowed to have one mat if I want to compete it at the intersquad, or any meet, for that matter.

I've also been doing layouts on floor and bars. Floor has been going well, but I land short whenever I do layouts on bars, even with a spot. Those will probably not be ready in time for season.

It's kind of fun to work on upgrades that don't have to be in the routine. It's so much less stressful than compulsories where we had to either have a skill or just not compete.

We have completed our conditioning list that Katie gave us when we finish our floor workout. We are dragging panel mats to the floor for stretching. I love the feeling of accomplishment at the end of a good workout. The hard part is done and I can sink into my splits and talk to my friends.

The quiet talking starts as girls slide into their splits. The Level 7s have thirty more minutes of practice than we do. They are just now done with their floor assignment and ready to start conditioning. Savannah comes over to get the list from Paige.

"Your fulls are looking good, Savannah; are you allowed to compete those?" Trista asks, referring to Savannah's layout with a full twist.

"They are a B, so I can compete them," she assures her.

"That feels like a hard skill for a B. Anyway, they look good."

"Thanks, I bet you'll be doing them soon."

"Sevens are you done with floor?" Katie asks, coming out of the office that she ducked into a few minutes ago.

"Yes, we were just going to start conditioning," Riley says.

"Gather round first and then you can go condition." They do as she says, coming over to where we are in our splits. "You guys stay in your splits," she says to us. "Anyway, I have a quick change in our agenda. The judge that was going to come to our intersquad Saturday morning was flying home Friday night from another meet. Her flight just got changed to Saturday. So, she can't come in the morning. The only time she can come when the gym is empty is Saturday night. I know that is less than ideal for your parents in the month of December, but it's all we have. I'll cancel Saturday open gym and we will crank out our meet as fast as we can."

The team is quiet as we take in this information. "What time?" Paige asks.

"I need to check with her, but late; like six, I think," Katie answers, looking at her phone. "I'll email your parents tonight." She looks around at us. "Everyone got that? This Saturday night, not morning."

We murmur 'yes' and the 7s stand up to get started on their conditioning.

"Switch sides," Carmen, who has the stopwatch for over-splits today, says to us.

We slowly and quietly switch sides. "Are you going to be able to make it?" Trista asks me.

"I think so, I don't see why not."

"What do you mean I can't go?" I shriek as soon as Paige is out of the car.

"Vanessa has her Christmas concert," my mom calmly repeats.

"That doesn't mean I have to be there," I reason.

"Yes, you do. Vanessa has been working very hard for this concert and it is her last one with Ms. Brooks."

I think about that for a moment. I like Ms. Brooks and want to go to her concert.

"Maybe Trista's family can take me to the meet and then bring me late to the concert," I try.

"This isn't an actual meet, right?"

"Right," I grumble.

"Marissa, if it was a meet then I would send Dad to the concert and take you. Or let you go with another family. But it is a practice meet and last time you did fine. I think the concert is more important."

"But I wanted to try my new skills," I pout.

"Do you have to?"

No. "Maybe," I fib.

"Tell you what, I will call Katie tonight and see what she thinks you need to do." I'm not sure how to argue with that one so I agree.

When we get home, all I want to do is eat, shower, and go to bed. I start with the dinner my mom has left out. While I wait for it to heat up, I find my laptop and pull up my unfinished assignments from today. I stare at the three assignments I haven't uploaded yet. I asked Trista today at practice how much homework she had. She said she finished everything in class. How come I can't do that?

The microwave beeps and I get up and get my dinner. Chow fun and bok choy tonight, which is a wide noodle stir-fry with cabbage. I work on my three assignments while I eat. The actual brain power it takes to do the work is easy. The time it takes to do the work feels like forever.

When I'm done, I shut my computer, set it by my backpack, and put my plate in the sink. It is silent down here so I assume everyone is upstairs. I find my parents in their room half watching the news, half talking to each other.

"Did you talk to Katie?" I ask, walking in.

"Oh Marissa, we were just talking about you," she says.

I am silent as I wait for her to continue. "Katie said it's not a big deal for you to miss. She said you did great at your first intersquad and that you are ready for your first meet in January."

"I did great because I did all the easy skills. What about if I add my B skills?"

"She didn't seem worried."

"Okay," I say, seeing no way I can go, now that Katie told her it's okay to miss. I stay standing in their room wondering how to bring up school.

"What is it, peanut?"

"It's school," I admit. "I'm doing everything Vanessa taught me. I'm trying hard to listen in class and do what the teacher says. But I still can't finish assignments in class. Not the way other kids can."

I watch my parents exchange a look. Then my eyes land on my mom's nightstand and there is an entire stack of books on ADHD with bookmarks hanging out.

"Marissa, some things are bigger than you. It might be time to try meds," she admits with a sad look on her face.

"Will they hurt me?" I ask, trying to gauge from the look on her face.

"No, but you may have side effects and we may need to try more than one before you feel good."

"Will I feel funny?"

"I don't know," she answers honestly.

"What do you think?" I ask my dad.

"I think you need to do what it takes to help yourself. We can try it and see if it improves your life. If it gives you side effects or makes you feel sad, then we stop."

"Will they make me feel sad?"

"It is a side effect Dad is worried about, but it isn't likely," Mom answers.

"What is the medicine supposed to do?"

"Help you focus," my dad answers this time.

"I feel like I'm focused," I say in frustration. "I just need to work faster."

"It might add up to the same thing," my dad reasons.

"Okay," I sigh. "I want to try it."

My mom stands up and gives me a hug. "I'll call the doctor in the morning."

CHAPTER 35

Lunchtime is my favorite time of the school day. I enjoy talking with my friends and getting a break from tedious classes. Today is the last day before winter break and also the last day of the semester. All our work, makeup work, and any retake tests had to be turned in by yesterday. Grades are finalized today. Since the teachers don't want to assign anything new, we have had a fun couple of days. In science, we played with mini robots and in history we're watching *Hidden Figures*.

I started taking medication to help with my ADHD and it *is* helping. The first day I tried them, I bit my lip all day and it was awful. Then my mom talked to my doctor and we got a different type of medication. I feel like myself on this one. I don't struggle as much to finish things in class or to turn in assignments on time. I will finish the semester with no zeros. As nervous as I am to see my grades, I'm glad the semester is over and there is nothing I can do about it anymore. I think I got a couple of As, three Bs, and a C. I'm embarrassed about the C and I really don't want my parents or Vanessa to see it; but I know they will. At least I know I don't have to tell my friends.

"They should just let us out now," Logan complains, sitting down and setting his lunch bag on the table. "All we're doing is watching movies."

He's right, of course, but I have noticed school is not always logical.

"What are you doing over the break?" I ask him.

"Mostly skiing, I think. I have cousins coming into town and they love to ski here."

"What about you guys?" he asks us.

"Practice," Trista says. "At least in the morning; I'm not sure what my family is doing the rest of the time. It's a busy time of year for my dad's work so we don't travel."

"Marissa?" he turns to me.

"My sister has a Christmas concert and we're going to the symphony. Other than that, just relaxing."

"The line was the shortest it has ever been. I think a lot of kids just didn't come today," Nate observes as he sits down. I look around the cafeteria and he's right; it isn't as crowded as it usually is.

"What are you doing for the break?" Logan asks him.

"We leave tomorrow to visit my aunt in Oregon," he says.

We talk for a minute about what Nate does when he visits family in Oregon and then there is a lull in the conversation.

"The semester is over, what kind of grades did you guys get?" Trista blurts out in a way only Trista does. I know she doesn't mean any harm, but I do not want to share my grades with anyone here.

"Mostly As," Logan answers. "I might have a B in

history because we had to give a speech and I'm really bad at that." No surprise that Logan has all As. That's how I expected middle school to go for me as well.

"How about you?" he asks Trista.

"Same, only I have a B in Spanish. And maybe in math. I don't test well in math. I do all of the homework and study for the tests, but then I second guess myself when we take tests in class."

"I don't know how I ended up at the nerd table. I pulled out three Bs and three Cs, and I'm proud of it," Nate declares. " I worked my butt off to manage a C in Cutler's class and I study hard for my Bs."

"Everyone learns differently, Bs and Cs are still good," Trista says, trying to make him feel better.

"I know. My parents are giving me $15 for each B and $10 for each C. I started the year with Ds and Fs; they're going to be overjoyed."

"You get paid for good grades?" I exclaim flabbergasted. *And since when are Bs and Cs good grades?*

"How much is an A?" Trista asks.

"Twenty bucks," he beams, even though he has no As to collect his twenty bucks.

"You're getting seventy-five dollars for nothing?" I marvel.

"Not nothing, for getting good grades," Nate corrects me.

The table is quiet at his declaration that a 2.5 grade point average is good. Maybe he's right; it's good for him. Just like my grades consisting of a mix of As and Bs will be good for me. They are not up to Vanessa standards, but clearly, I have more challenges than she does staying organized and paying attention. I worked really hard for each grade.

"I'm not sure of my grades," I tell my friends. "I think it will be mostly Bs," I admit. They all look at me gob smacked. All this time they assumed I had straight As and I never corrected them.

"I've been struggling to stay organized. In fact, I learned that I have ADHD," I share, squeaking out the last D in a little half cry. I take a breath to calm myself because I refuse to cry at school.

"Wow, Marissa, we had no idea," Logan says.

"I was embarrassed; I still am a little. You guys assumed I'm a straight A student and I'm just not."

"But you're so smart," Logan comments.

"It doesn't translate to good grades. Not anymore, anyway. Not when there is so much to turn in and keep track of," I explain.

Trista puts an arm around me and pulls me to her side. "Well, we still love you, even if you are a big dope." I lay my head on her shoulder and I chuckle while a single tear escapes at the same time.

"All Bs would be ninety bucks at my house," Nate announces, lightening the mood at the entire table. I smile and sit up and wipe at my one tear. Thankfully, no one says anything about it.

"Don't be so hard on yourself, Marissa, no one said you had to get straight As," Logan says.

He's right, no one put that one on me except my obsession to keep up with Vanessa. I'm learning we are much more different than I originally thought.

After Logan's mom drops us off, our mom calls and tells us she is taking us shopping to find something for Grandma and Grandpa for Christmas. We quickly have a snack and just sit in the kitchen, quiet and drained. I'm so glad I don't have to worry about school or homework for two whole weeks.

"Are you nervous for the concert tomorrow?" I ask Vanessa.

"A little. I'm excited to perform, but I'll also be glad when it's over," she admits.

We hear our mom honking in the driveway and we run outside to hop in the car.

"Why can't we shop online?" I ask my mom.

"Because that only works if you know what you want to get someone. I have no idea what to get my parents so we are going to the mall before it gets too crowded."

As we are buckling up, she reminds us, "I'm on vacation for a week!"

"And we have two weeks!" I add. We celebrate that thought for a minute as we back out of the driveway.

We drive in silence for a while before she asks us how school went. I let Vanessa answer that one and she chatters all the way to the mall about her classes, her friends, and her performance tomorrow. When we get to the mall, it's crowded and we have to park all the way at the back of the lot.

"Grab your coats," my mom tells us as we get out. It's a cold walk into the mall, since the wind is up. The Salt Lake Valley isn't that cold, even with the snow, because the air is so dry. But when the wind kicks up and whistles down from the mountains, it is frigid. I look up at the mountains as we walk in. They are huge and white. The snow is no longer on just the peaks but covering the entire massive mountains. Somehow, they look taller when they are covered in snow. Maybe it's the contrast to the blue sky.

When we walk into the mall, I'm reminded why I love Christmas time. The mall is decorated beautifully with trees everywhere. I can smell wonderful scents as we pass the different stores: Douglas fir as we pass the candle store, fresh chocolate chip cookies as we pass the bakery, and leather as we pass the luggage store.

"Where should we go?" my mom wonders.

"The jewelry place?" my sister suggests.

"Your grandma has so much jewelry already," Mom sighs, sounding defeated before she starts.

"Not anything from us. And she loves anything we do," Vanessa reminds her.

My mom laughs, "You're right, let's go."

In the end, we get a long necklace with a heart for Grandma and a little tile for Grandpa's key chain that will help him find his phone. My mom lets us stop and get cookies on the way out, because really, who can resist that smell?

I walk to the car enjoying the hot gooey chocolate chip steam in the cold air. I have to eat it fast though before it cools down too much. We get in the car and mom goes through the coffee shop drive-thru for a peppermint latte for her and hot chocolate for us. She is definitely vacation mommy today.

When we get home, my mom goes straight into the family room to wrap the presents we got. I grab my backpack and head up to my room. I shut the door, sit on my bed, and pull out my laptop. Final grades were to be submitted by our teachers by 3 o'clock today. It's 6 o'clock now; all my final grades should be in the computer. I slowly open my laptop and log in. I feel a pit in my stomach as I click over to the list of classes and grades.

Science – A-

Math – A

History – B+

ELA – B

Art – A

Spanish – B

I can't believe my eyes; I earned three As and three Bs! I pulled up my Ds in English and Spanish up to Bs and my Cs in science and math up to As. It may not be straight As, but I am beyond happy right now. If I was Nate, I would be getting over a hundred bucks!

I think my mom is going to be more surprised than I am. We worked so hard to get rid of all those horrible zeros. I grab my laptop and run down the stairs to show her, no longer afraid of what she will say if I don't have straight As. She knows that these grades are my best effort.

"Mom!" I call, running down the stairs. "Mom!" I yell again at the bottom of the stairs. I find her wrapping presents by the tree.

"What is it?" she responds with concern.

"I got my grades!"

"And?"

"And they aren't horrible!" I exclaim.

"Of course, they aren't." I don't know why she thinks 'of course.' I had Cs, and even Ds, before we started working on missing assignments, using planners, and taking meds. "Well?" she prompts.

I open my laptop and show her my list. "Three As and three Bs," I announce proudly.

"That is amazing, peanut!" she exclaims, standing up and giving me a huge hug.

"You aren't disappointed? Not even a little?" I look at her with skepticism.

"Why would I be disappointed? Those are wonderful grades."

"But they aren't straight As like Vanessa," I remind her.

"Who said you had to be just like Vanessa?"

"I don't know; I just thought it was expected," I mumble.

"Look, Marissa, I absolutely think you are capable of straight As in the future. But right now we are trying to get you the tools you need to succeed. You did your best. All we have ever wanted is your best. And I am very proud of these grades."

"Thanks, Mom," I say, giving her another hug.

Chapter 36

We drive up to Sarah's house to pick her up for Vanessa's concert. My mom tells me to jump out and get her. Before I get out Sarah is walking down the driveway toward us.

"Here she comes," I say, sliding over to the middle seat to make room for her.

"She looks nice," my mom comments. I look at Sarah in a red skirt and white sweater. She looks so sophisticated and fun at the same time. Especially since the outfit is complete with white tights that have red poinsettias on them and brown ankle boots.

She opens the car door and gets in beside me.

"Hi, Sarah," my mom greets her and my dad just smiles back at her.

"Hi, Mr. and Mrs. Li," she greets politely.

"I like your tights," Vanessa says.

"Thanks. I found them on this fun website; I'll show it to

you after your show," she replies as she buckles up. "Your dress is stunning," she adds.

"Thanks," Vanessa beams. It is beautiful. It's a festive red dress with a fitted tank bodice and a tulle skirt with little sparkles on the tulle. "Are you nervous?" Sarah asks.

"For the solo, yes. But the group songs are fairly simple. At least for strings."

"Have you ever done a solo?" Sarah continues.

"No. Ms. Brooks is super picky and she usually reserves them for her older kids, which is me now. Her Children's Orchestra doesn't go past eighth grade."

"What will you do after this year?" I inquire.

"Not sure," she admits. I can tell this thought bums her out so I try to think of a way to change the subject.

"When are you up? When should we be paying attention?" I wonder.

"Marissa, you should be paying attention the entire time," my mom says.

"Okay, but like, really pay attention," I qualify.

"My solo is the fourth song."

"We can for sure pay attention to the fourth song," I tease.

My Dad asks Vanessa what the ensemble pieces are, and I don't recognize many of the titles. Probably because I haven't been going to orchestra for two years now and Ms. Brooks has changed up her list.

When we get to the high school, we drop Vanessa off at the front and then go to find a parking spot.

"This school is huge. I don't think I've even been here before," Sarah says.

"Will you be going here next year?" my mom asks.

Sarah's eyes widen a bit as she says, "Yeah, I guess I am."

"Do any of your teammates go here?" my mom wonders.

"Not yet, I don't think. Maya might. It's weird that I don't know," I comment. It's kind of odd; we know our teammates so well in the gym. What makes them laugh, what motivates them, how they like to learn a new skill, how they overcome fear, how they handle pain, their favorite color (at least with leos), and favorite snack. But we don't always know what school they go to. "Maybe we need to put school mascots on our lockers," I add.

"Good idea, because it's embarrassing that you don't know," my mom teases.

We walk across the parking lot in the cold winter weather. We had one storm blow through that took the leaves off the trees and left snow on the ground. The snow has been plowed in the parking lot but there are still small patches we crunch on as we walk. It's light gray out as the sun sets over the mountains. It will be dark when we come out.

Since we had to get here early for Vanessa, we easily find a seat front and center. My dad is delighted by this because he can take pictures.

"You guys can go walk around if you want to," my mom offers. "They don't start for another twenty minutes. Just be sure to come back with a few minutes to spare so you don't disrupt anyone."

We agree and scoot out of our row and walk up the auditorium aisles to the exit. Out in the main hall, we are in awe at how big the school is.

"And I thought our school was big," I comment. We walk over to a glass cabinet full of sports trophies. It seems like every sport imaginable is here, except gymnastics, of course.

"No gymnastics," I notice.

"It's a hard sport for schools to have," she comments.

"But they have a ski team and mountain biking team," I point out.

"I mean, look where we live; it only makes sense," Sarah counters.

"Yeah," I agree, following her along the long row of trophies.

"They have a chess team," Sarah says, pointing to a trophy with a king chess piece on top.

"Really?" I ask, taking a step closer to her. I peer into the glass cabinet and look at the trophy and several pictures of teams from the last five years. "They haven't won for six years," I comment.

"You'll change that when you get here," she teases me.

We continue on past the glass cabinet to look at framed pictures on the wall.

"Hey, isn't this Trista's sister?" Sarah exclaims. "I recognize her from all the times she's picked up Trista from your house."

"Student Body Officers," I read aloud. "Which one?"

"Right here." As soon as Sarah points her out, I immediately recognize Madison. She slightly resembles Trista with her brown hair and hazel eyes. Her picture is under the words Sophomore Officers.

"Sophomore Treasurer, Madison Thompson. Yep, that's Trista's sister," I confirm.

"That's cool," Sarah says. "At least I will know a few people who go here."

"Who else?"

She looks down at me. "Your sister and Madison."

I laugh, "Oh yeah, I forgot you and Vanessa will be here next year. That's weird."

"Right?" she agrees. "We better head back."

I turn around and walk back down the large corridor with Sarah. There are three hallways off the main corridor and all of them have lockers lining the walls.

"Can you imagine this place full of kids?" I try to

imagine the hallways crowded with big kids.

"Not really. It must get loud," she laughs.

"Totally," I agree.

We get to our seats with about five minutes to spare. It's weird to think both Sarah and Vanessa will be going here next year. I cross my legs and jiggle my foot as I think about how much bigger this school is and how I can hardly handle middle school.

The orchestra is on stage warming up and I see Vanessa in a middle row of the strings group. Part of me is sad and part of me is relieved that I'm not up there with her. I guess as we get older and get good at something, we have to focus on only one or two things.

My mom reaches over and sets her hand on my knee to stop my jiggling, which I forgot I was doing. I still my foot just as Ms. Brooks comes up to introduce her orchestra.

She tells us the songs will be a fun combination of classic and contemporary music. Ms. Brooks always picks a song for the end that the audience will recognize. Vanessa said she picked music from *The Nutcracker* this time and I'm looking forward to hearing it.

After about halfway through, it is time for Vanessa's solo. I'm surprised she doesn't walk to the front. She simply stands up in her spot to start the song. When her group joins her after a while, I think she will sit, but she doesn't. I look over and my dad isn't in his seat. He's at the front of the aisle, squatted down, taking pictures of her on stage. When the entire number is over, she bows, and the audience claps for her. My dad slips back into his seat while my mom is clapping furiously. They share a glance and I know they are incredibly proud of her. She has worked hard all summer and fall for this moment. I sigh; she deserves it, even though I'm a tiny bit envious.

After the concert, Sarah and I wait while my parents take

several pictures of Vanessa with her friends, with Ms. Brooks, with her violin. We even take a picture of Sarah and me with her. Sarah offers to take one of our family and my dad is so pleased. He adjusts the camera for her and then runs over to us. I have a feeling this picture will become our Christmas card.

CHAPTER 37

   As I enter the gym Monday morning, I am dying to hear
from my teammates how the second intersquad went. It was
the first Level 6 intersquad for Carmen and Trista. We are
training in the morning all week since school is out for winter
break. As much as I love morning workouts, man oh man, the
gym is cold. I don't bother to go upstairs to our lockers since
no one is else will be in the gym today. The recreational
classes don't train during winter break so I throw my bag in
the cubbies in the lobby.

   "Morning," I hear Trista say from behind me.

   I spin around and find Trista and Savannah walking in,
"How did it go?"

   "Good. All my skills are the same except on floor so it
wasn't stressful. Mostly, I was worried about not
remembering my beam routine since I haven't had it very
long."

   "And did you?"

"I did," she smiles. "Optionals is seriously fun."

"It is," I agree. "Did you make your giants?" I ask Savannah.

"Yeah, but then I fell on beam on my series."

"Good job on the giants though."

"Where's Paige?" Trista asks me since Paige and I usually carpool together.

"At her aunt's farm for a few days. I think she'll be back Thursday."

"Hi, girls!" Katies trills, coming in from the training area. "The heaters are on; go ahead and start running."

We start on floor since it is too cold for beam or bars. Beam will sting our feet and bars will sting our hands. Floor and vault are the best places to start when the gym is cold.

"How about your layout in a routine today?" Katie asks me.

A layout? I guess my layouts have gotten stronger this fall and I could try it in a routine. "Okay," I agree hesitantly.

"The assignment is two full sets. I want you to do one with the back tuck and one with the layout. When you are done with both of those, I want you to work front handspring, front tuck onto an 8-incher."

I nod with a little pit forming in my stomach. I can't decide if it's because I'm excited about the upgrades or nervous. It seems awfully close to the season to be making big changes.

I take a little longer to warm-up my passes, since I need to warm-up a layout too. When I've finally done two good passes of both the tuck and the layout along with my front handspring front, I tell Katie I'm ready for a full set.

"Okay, you're after Alexis." I decide to rest and watch Alexis' routine. She is competing the same routine as last year, only now she has a front handspring, front pike at the end. In fact, the pike is so open its almost a layout. Her front tumbling has gotten good.

"You're up," Katie says to me as soon as Alexis' music stops. I watch as Katie scrolls though the titles on the gym phone. I know she will hit play as soon as I stand in my starting pose.

I walk to my corner and hit my pose. I see my teammates tumbling the diagonal out of the corner of my eye while I wait for my music. I take a deep breath. Layout. I can do this. My beautiful violin music comes on and I dance to the corner. I hear Katie yell out, "Nice and hollow, pull your toes!"

When my teammates hear this, they cheer for me, "You've got this, Marissa!"

I run, round-off, back handspring, set, and instead of lifting my knees, I lift my toes and try to stay as hollow as possible. I see the floor and I am lower than I thought. I land and have to take a huge step forward . . . but I landed!

"Nice job, Marissa!" I hear my teammates yelling. I smile as I run into my leap. Upgrading might be more fun than I originally thought.

I thought for sure I would have a similar assignment on beam as we did on floor. I expected half my routines with the back walkovers and the other half with the back handspring (with two mats). Instead, Katie tells me I am going to add my back handspring in my routine with one mat and to warm them up.

I warm-up my handspring on the medium beam with no problems and do them on high beam with two mats. Then Katie moves the second mat and leaves only one, making me nervous. I climb up onto the beam, look down at the one single mat under the beam, and I don't want to go. Not sure what to do, I step up and stand there like I intend to go and I don't.

Katie calls me over to her and I have a feeling I'm going to have to figure out a way to do this today.

"Marissa, you have been doing your back handsprings just fine for weeks now with two mats. It is time to move one of them," she tells me.

"I know," I say, looking at my feet.

"What happened up there?" she asks.

"It looks really high," I admit.

"Okay, your lizard brain thinks it's a bad idea. What does your logic brain think?"

"That I can do it. I know I can; it's just, it just is high," I repeat.

"What's your go-to for mental blocks or fear?"

I stare at her blankly. I don't know; I've never really had a big block. I've been afraid before, but it never lasted long.

When I don't answer, she asks, "Do you use visualization, positive self-talk, or do you need to do more numbers?"

"Visualization, I guess," I answer.

"Okay, go sit down and visualize yourself doing it correctly on the high beam five times."

I nod and head over to the low beams. Girls are rarely over here anymore since even their B skills are on the medium beam by now. I sit on a low beam, set my head on my knees, close my eyes, and try to visualize my back handspring. I immediately see myself doing it with the two mats. Then I stop myself; that is not what I want to see. I try to quiet my mind. I hear my teammates talking and Katie giving out corrections.

Block it out, Marissa, I tell myself. Then I force myself to imagine myself standing on the beam with one mat below. I see myself step up, raise my arms, and do my back handspring. I also see myself fall off to the side. *Seriously? I fell in my own visualization!* I start again. I conjure up an image of me stepping up and doing a back handspring. This time I make it. Not bad. Four more times. I have imaginary Marissa step up again and do another one. I stick it again. The image of one mat is less scary now that imaginary Marissa is doing it. After I correctly visualize my back handspring five times, I look up.

I'm a little disoriented when I look up. My team seems so loud right now. I watch as they are doing routines, moving mats, clapping, and laughing. It's so much going on at once. I slowly stand up and walk over to Katie.

"How did it go?" she inquires.

"I fell on one and stuck five," I answer.

She chuckles and says, "Falling in visualization happens more than you might think. Are you ready now?"

"Will you stand there?" I request. Katie rarely spots beam. Asking for a spot is a long shot but I know I can do it with her there.

"Yes, but only because I'm allowed to in a meet," she agrees.

As soon as Lucy dismounts from the beam with the one mat, we walk over. I climb up and Katie steps up onto the mat. I look down noticing that it looks a little more familiar now. My brain is not telling me not to go. Although, my stomach might be.

I step up, raise my arms, and hesitate.

"Just like you just did in your head. I am right here," Katie encourages.

Okay, okay, she is right there. I drop my arms and quickly wipe my sweaty palms on my shorts and raise them again.

"You can do this," Katie adds.

I nod and decide to go. I jump back, my hands connect, but I am off to the side. Katie lets me fall to my feet on the mat below. I don't say anything as I jump up again.

"This time think about more than just going. Big jump, shoulders open, look for your first foot."

Okay. I take a breath, step together, lift my arms up, and jump. I think about open shoulders as I watch my first foot connect with the beam. Then I lift my chest as my second foot comes down.

"Nice one!" Katie praises. I hear my teammates clapping and cheering. I look over and smile from my spot up on high beam. "Thanks, guys."

CHAPTER 38

I wish every week was like the week before Christmas. I had amazing workouts in the morning and relaxing afternoons with Vanessa. We played games, watched movies, and soaked in the hot tub. When she had to practice violin, I opted to play chess online with my teammates. Whenever I log in, I have at least two or three turns waiting for me.

Today is Christmas Eve and my family and I are going to the symphony. Every Christmas Eve, we either go to *The Nutcracker* or the symphony. I'm in a fitted deep green dress. It has a simple square neckline with fluttery sleeves and a ruffle along the bottom of the skirt. I pick up the purple clip I got from Grandma (Vanessa and I traded) and twist my hair the way Grandma showed me. Then I secure the clip in, also the way she showed me, but it doesn't feel secure. It feels like it is going to slip out at any moment.

I walk down the hall to my parents' room. "Mom? Can you help me with my hair?"

"Oh peanut, you look exquisite."

"Thanks, can you help with my hair?"

"Sure," she agrees, putting down her mascara wand. "It looks good to me, what's the problem?"

"It feels loose."

She walks over. "Yeah, when you have straight hair like ours it can slip out easily. That is what bobby pins are for." She opens a drawer and pulls out a little bowl full of pins. Then she selects a handful and starts sliding them into my hair and the clip, securing it more tightly to my head. "Does that feel better?"

I move my head slowly side to side. "It does! Thanks, Mom!"

"You are borrowing Vanessa's to match your dress?" she observes, looking at the purple clip.

"We traded; is that okay?" I ask, a little worried we are being disrespectful.

"It's fine. Grandma even asked me which one to give you guys and I told her you would like the purple. Then she mixed them up. She tries," she says, turning back to the mirror. "Your dad is downstairs waiting if you want to join him. He'll be glad someone else is ready."

The symphony is amazing and I love that they do several holiday songs that I recognize. The people are dressed up and the building has at least three Christmas trees and garland everywhere. The trees and garland are decorated in red ribbon and gold bulbs. My mom takes an obscene number of pictures, but to be fair, it is a very pretty setting.

Even with all the glitz and glamour of the symphony and the twinkle lights of downtown, my favorite part of

Christmas Eve is when we get home. My family gathers in our formal living room. Our tree stands at the window, decorated in traditional red and green. Our tree is music-themed, with ribbon that has music notes and ornaments of musical instruments. My dad walks in with a tray of eggnog for each of us. I lift my glass and take a sip; I love it when he sprinkles nutmeg on top. I set down my glass on a coaster that is sitting on the table next to me.

"Are you girls ready for a present?" our mom exclaims.

"Can we have one extra?" my sister asks.

Every Christmas Eve we open two presents. One is our matching pajamas and the other is a book. Vanessa is asking for a third.

"I'll think about it," Mom declares. "First, let's talk about what we have been grateful for this year."

I knew this was coming and forgot to think of something. *Think, think, what am I grateful for?* Vanessa says something magnanimous like she is grateful for learning to play music and reading music or for Ms. Brooks' program; I'm not exactly sure because I am trying to think of something.

"Marissa?" my mom turns to me, "What are you grateful for this year?"

I don't know. Little Miss Perfect took music, which my parents love. I'm grateful for chess? No, they would think that's silly. As I am trying to think as quickly as I can, my clip slides and I reach up to grab it.

"Grandma!" I shout. "I'm grateful for Grandma," I repeat a little more calmly.

My mom smiles, "Why?"

"She teaches us stuff, plays games with us, loves us, and tells funny stories," I say, proud I thought of something worthy.

"And buys us gifts," Vanessa adds, looking at me

suspiciously.

"That too," I admit because there is no denying it.

My mom is a little teary-eyed as she says, "I'm grateful for Grandma too."

"Let's open pajamas," my dad says, done with sentiment for now.

My mom hands us each a gift box. I rip open the package, pull back the tissue, and am surprised at what I see. Rather than Christmas-themed pajamas, I am looking at the cutest flannel set of gymnastics pajamas. They are pink with black silhouettes of gymnasts doing handstands and leaps.

I pull them out excitedly. "Mom! I love them!" I gush, standing up and holding the top up to my body.

"I thought you might," she grins.

I look over and Vanessa is holding a pair with music notes all over. The top reads 'Diva.'

"We don't match," I observe, surprised at this break in tradition.

"You guys are old enough to not have to match anymore. I thought you would like these better."

"I do!" Vanessa confirms, beaming at her Diva jammies.

I carefully fold my jammies back up and put them in the box and set it next to me. When I look up, I see huge fat snowflakes sticking to the front window.

"You guys, it's going to be a white Christmas this year!" I exclaim.

"Wonderful!" Dad exclaims, and I can't agree more.

"How was your Christmas?" Logan asks me at lunch.

"Good, I loved being off from school," I answer.

"Did you get anything cool?"

"A bunch of books and leos," I answer, opening my lunch, "What about you?"

"Games and clothes mostly."

"I hate it when I forget a lunch," Trista grumbles, sitting down next to us with a tray.

"Where's Nate?" I ask, assuming he was with her in the lunch line.

"In the fray somewhere," Trista says, opening her drink.

"How was your Christmas?" Logan repeats his question to her.

"Good, but I'm glad we're back," she says, befuddling both of us. Why would anyone want to be back at school?

"Why?" he questions.

"Because we get to compete this weekend. I can hardly wait," she explains.

"Both of you in the same meet? I thought you were different levels," he says, trying to keep up.

"We were, but Trista caught up and we are both competing Level 6 this winter," I explain.

"Starting Sat-ur-day!" she sing-songs.

"Why aren't you as excited?" Logan asks me as Nate quietly sits down.

"Glad you finally made it," Trista teases him.

"I picked a bad line," he grumbles.

"I'm not sure what skills I'm going to do and that makes me nervous," I answer Logan.

"What are we talking about?" Nate asks.

"Our meet on Saturday," Trista fills him in. "Marissa was just saying she's not sure what she is going to do."

"What are your choices?" Nate questions, digging into the problem.

"Well," I start, trying to figure out how to explain this to a non-gymnast. "My coach is letting me choose if I want to compete routines with simple skills versus hard skills. Hard

471

for me, anyway."

"What are the pros and cons?" Logan prods, always the logical thinker. Which I appreciate about him.

"The routines with the simple skills are less stressful and will score better. The pro of the harder skills is, well, that it would just push me to be better. Probably move me to Level 7 faster."

"Why would you score better with easier skills?" Nate frowns confused.

"I would have less mistakes," I explain. "They would be closer to perfection."

"Are you in this meet?" Nate asks Trista.

"Yes, sir!" she beams.

"What did you decide on the hard stuff versus easy?" he asks her.

"I only have two upgrades so far and they are solid for me. I don't have to stress about it like Marissa,'" she says.

"I vote go for it," Logan finally pipes up.

"Go for the more difficult skills?" I clarify.

"Yep."

"Why?"

"Because perfection doesn't seem like the point."

"Of course, it's the point. Ever heard of a perfect ten? That's a gymnastics thing," I sass.

"Yeah, but you guys are always talking about the next skill and the next level. It sounds like that's the point."

He has me there. I am quiet as he picks up a cookie and drives his point home, "Perfection is boring."

CHAPTER 39

As we drive from our hotel to our meet on the Utah State
University campus, I can't stop thinking about Logan's
comment. 'Perfection is boring.' It certainly is not. Perfection
is beautiful and amazing. Why would he think that? He's
supposed to be the logical friend. Logic says that the sport of
gymnastics is all about perfection. The perfect ten, perfect toe
point, perfect leo. *It's also about leveling up*, a voice reminds
me. That's true, I concede to my voice. Gymnastics is about
pushing yourself to the next level, the next skill, the next
combination. There isn't a limit on any of the skills in the
sport. The men are doing triple backs for crying out loud.

My family is chattering away as a knot forms in my
stomach. I'm going to have to tell Katie which routines I
want to do as soon as we get there and I still have no idea
what my answer will be.

When we walk into the arena, the Level 5s are
competing. Sessions have been going on all morning, starting

with Levels 1 and 2 at eight in the morning. I see James over at bars with his Level 5s.

"Katie said to meet her at the top of concourse C," my mom reminds me. We follow the letters around the top of the arena until we get to C. Right under the C, Katie is standing there in her Perfect Balance polo shirt. A few of my teammates are gathered around her. "We'll go find seats. Good luck," my mom says, giving me a side hug.

"Thanks, Mom," I say, and join my team.

We are a small group without our Level 7s. It's just Carman, Trista, Paige, and me. Savannah, Alexis, Lucy, Riley, and Victoria will be in the next session.

"We're all here?" Katie asks. We murmur that we are. "Okay, I just got a text from James. He said that this is their last rotation and that the sessions have been running on time. Since it is just the four of you, you will only be with me today. James and Melony need to go eat."

"Awards are up here in a banquet room. As soon as they are done competing they will come up here and we can head down there for open warm-ups. It's scheduled to start in fifteen minutes. Any questions before we start?"

"What is our order?" Trista asks.

Katie shuffles through some papers and says, "We are rotating with a team from Wyoming and we start on floor."

"Olympic order?" Carmen double checks.

"Of course," Katie confirms.

Olympic order is vault, bars, beam, floor. Which means that if we start on floor, we will be competing floor, vault, bars, beam.

"Has everyone decided what they are doing?" she continues. I suck in my breath; I haven't.

"Trista, the layout?"

"Yes, coach," Trista chirps.

"Carmen, your flyaway? Are you doing tuck or layout?"

474

she asks.

"Layout," Carmen confirms.

What? My teammates who just showed up a few weeks ago are already upgrading, and I have a stomachache about my upgrades? Why am I so hesitant? What am I worried about? Or maybe the question is, why aren't they worried?

"Marissa? Are you doing your layouts?" she asks me.

"Yes," I hear myself squeak.

"Good, and the back handspring?" I'm silent. I don't want to say yes, but I'm not sure I am a no either. She looks at me and I look at her. Then she finally says, "Beam is the last event. We can decide then."

"Paige, which front tumbling pass? Are you ready for the bounder?"

"Yes," Paige answers.

"Bold group today. This season is going to be fun," she smiles, making a note on her papers.

An announcer comes on the overhead speakers and tells us that the Level 5 session has concluded and that we have ten minutes before open warm-ups, when we will be allowed to warm-up on the floor.

"Go time," Katie announces, and we follow her down the steep stairs of the arena to the floor of competition. She helps us find a place on the edge of the floor for our bags. We sit down and take our shoes and socks off to prepare for warm-ups.

"I love competing here," Carmen comments.

"It is a fun arena," I agree.

"Do you see our parents?" Trista asks.

We search the stands and finally I see them in front of vault. "Over there," I point to them. We try to wave to our families, but they aren't paying attention.

"Open warm-ups begin," is announced over the speakers.

Paige leads us out to a strip of floor for a few laps of running. We take a small section so other teams have room too.

She leads us in our usual runs, chassés, and a short and simple complex. When we are done, we clear off the floor and go get our bags. We strip off our warm-up jackets and pants and wait in our new competition leos. I love this leo. It came just in time for the meet. Instead of several little snowflakes, we have one big snowflake on the side.

As soon as the floor clears off and timed warm-ups are announced, we know what to do without Katie telling us. This meet is a capital cup format which means that we will warm-up and compete as we go to each event.

I start with a round-off, back handspring, back tuck. Katie is standing along the edge of the floor watching us intently.

"The next one is a layout," she says to me as I walk by.

Really? After only one warm-up pass? I nod to acknowledge I heard her and keep walking. I can do it. Same skill just a different shape. I get to the other corner and realize that in this corner I will be doing my front pass so that is what I better warm-up. I run and do my front handspring, dive roll. It's a good thing this one doesn't take much warming up.

Now it is time for my layout. I get to the diagonal and my lizard brain starts in. *Why did I say I wanted to upgrade today? You have plenty of meets to step it up! Remember how fun the intersquad was doing easy skills? You could be perfect today if you just did what you know how to do.*

No! I shout to myself. I don't want to be perfect doing something that is too easy for me. I can do this; I can do my new skills.

I take a deep breath in my corner and run, round-off, back handspring, set, pull my toes, hollow, see the floor, and land. I land a little short and have to run forward. But I did it.

This is a tough call. Back tuck and stick, or layout and get a deduction for a giant fall.

"How do you feel?" Katie asks, seeming to appear out of nowhere.

"I can do it, but I may get a big deduction for landing short," I admit, being completely honest with how I feel.

"A deduction is okay. Early in the season is the time to make mistakes," she comments unconcerned. "Set a little longer and pull your toes faster and you won't land short."

I can do that; set longer, faster toes. Okay. I do one more of my front pass, leap passes, and by that time, timed warm-ups are over.

CHAPTER 40

We stand along the edge of the floor while they announce all the teams of the session and play the national anthem.

As soon as the national anthem is done, Katie calls us over for our order. "This is going to go nice and fast. Your order is Carmen, Marissa, Trista, and Paige."

"Oh, can I go first?" Trista pleads. "Is that okay, Carmen?"

Carmen nods and Katie says, "Fine, Trista, Marissa, Carmen, Paige."

She looks at me, "I want you to go second so you don't have time to sit and stew."

I don't stew. I don't think I stew. It's interesting how differently Katie sees me as an athlete versus James. He always told me I was the solid one and Katie thinks I'm a basket case. Maybe it's because with James our routines were set and I felt prepared. In optionals, routines are always changing and Katie is seeing a different side of me.

We sit along the edge of the floor while we wait for Trista to begin. Floor has always been her thing and she has a huge layout to show off in her first pass. I watch as Trista does a peppy routine, and as expected, a beautiful layout in her first pass and a nice front handspring, diveroll at the end.

I stand up and walk to the side of the floor where I start. Katie comes over to me after high fiving Trista. "The layout in the first pass, right?"

"Right."

"You've got this. Just take your time with the set," she reminds me. She pats me on the back and moves away from me so the judge knows I'm ready.

She salutes me from across the floor and I salute back. I walk to my corner and strike my pose.

"Show it off, Marissa!"

"You've got this, Riss!"

I hear my teammates cheering as my music starts. They continue as I dance to my corner, but I am able to block it out and focus on my pass. Here it goes: run, round-off, back handspring, set, toes, hollow, see the floor, and the floor is way too close. I know I need to pike down to land on my feet. I snap my feet around and land short, running several huge steps to avoid touching my hands to the floor. If my hand touches it would be considered a fall, half a point deduction. Although my huge steps are now probably four-tenths. I finally get my feet together and stand up in a finish position. I listen for my music and realize I am behind my music by about four counts. I hurry into my leap pass and rush the dance over to my other corner. I frantically get to my second corner for my last pass. I take a deep breath and I hear my teammates cheering again.

I run and do a nice front handspring, dive roll, and stand up. I rush my one and a half turn and stumble out of it. I get in a finish position after the turn. I've finally caught up to the music for my last little bit of dance. I hit my final pose when the music ends.

I salute the judges, but I can't bring myself to smile. That was a disaster.

I walk over to my teammates. Katie intercepts me before I get to them and gives me a hug. "I'm proud of you for going for it," she says. I'm not. I would have had a much better routine if I had just done the back tuck.

I don't say anything because I feel like if I do, I might shout at her in frustration or cry, I'm not sure which.

Thankfully, she has to be brief since Carmen is already waiting along the edge of the floor for her turn. Katie looks at me warily and then goes over to Carmen.

When I get to my teammates, Trista and Paige high five me and tell me what a great job I did. I know it's untrue and I wish they would just say nothing after a botched routine. I will be sure to remember that if a teammate has a bad routine; I will say nothing and leave her alone.

I sit down, find my water bottle in my bag, and take a needed drink. Then I settle in to watch Carmen. She does a solid routine (with a tuck, not a layout) and is pleased as she comes off the floor.

Paige is up last and floor is her thing. She is such a beautiful dancer she makes the judges sigh in happiness. I watch her execute a nice high layout with her long eighth grader legs and I'm envious. Like everyone, I'm captured by her balletic dance as she does her leaps and prepares for her last pass. I know this pass is new for her. I throw out a "You've got this, Paige!" when she is in her corner.

She runs and does a front tuck right into a second front tuck. She is low on the second flip and lands with her booty about three inches off the floor, but it doesn't touch. Which means her deep squat and quick jump into a lunge saved her from a fall. She will probably get three-tenths off for the deep squat and low flip, but she made it.

We clap as she finishes up her routine.

"Good save," Trista beams when she comes over to us.

"So pretty," I tell her.

"I love your layout," Carmen tells her..

"Great start, girls," Katie says. "Go to vault and I'll join you. I just have to get our music from the head table."

I put my water away and pick up my bag. Everyone lines up behind me (shortest to tallest) and I walk them over to vault.

Vault is already set up for us with all the mats behind the table. All Level 6s and Level 7s do timers for the more difficult vaults we will be doing in Level 8.

Paige, Carmen, and I all do Tsuk timers and Trista is going last with a Yurchenko timer. Her strong tumbling has translated over to vault and she has a nice round-off, back handspring entry.

"Trista, you are last since we have to change the table for you. Let's see, Paige why don't you start us off? Then Carmen and Marissa."

We walk to the end of the runway where we will watch our teammates compete. Katie will stay near the table to spot if anything goes wrong.

I watch Paige do two slow but clean Tsuk timers. Then Carmen does her two, which are not as clean, but she has a fast snap to her back on the back side.

I stand up and walk to the edge of the runway. This timer was fairly simple to learn and doing it to the mats is easy. Really these vaults are all about body position and learning to do them technically correct so we can add the flip on the back side. That is when it will get scary.

The judge salutes me and I calmly salute back. I step onto the runway, take a deep breath and start running. I hurdle, punch, twist in the air, hit the table and pop up to my feet on the mats that are as high as the table. Then I fall onto my back. I sit up and salute the judge.

I climb down from the mountain of mats and Katie is on the side waiting to greet me. "Your entry started out well, but I need you to look under your arm a little more. And lift your chest faster on the back side."

"Okay," I say. I can do those corrections.

"Great form on your legs and toe point." She pats me on the back and sends me down the runway for my second vault.

I am ready as soon as I get to my starting mark on the runway. I turn around and wait for the judge to raise her green flag. They use a flag on vault because they are so far away from us. We start at the back of the runway and they are sitting by the table where they can see our skill the best.

Twist in my shoulders, chest up, I tell myself as the judge raises her flag. I salute her back and run and do basically the same vault.

"Great job! We'll work on those corrections in the gym," Katie says, aware that I didn't make any changes. I did try; I just don't like big changes in a meet. I like to do what I've been trained to do in the gym.

Katie begins to change the setting of the table and I walk back down to my teammates.

Trista is already standing on the edge of the runway, looking nervous. This is a big, new skill for her. I'm impressed she's doing it. I watch as Katie puts the yellow mat around the springboard and gives Trista a thumbs up. Trista nods and looks to the judge.

The judge has been waiting for Katie to finish her changes to the table and is ready right away. She raises her flag; Trista salutes back and starts to run. She does a round-off onto the board and a back handspring up onto the table and lands on her feet on the mats behind the table. I see she is really happy she went for it and jumps down with enthusiasm. She gives Katie and hug and trots back down the runway. She takes a deep breath before turning back around for her second vault.

"Great job, Trista; same thing!" Paige yells.

"You've got this, Trista!" I join in.

She salutes and begins again. This time her round-off is a bit off to the side, making her punch the board on one corner. We all gasp knowing she may miss the table entirely on the back handspring. Katie jumps in and bumps her back to get her up to the table. Trista barely makes it up and falls to the side of the mats where Katie catches her around the waist and sets her down.

"That was some amazing spotting," Carmen says.

"It really was," Paige agrees.

"I will never question Katie again," I vow, making my team laugh.

Trista salutes the judge and we can see the judge is saying something to her. They have a brief conversation and then Trista gives Katie a heartfelt thank you hug. She walks back down the runway while Katie stays to help the next coach set up the table for his team.

"What did the judge say?" Carmen asks her.

"She wanted to make sure I was okay. I said that I was, although it was scary," she admits with a frown. "Then she said we would just take the score from the first vault."

"Of course, no need to even score the second one," Paige comments.

We all agree and give her a hug.

"You scared us," Carmen says. Even though we make mistakes like that in the gym, somehow it's scarier when it happens in a meet. Maybe because the gym has mats everywhere and meets just have the mats on the landing areas. Or maybe a big goof is so unexpected in a meet.

"I scared me!" she laughs.

"The Wyoming team needs to warm-up vault, let's get over to bars," Paige suggests..

We gather our stuff, my teammates line up behind me, and we go to bars.

CHAPTER 41

I decide that I hate arriving at a meet not knowing what skills I'm going to be competing.

"Start with push aways to get a feel for the set," Katie tells us as we put our grips on. We nod and walk over to the chalk tray and start chalking up our grips.

Paige goes over to the set first and jumps into a kip, pushes away into her second kip, and swings off the bar at the bottom of her kip.

"There's no chalk," she says, surprised. Katies comes over and looks.

"Who stripped these?" she wonders. She goes over to the chalk tray, grabs a block of chalk, a water bottle, and chalks up the bars perfectly.

"Push away kips on the low bar only while I chalk up the high bar," she instructs. Then she jumps up to the high bar and chalks it while she is swinging from it.

Carmen does her kips while Katie fusses with the high

bar. It looks like she is going to hit her, but in reality the bars are so far apart she's not even close.

I take my turn after Carmen and the bars feel normal to me.

"Jump to first halves," she says after Trista takes her warm-up turn.

I easily do my first half and Katie tells me to do a tuck fly away on my second half. I chalk up with mixed feelings about the flyaway. Part of me wants to play it safe and do the tuck and the other part of me wants to compete the layout like I did on floor.

I swing into my second half with my long hang kip, clear hip, swing down, tuck flyaway. I take a step forward on the landing, but other than that it feels good.

"You are letting go a little early on that flyaway. I want you to compete the tuck today." I nod, a little relieved.

Man, the A/B routine business causes a lot more angst at a meet than I'm used to. I am going to have a better handle on what I'm doing in a meet next time.

I chalk up, preparing for my full set and final turn in warm-ups. I walk over and wait for Carmen to finish her set. As soon as she lands, I jump into my glide kip. My routine is comfortable for me. The only part I worry about is the swing out of the clear hip and into the flyaway. I push out of my clear hip into a decent swing and let go for a tuck flyaway sticking the landing.

"Well done. Do it just like that; no more warming up," Katie tells me. I agree as I stand near her to wait for our order.

"Do you want to start us off?" she asks me.

"Sure," I agree. I know my teammates are almost done warming up so I go over to chalk up for my turn.

Katie gives them their order and they go sit down. Then she comes over to me as I move to stand in front of the low bar.

"This routine is getting easy for you. Have fun, swing big," she instructs.

I nod and turn to the judge. Since she has been waiting while we were warming up, she is ready and salutes me right away. I salute back and face the low bar.

I jump into my kip, pike-on, front sole circle, switch grip, kip, pike-on; *almost done*, I think as I jump to the high bar. Kip, clear hip, into a perfect swing down, tuck flyaway. I see the landing and easily stick it. I turn and salute the judge; that was the best routine I could hope for.

Katie comes over and gives me a big hug, "You really do like competing what you know, don't you?"

"Looks like it," I say, a little embarrassed.

Pleased with my clean routine, I walk over to my teammates for high fives. I get one from Paige and Carmen; Trista is standing by the low bar waiting for the judge.

It felt so good to do a routine I have been practicing for weeks, months even. I know this routine didn't exactly push me, but it sure felt good to hit. I sit down and take off my grips while Trista takes her turn. She surprises me by doing her layout flyaway at the end of her routine. Bars used to be a struggle for Trista. Clearly, it isn't anymore.

"Great job doing the layout," I compliment her when she comes over after her set.

"Thanks. James let me compete them in Level 5 so the only change was no tap swings," she tells me.

"You are no longer behind on bars, Trista," I point out.

"Thank goodness! It only took me four years," she laughs.

"True, but you did it."

"Carmen is going," Paige tells us, and we turn and see Carmen saluting the judge. Carmen does a simple routine, basically the Level 5 routine without the extra tap swings.

She is clean and only has a small step on the landing.

Paige also cranks out a solid routine. While she may not have her giants, she is almost to handstand on all her casts and her clear hip. Paige has improved a ton since she got to Level 6. Maybe not as fast as Savannah, Alexis, and Lucy, but she *has* improved.

"Last event. Nothing like ending on beam," Katie declares at the end of our rotation.

We grab our bags and follow her to beam. We have to wait for three girls to finish competing before we can warm-up. We quietly wait and try to keep our talking to a whisper or not at all.

"This is their last one; when she is done, I want you guys to line up. Two of each skill. You have thirty seconds per turn. Know what you are doing before you get up there."

Then she turns to me, "Are you doing your back handspring?"

"No. Yes. I don't know."

"Warm-up both and we'll see," she says.

I know she would let me compete either one. All I have to do is tell her. For some reason, I really don't know. I jump up onto the beam, walk to the front, and easily do my walkover, walkover. Then I leap back the other way, full turn, and jump down.

I walk over to the dismount mat and do a few back handsprings to warm-up. I know none of my teammates are dismounting right now, since we will do them together at the end of our warm-ups. I do another back handspring and feel ready. I think.

Katie has grabbed a mat that was sitting off to the side and slings it under the beam. Paige and Carmen help her straighten it out. I know it is for me. I slowly climb up, and without a word, I see Katie step up onto the mat.

I step together and before I can raise my arms, Katie

says, "I'm right here, you've got this." I lift my arms and immediately swing them jumping into my back handspring. I am slightly crooked, but my hands and first foot make it on and that is good enough for me.

"One more. Think about the mechanics of the skill this time. Jump, shoulders open, see your foot come down." I nod and climb back up.

I step together and pause. Then I think about what she just said. I raise my arms, jump, arms open. I see my foot come down and lift my chest and look at the end of the beam. I nailed it!

"There you go," Katie grins. "Jump down and set up for your mount."

I do as she says. I jump down and find the springboard sitting off to side next to the dismount mat. I pick it up and set it in front of the beam then back up and wait for my teammates to be done warming up. When Paige jumps down, I quickly do two mounts and then move my board out of the way so my teammates and I can do dismounts.

We know we get two each and we don't waste time talking. As soon as one person lands, the next person is already on the beam ready to go.

When we are done, we present ourselves to the judges and then gather around Katie.

"Marissa, you are throwing the newest skill so I'll let you pick your order. When do you want to go?"

"Um, I'm not sure," I stammer, surprised she is giving me the choice.

"First, middle, or last?" she presses.

Since I am all warmed up and ready to go, I say, "First."

"Oh, man," Trista groans.

"You can go second, Miss Impatient," Katie tells her. "Then Carmen and Paige."

Since I am first I head over to get my board.

"I'll set up your board, silly," Katie says to me. "You take a moment to yourself and face the judges when you are ready."

I nod and walk over to the end of the dismount mat where I will start the run for my mount. I watch as Katie puts the board in front of the beam and adjusts it. Then she walks around and adjusts the mat under the beam.

I take a deep breath; I can do this. I turn to the judge, she salutes me, and I salute back. I run, punch the board, and do my little straight jump. It really is harder than it looks. I pose and run into my leap pass. I pose again and pause. Time to do the back handspring. Even though I can't see her, I know Katie has stepped up onto the mat that is under the beam. She is here for me. If I go off to the side like Trista did on vault, she will catch me. I take a breath and step together. I raise my arms and jump back. I think about getting my arms open too late, but I do see my foot come down. Both feet make it on the beam, but I am off to the side a little as I lift my chest. I wobble, drop my chest, and almost fall, but I bend my knees instead and save it.

I can hear my team cheering as I stand up in a controlled finish position. I did it! My heart is pounding in my ears as I do my jumps. I take a breath and step into my full turn. Then I dance a little more, turning around on the beam. I see Katie has moved the board out of the way for my dismount. I step back to the end of the beam for my dismount. I easily do my cartwheel back tuck, landing with only a slight step.

As soon as I salute the judge, Katie picks me up in a hug. "See what happens when you take a little risk? That was a gorgeous routine!"

"But I wobbled," I say, confused with her excitement.

"So what? You wobbled on a new skill and rocked the rest. I'm proud of you."

So what? To a wobble? Confused I go over to my

teammates who are just as excited as Katie. I accept their kind words. It is exciting that I did my back handspring in a meet. I feel a huge sense of accomplishment and pride.

I watch Trista start her routine as I pull on my sweats. I can't believe I just competed my first Level 6 meet and added a few of my B skills. My pride in competing new skills might be greater than my need for perfect routines.

Trista does a clean routine with her two back walkovers. I know she will add her back handspring by the end of the season. Carmen competes a similar routine to Trista's, just with some different dance elements. Paige, however, does not have the shoulder flexibility for a back walkover or a back handspring. Instead, she does a round-off and a front pike dismount.

"Impressive first meet you guys, especially on beam," Katie says to us. "This session is running a little late so the 7s are already here waiting for open warm-ups. Head up to awards. Your parents will meet you there. I have to stay here for the next session."

She turns to Paige. "Paige, make sure no one leaves awards without a parent," she instructs.

"Got it," Paige agrees. "Let me just get my sweats on and we can head up," she says to the team. Katie doesn't wait for us to depart. She immediately goes to the head table to see exactly when the next session will be and to wait for her 7s to come down.

"Does everyone have everything?" Paige asks us. We look around to make sure we have all of our bags, grips, tape, etc.

"Looks like it," Carmen confirms, and we start walking to the edge of the arena where there are steps going up to section X, which is where Katie said awards are being held. As we are walking up, we hear the announcement that our session is over and the Level 7s will be allowed onto the floor of competition. A few stairways over, we see our Perfect Balance Level 7s coming down the stairs.

"Savannah!" Trista yells, and she catches Savannah's eye who waves and then gets the attention of the rest of the team.

"Good luck!" we yell. And they yell thanks back. It's a good thing we are between sessions and no one is competing right now because we are really loud.

"Do you think we'll be done with awards before they start?" Carmen asks.

"It's going to be close," Paige determines. "But we'll catch the majority of their meet."

CHAPTER 42

As always, awards are fun. We don't get a team award because this meet defines a team as five members and we only had four. I placed 5th on bars and 10th in the All Around for my age. I knew taking risks would hurt my scores. But the more I think about it, the more I'm glad I did the new skills.

We leave awards with our parents and join the Level 7 parents to watch our teammates.

"What did we miss?" Andrea, Trista's mom, asks the group as we sit down.

"They just started the first event. You missed Lucy and Alexis on beam. They both did their back handspring series. Alexis fell on hers, Lucy had a little wobble," Debbie, Savannah's mom, fills us in.

I sit next to Paige as she pulls out a packet of red licorice and passes it around.

"You had this in your gym bag all along?" Trista asks.

Paige grins.

"Good thing Katie didn't see," Carmen comments.

"I know. But I also knew that we wouldn't have time to go back to the room. And I wanted a snack while I watch this session."

"Because it's better than a movie," Trista teases.

I look at my teammates standing by the beam in the sparkling Perfect Balance snowflake leos. Lucy, Savannah, Alexis, Riley, and Victoria have all worked hard this fall. I hope they do well today.

I lean back and agree, "Totally better than a movie."

After the Level 7 session, we all go to dinner together and back to the hotel. We talk our parents into letting us swim in the hotel indoor pool before bedtime. When we walk into the pool area we find the compulsory teams and their parents.

"We all had the same idea," my mom notices, walking in and setting towels down by the other Perfect Balance parents.

"Are all the teams here?" Carmen asks, seeing that gymnasts have taken over the pool.

James is sitting nearby talking to some moms and he answers her, "The upper optionals are in their rooms. Hopefully going to bed soon. They compete in the morning. No pools or hot tubs for them tonight."

Actually, as I look closer, I see that he is sitting with a judge, not a mom. I think she was the beam judge today.

I step out of my shorts I was wearing over my swimsuit and lay them across a chair. Trista is faster than me and throws her clothes down before running and flipping into the pool.

When she pops up, James says, "No more, Trista; we don't want to get kicked out."

"But you know that we know what we're doing. We won't hurt ourselves," she reasons.

He smiles. "I know. The staff is already on to us. So until next year, you have to play it cool."

"So when no one's looking," she surmises, looking through the glass walls at the staff working at the front desk.

He has a twinkle in his eye when he says, "I don't know what you're talking about."

"Come on in guys, the water's great!" she yells over to us.

"I think I'll get in slowly," Paige decides.

I'm busy pulling my hair up into a ponytail while my teammates walk over to the stairs.

"I heard you had a good day today," James says to me. I look over at him, wondering how he knows that. And did I have a good day? I mean, I totally goofed on floor and beam, but those are also the events where I did new skills.

"I guess," I say, walking over to him and the judge.

"Katie said that you competed some of your new skills," he explains.

"I did. But I scored better on my bar routine with the easier skills," I point out.

"That is the problem with Level 6 and 7," the judge says to me. "You aren't as rewarded for doing your new skills. You'll be more rewarded on difficulty as you get into the higher levels," she explains.

"So, which do you like doing better?" James asks me.

"Which what?" I ask him.

"Do you like the safe skills or competing your new skills?"

I think about that for a minute as he watches me.

"Both," I answer. "I finally understand the fun of doing

the new skills."

"I agree, it is fun. Good job today," he says and turns back to the judge he is talking with.

I walk over to the steps and Paige is still there. Carmen is all the way in the pool swimming with Trista. They have started a game with the Level 5s.

I sit down next to Paige with James' comments in my head.

"What was the wisdom James was imparting to you?" she asks me.

"He wanted to know if I like upgrading skills at meets," I share.

"Do you?"

"I think I'm starting to."

"I think we all have mixed feelings on consistent skills versus competing an upgrade," she comments.

"Perfection versus Excellence," I summarize. I've been thinking about the difference between these two concepts since Logan told me perfection was boring.

"The gymnastics conundrum. What did your brilliant mind determine?"

"It seems like perfection is impossible, or almost anyway. You have to do something over and over to get it perfect and maybe even hold yourself back."

"And excellence?"

"With excellence, you are stiving for the best you can do. Pushing yourself every day. It's . . ." I pause searching for the word. "Attainable."

Paige steps down another step into the water, squealing a little at the cold.

"You've been perfect for a long time, Riss; this must be hard."

"I fell at state," I point out my one fall on beam at the end of our Level 5 season.

She looks at me sideways, "Once in how many years?"

Trista swims up to us. "Let's get in the hot tub."

"We aren't even in the pool yet," I laugh.

"Then you must need the hot tub," she reasons, getting out.

Paige and I laugh and follow her and Carmen into the hot tub.

I feel so lucky to be with these girls and I feel great about my day. As I watch the water and bubbles swirl around my teammates, I think I finally get what my parents and James, and even Logan, have been trying to tell me. I don't have to be perfect. I just have to be myself and strive for excellence. Try my best at school and at the gym. And try to learn the tools to help my ADHD. None of it means I can't be excellent. I like that word more and more as I let it roll around in my head.

"How's it feels to be an optionals gymnast?" Paige asks us.

"Easier," Carmen says.

"Right?" Paige agrees. "So much better creating your own routines."

"More exciting," Trista adds. "It was fun to watch you guys and the other teams. And the variety of music was awesome."

"What about you?" Paige turns to me.

"It's excellent!" I exclaim, and I know she knows what I am talking about.

THE COMEBACK

By MELISA TORRES

CHAPTER 1

I load my suitcase into my mom's car and say goodbye
to my friends in the hotel parking lot. It's Sunday morning
and I'm driving home with my mom from an amazing meet
weekend in Logan, Utah. On Friday I competed in my first
Level 7 meet. All my Level 6 and 7 teammates were there
and we had a great time in the hotel pool after our meet. Then
Saturday morning we watched our Perfect Balance
Gymnastics Level 8s, 9s, and 10s compete. We spent the
afternoon touring campus and the evening at the college meet
watching Utah State University versus Boise State
University. The college girls are so amazing. I can't believe
my mom ever did that.

"Ready, Alexis?" my mom asks me.

"I didn't say goodbye to Lucy." I locate Lucy across the
parking lot and trot over to give her a quick hug.

"See you tomorrow," she says.

Even though I don't go to the same school as any of my

teammates, I will see them all tomorrow at practice. We train four days a week now.

"Can I sit in the front?" I ask my mom as I open the front passenger side door. I shiver as I get in. It's cold out and just that quick jaunt across the parking lot made my face sting. Logan in the winter is next level cold since it's at an even higher altitude than Snowcap Canyon.

"Not yet, you have to be thirteen and probably a little taller."

Probably a lot taller. I'm small for my age. Sometimes I forget that fact because my teammates are all similar in size to me and my mom is petite. She stands at only five feet, two inches; three of my four brothers tower over her. Drew is the only brother left who is shorter than her, but he is only thirteen. I'm sure he'll pass her up by the time he's done growing.

"Fine," I pout and move to the back seat. It is such a waste; none of my four brothers are here and I still can't sit in the front with my mom. At least I have her all to myself. My mom backs out of the parking lot and we head home.

"Can we drive through McDonalds for breakfast?" I ask and my mom agrees. We get our food and I happily settle in for the two-hour drive.

We are silent as we drive away from the campus and onto the cute Main Street of Logan. It looks like the entire town has been frozen in time. Something from the 1920s. The sun is up and twinkling off the snow. We turn off of Main Street, leaving the stores behind and entering the rural part of town. We make our way to the canyon that will take us out of this high-altitude valley.

"Great weekend," my mom comments.

I nod as I bite into my breakfast sandwich.

"Are you pleased with how you did?" she asks me. We have been around teammates all weekend so I haven't really had time to discuss my competition with my mom. It's nice that Mom knows gymnastics and we can talk about it easily. I watch some of my teammates try to tell their moms about a skill and they have no idea what they are talking about. On the other hand, she isn't as impressed by my progress because she did it too.

"I'm bummed I fell on my series, but happy I made my giant," I say around the food in my mouth.

"I'm so proud of you for making your giant!" she exclaims.

"Yeah," I agree, "and I'm still just glad anytime I go for my series. I mean, it stinks to fall, but at least I did it."

"Is it getting easier?" she asks.

I think about this for a moment. "Not really."

"It will," she confirms.

I'm not so sure, but I don't say anything.

"You qualified for State," she says.

"I did?" I ask, shocked.

"Yes, you got a 32.00 All Around even with your fall. Impressive."

"Do you think I could make Regionals?" Regionals is what I really want to qualify for. In Levels 3 to 5, there is only a State Meet. In Levels 6 to 8 it goes up to Regionals. Level 9 has Western Nationals and Level 10 has Nationals. I didn't make Regionals as a Level 6 last season. I'm dying to go to a big meet like that.

"I absolutely think you can make Regionals."

"How do I qualify?" I ask her. Here is where her knowledge is handy. She'll know the answer.

"You have to score a 34.00 All Around at State," she says. See, very helpful.

I'm silent for a moment. A 34.00 is a lot harder than a 32.00. To make matters worse, scores are generally tighter at State Meets versus a regular season invitational.

"You can do it," she says, glancing in the mirror, checking on my silence.

"I'll have to start staying on beam," I muse.

"You need to be lighter on your hands on that handspring," she says.

"Mo-um," I roll my eyes in major annoyance.

"Sorry," she mutters. "Years of coaching doesn't just go away, Alexis. It's hard not to say anything."

"Try," I say. We drive in silence for a while and I feel bad that I hate getting corrections from her. She and I made an agreement a long time ago for her to just be my mom and not my coach. Generally, she is good at sticking to that rule. Mostly because she's so busy with my brothers.

"How do I become lighter on my hands?" I ask quietly.

"Jump harder," she says. "Do the drills where you do a back handspring up onto a panel mat."

"Okay," I say and we leave it at that.

"How's school?" she asks, purposely changing the subject. Happy to be on to a new subject I tell her about how I got one hundred percent on my spelling and vocabulary test.

Even with the gymnastics corrections I'm happy to have my mom to myself all weekend. Regionals will be like that. If I make it, not only will it be an amazing meet with athletes from five states, but I will get another fun weekend with my teammates and my mom. I think I'll even get a gorgeous leotard that says Utah on it to represent our state at regionals.

I can't wait to get back into the gym and fix my series so I can score consistent 34.00 all arounds before State Meet.

CHAPTER 2

We get home at about noon from our road trip and the boys are just getting back from their two hours of church. The house is noisy and they are yell-talking to my mom as soon as she enters. They want to host a Dungeons and Dragons (D&D) game when our cousins come over for family dinner.

Two of my mom's seven siblings live in Snowcap Canyon. They usually come to our house for Sunday dinner since our house is the biggest of the three families. Her sister, Aunt Josselyn, has two kids, Ronan and Oakley. Her brother, Uncle Jeremy, has three kids, Ashtyn, Liam, and Harper. They also attend Mountain View Charter School with us. Ronan is in 7th grade, Ashtyn is in 6th with me, Oakley is in 5th, Liam is in 3rd, and little Harper is in 1st. I rarely see Liam and Harper because they have a different lunch time than we do.

"Let's play now so I can practice as DM before they get

here," Will says. He loves being Dungeon Master, probably because he's a middle child. Drew and Ethan nod in agreement.

"Are you playing?" Will asks me. "I think you leveled up last time."

I think about it for a moment. D&D can be fun sometimes, but it can get so long and my brothers can be a bit much when they talk all at once.

"I'll join you when they get here. I'm just going to go read or something," I say.

"Sounds boring," Ethan grumbles. Maybe. But at least it will be quiet.

I head up to my room, dragging my suitcase behind me. I go back down for my gym bag and find it by the garage door. I take it up to my room and remove the medals I got for floor and vault. I hang them up on my medals rack. After four years of competition it is getting pretty full. I pull out my phone and flop on my bed. I'm lucky to have a phone. None of my brothers got a phone until 7th grade. Last Christmas my mom got Drew and me both one; something about a deal for two new lines. Drew is in 7th grade and I'm in 6th, so he was excited and furious at the same time. Then all my brothers ganged up on me for being the spoiled baby. I hate it when they say stuff like that. But I got a phone a year early, so maybe it's worth it.

I quickly text my mom.

Me:
> Can you send me videos?

I lay back and look at the ceiling, surprised at how tired I am. It was a big weekend. I hear my phone ping and I pick it up. My mom has sent me videos of all my routines along with some that she got of my teammates. She was a bit haphazard about who she filmed besides me.

I carefully watch each routine. Vault looks good. My vault is a front handspring, the same vault I have been doing for years. Only now I do it up onto mats, so it must have more power and height. The idea is that I will add a front flip to it in Level 8.

Bars looks good, except I barely made my giant over. Watching the video I see that my body shaping is wrong and I am arching over the top of the bar. My coach Katie has been telling me that. Now I can see what she has been talking about.

Beam looks good. My leaps are finally close to split and I am not holding back the way I used to. I split the beam on a leap years ago and it took me forever to forgive beam. Plus, I've had a lot more falls since then and am used to it now. I watch my incredibly crooked series. There was no way I was going to stick that even if I'd tried, and I hadn't. I was only focused on going for it. I go back and watch my series again. I put the video in slow motion and watch my crooked back walkover into a back handspring. I am heavy on my hands; my mom is right. I sigh as I open the floor video.

I love my *Beauty and the Beast* routine; my dance looks good. Not like Paige good, but decent with minimal deductions. I do a front handspring, front pike in the first pass that I'm really proud of. But my full in my last pass is all wrong. I twist so late. Katie taught us to spot on our set, but clearly, I was waiting too long. I watch my full again; it's borderline scary. I'm surprised Katie let me compete it. I could have just done a layout like I did last year.

Last year I was a Level 6. A Level 6 who didn't make Regionals. This year I'm a Level 7. The skill requirements are a little harder and the competition is tougher. The scoring is supposed to be similar, but I swear it's harder. Even with these challenges, I still want to make Regionals. I have to have that Utah Team leo!

I stare at the screen. I have a lot to work on. I still have two weeks before the next meet. I can do it.

I hear a knock on my door and I look up from my phone.

"I came to help you unpack," my mom says.

"Do I have to?" I ask.

"Yes, otherwise we'll forget about it and I need to wash your comp leo so hand it over."

I get up and pick up my suitcase and throw it on my bed. Together we start taking things out. I hand her the bag of dirty clothes along with my leo that I had carefully put back in the plastic garment bag. She throws the dirty clothes bag into the laundry room and walks across the hall to hang the leo on Drew's pull up bar.

"Why didn't you want to play with the boys?" she asks as she grabs a shirt and turns to my closet to hang it up.

"I'll play when the cousins get here. Their yell-talking was bugging me I guess," I admit.

She laughs, "An entire weekend away and they're still too much for you."

"They're just so loud," I grumble.

"It's a good thing you are at the gym a lot," she teases me.

"I can't wait to get back in and clean up my routines."

"I remember feeling like that. Especially after a fall," she says, hanging another shirt I didn't wear. I think we overpacked.

"Does competing optionals get easier?" I ask her.

"Not really. If it gets easy, you're probably in the wrong level. You could have stayed Level 6 this season, but it would have been too easy. That's the thing about gymnastics, as soon as you get the hang of a level, it's time to move up."

I nod in understanding. It's okay, I'm happy I got my Level 7 skills and moved up with Savannah and Lucy. Paige is the only one that is repeating Level 6. I'm glad we work out together with the Level 6s, especially since Carmen, Trista, and Marissa are now in Level 6. I love that we are all training together again.

CHAPTER 3

Monday afternoon Mom drops Drew and me off at the front door of Perfect Balance Gymnastics Academy. We hop out, tell her a brief goodbye, and walk in. "Dad's picking you up!" she yells after us.

Drew opens the door to the gym and I follow him in. Katie greets us both and we head upstairs. As an optionals gymnast Drew is allowed in our optionals study room. The boys' lockers are in the men's locker room, so they usually just hang out briefly in there before their workout. Sometimes if a guy from the men's team has homework they will do it in our room. They don't use the optionals room like we do. I feel bad about that.

"Have a good workout," he says to me as he heads into the men's locker room.

"You too," I say and keep walking to the optionals room. Once inside I head to my locker. Savannah and Trista are already there.

"Did your mom record the Florida meet too?" Trista is asking Savannah.

"Yes, and Oklahoma."

"Who did they compete against?"

"I'm not sure. We can just find out when we watch them," Savanah says, making Trista frown.

"Trying to catch what you missed over the weekend?" I ask, opening my locker.

"Yeah, we're going to watch them tomorrow at Savannah's house if you want to come," Trista says, taking the liberty of inviting me to Savannah's house. To be fair, Savannah's mom, Debbie, probably would be fine with it. Savannah is an only child and her mom loves it when she has friends over.

"Sounds fun, I'll ask my mom," I say, taking off my boots and throwing them in my locker.

We hear the clock on the wall chime that it's four o'clock. We need to get downstairs and start warming up.

We run our laps with all the optionals girls today, Level 6 all the way up to Level 10. Melony is coaching with Katie, and when James is done with the Level 3s in another hour, he will join us. While we are stretching Katie comes out with Melony; they are talking quietly and looking at Katie's clipboard. Katie has to keep track of all our routines. In optionals we have different routines and each routine has to have certain requirements to earn a 10.0 start value. That is the easy part. The hard part is that Katie also has B routines for each of us. These are routines with harder skills in them that we are aiming to have by the end of the season.

"Are you guys about done stretching?" Katie asks.

We say that we are and she looks around the gym at the classes going on.

"Level 6 and 7 with me on beam. Upper optionals on vault with Melony."

Girls start getting out of their splits and getting up to go to their first event. I start on beam. I fell on beam at the meet in Logan so this is going to be a tough workout.

"Ten of everything you fell on and five stuck routines," Katie announces.

Ten? I fell on my flight series (back walkover, back handspring). Ten of those may take me the entire workout.

I find a line on the floor to warm-up my back walkover, back handspring. Then I jump up on a beam and warm-up my back walkovers and my back handsprings. Girls who fell on leaps or jumps are already done and moving on to warming up their series for routines.

Connecting a flight series on beam is still new for me and it still scares me. It takes me a long time to warm it up and that's why I get rattled and fall at meets. We have such a short amount of time to warm-up all of our skills during competition.

"Alexis, it's time to start throwing your series," Katie tells me. I knew that was coming. I nod and choose the far beam that has one mat under it. Not that one mat is going to do me any good, but it feels nice to have an extra layer of squish under the beam. I do a back walkover and pause, then I do a back handspring.

"Not connected," Katie yells up to me. I nod, I knew it wasn't.

I walk to the front of the beam and try again. I reach up, arch back, connect my hands to the beam, watch my feet come down one at a time, and immediately jump into my back handspring. I fall off to the side of the beam. But I connected it.

I look over and Katie is busy talking to Carmen. So I jump up to go again. This time I connect the two skills faster and almost make it. The next one I complete the skill, getting both feet on the beam, but then I fall to the side. I decide to

511

take a small break and let another teammate on the beam.

Three connected series and I am still at zero. I need to stick ten.

"How many have you truly connected?" Katie asks me.

"Three."

She looks up at the clock, "Stick ten or do fifteen, whichever comes first, okay?"

"Okay," I agree relieved. I may get to routines after all.

"Jump harder into that handspring," she adds.

I can't decide if it's helpful or annoying that my mom is always right. I sigh and decide to pull over a panel mat for my handspring drills. I do a few back handsprings up onto a mat and go back to my series. I don't want to fall on this skill ever again, the post fall workout is brutal.

In the end, I did all fifteen flight series and stuck only five. Not great odds. At least I'm done with them. I walk to the end of the beam to warm-up leaps. Katie sees this and calls me over to her.

"You did fifteen?" she asks.

"Yes."

"How many did you stick?"

"Five." I mumble, knowing this is not good.

She is quiet for a minute and finally says, "You know the back handspring, back handspring might be easier."

My eyes fly up to hers, "What?" I ask.

"Well the back walkover to back handspring is slow, so it's easy to get off to the side. You may have better success with the back handspring series."

"But it's so much harder."

"Not really. Look, we only have ten more minutes until you go to vault. Skip routines for today and do some back handspring series on low beam."

I walk over to the low beams with a combination of excitement at getting to work my back handspring series again (I haven't since November) and frustration that I didn't get to even one routine today.

Thankfully, it's early in the season and I have two weeks until the next meet and several meets before State. I plan on having a great State Meet and making Regionals. A back handspring series will help me score better at State. I am sure of it.

The problem is that the back handspring series is even scarier to connect than my current series. Katie is right, it is faster. I'm not sure how that will help me stick it, but I am going to keep that thought to myself since I get to work a B skill while my teammates finish routines.

CHAPTER 4

"It's like rolling a penny on its side," Drew explains
when I tell him and my dad that I'm trying the harder series
in an effort to stay on beam.

"Yeah," my dad chimes in. "Have you ever tried to roll a
penny slowly? It falls over. But if you roll it quickly, it stays
on its teeny tiny edge."

I twist my hair around my finger as I think about what
they are saying. I'm going to have to find a penny when I get
home. I need to see what they are talking about, because
doing a back handspring series does not seem any easier than
a back walkover, back handspring. I'm not sure I care
though. I'm just happy Katie is letting me train the harder
series, and hopefully, I can do it at State Meet.

When we get home my mom and Ethan have just arrived
and she is bustling around the kitchen trying to throw a
dinner together.

"Mark, can you go pick up William in thirty minutes?"

"Yes, I hate that he doesn't just practice when you do,"

my dad comments to Ethan.

"That's what he gets for not making JV," Ethan remarks with no empathy at all. William was bummed when he didn't make the Junior Varsity basketball team.

"Freshman rarely do, that's why there is a fresh-soph team," my mom reminds us.

"Josh and I did," Ethan points out. Josh is our oldest brother who is a freshman in college at the University of Utah. He wasn't quite good enough to make their basketball team, but he is playing what he calls intermural basketball, and apparently, is really good at it.

"You two were bigger. William will get there; he just needs a year. This team is perfect for him," she says, unconcerned.

"Still annoying they can't use the gym at the same time," my dad grumbles. "Ethan you need to get your driver's license and just stay at school and wait for him. You could do homework."

Ethan nods and slides out of the room. For some reason, he doesn't want to drive, even though he is already sixteen.

"Alexis and Drew, why don't you two get started on homework? We'll have dinner when Dad gets back with William."

"But I'm hungry now," Drew complains.

"I know it's late. You can have a small snack. It's so hard when you all get home so late."

"You used to make save plates for us. Why don't you do them for Ethan?" Drew asks.

"I do sometimes, but we all hit the house late on Mondays, so we might as well wait and eat together."

He doesn't say anything but takes the box of crackers and baggie of cheese she is offering him. My stomach growls so I climb up on a bar stool next to my brother and join him.

He tells my mom about his practice and she quietly

515

listens. I notice she makes less comments about his gymnastics than mine. Maybe it's because men's gymnastics is so different and she doesn't know it as well.

"Okay you two, you have stalled long enough. Homework," she says.

We reluctantly go into the dining room where we do homework. The hard thing about gymnastics is that it doesn't leave much time for homework at night. Or much of anything else. I usually try to do as much homework at school as possible.

Drew and I both quietly get to work. I think we are both too tired to goof off like we sometimes do. I pull out my math workbook and flip to the unit we are working on and get started.

I'm on the last problem when we hear William hit the house and my mom tells us to clear up our papers and set the table for dinner. We used to only eat in the dining room on Sunday. Lately we have been eating in the dining room during the week. Maybe because our sports schedule are matching up more than they used to when we were younger.

I set the table as I listen to my mom ask William about practice. He gives one-word answers to my mom and I feel bad for her. I glance at William; he looks pretty down.

"I thought you liked basketball," I say, grabbing a stack of plates from the cupboard.

"I did when all my friends were on the team. They made JV and I'm the only one left behind."

"You have new friends on the team; you just don't know them yet," my mom quips.

I think about how awful that must feel. I would be sad if Lucy and Savannah and even Paige moved up without me. It was hard when we moved up and left Trista, Carmen, and Marissa behind in Level 5. It must have been harder on them than it was on us.

CHAPTER 5

Tuesday night we don't have practice so I get to go to
Savannah's house to watch college gymnastics. My mom
couldn't take me until it was time for her to go get Ethan
from basketball so when I show up they have already
watched the first rotation.

"You only missed vault, most of them did Yurchenko
fulls anyway, it's early still," Trista says, as she, Savannah,
and Marissa meet me at the door. She's right, it is early in the
gymnastics season. By the end of the season, college
gymnasts will be doing bigger more complicated vaults
because they will be trying to peak at Nationals.

"Hi, Alexis," Savannah's mom greets. "Come on in, the
girls just barely started," she repeats. I nod and follow them
all into the family room.

"Is anyone else coming?" I ask.

"Not tonight, school nights are hard. Maybe we can do
this again this weekend," Savanah comments.

"I'm in," Trista says, sitting down.

"Who's competing?" I ask as Savannah picks up the remote and resumes playing the first session. "It's an SEC meet, Florida versus Alabama."

"What is SEC?" Marissa asks and I am wondering the same thing.

"Southeastern Conference," Savannah and Trista say at the same time.

"That's why we have to watch it here. Local TV only shows PAC12, but Savannah gets all the channels," Trista says.

"You could watch it online." Marissa, always the problem solver, points out.

"This is more fun," I say when I see Savannah's face fall at that suggestion.

We watch the last few routines on bars and vault and then the teams switch events. They are so incredibly good. Some of the Level 10 girls in our gym do the same skills as these college girls, but the college gymnasts do them so much higher, cleaner, and more gracefully.

I love watching them on bars. They make giants into their flyaways look easy. After watching them I can't wait to get into the gym and try again.

"Whoa, did you see that? She did her dismount right out of a full pirouette," Marissa marvels.

"No swing," Savannah says.

"Incredible," Trista adds.

I smile at my teammates. The only thing better than watching gymnastics is watching with my teammates. They are as engrossed and inspired as I am. When my mom and I try to watch at home my brothers constantly interrupt and ask when we will be done.

"Who do you think will make Nationals?" Marissa asks.

"It's hard to tell this early in the season. Utah will, of

course. They're the only team in history that have made it to every Nationals." Savannah states. I can tell she and her mom have been following college gymnastics for a long time.

We all start talking at once about which teams we think will be the final eight to make it to Nationals.

"Wouldn't it be amazing to watch live?" Savannah sighs.

"We'll go someday," Trista says.

"As a spectator or athlete?" Marissa asks.

"Both!" Trista says, making us laugh.

"I hope we get to work on upgrades," Trista says as we start warming up in the cold gym on Saturday morning. I had a great week of workouts. My A routines are getting easy and I can get through them with time left over in most rotations to get to my B routines. Trista has not been getting to her B routines in practice so I can see why she wants to work upgrades today.

"Usually Saturday is more relaxed, even during season," Paige comments.

When Katie comes up to us while we are stretching, Trista's wish comes true as she tells us we are going to work B routines today.

"Yes!" Trista says, making a fist and pulling it back.

Katie walks around with her clipboard reviewing everyone's upgrades. Then she comes to me.

"Back handsprings for the flight series," she says to me and I nod. "Front handspring, front layout on floor and let's keep working your fulls. On bars I want you to work two giants into a layout flyaway over the pit today."

My stomach sinks a little. I hate flyaways out of giants. They feel so out of control.

By the time she is done telling us each what we are working on we are done stretching. As we slowly stand up, James walks in with coffee in his hand and his baseball cap pulled down low. I'm glad the compulsories season is over so he can coach us on Saturday again.

"James do you want to take the pit bar while I take the comp set, or do you want to split events?" Katie asks as he walks up.

He looks around the busy gym and says, "I don't think there's room for us to split up. I'll take pit bar."

We get to work upgrades on Saturday because the gym is just too busy for us to run routines. Recreational classes used to start at nine in the morning. But Katie started opening up classes as early as eight o'clock. Now it feels like a zoo all the time on Saturdays.

I get my grips on and go to the pit bar since she said I was to work giants into flyaways. When I get to the pit bar, James and Lucy are already there and James has set up a mat with a block on it along the edge of the floor.

"What are you working?" I ask Lucy.

"Flyaway fulls," she answers with a shy smile.

"Are those allowed in Level 7?" I ask.

"It's a B," she tells me.

In optionals gymnastics skills each have a letter. They start at A for the easiest and go all the way up to E for the hardest. In Level 7 we are only allowed to compete As and Bs, which sounds easy, but the Bs are seriously difficult.

"I feel like it should at least be a C," I say, taking the chalk block she hands me.

"But then I couldn't compete it this season," she says as she climbs up. That's one way to look at it.

I listen and James gives her pointers before she goes and she pushes out of her support position and does a layout flyaway.

"You forgot to twist!" James yells.

She looks up at him from the pit, "I didn't know when and by the time I was done debating, I was done flipping," she explains making us both laugh.

"What are you working," he asks me, as Lucy climbs out of the pit.

"Giant to layout flyaway."

"Don't you already have that?" he asks me.

"I can do giant into a tuck flyaway but not into the layout," I clarify.

"What is the difference to you?" he asks.

I think for a moment. "It feels too fast," I admit.

He nods and says, "Let me see what you've been doing."

I climb up to the pit bar, pump into a kip, and pause at the top of the bar in a support position. Then I cast up into an (almost) handstand and swing down into a giant. When I am coming down from the handstand in the giant I pike down to slow my swing into my tuck flyaway.

"I never thought of you as a cautious bar worker. When did that happen?" he asks me.

"I'm not cautious," I disagree.

"Then what was that?"

"A giant to tuck flyaway."

"A giant that you slowed way down for your flyaway. There's no need for that, Lex."

I hate it when he's right.

CHAPTER 6

"I did my layout flyaway out of a giant!" I say as I get in the car. "And back handspring series on the medium beam, with mats though. I love Saturdays."

"I'm glad, baby girl," my mom says, pulling away from the curb.

"Your clothes are in that bag next to you and I have a snack up here when you're ready."

"Are you sure no one can see me?" I ask.

"Those back windows are tinted so no one can see in. But you can wait until we're on the road up to the ski resort. It's a two-lane road so it will be even more difficult for anyone to see in."

I think about this and decide it's probably fine. I can never see in these back windows when I've watched my mom pull up.

"When did the others go?" I ask her.

"This morning. We'll probably catch them having lunch

and we can ski the afternoon with them."

I pull off my leo and wiggle into my long underwear pants. Then I put on the matching shirt. They are both black with teal stitching at the seams. I dig in the bag and find my fleece vest and put that on. All that is left are my puffy ski pants and puffy coat. I decide to wait until we get there to put both of those on because it can get hot in the car.

"I'm all dressed, can you pass back the snack?" I ask.

"You have to change socks too," she reminds me passing back a lunch bag. I take it from her and see it has a banana and almonds, nothing too exciting, but I'm hungry enough to eat it. I look down at my feet in my white cotton socks. I do need to change socks. For skiing we have special wool socks that have extra padding where the ski boots press into your shins. I change socks before I forget and then I dig into my too-healthy snack.

"We get to eat at the lodge, right?" I ask with my mouth full of banana.

"Yes," my mom laughs, "we'll have lunch at the lodge."

Just as my mom predicted, by the time we parked, put on our puffy pants, jackets, and ski boots, and walked to the resort, my dad and brothers are having lunch. Except they are having lunch at the lodge at the top of the mountain.

We quickly put on our skis and get on a chairlift. Then as soon as we get off that one, we ski across to another chairlift that takes us to the top of the resort.

"Now I want to ski," I comment to my mom. All the work of getting bundled up, riding the cold lifts, only to sit at the lodge.

"Me too, but we might as well catch them and you said

you wanted lunch," she reminds me.

I do love ski resort chili.

We find the rest of our family, but the lodge is so busy we don't get to sit next to each other. After lunch Dad decides to take Ethan on some difficult black diamond runs and Mom is left to take me, Drew, and William on some fun blue cruisers.

Since the lodge is at the top of the mountain we get to ski down from there. But we have to decide which chair we are skiing to. Drew suggests a rare double chair. We all agree because we like the jumps between the trees under that chair.

Drew heads down the mountain, followed by William, me, and my mom bringing up the rear so she can keep an eye on all of us.

I feel good on my skis as I make my turns behind Will. The sun is out, the sky is blue, and I love the smell of snow. The sun is shining between the trees and glinting off the snow. My goggles have a special yellow tint, otherwise the sun reflecting off the snow would be so bright it would be hard to see. I take a deep breath in, enjoying the thin crisp air. I wish I could feel the wind in my hair, but I have a helmet on instead. It would probably be too cold anyway. I ski fast enough to keep up with my brothers and I don't have to look behind me to know my mom is right on my tail. I watch as Drew turns onto the trail that will take us to the old two-chair lift. William is right behind him and they get in the short line. I ski up and get in line behind them. When my mom skis up, she announces that she wants to ride up with Will. He drops back and I get in line with Drew.

Drew and I don't say anything as we wait in line and watch a few people get on the chair in front of us. When it's our turn we ski up, stop, and stand in place on a red marker. Then we let the chair come and scoop us up. Once we are up the air, Drew asks me, "What do you think that was about?"

"She must want to talk to him about something."

"I thought that was Dad's trick."

"It is. Guess she got it from him."

"Will has been grumpy lately," Drew observes.

"Yeah," I agree.

"How was practice?" he asks me, abruptly changing the subject. His team doesn't practice on Saturdays and I know he misses it.

"Good, I got to work upgrades."

"What are your upgrades?" he asks.

We talk about gymnastics all the way to the top of the mountain. We quiet down when it's time to ski off the chair lift. Then we wait to the side for Mom and Will. They quickly join us and we are off to ski in the trees. This time Will is leading the group and I'm behind him.

I recklessly follow him over bumps and jumps and have the time of my life. I really do love skiing. Especially with my crazy brothers.

"Wha-Hoooooo!" I hear Drew behind me and I just keep skiing so I don't get landed on.

When we get to the bottom of the run we have the choice to keep skiing to a quad chair that will take us to some bigger runs or to stay here. We look at each other, Will says, "Again?" We agree.

Will heads into the line and I follow him with Drew and Mom behind us. Once on the chair I take the opportunity to find out what Mom wanted.

I immediately ask as soon as we are in the air.

"You are such a busy body."

"No I'm not, I just want to know what she wanted to talk to you about."

"That is literally the definition of a busy body," he fires back at me.

I don't know what to say to that so I am quiet.

"She's just worried, I guess," he says.

"About what?"

"About me, you ding-dong."

"Oh," I say, feeling dumb. "Should she be?" I ask. "Should we be?" I amend.

"No," he sighs. "I'm fine. I told her I'm fine."

"You *have* been grumpy," I point out.

He is quiet for a moment.

"Can you keep a secret from Mom?"

"Maybe," I venture. I want to know Will's secret, but I'm worried it's one of those secrets adults warn you about where you have to tell someone.

"Never mind," he snaps.

"No, tell me. I won't tell unless . . . unless you are going to do something bad. Like hurt yourself."

"You watch too many movies, I am not going to hurt myself," he says, exasperated.

"Then you can tell me," I say, seeing that our ride is more than halfway over. Once we're off this chair I know he won't speak of it again. Mom and Dad are on to something.

"I don't like basketball anymore," he confesses.

"That's it?"

"What do you mean, 'that's it?' It's a big deal. I don't want to be the basketball star like Josh or Ethan."

"Okaaaay," I say slowly, still not really understanding.

"And I'm afraid to tell Mom and Dad."

"I think they would understand."

"You could tell Mom you want to quit gymnastics? Her *baby girl* quitting her favorite sport?" I never thought about it before because I've never wanted to quit. But I can see now how that might be scary.

"What are you going to do?" I ask.

"I dunno," he mumbles.

"And you didn't tell Mom when she asked?"

"I didn't tell Mom," he confirms.

"You might want to just so she doesn't worry. Not knowing what is wrong is so much worse."

He looks at me sideways, "You're pretty smart for a spoiled little pipsqueak."

I shove him at his compliment that wasn't a compliment and almost make him lose his poles over the edge of the chair. It would serve him right for calling me a spoiled pipsqueak.

CHAPTER 7

It's meet week. Three days of workout and then we compete this weekend in Park City. Park City is a fun meet because the theme is skiing. After the meet our team usually goes out to dinner on the quaint Main Street of Park City. Trista says she wants to spot a movie star. The easiest way to tell is if they are overdressed for the weather. Movie stars wear huge boots, fur coats, and hats when a puffy coat will do. I can spot them, but I never know who they actually are.

"Level 6 and 7, to floor!" Katie announces, pulling me out of my thoughts of the upcoming weekend. I do as she says and walk over to floor where Melony will be coaching us. Katie is headed to vault with the upper optionals team.

"Good afternoon," Melony greets us when we walk up to her, ready to hear our assignment.

"Three of each pass and two full sets. When you are done with your sets then ten of each of your leaps and turns."

We nod and head to the different corners to start our

tumbling. I decide to do my back tumbling first to get it over with. I like front tumbling much better. Coaches talk about how the landings are difficult out of front tumbling, but I disagree. I always know where I am and it feels so much more natural than back tumbling.

Since our warm-up complex was quick and simple today, I start with a round-off, back handspring, back tuck. Then I do my layout. I should be ready to do my full, but for some reason, I don't feel ready. I decide to do one more layout. I know my set isn't great, which is giving me less time in the air to twist.

"Is anyone ready?" Melony asks us.

Carmen volunteers to do a routine. The Level 6s are usually ready for full routines before we are because they can warm-up their passes faster.

I wait in a corner as Carmen begins her routine. After her first tumbling pass, I take my turn. I know she will be dancing in the adjacent corner for a few seconds and I have time to tumble without getting in her way.

I do a nice high layout and now I'm ready for my full. I wait again in a corner. This time I'm behind Savannah. She watches Carmen carefully and takes her turn when Carmen is out of the diagonal.

By the time I am up, Carmen is done, and Marissa is standing in the corner waiting for her music to begin. I know I can get a pass in before she starts.

I run, do my round-off, back handspring, set, and twist. But before I can finish the twist and look for the ground, my feet hit, and I fall to my hands.

"Longer set and twist sooner, Alexis," Melony says to me from the other corner. I nod that I heard her. "Actually, come here."

I do as she says and walk over to her. "Show me your arms in a set and pull," she says to me when I am standing in front of her.

I lift my arms and one leg slightly off the ground (both legs would go up if I were in the air) as if I am setting. I am in a hollow body position and she says, "One, two." And I know to pull one arm down and turn my body and then the other arm. In the air this makes me twist.

"That's not the timing you are doing in the air. Try again. Set, toes, one, two," she says as I do the actions with her. "Do that a couple more times and I want to stand there on your next one."

"Okay." I agree and walk over to a corner to wait to tumble. I say in my head, *set, toes, one, two* as I do the arm motions.

When it's my turn, I to call Melony and she stands in the opposite corner. She waves for me to go. I run, round-off, back handspring, set. I feel Melony bump my back up to help me get more height. Toes, one, two. I feel her grab my waist as I land.

"Better timing, but it would have been short if I wasn't spotting it." I look at her, not sure what to do. Does that mean she needs to spot me in routines?

My fulls have always been a little low. I'm not sure why she's worried about it now. I decide to move on to front handspring, front pike. These are easy and fun for me. Once I learned how to get a good lift out of my front handspring and flip through my upper body (not my hips), they have been high.

I quickly do two of my front tumbling pass and I'm ready for routines. My *Beauty and the Beast* routine is graceful and fun. It has some slow parts and some sections that are moderate speed, which I like. I easily do my front tumbling in the first pass. When I get to my second and last pass, the full, Melony is standing there to spot me. I'm a little annoyed, but I don't have time to say anything or argue since

I'm in the middle of a routine. I do my full easily . . . or was it easy because she bumped me? Then I do my ending dance and strike my ending pose.

"Your routine is improving. Your front pass seems easier for you than your full. Is there a reason it's not at the end?" she asks me.

"I think the front pass was harder for me when we made up my routine and I was just doing a layout," I explain.

Melony chuckles, "It's funny how it can change sometimes. You may want to consider flipping them and putting your full at the beginning. When you have a little more energy."

"But I face out after the first pass, my dance will be all messed up."

"That would be simple enough to fix. I would just change a few things in your choreography after each pass."

"Maybe we should wait until after the meet this weekend so I have time to work on it."

"Are you sure? It would be minor changes, I promise."

"Next week," I plead.

"Okay, next week," she concedes and starts the music for Victoria.

CHAPTER 8

"Are you competing this weekend?" Aaron's mom asks me. Aaron is one of Drew's teammates. His mom is driving us home from practice tonight since our parents are at a basketball game.

"Yes, I have a meet in Park City this weekend," I answer her.

"It's too bad you guys don't have the same meets. It would be so much easier on your folks," she comments.

"We have one together this season," Drew reminds her.

"Really?" Aaron asks.

"Yeah, the Capitol Hill Meet is a Men's and Women's meet this year. It's our meet after this one. In two weeks."

"That will be fun," Aaron's mom says, pulling into our driveway.

She's right, competing at the same meet as Drew does sound fun. We get out of the car and thank her. She waits as we walk up the drive and watches to make sure we get ourselves into the house. Once we open the door, we wave, and she drives away.

"Why didn't we do that meet last year?" I ask.

"I don't know, but I'm looking forward to it," he says, walking to the kitchen to find food. He has started to be hungry all the time like my other brothers.

Mom has put a giant sticky note on the pantry that tells us to eat the save-plates before junk food.

"As if we have any junk food," he mumbles.

He goes to the fridge and gets out both plates and hands me mine. I set it on the counter and wait while he puts his in the microwave.

I hear a thump from upstairs and freeze. I know Drew heard it too because he looks at me in surprise.

"Isn't everyone at the game?" I whisper. Drew nods and motions for me not to say any more. He quietly walks out of the kitchen and to the stairs. I follow him wondering what the heck he is doing.

"If there is someone here you don't want them to find you," I whisper.

"Shh!" he retorts, barely audible.

We stare upstairs for a moment not sure what to do when William appears at the top of the stairs.

"Oh, you guys are home," he says, pulling out an ear bud.

"Geez man, you scared us!" Drew exclaims.

"How? I'm just up here doing homework."

"And thumping around," Drew accuses.

"Sorry, I thought I would hear you when you got home. I figured I would open the door for you."

"Why are you here? Don't you have a game right before JV?" I ask.

"I told them I wasn't feeling well," he says quietly. So he still hasn't told Mom and Dad, or his coaches for that matter, that he wants to quit.

"Bro, just tell them," Drew says and goes back to the kitchen to pull his plate from the microwave.

"You told him, too?" I ask, feeling a little less special.

"You told him?" Will accuses at the same time.

"No!" Will and I both say.

"He must have figured it out," he finally concedes.

"When?" I ask.

"Just now." He frowns.

"Mom will soon, too!" Drew yells from the kitchen. William looks at me with a worried look on his face and walks down the rest of the stairs.

"You promise you didn't tell him?" he asks me as he reaches the bottom of the stairs and steps a little too close and looks down on me. He's trying to intimidate me but it won't work. I stand as tall as I can and am sure not to take a step back.

"I did not! He just figures stuff out because he listens when no one thinks he does."

"I heard that!" Drew yells.

"See."

Will backs up and nods then turns to go into the kitchen and I follow him.

I watch as Drew puts my plate in the microwave and goes and sits at the counter to eat. "Have you eaten?" he asks Will.

"Yeah, but I could eat again," he says, opening the fridge and just staring inside.

"What did you tell your coach?" Drew asks, digging into his food.

"That I wasn't feeling well," William sighs.

"How long do you think that will hold?" Drew asks around his food.

William shrugs. I look at Drew. I think the shrug means

he doesn't care if his coach figures it out. I can't imagine telling Katie I don't feel well when I'm fine. Then again, I like being at the gym.

"You didn't even want to go watch?" I ask, that doesn't seem like Will. He's usually pretty supportive of all of us.

"If I don't feel well, I can't watch a game, genius," he retorts.

"Then another reason to come clean," Drew fires back, saving me from having to defend my oversight.

The microwave beeps and I pull out my plate and sit down. As soon as I sit I focus on my lasagna and let Drew and Will continue to discuss what Will is going to do from here. It seems simple to me; he should just tell Mom and Dad. For some reason it's not simple to William.

CHAPTER 9

It's the last practice before meet day and I have decided to do one more meet with my A routines before moving on to adding in my B routines. Since I've already qualified for State, my goal is to increase my skills so I can qualify for Regionals.

I need to get through my assignment with A routines so I can work B skills at the end of each rotation.

We start on beam today and my back walkover, back handspring is getting more consistent. Our assignment is five stuck routines or ten total, whichever comes first. It takes me eight routines to get to five stuck. When I jump down from my last set, Savannah jumps up.

I walk over and stand next to Victoria as she is waiting for a beam too.

"Your routine is looking good," she comments.

"Thanks," I smile. "The series is getting easier."

"Then it's time for an upgrade," she teases.

I nod in agreement, "That's my hope. In fact, I'm headed to low beams now," I say.

"Good luck," she says, walking over to the beam Marissa just jumped off of.

I make my way over to Katie, knowing I need to check in with her before I work something else.

"I stuck five," I tell her.

She is watching Paige and quickly glances at me and back to the beam again. "Out of how many?" she asks.

"Eight," I say, proud of this number. Just last week I couldn't even finish the assignment.

"What did you fall on?" she asks.

"Series, and in one routine I fell on series and full turn," I admit.

"Okay, stick three more series on high beam and we'll rotate," she says.

I pause, debating if I should speak up or just do as I'm told. Paige dismounts and Katie looks down at me, "What is it?" she asks.

"I was hoping to work my back handspring series. You said it might be a better series for me," I remind her.

"Something has seemed to click for you on your back walkover, back handspring. I think we stick to that for now. You're still welcome to work your back handspring series at the end of rotations. But we rotate soon and we have a meet Saturday. I need you to feel comfortable with your walkover series," she reasons.

I have no argument for her so I go do as she says. I jump up on a high beam to stick three more series. I'm bummed I can't work on upgrades. But she's right, we have a meet the day after tomorrow. I only have time to do three series (stuck two) before we have to rotate to floor.

Our floor assignment is the same as it has been the last few weeks. We have two routines and three of each pass.

537

Most of us use the three of each pass as an opportunity to warm-up our tumbling for routines. Trista and Carmen prefer to do their routines cold and get them over and done before working on tumbling. I like to do at least two of each pass before doing a routine. I appreciate that Katie lets us take either approach.

We do a quick complex then Melony joins us and sends Katie over to vault where the upper optionals are training. "Anyone ready?" she asks, and true to form, Trista volunteers.

I stand in the corner and tumble as soon as Trista dances out of the way. I start with back tumbling because my fulls are hard for me. I run and do my round-off, back handspring, layout. Then I walk to the other diagonal and decide to warm-up just a front handspring as Trista finishes her routine.

When I get back to the first diagonal I know I need to do my full or I will never have time to work front layouts at the end of the rotation.

"Alexis, you are skipping the set and waiting too long to twist." Melony says.

I nod to indicate that I heard her. Then I wait in the corner for Marissa to do the first tumbling pass in her routine. *Set, toes, twist,* I think, as I wait and mentally prepare to do another full.

As soon as Marissa is out of the way I run, round-off, back handspring, set, whoa, that was a weird set. *Just do a layout*, a voice in my head says. *No, don't change in the middle, twist!*

I pull one arm and then the other into a twist that I now realize is way too late. Usually I twist, see the ground, and land. I have no idea where I am in the air or where the ground is. I feel my feet hit the ground and since I'm only about three-fourths of the way around I'm pulling for the twist when I hit the ground. My feet are planted on the floor and my upper body is still twisting. I feel a pain in my ankle as I fall forward on my hands and knees. The pain is searing. I hear a yelp of pain and realize it came from me as I turn myself over so I am sitting on my bum.

"Oh man!" I whisper and grab my ankle rocking back and forth in pain. *It's fine. It's probably fine,* my voice says. And even as my voice is trying to convince me it's fine, I know it's not. I hear my teammates yelling as Melony stops Marissa's music.

CHAPTER 10

Melony is kneeling by my side and gently touches my ankle. "Can you move it for me?"

I wince as I do as she says. She gently holds my heel in her hand and looks from all angles. "I don't see such an obvious break that I would need to call 911. Let's see how it feels after some ice."

I nod, trying not to cry. I look up and three teammates are around me, which is rare after a fall. It must have been bad.

"Can you stand?" Paige asks.

"Yeah, I think it's fine. It just surprised me." I say, getting up. But as soon as I put weight on my ankle I collapse back down in pain.

I feel a teammate pull me up from either side and I'm able to get up and hop over to a panel mat on the side of the floor. The pain radiating through my ankle from trying to stand on it has me blinking back tears of pain and fear. *This can't be happening. Not in the middle of season.*

Victoria and Riley set me down on the panel mat as Savannah walks up with ice and a towel. I take them from her and set them on my ankle.

"Fifteen minutes with the ice and I will come back and check on it," Melony says to me. Then she turns to my teammates, "Back to work."

I watch as they disperse to the four corners to tumble the diagonal. Marissa starts her routine over. The ice stings, but I know it will help my ankle feel better soon. I notice I am still rocking back and forth. I'm in pain, it's a deep achy pain now that I am off of my foot and icing.

Maybe it's not that bad. Maybe the initial impact was the worst. Maybe I'll be fine after I ice. I can't be hurt. I don't have time to be hurt. I have a meet in two days! It's fine. I'll be fine.

The ache is subsiding as the ice numbs me and I'm feeling a little better. I will be fine by the next rotation.

I watch my teammates practice their floor routines. As I watch, I run through my head what happened. How did my full get so off? I waffled in my head. I know what happened. I was going for a full, decided in the air to do a layout, and I changed my mind back again. The absolute worst thing a gymnast can do. My brain was confusing my body. My brothers are right, I can be such a ninny. This was a big screw up. I know better. I would have been better off doing the layout if the set felt wrong.

I look down and lift the ice off my ankle to see if there is evidence of my pain. Of course, it's just red and looks nothing like how bad it feels. This might be bad. Melony said it didn't look like an obvious break, but what if it's an unobvious break? No, it's probably nothing. I'm fine.

My head is spinning back and forth between deciding I am going to be able to join practice after I ice to I broke my ankle.

I take a deep breath and am forced to wait my fifteen minutes of icing. It feels like eternity.

Finally, Melony comes back over to me. She sits next to me and says, "How's it feel?"

"Okay, I think. I'm not sure," I admit.

"Still in pain?"

I'm quiet for a moment and nod, yes, I'm still in pain.

She lifts up the ice pack and peers at my red ankle. "Hmm, let me see your other one," she says. I move to put my ankles next to each other. "It's swollen already, even with the icing."

I look at my ankles together; it is swollen. Alarmingly swollen. I turn it to see if the side is swollen too. I wince at that bad idea and stop trying to move it.

"Push on my hand," Melony says with her hand on the bottom of my foot. I try to push but I can't. "Like you are moving from flex to point," she says.

"I'm trying," I say. The tiny movement is impossible. Well, not impossible, it just hurts. I move her hand a little bit and can feel the pain send shock waves to my brain. *Stop*, it says, *that hurts!*

"It hurts to do that. A lot," I say through watering eyes.

"Okay," Melony squeezes my shoulder. "Let's call your mom or dad."

"For what?" I squeak past the lump in my throat. This can't be that bad. It just can't.

"Your workout today is done. Stretch a little if you can get in the stretches without causing your ankle pain and I will get the gym phone," she says, standing up.

I'm going home. I've never been sent home from the gym. Even when I straddled beam, I kept working out.

Marissa comes over and hands me the gym phone. "Thanks," I manage.

"How bad is it?" she asks.

"I don't know. It's probably fine. Melony is just being cautious." She looks unconvinced but nods and gets back to work.

I dial my mom and I can tell she is in the car when she picks up. "Hello?" she says in a formal voice she doesn't use for me. Then I remember I'm calling from the gym phone and not my phone.

"Hi, Mom," I say, and my voice cracks.

"Hi, Alexis, what's going on?" she asks, knowing it's the middle of practice.

"Can you come get me?" I ask.

"Of course. I just have to drop off your brother and then I can come get you. It will be about fifteen minutes. Is everything okay?"

"It's fine. I crunched my ankle a little on a full and it hurts too much to finish practice."

"Oh no, how bad?"

Why does everyone keep asking me that? I have no idea how bad it is. And what does that mean anyway? Miss practice bad? Miss the season bad? I'm in terrible pain bad? Well two for sure, so I guess it's bad.

"I mean, it hurts to stand," I say and sniff up a tear. I will not cry. "But I don't think it's broken or anything," I quickly add. It's not broken, Melony said. Plus, it can't be. Breaks require casts and time off. No, it can't be. It's not.

"Okay, I'll be there as soon as I can. Are you icing?"

"Yes. Well, I was."

"Good, okay. I'm so sorry, baby girl."

"It's fine, it'll be fine," I reassure her.

She is quiet and then says, "Okay, put ice back on it after fifteen minutes, see you soon."

"See you soon," I say and hang up. I set the phone next to me on the panel mat.

543

I know I'm supposed to ice for fifteen and rest for fifteen and ice again. But I have no idea how long I have been without ice.

I can tell my team is just about finished with the floor rotation. That means it has probably been fifteen minutes. I try to stand up. If I put all of my weight on the other foot I'm okay. I pick up the ice and try to take a step. I end up catching myself with the good foot. I guess that is what limping is. A slow shuffle with all your weight on one foot and a nano second on the injured one and back to the strong one again.

Paige comes over and grabs the ice from me. "I'll put that back for you," she says.

"Thanks," I say, truly grateful. She walks off to put the ice away. I take two more shuffles and see this is going to take forever. I look across the floor and the tumble strip that I have to pass to get to the glass doors. The gym has never felt so big. I make my way to the side of the floor so I am not in the way of my teammates, but now I still have to walk the length.

"Is your mom coming?" Melony yells across the gym.

"Yes," I answer. I'm less emotional now that I am focused on getting across the gym.

"I'll text her tonight to see how you're doing," she says, walking over to me.

"Okay," I say, eyeing the distance between me and the doors. I have an idea.

"Do you need help getting out of here?" she asks, watching me limp.

"No, I think I got it," I say. Then I kick up into a handstand and walk across the floor on my hands much faster than I was moving on my feet. I can hear Melony laughing.

"Great problem-solving skills, Lexi, I like it."

When I get to the edge of the blue floor I step down

easily out of my handstand onto my usual right ankle, my left is the one that is hurt. I hear clapping when I step down and look over my shoulder.

Melony and my teammates, and even James, and Katie are clapping for me. This makes me smile and I kick back up to get across the red floor. When I step down again, Katie is holding the glass doors open for me. She helps me limp through.

"Tell me what happened," she says, following me into the lobby.

"I have to go up to get my things."

"Let's have someone else do that. Sit down," she says, gesturing to one of the few chairs in the lobby.

Since my ankle is throbbing, I do as she says. Then she sticks her head back in the lobby and yells, "8s, 9s and 10s, come get your grips on!" Then she turns to me, "They need to rotate anyway. One of them can get your stuff."

Brooklyn is the first to come through the lobby doors and Katie asks her to bring down whatever is in my locker.

Then she turns back to me, "What happened?" she asks softly, squatting down and turning my ankle in her hand.

"I hesitated on a full and twisted late. I lost where I was in the air and was still twisting when I landed."

"Oh man, Alexis, that will give you a good sprain," she confirms, tilting her head to get a closer look. "It's already swelling and bruising. Keep up the icing tonight."

I nod that I will. "So just a sprain? It'll be fine, right?"

"I'm not a doctor, but I'm guessing a sprain. You will be fine eventually. But it might take some time." She lets go of my foot as Brooklyn comes down with my gym bag and shoes and sets them next to me.

"Sorry about your ankle, Lex," Brooklyn says with empathy only another gymnast who has hurt herself could have.

"Thanks," I mumble.

"Is your mom coming?" Katies asks, standing up.

"Yeah."

"Have her come in and talk to me. Plus you will need help getting to the car. The handstand walks won't work in the parking lot," she teases, making me smile.

"Okay, I'll text her." I lean over to my gym bag that Brooklyn set next to me. I find my cell phone and text my mom.

Me:

Katie wants you to come in and talk to her

Mom:

I am driving and will respond to you momentarily.

"I got her auto response. Hopefully she'll see it when she pulls up."

"One more round of ice while you wait," Katie says, handing me a new ice pack and pulling another chair over to me. She props my leg up on the second chair and adds the ice. Then, to keep it in place she wraps both my ankle and the ice with a cloth ACE bandage.

"I want you to RICE the rest of today and for the next three days,"

"RICE?" I ask.

"Rest, ice, compress, elevate. When you are not icing, wrap it in this bandage to keep the swelling down. And keep it elevated like we have it now as much as possible. That will also help with the swelling."

"But my meet is in two days!"

Katie is quiet and finally says, "I doubt you'll be competing this weekend. But since we are past the deadline of getting your money back, I can wait until that morning to scratch you. I'll call your mom and check on you tomorrow to see how it's going."

I have to be better in two days. I have been training for nine months for this season. Competing is the best part of gymnastics; I can't scratch.

"I have to get the upper optionals started on bars. I'll come back out in a few minutes to talk to your mom. Don't leave until I have a chance to talk to her."

I nod again in agreement. Katie understands my untalkative mood and goes back into the gym.

I adjust the ice and my foot on the chair to get more comfortable. Then I watch my teammates rotate from floor to beam. I'm frustrated and angry at myself that I'm not with them right now. Why did I have to be such a ninny and second guess my full? It was scary to not know where I was in the air. I don't want to feel that again. The one thing about being hurt for real is that no one is making me get up right now and do a full. Although, that may backfire later.

This stinks.

"Hey," I hear and look up to see Drew has poked his head through the doors. "I saw you limp over here. Is Mom coming?" he asks.

I nod.

"You okay?" he asks and I can tell he is concerned for real.

"I don't know," I admit.

"Sucks," he says. Yep. "Tell Mom Aaron's mom can bring me home."

"Okay," I agree. He nods and goes back into the training area. I know he doesn't have time to talk since he is in the middle of practice.

"Alexis!" my mom says coming into the lobby. There are younger kids in the lobby waiting for their recreational class to begin. Normally I would be embarrassed by her yelling out my name, but right now I don't care.

"Hi, Mom," I manage as she comes over and gives me a side hug while I still sit in the chair.

"What happened?" she asks.

"I lost where I was on a full and landed short," I say, leaving out the part where I hesitated.

"How bad is it?" she asks, unable to see my ankle under the bandage and ice.

"It'll be fine I think. I might even be fine by Saturday," I lie. I know this is a lie, but I can't seem to admit that I'm out for the weekend.

My mom hugs me again and kisses my head.

"Hello, Amanda," Katie says coming back into the lobby.

"Hi, Katie."

"I imagine you're pretty familiar with how to care for her injury," Katie begins, knowing my mom was a gymnast.

"Unfortunately, I do," my mom confirms.

"RICE the next three days," Katies says and my mom nods.

"So you're thinking a sprain?" my mom asks.

"That's my guess, but I've been wrong before. I would get it checked out as soon as possible and rule out a break or fracture. It's already swelling and coloring, so it could be. Then again, I've seen sprains do the same."

"It's not broken," I say, willing it to be true. I know from watching other kids that casts stay on for weeks. It would take me out for the season.

"I hope you're right," Katie says. "Text me after you see a doctor and let me know. Keep the bandage and ice bag, you'll need both this weekend."

My mom nods and thanks her. Katie goes back into the training area to coach.

My mom picks up my gym bag and puts it over her shoulder. "Ready?" she asks me. I stand up on my good leg and lean on her to limp out of the gym.

We are silent as we shuffle out to the car, both just focusing on getting me there.

She slides open the van door and helps me hop in.

"Drew said he can get a ride home from Aaron," I remember to tell my mom as I climb in.

"Okay, I'll text his mom to make sure," she says and shuts the sliding door.

I watch her walk around the car and get in.

"Do we have to go pick up the rest of the boys?" I ask, knowing they are at basketball and that they will need rides soon.

"Your father is going to do that tonight. I'm taking you straight to urgent care to make sure that isn't a break," she says, backing out of her parking space.

CHAPTER 11

My mom helps me limp through the doors of urgent care and into a waiting room that is about half full. She sets me down in one of the first chairs and goes up to the counter to check me in. I look at the other patients. One has a bloody finger, one is coughing a ton, and I can't tell what is wrong with the other two.

My ankle starts throbbing and I realize it's because I don't have it propped up. I turn my body sideways in my chair and prop up my foot in the seat next to me. After a few moments, it does feel a little better.

My mom comes back and sits across from me. "It might be a while."

"Only four people in front of us, that shouldn't be too long," I say, trying to be positive.

"It's triage and they are short-staffed tonight."

"What's triage?" I ask.

"It means they don't take you in the order you came in,

but in order of urgency. Since you are able to sit here in relative comfort, it might be a while."

"Oh. Can I play on my phone?" I ask.

"We left it in the car," she says. "But I brought us both books," she says, pulling out a book for each of us. She didn't have time to grab the book I have been reading from my nightstand; this book was in the car.

"You knew it was going to be like this?" I ask.

"I figured," she says, handing me my book.

"How did your purse fit both?" I ask.

"Magic of the Mom Bag," she says and opens her book.

I try to read mine, but I can't get comfortable. My ankle is throbbing and I'm sitting at a funny angle.

"Can I unwrap it?" I ask my mom.

"You need to keep it compressed as long as you can."

"But the ice is melting under it," I complain.

My mom gets up and unwraps my bandage then pulls off the ice. I'm surprised to see it's turning purple now along with the bright red. Without a word she walks over and throws away the plastic bag with ice. Then she comes back and rewraps my ankle with precision.

"How do you know how to do that so well?"

"Personal experience," she says.

"Did you hurt your ankle too?"

"Yes, I sprained my right ankle twice and my left three times. I am sorry to say, but you get your weak ankles from me. The good news is our knees and backs stay intact."

I think about this. I'm probably like her and it's just a sprain. I'll be fine in a few days.

My mom finishes wrapping it. It does feel better with the lumpy cold ice off of it and wrapped securely.

"Thanks," I say as she sits back down.

We watch as the four people in front of me get called back to see the doctors and leave us in the waiting room alone.

"Now we hope no one else comes in and gets in front of you," she says as another patient walks in. He doesn't look like he is about to die so hopefully I get in before him.

No such luck. Whatever his problem is, they let him in back right away.

I sigh and try to read my book again. I keep reading the same paragraph over and over. Is this what Drew and Ethan, and even Marissa, feel like when they say they have ADHD?

"Alexis?" I hear a medical assistant call out my name.

I stand up on my good leg and my mom helps me limp over to the door as we follow the medical assistant to an exam room. She has me sit on the exam table and immediately puts a blood pressure cuff on my arm and a little heart rate reader on my finger. When she is done taking my blood pressure, she unclips the finger monitor. Then she puts the numbers in her computer. When she is done she looks at me and says, "What are you here for today, Alexis?" *Isn't it obvious?*

"Um, I hurt my ankle."

"How did you do that?" she asks, typing away.

"Doing gymnastics."

"So you fell?" she asks.

"I landed wrong and then, yes, fell," I answer. This is such a difficult thing to explain to non-gymnasts.

She nods and types a little more and stands up, "The doctor will be in soon," she says, departing the room.

I look around the little room. Not much to see here. I look at the clock and realize we've been here for more than an hour.

"Practice is almost over," I comment.

"Yeah, we're going to get home late. Do you have much homework?"

"No," I say, even though I'm not entirely sure. I've

gotten used to using our planners at school. I remember writing something down today, but I would have to look to remember.

Finally, the doctor comes in and introduces himself and shakes my hand and my mom's hand.

"Your ankle huh?" he asks. He slides out a tray under the table I'm sitting on and props my leg up. "May I unwrap it?" he asks. I nod that he can. "What'd you do?"

"I fell in gymnastics," I explain. I know he won't understand the specifics, so I don't bother.

"When?"

"Just now. Like an hour ago."

"Did you hear a snap or pop or any weird sounds?" he asks unwinding the wrapping.

"No," I answer.

He examines my ankle by gently touching it in different locations and asking me when I'm in pain.

"Can you put weight on it?"

"No," I answer honestly.

"Ankle x-rays aren't always needed. But in your case you are hurt in some places that are important to us doctors. I would like to get an x-ray to rule out a break. Is that okay with you Mrs. Bingham?"

"Yes," my mom consents.

"Okay, then hang tight and I'll put in the order for x-rays," he says and leaves the room.

"That hurt," I complain as soon as he leaves.

"He was being as gentle as possible," my mom comments.

"Do you really think it's broken?" I ask.

"I don't know, baby girl; that's why we're here."

"I hope not," I whisper.

We sit in silence for a moment. Then we hear a knock on the door and a woman in blue scrubs steps in, "I hear someone in here needs an x-ray?"

"Yes, me," I say. Again, forcing me to state the obvious.

"Hop down and follow me," she instructs as if it were that simple. Did she forget I'm in here for a possible broken ankle?

My mom jumps up and helps me down while the lady waits with the door open.

"You can come too, Mom," she says. Of course my mom has to come; how else am I going to get out the door of this office? I lean on my mom and we do the limp hop thing we have been doing all evening.

We follow the x-ray tech down what feels like the longest hall ever. Then we turn and go down another hall. This is miserable. When we finally get to the big x-ray room she has my mom sit in a room behind a glass window. Then she has me sit on a giant white hard flat table. Next she drapes a heavy apron over me and attaches the Velcro at the back.

"No possible pregnancy?" she asks me. What the heck? I'm twelve and haven't even gotten my period yet.

"No," I say, embarrassed by the question being asked at all.

She picks up a black square, puts letter magnets on it.

"What are the letters for?" I ask her.

"They are your initials and the L is for your left ankle," she explains. Sure enough it says AB for Alexis Bingham and an L for left.

"Bend your knee and put your foot flat on here," she says referring to the black tray. I do as she says, she tells me to hold still and then runs to the room my mom is sitting in. I hear a click and then she comes back. Next she tells me to drop my knee so she can get the side of my ankle. This position hurts, and she fiddles with my foot with no mercy to get it on the tray just right. The pain is shooting up my body and tears are stinging my eyes.

"Hold still," she says and runs to the room. I am in so much pain! I want to move my foot so badly. I'm afraid if I do she will have to situate me all over again.

Then she comes back out and moves my knee to the other side and fiddles with my foot again. Has this woman never touched a broken ankle before?

"Ouch!" I finally say out loud in hopes that she will be more gentle.

"I know, but I have to get this angle so we can see your foot from all sides," she says with absolutely no remorse. I grit against the pain of the awkward position she has put me in and hold it while she goes into the other room again.

I look over to my mom and she is wringing her hands. At least she knows this is excruciating. The demon woman comes out and adjusts me again.

"This will be the last one if we get a good picture," she promises.

All I can do is nod and grit my teeth while she moves my foot. I hold the awful pose while she runs and takes the picture.

Then she comes out and says, "All done! Great job!"

I have no response to her cheery mood and just swivel my body sideways on the table and wait for my mom to help me down.

My mom comes over and says to the tech, "Do you guys have crutches?"

"We might somewhere around here. Follow me back to the room and I'll see if I can find some."

The struggle back to the exam room is even worse than before because now my ankle hurts so much I can't even put a little weight on it.

"Can I just do handstand walks?" I whisper to my mom.

She giggles and says, "Not a bad idea, but they would

probably tell you to stop. We're almost there," she lies.

When we finally get to the room the tech is holding the door open for us. Gee, thanks.

My mom helps me to the table. "The doctor will be in as soon as he has time to take a look at her pictures," she says and shuts the door.

"That hurt so bad!" I yell as soon as she shuts the door.

"I know, baby," my mom says, pulling the compression bandage I was wearing before from her purse. "Let me wrap it back up, that will help with the pain."

"I don't see how," I moan. She ignores me and tells me to scoot back on the table so my leg is all the way on the table and my ankle is in front of me. She proceeds to wrap my ankle expertly.

I take deep breaths trying not to get mad at my mom for the movement. When she is done, she is right. The pressure on it does feel better. I look up at her.

"Mom, if you think it's sprained, why did I just go through that torture chamber?" I exclaim.

"The doctor said we had to first rule out a break," she reasons.

"This royally stinks," I say, leaning back on my hands.

"I know," she says.

Then her phone pings. She goes to her purse and sits down.

"Practice is over. Katie and Melony want to know how you're doing," she says.

"Really? They're already done? We've been here forever," I comment.

"Waiting on x-rays," she says out loud as she types. "Your teammates have been texting you. They seem pretty worried. That's so sweet."

I nod in agreement.

"You can text them back when we get in the car and we

know more," she says.

I nod and my arms are tired of supporting my weight so I sit up. I can't seem to get comfortable. How long do we have to stay here?

Finally we hear a knock on the door. Hooray! An answer to the x-rays and we can get out of here.

The x-ray tech comes in with crutches.

"This is all we have, they are men's size," she says, holding up crutches made for someone six feet tall. Is she kidding?

My mom is more gracious than me and nicely says, "I don't think that will work for Alexis, but thank you for trying."

I say nothing because if I say something it is going to be extremely rude.

"She is a complete ninny," I say as soon as she leaves. "Why am I so grumpy?" I usually like people.

"Because you're in pain. And probably hungry too. And, she is a bit of a ninny," she says, making me laugh. My mom rarely says anything negative about anyone.

"You probably need dinner as soon as we get out of here."

Dinner doesn't sound good right now.

We hear another knock on the door, "It better not be that ninny with toddler crutches," I whisper.

Thankfully, it's the doctor.

"The good news is that it's not broken," he says.

Thank heavens! Phew! Maybe I can even compete this weekend. If not this weekend, then for sure next weekend.

"But you do have a sprain," he says. "You need to stay off of it for six-weeks."

"Six weeks! No, that's not possible."

"Unfortunately, you must. It's the only way you will heal."

"I can't! You don't understand - "

"Thank you doctor," my mom cuts me off. "I will make sure she takes care of herself."

I turn to my mom, incredulous. I know for a *fact* my mom never took six weeks off from gymnastics. Why is she agreeing to this?

"Is there anything else?" my mom asks sweetly.

"I recommend you rest and ice. You can get some crutches at the drugstore that are her size. And you can give her ibuprofen for the pain," he tells her. They talk about dosage for a moment and my ears are ringing.

Six weeks.

That's the entire season. If I'm going to miss the entire season I might as well have a broken ankle. At least then I would have a cool cast.

"I see you know how to wrap it. Are you a doctor or trainer?"

"Just a former athlete," my mom says.

He nods and gives her a few more instructions and leaves.

"Mom! Six weeks!"

"Shh, Alexis, let's talk about it in the car," she says and helps me down.

CHAPTER 12

We quietly struggle to the car. I can't put weight on my ankle now that the x-ray tech moved it around so much. As soon as we get in the car I start my argument again, "I can't be out six weeks. It's not that bad. I'm sure I will be fine in a week."

"I don't think you will be fine in a week, but I don't think you need to take six weeks off either," she agrees.

"You don't?" My mom always complies with doctors and experts, so this surprises me.

"But you agreed with him back there."

"No, I didn't. I told him I would make sure you would take care of yourself. Alexis, most doctors have no idea what it means to be an athlete. They see an injury like yours and always say 'stay off of it for six weeks.' A sports doctor will be able to rehab you faster."

"Then why did you take me to a doctor that knows nothing about sports?"

"Because we needed to see if we had to rule out a break."

"So what will a sports doctor say?" I ask.

"Probably that you need to stay off of it for a week and then physical therapy will begin. Maybe sooner. I'm not sure exactly of the timeline. Medicine has changed since I was an athlete."

"When can we see a sports doctor?"

"I'll make some calls tomorrow morning. They are closed by now. Do you want some dinner? We can drive through somewhere?"

This is a rare offer. With so many kids in our family, going to a drive through for dinner is expensive. But I guess my dad and brothers have already had dinner and it's just us.

"No, I'm kind of nauseous," I admit. I feel exhausted and queasy and I just want to go home.

"You do?" she asks glancing back at me.

"Yeah," and as I think about it, I feel even worse; seasick and icky feeling. I definitely do not want food. "No food- can we just go home?"

"I was going to stop and get you crutches, but that can wait," she comments.

"It's getting worse. Why am I getting carsick?"

"It's not carsick, you're nauseous from the pain. Oh honey, we should have given you something at the doctors office. That tech must have really yanked around your ankle."

"She really did," I agree. I feel a wave of nausea. I try to get comfortable in my seat and can't.

"We'll be home soon and you can lay down and put your foot up. Then I can give you some ibuprofen for the pain."

I nod and lean back. I close my eyes and will myself not to throw up. How did this happen? One little hesitation on a dumb full and I'm out for the season?

Maybe not the season. For sure Saturday and maybe even the next meet after that. I take a deep breath, one thing is for sure, it will not be six weeks.

By the time we get home I feel like I actually might throw up. My mom helps me into the house and deposits me on the couch. I immediately lay back as she props up my leg on several pillows. My dad comes over and asks what the doctor said. I just can't answer him.

"You don't look so good," he comments, and all I can do is nod in agreement.

"We need to get her pain under control. Go get some ibuprofen," my mom orders. My brothers come around and all talk at once at me and I can't answer any of them either.

My mom shoos them away and hands me a glass of water. "Try to sit up and drink it, baby girl," she instructs.

I do as she says, unable to take more than a sip before I lean back. Then she goes back to the kitchen to get ice and my dad arrives with the pills. I take two and lay back again and close my eyes. I might throw up for real.

"Ethan, can you get me a garbage can?" I ask in a weak voice.

"Why?" he questions.

"She's not feeling well, Ethan, please just get it," my mom says from the kitchen.

Drew is faster than him; he sets a garbage can next to me then sits down near my head.

"What did the doctor say?" he asks.

"Not broken," I mumble.

"How long are you out?"

"Doctor said six weeks, but I think he doesn't know what he's talking about."

"We're going to see a sports doctor as soon as possible," my mom interjects. "We'll see what they say about recovery time. She'll be fine no matter what. There's always another

561

meet," she says, trying to make light of this disaster.

She unwraps my foot and my brothers groan. "What?" I ask lifting my head.

"That looks bad," Will says.

I look down at my foot. It's much more swollen than before and the bruising has spread. The light purple stretches along the outside of my ankle and travels under my foot. Even my toes are puffy.

"It's fine. It'll be fine, " I say, like I have been saying all day. Now I don't believe it.

"We'll get the swelling down. You went too long without icing," my mom says as she places the ice on my ankle and wraps it back up to keep the ice in place. Then she adds more pillows to make sure my foot is elevated above my heart.

"Do you want to watch something?" my dad asks.

"On a school night?" Will asks, surprised.

"She's not going to school tomorrow," my mom says.

Well, at least there's that, I think as I close my eyes and try to rest. It hurts too much to sleep, but I just can't converse anymore.

"Let's let her rest," my mom says as she herds everyone out of the room.

I must have dozed off, because the next thing I know my mom is unwrapping my ankle and taking off the ice. My dad is sitting me up and asking if I can eat.

My stomach does feel better so I nod yes. He brings me a turkey sandwich and chips and I devour both.

"You ready for bed?" he asks me. Then he picks me up and carries me to my room. I wish he could just plop me down and I could go sleep, but I have to change into my jammies, brush my teeth, and use the restroom. Since I'm feeling a little better, changing into my jammies isn't too difficult. I call for my mom and she helps me to the bathroom. After she gets me back to my room I climb into bed.

"Try to keep it elevated all night, okay?"

"Okay," I say. I watch as she arranges pillows under my foot.

"Mom?" I ask.

"Hmm?"

"How long were you out when you sprained your ankle?"

"Not long enough," she says.

"What does that mean?"

"Well," she begins as she finishes fussing with my tower of pillows and sits next to me. "I only was out two weeks. Then I trained on a taped-up ankle."

"Two weeks, that's great news!" I exclaim, feeling a little more hope for my situation.

"No, Alexis, it wasn't great. I was in a lot of pain and I worked out and competed anyway. At the time it seemed worth it. But now I wake up with swollen ankles every morning."

"Really? I didn't know that."

"Running hurts, walking too much in a day hurts, walking on uneven surfaces hurts, high heels hurt after a short time. Long term, it was not worth going back into the gym before my body was ready."

I look at my ankle and feel angry. How could I let this happen?

"Sprained ankles are tricky because there is not a specific healing time like with a break. It may take three weeks; it may take eight. You are going to have to listen to your body and be honest with yourself. Can you promise me that?" I nod in silence.

She leans over and kisses my head. "I know it doesn't seem like it now, but there is life after gymnastics. We need to do what is best both for your season and your future after gymnastics."

I force a smile and nod. She stands up and flips the light off as she walks out.

I lay in bed looking at the ceiling. I can't roll to my side because of my stupid ankle all propped up. Instead, I take a shaky breath and feel the tears on my face. I'm not sure if they are from pain, frustration, sadness, or what. Whatever the reason, I have a lot to cry about, because I cry for a long time. By the time I'm done, I'm exhausted and quickly fall asleep.

CHAPTER 13

The next day my mom lets me sleep in, but I wake up anyway because my brothers are so loud as they get ready for school. I lay in my bed; glad I don't have to get up. My ankle moved off the pillow in the night. The bandage itches and is constricting. I sit up and take it off.

As I unwind the bandage I see that it has left red marks and indents on my skin. My good spirits drop as I see black and blue on my ankle. The bruises are now on all sides of my ankle and foot. I sure did a number on myself.

"You're up," my mom notices as she pops her head in. "I have to run the boys to school and then I will get you crutches. Depending on how many stops I have to make to find a children's size, I might be gone up to an hour."

"Okay," I say.

"How is it?" she asks, walking in farther. "Oh, Alexis, that bruising looks like it hurts. The swelling has gone down a little," she says, peering at my foot.

I nod, unable to say anything.

"I have to go. Dad will make breakfast for you before he heads out. Try not to walk on it except to go to the bathroom," she says on her way out.

I hear the chaos of her rounding up my brothers and getting them in the car. Then a door slams, I hear the garage door go up and down and then silence.

I have to use the restroom. "Daaaaaad!" I yell.

After a few moments without hearing anything I yell again. Finally he pokes his head in.

"Alexis, good morning. I'm just making you breakfast."

"Can you help me to the bathroom?" I ask.

"Oh, of course," he says walking over to me. Instead of helping me up and having me lean on him while I hop, like Mom did, he just scoops me up and carries me out of my room and to the bathroom I share with my brothers.

He sets me down on the toilet, "Can you take care of it from here?" he says with a worried look.

"Yeah, I've got it," I say, knowing I can lean on the side of the bathtub if I need to.

"Okay, I'll be just outside when you're done," he says.

I nod and he leaves. I use the restroom and easily hop over to wash my hands. When I'm done I hop over and open the door and he is waiting for me.

"Ready for breakfast?" he asks. I nod and he picks me up again. This time throws me over his shoulder like a sack of potatoes, making me laugh.

"Are you going to do this all day?" I ask.

"No, I have to go to work. Once I get you settled on the couch you are on your own. No bathroom breaks for you!"

He sets me down on a bar stool at the counter and resumes mixing pancake batter.

"Are you hungry?" he asks.

"Very," I answer.

"Good, because, as you know, I make amazing pancakes. Other than hungry, how are you feeling?"

"Better. My stomach is better and my ankle is okay. It hurts less," I share.

"That's good," he says sliding a plate of pancakes in front of me.

Once we're done with breakfast my dad gets me settled on the couch and leaves for work. He put my laptop next to me and the TV remote far away. I'm supposed to see what schoolwork I can do from home before turning on the television. I sigh, staying home from school was a good idea. I'm glad it's Friday. By Monday I should be able to get around easier.

My foot is propped up and wrapped with ice. My dad is not nearly as good at wrapping it as my mom and it keeps sliding out of place any time I move.

I'm glad the house is finally quiet. Our house is rarely quiet. I reach for my laptop and log in. None of today's work is posted so I have nothing to do. My book is in my room and the remote is across the room. My phone is next to me. The only games we are allowed to play on our phones are solitaire and a scrabble type game we play with each other and Grandma. If I play my brothers, they can't play back because they are in class. If I play my parents they will know I'm not doing homework. If I play grandma she will ask why I'm not in school. I just don't want to talk about it yet. I feel like I don't have answers. I don't know how long I will be out of the gym or if my season is over.

I keep telling myself it's not over, but a little voice in my head keeps saying, 'it might be.' I hate that voice sometimes.

I play a few terrible rounds of solitaire on my phone before I hear the garage door opening. I set my phone down and pick up my laptop. Then I realize I can't fool my mom, so I just set them both down.

She comes in the door with her arms full. Normally I would help her, but clearly, I can't.

"Hi, Mom," I say,

"Hello! How are you doing?" she asks.

"Bored."

"No assignments yet?"

"Not yet."

"Okay, well, let's take off that ice and practice with the crutches," she says, setting bags on the kitchen counter and heading back into the garage. She comes back in with crutches that look much more appropriately sized for me than the doctor's office offered yesterday.

"Those look better," I comment.

"I agree. We can adjust them too, so they can be as comfortable as possible." She comes over and unwraps my bandage taking off the melted bag of ice. Then she lifts the towel that was between my foot and the ice to take a good look at it for the first time today.

"Oh, Alexis," she says.

"That bad?" I say, biting my lip. She would know and by the look on her face, it's bad.

"It's bruised everywhere," she says, picking up my foot and turning it gently.

"I know. If I wasn't so bummed I would think it looked cool."

"I called the sports doctor this morning. They can get you in on Wednesday."

"Wednesday? Why so long?"

"Alexis, I had to pull strings to get you in on Wednesday. Some people have to wait weeks."

"What do you mean pull strings?"

"I mean, one of the physical therapists there used to be our trainer in college. She did the best ankle tape jobs. Anyway, I texted her and she got you in. I don't know the doctors, but I know the entire office works with athletes."

"Like who?"

"Kids like you and adults who get skiing injuries, stuff like that."

"Not the college athletes?"

"No, their schools take care of them. But probably retired college and pro athletes. Athletes in general just need different care. More aggressive rehab."

"Faster than six weeks?" I grumble.

"Let's hope so," she says, rewrapping my ankle without the ice this time.

"Alright, stand up. Let's adjust these crutches for you," she says, holding them up to me. I stand up on one foot and she holds them up to me adjusting them slightly to be taller. They are kids crutches and they were on the lowest setting. "Okay, try that."

I put them under my armpits and stand on one leg. I put the crutches in front of me and they help me swing forward and take a step on one foot. "This is so much better than hopping," I say getting the hang of it and making my way to the kitchen and back.

"Good. Now, how is your pain?" she asks.

"Better than yesterday. But not great when I don't have my foot up."

"Let's keep it elevated as much as possible today. And we still have to rotate the icing."

I crutch my way back to the couch. "When do you think I can walk on it?" I ask. Once I am walking, tumbling can't be too far behind.

"You are going to be the judge of that. You're going to have to listen to your body. If it hurts to walk on it, don't do it. The only place I want you pushing yourself is when you are in physical therapy and the therapist can make sure you aren't making anything worse."

I get to the couch, set my crutches against the coffee table, and try to put weight on my ankle before sitting. I'm shocked at how weak it is. It physically cannot hold my weight.

I plop onto the couch. "My body says not today," I say, trying not to panic.

CHAPTER 14

I spend the day on the couch with my mom coming in and out to rotate my ice all day. She lets me watch a movie in the morning and in the afternoon I'm able to get some schoolwork done. Only my math and English teachers are organized enough to already post today's assignments. I get them done much quicker than I would have in class and I find I'm bored again. I look at the clock on the wall; my brothers will be home from school soon. Having some noise in the house will be nice.

They hit the house in a storm, and as always, head to the kitchen arguing.

"I can't believe you got to stay home, faker," Ethan says.

"Leave her alone," Drew says, shoving him as they trip over each other getting to the kitchen. My mom puts them to work emptying the dishwasher while she prepares a snack.

There is so much talking on top of each other that I can't even follow the conversation. I pick up my phone to play each of them on the word game and get the satisfaction of hearing their phones pinging.

"Oh it's just you," William says.

"Are you waiting for someone to text you?" Ethan asks.

"No, are you?"

"Always," Ethan says, unruffled.

After my mom gets them to eat something healthy they raid the pantry eating whatever they can find.

"I'm so glad it's Friday and no one has practice or games tonight," she says, coming over to me to hand me a plate of celery and peanut butter.

"Can I go to PNO?" Drew calls to her from the kitchen.

"Only of you can get a ride, I need to relax tonight."

"Are your teammates going?" he asks me.

"Probably not, they have a meet tomorrow," I answer. "Did you call Katie? To tell her I can't come tomorrow?"

"I did, when I was driving to get the boys from school."

"What did she say?"

"She figured as much. She told me to tell you to take care and to keep us posted on your progress."

"What progress? I'm just sitting here," I pout.

"Alexis, it hasn't even been twenty-four hours. This is going to take time."

"Can I see it?" Drew asks.

I nod and sit up to unwrap my mom's perfect wrap job. As I unravel the bandage, I start to see the bruising has traveled up my leg and down my foot. And the purple is darker now.

"Oooh, that is gnarly!" Drew says, covering his mouth.

"Really?" Will asks, running over. "Let me see," he says, jumping over the back of the couch to take a look.

"Holy Moses! That's legit, Lex," he admits.

I understand that to William this is a compliment. "Thanks," I say.

"What does the other side look like?"

I rotate my entire leg rather than my ankle so they can see the other side.

"Damn, Lex," Ethan says.

"Ethan, language," my mom chides and gives him a look. My mom is a stickler for language and he is going to have an extra chore for that tonight. I don't think he cares.

"So no meet tomorrow or probably the next one," Drew says quietly. Being a fellow gymnast who is also in the middle of competition season, he knows how devastating this is for me.

"I might be able to do the next one," I say, desperately trying to believe it.

"She has an appointment with a sports doctor on Wednesday. We'll see what that doctor says," my mom comments.

Drew grabs my crutches and starts using them around the room. "These are pretty cool."

"Can I try?" William cuts in and they start doing laps around the kitchen and family room until I need the crutches to go to the bathroom.

"Ethan, come take out the garbage," my mom says from the kitchen as she is putting away their snack mess.

"Why me?" he whines.

"Because you forgot to respect our home," she comments. I knew it. At least she's predictable. I smile to myself as I take my crutches from Drew and make my way across the room to the guest bathroom.

When I get back to the couch everyone is gone, probably to their rooms. I pick up my phone to see if any of my brothers have played me back. They all have, also predictable.

I see I have a text message. I open it up.

Paige:

How are you doing? Katie said you are not going to
make it tomorrow. So sorry Lex. Can we come visit?

"Mo-um!" I yell and I hear her yell back from upstairs.
"Can my teammates come over?" I yell. I wait for a response,
but she doesn't reply. Then I hear someone coming down the
stairs and I assume it is her because they aren't running.

She comes into the room talking. "That would be lovely
if your teammates came over. Why don't you invite them for
pizza?" she asks.

"What time?"

"Well, it can't be too late because they have their meet
all the way in Park City so it's going to be an early morning.
How about five-thirty and their parents can pick them up at
eight or eight-thirty?"

I nod and type back to Paige.

Me:

I would love that! 5:30? And we will feed you pizza.

Paige:

Okay, I will tell the others.

I look up when I'm done and see my mom is texting.

"Paige said she would tell the others so you don't have
to tell the moms."

"I'm texting Dad and telling him to get pizza on the way
home. I just really don't want to do it tonight."

"Thanks for getting me the crutches and changing my ice
all day," I say, realizing how busy she was today.

She walks over and hugs me, "You are welcome. We are
going to get you better in no time."

"Faster than six weeks?"

"That can be our goal," she deftly says, never one to

make promises she can't keep.

I agree and lean back into my pillow pile.

"Why don't you rest until your friends get here?" she suggests.

I nod. But I can't really sleep, so I pick up my phone when she walks out and play my turn in my game with my brothers.

I hear the doorbell promptly at five thirty. I stay where I am because it is such an ordeal to get up and move around. I hear my mom greet them and say, "Oh, that is so sweet, Alexis will love it." Now I'm wishing I'd gotten up. I can't hear anything else they are saying because there's a lot of talking at once.

Debbie and my teammates walk in. Savannah is holding a balloon bouquet. It has one mylar balloon in the middle that says, 'Get Well'. The other four balloons are red, blue, green, and yellow, to match the 'Get Well' balloon.

Savannah hands me the balloons. "They're from all of us, Riley and Victoria, too. They're sorry they couldn't come tonight but told me to tell you hi."

I take the balloons and thank them. But I don't know what to do with them. "Why don't you tie them to the lamp?" my mom suggests. I look over to the floor lamp and I can't quite reach it.

"I can do it for you," Paige offers and takes the balloons from me.

It's a little awkward as they all stand above me. "Do you want to see it?" I offer.

They all say yes and I sit up and start unwrapping my ankle.

"I didn't even see you do it," Marissa says.

"I think you were doing your routine," I comment.

"I saw it," Lucy says. "You were in so much pain when you first hit the ground. It was awful."

I think back; it was bad. I'm glad it doesn't hurt that bad now. As I unwrap my foot, the bruises start to reveal themselves.

"Oh my gosh, Lexi!" Trista says. "No wonder Katie told us to come see you."

"Trista!" Savannah exclaims.

"Was that a secret? Sorry. Katie was worried is all," she says.

"Is it like that all the way around?" Carmen asks.

I turn my leg, and therefore my foot. "Yeah, all sides."

"And you are sure it's not broken?" Debbie, Savannah's mom, asks.

"Not broken," I say, leaning back.

"When will you be able to come back?" she asks.

I look at my mom to help me with this question. I don't want to say six weeks to my teammates. One, because I don't believe it, and two, because that would mean I'm missing State and letting them down.

Thankfully, my mom sees me turn to her and says, "We are seeing a sports doctor on Wednesday. We'll have more information after that."

There is silence for a moment and I can tell my teammates don't know what to say.

"Why don't you girls sit down. I'll bring in drinks," my mom says, breaking the silence.

"I'll help you," Debbie offers.

My teammates back away from me and sit around the room.

"We'll sure miss you tomorrow," Carmen says.

"Can you come watch?" Trista asks.

"I don't think so. My mom said it's best if I keep icing and keep it elevated. That would be hard to do at the meet and even on the drive. Apparently, this is important for the first three days."

"Is your mom a doctor?" Marissa asks.

"No, she knows what to do from being a gymnast," I say, making them laugh.

"We can send you videos," Savannah says. "Of the meet tomorrow."

"Would you please?" I say, brightening a little. "I would like that."

My mom and Debbie come in with big bottles of soda along with plastic cups and several black markers. They set everything down on the coffee table and my mom says, "Take a cup and write your name on it, then you can get a drink." Then she hands the stack of cups to Lucy who takes one and passes the rest. My mom gives the markers to Carmen and she also takes one and passes the rest. Pretty soon we each have a cup and marker. Instead of just writing our name we spend a bunch of time decorating our cups and writing our names as fancy as possible.

"Next time remind me to get you girls an art project to do," my mom says, leaving the room with Debbie.

We are drawing on our cups and talking about our brilliant designs. It's an easy conversation and companionship. They almost make me forget about my pain.

"Why was Katie so worried?" I finally ask.

"She just knew your injury might be serious and asked us to check on you," Carmen explains.

"What makes it serious?" I ask and everyone is quiet.

Finally Paige says, "She knew you'd be bummed you're missing a few meets."

"One meet," I say, a little angrier than I intended to. "One meet for sure. We don't know about the rest," I say in a more normal tone.

"Who's ready for pizza?" my dad yells, bursting in from the garage door. He breaks our awkward moment and my teammates yell that they are ready for food.

My brothers materialize from upstairs and my teammates go to the kitchen to get their pizza. They bring it back into the family room to eat with me.

"What kind do you want?" Trista yells to me from the kitchen.

"Pepperoni," I yell back. She delivers me a plate with two slices of pepperoni and I thank her. We eat in happy silence until my brothers come in and start talking to us.

"Where do you guys go to school?" Ethan asks.

"Snowcap Middle School," Trista says.

"Same," Marissa says.

"St. Mary's," Paige says.

"Is that a pretty hard school?" Ethan asks her.

"It is. We have a lot of homework and projects but the tests aren't too bad."

"What's Mountain View like?" Marissa asks.

"I think a little like Snowcap but we rotate classes less," William says.

This goes on for a while, comparing the schools. Which sports they have, which clubs. If the teachers are nice. I'm pleased my brothers are being polite to my friends. When we are done eating William suggests we play a game, but it's hard to think of something with this big of a group. In the end we play a trivia game that we play on the big television screen through our gaming system.

We split into three groups. One with Lucy, Trista, and Ethan, one with Savannah, Paige, and Will. The last group is Drew, Marissa, Carmen, and me.

The first question comes up on the screen.

What do Humpback Whales eat?

    A – fish

    B – seaweed

    C – krill

Each team has to select A, B, or C on their remote. My group easily gets that it is krill and we wait for the other teams. They get this one right too and we have a three-way tie. I know that the game will come up with harder questions if all three teams keep getting them right. Finally we get to the hard questions.

Who was Henry VIII's third wife who also died in childbirth?

    A – Kathryn of Aragon

    B – Anne Bolyn

    C – Jane Seymore

All of us are stumped on this one, but we recognize the name Anne Bolyn and start to select her.

"Wait," Marissa whispers to our team. "Didn't Anne Bolyn die at the guillotine?"

"Gross, I don't know," Carmen says.

"I think she did. It's not her. And Kathryn was his first wife who he divorced. I saw it on the History Channel. Do the third one, Jane Seymore."

We know better than to question Marissa so we select C, winning the round for us.

"No fair, you guys have four people," Ethan complains.

"I don't think they are winning because they have four people. It's because they have Marissa," Trista comments.

"Then you trade with her," Ethan suggests. "We shouldn't have her on a four-person team."

"Fine," Trista agrees and comes over to our team.

This time Marissa wins the round by knowing Pi out five places past 3.14.

We mix the teams up again, but whoever is on Marissa's team always wins. That girl has endless trivia in her brain.

"You are crazy smart," William says.

"She totally is," Lucy agrees.

"Girls, about five minutes and Kay will be here to get Paige and Marissa and I have to take the rest of you all home," Debbie tells us. Paige and Marissa live near each other, so they probably carpooled because Debbie's car can't fit everyone.

Wow, it's already eight o'clock. My teammates have to go home and get a good night of sleep before tomorrow.

After our five minutes, I get up and use my crutches to walk them to the door. "Thank you for coming. You really helped cheer me up." Savannah gives me a hug and the others do the same after seeing her do it.

"Bye!" they say, piling in the two cars.

"Good luck tomorrow!" I say and wave. When the words and their full meaning come out I feel a lump in my throat and I'm glad I didn't feel this way until just now. My teammates were so nice to come over and visit me. I'm glad I didn't ruin it by crying and making them feel bad.

I slowly make my way back up the driveway after they drive away. My mom is holding the door open for me and I crutch my way in.

"That was sure nice of them," my mom comments.

"It was. Are you sure we can't go to the meet?" I plead.

"Like I told you before, the first three days of a sprained ankle it is best to ice and elevate. It will give you the best odds of coming back in less than six weeks."

"Do you think that's possible?" I ask, getting a little choked up.

"If you work hard enough."

"Seems the only thing I have to do is sit on my bum," I grumble.

"You'll see," she says, shutting the front door behind us.

CHAPTER 15

The next day I'm very mopey knowing my teammates are competing in Park City without me. My dad is gone all day taking my brothers to basketball games. Drew is home but sleeping in. I don't know how he does that.

My mom settles me on the couch just like yesterday.

"I don't think I can handle another day on the couch," I moan.

"Well, this is day two. You go to school Monday and to the doctor Wednesday, so enjoy it while you can," she says, wrapping my ankle with the first round of ice for the day.

"Can I watch movies?" I ask.

"I got you something better," she says.

"What?" I ask. What could it possibly be that's better than movies? She doesn't answer, but when she is done wrapping my foot she leaves and comes back with our family handheld video game device.

"I got you a game."

"I don't really like games." I never got into video games because, for one, my brothers are terrible at sharing games, and two, I just never got into the games like they did.

"You'll like this one. I loved this game when I was your age."

"Ugh, an old game?" I'm not going to like it.

She ignores me and sits next to me and turns on the player. "Tetris," she says. "It's a game testing your spatial awareness and speed. You'll love it."

I watch over her shoulder as she plays and it is interesting. More interesting than I thought.

"Can I try?" I ask. She shows me which buttons do what then passes it over.

"This is cool." I'm immediately sucked in.

"You're welcome," she says, standing up. "I have to run some errands. Take your ice off in fifteen minutes."

I agree and she leaves.

I sit in the eerily quiet house and play my game. I look up at the clock between each game to see if my teammates are competing yet. It's nine-thirty, they're probably done with the first rotation by now. I thought they were going to send me videos. I should have gone. I would have propped my foot up and just iced it when I got home.

Since there is nothing I can do, I pick up the hand-held player and start another round of Tetris. When my phone pings, my heart leaps, expecting meet videos.

Mom:
  Stopping at the store, do you need anything?

Oh, just my mom. I sigh. Do I need anything? What sounds good right now?

Me:

    Ice cream, peppermint if they still have it.

I love peppermint ice cream, but it's only sold at Christmas time. Since it's January, there's a chance they might still have some at the store.

Mom:

    Second choice?

Me:

    Caramel ribbon

I go back to my game and my phone pings again, I roll my eyes, assuming it is my mom.

But when I look at my phone I see it's Savanah's mom.

Debbie:

    Hi Alexis! We just finished beam, here you go:

She has attached six videos, one for each of them. I watch the videos. Paige fell on her round-off and Savannah fell on her series. Everyone else stayed on. That's an improvement for us.

Me:

    They look great. Thank you! Go PBGA!!!

She sends me back emojis of a gymnast and balloons. I smile to myself and lean back. I'm glad my team had such a good start. And I'm glad they remembered to send me videos. I pick up my hand-held gaming device and happily play some more Tetris.

My mom comes in with her arms full of groceries and, once again, I feel bad I can't help her.

"How's it going?" she asks me, dumping her bags on the

counter.

"Fine." I answer as she goes back out to the car for another load.

"Time to ice," she says when she comes back in and I groan. "Have you heard from your team?" she asks.

"Yeah, they just finished beam," I say. "I feel bad I didn't go," I admit.

"Oh, baby girl, I promise this will be worth it. You have to take care of yourself if you want to be back with them as soon as possible."

"Yeah," I say, unconvinced.

It really, really, cannot be like this for six weeks. My mom keeps saying I will be doing rehab, but I don't know what that means.

"Mom, what is rehab like?" I ask.

"It's like conditioning only it only focuses on your ankle. It will be a lot of exercises for your ankle."

"Will it hurt?" Just moving my ankle hurts.

"Sometimes, and you will be sore like conditioning."

Doesn't sound very fun. At least I will be off the couch.

The weekend crawled by with me sitting on the couch both Saturday and Sunday. My brothers are jealous I missed school and church. Every tragedy has an upside.

Getting ready for school on Monday was an ordeal even though I'm getting around better. I can put weight on my foot now, but it causes pain and my mom keeps telling me not to push it.

I thought school would be fun with crutches because of all the attention. It wound up being way harder to get around than I anticipated. It wasn't worth the attention. What's worse was that kids didn't understand why I had crutches if my leg wasn't broken. They kept telling me that sprains aren't as bad. It made me feel like a faker.

By lunch time I'm sick of answering questions and my armpits are throbbing.

I get over to my usual table with Oakley and Ashtyn and lean my crutches on the table and sit down.

"Oh no, our mom told us you hurt yourself," Ashtyn says with real sympathy in her voice.

"Why didn't you come over last night?" I ask them.

"Aunt Jane hosted last night," Oakley answers. Our Aunt Jane lives about an hour away. Every once in a while she hosts Sunday dinner.

"I wonder why we didn't go," I say as I get out my lunch.

"Your mom said you had to stay home and ice," Oakley comments.

"Oh, yeah, I guess that's true. According to my mom the first three days of icing are super important. That was Friday, Saturday, and Sunday."

"How long will you have crutches?" Ashtyn asks.

"I don't know. I'm seeing a doctor later this week to find out more."

"And gymnastics?" she asks.

"Out for now," I say, trying not to cry at school.

They are silent at that and I don't know how to lighten the mood.

"It's not broken," I manage.

"Well, that's good. Maybe you won't be out very long then," Ashtyn says.

I smile at her hopeful face. "Maybe."

That night Katie calls to see how I'm doing and my mom tells her we have an appointment with a sports doctor on Wednesday.

Tuesday night Katie emails my mom a conditioning list.

"What's this?" I ask, taking the list my mom is holding out for me.

"A conditioning spreadsheet from Katie," she answers.

"Conditioning?" I ask, scanning it.

"Yes. If you don't condition you'll lose muscle. Coming back will be so much harder."

"Oh," I say, scanning the list. It includes hip flexor work, presses against the wall, pull-ups, V-ups, and more.

"All things you can do from home and that you don't need your ankle for," she says.

The spreadsheet has the exercise name, number of reps, sets, and a place for me to put in the date that I did it.

"When am I supposed to start this?" I ask.

"Today. She will give you a different one in a few days depending on what the doctor says tomorrow. It looks like she is being really cautious with her list," she observes, looking at it over my shoulder.

I don't know what to think of the list. I guess it's nice Katie thought of me and put it together. But it means that no one thinks I'm going to be back anytime soon.

"I guess I'll get started, since it's late already," I say slowly.

"Do we need to move the coffee table out of the way?" she asks. Normally this is something I would have done in the basement. However, stairs are such an ordeal for me, the family room is probably better.

"Yeah," I say. My mom is deceptively strong and she easily moves the coffee table out of the way to sit along the couches. "I thought I would leave the wall open for your presses."

I nod and start with the hip flexors. I sit down with my legs in front of me in a 90-degree angle, like a pancake sit. Then I put my hands on either side of one knee and lift my leg with a straight knee and a pointed toe. I do this twenty times and then move to the other leg. Then I put my hands in the middle and lift both legs at the same time. I can definitely feel my hip flexors working hard. I have three sets of twenty each way: right, left, middle.

Then I have twenty press handstands. I can do these without the wall. Maybe she wants to make sure I don't put any pressure on my ankle when I start. I make sure I have space around me and put my hands on the ground and my feet a little wider than shoulder distance apart. Then I lean my shoulders forward and lift my legs into a handstand and gently come down onto my good foot. I can feel my shoulder, lat, leg, and core muscles working.

I complete five and look at the paper again. I have twenty! I may have to work up to that. I do five more for a total of ten and decide to take a break and do something else.

I do my three sets of thirty V-ups and arch-ups. Those aren't a problem, but to be honest, my ankle is starting to throb from the movement.

I look at my list. I have a few more core exercises and then pull-ups. How does Katie know Drew has a pull-up bar in his doorway? My mom must have told her. That means I have to finish the presses because once I go upstairs for pull-ups, I'm not coming back down.

I finish the presses and I can feel my armpit muscles are going to be sore. I grab my crutches and make my slow progress up the stairs.

"I hear Alexis coming," my mom says.

I get to the top of the stairs. "This is hard."

"Hopefully you can ditch the crutches tomorrow," she

predicts.

"It still hurts to walk on it though."

"You might get a boot or air cast or something. Crutches aren't needed for long term anymore."

"When do we go tomorrow?"

"Nine, you'll miss your morning classes."

At least I get to miss school. I make my way over to Drew and William's room. Their door is open and they are each chilling on their beds. Drew is listening to music and Will is reading a book.

"Can I use your pull-up bar?" I ask them.

Will is the only one who hears me and he nods. I set my crutches against the wall and set my paper down. I reach up and do ten pull-ups. I gently let go and come down on one leg. I rest and do two more sets, as my paper says.

Then I take my crutches and go to my room. As soon as I get to my bed, I toss my crutches and lay down. That was an easy conditioning list and yet somehow it was hard. Did I already lose some muscle? That thought is depressing.

"How did it go?" my mom asks, coming in and putting away clean laundry (something I would normally do for myself).

"It was an easy list, but still hard," I whine.

"Your body is busy healing. It will get easier. Give yourself some grace."

Give myself grace. I'm never sure what that means. I think maybe it means to be patient or maybe not be hard on myself. It's hard not to be frustrated. I thought I would be able to put weight on my ankle by now.

When I don't say anything she moves on. "Why don't you get your pajamas on and brush your teeth. Then we can put you in bed and ice you one last time before you go to sleep."

I haven't been icing as much now that the three days are

up, so I'm surprised she wants me to. "I thought I didn't need to anymore."

"You need to after workouts and you just had a mini workout."

"I didn't use my ankle though," I counter.

"It still had blood pumping to it and still may swell up. Ice won't hurt," she insists. I nod and pull myself up and hop over to my pajama drawer.

"This is a royal pain," I mumble as she walks out of the room.

I get my pajamas on, brush my teeth, and snuggle in bed. I don't yell to my mom that I'm ready. I know she will be in when she can. I pick up the book on my nightstand and start reading.

"Hey, sport," my dad says, coming in with a bag of ice. "I hear you need ice."

"Mom says so anyway."

"Well, she's pretty smart when it comes to this stuff, so let's listen to her," he says, walking over to me and grabbing pillows from the top of my bed. "Do you want the pillows under the covers or your foot out?"

"Foot out," I say, pulling my covers down and getting my leg out to set on top of the covers. He props my foot up on three pillows and starts unwrapping my bandage.

He pauses to look at the bruises for a moment. He gently turns my ankle. "I didn't know a sprain could do this," he says.

"The swelling is down, but yeah, the bruises are legit," I say, using Wliiam's word.

He puts the ice on and I sit up to wrap it back up. I have watched my mom do it enough times. I'm sure I can do a better job than my dad.

"I got it," I say, taking the bandage from him.

"Don't trust me, huh?"

I smile, "I've just watched Mom do it a lot."

He sits on the bed next to me and watches me for a minute.

"How are you feeling?" he asks.

"It doesn't hurt as bad."

"No, Lex, how are you *feeling*?"

I pause and look at him. I think about it for a moment.

"Frustrated. Angry. Disappointed," I answer.

"That's all understandable. I'm sorry this happened, it must be really hard." I nod that it is. "But Lex, this is just a bump in the road. I know it seems like a huge deal right now, but there is more to life than gymnastics."

"No there isn't," I disagree, frowning. "I have worked so hard for this season, and now, well, I don't know what is going to happen now. I thought I would only miss one meet, but I don't see how I will make the next one either."

He rubs my back and says, "All you can do is focus on getting your ankle better and then see where the season is at."

Over probably, a pitiful little voice in my head says.

"Tomorrow is a big day. Let's see what a sports doctor has to say about your timeline."

I nod, mostly because I can't speak. I lean back on my pillows. I have to stay on my back while I'm icing so I might as well read. I don't want to talk about my ankle anymore so I pick up my book. My dad gets the hint and stands up. He leans over, kisses me on the head, and says, "Night Lex."

"Night, Dad," I manage.

CHAPTER 16

"She gets to miss school again?" Ethan complains.

"She has a doctor's appointment and will join you later. Now go get in the car. Dad will be out in a minute," my mom orders, herding my brothers out the door.

I can hear them loud and clear even though I'm upstairs in the bathroom brushing my teeth. The garage door shuts and suddenly it's silent. Whew, are we always like that?

I limp out of the bathroom to go get my crutches. I have been using them less around the house. I can feel my ankle has gotten a little stronger. I can put just enough weight on it to limp, which is easier than the crutches. Unfortunately for longer distances, like getting to the car and to the doctor's, I need crutches.

I slowly make my way downstairs and find my mom in the kitchen making us breakfast.

"Morning, Alexis," she says.

"Morning," I say back. "Are we always like that?"

"Like what?"

"So loud leaving for school?"

She laughs, "Always."

I sit at the bar and start drinking the milk she set out. Since we have a little extra time she is making eggs and toast. The variety is a treat and so is being alone with my mom.

"Are you ready for this?" she asks, sliding two eggs on my plate.

"Yes. I'm anxious to know when I can start training again."

"It will be nice to have a plan of action, that's for sure."

I'm not sure what action she is talking about. It seems like all I can do is sit on the couch and play Tetris while I wait for my ankle to get better.

The special sports doctor facility is about thirty minutes away in Salt Lake City. When we pull into the parking lot there are pictures of Olympic skiers on huge banners on each of the light posts. A few Olympic ice skaters, a golfer, a tennis player, and more.

"Are these some of their patients?" I ask my mom.

"Some of the more famous ones, yes," she confirms.

This doctor may get it after all, instead of telling me to rest for six weeks.

We walk in and I sit and wait while my mom signs a bunch of forms on a tablet. I look around the waiting room and it is huge. There is a long desk in front and two doorways, one on either side. One doorway leads to a long hallway of doors. I assume they are exam rooms. The other doorway goes down a hall and to a large workout room on the right. The entire right wall of the waiting room is glass and I can see patients working out. Not like gymnastics working out, just conditioning type working out and weightlifting. Most of them are adults, which is intimidating.

People from the waiting room don't wait long before

someone in khakis and a green polo shirt comes to get them. I can see through the glass that they go to the workout room. I'm surprised each athlete has a coach. It is all one-on-one in the gym area, instead of eight-to-one like we have at Perfect Balance. That is intense. There will be no cheating in conditioning around here.

"Alexis?" I hear my name called by a man in scrubs. I stand up and grab my crutches and slowly make my way to him then follow him down the hall to an exam room. I sit up on the exam table and he takes my vitals and leaves.

We wait some more. "All this waiting," I groan.

"I know, but these doctors are worth it. I promise."

Finally, we hear a knock on the door and a man in a white coat comes in. "Hi, Alexis, I am Dr. Jensen," he says, extending his hand. I tentatively take it and he shakes my hand. That's nice; most adults don't address kids.

"I hear you hurt your ankle," he says.

"Yes," I confirm.

"May I take a look?"

I nod and he pulls out the familiar tray under the exam table so I can prop up my leg like I did at the last doctor's office.

"Nice wrap job." He gently unwraps my bandage and takes a look.

"When did you do this? About a week ago?"

"Thursday, how'd you know?" I ask.

"The color of your bruises are about a week old. How did you hurt yourself?"

"Doing gymnastics."

"A gymnast! I love working with gymnasts. You are tough kids," he comments. "Tell me exactly how though."

"Tumbling."

"Did you land short or in a hole in the mats?" I'm impressed he knows enough about gymnastics to ask these questions.

"I landed short while I was still twisting."

He whistles, "That'll do it." Then he gently pushes in on the swollen parts of my ankle and moves it around a little. It doesn't hurt nearly as much as the last doctor. Probably because my ankle is a little better than it was six days ago.

"How have you been taking care of it?"

"We aggressively did RICE the first three days and now we have been icing a few times a day," my mom answers.

"Were you a gymnast?" he asks, clearly knowing the look of a former athlete.

"Yes, for BYU," she confirms.

"So you are a legacy athlete," he says. "I better take good care of you."

I smile, not really sure what the significance is. Except that Mom knew to bring me here.

"You have a second-degree sprain, which means that your ligaments probably have some partial tears."

"How do you fix it?" I ask.

"Surgery is not needed so I'm not going to fix it, you are."

"Me?"

"Yes, you're going to do a lot of physical therapy to strengthen the muscles around your ankle. Since your ligaments are hurt your muscles are going to take up the slack."

"How long do you think it will take to rehab her?" my mom asks.

"Let me try to see how weak it is. Can you push against my hand?" he asks as he puts a flat palm on the side of my foot. I try to push but get very little movement and it hurts.

"How about this side?" he asks, putting his palm on the other side of my foot. I get a little more movement, but not much.

"How about now?" he asks, putting his palm on the bottom of my foot. I can get to a toe point okay, but not with the resistance of his hand.

"And up?" he asks as he puts his hand on the top of my foot. That one I can't do at all.

"When is your next competition?"

"Next weekend, in a week and a half," I say.

"You're not going to make that one. What is after that?" he asks.

My mom pulls out her phone and looks at our schedule. "She has one in a week, like she said. Not this weekend, but next weekend. Then one the following weekend after that. And the next two are two weeks apart."

He picks up a flip calendar that is sitting on the counter. "What was the date of injury?"

My mom tells him again and goes over the dates on her phone again.

"So you have one two weeks from injury, three, five, and seven, is that right?"

Mom my swipes on her phone and says, "Yes."

"Alexis, if you work really hard in physical therapy, you might be ready for your last two meets."

"Five weeks out?" This doctor isn't any better than the last one!

"Your injury has left your ankle weak and gymnastics puts a lot of impact on your ankles. Your entire body, really. What we don't want is for you to return before you are ready and do long-term damage to your body."

He looks at my mom, "I bet you returned too early after injuries. What hurts now?"

"My ankles," she admits.

"How often?"

"Every day," she says.

"Thankfully, we know a lot more and don't make that

596

mistake of long-term damage anymore," he says.

"What meet is in five weeks?" I ask, changing the subject back to my season. I want desperately to grasp onto a goal.

"The Winter Classic Invitational. It's in four weeks, five weeks from injury," my mom says.

"And after that?"

"State," she says.

I would only have one meet before State?

"You'll for sure get to compete in that one, seven weeks out," the doctor smiles.

"Good thing you already qualified," my mom says. That is good, but without the entire season to improve, my shot at making Regionals is officially shattered.

"Let's get you a better system to get around than these crutches," Dr. Jensen says. "Mrs. Bingham, why don't you rewrap her ankle while I get a boot. Are you a trainer?"

"No, I just took a class in college," my mom says.

"You do a perfect wrap job. Can you tape her up, too?"

"Yes, I used to tape my own ankles," my mom answers.

"You are in good hands, Alexis, I'll be right back." He leaves the room.

"Good news, huh?" she says, standing up and grabbing the bandage off the table next to me.

"No. He's no better than the last guy," I pout.

"You will still get to compete in a couple of meets this season," she tries again.

"I won't make Regionals!" I yell, choking back tears. "This stinks!"

"You don't know that," she says, wrapping my ankle.

I don't say anything because I want to scream. Or cry. Or scream and cry.

"Okay, I have a couple of sizes here," the doctor says, coming back into the room. He has two black tall medical boots in his hands. He holds one next to my leg and it reaches past my knee. "Way too big," he says and holds up the other one, it reaches to about three inches under my knees. "Let's try this one on."

He un-Velcros it, lifts my leg, puts it in, and Velcros it back up. "Okay, stand up," he says.

I slide off the table and stand in the boot. The base of it feels chunky and high. Somehow the boot makes it so it doesn't hurt to stand. It's supporting my ankle on all sides.

I take a little step and I can do it without too much of a limp.

"Better than crutches?" he asks.

"So much better," I agree. Finally, this guy is helpful.

"Great, let's have you practice walking while I show you around our facility."

"Will I work out with you?" I ask.

"No, I'm the sports doctor. I asses the injury and tell the physical therapist what you need."

He opens the door and I limp-walk out of the room. We follow him down two halls while he talks to us. "I want you here at least three days a week if you want to compete in four weeks. Plus you are going to have to do some home conditioning for the rest of your body."

"Her coach is already on that," my mom says.

"Good. You can probably get back in the gym next week for a limited workout," he says, surprising me.

I stop. "Next week? Well, how long am I in the boot?"

"Oh sorry, you will need to be in the boot at least a week, but you can do bars in that right? Over the foam pool thing."

"The pit?"

"Yes, the pit! You could do bars over the pit so nothing can hurt your ankle," he says.

I hadn't thought of going back to the gym with my

injury. I'm not sure why, because I've seen several of the upper optional girls come in and work bars with a foot injury or beam with an arm injury.

We go into the huge workout gym and there are athletes everywhere working with trainers. Some are using dumbbells and lifting weights, some are on stationary bikes or treadmills, some are using TheraBands, yoga balls, and some are stretching on the floor on yoga mats. There are also big tables along a wall that people are sitting on getting what looks like ultrasounds or massages on a specific body part.

"Here is where the hard work happens. We'll match you with a trainer and they will spend thirty minutes with you to strengthen your ankle. Mrs. Bingham, you can come in or watch from the windows."

He looks at me, "Do you have any questions?"

"No," I say a little overwhelmed.

"Mrs. Bingham?" he asks.

"I assume she needs ice after each session?"

"Yes, we will do the heat before, there is an icing room for after," he confirms, as he walks us back to the waiting room. He walks us over to the reception desk and says to the worker behind a computer, "Can you set her up three times a week with Bobbi? If Bobbi doesn't have room then I think Janice."

The receptionist nods and starts clicking on her computer.

"Starting when?" she asks.

"As soon as possible," he says. Then he looks at me. "Alexis, I look forward to seeing your progress. Mrs. Bingham, thank you for bringing her in."

My mom thanks him back and he pats me on the shoulder. "Good luck this season!" Then he walks away.

"I have a recurring two o'clock with Bobbi starting tomorrow. She can do Tuesday, Thursday, and Friday."

"Do you have anything after three thirty?" my mom asks. "She has school."

"No, afternoons and evenings fill up far in advance."

"I have to leave here by two to pick up her brothers from school. What else do you have?"

"Janice has a twelve-thirty? Monday, Tuesday, Thursday."

"Twelve-thirty works," my mom says. More missed school. It has been kind of fun, but three days a week might become a homework nightmare. She puts us in her computer while my mom schedules it in her phone.

"No aspirin before sessions, wear workout clothing, tennis shoes, and hair up. If you miss a session with less than twenty-four hour notice you will be charged the full amount. If you are late it will cut into your session and you will be charged for the full session. We will bill your insurance. We recommend you call ahead to understand your co-pay. It is usually different than doctor visits."

The lady drones on with instructions for my mom. While we are standing at the desk, the medical assistant that put us in the exam room comes running over to me with my crutches. "I'm glad I caught you. Here are your crutches," he says, handing them to me.

I take them, wondering what I need them for now. My mom looks over, "Oh thank you! We did forget!"

"But we don't need them now," I point out.

"Might as well keep them, your brothers or cousins might at some point," she says. The lady is finally done talking. My mom thanks her and we leave.

I'm faster in my boot, but not much. I'm grateful to not have crutches under my armpits. When we get in the car my mom says, "How about we go to lunch and then I will take you to school."

I agree. "He didn't have much better news," I point out.

"All you can do is your best. You just have to do what they say and see what happens."

CHAPTER 17

After my doctor appointment my mom takes me to a great Mexican restaurant downtown. We don't have food this good in Snowcap Canyon. While we are waiting to be served I ask to see her phone and I study when my next three meets are. One week, two weeks, four weeks, and State in six weeks.

"Think I can compete in four weeks?" I ask.

"I think it's up to you. I think you have to put the work in with the physical therapist and see your progress."

I whirl the lemon in my water with my straw and think about that.

"What about school?"

"You're going to miss a lot of school, but you will be at the gym less so I think you can keep up."

"I won't be at the gym at all," I pout.

"Alexis, you can go into the gym with an injury. There are less things you can work while you wait for your ankle to heal, but you can still train."

"I guess," I agree even though I don't believe her.

She changes the subject and asks me about school and what classes I missed this morning. Then we talk about how I need to tell my teachers that I'm going to miss the class after lunch on a regular basis. I think my mom should tell them but she insists I should talk to them today and she will email them tonight to follow up. We look up the bell schedule and it turns out I will be missing lunch time and 4th period, which is math. That is a relief. I'm not great at math like Marissa, but math teachers tend to be the most organized and have the easiest work to make up.

We time it so that I get to school as the lunch period is almost over. We walk into the office, she signs me in, and we say goodbye. I slowly join the fray of the hallway in my boot. The boot is much easier than the crutches were and that alone was worth going to the doctor. By the time I get to math class I'm not early enough to talk to my math teacher. I quietly and ungracefully get to my seat just after the bell rings.

I try to pay close attention to the lesson, knowing I'm going to miss tomorrow's lesson. When class is over I make my way up to my teacher.

"Alexis, I have been meaning to ask what you did to yourself?"

"I sprained my ankle." For some reason this explanation always feels lame. A break would be so much more real. And I'm out six weeks either way.

"It must have been a pretty bad sprain," she comments.

"Yeah. I'm actually going to have to miss your class a lot for physical therapy because they didn't have any times after school."

"Okay, how much time?"

"Monday, Tuesday, and Thursday for a few weeks. Or maybe it was Tuesday, Wednesday, Thursday. I can't remember. My mom will email you."

"That is a lot, Alexis. You are going to have to do a lot of work at home and maybe plan to stay after school a few days a week."

"Okay."

"Thankfully, we stay on track well in this class and I put all the assignments for the week online on Sunday night."

"We will try to get afternoon appointments," I say.

"Good idea. You should be okay if you work to make it up each day. As you know, all assignments are due Friday and quizzes are on Friday. Try to finish your assignments before the quizzes."

"Okay."

"I'm here every day for an hour after school if you need help catching up."

"Okay,"

The second bell rings and I mumble thanks and scurry (well, a slow booted scurry) out of class to my science class. Thankfully, the teacher takes pity on me and doesn't mark me tardy for being a few minutes late.

That night my mom is trying to figure out the logistics of getting me to physical therapy three times a week.

"Maybe we should get a morning appointment," she thinks out loud. "What class do you have first?"

"Homeroom, which is reading and English. And all the important announcements."

"You would rather miss lunch and math?" she asks.

"Yeah."

"Maybe we keep it this way. You're only missing one class. If we go in the morning you would miss two classes."

We just finished a late dinner because the boys had basketball and my mom is sitting at the counter with her planner while my dad is cleaning up the kitchen.

We hear a ruckus upstairs and my mom says, "Mark, I can't even deal with them tonight."

"Then you have to finish here," he says, tossing down the towel.

"Gladly," she agrees, and he heads upstairs to yell at my brothers.

"Is this is a lot for you? Driving me all the way downtown three times a week?"

"Oh, baby girl, don't worry about it. It's life. Sometimes you have to dig in and do what needs to be done."

"Did you email my math teacher and the school?" I ask.

"No, I will do that right now," she says, opening her laptop that was sitting next to her. "Thanks for reminding me. Why don't you ice while I do this and finish the kitchen. Then we can head up to bed."

I nod and hobble over to the freezer. I'm not wearing my boot right now. It got heavy and itchy. At home I can walk okay, just very slowly. My ankle is more tender and weak than excruciating when I put weight on it now.

I select a pre-made bag of crushed ice and pull it out of the freezer, grab a towel, and sit at the counter with my mom. I sit on one bar stool and prop my ankle up on another. I set the ice on it and don't bother to wrap it because my bandage is all the way over in the family room with my boot.

"Katie emailed me to see how you are doing and what the doctor said. They sure are worried about you."

"Can we watch the meet next weekend?" I ask, knowing I am going to miss this meet too.

"Of course, Drew is competing."

"Oh yeah, the one with boys and girls. I'm bummed to miss that one. I've never gotten to compete with Drew before."

"I know, that would have been fun," she says, typing away.

"Are you writing to Katie or my teacher?" I ask.

"Katie. I'm giving her the timeline the doctor gave us so she has an idea. She wants you back in the gym on Monday."

"But I can't do anything!" I yell in frustration.

"You can do bars, strap bars, and conditioning. You'll only go for about an hour each time because you have to make up the math class you're missing."

I am silent at that. I don't want to go in just for strap bar. That's not going to do me any good. I need to just get better. I miss the gym and my friends, but I'm embarrassed to go in late and leave early. It seems so dumb.

I take the ice off my foot. "I'm done," I announce.

"Already?" my mom asks.

"Yes!" I yell and make my way out of the room as fast as possible, which isn't very fast. I'm so angry this is how my season turned out. Doctor appointments and extra math after school instead of just training like everyone else. No one on my team has ever gotten hurt like this. Why did I have to go and be the one to get hurt? It's not fair. And why couldn't I have gotten hurt in the middle of summer when we aren't in season and there's no school to make up?

I limp up the stairs getting more and more mad. I see Drew come out of the bathroom showered and in his PJs. I go into the bathroom without a word and shut the door. I don't know if William or Ethan were waiting, but I don't care. It was fairly quiet up here, which means they are probably all done. I turn on the shower for the first time since I got hurt. I have been taking baths since standing has been so hard. But I can stand now. I can.

I strip down and step into the warm shower stream. After a few minutes my ankle is throbbing and I can't stand anymore. Well, I can; it just hurts. I grab the shampoo and plop down on the tub floor of the shower. I try washing my hair sitting on the ground. The water is spraying everywhere because it gets wide this low to the ground. Rinsing out the soap is a challenge but I finally get all the soap out. Then I just sit there feeling angrier and angrier. I can't even stand for a shower! How am I going to ever compete again? I pull my knees up to my chest, wrap my arms around my legs, set my forehead on my knees, and cry.

I don't know how long I sit there crying. The water starts getting cold, which snaps me out of it. I reach over and turn off the faucet even though I never conditioned my hair. I'm not doing it in the cold.

I slowly stand up and grab a towel. I dry off balancing on one foot, which doesn't work very well. I sit on the edge of the tub to finish drying. I didn't bring my robe in like I usually do so I wrap my towel around myself to dash to my room. Then I remember I can't dash.

I get to my room and change into my jammies and climb into bed. I'm so tired now from the day, especially from crying. My mom comes in and sees me in bed, staring at the ceiling with the lights on.

"You okay?" she asks.

"Yeah. Can I use your leave-in conditioner?" I ask.

"That long shower and you didn't condition?" she questions.

"Nope."

"I'll get it."

She comes back with her leave-in conditioner and a brush. "Sit up," she says.

She puts conditioner in her palm and begins rubbing it in my hair.

"I can do it."

"I want to. You've had a big day," she says, looking at

my puffy eyes. "Do you want to talk about it?"

"No."

"I guess I've been so busy with the logistics of taking care of you, I forgot to take into consideration how you are feeling." She gently starts combing my hair to get the conditioner in and the snarls out.

I'm quiet so she continues. "Sports are hard. This kind of setback is what builds character."

"I don't want to build character. I want to make Regionals," I grumble.

"God may have a different plan," she says, calmly brushing my hair.

Then I'm mad at God right now, too. I hate His plan; it's mean. I know better than to say this out loud. Instead, I try to relax and enjoy my mom brushing my hair.

"Take it one day at a time, okay?"

"What is the plan for tomorrow?" I ask.

"You go to school. I'll pick you up at lunch time and we'll go to your first session of physical therapy. Then I'll take you back to school," she answers.

"And make-up math after school," I add.

"You got it. See, not so bad."

"Does physical therapy hurt?" I ask.

"Not usually. Their goal is to make your ankle stronger as fast as possible. There will be exercises that will push you a little. But be sure to tell them when you have pain."

"Will you stay with me instead of behind the glass?"

"Sure, whatever you are comfortable with."

"I want you there," I confirm.

She nods in agreement and sets the brush down in her lap.

"I hate to see you this angry and frustrated at the same time. All I can say is, it will get better."

"My ankle or how I am feeling?"

"Both," she says. "You have been so brave this far, I guess I took it for granted. You are allowed to be upset. It's normal."

"That's good." I'm glad to hear that my roller coaster feelings are normal. She gives me a hug and kiss goodnight and flips off the light on her way out.

I roll to my side; glad I don't have to wrap my ankle at night anymore.

CHAPTER 18

Thursday morning I notice my boot is next to my bed along with my bandage. I don't bother putting either on until after I'm dressed. Leggings and a sweatshirt are my only option with the boot because jeans don't fit under it. Plus, I have physical therapy today, so I might as well be in tights.

We have the usual morning chaos with the four of us getting off to school. My mom drives Ethan and William to the high school and my dad drives Drew and me to Mountain View.

I start off in homeroom. My teacher and several students comment on my transition from crutches to a boot. I'm still getting 'How'd you break your foot?' I don't bother correcting anyone anymore.

While it's nice that my classmates are concerned, all their questions just remind me that my season got interrupted. All my hard work over the summer is down the drain.

In homeroom our teacher introduces us to our next book,

The Diary of a Young Girl by Anne Frank. Let me tell you, she was my age and her problems are way bigger than mine. Her entire family is hiding to stay alive. I can't imagine being stuck in a small space with my big family. I would be happy and unhappy to have them with me at the same time. Now I'm curious to see what Anne thinks.

Before I can get very far in our new book the bell rings and we rotate to science. In science we are learning about plants and I don't find it nearly as interesting as my other classes.

About five minutes before class ends, a student office worker brings in a slip of paper to my teacher. My teacher reads the paper, looks at me and says, "Alexis, you are being checked out." I nod, pack up my backpack, and leave. Even though the teacher resumes talking about her plants, I know many of the kids are watching me.

I walk down the empty hall to the office where my mom is waiting. When I get there she greets me and we leave. She has already signed the form on the desk checking me out while she was waiting for me.

As we walk out the doors the bell for lunch rings and I know it is going to be a zoo in a matter of seconds.

"Good timing," I say.

"That was the idea. I brought you lunch to eat in the car. We will arrive about ten minutes early. Hopefully they can get you started sooner so you don't miss anything more than math."

She passes back a sack lunch with a peanut butter and jelly sandwich. Exactly the lunch I would have had at school. I guess it was not realistic to think I'd get to go to the Mexican restaurant every time we go to PT.

I eat my lunch as we drive and we get there fairly fast. It's the middle of the day and people aren't on the freeway as much.

We arrive ten minutes early and only wait for five. A lady wearing the green physical therapy shirt comes to get me. She is tall and has warm brown eyes and dark brown hair pulled into a messy bun like the athlete that she probably is.

"Alexis?" she calls. I stand up and walk toward her with my mom following.

"Hi, Alexis, I'm Janice. Looks like we will be working together a lot over the next few weeks." I nod in agreement and follow her down the hall to the big workout area. Rather than going to the middle where all the activity is happening, she leads me to one of the tables along the wall.

"Jump up here for me," she says.

I climb up onto the table because jumping isn't really an option yet.

I swing my legs up in front of me. She gently takes off my boot and unwraps my foot.

"What sport are you in?" she asks me as she unravels my bandage.

"Gymnastics."

"And did you do this doing actual gymnastics or running across the gym?" she asks.

"Doing gymnastics," I say.

"What were you doing?"

"Tumbling," I say and she nods, taking a look. She presses in on the swelling like the doctor did yesterday.

"The doctor has asked for heat before you begin, so let's do some stim," she says. "Stim is short for electrical stimulation."

I have no idea what that means and I look over to my mom who is sitting quietly in a chair next to me. Janice rolls over a cart that has medical equipment on it. She grabs a thick wand, turns a knob on a gray box, and grabs a plastic bottle.

"This is going to be a little cold," she warns just before

she squirts cold gel on my ankle. "And this is going to be warm and feel tingly," she says, putting the wand over the gel. Then she rubs it around like mushing paint. I feel what she means by tingly. It feels like a wave of heat is going deep into my ankle.

"What is this and what does it do?"

"It loosens up and warms your muscles so they can handle the workout and heal. They are probably stiff as they overcompensate for your ligaments that can't do their job. How does it feel?"

"Weird."

"It is kind of weird. How is the temperature?" she asks.

"Okay, warm for sure."

"Painful warm or are you okay?" she asks.

"I'm okay."

She nods and continues to rub the goo all over my ankle on all sides. My bruises are faded now, only some brown and green ones are left.

When she is done she takes a tissue and cleans off her wand and cleans off my ankle.

"Roll your ankle around for me." I do as she says. It is easier to move than it was before we walked in here. I roll it in a circle. It is stiff but not painful.

"Good. Let's do our first exercises right here. Slide back on the table until your back is against the wall and both feet are straight in front of you."

I lift my other leg up onto the table and then I slide backwards until my back hits the wall and I am sitting in a pike position. She hands me a giant blue stretchy ribbon.

"Loop it around your foot and hold it with both hands," she instructs. She helps me loop the band around the bottom of my foot as I hold an end in each hand. She adjusts the band so it's flat across the bottom of my foot.

"Move your foot slightly to the side like you're waving

with your foot. Keep your foot flexed." I try to do as she says but my foot hardly moves. "Hmm, I think we need a different color," she says and walks a few feet away to a wall where red, yellow, green, and blue bands are hanging. She grabs a red one and comes back. "Try this one."

I do as she says and take the red one from her and loop it around my foot. This one is not as tight; it's easier to move. "Try staying flexed and moving it slightly to one side."

I try again, and this time, I'm able to move my foot within the band. I'm doing tiny movements, but she seems pleased, so I guess that's all I'm supposed to do.

"Do eight more," she says and I start to count the little movements of my foot. While I'm counting she turns and talks to my mom. She asks where we are from and how long I've been doing gymnastics. When I'm done I look up at her and she says. "Rest and then one more set of ten."

"It doesn't hurt. I'm not sure I need to rest."

"Your ankle is working harder than you think. How exactly did you hurt it?" she asks.

"Tumbling, on a full."

"What's a full?" She asks.

"A back flip with a straight body and a full twist," I explain.

"You gymnasts are brave. I don't think I could do a sport in flight."

"What did you do?" I ask, figuring it's a safe bet that she was an athlete since this place specializes in sports.

"I was on a ski team. Giant slalom."

"What does that mean?" I ask.

"Do you ski?" she asks me.

"Yes."

"Okay, you know how you make the letter S to get down the hill?" she asks and I nod. "In Giant Slalom the flags are really far apart and the S curves are giant as they go down the hill. We are going for speed."

"So basically, going straight down the hill?"

"Basically," she says. "Do your other ten."

I do as she says and start my other ten. I know that the US Ski Team trains in Utah and I want to ask her if she was in the Olympics. But I hate that question so much I want to think of a different way to ask it. Any time someone finds out I am into gymnastics they ask if I am going to the Olympics. No one asks kids who do soccer and basketball or basically anything else if they are going to the Olympics. It's like they know the odds for other sports but think all gymnasts get to go just for being a gymnast. When in fact our odds are just as slim.

"Who did you race for?" I ask when my ten are done.

"I raced for Snowbird Ski Resort when I was your age and then for the University of Utah. I was never quite fast enough to train with the national team," she says. "So I knew I needed to find something else to do and here I am," she smiles.

"Do you still ski?" I ask.

"Every chance I get. Other side."

I look up to her questioningly and she instructs, "Move your foot to the left. You were waving middle to right, now do middle to left."

I do as she says and look to her when I'm done. "Ready for the next one?" she asks and I say that I am. "This one is harder, but I want you to go from the bottom of your foot facing the end of the table to curving your foot in so that the bottom of your foot is facing a little to the right." I try it and my foot moves just a fraction, but I can feel it pulling a bunch of muscles along my ankle bone. "Good, try to do five." I nod and do five and then she tells me to go the other way. It takes huge amounts of concentration, but I'm able to make a fraction of a movement the other direction. "Good, only five."

"Okay, now forward and back," she says, adjusting the band on my foot. "We call it dorsiflexion and plantar." I'm not sure what she means until she moves my foot. "This way,'" she says.

"Oh, you mean point, flex," I say, understanding.

She laughs and says, "Oh yeah, that's how gymnasts and dancers know this one." The point flex is a little easier than the side to side, but not much.

"So we are going to call the first two a 'right left wave' and then 'twisting to both sides', and the third 'point and flex'." I nod, remembering the names as she types into a tablet she is holding.

"Okay, let's have you stand up. Can you stand on it?"

I nod and slide off the table. She stands in front of me and holds my hands. "Try to balance on both feet evenly." I didn't even realize I was putting all my weight on my right foot. I shift my weight until I am standing evenly on both feet. It hurts a little, but I can support my weight. "How are you doing?" she asks.

"I'm okay; I can feel it straining though."

"Straining is fine. Working your ankle is good. If you are in sharp pain, let me know," she instructs and I nod. Then she stands directly in front of me and takes both my hands in hers. "I want you to hold on to me and slowly put all your weight on your left leg." I look at her wide-eyed. All my weight on my bad ankle? That doesn't seem like such a good idea.

"I've got you. You can put some of your weight on my hands. I will be able to feel how much support you need."

I nod and slowly transfer my weight to my left leg. It doesn't hurt like I thought it would but it's unstable and weak. I press into her hands, scared I'm going to collapse.

"Good, and back to center," she says and I quickly move

my weight off my foot. "Let's do three more." I transfer my weight three more times using her hands less than I did the first time. "Great! Now turn and face the table." I do as she says. "Put your hands on the table and do the transfer drills. Don't use the table more than you were using my hands."

It is tempting to put all my weight on the table and just move back and forth. Knowing I will not get better that way, I try to transfer my weight exactly as I was before using the same amount of support I was using with her.

"Two more sets of five and I will be right back." While she is gone I get one set in and am resting when she comes back. "Okay, Mrs. Bingham, let me show you what we did," she says.

She shows my mom her tablet and says, "We did five motions with the TheraBand. I want her to do two sets of ten each way at home twice a day when she is not coming here. Once a day on the days she is coming here. I will print this out for you," she says and my mom nods.

"I did both sets," I say.

"Great! Jump back up," Janice says.

I climb back up on the table grateful to not be standing on my ankle anymore. She pats the table in front of me and I straighten my leg and give her my ankle.

Then she puts lotion in her hand and begins massaging my ankle. This feels weird but good. I can feel her squishing the swelling around. Maybe she's breaking it up. I'm not sure what she is doing.

"How do you feel?" my mom asks.

I shrug. I feel exhausted but I don't want to admit that this tiny session wore me out. "Fine," I finally answer.

My mom rubs my back as Janice finishes her ankle massage. Then she says, "Okay, you are going to ice to finish up. Follow me. Mrs. Bingham, grab her boot."

CHAPTER 19

I limp behind my physical therapist as she walks out of the large training area into another room. It has a huge silver ice machine along the wall. Along the other wall there are tables like the one I was on and several big silver tubs with water swirling around.

"You can pull over that chair, Mrs. Bingham," she says, walking me to yet another table. My mom sets my boot on the floor next to the table then grabs a chair and pulls it over. I climb up onto the table and sit with my leg in front of me.

I watch as Janice goes over to the ice machine and scoops ice into a big plastic bag. She spins the bag and ties a knot at the top as she walks back to us.

"I am not going to have you go in the whirlpools today because I want to you to come back," she says, putting the bag of ice on my ankle. It is made up of tiny pebble ice so it conforms around my ankle way better than the big cubes we have been using at home. It's colder too, because she put it directly on my skin instead of using a towel.

I wince a little and straighten up as she adjusts it. "Fifteen minutes here and you are done. I'm going to go get the printout of what we did. I'll be right back."

When she is gone I look at my mom. "What do you think?" she asks.

"I thought it would be harder because you said it was like conditioning."

"It will get more like conditioning as your ankle gets stronger."

"I mean it was hard. Like the movements were so tiny and they were hard to do. It was kind of pathetic," I say.

"Not pathetic, Alexis, your ankle is weak. It's up to you to make it stronger."

"At this rate it's going to take forever," I complain.

I see my mom's frown and then I feel bad. It was a lot of work for her to get me out of school and drive all the way here.

"Thanks for bringing me. I know it's a big pain."

"It's the only way for you to get better before the end of season, Alexis. If you just wait to get better it would take even longer."

"I know," I say quietly. I really do feel grateful she is bringing me here. I'm just frustrated at the entire situation.

Janice comes back with one of the red bands and hands it to me. "I want you to do everything we did today at home. Two sets of ten each way. Then use a table or your bed to work on standing with your weight centered and then all your weight on one leg. Here is a printout of what we did." She hands me a paper with pictures of each of the exercises.

"I forgot to ask you what your goal is?"

"To get better."

She laughs and says, "No, I mean, I have in my notes that you are in season. What game, or meet I should say, are we aiming for?"

"The Winter Classic is in four weeks,"

"That's ambitious. You have youth on your side." She sits on the edge of the table where my foot is and adjusts the ice. "Eat healthy, sleep well, come here three times a week, and do the extra work I give you in between and you will have a fighting chance." I nod. "Heat before you use your ankle, ice after. Wrap it if it starts swelling. When do you go back into the gym?"

"Monday," I say.

"I want it taped up even though you won't be using it. You don't want to roll it just getting around. Do your coaches know how to tape?"

"They all do and I do, too," my mom says.

"Were you a gymnast, too?" she asks.

"I was." Janice nods, obviously used to the parent-child athlete combo. "And I took athletic training classes in college."

"Have your mom tape you up before practice." Then she pauses and leaves the table again. She comes back with an ankle brace. "I want you in the boot when you're going to school. Wear this over tape when you work out. You can rest from both when you're at home. In fact, going without when you are at home will force your ankle to get stronger. Listen to your body. If it's hurting, don't force it."

I take the soft-sided brace from her. "Normally I would leave you to ice on your own and Gary would take care of you. We had a lot to go over today."

"Who's Gary?" I ask.

"You are going to love Gary. He's great." She spots him over by one of the whirlpools and calls him over. I see that there are several people in here but none of them have their trainer with them like in the workout room. Gary and Janice are the only workers in here.

Gary comes over and I see he is a little different than I'd expect. He looks like my friend's brother from church who has Down syndrome. Janice says, "Gary, I would like you to meet my newest athlete, Alexis. She is a gymnast trying to make it back to her competition season in a few short weeks. Alexis, this is Gary. He is the man in charge of post-workout icing for all of our athletes. He makes the perfect bags of ice and helps people survive the first five minutes of whirlpool."

"Nice to meet you," I say and hold out my hand the way my mom taught me. He shakes my hand and gives me a huge grin.

"Sorry you hurt your foot," he says with a little slur, although I understand him just fine.

"Thank you, it's a bummer."

"Janice will get you better. And I will make sure you have a friend at whirlpool," he says.

"What is whirlpool?" I ask.

He points to the huge silver tubs of water. "They are ice water baths and they sting when you get in."

"She'll do it next time," Janice tells him.

Then someone calls out, "Gary, I need you!"

He smiles and says, "Nice to meet you Miss Lexis, see you next time," and he runs over to the man that called him over.

"So that's Gary and he makes this area the best." I watch as an athlete climbs up wooden steps and sits on a bench at the top of the whirlpool. Then he takes Gary's hand and puts his legs in. I can tell by the look on the man's face that it hurts. Gary holds his hand, pats his back, and talks to him.

"I don't think I want to do that," I say.

"Smart girl. But you will next time. Big goals means pushing your limits. You already know that," she says, taking my ice off. "You are done for today, Alexis. See you next week."

"Thank you," I say.

My mom thanks her too and stands up. She hands me my sock and I put it on. Then she helps me with my boot and we walk out. My ankle is cold in the boot from the ice. I feel a little better now that there is a plan to get me to the Winter Classic. Janice seems to know what to do to get me there.

CHAPTER 20

My mom checks me back into school only ten minutes before history class, which is held in homeroom. My homeroom teacher is nice and she quietly nods to me as I walk in. After school I sit in the dining room trying to figure out how to do the math assignment I missed. Maybe missing math isn't such a good idea. My brothers know how to do this stuff, but they'll only help me if I do their chores. Marissa would know how to do this. Then I remember she's at practice right now. This thought makes me sad. It's Thursday night and I haven't seen my friends since they visited almost a week ago last Friday. Maybe Katie is right and going back into the gym next week is a good idea. At the very least I'll get to see my friends.

The house is suddenly quiet and I realize my mom has left to take Ethan and Will to basketball and Drew to gymnastics. I could play Tetris. No, no, I should finish math and then play Tetris while I ice. They'll be gone long enough for me to do both. I go back to the math instructions my teacher has left online and decide to read them. I tried to solve the problems without reading it like I usually do, but missing class made skipping that step impossible.

"You are actually doing homework while everyone is gone?"

I jump in my seat startled by another human in the house.

"Will! You scared me!"

"Sorry," he says coming in a little farther.

"Why are you here? Don't you have basketball?"

"I jammed my finger."

"Did you really or are you faking it again?"

"Are you faking it?"

"Of course not." Imbecile, he's seen my bruises.

"It's jammed a little. If I really liked basketball it wouldn't stop me," he admits, sitting down.

"When are you going to tell Mom and Dad you want to do something else?"

"When I figure out what that something else is. They're kind of weird like that. We all have to do something."

I think about this and shrug. "Maybe, but maybe Mom would help you find your new thing."

"Could you tell Mom you don't want to do gymnastics?"

"I do want to do it so I don't have to worry about that."

"Are you sure? Do you love gymnastics or do you just love that Mom gives you all this attention for doing gymnastics?"

"Mom gives me attention because I'm a girl," I try.

He shakes his head. "She always picks driving you and Drew if she has the chance and leaves basketball to Dad."

That's true.

"Well Dad always picks basketball games over gymnastics meets so we're even."

"We are, but that's why it's so hard to tell Dad. All I'm saying is you would have a hard time, too so stop giving me a hard time for stalling." I nod in agreement. "And I'm saying you don't even know if you like gymnastics over other things. You've always just done it because Mom wanted you to."

"That's not true." *Is it?*

"So you've missed it this week?"

"Of course," I say, rolling my eyes at him. Although today was the first day all week I thought about practice. I have been so busy focusing on my ankle I didn't have time to miss it until today. And today all I missed were my friends, not the sport.

He looks at me for a moment with intense blue eyes and I hope he can't read my mind. He will badger me more about my choices if he senses I'm confused.

"Wanna play Mario Kart?" he asks.

I smile and nod. Math can wait. We have the house to ourselves, a rare Mario Kart opportunity. I slowly limp over to the family room while he runs ahead and sets up the system.

"You really are hurt," he observes as I wince while walking without my boot.

"Of course I am, you jerk."

"I wasn't sure."

"Did you not see the giant bruises last week?"

"They could have been only skin deep. You love attention so much I thought maybe you were playing it up. But since you can't even move fast for Mario Kart, you are legit."

"I was always legit," I say, plopping down and picking up a remote. He sits next to me and we choose our players.

Mario Kart is fun because we both get to be on the screen at the same time while we race each other. Will is always Mario now that Josh is gone and I usually pick one of the mushroom characters. I like playing Will. He plays less dirty than Ethan and just wants to drive fast. After about three rounds I notice it's getting dark.

"Mom is going to be back soon. We should shut it down and start icing or something," I tell him.

"She said she's stopping at the store. We have time for one more," he says, selecting a new car.

I smile; it is fun having Will here. I rarely get to hang out with him. Maybe there is something to be said for taking a break from sports.

CHAPTER 21

Everyone goes skiing on Saturday except for me. Obviously, I cannot go skiing yet.

"Are you sure you're going to be okay all alone?" my mom asks.

"She'll be fine," Dad says, grabbing ski boots that were drying by the door and heading out to the car.

"You have books. You are welcome to watch Disney Plus or you could do homework. Where's your phone?"

"In my room."

"DREW!" my mom yells, "Bring your sister's phone when you come down!"

"I don't want Drew in my room," I complain.

"It'll be fine, he doesn't have time to mess with anything."

"Why do I need my phone?" I ask.

"So you can text if you get lonely. Or if there's an emergency, you can call us."

"Mom she's twelve, I was babysitting all of them when I was twelve," Ethen reminds her as he walks by.

"I know, it's just that with such a big family she has never really been alone all day," my mom comments.

"I'll be fine," I say again. "I'll get to watch what I want."

"You always get to watch what you want because you're the favorite," Drew says, handing me my phone.

"That's not true," I defend. It really isn't. I always get outvoted on movies and have to watch intense action movies. Although now I kind of like them.

"Okay, you have your phone. There's lots of leftovers in the fridge. Do your TheraBand exercises and then ice, don't answer the door for anyone. Pretend you aren't home."

"Got it. No answering the door," I repeat.

"I love you, enjoy the quiet," she says, as she gives me a kiss and runs out the door.

Almost every single one of them comes back in for one more thing before they actually leave.

Then it's finally quiet. I sit for a moment wondering what to do with myself. Finally, I decide to watch a movie. I thoroughly enjoy the movie with no one talking and no interruptions. Then I decide to do my ankle exercises. I slowly make my way up to my room to get my exercise band Janice gave me on Thursday. I sit down against my bed and do the five different motions she taught me. It's a lot to keep track of; I should write it down. I get up and look through my desk until I find a plain red notebook and I write down the date and the exercise I'm doing today. For some reason writing it down makes me feel better.

I do two more sets of the ankle exercises and then lean my head against my bed. That was unexplainably tiring. I'm hardly moving, but it wears me out. Maybe Mom is right. It takes the entire body to heal.

The house is quiet. Too quiet. I look at the clock on my

desk. It's still only morning time. They won't be back until almost five o'clock tonight. This stinks. I should be skiing. I was so busy this last week thinking about gymnastics that I didn't realize I'm going to miss the rest of the ski season, too.

I see it has started to snow. I climb up onto my bed and look out the window. I watch the snowflakes for a long time. Do I only like gymnastics because it makes my mom happy? Maybe I like skiing better? Or do I only like that because it makes my dad happy?

I pick up the book on my nightstand and try to read. I can't concentrate because my ankle has developed its own heartbeat and hurts. I should probably ice. I don't want to go all the way back downstairs. I slide farther down on my bed and look at the ceiling. Maybe I should have gone with them and hung out in the lodge. There's a giant fireplace there and all sorts of people coming and going that I could have watched.

We need a dog. Or a cat, like Paige. If I had a dog or a cat here I wouldn't be lonely. I don't think I've ever stayed home alone this long. No wonder my mom was worried. Ethan was right, lots of kids babysit younger kids at my age. I can do this. I could play Mario Kart. That's no fun without other people. I could go get my phone and see if anyone responded to the word game. I could do the math homework I never did Thursday night.

I decide to go get my phone and ice my foot since I have to go all the way downstairs anyway. Like always, I slowly make my way downstairs. I go to the freezer and grab a bag of ice my mom already prepared for me. Then I grab a kitchen towel and go sit on the family room couch where I left my phone. I prop up my foot and set the ice on it. Then I grab my phone and go to the word game app. It looks like all my brothers played their turn late last night. I play each of them and then stare at my phone wishing for someone to respond to me. Of course none of them do since they are busy skiing. Maybe I can text a friend. Trista and Savannah don't have phones yet. I can't remember if Lucy or Marissa do. I know Victoria and Riley do, but I don't know them as well. I'll text Paige to see how practice went.

Me:

Hi Paige! How did practice go this week?

I set my phone down and wait for a response. I look at the clock. It has been fifteen minutes since I started icing, so I take the ice off and plop it on the floor. I hear my phone ping and I quickly pick it up and see its Paige.

Paige:

Hey Lexi! Practice was great! Lots of upgrades.

Me:

Like what?

Paige:

I did my bounders today and Savannah was working her back handspring series. Trista too, she may compete her series next weekend.

I stare at my phone with mixed emotions. I'm happy for my teammates; I really am. Yet, I feel anger boiling up inside me. I can't think of a single thing to say that would be appropriate. I certainly can't type 'well la-de-da for you' even though that's how I feel. My phone pings again and I look down. Paige has sent another message.

Paige:

How's the ankle?

Me:

I can almost walk.

Paige is doing bounders, Savannah and Trista are tumbling on beam and *I can almost walk.*

Paige:
> What did the doctor say?

Me:
> It's going to be a few weeks. My goal is to compete in the Winter Classic.

Paige:
> When will you be back in the gym?

Me:
> Monday

Paige:
> Oh good! we miss you.

Me:
> Miss you too.

I leave it at that because I don't feel like talking to her anymore. I reached out to Paige hoping to connect with a friend and feel better. All it did was make me feel worse. How did my teammates come so far in upgrades in one week?

I guess it hasn't been one week. They've been working on those upgrades for a while now. Somehow, I still feel cheated. Betrayed even. I toss my phone on the couch. What I really want to do is throw it across the room. I groan and lay back on the couch. This is the longest day ever!

I look out and it's still snowing. They are going to ski until the last chair closes and then take forever getting down the canyon in this weather. Maybe I'll watch another movie. Instead of getting up and grabbing the remote and selecting a movie, I continue to lay there and watch the snow. What am I going to do? My teammates are busy focusing on upgrades, which is what I was doing two weeks ago. Now, here I am excited when I can put all my weight on one foot. It feels unfair. It feels mean. I didn't do anything to deserve this. God has a plan? *A plan?* I think He goofed and that is His great cover up, to say there's a plan. To learn a lesson. Well, I don't want to learn a lesson. I want to be training with my teammates and getting upgrades to add to my routines. Instead, I'm sitting here watching the snow.

I pick up a pillow and throw it across the room. It hits the TV and for a split second I panic that the TV is going to topple over and shatter. The pillow just bounces off of it and falls to the ground. The narrow TV moves a little, but it's stable. Thank goodness for earthquake safety straps.

What else could I do to let out some anger? I grab another pillow and scream into it. This feels a little better. I realize I'm here all alone. Why am I screaming into a pillow? I try to scream out loud. A little squeak comes out. That was weird. Why can't I scream? I ball my fists together and try again, letting out a scream at the top of my lungs. When I'm done, nothing happens. I'm not sure I feel better. Now my throat just hurts. I look at the snow again; it's so quiet and calm. The opposite of how I feel. I feel agitated and annoyed.

My phone rings and I see it's my mom. I slide the green dot over on my phone and greet her, "Hi, Mom."

"Hi, hon. How is your day going?"

"Boring," I admit.

"Oh no, I thought you might like the house to yourself."

Hearing her voice my throat starts closing up. I don't want her to hear the frustration and near tears in my voice.

"Not really," I manage to say as normal as possible.

"Did you watch a movie?"

"Yes"

"Do your exercises?"

"Yes"

"Ice?"

"Yes"

"Well, why don't you get yourself lunch and take a bath?" she suggests.

"I'm not hungry," I say and my voice cracks.

"Oh, Alexis, are you okay?" She heard it in my voice.

"I'm just frustrated," I say.

"Frustrated we left you?"

"No, frustrated I can't do anything. I can't ski, I can't train. I texted Paige and they all got upgrades this week and I can't even walk!"

I hear a commotion in the background and my mom saying, 'just a moment' and I know my meltdown is bad timing.

"Alexis, listen to me. I know it's hard. Trust me, I know more than anyone that it's hard. All you can do is be happy for your teammates and focus on your road to recovery."

I nod with tears starting to come down my face.

"Okay," I squeak.

"Why don't you have lunch and do something relaxing like take a bath or color. I got you the Tetris game that got me through some tough times," she reminds me.

"Okay," I say again, getting a grip. Lunch and Tetris is a good idea.

"Do you want us to come home early?"

"No. No, Mom, it's fine. I'm fine. I just had too much time to think I guess."

"Okay, I'll check back with you in a couple of hours, okay?"

"Okay. Thanks Mom."

"I love you baby girl."

"I love you, too," I reply. We say goodbye and hang up. I lay back and stare at the snow and wipe away my tears, feeling a little silly for crying at all.

A few minutes later I start getting funny videos and memes from my brothers. I can just picture them in the ski lodge at the lunch table playing on their phones and trying to find things to cheer me up. I'm certain my mom told them I'm having a bad day and they are all trying to fix it. I think I will do what my mom says, lunch then a bath. Then I should probably do the math homework I blew off on Thursday. I sigh. Long day.

CHAPTER 22

Today is a big day. I have school, physical therapy, and practice after a week out of the gym. My boot seems excessive now that I can walk okay without it. However, a long day at school is different than getting around the house, so I put it on anyway.

I hustle out the door with my family and walk into school with Drew. We walk down the hall and Drew says, "See you at lunch."

"No, I won't be at lunch," I correct him. He stops and raises his eyebrows. "Physical therapy at lunch again," I remind him.

"Oh, yeah. See you after school then." And he is off down the hall. It's weird to be at this school with just Drew. Mountain View is a Kindergarten through 8th grade school. All of my brothers used to go here with me. But now that William is in 9th grade, Ethan is in 11th grade, and Josh is in college, it's just Drew and I left.

I make my way to homeroom, sit down, and open my planner. I see my note to make up Thursday's math class that I never did. Not great especially since I'm missing math again today. And tomorrow and Thursday.

The bell rings and I'm forced to focus on English and language arts and worry about math later. I enjoy this class. I don't really like when we have to learn how to write a paragraph, but I like reading. Two hours of homeroom goes fast and I'm off to science. My mom will be picking me up ten minutes before the bell rings for lunch. I don't particularly like science, so the entire time I'm watching the clock for when I get to leave.

Thankfully, a student comes to check me out fifteen minutes early and I'm grateful for my mom's over-the-top punctuality. I gather up my stuff and go to the office where my mom is waiting.

"Off to the doctor again?" the office manager at the front desk asks. I nod yes and she buzzes us out.

"Thanks for coming early," I say as we walk out.

"Well, I figured out that if the icing after is not part of the thirty-minute appointment we need a little longer. You will miss fifteen minutes of science, lunch, math, and hopefully just a few minutes of 4th period. What class is that?"

"Social studies, history," I answer.

"Math is probably the easiest one to miss but I will still try to get an after-school appointment. Although then I don't know how I'm going to get the boys to basketball. Ethan needs to get his driver's license."

I'm quiet as I listen to my mom go through everything to make it right in her head. We get in the car and she passes back the lunch I need to eat during our drive.

We get to physical therapy and we hardly have to wait at all since my mom doesn't need to talk to anyone or sign anything. Janice comes and gets us and we get started the same as last Thursday. She does the stim heat on my ankle while she talks to me and my mom. The stim feels good in an odd tingly sort of way.

"It's looking better,'" she comments. "How did your walking around the house go?"

"Good, I still favor it though," I tell her.

"That's normal. Did you do your TheraBand motions?"

"Yes, Friday, Saturday, and Sunday," I proudly answer.

"Awesome! You will be back to training at 100% in no time with that work ethic."

She puts away the stim wand and wipes off the gel. Then she massages my ankle for a bit, especially around the swollen spots.

"Okay, let me see a set of each of your TheraBand exercises," she says, handing me a red band.

I take the band and know what to do. I do the flexed foot middle to right ten times then middle to left.

"You have a little more strength already. See how you are getting more motion?"

"Not really."

She laughs, "Well you are. Let's see the side movements."

These are the ones where I have to turn in my foot and they're really hard for me.

"You are stiff and weak on these," she says, making a note on her tablet. "Okay, now forward-back or point-flex as you like to call it."

She watches my motion and makes more notes. Then she sets her tablet on the table and says, "Jump down and let's do the balancing one."

I slide off the table and stand to the side of it. I take her hands and successfully stand evenly. "Great progress! You did work hard over the weekend!" I smile, pleased I made progress. I did everything she told me to do over the weekend, but it didn't seem like it was doing any good. I'm happy to learn that it did make a difference.

"Now transfer your weight." I do as she says, and slowly move my weight to my left ankle. I can feel my ankle straining to hold all my weight, but it doesn't feel like it's going to collapse like last week. "Good, and back."

She turns me to the table, "You can do these using the table now. Five more and I will be back."

When she is gone my mom says, "How does it feel?"

"Way better than Thursday," I comment, slowly shifting my weight.

Janice comes back and sets down a small round trampoline next to me. "How many have you done?"

"Three," I say, trying not to put too much weight on the table.

"Tell me when you're at ten." I nod and keep shifting back and forth.

"Did you get to ski over the weekend?" my mom asks her.

"Yes, the snow was amazing. How about you?"

"We went up Saturday. It was a perfect day."

"Do you ski, Alexis?" Janice asks me. I nod yes, but don't say anything because I'm busy counting.

"She had to stay home Saturday and take care of that ankle. I felt so bad. I should have stayed home with her," my mom says.

"It was fine," I say. "Ten."

"Good. Come over here." I do as she says and walk a few steps over to her. "You are going to do the same thing only on this little trampoline."

I take her extended hand and step up onto the trampoline. As soon as I am on it I lose my balance, but Janice takes my weight and helps me stay standing.

"Harder on here?" she asks me.

"A lot harder," I confirm and stand still so I don't lose my balance again.

"I got you. Stand up straight, take both of my hands, and find your balance." I do as she says but it feels like the ground is rolling under me even though it is just a little trampoline bed. When I find my balance she tells me to transfer my weight to one leg.

"I can't," I say. She has no idea how hard it is just to stand here.

"Engage all those tiny stabilizing muscles around your ankle."

I put a lot of weight onto her hands and shift my weight to my left ankle. My ankle rolls around and wobbles all over the place so I quickly shift back.

"Great job! Did you feel that?"

"My ankle wobbling all over the place?"

"It was working hard! Again."

I do it nine more times, and it never gets easier. It feels like when you are in relevé on beam and you are trying to keep your ankle up high without falling. Only I'm not in relevé; I'm just standing flat on a trampoline. It's discouraging that I have so far to go. Just when I feel a little stronger, she brings out an exercise that makes me feel even weaker than before.

"That's ten, step down and follow me."

I carefully step down and follow her across the training area, walking pretty good without my boot, I might add. She stops in front of a square mini trampoline that is standing vertical. She grabs a ball and says, "I want you to stand sideways to the trampoline and throw the ball at it." She throws the ball to the center of the trampoline and it bounces back to her. "And catch it."

I nod. "Watch again. Your feet will be planted and I

want you to twist your body when you throw it. When you catch it, twist back to center. Keep your balance evenly distributed." She twists and throws the ball again. It bounces, and she catches it and twists back to face me. "Got it?"

"Got it," I say stepping forward and taking the ball from her.

"Okay, line up facing me sideways to the trampoline. Feet a little farther apart, bend your knees." I do as she says, making sure not to favor my left ankle. "Now twist and throw."

The ball is light and I easily throw it, watch it bounce, and catch it. "Ouch!" I say.

"Did it hurt?" she asks.

I hold the ball to my chest and say, "More like straining or stretching and yeah it hurt a little. I definitely felt it."

"The turning motion is what you are feeling," she explains. "Why don't you try doing five. If your pain gets any higher than a strain, I want you to stop."

I nod and do five more. Then she has me turn around and do the other side. For some reason these hurt less. My bad ankle is closer to the trampoline on this side so I guess it isn't twisting as far.

When I'm done with five on that side she says, "Alright, that's enough for today. Let's get you to the icing room."

I follow her back to the table where my mom is. "I want her to still do the TheraBand exercises at home and I want to do a version of the trampoline ball throw. Squat a little, hold your hands in front of you, and twist," she says, doing the motion for me. "It's easier than throwing the ball so I want you to do twenty."

Then she looks at us. "Any questions?"

"She is going to practice today to do bars and conditioning. What do you want her to wear on her ankle?"

"Wear the soft brace with tape under it. For school, I

want you to wear the big boot one more week, then the soft brace. But outside of school you can try to challenge yourself and wear the smaller one. Let's get you started on icing and I will get you the printout of what to do at home."

We follow her to the icing room and I'm surprised at how fast the session went compared to conditioning at the gym. Probably it's a little easier for my overall body.

"Over here today," Janice says, leading us to a bench at one of the silver tubs. She pushes a button and water starts swirling around like in a hot tub. I climb up the few steps to the bench. My mom stands next to me.

"You are going to put just your left foot in and it's going to be hard to keep it there the first several minutes."

"Why?" I ask, looking into the water.

"It's ice water. We keep it about fifty degrees. It will sting at first."

I look into the clear water, pull my leggings up to my knee, and swing around so I can dangle my left leg in. My mom grabs my hand before I put my foot in and I look at her, "That bad?" I ask.

"At first yes, but then you get used to it," she answers honestly.

I take a breath and put my foot in and I let out a yelp. "Oh my gosh that's cold!" I yell. My mom takes my hand and I squeeze it. "Why am I doing this?" I ask.

"It gives you a much deeper icing than just putting ice on top. If you're okay here with your mom, I'll go get your home assignment." I nod and she is gone.

I start rocking back and forth, "Why didn't you warn me?" I start whining.

"What could I have said? It's like nothing you've felt before."

"I don't know, I don't know. Oh my gosh, when does it get better?"

"When your foot gets numb."

"Hi, Miss Lexis," Gary says coming over, forcing me to look up but I'm still rocking back and forth. "Janice told me to check on you. Are you okay?" he asks.

"No!" I yell and wrap my arms around my stomach, letting go of my mom's hand. Gary moves over to the other side.

He starts rubbing my back and asks, "What is your favorite color?"

"I don't know. Pink. No teal. Does it matter?"

"Mine's red," he says, not at all worried about my rocking and wincing.

"Hey, Gary," a man calls from the other side of the whirlpool.

"Hi, Paul," Gary replies. Then Paul climbs into the whirlpool all the way up to his chest!

"How are you doing that?" I exclaim.

"A whole body of injuries I have to heal before spring training," he answers with a smile.

"Football?" my mom asks and he nods. "For the U?" she asks, referring to the University of Utah.

"Yep," he says, sinking down lower.

"They don't have a training facility on campus?"

"They do. A really nice one. This is just closer to my apartment. I come here on days I'm not up on campus. I do have to lift with the team later today, but I wanted to get this done."

The pain from the cold subsides a little and I'm able to stop rocking. "How do you put your entire body in?" I ask.

"It hurts more if I don't," he says simply. "What are you in for?" he asks me.

"Ankle."

"Surgery?"

"No, just a sprain."

"Sport?"

"Gymnastics."

"You guys are crazy," he says.

I eye him with his entire body in an ice bath and say, "Not compared to some."

This gets a roar of laughter from him, "How old are you?"

"Twelve, 6th grade."

"I look forward to watching you compete for Utah. We have one of the best teams in the nation."

I smile. "I look forward to being there."

He looks at my mom, "You have a sharp one there."

"I do," she says.

Then he turns to Gary. "Gary! She gets all the attention today?"

"She's new, Paul. She needs me."

"Fair enough," he says, leaning back and resting his arms over the sides as if he is in a hot tub. He looks comfortable. I know he's not. He can't be. I can barely stand it now that I'm numb. I know he's not at the numb stage yet.

"How much longer?" I ask my mom.

"About ten more minutes Miss Lexis," Gary says. I look at him and give a weak smile. Ten seems like a lot. "Are you okay now?"

"I'm okay," I say and he gives me one more pat and goes to the ice machine to fill bags for a patient that just walked in.

Janice comes back in. "Here is her printout for the exercises at home this week. Do them once tonight and I'll see you back tomorrow."

I don't see how I'm going to get to them tonight. I still have the rest of school, gym, and homework from what I missed today, plus regular homework.

Being injured sure takes a lot of time.

CHAPTER 23

I'm excited to go to practice tonight. I'm not sure what I'm going to be able to do, but I'm excited to go.

"Do I tape up now or when we get there?" I ask my mom.

"When we get there," my mom says, grabbing her purse. "Where is Drew?"

"Coming!" my brother yells, rounding the corner.

"Let's go." We go out front to the car and my mom yells to Ethan and William that Dad will be picking them up in twenty minutes.

We get to practice just as my team is starting to warm-up and I still have to tape up. I can't do the usual run to warm-up anyway, so I guess it's okay. My mom asks Katie if she wants to tape me up or if she should do it.

"I'll do it," Katie says. "I want her used to my tape job." My mom hands her a roll of tape and Katie tells me to go into the training area.

I walk in without a limp and as soon as I'm in the doors Savannah yells out to me and waves. I wave back to my teammates who are running around the floor.

"Sit on this block over here," Katie says. She has me sit on a spotting block with my leg straight out so my ankle is off the edge. "Flex your foot," she says and then she starts taping. First she does two strips of tape around my shin and two strips just below my toes. Then she does a strip that goes from the shin strip under my foot and up to the other side. Then one from the toes strip around the back of my ankle. Then she does complicated figure eights around my ankle. She is fast and there seems to be a very specific pattern to what she is doing. By the time she's done my entire ankle is covered in tape.

"How does that feel?" she asks. I wiggle my toes and try to point my foot and I can't.

"I can't really move it," I comment.

"That's the idea."

I hold up my brace, "I'm supposed to have this over it, too."

"Good idea. Put it on then come over and stretch with the team."

She leaves me to put my brace on and then I slide off the block and join my team. I don't have a limp when I'm in a brace or boot so I easily walk over to them.

They greet me at once.

"Welcome back!" Savannah says.

"How do you feel?" Marissa inquires at the same time.

Before I can answer Trista asks, "What are you allowed to work today?"

"Are you competing this weekend?" Riley asks.

I smile and try my best to answer as I slide into my splits. "No, I'm not competing this weekend and I think I'm just working bars today."

It's weird to be in my splits and unable to point my foot in front of me. But I do like how secure my ankle feels in the tape and brace.

"How does it feel?" Marissa asks again.

"Better, but still very weak."

"We missed you," Carmen says.

"Thanks," I answer, leaning forward into my stretch.

I listen as Katie starts giving instructions. "Let's start the 6s and 7s on bars so Alexis can work out with her team. Upper optionals, you can start on beam."

We finish stretching and then the girls stand up for complex. I'm not sure what to do. All I know is that I absolutely cannot do complex.

"Alexis, here is a conditioning list for you. Go down the list until we get to bars and then you can stop."

I take the list from her. Lots of pull-ups, push-ups, and core work such as V-ups, walk-ups, and leg lifts. It's a long list and I wonder if I'm expected to do all of it tonight or if it's just to keep me busy while they're doing complex.

I decide to do the floor work on a corner of the floor so I can at least be near my teammates. I sit down by a line of four girls: Victoria, Riley, Maya, and Carmen.

"It's good to have you back," Carmen says as she walks to the back of the line.

"Thanks, it's good to be back."

"Are you staying the entire time?" she asks.

"Probably not," I say, realizing how much I still can't do. She stops talking so she can listen to Katie's next instruction.

I get started on my three sets of twenty walk-ups.

"You're going to have a nice six-pack before this is all over," Riley comments as she gets to the back of the line. I nod and smile, but don't talk since I am in the middle of both counting and using my stomach muscles.

I do the walk-ups and V-ups, then look at the list. Push-ups. I get in a push-up position and I am worried about putting pressure on my ankle. I hook my left ankle on my right one and I'm able to do the push-ups on one leg.

Next are leg lifts and pull-ups. I get up and walk over to bars and Katie yells over to me. "Alexis! Do your pull-ups on the low bar, bent knees!"

I'm surprised she even saw me get up and walk toward bars. She is doing complex with all the optionals teams right now. I give her a thumbs up that I heard her and keep walking.

I get to bars and understand that jumping up to the high bar and falling down from the high bar for pull ups would have been a bad idea. Okay, so I have pull-ups on the low bar with bent knees. I can do that. I grab the bar in front of me and hang down. I can hang straight down and with my knees bent, I don't touch the floor. I start doing my pull-ups feeling a little frustrated that all I'm doing is conditioning. It's difficult and boring.

After I do two sets of ten my teammates are done with complex and they break off into two groups.

"Saved by the bell," Trista says, "Time to get grips on."

I smile, I'm ready to do some gymnastics! I go into the lobby for my grips while my teammates go upstairs to the Optionals Room for theirs. I knew walking upstairs would be slow; so I just used one of the cubbies in the lobby.

I see my mom in the lobby reading. "You're still here," I say surprised.

She looks up, "You thought I was leaving?"

"Well, yeah, you never stay."

"I figured you wouldn't be here long and it wasn't worth driving all the way home just to come back." Oh. She's right, I probably won't be long. For sure not the usual three and a half hours. "How's it going?"

647

"I haven't done anything but conditioning yet. But we're going to bars now."

"Listen to your body," she reminds me.

"I will," I say, as I pull my wrist bands out of my grip bag and start to put them on. Then I take out my grips and hold them in one hand while I shove the bags back in the cubby. I walk back into the training area as I am putting my grips on.

Katie is moving mats around under the bars. When she sees me walk up she starts giving me my assignment.

"Start with push away kips, but on the third one instead of pushing away and landing on the panel mats I want you to end in a support position. Then you can come down carefully."

"So basically two push away kips and one kip at the end?" I clarify.

"You got it. Do that three times."

I go to the chalk tray and my teammates come down. They are full of their usual chatter and I love it.

"Push away kips," Katie yells as she throws one last 8-incher in place under the high bar. Since I'm already chalked up, I walk over to a low bar. I step up onto a panel mat and jump into a kip. As soon as I jump I feel searing pain in my ankle. That was stupid. Why did I think I could jump? I kip and do a small cast into a push away. I do my second kip and cast a bit higher, and I do my third kip and stop. I hop down onto one foot.

Then I walk over to the chalk tray trying not to show a limp.

"What did you do last week without practice?" Victoria asks.

"Video games, doctor appointments, and physical therapy. I have to go three times a week until my ankle is better."

"What do they do for it?" Marissa asks.

"They have me do strengthening exercises," I tell them.

"That's smart," Marissa decides.

"Yeah, it should speed up my recovery," I say, mostly trying to convince myself. I chalk up for my next turn and listen to the girls talk about some of the college meets that took place over the weekend. Why didn't I watch any college meets when I was bored over the weekend? I'm going to have to remember that this weekend.

I go to do my second set of kips and I'm not sure how to get started. I can try jumping off one foot or glide from a stand, but either way doesn't give me much swing. I decide to try to jump off my right foot. This works even though I don't have much swing into the first kip. I push away well and have decent swing for the next two. I jump down again on one foot.

Now that I have the hang of how to stay off my foot I'm having fun on bars. I do my third set and cast high on all three.

"Very nice, Alexis, is that your last set?" Katie asks. I nod that it was.

"I want you to go do giants on the pit bar."

"I think I could do routines and just not do the dismount," I suggest.

"I thought of that. If you fall out of your giant on the comp set it will be a big impact on your ankle. And based on how you are babying it on push away kips, I think it's best to start on the pit bar."

She has a point. As much as I would love to do routines with my teammates today, falling onto my ankle from the high bar would be excruciating.

"I want you to work your body position on giants. You fall on your second giant because you are arching over the top. Work on staying hollow and pulling your toes over. It's also what is making a flyaway out of your giant difficult."

"Can I work those, too?"

"Yes, but hollow giants first. Do sets of four."

"Four? I've never done that many anywhere besides strap bar."

"Really? Can you do three?"

"Maybe, I've only ever done two in a row."

"Well, there's your new goal. Do three sets of three then come get me."

CHAPTER 24

I'm all alone at the pit bar because my teammates are busy doing routines. They are in season and will only come over here if they finish their assignment. I know better than to jump up to the high bar like I would normally do. I use the stairs that coaches use to get to the spotting block. Then I grab the bar and pump a swing so I can kip up. Once in a support position I decide to warm-up with my usual two giants. I cast up into an almost handstand and do one giant and on the second one I arch and don't make it around. I twist and fall into the pit.

"Hollow over the top!" I hear Katie yell.

I chuckle to myself. How does she see everything? I climb out of the pit and sit on the edge of the floor. I think about how easy it is to do multiple giants on the strap bar. I want it to feel like that over here. I stand up, I can do that. *Saty hollow,* I remind myself.

I chalk up, climb up again, and kip up. I stay in a support

position for a moment thinking about how I want this to go. *Arch on the bottom, tap to hollow over the top.* I cast up to an even better almost handstand and do a nice first giant and focus on doing a second one the same way. I fall, tap from arch to hollow, and make it over easily. Then I let go on the bottom and fall into the pit.

"Beautiful! Do three!" she yells.

Three? I didn't even think about three! I was just trying to make two. I climb out of the pit and think about what it will take to make three. The second giant will have to be a good body position to make the third. And will I be able to hold on for a third?

I take my third turn, trying to talk myself into three. I cast up, do one solid giant, a second one, and when I swing down for the third one I freak out a little and pull my shoulders closed and change it to a baby giant.

I wait in a support position for Katie to yell a correction over to me. I look across the gym and she is busy watching Paige do a routine.

I sigh. I'm already here; I could go again without chalking up. I look at my hands one at a time. They're still chalky. I decide to go again from right here. I cast up, giant, giant, baby giant. What is wrong with me?

I swing down and fall into the pit because now I for sure need chalk.

I really shouldn't change my mind in the middle of a skill. That's how I got hurt in the first place.

I do giant, giant, baby giant for several more turns. Lucy comes over to me and says, "Katie says to work giant flyaway."

"Okay," I agree, relieved. I undo the Velcro on my grips and readjust them. "What are you working?"

"Flyaway fulls."

She jumps up to the bar and easily kips up. Then she

casts to a handstand and does a gorgeous giant right into a layout flyaway.

"How do you do that?" I ask as she starts climbing out of the pit.

"What?"

"The flyaway right out of the giant."

"Oh, we did a ton of drills at my old gym." Then she thinks about it for a moment. "It's faster than out of a cast so you have to be ready and I guess when you know the timing well it's not a big deal. Also, for the layout you wait a little longer than is comfortable."

"I'm always afraid my shoulders won't be open enough to wait that long," I comment, rubbing chalk on my hands.

I jump up and warm-up with just a cast flyaway.

"Those are fine, nothing to worry about."

I smile as I climb out of the pit. At this point giant flyaway seems less scary than three giants in a row. I better do it so I feel like I accomplished something today.

It feels good to be back in the gym challenging myself and talking with my teammates.

"Are you ready for this weekend?" I ask her.

She nods. "This season is a lot of fun for me. My A routines are solid so I'll get to add upgrades when I'm ready."

I nod, trying not to feel sorry for myself. That's where I was just a few weeks ago.

"I'm finally used to how PBGA does things. I'm less nervous this year."

"What do you mean?"

"Well, at my old gym, whatever your routine was at the beginning of the season, that was your routine all season. Upgrades were rarely worked in season and never added to a routine during season. It was more strict. It took me time to get used to throwing a new skill in a routine. I'm still slower than everyone else on being ready but I'm getting better."

I nod in understanding. I have to admit, Lucy's basics are impeccable so they were doing something right at her old gym.

She takes another turn and this time twists her layout flyaway.

I jump up right after her and am determined to go for it. I cast up and do a giant. When I hit the handstand out of the giant I pike down to slow my swing for the flyaway.

"Great job!" she says, acknowledging that I went for it.

Then she takes her turn and does a beautiful flyaway full.

"You could totally do those with a mat," I comment.

"I know, one more."

I nod and go again. Giant, pike down, flyaway.

Lucy goes again, perfect full and then Katie yells over to us that she needs a mat.

We laugh since we were one step ahead of her. I help Lucy walk over and get an 8-incher from floor. We drag it across the floor and toss it in the pit. The motion kind of makes my ankle uncomfortable.

"Do you want to go first?" she asks me.

"I can't land on that yet."

"Oh yeah, oh my gosh, I'm sorry. Should we take it out?"

"No, do your turn and we can pull it out for me."

"Okay," she says, climbing up. "It's that tender?"

"It still hurts to walk. So yeah, a landing, even on a soft mat, would be bad."

She gives me a look, then says, "I'm so sorry Lexi, it must be hard to be here."

"Yes and no, it's good to be back," I answer. If I tell her the bad parts I might cry so I leave it at that.

She nods, jumps up to the bar and kips up. She casts,

does a perfect giant, and then lets go just a tad earlier than usual and her full is a little wonky. She doesn't rotate all the way around and lands short with her head in front of her feet. She bounces forward on the mat and lands on her stomach and then slides off the mat like a penguin headfirst into the foam pit.

I start laughing immediately. I know she's not hurt so it's okay to laugh. She rights herself and is laughing, too.

"What'd I do?" she asks me.

"You let go too early and twisted funny."

"I lost where I was after I let go. I just pulled."

"Good call. I wish we had that on video. You should have seen the slide," I say, making us laugh all over again.

We hear Katie yell over that it's time to rotate. Lucy's eyes get big, "I can't end on that one."

"Go," I say, gesturing for her to skip me. "I have a feeling I'm going to be here for a while."

She quickly chalks up and does a textbook giant layout full and lands it upright. "Beautiful," I say. She nods and jumps off the mat over to the floor and starts taking off her grips.

"That felt much better," Lucy says.

"It was awesome!"

"You're staying here?"

"I can't do anything else except condition," I answer and see her frown.

"Okay, well, it was fun over here with you."

"Thanks." I smile and she goes to put her grips away and get ready for whatever event they have next.

Katie comes over to me. "I can work with you while they are putting away their grips." I remain quiet, waiting to see what she wants me to work on. "Let me spot you on the giant flyaway," she says.

"I need the mat out," I say. She reaches down and is able

to pull the mat out before I have a chance to help her. Then she reviews the body and arm position I need to be in going into the flyaway.

"You don't need to slow it down," she advises.

"It's just so fast and scary," I admit.

"That's why I'm here. To give you a little more confidence for the skill," she says as she climbs up to the spotting block. "I won't let you come back into the bar; I promise."

I do trust what Kate is saying and I know she'll keep me from getting hurt. For some reason that understanding still doesn't make the fear go away. I don't want to disappoint Katie and I really do want to get my layout flyaway out of my giant. I take a deep breath and start telling myself I can do this.

I jump up to the bar and kip up. When I'm in a support position Katie gives me one more brief instruction. "Stay open. Let go on the upswing."

Stay open. Stay open. I know she means that I want to be straight from my hands all the way to my toes. Having an angle at my shoulders is what she means by closed.

I cast up and she gets me all the way to handstand, then I swing down into a faster giant (because I started in handstand). I come over the top of the bar and Katie adjusts my body position and then I swing down for the flyaway. I stay open and I feel like I'm going too fast. I feel my toes come up and I let go and fly up into the highest flyaway I have ever done.

"That's it!" Katie yells as I land in the pit.

"That was awesome!" I exclaim looking up at her.

"Great job," she says. I see that my teammates are headed over to beam and the upper optionals girls are coming over to bars. I'm not sure I have time to get another spot from Katie. She has to get her team started on their assignment.

"Do I have time for one more?"

"Yes, chalk up fast and jump up," she says. "How's the ankle doing?"

"It's . . . sore, achy, I guess."

"Then you stay on bars. There's plenty for you to work."

I jump up to the bar. I kip up and this time she says, "Same thing as last time." I cast up, and again, she gets me to handstand. Then I swing into a giant right into the flyaway. I can't believe how high and floaty my flyaway is when I do it like that.

"Looking good, Alexis," she says. "Getting your cast all the way to handstand will help with these, too."

I smile and climb out of the pit. I see the upper optionals have started their push away kips without even being told and my teammates are doing beam complex with Melony. I'm not sure if my workout is done.

"Do three more exactly how we just did and then I'm going to have you do some drills," she says. I guess I'm working out for a little longer.

I chalk up as she walks back over to the upper optionals girls. I jump up again and try to do what I just did. I still pike down a little out of fear but not as much as before.

I take three more turns and they are an improvement so I feel good when I go over to Katie to tell her I'm done. Which is a good thing because my hands are burning. I have been on bars longer than usual and I can tell.

Katie sees me walking over and instructs Maya to help me set up a drill that I'm not familiar with. She tells her to get an 8-incher, a cheese mat, and a mini trampoline. I move to go get the cheese and Katie tells me not to.

"You're on that ankle enough. You don't need to be moving mats." I do as she says, feeling bad about making Maya move mats for me. Katie comes down from the spotting block to help Maya situate the mats.

"Can I take my grips off?"

"No keep them on for this one," Katie answers. "Alright," she says, setting the floor bar over the 8-incher. "Come on over and I'll walk you through this drill. I can't believe we haven't done these with you." I walk over and wait for instructions. "Do a handstand on the bar with your belly to the cheese mat," she says. The cheese mat is propped up along the wall with the thick end on the floor and the thin end at the top. I do as she says and get into a handstand on the floor bar with my belly against the cheese mat so I am at a slight angle.

"Okay, now fall slightly rounded and hit your back on the center of the mini tramp and bounce back up to a handstand." This sounds a little awkward and I don't move. She grabs my thighs and says, "Maya and I can help you do one in slow motion so you understand." I feel Maya grab my thighs from the other side. They slowly help me up into a straight handstand then they lower me onto the mini tramp. "Arms stay straight, slightly rounded." I do as she says and I feel my upper back hit the small trampoline. Then they pull me back up to handstand. It is exactly the motion on the very last part of a giant when I come up over the bar. Then they lean me against the cheese.

"How did that feel," Katie asks.

"Weird," I admit.

"Did you feel the back side of a giant?"

"Yes."

"Let's do it again." I tighten up my body and push away from the cheese so I am in a handstand directly over the bar. Then they lower me a little faster and I bounce back up to handstand. "That one was mostly you. Come down and rest." I twist and step down out of the handstand onto my good foot. "Thank you, Maya, I can spot her for a few more on my own." Then she looks at me. "Rest and I will be back."

I shake my arms out while I wait for her. This entire-workout-on-bars thing is intense. I look out the training window at my mom reading. I'm probably working out longer than she anticipated. I decide to go get a drink and walk over to her in the lobby.

She looks up when I walk through the doors.

"How's it going?" she asks me. I reach for my water bottle in the cubby next to her.

"Better and worse than I expected," I answer.

"You can tell me the details of that later," she says. "Your giants looked good."

"Thanks," I say, taking a long drink. "It feels good to be in the gym."

"I bet."

"It's going longer than I expected. I feel bad you're waiting."

"Don't feel bad, this is what I expected. Plus, I wanted to be here."

"I better get back," I say, setting my water back in my cubby.

"Have fun," she says, returning to her book.

I walk carefully back to my drill and wait for Katie. I don't wait very long before she comes over to spot me again. I do three in a row and on the last one I do it almost by myself.

"You have the timing right. You can do these on your own. Do three more sets of three."

I don't mind drills. They are less stressful than giants and I'm still learning. I can definitely feel the hollow body position I have to get to between the trampoline and the cheese mat. I know I'm not doing that motion in my giants and I hope this helps. I do three more sets of three and tell Katie I'm done.

"Strap bars," she says. More bars? I thought for sure I

would be finished. "Your hands have probably about had it so strap bars are best. Practice the body position on the back side you just learned."

I take my grips off and drop them on the spotting block next to the strap bar. I find the straps on the floor next to the block and grab them. I climb up onto the spotting block and slide the PVC pipe that is over the metal bar toward me. Then I strap myself in, slide my hands to the center of the bar, swing down, and start pumping tap swings. When my tap swings get high enough I start doing giants. Strap bar giants are easy for me and I haven't done them in a while. I try to focus on my body position on the back side of the giants. I easily do five and slow my swing to take a break. I stand on the block resting and watch the upper optionals girls run routines on bars and my teammates running routines on beam. How far behind am I getting dorking around on bars for an entire workout?

I feel myself getting discouraged and I try to push the thoughts from my mind because I do not want to get frustrated and cry here at the gym.

I do two more sets of five before Katie tells me to be done. I gratefully unstrap myself and climb down. The bars rotation is done for upper optionals and they leave to go put their grips away. I just did bars for two entire rotations.

"Here is a list of conditioning for you. You can do it here or at home. It's mostly legs since your arms are probably exhausted."

"What leg exercises can I do?" I ask looking at the list.

I see hip flexors lifts (which you do sitting), wall sits (I hate those), and hamstring leans (which I will need a partner for).

"You may not be able to do the wall sits yet because it will put pressure on your ankle. If it hurts then stop."

"I think . . . I think I'll do these at home," I say.

"Sounds good. Let me go talk to your mom," she says as some upper optionals girls come back down and look at her.

"Set up vault," is all she says and they know what to do.

She follows me into the lobby to talk to my mom.

"Hi Amanda," she greets my mom. "She had a great workout and I'm happy to see her back in the gym."

I put my grips away while I let them talk. Katie tells her about the conditioning that I have left and my mom tells her about my physical therapy. I put on my sweatpants as I listen to them discuss my training.

"Make sure she ices tonight. We didn't do anything on her ankle per se, but just the jostling around and walking around has probably irritated it. Oh, and be sure to stretch," she says over to me.

"Okay," I say, as I put on my hoodie sweatshirt and zip it up.

"Great job today! See you Wednesday!" she sings and walks through the training doors. I look through the glass to where my teammates are tumbling on the diagonal of floor and I want to cry.

That night I lay in bed thinking about all the things I have done to try to heal and stay up with my training and it still seems so slow.

I'm not mad at you, God, I try. *I'm sorry I said I was mad. My mom says you help people who help themselves. I am trying to help myself. So can you maybe help me, too? Could you make healing go faster. Please? I will do all my chores and not complain and listen in church.*

There, maybe that will help.

CHAPTER 25

I'm happy to see my cousins as I sit down at our lunch table. I'm also happy it's Friday. It has been a long week of physical therapy and practice. I did the TheraBand and balancing stuff at PT and nothing but bars and conditioning at practice. An hour and a half to two hours of bars every workout is brutal and I have three rips to prove it.

"You're here today," Ashtyn says as I sit down.

"Of course, I'm here," I say, pulling out my lunch.

"No 'of course', you haven't been here all week."

"I was here Wednesday," I comment. "I'm at physical therapy on Monday, Tuesday, and Thursday. So yeah, I guess I'm only here Wednesdays and Fridays."

"Like I said, not here," she repeats and I frown.

"We just miss you," the ever-diplomatic Oakley says.

"What are you guys doing this weekend?" I ask, trying to change the subject away from me.

"I think we're going to the cabin," Ashtyn says, referring

to the cabin that our grandparents own. It's in a different canyon than Snowcap. It's not a ski cabin. Instead there are a lot of trails for snowmobiling and snowshoeing. And it's near a lake which is epic in the summer when we all get together.

"You are? I wonder if we are," Oakley says.

"Oh, beg your parents tonight. It would be so much better if you and Ronan were there."

They continue to talk about the cabin while I eat lunch. It makes me kind of miss the cabin in the winter. We haven't been to it the last year or two because of basketball and gymnastics.

"Can you go?" Oakley asks me.

"Probably not. My brothers have games tonight and Drew has a meet tomorrow."

"What about you?"

"What about me?" I ask.

"You could come with us!" Ashtyn exclaims.

"I could," I ponder. "But I promised Drew and my team I would be at the meet tomorrow."

"Oh, we would have so much fun. You haven't been to the cabin in for-e-ver."

"Maybe," I say, mostly because I know she won't stop if I don't at least consider her request. Then I get out my laptop to finish up my math homework.

My cousins keep talking about the cabin and pretty soon Ashtyn is texting Oakley's mom. This occupies them while I work. I have a quiz in math today which means all of my math homework for the week is supposed to be done. Since I have missed six math classes in the last two weeks, I am nowhere near done with the homework. It sure piled up on me quickly. Thankfully, I understand most of it and I am cruising though the assignments. One section stumps me though. Clearly, I missed the day we were taught how to do these problems and I can't seem to figure it out on my own. I should have looked at this sooner, then at least Drew could have helped me. Now I have to take a quiz with an entire section that confuses me. And I have to turn in homework with a section missing.

"What are you doing?" Oakley asks.

"Just trying to catch up in math. I miss math when I go to PT," I try to explain without looking up. I frantically try to finish as many problems as possible. She sees I'm busy working and goes back to talking to Ashtyn.

The bell rings for lunch to be over and I decide to hit submit. I was missing at least ten problems, but turning in what I did is better than nothing. I shove my laptop into my bag, stand up, and follow my cousins out of the cafeteria. They say goodbye to me and remind me to talk to my mom about the cabin and then we split off into separate halls.

I turn into my math class dreading my quiz. This is going to be bad.

The math quiz was awful and I'm afraid to pull up my score. Thank goodness the week is over and I'm home now. Drew and I chose not to go to the basketball games tonight. Drew wanted to go to bed early because he competes tomorrow morning. I decided to stay with him because I just didn't feel like sitting through two basketball games.

"Do you want to watch a movie?" I ask him.

"Sure, if we can agree on one," he says, knowing he and I don't have similar taste in movies.

"I wonder if there is a gymnastics one we would both like?"

"Doubt it, but we could try," he agrees.

We couldn't find a gymnastics movie that had men's and

women's gymnastics so we settled on *McFarland*, a movie about cross country running. The streaming system saw we were looking for a sports movie and it recommended that one. It ended up being better than I expected and it made me miss my teammates. I'm glad I'm going to watch them tomorrow instead of going to the cabin with my cousins.

CHAPTER 26

We get up early to head downtown for the meet. Drew is in the second session of the day. My teammates are in the same session since all the Level 7s are competing in the same session. I may miss seeing the Level 6s compete. I think they're in the session before.

"Hey Mom, can I see the schedule?" I ask, as my mom, Dad, Drew, and I pile in the car. Ethan and William opted to sleep in this morning.

She hands the schedule back to me and I take a look. Yesterday Level 1-5s competed and today they are starting this morning with Level 6 in the first session. Level 7 is second, then Level 8, and at the end of the day the Level 9s and 10s are together in the last session. This is normal because there aren't a lot of Level 9s and 10s.

I may get to see the last rotation of my Level 6 teammates. I hand the paper back up to my mom and get out my book. We have a thirty to forty-minute drive to get to downtown to the event center Capitol Hill Gymnastics has rented out this year.

Drew puts in his earbuds and closes his eyes. This is his pre-meet ritual. The music is to block everyone out while he visualizes all six of his routines. The men have six events. I can't imagine; four is hard enough.

We walk into a huge arena and Drew checks in. I love seeing the men's events mixed in. The floor is in the center of the giant room. To the left is the men's high bar, men's parallel bars, and the women's uneven parallel bars. To the right of the floor are beam and rings. In front of the floor is both a mushroom and a pommel horse. The mushroom is circular and lower to the ground. It's what the lower levels use to train up for pommels. Way in back is vault. Both the men and women use vault and floor, so I wonder how sharing the equipment for those two events will work.

"I'm going to go find my team," Drew says, spotting groups of athletes coming in and stretching in a room just outside the room we are in. There is seating all around the gym. Since this is a giant conference room there isn't stadium seating we are used to, but three rows of chairs all the way around the equipment.

"Well, which event would you like to sit by?" my mom asks me.

"We could sit in the middle, by floor?" I suggest. She makes her way to the center of the room. We end up in seats in the third row and can hardly see.

"These aren't great seats," I comment.

"When this session is over, these parents will clear out and we can move up," she says. I nod. She has done this before.

"There's Perfect Balance," my dad points out. They are standing at the far end of the room over at vault. I'm not sure if they just finished vault or are doing vault next. I see Katie talking to them and they start to walk over to floor. So they were finishing vault and have floor next. In that case we are in the perfect seats.

I watch as they prepare to warm-up and I feel pride at how great they look in their snowflake leotards. I see Paige, Carmen, Trista, and Marissa walk over to the same diagonal and a group of boys take the other diagonal. Then they are given a nod that their one touch begins.

How fun, they get to compete with the Perfect Balance boys' team. There are four of our girls and three boys. All of them know how to tumble the diagonal and warm-up smaller skills along the edges without getting in each other's way.

When they are done they all sit together and I watch as Marissa starts them off. Marissa does a clean routine with her layout on floor which is a small upgrade for her. Then an athlete from our boys' team salutes immediately after Marissa is off the floor. How is that possible? Usually it takes a few minutes for the judges to be ready. I look at the tables along the sides and I see at each table one judge is looking at her notes and one judge is intently watching Matthew walk onto the floor. They must have two women's judges and two men's judges and they are alternating to make the event move faster. So that's how they share the floor.

About the time the judges post Marissa's routine, Matthew is done competing and walks off. Paige is immediately next. She does a gorgeous routine with her new bounders in the first pass. Then one of our boys competes while Trista prepares to be up next. Trista loves floor and her tumbling is so good I don't think there are any more upgrades for her to do.

I'm wrong; she does a full in her first pass. When did she get that? When she salutes and walks off the floor she high-fives the boy standing on the edge of the floor waiting to compete next. It looks so fun to have the boy's team with them, and it makes the rotation fly by.

Carmen is up last and she does a solid routine with a layout and a front handspring front. I let out a breath I didn't know I was holding. Was I just hoping she didn't have an upgrade? What is wrong with me? I should be happy for my teammates.

As soon as they are done competing the meet director ushers them into a separate room for awards and Drew's session is allowed to warm-up on the floor for the next fifteen minutes.

I watch as Savannah, Lucy, Victoria, and Riley warm-up. I can't believe I'm missing a second meet. Maybe it was good I didn't go watch the last one, it kind of hurts my heart a little to see them out there without me.

When they are done warming up they go to vault with the boys. They do the same thing as floor. They warm-up together and it looks like there are men's judges and women's judges. I think the judging is really different for men's versus women's so they need different judges, plus it does seem to make things go faster. Vault is fast and my teammates do all the timers I expect them to do. There really aren't upgrades you can do on vault other than learn an entirely new timer.

Then the girls go to bars and the boys go to high bar. I notice their judges follow them to high bar since the next rotation to vault doesn't have a boy's team.

My teammates don't have upgrades on bars either, but they are swinging higher and making their handstands, something none of us were doing consistently at the beginning of the season. I have to admit I missed a few of my teammates' routines because I'm having so much fun watching the boys. Drew did a great bar routine and his giants into his flyaway is amazing. Maybe I should ask him about that.

Somehow the boys manage to do both high bar and parallel bars in the time it took the girls to just do bars. Then they rotate to beam and the boys go to rings. I thoroughly enjoy watching the boys compete. Their gymnastics is just different enough to be interesting. Plus, I'm struggling to feel anything but jealous when I watch my team.

I'm not proud of it, in fact I'm embarrassed. I stay quiet so my parents don't guess my feelings. I stay focused on Drew and my parents don't question my interest in his meet.

I watch as my teammates warm-up beam and Drew and his teammates warm-up rings. I notice both Savannah and Lucy are warming up their back handspring series. How did everyone get so good? I have only been out for two weeks. I know the answer. They have been working on these upgrades all fall. We are now in the middle of season and it's time for them to throw their new skills if they want to do them at State. If I had not gotten hurt I'm sure I would be doing a back handspring series too. But I did get hurt and I don't even know if I can still do a back walkover series. How long will it take me to remember to do my skills again when I do heal well enough to do a full workout?

"Drew's up," my mom whispers to Dad and me. I turn my head and see him salute the judge back with one arm. Then his coach lifts him up to the rings to begin his routine. I am so proud and impressed with my brother. Men's gymnastics takes so much strength, technique, patience, and control. They have to be brave too, like we do. I honestly don't know why everyone makes a fuss over my other brothers for doing basketball and baseball when Drew is the real athlete. He never gets any attention for doing gymnastics. None of the boys do, at least not like we do. That makes them even cooler to me. They are doing it because they love it.

I watch as he does a dismount that is kind of like a giant

flyaway, only on rings. He sticks the landing and bows to the judges. The boys bow at the end of their routine instead of salute and I think it is so classy.

I glance over to beam and I see Victoria starts my team off with a solid beam routine. She is for sure making Regionals and moving up to Level 8 next year. Level 7 looks easy for her.

The boys rotate to pommel horse. They walk over to a horse that does not have pommels on it. That is how the Level 6 and 7s compete pommel horse, with no pommels. In Levels 4 and 5 they compete on the mushroom, so they are improving. Pommels are kind of like vault. It looks like a whole lot of nothing until Level 8 or 9, and then it is super cool all of a sudden.

Then again, pommels are starting to look impressive for Drew. He can do flairs and circles on the horse and they look amazing. I keep trying to get him to teach me flairs so I can do them on beam like Peng-Peng from UCLA.

I watch Drew warm-up and I miss seeing Savannah and Marissa compete. Was that on purpose? I sigh, glad I'm not sitting with their parents.

The boys compete pommels so fast they are ready for floor when the girls are. I guess there are only three of them in their rotation. There is another boys' team here that has seven boys and another team has five. They are all somewhat rotating with their girls' team. I think it's awesome the meet tried to keep them together.

I watch as our men's and women's teams warm-up floor together. My heart squeezes as I watch Drew. I'm the one that did endless tumbling with him on the grass in the back yard. I'm the one that always went to Open Gym or Parents' Night Out when he had something extra he wanted to work.

And now, the one rare time men and women get to be in the same meet, I'm in the stands. I can feel myself getting choked up as Drew and my teammates sit together and I can see them talking and laughing. Why am I so emotional about this? Yes, it was something I was totally looking forward to, but it's certainly not something to cry about.

Maybe we'll do this meet again next year. *Yeah, but you will still be a Level 7 and Drew will be a Level 8 by then.* What a horrible thought. One I hadn't let myself think about until now. I may stay back in Level 7 because of my injury. All my friends and my brother will move up and I will be right where I am. Continuing to be afraid of fulls and giant flyaways.

Thankfully, Savannah's music starts, pulling me out of my downward spiral of negative thoughts. Savannah's routine is fun and lively and I can't help but be in a better mood after watching it.

Then Drew's teammate, Aaron, competes. Directly after him Riley does a gorgeous routine with a front handspring pike instead of a tuck at the end. More upgrades.

"He's up," my mom says to us as we watch Drew salute the floor judges. The guys don't have music on floor. They tumble and must show strength and flexibility at some point in their routine between tumbling passes. Drew does flairs and a press handstand to show his strength. He really needs to teach me flairs. His tumbling is a little harder than the girls do in Level 7. I can already see how the strength guys get as they go through puberty is improving their gymnastics and I'm a little envious.

When he's done he bows to the judges and my parents stand up and clap. He had a great meet. In fact, he hit six for six. I'm positive he's never done that. No wonder my parents are on their feet. I'm happy for Drew. I really am. I would just be happier if I was out there with him.

CHAPTER 27

I'm in a mopey mood Sunday night. My mom calls it the Sunday-night-blues. The idea of the week in front of me is daunting. Usually I'm excited for the week ahead. But this week looks like it's going to be like last week; a lot of physical therapy, conditioning, and driving. It also means a lot of homework since I'm missing so much school.

That reminds me; I never looked at my math score. I sigh and pick up my laptop off my dresser and walk over to my bed. I sit down and scoot back until I am leaning against the headboard. Then I open my laptop and log in to see my grades. I got a B on my test, which is better than I expected. But I have a C in the class. Whoa, no one in this family gets Cs, not even Ethan. How did that happen? I scroll down to look at my assignments and I have four missing assignments from the last two weeks. I guess I did only make up two of my missing days. And three times a week times two weeks is six missing days. That added up. Since we already took the test, the missing assignments are locked. I could maybe email my teacher. Honestly, I don't really care. So I get a C, so what?

The worst that will happen is my parents will make me stay home from gymnastics. Well, newsflash, I'm already basically staying home from gymnastics.

I shut my laptop and lean back. I don't want to go to PT this week. I don't even want to go to the gym this week. Fine, they can discover my C and keep me home.

William pops his head in, "Are you done with homework?"

"Yeah, why?" I lie.

"Because mom said we can play Mario Kart if you're done."

I don't really feel like Mario Kart either but he looks so hopeful. I nod and scoot off the bed.

"Sweet," he says and runs down ahead of me as I slowly make my way downstairs. I'm not wearing a brace at the moment so I have to be gentle when I move. By the time I get downstairs he has the system all set up and hands me a remote as soon as I sit down.

"I want in," Drew says, walking in.

"Great," Will says, handing him a remote. What I like about Mario Kart is that all of us can play at the same time. Each of us are on the screen at the same time. I love that no one has to wait for a turn and it eliminates bickering. Plus, my brothers are the worst at skipping me when they have to wait for a turn.

We begin and Drew wins the first race and William the next one. I usually get competitive with them and can beat them. Today I'm off and don't seem to care. I continue to play anyway as they continue to win.

My mom comes in with a book, and of course, starts in on me. "Have you done your ankle exercises today?"

"I will after this," I promise.

She turns to Drew, "Did you finish your history reading?"

"Yep," he says, keeping his eye on the screen.

This satisfies her and she settles onto the couch to read. Sunday is one of the rare days I see my mom sit down and relax. Probably because we don't have any sports or school stuff on Sunday.

"Alexis, you are a terrible driver today. Here, pick a new car," William says, going back to the selection screen.

"It's not the car. Go back," I order.

"You're never this bad. Get a new car," he insists.

I scroll through the selections but I can't seem to pick one. None of them are that exciting to me. Finally, I pick one I haven't raced in a while and he is satisfied and gets us back to the racing screen. We play a few more rounds and I just don't feel like playing anymore.

"I think I'm done," I say, exiting my player out of the game.

"Really?" Drew says, turning to look at me.

"Yeah, I need to go do my exercises." I go back up to my room and grab my TheraBand and sit on the floor with it. I can't seem to get myself to do the dumb movements. They're tedious and difficult and sometimes they hurt. I lean against my bed with my legs straight out in a pike sit, as if I am going to loop the band around my foot and begin. Instead I lean my head back on my bed and just sit.

I think about the meet yesterday. It was both fun and painful to watch my teammates compete. They have improved. They should be improving; it's midseason. Why did I have to hurt myself smack dab in the middle of season? Why couldn't I have hurt myself over the summer? That would have been better.

I don't want to go to PT tomorrow or gymnastics for that

matter. I close my eyes and think of the torture of the last three weeks. First the pain of the injury, then the pain of physical therapy, and then the agony of being in the gym and just conditioning while my teammates throw upgrades left and right.

I keep my eyes closed as I listen to my brothers yell at the television while they play their video game. It sounds like they've changed games.

I must have drifted off because the next thing I know my mom is in my doorway, "Alexis?"

I open my eyes. "Hmm?"

"Were you asleep?"

"I must have been," I say, sitting up a little. She comes in and sits next to me.

"You fell asleep doing your exercises?" she asks, seeing the band looped around my foot.

I shrug, not wanting to lie to her. "I don't want to go to PT or practice tomorrow," I blurt out.

"Really? But you're making so much progress."

"No I'm not. And it's all too much. Can I just let it heal?"

"You can," she says slowly. "It will just take longer."

"The first doctor said six weeks. It seems like that is how long it's taking no matter what I do."

"Maybe, but you would have to start over in the gym. What we are doing is keeping you ready to jump back in as soon as you can."

"Well, I don't like it and I'm tired of both."

"Why don't you sleep on it? I would hate for one bad mood to make you lose all the hard work you've put in so far."

"I'm not in a bad mood," I grump.

She puts her arm around me and hugs me. She leans her head over and touches mine. "I know it's hard baby girl."

676

"It's not hard, it's impossible," I choke.

"I know it feels that way. You have to trust that what you are doing at physical therapy is getting your ankle stronger and what you are doing in the gym is keeping your body strong for when you're cleared for a full workout."

"For what? The season is going to be over by the time I'm ready," I croak as tears start rolling down my face.

"Maybe. Maybe not. That's up to you and how well you take care of yourself," she says, squeezing me a little tighter. "Maybe I have been pushing you too hard. You don't have to be in the gym. I thought you wanted to be there. I thought you wanted to do what you could do and see your teammates."

"I thought I would like being there too, but I don't," I sniffle. I don't tell her how insanely jealous I get when I watch them run routines and add in upgrades.

"I know it's probably not easy to just condition and do drills. Gymnastics has always been fun for you. You're experiencing the hard part of athletics. The part that teaches you character."

"I don't need character," I pout. "I need a break. I don't want to do either this week."

Mom is quiet for a moment and says, "You don't have to go to the gym, but you do have to go to physical therapy. You are making more progress than you think and recovering from your injury is important."

"Okay," I agree, glad I don't have to go to the gym tomorrow. I have never felt like this before. I have never dreaded the gym. Is this how Will feels about basketball?

"Let's get you ready for bed." She stands up and puts out a hand to help me up. I take her hand. She gives me a big hug and tells me everything will work out. I don't believe her but I enjoy the hug.

CHAPTER 28

As usual, my PT starts off with Janice using heat on my ankle. I can feel less swelling squishing around when she pushes the wand around my ankle bone. It is kind of relaxing to sit here and let her work on my foot while she and my mom talk.

She turns off the heat machine and sets the wand in the cradle and begins her massaging. "It's healing nicely. Does it feel better?" she asks me and I nod. "We get to do some different things today to challenge you."

I've learned that is not what I want to hear around here. She finishes the ankle massage and goes to get a TheraBand. Instead of the usual red she is holding a blue one. "Same exercises, but we are going to try a tighter band today."

Janice hands me the band and I know what to do. I sit in a pike on the table, flex my foot, and loop it around the bottom of my foot, holding the ends in each hand. "Start with the right and left waves," she instructs.

I begin to move my foot and the band is so tight I can barely move my foot. I look up at her in frustration. "How does it feel?"

"Like it felt on my first day. I can hardly move it."

"The fact that you can move it at all proves your ankle is stronger. This is a tighter band so you'll have to work harder to get motion."

I focus a little harder and move my foot against the band. The motion is smaller than I've been getting with the red band. It's truly like the motion I got on the first day. I guess I'm making progress, as minuscule as it may be.

When I'm done with the five different motions on the TheraBand she brings over a half ball and sits it on the ground. It is a big round blue exercise ball on one side and flat on the other. It sits flat and stable on the ground.

"Jump down," she says and I slide off the table. "We are going to do the balance exercises we have been doing, only today you will stand on this."

The first week I stood with her helping me put my weight on one foot. Last week I successfully stood on my bad ankle and was able to balance my weight on the trampoline bed. Now this.

"On one foot?"

"Yep. Why don't you do it first on your right leg to get the hang of it, then we'll try the left."

I step onto the ball with my good foot and she grabs both of my hands to help me. At first it's a little wobbly, and I feel my ankle moving slightly to find balance. I quickly find my balance and the wobbling stops. "Your stabilizing muscles in that ankle are amazing. That is what we are working toward in the other one. Let's see if you can go ten seconds without holding my hands." She slowly lets go of my hands and I stay standing on one leg with my other foot at my ankle. I steady myself on the half ball as she slowly counts to ten. "Great job," she says taking my hands and telling me to step down.

"Rest for a second and we'll try the other side."

"Why did we do my good side?"

"I wanted to see your normal level of balance. It's amazing by the way. Gymnasts and dancers usually are incredible with balance."

I smile at the compliment. She has all these world-class athletes here. It's fun to get a compliment specific to gymnastics.

"Ready for the other side?" I nod and she takes my hands. "Step in the center."

The ball has rings on it and the very center has a little circle. I'm sure to step on the little circle with my foot. My ankle immediately starts rolling around and I cannot catch my balance. I lean heavily on her with my hands and look down at my foot that will not stop wobbling. I am horrified at how hard it is to stand still on one foot.

"Try to stand up straight," she says. With my ankle still rolling around I try to straighten up. "Five seconds," she says and I nod. She counts out five even though my ankle never stops wobbling. "Step down."

I step down and feel relief at getting off of that torture ball. "That was hard," I tell her.

"You did great. You held on for the full five seconds."

"I never found balance. I never stopped wobbling."

"Your ankle is weak. This will help; I promise."

All this exercise did was show me just how weak my ankle really is. There is no way I'll be able to stand on beam in a relevé any time soon. I thought I was closer to recovery than this. The ball exercise just showed how far I have to go. My right foot was so much stronger, so stable. My left was pathetic.

She has me step up on the ball three more times and I improve a little if I concentrate really hard on not letting my ankle wobble. For the most part, it has a mind of its own, but I do improve a tiny bit.

After that torturous exercise, we go to the trampoline. Today Janice gives me a heavier ball and has me twist my upper body a little more.

Normally I'm done after this. However, today she has me do air squats. I can feel the strain on my ankle as I squat down and my knees bend forward over my foot, putting my ankle at an angle. I do ten air squats before she tells me I am done and that she will add squats to my list for home.

By now my ankle has been worked so hard I limp to the icing room and happily put my foot in the ice water. I don't squirm as much when I put my foot in. It still hurts like crazy; I just know what to expect.

"How are you today, Miss Lexis?" Gary asks, coming over to me.

"It was hard today," I tell him as he begins to rub my back.

"But it will make you better. The doctors here make athletes better," he says. I nod. "What's your favorite animal?" he asks.

"I don't know," I laugh.

"Just pick one you like. You can change your mind tomorrow."

"Cats, I guess."

"I like cats, mostly kittens," he says.

"What is your lucky number?" he asks.

"I don't know that either!" I say making both of us laugh. My brothers always have lucky numbers. It's whatever their jersey number is that season. Since we don't have jerseys, I never really thought of a lucky number. We do have the perfect ten. "Ten!" I finally say.

"Ten is a great number," he agrees. "Are you numb now, Miss Lexis?"

"I am," I say, surprised he could distract me that long.

"Good job! Keep soaking. I have to get ice for Mr. Michael," he explains. I watch as he goes over to the ice machine and grabs a plastic bag off the wall. He opens the lid to the ice, picks up the giant silver scooper, and starts scooping ice into a bag.

"I have your ice, Mr. Michael," he says to a man who comes in with a knee brace on.

"Thanks, Gary, you make the best ice bags," he says, sitting on one of the many tables along the wall.

I look down at my foot and move my leg around. My mom is at the front desk trying to get us a new appointment so I have no one to talk to.

I watch as the water swirls around. I can't believe I thought this was a hot tub on my first day.

"I can get us an afternoon appointment," my mom says walking back into the icing room. "But it will be with a different therapist. What do you want to do?"

"Stay with Janice," I say immediately.

"You are doing okay missing math?"

"Yeah, it's fine," I lie. It can be fine. I can catch up. It's fine. I don't want a different therapist. I am finally used to Janice.

"Okay, we'll keep what we have then," she says, taking a seat in a chair next to the whirlpool. "How much longer do you have?"

"Like ten minutes or less. I'm already numb, so not that long,"

My mom looks at her watch and nods. "Do you still want to miss practice today?"

"Yes," I say. Because, really, what's the point?

CHAPTER 29

The week crawls by and I spend most of it not knowing what to do with myself. I try to do the math class work I am missing. My attempts are half-hearted and I end up doing a small portion of it. Then I skim my other homework and decide none of it is urgent. I don't have practice since I requested not to go. I could do my TheraBand exercises but I don't feel like it. I could do my conditioning list from Katie. I don't feel like doing that either.

I don't even want to do Mario Kart when Will asks me to play.

"So you are just going to sit there?"

"Why do you care?" I retort.

"It's eerie," he says. I drag myself off the couch to go lay on my bed in my room. Then I don't have to listen to him nag me for video games or tell me I'm eerie.

I look at the ceiling for a while until I finally roll over and look at my nightstand. There are a stack of books sitting there that I could read. I don't reach for any of them. I stare at the wall and see my gymnastics medals hung on four hooks that my dad put up for me. It seems like so long ago that I stood on a podium and received a medal.

I look at the hot pink wall and wonder why my room is so pink. Do I even like pink? Gary keeps asking me these simple questions I don't know the answer to. What is my favorite color, animal, or number? Why don't I know these things? Do people just pick one, like he said, and see how it fits? I don't think I like pink.

I roll onto my stomach and decide to take a little nap.

I wake to a knock on my door. "Come in," I respond.

Drew cracks the door and says, "Mom wants you to come down and have dinner with me." I sit up, not sure what time it is. Sometime after Drew's practice ended.

I swing my legs off the bed and follow him down to the kitchen. I don't even know what day it is. I know it's a school day.

He microwaves both of our save-plates and puts mine in front of me. I don't feel like eating so I just move the food around on my plate. It's a trick I haven't had to use in a long time. I'm not sure why I'm bothering since neither of our parents are here.

"Where's Mom and Dad?"

"Mom went to pick up Ethan and Dad is working late."

I stop pushing my food around and set my fork down. Drew is being so nice I should try to make small talk. "How was practice?"

"Good, your teammates asked about you. Why aren't you going anymore?"

"There's nothing for me to do."

"You could do bars," he counters.

I don't say anything to that. "I'm not sure I even like gymnastics. Mom just put us in it. Will was saying the other day that I just like it to please her and maybe he's right."

"Don't let Will get in your head. He's dealing with his own stuff. I've seen you in the gym; you like gymnastics."

"Maybe. At least I probably used to," I agree.

"You just have to come back. Remember what it feels like to learn a new skill."

I sigh, "There are no new skills in my near future."

"There for sure won't be if you keep skipping," he says, getting up and taking his plate to the sink. "I'm going to go shower. You should stop feeling sorry for yourself and do something."

How rude. I'm not feeling sorry for myself, I'm just being realistic. What something does he expect me to do anyway? I drag myself back up to my room and shut the door so everyone will leave me alone. I sit in the middle of my bed and look outside. It's dark out with cloud cover so there are no stars to look at. Even the sky is boring. Everything feels black, white, and gray; nothing is in color anymore. No wonder I don't know my favorite color.

I shuffle off to school and I can't remember if it's a therapy day or not. I wear black tights, a sweatshirt, and fuzzy boots just in case. I can now wear just the cloth bandage if I am wearing boots over it for extra support. If I'm wearing sneakers, I need the soft brace.

"Happy Friday," Ashtyn says as I sit down for lunch. Huh, it's already Friday. This week crawled by and yet I'm surprised it's Friday.

"Are you okay?" she asks.

"I'm fine. Just tired," I answer. She accepts my answer and turns to our cousin, Oakley, and asks her if she got the invitation to our grandparents' upcoming anniversary party. It does sound like a fun event and I'm looking forward to it.

"Are the St. George families coming?" Oakley asks.

"Everyone is coming. Grandma says they have to," Ashtyn answers.

I take a bite out of my sandwich and realize I don't feel like eating. I shove it back in the baggy and put it back in my lunch bag. I don't even look to see what else my dad packed. I don't feel like eating anything.

I lean back and listen to my cousins talk and I don't feel like joining the conversation. I'm worried they will notice, so I decide to leave.

"I'm behind on math because I keep missing, so I'm going to go to the library to make up some work," I say, standing up.

"Okay, maybe we'll see you this weekend after church," Ashtyn says. I nod, maybe. I don't really care either way. I walk slowly to the library. I don't really want to do math homework; it was a good excuse though. I better stick to it or they're going to tell my mom something is wrong. Is something wrong? No, I'm just tired and people are just particularly annoying these days.

I enter the library and walk by the rows of books to the back. The back of the library looks out at the front of the school. There are huge windows that give great natural lighting. There are tables for studying along the windows. I sit at one of them and look out. The sky is white- that means snow this afternoon. Fresh snow means everyone in my family will ski tomorrow. Except me. Again.

When my mom picks Drew and me up from school Drew is busy talking about a speech he had to give in English class. I'm happy to let him talk, since it's an unusual switch in roles.

"And how was your day, Alexis?" my mom asks me.

"Fine," I answer.

"That's it? Just fine?"

"Yep," I say. I honestly have nothing to add. The day was uneventful.

"Are you okay?" she asks me. Why is everyone asking me that.

"Just tired."

My mom doesn't say anything to that and starts talking about the snow coming down (called it) and how we will have a nice ski day (called that too).

"You can go too, Alexis," she adds.

"I can?" I look up at her in the mirror.

"Yes, Janice said that ski boots are so secure that if I tape your ankle you'll be fine."

"Okay." Although, I'm not even sure I want to go.

When we get home she makes us a snack that I don't eat. Thankfully, she leaves to go get the older boys from high school and I go up to my room. I flop on my bed, glad the week is over. I stare at the snow for a while when I hear a ping from my phone.

Paige:

    Rounding up a group for PNO, want to come?

Me:

    Don't you have a meet tomorrow?

Paige:

    That's next weekend. Are you in?

I stare at the screen. Am I in? Do I want to go? I don't even know if I want to go or not. When I don't respond my phone pings again.

Paige:

    We miss you.

I set the phone down and roll over to my side. I don't feel like going. Does that mean I never really liked gymnastics? Or maybe I don't like it anymore? Did I always do it for my mom?

"Want to play Mario Kart?" William says, interrupting my thoughts, or was it sleep?

"You are obsessed," I groan.

"And you have become lazybones."

"No I haven't."

"Then you've just become boring."

"At least that's better than being a liar pants," I retort.

"What do you mean?"

"I mean why don't you tell Mom and Dad you hate basketball?" I shout.

He comes in the rest of the way and shuts the door, "Alexis!"

"What? Just tell them."

"I will if you will," he bargains.

"I will what?"

"Tell them whatever is wrong with you."

"Nothing's wrong with me," I deny.

"Something is," he insists.

I hate him for talking about something I don't understand. "Leave me alone!" I yell at him. And surprisingly, he does.

I hear him yelling down the hall to Drew, "She doesn't want to play. She's grumpy and sleepy again!"

I don't appreciate him yelling that down the hall. I know he did it because I yelled his secret. Maybe I will go play. I pull up to a sitting position and just sit there. That is how my mom finds me, sitting on the edge of the bed wondering what to do with myself.

"Hey, Alexis," she says, coming in and sitting next to me. "You don't want to play with the boys? It's one of your favorite Friday night activities."

"I was thinking about it," I admit.

"How has your week been?" she asks me.

"Dumb and boring," I sulk.

"Why do you think?"

I sigh and look away from her. "Because I can't do anything."

"You can do plenty. You are just choosing not to." I'm silent about that and she continues. "Look, I let you take a break from the gym because you expressed that PT and gymnastics was too much. However, I have watched you this week. Not going to the gym has put you into a funk."

"I'm not in a funk. I'm just tired," I try.

"Being tired is part of your funk or feeling blue. You haven't done any of your PT exercises, conditioning from Katie, or even homework. You aren't eating and most of all you aren't your smiley happy self," she finishes.

"How do you notice all this with five kids?" I say, trying to be funny, but she doesn't laugh.

"A mother notices."

"What do I do?" I whisper.

"I think maybe you start small. Start doing things you like to do. Do you want to ski tomorrow?"

"Not really."

"I can stay home with you and maybe we can think of something that will make you feel like yourself."

"What about skiing?"

"The boys can go with Dad. Actually, I think Will has a game tomorrow. Either way, Dad can be in charge of the boys tomorrow."

"It's weird, I don't know what I like anymore."

"Well, that's what we can try to figure out."

CHAPTER 30

On Saturday the boys go skiing right after morning basketball games and Mom stays home with me. I help her with laundry and I don't mind the task. It's quiet in the house as we fold laundry.

"Josselyn, Brandon, and your cousins are coming over for dinner tomorrow. Will you help me with dinner?"

"Sure." I shrug as I pick up a shirt and shake it out. "Will or Ethan?" I ask.

"Ethan," my mom says, and I put the shirt in a pile of Ethan's clothes.

"What would you like to make? You can pick and I will go to the store later today."

"I don't care," I tell her grabbing another shirt from the basket. This one I know is Will's because I remember seeing him in it.

"I need you to care Alexis. About anything. Now think, what is your favorite dinner?"

"Chicken and rice," I say, not because it's my favorite but because I know it's super easy to make.

"What veggie?"

"Sweet peppers," I decide.

"Do you want to go to the store with me?"

"No." I answer a little too quickly, making my mom frown.

My mom switches out the next load and comes over and helps with the basket I'm working on. When we are done she says, "Why don't you go do the exercises Janice gave you? She will be pleased if she sees some improvement by Monday."

I nod and shuffle to my room. My mom is not usually this direct on what I must do in a day. I guess since I haven't been doing what I'm supposed to, now she is managing me every minute of the day.

Since I'm the only child in the house I don't see how I'm going to get out of doing exactly what she says. I walk into my room and grab my new blue TheraBand and sit on the ground against my bed and begin my exercises. The blue is difficult. I can hardly move the band, yet I can feel my ankle working.

I finish a round of all five exercises and rest. For the first time I feel sorry for Savannah for being an only child.

When we get home from church on Sunday it's almost noon. Sunday dinner is more like linner, lunch and dinner together. Josselyn and her family will be here at one o'clock and we will eat at about two o'clock. Since the dinner I picked takes an hour to cook my mom asks me to change and get started right away. If grandma was coming to dinner we

691

would have to stay in church clothes. Since it's just my mom's sister coming over we will all be casual and changed out of our nice clothes.

I change into jeans and a BYU gymnastics sweatshirt and run back downstairs. Well, not run, I still can't run, but I'm getting around a lot quicker these days. I get to the kitchen and my mom has already pulled out all the ingredients I need. She sets the recipe out on the counter and pats me on the shoulder.

I get started on the dinner while she and Will get started on an apple pie.

"What are the others doing?" Will asks.

"Homework," my mom answers and I roll my eyes. Yeah, right. They probably both said they have homework to weasel out of cooking. Will knows that trick, too. I wonder why he didn't use it.

I look down at my recipe and get started. I take the casserole dish my mom set in front on me and place six chicken breasts along the bottom.

"Is this going to be enough?" I ask.

"You're making two," she says, setting another casserole dish on the counter.

"Oh," I say. That makes more sense.

I place six more breasts in the other dish then I set to work preparing the chicken with salt and pepper. Then I make the mixture of water and cream of mushroom soup. I have to read the recipe to see how much of each I need to make. I don't double the recipe. I just make two mixtures since I have two trays and I don't want to get it wrong.

I pour in uncooked rice and sprinkle the onion soup dry mix all over my chicken and then add my soupy mixture on top. I repeat that for the other dish.

I look at my dishes, proud of myself. I look up and my mom is busy peeling apples and Will is making a crust.

"I'm done," I announce.

"Great, now just cover it," my mom answers.

"Where's the lid?"

"Those dishes don't have lids. You have to use foil," she says, not moving to help me.

I open the drawer where the foil is and take out the roll. I pull out way too much foil and wrap it around one of the trays. Mom doesn't say anything but she raises an eyebrow. I pull out less for the next one and it doesn't fit so I have to add an extra square to cover the second tray. Again, my mom just lets me make a mess of things and when I'm done she tells me to set my casserole dishes on the stove.

"I'll put them in the oven when they get here."

"Great, can I go now?"

"You have your veggies to prepare," she says.

"But I can't cook them yet."

"You can cut them. They're in the bottom drawer."

I sigh and go to the fridge to get out the three peppers she bought. One yellow, one red, and one orange. I wash them and set them on the counter. I get out a knife and cutting board and set up at a seat at the bar so I don't have to stand. Will is already sitting at the counter now that he is slicing up his apples.

I climb onto a bar stool next to him and start cutting my peppers. My mom's phone rings and she picks it up. I can tell by how she is talking that it's her sister. She leaves the room to continue her conversation.

With the room quiet I take the opportunity to ask Will why he didn't try to get out of cooking.

"I like it," he shrugs.

"You do?"

"Yeah."

"Does Mom know?"

"I think she must, I always volunteer."

I guess he does always seem to pick cooking chores over other chores. And it does get him out of a lot of other chores.

"Have you told her you don't like basketball?"

"Have you told her you don't like gymnastics?"

"I do like gymnastics."

"Could have fooled me," he retorts.

"I'm just having a bad week. Or season. I don't know."

Thankfully he doesn't say anything to that and keeps slicing. Do I like gymnastics? I used to. Now I'm not so sure. It got hard. Really hard.

CHAPTER 31

When my aunt, uncle, and cousins arrive my mom puts my casseroles in the oven. I know I have to grill up my peppers about fifteen minutes before we eat. Until then, I'm free to play with my cousins. It is too cold to play outside, so we decide to make an epic Hotwheels track that starts at the top of the stairs and runs down to the bottom of the stairs. Ethan is still in his room doing who knows what and Will is still working on his pie. That leaves Ronan, Oakley, Drew, and me to work on the track. It takes us a while to engineer a working track. Each time we test it a car flies off and it doesn't finish the course. We have to redesign how we have it set up. Pillows are brought in to prop up the track in certain spots and we retest. Before we are done my mom calls me back to the kitchen.

"Why doesn't Drew have to do anything?" I whine.

"Because you're in charge this week. Drew can be in charge another time."

"Here, this pan is ready. Start with the red peppers, then add in the lighter colors."

I do as she says, dumping in the red peppers and listening to them sizzle. I stir them around for a few minutes and then add in the yellow and then the orange. Now my huge pan is full of peppers and I can barely stir them. My mom comes by and drops a pat of butter in my pan and tells me to stir it around.

"These look great! You can turn it off and cover them." I do as she says and turn off the burner and put a lid on my pan to keep the peppers warm. "Now help Josselyn set the table."

"But I'm the cook!" Usually if you are the cook, someone else sets the table.

"You are short on chores for the week. Set the table," she says, putting plates in my hands.

She might be right. I didn't do much this week and I know that's why she has been hard on me the last couple of days. Lazing around is just not permitted in this family.

I walk into the dining room and start setting plates around the table. My aunt comes in with silverware and napkins and starts setting them out.

"Do we need a kids table?" I ask, knowing we sometimes pull out a card table for kids to sit at because our family gatherings are so big.

"How many does this table fit?" she asks and starts counting seats. "Ten. How many do we have?"

I think. "My family is seven. No wait, six without Josh. And you guys are four, so ten."

"Your mom probably already knew that; that's why the card table isn't in here," she comments.

I nod and we quietly go around the table. I set down plates and she sets down silverware.

"How's life, Alexis?" she asks me.

"Fine." I say, falling back on my usual answer.

"That's not what my kids tell me."

I look up from what I am doing. "What do they say?"

"That you're not yourself. You're missing a lot of school and are out of sorts."

"I am missing school. Mostly lunch and math for physical therapy." She doesn't say anything and I know she wants me to continue. "Sometimes I have to catch up on math at lunch time is all."

"Your mom is worried, too," she adds as she continues to set out silverware as if we are talking about the weather.

I'm silent because I absolutely do not know what to say about that. This is my mom's sister; she probably knows everything already. There is no evading her.

"Your mom has come to me with her concerns," she admits. I knew it. I slowly set out another plate and don't meet her eyes. "You know I'm a social worker, right?"

"Yes," I say quietly.

"My job is to help people who hit hard times in life. I help them get back on track." I nod. "Anyway, from what your mom tells me it sounds like you are just going through the five stages of grief."

"Grief?" I ask, looking up. "No one died."

She smiles. "You can grieve for things other than people. You could be grieving your season, or your gymnastics career."

"My gymnastics career isn't over."

"Not if you don't want it to be."

"I don't."

She nods and quietly starts setting out bread plates and hands me salad plates to put on top of the dinner plates I just set out.

"What are the five stages?" I ask, incredibly curious.

"Denial, anger and frustration, negotiation, depression, and acceptance."

I think about that while I carefully set out a salad plate. Was I in denial in the beginning? I think I was. I remember thinking I would only miss one meet. I was definitely frustrated and angry.

"What was the one after anger?"

"Negotiation."

"I'm not sure I did that one."

"They don't always happen in that exact order. It's just the most common order."

"Maybe I did. I asked God to help me. I thought I was praying, not negotiating."

"It can be both," she says gently.

"And depression. Like being sad?"

"Yes, sad, tired, irritable," she explains. It is unsettling how she just described my exact mood for the last week.

"How do I get out of that one?"

"You move into acceptance."

"How do I do that?"

"You have to accept that your season is over or accept that you have to work hard if you want to compete in one or two meets this season."

"Accept that my season is over. Or accept that I have to work hard to compete again," I repeat.

She nods. I know my mom put her up to all of this, but I don't mind. I was getting tired of talking to my mom about it.

"I guess I have kind of given up," I admit.

"On what?"

"Everything."

"That doesn't sound like you."

"It isn't me and it doesn't feel very good. It doesn't feel right."

"Then change it," she says simply.

I set out the last salad plate. Just change my mood? Just like that? Can people do that? It seems like these emotions are bigger than me. I'm not sure Aunt Josselyn knows what she's talking about. Although, the five stages of grief stuff is interesting.

"I brought you some books that might inspire you to the next step."

"To acceptance?"

"Yes, to acceptance. I will give them to you after dinner." Then she stands back and surveys the table. "What are we forgetting?"

"Glasses."

"You're right; let's go get the glasses."

We both enter the kitchen to get glasses out of the cupboard and I see my mom has pulled my chicken casseroles out of the oven and is tossing a salad. Will is cutting the fresh bread and setting it in a basket.

"I think we are ready. Will, please tell everyone we are ready for dinner."

Will walks to the base of the stairs and yells up to the kids at the top of the stairs that dinner is ready. I see my mom sigh because she has told us a thousand times not to yell when getting siblings for dinner. Then we hear Will walk over to the garage where the dads are fixing a garage door remote. He opens the door and yells to them, too.

Everyone appears in the dining room in a matter of seconds. My parents sit at the ends of the table and everyone else sits along the sides in no particular order. My dad says a prayer and then we all start filling our plates and talking at once.

"Alexis made the main dish," my mom brags. I get several 'great jobs' and 'I can't wait to try it' before my mom adds, "And Will made the dessert."

I see this praise makes him far happier than it does me. I do not want to be considered a good cook around here and I think he does.

The conversation moves to basketball and mostly Ethan's season since he is on varsity and plays more. I watch Will and he doesn't seem bothered by Ethan getting all the attention. Then my uncle asks why Josh isn't at dinner. Since his college is only thirty minutes away, sometimes he comes home for Sunday dinner. "He said he had too much homework today."

"I bet he went skiing," Ethan says.

"We don't ski on Sundays," my mom says.

"Exactly," Ethan says, making her frown.

My aunt laughs and says, "That's what college is for. If that's the worst thing he's up to then you're winning."

We talk about Oakley and Ronan's skiing lessons and find out that they get to do a race with gates at the end of the season.

They ask Drew how his season is going and then ask me how my ankle is doing. I decide to be more polite than 'fine.'

"It's doing better. I go to physical therapy three times a week and they are helping me get stronger every day."

"What do you do at physical therapy?" my uncle asks with genuine curiosity.

"Heat, strengthening exercises, then stabilizing exercises, and then ice. I have to stick my entire foot in a whirlpool of ice water."

"You are one tough athlete," my uncle says before the conversation moves to my dad's work. I catch my mom smiling at me. Clearly, she understands the significance of me answering the question with a real answer other than fine. I feel like myself for the first time in a while.

"Who is ready for dessert?" my mom asks, standing up. Of course everyone moans that they are full, yet they all say they want a slice when Will carries the pie to the table. It has a beautiful perfectly browned crust and it smells amazing.

My mom cuts slices and Will passes them down the

table. When people start oohing and ahhing over the pie I see William beam. This is his thing. Not basketball, not baseball, but cooking.

I take a bite of my pie and it is a mouthful of apple-brown-sugar-buttery goodness. "Wow, Will," I say with my mouth full of pie. "Thish ish amashing!"

He dips his head and says, "Thanks, Lex." Somehow he is happy and embarrassed at the same time and I don't understand why. Maybe he just doesn't like all the attention. Whatever the reason, I don't care, as long as he keeps baking pies.

The upside to cooking in our house is that you don't have to do the dishes. Drew and Ethan are given the task of clearing all the dishes from the dining room and the dads are rinsing and putting them in the dish washer. Ashtyn and Ronan are the only ones that get out of doing anything.

We tire of the Hotwheels game and move on to standing in front of the game closet and arguing over what to do next.

"You guys don't have time to start anything else," my aunt says. "We have to get going. Besides, you still need to clean up the Hotwheels and racetracks." This gets a collective moan from all of us as we go to the stairs and start cleaning up tracks. "Alexis, come with me."

I happily follow her because it gets me out of cleaning. I follow her outside to her car. She opens the trunk and grabs a cloth library bag. "Here are some books that may inspire you to move to the acceptance stage."

I take the bag and peer inside. The book on top has an ice skater. "Thank you."

She gives me a big hug and kisses me on the head and

says, "You know we don't care if you do gymnastics or not, right?" I nod into her sweater. "We just want you to be happy. We love you no matter what." I nod again, unable to say anything because if I do I will cry. I know that; I really do. Somehow hearing it squeezes my heart and gives me permission to just be me, whatever I am. "We don't care if you change your mind a million times, just be happy, okay?"

"Okay." I say and back up. "Thank you," I repeat, surprised I'm not crying.

"And seriously, Alexis, take a look at those books. I don't think any of us can relate to what you are going through. But you might relate to the people in these books."

"I promise to look at them."

She hugs me again and we walk back into the house. By now everyone is in the entryway saying goodbye to one another. The room is loud and chaotic until my aunt, uncle, and cousins leave.

"What have you got there?" my mom asks, even though I am certain she knows.

"Books from Aunt Josselyn."

"That was nice of her. Why don't you go up to bed early and take a look at them." I do as she says, mostly because that is what I wanted to do in the first place.

I get to my room and shut the door. I sit on my bed in a pancake sit and set the bag of books in the middle. I pull out the first one. *Nathan Chen One Jump at a Time*. Huh, ice skating. I'm surprised she didn't get me gymnastics books. I turn over Nathan Chen's book and read about how he had to overcome cultural differences and financial problems to compete. Interesting. Those sound worse because they would maybe never get better like an injury can. I set it aside and pull out the next book, *Rudy*. This one is about football and he had to overcome his small size. That also seems harder than an injury. I set Rudy down next to Nathan. The next one is Abby Wambach's story. She had to overcome being told she couldn't play soccer because she's a girl. That would be awful and frustrating. I set Abby next to Rudy forming a neat line. Then I pull one out with pictures of wheelchairs on the front *A Sporting Chance: The Start of the Paralympic Games.* Just looking at the cover of this one makes me feel like a terrible person for even entertaining feeling sorry for myself. I smile as I pull out the next one, *Courage to Soar,* Simone Biles' book. She did think to include a gymnastics book. I turn it over and the back says that Simone had setbacks and I wonder what they were. She is such a magnificent gymnast I can't imagine her ever having a hard time. Then I reach in for the last book, *Comeback Quotient.* I turn it over to read the back. It has several short stories of many different athletes and their comeback stories. It talks about the mental toughness involved.

I carefully set down *Comeback Quotient* next to the others and look at them. I haven't been very mentally tough these last few weeks. I lean back and stare at the books. Then I pick up *Comeback Quotient* and immediately get sucked into one of the stories.

"Are you ready for bed?" I hear my mom say. I look up and see her in my doorway.

"No, I haven't even started," I admit.

"Did you find a good one?"

"They all look good," I admit. She comes in, sits on the edge of my bed, and looks at the books I have lined up.

"She picked some good ones," she says, picking up Abby's book and flipping through it.

"She did. Can I stay home from school and read them all?"

"Nice try. You can read for another hour before lights out," she says, giving me an extra half hour I notice.

"Deal," I say, looking back down at my book.

"You have PT tomorrow," she reminds me and I give her an absent 'yeah.' "You also have practice tomorrow. Do you want to go this week?"

I look up at her and take a deep breath. "I want to go."

To her credit, she doesn't show a huge reaction, she just says, "I think that's a great idea." Then she hugs me good night and leaves.

I scoot back on my bed and settle in to read my new stories.

CHAPTER 32

After spending the evening reading comeback stories of other athletes I feel like a big wimp. I can't believe I let one little sprained ankle get me so down. I really want to turn around my attitude and I am finding it's harder than I thought. I'm so used to being grumpy and mopey that just choosing to be in a better mood felt weird at first. Almost fake. One of the books talked about faking it until it feels real. That's what I've decided to do today. Fake being a happy amazing comeback kid until it feels real. It starts with practice today.

Physical therapy went well and Janice noticed my improved mood. Standing on the half ball is still difficult and it was hard not to get frustrated with that one. I succeeded in keeping my frustration to myself and just did my best. Icing of course was difficult but I had answers for Gary today when he asked me my favorite color.

"Yellow! My favorite color is yellow."

"You changed your color Miss Lexis, good for you."

"Why yellow?" my mom asks from her chair nearby.

"It's a happy color," I say, making her smile. "Can I change my room to yellow?"

"Of course, I knew you were growing out of the pink. We haven't changed that room since you were a toddler."

I smile and swirl my foot in the freezing cold water. The new me or new attitude already feels better.

Back at school I try to pay attention but my mind is on practice. It was dumb of me to miss practice last week. I could have been doing bars and supporting my teammates. I'm a little embarrassed to show up today after missing for no reason.

Once again, my mom takes Drew, Aaron, and me to practice and she has decided to stay until I have to go home. Drew will have Aaron's mom take him home.

I can go upstairs now to the optionals room. When I walk in, Carmen and Victoria see me. "Hey, Alexis, welcome back," Carmen says.

"Hi," I say shyly and walk over to my locker.

"How's your ankle?" Victoria asks.

"Better," I say, and I'm happy to realize it really is getting better.

Savannah and Trista come in next and they greet me warmly, too. Why did I stay away? What was I avoiding?

We all head down together and the girls get started on their run. I find Katie and she tapes me while they warm-up. When I am done I sit down and stretch with my team. They are their usual lively selves talking about school and family and trying to guess what event we are going to start on.

Katie comes over and tells us to line up for complex. I stand up with my teammates and she turns to me. "You can do handstand walks with us and then you should head over to bars."

I get in line behind Riley and Paige and easily do handstand walks when it's my turn. My ankle is at no risk of getting hurt because if I lose my balance I can come down controlled onto my right foot.

When we are done with those, I leave complex and go upstairs to get my grips while my teammates continue. I come back down and know I have to warm-up with push away kips. I do them like last time, where I don't push away on the third kip so I can jump down lightly onto one foot.

After my three sets of three I go to the pit bar without being told. By now my team is done with complex and they break into two groups. Today they go to vault and bars. It looks like the upper optionals group is starting on bars. I warm-up my giants and they feel good, as if I haven't been gone at all. Then I warm-up my flyaways. I'm hesitant to put them together. I've always struggled with this combination, which is why it isn't in my routine.

Katie comes over to me while her girls are warming up with push away kips on low and high bar.

"Happy to see you in the gym, Alexis," she greets.

"Happy to be here," I smile.

"Do you need a spot on your first giant flyaway?"

"Yes, please."

She walks up the narrow stairs to the spotting platform. Once she is up there I jump up to the bar and kip up. I pause in a support position. "Keep those shoulders open and keep your giant swing going into the flyaway. There's no reason to slow down. Just stay hollow."

Keep my shoulders open, stay hollow, I repeat to myself. I cast up, she gets me to handstand, and I giant. Determined to do as she says, I stay open in a straight body right into the flyaway. I can feel her holding my shoulder open as I let go at just the right time, stay hollow, and float up in a perfect flyaway.

"Gorgeous!" she yells from the platform.

I smile as I climb out of the foam.

"Again as fast as you can," she instructs. I quickly chalk up and jump up again. I do the same exact thing and it is so fun!

"Keep doing them just like that," she says, climbing down from the platform. "I want five more like those last two and then three sets of three giants."

"Okay," I say adjusting my grips. She leaves to go watch her upper optionals run routines. I jump up and go again. I'm nervous. *Alexis, do it just like last time.* I cast up and without Katie here I don't make it to handstand, therefore my giant is slower and I arch over the top. I'm not in a good body position going into the flyaway. I let go a little early, but not much. I still land feet first into the pit. It was an acceptable flyway, just not as high as the two with Katie. I need to get my cast handstand.

I do four more. They are all about the same but mentally they get easier. By my fifth one, I feel like I could do this onto a mat into the pit. Of course, I can't yet because of my ankle. It's nice to know I will be ready when my ankle is strong enough.

I move on to giants. Three in a row is hard for me. I don't cast to a handstand and I don't have a lot of swing in the first one to keep going. I do two sets of two giants and on my third try I manage to get a third giant around. When I swing down and drop into the pit I hear cheering from over on vault. I see my teammates clapping for me.

"Thanks!" I yell back at them.

Brooklyn, a Level 8, comes over to the pit bar. "How's it

going over here?"

"Good. Glad to have company though. What are you working?"

"Releases. Jaegers. I finished all my sets so I get to work these."

"A nice break from sets."

"For sure," she says jumping up. I watch as she kips up and stops. She changes her hands into a front grip, casts to handstand in a front grip, does a forward giant, and on the back side lets go of the bar and does a front flip in a straddle position. She is supposed to catch the bar when she rotates around, but she is about a foot and a half away and falls to her belly in the pit.

"I am so far away," she laughs.

"You can't compete it anyway, can you?"

"No, it's a D, so only in Level 9. Even then, it will only count as a C," she confirms, climbing out. "I don't have any upgrades I can add in this year, so Katie lets me do these if I finish early. What are you working?"

"Giants. Specifically, doing three in a row."

"Cool, let's see."

I jump up to the high bar, kip up, cast (almost to handstand) and swing down into a giant that arches over the top, making my next two slow as well. After my third one I swing down into the pit below.

"If you can get your body position to hollow over the top on the first one the other two will be easier," she comments.

"Yeah," I agree.

"You might have to tap harder on the bottom to make up for not casting to handstand. It will get you to hollow on the back side." I nod as I pick up the chalk block.

She jumps up to take her turn. *Tap on the first one*, I know I have been told that before. I just forgot that correction.

When it's my turn I cast up and try to do what she says and arch a little in a tap on the underside of the bar to try to get into a hollow position on top. It works and I pass through handstand straighter than I ever have without a spot.

"That's it!" I hear her yell just like a coach. I do two more perfectly straight giants and come down. "Those were perfect."

"Thank you," I say, beaming as I climb out. "They felt good."

By the time I finish my three sets the bars workout is over for the Level 8s, 9s and 10s and my teammates are coming over to bars. When everyone is either putting away grips or putting on grips, I go over to the comp set to talk to Katie.

"You read my mind. I want you over here for now. You are going to do cast handstands with me while they do push away kips, then I want you to do some cast handstand drills. Come help me set it up."

I follow her to get blocks and she sets them on the floor by bars about three feet apart from each other. "I want you to you to start here in front of the blocks. Get in a mini straddle with your hands between your feet similar to how you would start a press handstand. Now I want you to press up and get your feet up to the blocks. Do one with me and let's make sure it doesn't hurt your ankle."

She spots me on the first one and these aren't hard because I can do press handstands. "Great, do them between turns with me."

I do three and then take a turn on the low bar with her where I kip and she helps me cast to handstand. I come down and cast back up two times. Then I jump down to one foot. My teammates come out and they are loudly talking as they chalk up and start push away kips.

"You have another rotation of bars?" Savannah asks.

"Looks like it," I say.

"Your hands are going to be hamburger meat," Trista comments.

Now that she mentions it, they are starting to sting. I go over to my drill station and easily get my feet up to the blocks. Sometimes drills are easy and they teach us muscle memory more than anything.

I go back to the chalk tray, chalk up, and wait for my turn with Katie.

"Are you coming to watch the meet this weekend?" Marissa asks me. She correctly assumes I'm not competing this weekend, which I guess can only be blamed on me.

"Where is it?"

"I can't remember, Provo maybe? I remember it's not an overnight one."

"Then I will probably be there. Although it depends on where Drew is competing this weekend. And basketball, too."

"You could get a ride with us if your family can't take you to the meet," Savannah offers.

"Okay, thanks, Savannah," I agree.

I take my turn with Katie and then do my drills. It feels good to be with my team again, even if it's only for one rotation.

After my third turn with Katie she comes over to my drill station and adds a floor bar in front of the blocks. "Now do it with the bar. If you can't control it and you're jumping to that ankle we can use panel mats. You should be getting your hips over your head and controlling it down."

This looks a lot harder. "Can you spot the first one?"

"Only because you are injured."

She stands behind me so when my hands are on the bar, my back is facing her. When I lift into a press she grabs my hips and gets them over my head. When my hips are high enough, my feet clear the mats and I am able to gently set one foot on each block.

"Good," she says, and I drop my feet down, letting my right foot come down before my left.

"It's harder," I say, standing up.

"Since you have your press handstand there's no reason you shouldn't be making straddle up cast handstands. Do fifteen of these and you can go to strap bar."

Fifteen takes me a while. They require a lot of arm, shoulder, and core strength and I have to rest after every couple. If I concentrate on getting my shoulders in the correct position over the bar, my stomach and hip flexors don't have to work as hard.

When I'm done with fifteen I'm spent. Thankfully, strap bar is pretty easy. It basically swings for you and all I have to do is focus on body positioning.

Without a word I leave my drill station and go to strap bar. My workout is still a little isolating because my teammates are on the competition bars running routines while I'm at the pit, doing drills, or at strap bar. I slowly take off my grips and throw them over by the wall by strap bar. As I am strapping myself in Katie yells over to me, "Three sets of five and you are done."

My arms feel like Jello. I have been on bars for almost an hour and a half without stopping. I strap myself in and swing down and pump into giants. I do three and I can feel my arms shaking. It scares me so I slow my swing to a stop. I swing over to my block and I'm not sure what to do. I don't think I can do more. Do I tell Katie I'm hammered or just tell her I did three sets? She will probably notice if I only do one set so I decide to come clean.

"Katie?" I interrupt as soon as she is done spotting a dismount. She turns toward me and waits to hear what I need.

"My arms are Jello and it didn't feel safe."

"Be done then. Move on to conditioning. Start with hollow body rocks."

I nod and start taking my hands out of the straps, relieved she didn't make a big deal out of it.

I find a spot to do my hollow body rocks near bars so I can at least listen to my teammates and watch their bar routines. I do three sets of ten on my back using my tummy muscles, then I do three sets of ten on each side, and finally three sets on my belly for my back muscles.

By the time I'm done with hollow body rocks, they are done with bars. When they go upstairs to put their grips away Katie disappears into the lobby. I take a moment to just sit with my legs crossed and rest. It was a hard workout. Training only one event is brutal.

Katie comes back out with a paper and sits down next to me. "Here is the rest of your conditioning for today," she says, handing it to me.

I take it and scan the list: pull-ups, rope climb, push-ups, squats, single leg squats, wall sits, and more.

"Have you been doing the list I sent you at home?" I'm not sure how to answer this. I did her list only once and then gave up. "I take your hesitancy as a no. I also can guess that since your arms gave out at the end of your workout. You would have made it through if you had been doing my list at home."

I remain quiet, there is nothing for me to say.

"Alexis, coming back from an injury is hard work, mentally and physically. I hear you have been going to physical therapy."

"Yeah, three times a week."

"That is very good. If you keep coming to practice I think you could compete bars in two weeks."

"Really?" I say, feeling hope for the first time in a long time.

"Sure, we can throw down an 8-incher for your dismount and if I have to spot you to help with the landing I can. You'll just take the deduction for it."

"I won't need a spot," I declare.

"Maybe not but healing well is the first priority."

"I know."

"Alexis, I need you to keep coming and do your extra conditioning here since you didn't do it at home. That is the only way to salvage your season."

"What season?" I pout.

"You already made State. Regionals is not out of the question just yet. Fight for it."

"It's not that easy," I whine.

"Oh honey," she says, putting her arm around me, "I know it isn't. But I know you have fight in you. I know you can do this. Find the fire in your belly for the sport and do what you need to do to be ready in two weeks."

"What do I need to do?" I sass.

"I just told you, silly!" she says standing up and not even bothering to repeat herself. "Now go do that list."

I reluctantly stand up and walk over to the rope to start my rope climb. This ought to be fun with Jello arms.

CHAPTER 33

I wake up Tuesday incredibly sore. My arms are sore, my hands are sore, my ankle is sore, my stomach is sore. Generally, our conditioning during season doesn't make us sore. I guess I'm not training for the upcoming meet. I did the same event for two rotations plus conditioning. I only left practice an hour early from our three-and-a-half-hour workout. I think tomorrow my mom will just leave me for the entire time.

Today PT is the usual exercises plus one. Janice always seems to add one exercise. Just when I think I'm getting stronger she busts out some tortuous thing, like the half ball, that points out just how weak I am.

"Your mom tells me you went to practice yesterday?'" Janice begins as I step up onto the hated half ball. I nod, concentrating on not letting my ankle wobble around. I'm only holding onto her with one hand. "How was it?" she asks.

"Good. Great actually. I wonder why I didn't go last

week."

"Sometimes people need a minute to take a step back," she says kindly. "Okay, step off and rest." I do as she says and step down.

"When will I be able to test landings?" I ask.

"We can try some jumping today and see how you feel."

Oof, that sounds like it might hurt. "I mean like soft landings. Like a big soft mat that is sitting in the pit," I try to explain.

"I love your sport for that reason. You have a lot of options for rehab. You could probably land on a mat in the pit because it will absorb the force for your ankle, not jam it. But no hard mats yet."

"Of course not," I say rolling my eyes.

"You'd be surprised what athletes will do when they are dying to get back to their sport."

When I'm done with balancing on the ball five times she walks me over to a small round mini trampoline. "Try some small jumps on here."

I step onto the trampoline and stand in the center. "Just bounce?" I ask, scared to hurt my ankle.

"Small bounces and see how it feels."

I bend my knees and do tiny bounces. It feels okay! I can't believe it feels okay. I smile at Janice, "It doesn't hurt!"

"Good, a little bigger," she says, taking my hands. I'm hesitant to go bigger. I look at her face and she gives me a little nod of encouragement. I bounce a little bigger and it still doesn't hurt.

"How does that feel?"

"I can feel my ankle working hard, but it's not in pain, just straining maybe?"

"That's a good word for it. Okay, rest." I slow my bouncing to a stop and step down. "I want you to go again and let's see how high you can go before it hurts. If you are wanting to do landings, I need to see where you're at."

I take a moment and then step up again and this time start right away with where I was jumping before and jump even bigger. Then I feel it start to hurt.

"That hurts," I say, and Janice immediately tells me to stop and get down.

"Given what you did today, you can do your dismounts into the pit with a 4-incher, not the 8-incher yet."

"I'm impressed you know the difference," I comment.

"I graduated from the U's PT program. We got to work with the gymnasts in their training center. Your sport is amazing."

"It is," I agree.

"So, Mrs. Bingham, did you hear this? She can try dismounts into the pit with a 4-incher today and tomorrow. I want to see how she is doing on Thursday before she moves to an 8-incher."

My mom nods in understanding and smiles at me, "Progress," she says to me.

"Progress," I agree with a smile.

"Time to ice," Janice says, making me groan.

"No groaning, Gary is excited to see if you have a new favorite color," she says, walking me to the icing room.

"Gary, I have Alexis for you!" she announces as we enter the room.

"Hi, Miss Lexis," he says, "I will turn on the whirlpool for you," he says, walking over to the big silver tubs to turn on the mechanism that swirls the freezing water around.

"Thanks," I say, climbing up and pulling up my legging.

"I leave you in Gary's hands, see you Thursday!" Janice says and leaves.

I stick my leg in and have my daily extreme discomfort in the cold water. It's something I don't think a person can ever get used to.

Gary comes over, "What's your favorite color?" he asks, trying to get my mind off the freezing water.

"Still yellow," I screech. "I'm going to redecorate my room in yellow," I say, rocking back and forth a little.

"And what else?"

"What do you mean?"

"My mom says a room has to have two colors," he says.

I look at my mom, "Is that true?" She nods. "Then why is my room all pink?" I ask.

She answers in a southern accent and says, "It was two distinct shaaades of pink, blush and bashful."

"Why are you talking like that?"

"It's from a movie, *Steel Magnolias*. I have failed you. We need to watch that movie."

"Is it older than 2000?"

"Yes."

"Please don't make me watch it," I say, making her sigh. "What other color can I put with yellow?"

"Maybe a black and white?" she suggests.

"Like a bumble bee?"

She frowns, "Maybe gray and white?"

"Ooh, that would be cute." I look over at Gary filling an ice bag. He succeeded in making me forget about my pain before I got numb. He's good at what he does.

Since I don't have practice tonight I go to my room to keep reading the books Aunt Josselyn brought over. All of these athletes have way bigger problems than I do. It makes me feel both inspired and silly for feeling so down.

I tire of reading so I go to my desk and pull out a blank notebook. I have a really cute one with gymnasts all over it that my mom got me for Christmas. I've never even written in it. I open it up to the first page and write the word *goals*.

What are my goals? At the beginning of the season I wanted to make Regionals. Now I would just be happy to get to compete at State. I write down *Compete at State*.

Then I stare at the sentence. How long do I have until State anyway? I know I wrote down all my meets in my planner at the beginning of the school year. I go to my backpack and find my planner. I flip to the month view at the back.

This weekend we have Aerial's Invitational. Clearly, I am not competing in that one. Then we have the Winter Classic the following weekend. Yikes, that is a big fat maybe. Although if I am doing landings onto a mat this week, maybe I can land on an 8-incher next week.

I write down *Compete bars at the Winter Classic*. That would be really fun to be able to compete again. I write down *land on 8-incher in pit* next to Friday's square. Then I write, *dismount on comp set* next to Monday. And then I write, *full sets* next to Wednesday. I look at it; it seems fast. Maybe it's possible since I'm doing two rotations of bars a day and I'm basically doing my second half on the pit bar.

It seems far-fetched. Then I think about the stories I've been reading and so many of the comeback stories are unbelievable. I can do this; my goals are within reach. I look at the calendar and see the word State three weeks from now. I could for sure do bars by then. I might as well aim for next weekend and worst-case scenario I can compete at State. I let out a breath; it's a good thing I made State at the very first meet of the season.

Now that I have that figured out in my head I get up from my desk and sit on the floor to do my TheraBand exercises. I notice I am getting more range of motion with the blue band. My ankle is getting stronger. It's such small gains, it's hard to see progress sometimes. It's there though. I do the hardest point-flex motion and for the first time since I injured myself I feel good.

CHAPTER 34

Today is the day. I'm going to do dismounts onto a mat into the pit today. As soon as I walk into the gym I find Katie in the coaches' office.

"I can land on a 4-incher today!" I blurt out.

"You can? Says who?" she asks smiling.

"My physical therapist."

"That's a big jump," she says slowly.

"Oh, sorry, 4-incher in the pit. I can land onto a mat in the pit. Can you tape me?"

"That makes more sense," she says chuckling. "I'll be there in just a moment; start stretching."

I happily leave the office and head up to the optionals room. I open my locker and put my boots in, then I get out my brace, a roll of tape, and my grips before putting my bag away. I might as well have my grips since I know I'm doing bars as soon as I'm warmed up.

When I walk into the training area I'm one of the first

people here since Aaron's mom had to drop us off early today. I sit down in my splits and set all my stuff next to me.

Riley comes up and sits next to me in a pike stretch. "How's your ankle?"

"Getting stronger."

"Do you think you'll be able to do more than bars soon?"

"Probably not for a few more weeks," I answer, even though I have no idea when I'll be strong enough for the other events. I'm going with a few weeks in my head. The athletes in my books pushed big goals, even if they were outlandish.

More of my teammates show up and they start running. Katie comes over to me and I know to find a block to sit on. There is one on the other side of the floor so we go over to it. I sit down and hand her the roll of tape.

"So dismounts onto a mat in the pit, huh?"

"Yes," I say, feeling very excited about today's workout.

"Pay close attention to how it feels," she warns.

"I will."

"I'll spot the first one so it's a good landing and then we'll see from there."

"Okay."

"Start with push away kips then giants to flyaway. Then you can do cast handstands with me."

She finishes taping and my team is done running, jumping, and stretching. They are forming lines for complex. I join them for handstand walks.

I get in line behind Carmen and do handstand walks across the floor. I don't fall once. I'm improving at these, probably because all the handstands on bars and body shaping drills are doing their job.

When I'm done with the walks I go back over to my block to put on my ankle brace and grips. I go to bars all by myself and warm-up with push away kips. Then I get to go over to the high bar above the pit. I warm-up my giants with a set of three, which has become easier for me.

Then I do a flyaway and I feel ready to throw a mat in. I find extra 4-inchers over by beam. I get to the beam area and James is over there with the Level 3s.

"Can I take your 4-incher that's under the medium beam?" I ask James.

"Hi, Lex. Sure, we don't need it today." I move to grab the 4-incher and he asks me, "How are you doing?" I notice he asks about me, not my ankle.

Either way, the answer is the same, "Better," I say with a smile, dragging the mat out from under the beam.

"Keep coming in and doing what you can do," he says. Solid advice. Something everyone else seemed to know except for me.

I get a hold of the two handles and pull the mat behind me. "Thanks, I will," I say, and drag the mat over to bars.

By now my teammates are on bars and warming up with their push away kips. I throw the mat into the pit and lean over and straighten it out. I grab the block of chalk we keep by the pit bar. I remember Katie wanted to spot my first flyaway into the pit. I look over and she is by the competition bars reading a list on her clipboard, probably reviewing all our routines.

"Katie!" I yell over to her and she looks up. I don't need to say anything else because she knows what I need.

She comes over and says, "Start with just a cast into a flyaway."

"Okay," I agree and let her climb up first. Then I jump up and swing into a kip. I stop in a support position. "I'm a little nervous."

"Understandable. I think your ankle is ready though. It is taped up and in the brace, I don't think you can do more than

723

make it sore," she reasons.

I take a breath and cast up. As always, she makes me go up to handstand, then I swing down and do a nice layout flyaway. I land correctly in a straight up and down body position and bounce forward taking a big step because the thin mat over the pit is unstable.

It didn't hurt! I let out the breath I was holding.

"Woo-Hoooo!" I hear yelling from over by bars. My teammates across the gym at the competition bars are yelling and clapping for me. I smile and then pump my fist. I turn back to get more chalk to go again. I take a moment to take stock of my ankle. I can feel it but it doesn't hurt. Uncomfortable maybe, like a new muscle group in conditioning.

I mentally gather myself to go again. This time I want to do my flyaway out of a giant. I have done so many of these over the last several weeks into the pit that I am more than ready to do the skill onto a mat.

"Next one on your own?" Katie asks me and I tell her I am ready. She jumps down to watch me from the floor.

I climb up to the bar, kip, and pause in my support position. I cast up, and it might have been all the way to handstand, then I giant, and easily do my flyaway and land in a good upright, non-ankle-crunching position.

"Gorgeous, Alexis!" Katie confirms.

This is what I missed about gymnastics. Pushing myself to do something new. Being hurt, you are pushing yourself to do basics and it is boring and frustrating.

"I have to go back to the comp set. Do three more and then join us over there."

I easily do three more, and honestly, I don't want to go to cast handstands. I want to try my flyaway out of two giants. When I'm done with the three Katie told me to do, I walk across the floor over to her and ask if I can do one out

724

of two giants.

"Sure, just once though, it's time to move on to casts."

I go back to the high bar and easily do my flyaway out of two giants. I did it! I can't believe I just did my layout flyaway out of two giants!

When I go back to the competition bar to work cast handstands with Katie she says, "Your body shaping is textbook. Do they feel good?"

"They do, they're easier."

"Giants are definitely easier with the right body positioning over the bar. Okay, three sets of three casts."

I kip up and easily do a straddle up to handstand, surprising myself. Katie helps me come down to a support position and I cast back up and make it again on my own. The third one I need a small spot from her. When I come down after the third one and jump down to the ground she says, "You did two all on your own. Everything is coming together for you, great job."

"Thanks," I say and go to the chalk tray.

"Your bars are looking great," Trista says.

"Thanks Trista."

"Maybe I should have done two-hour bar workouts with you," she teases.

"I don't recommend it," I say, making her laugh.

My cast handstands continue to be solid and go all the way up with little or no help from Katie. Then I do my handstand drills along with pirouette drills on the floor bar.

By the time I'm done with my bars assignment I'm ready to rest my burning hands and get to conditioning. I happily go through the conditioning list floating on the happiness of my cast handstand and dismount into the pit.

I missed this; I do love gymnastics. It's not because of my mom. It's because it's the best feeling to push yourself and learn new skills, to accomplish something that seemed impossible months before.

When I'm done conditioning I have thirty minutes before the end of practice. My mom is no longer coming early for me so I decide to ice here rather than at home. I get ice from the coaches' office and sit down on a panel mat with the Level 6s who are stretching over splits. They are done with their workout thirty minutes before Level 7. The Level 6 practice is almost over and my Level 7 teammates are finishing up on beam before they do light conditioning.

I enjoy sitting with Carmen, Trista, Marissa, and Paige. I quietly listen to them as I take off my brace, cut off my tape, and finally put the ice on my ankle.

"Is it getting stronger?" Carmen asks me.

"Getting a lot stronger."

"Your giants to flyaway were beautiful," Paige says.

"They felt good. In fact, it was the best workout I've had in a long time."

CHAPTER 35

Saturday's workout goes much the same, except I have been cleared by Janice to land on the 8-inch mats. I start out by doing a lot of pirouette work on the floor bar.

Katie has me do first half bar routines on the comp bars since I can safely jump down to the mats below.

I do my kip, handstand, clear hip, kip, squat on. Then Katie has me do the first half without the clear hip.

"Don't I have to have it?"

"No, you need a circle, which your giants are. Now that you have consistent giants, we don't need to put your clear hip in. Especially since you aren't doing them to handstand."

"So my routine is just kip, squat on, kip, giant, dismount?"

"No, it's kip, squat on, kip, giant, giant, dismount."

"I'm adding a giant?"

"I think you should. Your giants have gotten easy for you."

I think about it for a moment. "I can do it," I decide.

"Great, three first halves with the clear hip and three without, and then come see me."

I easily do this assignment while my teammates are running full routines. As much as I love doing dismounts into the pit, it's nice to be over here with them today.

I tell Katie when I'm done with the six first halves and she starts pulling over a spotting block to the low bar for my turn. I assume it's for cast handstands.

I stand in front of the bar, ready to do my kip. Before I begin she says, "Cast up and half pirouette."

"What?"

"I'll spot you." I stand there stunned.

"I don't know how to do that."

"Alexis, I've seen how controlled they are on the floor bar. You've got this."

"Yeah, but we've been doing them on the floor for a year. I never thought I would be bringing them up today."

"I will help you, a lot. I promise."

This is like taking a skill from low beam to high beam. I usually tell myself it's the same beam. This is the same bar; I can do this. I take a deep breath and begin my kip and cast up to handstand. Katie holds me in the handstand and says, "Change your grip."

I slowly change my right hand, then she helps me rotate my body in a half turn. "There you go," she says, lowering me down to a support position.

I jump down and look up at her, "How was it?" she asks.

"Easier than I thought it would be."

"The power of wax on, wax off," she says. I have no idea what she's talking about and I stare at her confused. She sighs and says, "Never mind. I was just trying to say that all your drills and conditioning made it possible. It's starting to click for you. Great job."

"Thanks," I say and head back over to the chalk tray.

"That was pretty. Are you adding them into your routine?" Savannah asks me.

"I have no idea."

At physical therapy on Monday I happily tell Janice that I landed on the 8-incher in the pit with no problem and that I am doing first halves on the comp set.

"Can I compete this weekend?"

"The only problem is that if you fall from the high bar onto your ankle, it will reinjure it."

I hadn't thought of that. "My coach can catch me," I say, even though I'm not sure if that's possible.

"What do you think Mrs. Bingham? Can a coach do that?"

"Yes," my mom says. "She can also compete with 8-inchers under the bars. They're allowed for safety of the gymnast if needed."

"Like all the way under the high bar?" I ask.

"Yes." my mom confirms.

"But then my feet will hit it when I glide into my kip on the low bar," I say, trying to imagine an 8-incher under the high bar.

"You have teammates slide it under during your squat on," she says. In that moment I'm so glad my mom was a gymnast.

"Then I think you're good to go," Janice says.

"So I can train on the comp set?" I ask.

"With an 8-incher under the high bar," she qualifies.

"And I can compete this weekend?"

"On bars only," she says.

"Duh," I say.

"I also think you can probably try beam next week," she adds.

"Really?"

"Yes, you have worked hard and your ankle is getting stronger. In fact, we are changing to a yellow band today," she says, handing me a yellow band.

"Keep doing these at home," she says.

Oh, I will.

I walk into the gym and the minute I see Katie I say, "I can do full sets!"

"Well, hello, Alexis. Is that so?"

"It is if you can catch my fall out of a giant," I explain. "And an 8-incher under the bar."

"I can do that, and an 8-incher is fine," she says. I'm so happy that I run and hug her.

"Oh, you sweetheart," she says, hugging me back. "We will be careful and stop if it hurts. Sprains easily reinjure or have a back slide, so be smart, okay?"

"I promise," I nod into her sweatshirt.

"Let's tape you up," she says. I let go of her and walk over to my usual block so she can tape my ankle.

The optional team is warming up without being told. She takes the roll of tape from me and begins with the usual strips on my shin.

"I want you to warm-up with push away kips on the low bar. Then first halves. Then we will try second halves. We will for sure put mats under the bars and I will spot you." I nod. I'm so excited I can hardly stand it. "If you're done with push away kips before I get there, start setting up mats. You are going to need two 8-inchers and a 4-incher. I want an 8-incher under the high bar and at the dismount. Then a 4-incher over the dismount mat. It will be a higher landing than you've been doing into the pit so I'll be sure to bump you until you're used to it."

"What do you mean by higher landing?"

"You're landing below the floor level on the pit bar, so you have more time in the air. If we stack up two mats on the comp bar your distance to the floor is shorter. Your height has been fine, but you may just not be ready for the landing. Make sure you look for it."

I look over at the pit. The landing mat is well below the edge of the floor. It will be an adjustment. Now I'm a little nervous.

She finishes taping me and goes over to talk to my team while they stretch. We have a meet this weekend and I'm guessing she is bumping up the workout on them. I put my brace on over my taped ankle and walk over to join them for the handstand walks of complex.

My team stands up and forms lines along the floor. I join Lucy and Brooklyn in the line nearest to me. When it's my turn I kick up to a handstand and walk across the floor without falling once.

"Well done, Alexis!" Katie yells, and I'm pleased she saw it this time. "Those handstands are getting solid. Great body position."

I smile and step out of line to go set up bars. There's already an 8-incher at the dismount spot. I pull that one under the bar, then I go hunt for another 8-incher. I find a second one in a stack at beam. Since no one is at beam yet, I pull it off the stack and drag it over to bars. Then I remember I still need to do push away kips and the mat under the bar will be in the way. I stack them on top of each other at the dismount spot and then put my grips on.

I easily do my push away kips and first halves before my teammates arrive at bars. I'm glad they have bars first instead of the Level 8s, 9s, and 10s. I'm scared, and it is more comforting to have my team with me.

"What did you get done?" Katie asks me.

"Push away kips and first halves."

"What did you do for first halves?"

"Kip, clear hip, kip squat on."

"Remember, you can ditch the clear hip."

"But then my first half is so short."

"For now," she says and walks away, leaving me to wonder what that means. I go over to chalk up. I know I have to do my last half. I haven't done giants over at the comp bars for weeks. I haven't done flyaway over here either. What if I land and reinjure my ankle?

Katie comes back with a 4-incher and throws it over the 8-incher. She moves the other 8-incher under the bars. "You ready?" she asks, pulling a spotting block under the bars. I should have warmed up on the pit bar. Now all the mats are set up and Katie is standing on the spotting block looking at me expectantly.

I stand there frozen. I desperately want to go even though I'm not moving. "Just climb onto the low bar and start with your jump to the high bar," she says. I still stand rooted to my spot. Out of the corner of my eye I see my teammates coming over to bars with their grips on and heading to the chalk tray. Mostly I hear them, they sound extra loud today.

"Alexis?" Katie says. Then she jumps down and stands in front of me. "Alexis, you have improved a great deal on bars these last several weeks. Your giants are clean, your flyaway has perfect timing, this will be no problem for you."

She's right, I've done so many giants and flyaways in the past month, my body knows what to do. I know what to do.

"Yeah," I say and move over to the low bar and do a pullover to get up.

"You've got this, Lexi!" I hear one of my teammates say. Then I hear them all start to yell encouragement.

I stand up on the low bar, jump to the high bar, do a long hang kip, and surprise myself by casting all the way to handstand. Then I easily do a giant and as soon as I make it to handstand I see out of the corner of my eye Katie jump down to the landing mat so she can catch my dismount. I swing down, watch my toes come up, and let go in a hollow body. I see the landing and I know I am plenty high enough. I feel Katie catch my waist and I land.

"Woo-HOOOOO!" I hear my teammates yell. And before I know it they are surrounding me in hugs.

CHAPTER 36

"How did the dismount go?" my mom asks me when we get home from practice.

"Great! Katie only let me do three of them, but they all felt okay."

"They looked good, too." Drew adds.

"Thanks," I say, stepping up to the kitchen sink to wash my hands. The rest of the family has eaten dinner and Drew and I have save-plates in the fridge. I see Mom go to get them and put one in the microwave.

"I have a new first half, too. Well, I have a whole new bar routine."

"You do?" they both ask.

"Yeah, I ditched the clear hip since I never go to handstand and I added two giants into the flyaway."

"I saw you doing only one giant into the flyaway."

"I did it both ways tonight, but my routine will have both," I explain.

"Are you competing this weekend?" Drew asks me.

"I hope so. Mom, did we pull me from the meet?"

"No, you're still registered."

"So I can compete bars, right?"

"You have to talk to Katie about it," she answers.

"I think Katie's planning on it, but I'm not sure."

I frown, I guess I can I ask her at Wednesday's workout. "Can you email her or text her?" I ask my mom not wanting to wait until Wednesday.

"Yea, you sit down to eat and I can text her real quick,'" she says pulling out her phone.

Drew and I sit down to eat and I ask him about his workout. "A good workout, but brutal on my hands tonight," he says.

"I don't know how you guys do it," I comment.

"You've been doing it all month. Two hours of bars every day. How are your hands?"

"Better than they were two weeks ago."

"See, you just get used to it. Tonight was rough though because we didn't rotate to floor or vault, so there was no break for our hands."

We are silent as we eat and Mom looks up from her phone, "She's planning to compete you on bars." She grins. "Great job, baby girl, your comeback has started."

"I knew you had something to do with those books!" I say, making her laugh.

"Josselyn and I may have picked them out together, but she's the one that went to the library for you."

After dinner I do my homework and my TheraBand exercises. Now that I see there is a path to getting better, I'm more motivated to do all the exercises Janice tells me to do at home. I go down to the kitchen to ice my ankle before bed. I grab a pre-made bag of ice from the freezer, a towel, and find my hand-held Tetris game. I sit on the couch, adjust my ice, and turn on my game. I'm not sure if I'm allowed to play right now, but no one is around to ask. I figure I'm done with homework and just sitting here, so I put the game on silent and settle in for my fifteen minutes of icing.

I hear my mom come into the kitchen for a glass of water. I'm engrossed in my game so I don't say anything.

"Mom, can I talk to you?" I hear William say quietly. Is he finally going to do it? I sink lower in the couch so my presence doesn't ruin his nerve.

"Sure, honey, what is it?"

"I . . . I don't know how to say this," he stammers.

Now he has her full attention. "Whatever it is, we will help you," she encourages.

"I'm not in trouble or anything. I just, I just don't like basketball," he blurts out.

There is silence for a moment before my mom says, "Do you not like the fresh/soph team or do you not like basketball?"

"I don't like basketball."

"Or is it the coaches?"

"Mom! I don't like basketball! I never have! I just did it because it made you and Dad so happy."

"Oh, honey, I'm sorry you felt you had to keep playing for us," my mom says, finally getting it.

"So, I don't have to keep playing?"

"Of course not. You have to finish the season, but you don't have to keep playing after that."

"My team doesn't need me," he says quietly.

"You don't know that," my mom says. "Talk to your coach and see if he needs you to finish up the season. You committed to this team, so finish what you started and then you don't ever have to play again."

"Okay," William agrees.

"Well," my mom sighs, "you have to do something other

than Mario Kart and D&D. Is there something else you like to do?"

"I like to cook. Well, I like to bake specifically."

"You do?" she asks, surprised.

"Yeah, haven't you noticed I always volunteer for Sunday dinner as my chore?"

"Oh, Willliam, I wish you would have told me sooner. How long have you been miserable?"

"You mean you don't care if I quit?" he asks, surprised.

"Of course I don't care. I just want you to be happy."

I hear him walk across the kitchen and they are quiet for a moment. I assume they are hugging.

"Will you tell Dad?" I hear him ask.

"Yes, but I promise he just wants you to be happy too."

"Can you still tell him?"

"Yes."

"And can I take baking lessons after school?"

"Of course. A chef in the family, how fun!"

"Pastry chef," he corrects making her laugh. She asks him what his favorite dish is to make and they start talking about desserts. I smile to myself as I keep playing my game. I'm glad Will finally got that off his chest. Now I know how my mom would respond if I ever wanted to quit. I pause for a moment realizing that I don't want to quit. Will was wrong. I don't do gymnastics for my mom; I do it for myself.

Thankfully, Will and Mom are done with their chat before I'm done icing. When it's time for me to take my ice off, they have left the kitchen. I stop by Will's room on my way to bed.

"Feel better?" I ask him.

"Man, news travels fast around here," he complains. I lean against his doorframe. "Cooking, huh?"

"Don't make fun of me," he orders.

"I wasn't going to. I think it's cool."

"Thanks," he says and I turn to leave.

"Lex?" I turn back and look at him. "I know you don't do gymnastics for Mom."

"How?"

"It looks way too scary of a sport to do if you don't love it."

I smile, "You're right," I agree and head to my room to get ready for bed.

I climb into bed with one of the comeback books. I lean back on my pillow and think about my workout. I did three second halves with the giant to a dismount. I feel good about that part. Then Katie had me work half pirouettes on the low bar. She wants me to kip, cast to handstand, half pirouette, kip squat on as my first half. I made four of them without her help. It's surprising how easily I have learned that skill. It makes me a believer in drills. I'm not sure about all of it going together in a routine by Saturday though. Knowing Katie she will let me decide if I want to do the pirouette or not. I know I have to do a giant into a flyaway. She has been clear about that. It's the first half I'm now worried about.

I close my eyes and visualize both versions of my routine. I do love the one with the pirouette. It would be so cool to be able to pull it off. Might as well, the season is almost over and I already made State. I want to do it. I'm going to do it. I know Katie will ask me about it at my next practice, and I'm glad I have an answer ready.

As soon as I am done with push away kips on bars Katie tells me to warm-up one first half and one second half and do three routines.

I start with my first half. I face the low bar with the high bar behind me. I kip, cast up to handstand, switch one hand, start to fall, and force my toes back over my head. I rotate my body in a half turn and come down and kip, squat on.

"Way to fight for that one," Paige says, walking by me as I walk to the chalk tray and she is walking to the bar.

"Thanks." *It was a fight*, I think, as I go to the chalk tray. My second half is next. When it's my turn I slide the dismount 8-incher all the way under the bars in case I fall out of a giant, then I move another 8-incher that I had off to the side to the dismount spot the other one was just in. I wonder if I still need the 4-incher.

"You get one or the other in a meet, so let's try it with just the 8-incher. I'll spot you," Katie says, reading my mind.

I nod and walk over to the low bar to begin. I do a pullover, climb into a squat, and jump to the high bar. Katie is standing between the bars for me and is no longer using a spotting block. I know if I fall she will catch me. I also know the giants are up to me and she can't help me from down there.

I do my long hang kip, cast to handstand, giant, giant, flyaway. Katie catches me around my waist on my landing and sets me down. "How did that feel?"

"Fine. Good," I answer.

"Now add the easier first half for a full set."

"Just kip, squat on?"

"That's it," she says, walking over to move mats. "It will be no problem for you," she says, grabbing the two handles on the mat and sliding it back. I step over and pull the other one out from under the bars. No one else needs the mat like that, so I should help move it. "Thanks," she says, and starts yelling that no one is going.

I go over to the chalk tray to gather my thoughts that I am going to be doing a full set next. I'm only adding one skill basically, but still, the thought of it rattles me a little.

"Your handstands have gotten so good." Carmen says when I walk up to the chalk tray.

"Thanks. Glad something came out of two hours on bars every day."

"Has it been awful?" Savannah asks.

I think about this for a second, "It got lonely doing a rotation without you guys or being over at the pit bar. And my hands have been hurting every day. But it's been fun to improve so fast on one event."

"I bet, seeing your progress makes me want to come in extra," Trista says.

"Not during a meet week Triss," Paige reminds her.

"I know," she says and rolls her eyes, Although none of us put it past her.

"Will you guys help me with the mats on my next turn?"

"What do we need to do?"

I tell them I need to slide an 8-incher under the high bar after my kip and then the other 8-incher put in place for the dismount. They agree and go over and grab one end of the 8-incher that is in the dismount spot.

Katie sees that I'm ready to go and comes over to stand between the bars. I glide into my kip and as soon as I am casting for my squat on I can see my teammates sliding the big mat under the high bar. I jump to the high bar into my long hang kip. I can see them slide another mat from the side into the dismount spot. I have mats everywhere and don't need to worry about hurting my ankle if I fall. I cast up to handstand and make sure to have correct body position as I swing into my first giant. I can hear my teammates cheering as I do my second giant. I see Katie move to the other side of the high bar for my dismount, I swing down, wait for the correct time, and let go into what feels like a perfect flyaway. I land with a perfectly upright landing. I don't even need to take a step. I hear my teammates cheering. I look over to

Katie in shock and she holds up both hands for a double high five.

"Welcome back to season, kid. That was a great set."

"That was easier than I expected," I admit with a laugh.

"I am telling you, all the hours you spent at the pit bar were not wasted." I give her hug while trying not to get chalk all over her. Then I put the mats back for someone else to take a turn. My teammates help me and with three of us we easily slide one mat off to the side and the other to the dismount spot.

"That was so clean." Marissa says as I get back to the chalk tray.

"It felt good," I say. "I don't think bars have ever felt this good."

"Are you competing on Saturday?"

"That's the plan but seeing as that was my first set in weeks, I'm nervous."

"It looked great! The judges will never know you've been out."

I smile, leave it to Marissa to think of the logistics. I chalk up as I watch Marissa take her turn, she has improved too. It's fun to see the progress of the entire team.

I step up to the bar again. I don't even have to ask my teammates to help with the mats. They know I am up and mats need to be moved.

I do another set just like the last one and it feels great.

"One more like that and let's add the pirouette."

I nod nervously, sometimes Katie moves too fast for me. Now I understand what Lucy has been talking about.

I'm exhausted after the third set and I really don't think I can do a full set with the pirouette.

"Katie? May I just do the pirouette in first halves?"

"Yes, that's fine. You did some great sets today. Let's plan on that set this Saturday and you can train the pirouette for State. Do pirouettes on the floor bar until we rotate."

I do the handstand and pirouette drills on the floor bar by myself. When my teammates rotate to vault Kaite gives me a light conditioning list. I'm done conditioning and stretching before my team is even finished with vault.

I decide to text my mom to pick me up early rather than hanging out here. I need to go home and do my missing math assignments. I ended up emailing my teacher and asking her if I can turn in the four missing assignments. She said yes, but I must get it done this week. I can go home and finish it up while I ice my ankle. I need to pull up my grade to a B after all because I do care if I stay home from gymnastics. Also, it feels better to do my best in school.

CHAPTER 37

It's meet day, it's meet day, it's meet daaaaay! I'm so excited I wake up way too early. I know I'm only doing one event, but at least I am doing something!

My mom is up and she makes me a hearty meet day breakfast of eggs and potatoes. Then Drew wanders in and she does the same thing for him. "We need to head out for your meet in an hour," she tells him. "We'll need to take two separate cars so I can take Alexis to her meet if yours isn't done in time, which it probably won't be."

"Are Ethan and Will coming?" he asks.

"No they have basketball games this morning." Will talked to his coach and his coach asked him to finish the season. Will seemed okay with the request and is talking about his last games with a good attitude.

I finish breakfast and go upstairs to get ready. I get dressed in jeans and a Perfect Balance sweatshirt to cheer for Drew. Then I pack up everything I need for my meet. I pull out my competition leotard from my closet. I lay it on my bed leaving it in the plastic garment bag. I pick up my gym bag off the floor and check it. Grips, check. Tape, check. Brace, check. What else? Meet hair.

"Mo-um!" I yell and I hear her yell back from her room.

I go find her in her bathroom putting on makeup.

"Should we do meet hair now?" I ask.

"I think it will hurt if it's in all day. Let's do it at Drew's meet. Bring all the stuff."

I go back to my bathroom and the door is shut, one of the boys is in there. I lean against the hallway wall to wait. I should keep my hair stuff in my room. I can never get into the bathroom.

I hear a honking from outside and happily yell, "Your ride is here!"

"Can you tell them I'll be a sec?" I'm not sure if it's Ethan or Will and I don't I want to deliver the message.

"I'll tell them," Will says, trotting by in his basketball uniform.

"Good luck," I say to him as he runs by.

"You too," he yells and runs down the stairs and out the door.

A few minutes later Ethan bursts out of the bathroom and runs past me without a word.

I run into the now stinky bathroom to get my stuff. Someday I'm going to have my own bathroom.

My hair is long enough for a ponytail now and I grab two bands, hair clips, and hairspray and run back to my room to dump it all in my gym bag.

By the time my mom is ready, so am I. I even thought to grab a book. Although, I do like watching Drew compete so I may not need it.

I ride with my dad and Drew rides with my mom to his meet. He asks me how things are going and I'm happy to tell him about my progress on bars.

"When will you do the other events?" he asks.

"Beam, next week. Floor and vault might be a few more weeks. I will probably only be able to compete bars at State."

We get to Drew's meet and it's not at a big event center like our meets. It's held at a gym. There are so few boys in gymnastics that they don't get big meets very often.

We get out and see Drew trot in ahead of us. I walk in with my parents and we find seats in the gym's viewing area upstairs.

The meet starts quickly with the Perfect Balance boys starting on rings. As much as I'm enjoying myself I'm feeling restless and keep squirming in my seat. I wish my meet was the morning meet.

When they get halfway through the events, my mom tells me it is time to do my hair. We depart to the bathroom.

"Do you want a high pony or a French braid to a low pony?" she asks me.

"High pony," I tell her.

"Easy enough," she says, and picks up a brush and starts brushing my hair back into a ponytail. Once she has it secure she grabs the clips and pulls up the wispy hairs that didn't fit up in the ponytail. "Do you feel ready today?"

"Yes. I know I've only been doing routines this week, but my routine is short and the hard part is on high bar, which I've been doing this entire time on the pit bar."

"Well, I'm proud of you for working so hard and making a comeback," she says.

"It's not a comeback until I am doing the All-Around," I argue.

"You are competing today. It's a comeback."

I walk into the large event center and find the gymnast check-in table. Once I'm checked in and find my teammates my mom vanishes into the stands.

"It's capital cup," I hear Savannah say as we walk up.

"Do we know our order?" Lucy asks.

"Not yet."

"Hi, Alexis," Lucy greets me.

"How did the 6s do?" I ask, knowing our Level 6 team was in the session before us.

"They just went to awards, so we don't know exactly where they placed. But they looked good," Savannah answers.

"Have you both been here the entire time?"

"I just got here," Lucy says.

"Riley and I watched the Level 6 session," Savannah tells us.

We see the timer set to ten minutes on the wall. This means we have ten minutes until open warm-ups.

"I need to find Katie and get taped," I say.

"Okay, we're going to find a spot near the floor for our bags," Victoria says.

"I'll find you," I say and go looking for Katie. I find her standing in a circle with a bunch of coaches talking to the meet director. I know I can't interrupt that and I just have to wait.

I anxiously watch the timer and watch my teammates set their bags down, take their slides off, and prepare to get on the floor and start running as soon as the meet director says they can.

When there are about thirty seconds left on the clock the coaches meeting breaks up. I immediately go to Katie.

"Can you tape me?" I ask, slightly panicked.

"Sure, let's go over here to the bleachers and you can sit

sideways and hang your leg off the end. There's a training room in the back but I want to watch warm-ups."

I follow her to the edge of the bleachers. "I only have thirty seconds."

"You can't run. You'll be fine."

Oh yeah. I won't be doing the entire warm-up sequence with my team. I climb up to the third row of bleachers, sit on the end, turn sideways, stick out my foot, and hand Katie the roll of tape.

She immediately starts taping my ankle. The meet director announces open warm-ups and it's weird to not be out there with my team.

"We start on floor, so you have lots of time. You can stretch along the edge while they tumble." By the time Katie finishes with my ankle, my team is done running and are on the floor in a circle stretching. I walk over to them with Katie. When we get to the edge of the floor I sit down with all the PBGA bags to put on my brace. I'm glad Katie explained to me I have time, so I'm not panicking that I am missing open warm-ups.

"We start on floor today. Capital Cup, no march in. They will just announce you at your events. We rotate with Flips today."

No one says anything, so she starts addressing each athlete and checking in with how they are feeling today.

I finish securing my brace in place, zip up my bag, and go over to sit with my team.

They are at the end of their stretches. I join them in stretching my wrists and neck. I will have to go back and stretch everything else when they start tumbling. I think about what Katie said, we start on floor. That means we will rotate floor, vault, bars, beam. I have to wait until the third event to compete.

The meet director announces that open warm-up is over

and timed warm-ups will be in five minutes. We know we have to clear the floor even though we will be on floor first. We go over to our bags and my teammates take off their sweats to prepare to tumble in a few minutes.

I start to do the same. "Keep yours on until bars. I want your muscles to stay warm," Katie tells me.

I zip my jacket back up and wait until I can get back on to the floor to stretch. Katie instructs us to drink some water while we are waiting.

My teammates see that the clock counting down to timed warm-ups has thirty seconds and they make their way to the corners of the floor so they can tumble as soon as it begins. The Flips girls are in the corners, too. Everyone knows what to do at this level.

When the meet director says timed warm-ups begin, girls immediately start tumbling on the diagonals. I go to the edge of the floor where I will not be in the way and I stretch. I feel like such an oddball in my sweats, stretching on the floor while everyone else is tumbling. At least I'm in my PBGA warmups and I have a noticeable brace on my ankle, so I guess it's not a secret what I'm doing sitting while everyone else is tumbling.

I sit in my splits and watch my teammates. Their tumbling has gotten cleaner and higher since I last watched them. It's easier to see improvement when you don't watch everyday. This is their last meet before State and they look great.

Their last meet before State. Has everyone made it to State? Riley and Victoria probably got their 32.00 early on since this is their second season in Level 7. I look at my teammates. Savannah is the only one that looks nervous. Of course, Savannah always looks nervous at competitions.

Katie is standing not far from me along the edge of the floor. She no longer needs to stand on the diagonal and spot since everyone can do their passes with no problem.

I move to my middle splits and look over at Katie, "They've all made State, right?"

"Savanah needs to get her 32.00 today. Her high score this season was a 31.75."

How did that happen? Savannah is so good. I think back to our first meet. She fell on her back walkover, back handspring series, so that would have been hard to get a 32.00. I don't know what happened at the second meet since I missed it. The third meet I was watching the boys more than the girls. Did she fall? She must have. When all four events just don't come together in one meet it's difficult to score at 32.00.

I watch Savannah and see she is warming up her full, which she can do well. She is also warming up her front handspring front rather than the front handspring pike she has been working in practice.

My guess is she is going back to A routines to perform clean routines without falls. Oh man, big day for her!

I finish stretching my legs and move on to my shoulders. Once I am done stretching I want to do my usual handstand walks. Since I don't have an entire floor to do handstand walks, I just do a few handstand-holds in place. Then I go over and stand next to Katie.

She looks down at me and says, "And now you wait."

CHAPTER 38

Katie wasn't kidding when she said I had to wait. A meet feels so long when you have to sit out events. The floor rotation went great, everyone except Savannah did their upgrades. Savannah scored a solid 8.55. Since she needs to average an 8.0 on each event, the 8.55 gives her room to not score as high on vault, which is her weakest event.

My team looks amazing on vault and even though there are no upgrades, they are all getting great height and body position off the table. Savannah is the only one without amplitude. Fortunately, her body position is good and she pulls off an 8.00.

Now we are gripping up for bars. Katie is across the gym getting us the extra mat I need on bars.

I line up last, knowing I need the mat under me for my jump to high bar. When it's my turn I see Katie waiting with the mat. I jump into my kip, as I squat on Katie slides the mat under me, I jump to high bar, and with my first half done fall to my feet on the mat.

As soon as I step off, she pulls it out from under the bar. I help her slide it off to the side since Victoria is already starting her last half.

I go and chalk up and I hear Katie telling Victoria and Riley that they are going to help with mats for my turn.

Then it's my turn for a second half. When I walk up, Katie slides the mat under the bar. I pull over, climb up, jump to the high bar and long hang kip. The bars feel good, just the right amount of chalk and not too bouncy. I cast into a handstand, giant, giant, and flyaway with Katie lightly spotting me on the landing.

"How'd it feel?"

"Fine. Good."

"The next one is you," she says.

One more turn before the competition routine. A full set this time. I walk over to the chalk tray and quietly chalk up with Savannah.

"How are you doing?" I ask her.

"Good. Bars isn't a problem for me; it's beam."

"Oh, man, and it's last," I comment, spraying one of my grips with water and dipping it in the tray.

"I know, trying not to think about it," she says.

"Good plan. Focus on bars," I advise.

"Are you excited to compete?"

"Yes, it's been a long season on the sidelines. I'm extremely happy to be here today."

She smiles. "I'm happy you're here, too."

Then she goes over to the bars for her full set and it's beautiful. She's right; she has nothing to worry about on bars.

I step up to the low bar and wait for her to finish. As soon as she dismounts and steps off the mat, Katie gets ready to slide it under the bar for me. She picks up the end and dips her head to me telling me to go.

I jump into my kip, squat on, mat slides under, jump to high bar, long hang kip. Feeling good, just like the last turn. Cast handstand, giant, giant, and the second giant arches a little over the top. I pull my toes over and tighten my core to straighten it out before I swing down for my dismount. I easily do my layout flyaway and Katie keeps her word and doesn't assist with the landing.

"First giant was nice, second giant you got a little sloppy. Stay tight, tap to hollow."

She's right, I knew all of that. The good news is that even with my sloppy second giant it was a decent routine that I would be happy with in competition.

We sit down to wait for Flips to compete before it's our turn. Level 7 routines are short and we don't have to wait long. Katie has Victoria and Riley go first, then me, Savannah, and Lucy. I watch Victoria salute and begin. She does a perfect routine even with her new stalder circles on the low bar. We all high-five her and sit back down to let Riley compete next.

I take a deep breath. I'm next. I'm ready. My hair is up and looks good. I'm in my beautiful Perfect Balance snowflake sequined leo. My grips feel good. The bars had the right amount of flexibility and chalk. Everything is good. Why am I so nervous?

It's just been a while. Maybe that's it. I forgot about competition jitters. I walk over to the chalk tray as Riley begins her routine. I chalk up alone, which I hate at meets. This is when it feels lonely and you know everything is up to you.

I've been training bars alone so much this should be no big deal. I chalk up both hands and wait for Riley to finish. As soon as she dismounts I walk over to stand by the low bar. I watch as Katie gives Riley a high-ten and then briefly talk to her about her routine. Then Katie picks up the dismount mat and holds the one end up, ready to slide it under the bar as soon as I finish my firt kip. No words of wisdom before my set I guess. I have her too busy moving mats to give me a pep talk.

I can give myself a pep talk, I think as I watch the judge calculate Riley's score. I have been doing nothing but bars for weeks. I'm ready. I've improved and am going to hit this event. I came for one reason and this is it.

"Alexis?" the judge asks, raising her arm.

I smile to indicate that I am Alexis. I salute and walk over to stand in front of the low bar.

"You've got this, Lexi!" I hear my teammates cheer before I even begin.

I jump into my glide kip, squat on, the mat goes under, I jump to the high bar and see Katie stand under the high bar for me. I do my long hang kip and I can see Riley and Vicotria move the dismount mat into place. I cast all the way up to handstand and for a moment I think I am going to fall over the other side. I tighten up, getting control of the handstand, and swing down into my first giant, making sure to have excellent body shaping. The giant feels good and I swing down into the next one. The second giant has much better body shape than in warmups. Then I swing down for my flyaway. Katie moves to where I will be dismounting and I swing up, see my toes, keep my shoulders open, let go, float up, and execute a large layout flyaway. I come down in the correct position for a stuck landing and I do just that, surprising myself. I salute in the stuck potion, then turn and salute the judges. Then I turn for my high-ten from Katie and instead she gives me a big hug.

"That was beautiful! All those hours alone at bars just paid off!"

That felt great! I run over to my teammates who quickly give me high-tens before they turn their attention to

Savannah. I sit down and notice I'm breathing heavy. I grab my bag to find my water. I hear someone cheering for Savannah and I stop what I am doing to look up and watch her.

She does a kip, clear hip to handstand, toes on, back sole circle, jump to high bar, long hang kip, giant, giant, flyaway. When did she add the sole circle? She obviously went for the harder routine on bars, not worried about playing it safe like on floor.

I sneak a quick look at the huge score screen on the wall of the arena. I need to check for my score before they post Savannah's. I find my name and it says 9.20. What? That can't be right, a 9.20? That is the highest bar score I have ever received!

I turn back and watch as Savanah gets her hug from Katie and runs over to us. "You have really improved on bars," I tell her when she gets to me and sits down.

"So have you," she says, sharing the compliment.

I take a drink of water and peel off my grips before Lucy takes her turn. Lucy has a similar routine as Savannah only she does a stalder circle instead of a sole circle. Both girls are going to be ready for Level 8. In fact, this entire team will be ready for Level 8. Except me.

Before I slide down the pity path, I remind myself that just being here is a comeback to be proud of. My 9.20 is a huge bonus. I shove my grips in my bag and realize my meet is over. I stand up with my teammates to march over to beam.

When we get to beam we have to wait for Flips to finish competing before we warm-up. Katie takes that moment to come over to me.

"There is a trainer over by the head table. Go ask her for ice. You took a lot of landings this week. I want you to ice right away."

I do as she says, glad I don't have to miss watching my

team while I go get ice. I walk over to the judges table making sure not to get in the way of other events. I find the trainer standing by a large first aid bag.

"Hi," I greet her.

"Hello."

"May I get some ice?" I ask her.

"Sure," she says and turns and leaves to a room behind the judges' table. I'm not sure if I'm supposed to follow her or not. I decide to stay put. She comes back a few minutes later with a bag of ice like they have at physical therapy in one hand and a big plastic wrap wand in the other.

"I assume it's for your ankle?" she asks me.

"Yeah."

"If you take off your brace, I can wrap the ice on so you can walk with it."

"I don't have tape scissors over here."

"Oh, you're taped under the brace. Here you go," she says, handing me tape scissors she had in her back pocket.

"Nice," I say and sit down on the ground next to her.

I pull off my brace, cut off the tape, and look up at her. She crouches down next to me and situates the ice on my ankle. Then she wraps the plastic wrap around and around my ankle, securing the bag of ice in place.

"There you go."

"Thanks," I say, standing up and tossing my tape in the garbage.

I walk back over to beam with my brace in one hand and ice around my ankle. I see Flips is done competing and my teammates are warming up beam. I don't interrupt when I get to beam because I know they have limited time.

I sit down on a panel mat by beam where all of our bags are sitting. The ice makes me cold, so I find my bag and pull out my jacket and put it on. I wonder what Savannah got on bars and what she needs to get on beam to make State.

Marissa is probably in the stands and knows. I look up and try to find the PBGA parents. They are sitting all the way across the arena and there is no way I could pretend-sign to Marissa.

My team is done warming up and comes to sit next to me. I have no idea how warm-ups went so I stay quiet. They plop down on either side of me. We no longer sit in the order of competition like we did when we were little. Now we can remember who we're after.

I notice Lucy doesn't sit, which means she is starting us off. The judge is immediately ready since she was waiting for us to warm-up. Lucy mounts, does a nice leap, and then her back handspring series.

It's so fun to watch my teammates compete all of their upgrades. It's weird to not have all of their routines memorized like I would if I was training every event with them every day. This must be what it's like for the parents when they only see us compete. The improvement must be much more noticeable.

I watch as Lucy does a back handspring layout dismount. Another upgrade.

Lucy is happy with that routine as she gets her hug from Katie and runs over to us. Everyone greets her except for Savannah who is waiting by beam for her turn.

Savannah salutes the judge before we are done congratulating Lucy. We quiet down right away. Savannah mounts and as soon as she stands up I know she is terribly nervous. She steps into a pose, then does her jumps. She slowly walks to the end of the beam and raises her arms for her series. I can tell by how she is standing on one leg that she is going to do the easier back walkover back, handspring. She pauses longer than we are supposed to. Finally, Katie yells, "You've got this Anna!" The rest of us jump in, yelling encouragement. Savannah finally reaches back into a nice and straight walkover and she connects her back handspring. All of us erupt in cheers. I have no idea how that has been going in practice for her, but she was sure nervous to compete it.

She looks more relaxed now that that skill is complete. She easily does her leap, full turn, and prepares for her dismount. She takes a deep breath and does a clean front pike off the end of the beam. An easier dismount than her usual cartwheel, back layout.

When she lands she salutes facing forward then turns and salutes the judge. When the judge looks down she runs and jumps into Katie's arms.

She doesn't know if she made State or not, but she does know that she hit all four events and did her best. That's all any of us ever want.

The rest of the team hit beam as well and Katie is grinning with pride.

"You guys peaked at just the right time, great job," she says at the end of the beam rotation.

Then she looks at Savannah and says, "You did it, all of us will be at State. We might even all make Regionals." Savannah doesn't say anything, her face shows she is pleased.

"All of us? I'm only competing bars at State." I remind her.

"You can qualify to Regionals as an event specialist."

"What?" I had no idea!

"Keep slaying bars all day and you'll make it."

"Do you think I really can?"

"Not only can you make Regionals; I think if you add in

your pirouette you will be able to place."

My head is reeling. Competing at Regionals is a real possibility again. I can do this; I know I can!

She turns to the rest of my team, "You can say hi to your parents. Awards are in a separate room; follow the signs. The Level 8s start in ten minutes."

Before I go to my parents I walk over to the trainer and she helps me cut off the clear wrap and takes my ice and dumps it for me. By the time I walk across the floor I see the timer is on and the Level 8s are waiting for open warm-ups.

I find my family and my mom gives me a hug. I see my Dad and Drew made it to the meet. I ask Drew how the rest of his meet went. "Fifth all around, third on pommels," he says.

"Wow, Drew, great job!"

"Nice bar routine," he says.

"I second that," my mom says.

"Thanks," I say, beaming.

"Let's get to awards and see what happened," my dad says and herds us to the awards room. When we get there, they've already started. Since I didn't compete vault, we didn't miss hearing my name.

I walk up to the front and sit with my teammates. They are quiet since the awards are being announced fast. I lean into Savannah and she turns to look at me. "What was your All-Around?" I whisper.

"32.75," she whispers back with a grin.

I give her a side hug. "Way to go," I say quietly.

I survey the rest of the group and see that Riely and Victoria have medals around their neck, obviously for vault. The announcer finished with the older age group on vault and moves on to bars.

"Starting with the child A group, in 8th place with an 8.50, Emma from Flips."

I'm not sure what age group I'm in, but I'm twelve, which is usually in the middle of the pack. Based on the scores of the kids in the two child age groups, I will probably place in my age group. Lucy and Savannah both place in the Child C age group, which means I am probably in the next one since I am only a year older than them.

The announcer starts with Junior A and it begins with 8th place at an 8.25. If I'm in this age group I placed for sure.

"In 4th place, with an 8.70, Victoria from Perfect Balance." I am usually in the same group as Victoria. Placing above 4th seems impossible. "In 3rd place, with an 8.95, Ann Johnston from Flips. In 2nd place with a 9.05, Olivia Martinez from Salt Lake Gymnastics."

No way.

"In first place, with a 9.20, Alexis Bingham from Perfect Balance." When I stand up my teammates are cheering so loud. I happily make my way up to the podium and stand on the 1st place spot. I look across the room and find my parents. My mom is frantically taking pictures.

As the volunteer puts the gold medal around my neck I can hardly believe it. Bars used to be my mediocre event and I just won at a big meet. As I raise my arms, I know that my comeback story has just begun.

About the Author

Melisa Torres is the best-selling author of the Perfect Balance Gymnastics Series. She grew up in San Jose, California where she trained at Almaden Valley Gymnastics Club and competed in USA Gymnastics' Junior Olympic program for ten years. Melisa then earned her BA at Utah State University where she studied Psychology and Literature and competed for their NCAA Division 1 Gymnastics Team. Melisa was a two-time Academic All-American and team captain.

Melisa currently lives in Utah and is a single mother to two active boys. She enjoys attending their soccer games and taking them to the library. When Melisa is not parenting or writing she can be found weightlifting or partner dancing.

READ ALL OF THE
PERFECT BALANCE GYMNASTICS BOOKS!

I've Got This!
Nothing Better Than Gym Friends
Dance is the Secret Event
Brothers Have Talent, Too
The Kip
Score Out
Courage to Fly
Season of Change

PERFECT BALANCE GYMNASTICS OPTIONALS
NEW CHALLENGES
STRIVE FOR EXCELLENCE
THE COMEBACK

PERFECT BALANCE GYMNASTICS
GRACE AND CONFIDENCE FOR LIFE!

MELISATORRES.COM
VISIT OUT SITE FOR UNIQUE GYMNASTICS GIFTS,
BOOK SIGNING DATES, AND TO APPLY FOR OUR
READER OF THE MONTH PROGRAM.

FACEBOOK.COM/PBGSERIES
@PERFECTBALANCEGYMBOOKS
FOLLOW US TO SEE BEHIND THE SCENES AND TO
GET UPDATES ON NEW RELEASES.

If you enjoyed this book please consider leaving a review.
Our small family business relies on positive reviews from
readers like you.
Thank you!

Made in United States
North Haven, CT
06 September 2024

57040937R10461